River...

A Novel

by
Tim Anderson

(Formerly *Cherokee River Wolf*)

Paperback Edition – ISBN: 9798362392468

© Copyright 2022, Tim Anderson. All rights reserved. No part of this book may be reproduced, stored in a retrieval system, or transmitted by any means, electronic, mechanical, photocopying, recording, or otherwise, without written permission from the copyright owner.

This book is a work of fiction. Names, characters, places, and incidents either are products of the author's imagination or are used fictitiously. Any resemblance to actual events or locales or persons, living or dead, is entirely coincidental and unintentional.

While the herbal preparations contained in this book are mostly historical, the Author and/or Publisher make no recommendations, claims or endorsements regarding their safety or effectiveness in treating health problems of any kind. Many of the plants described in this book are widely known to be harmful and/or poisonous, and consumption could lead to sickness, permanent injury, or death. All plant substances, whether used internally or externally, may cause allergic reactions in certain people. We recommend that you consult a qualified healthcare professional before making any decisions about treatment for any illnesses. The Author and/or Publisher are not responsible for persons harmed by using plants and formulas described in this text. This fictitious story is for entertainment only.

For Susan Canaday.

Table of Contents

Characters You Will Meet...7

Prologue: The Arrival...15

Chapter 1 – Green Rock...19

Chapter 2 – Raid...49

Chapter 3 – Shaman...74

Chapter 4 – Crystal Vision...98

Chapter 5 – Rites of Passage...127

Chapter 6 – Thunder River...149

Chapter 7 – Bald Eagle...172

Chapter 8 – Journey...195

Chapter 9 – Good Medicine...218

Chapter 10 – Panther...243

Chapter 11 – Medicine Wolf...263

Chapter 12 – Canoe...282

Chapter 13 – Cahokia...305

Chapter 14 – Lost & Exiled...325

Chapter 15 – White Feather...346

Chapter 16 – Wedding...358

Chapter 17 – Booger Dance...380

Chapter 18 – Warrior...401

Author's Note...425

References & Suggested Reading...433

Characters You Will Meet:

(in alphabetical order, for use as a reference)

NOTE: Unless otherwise mentioned, all characters are clan members of the Cherokee.

Acorn – Green Rock's Bird Clan aunt, Squirrel Fur's sister.

Alligator – Leader of the Karankawas River Wolf stayed with.

Antler Tine – Titmouse's boyfriend.

Arrowhead – Tickanwatic (Tonkawa) hunter that River Wolf meets after leaving the Karankawas.

Autumn Leaf – Panther's first wife (Muskogee) – lives in the village of Good Medicine.

Badger – An acquaintance of Fox Claw and Buck.

Bald Eagle – Muskogee tribe trader who frequented the village in his dugout canoe, and later took River Wolf on his first trading excursion, during which Bald Eagle was killed.

Bear Claw Necklace – Chickasaw hunter – Walking Thunder's son.

Beaver Pelt – River Wolf's (Green Rock's) first wife. Long Hair Clan.

Beaver Tooth – Young Bird Clan boy who schemed with Running Fox during a childhood war game. Excellent at tracking.

Bent Stick – Muskogee (Creek) younger brother of the little girl, Red Stone.

Birch Trunk – Father of Frog and Fawn. Fishbone's husband. River Wolf stayed with them in Dogwood Creek after finding Buck dead.

Blue Jay – Shaman from Eagle Peak, who commissioned River Wolf to make a chunkey player effigy pipe for his village.

Bone Flute – Calusa trader who Buck and River Wolf travel with out to sea.

Broken Spear – Sparrow's second husband, Wild Potato Clan.

Buck (The Buck Kicks the Drum) – Wolf Tail's adult name. A flintknapper, and a traveling trader, best friends with River Wolf (Green Rock).

Buck Horn – Muskogee (Creek) Red Stone's other boyfriend from the village of Good Medicine.

Catfish – Karankawa hunter who River Wolf first meets after hurricane.

Clam – The Calusa, Watersnake's dead wife.

Corn Leaf – Elder Bird Clan woman, who held the title of Honored Woman before being replaced by Sparrow. Tanager's mother was Corn Leaf.

Cottontail – Karankawa woman who River Wolf befriended.

Crooked Arrow – Blue Clan boy who would grow up to be renamed, Song of the Wind, a mighty warrior.

Dances Like the Deer – Eagle Medicine's Wolf Clan wife. White Feather's mother.

Dead Buzzard Warrior – Muskogee (Creek) enemy of Panther and River Wolf. Also lived in Good Medicine.

Deer Skin – Muskogee (Creek) the mother of the little girl, Red Stone.

Doe – Stone Spear's long dead wife.

Eagle Medicine – The Shaman who was taught by Red Talon, and who later succeeded him. Upon his death, he was replaced by Three Crows. Eagle Medicine was of the Paint Clan and was Green Rock's instructor during his training for the priesthood. Father of White Feather.

Eagle Tail Feather – Unknown clan – made the blowgun that Elk Antler gave to his son, Green Rock.

Elk Antler – Green Rock's (River Wolf's) Blue Clan father.

Fawn – Timid daughter of Birch Trunk and Fishbone. River Wolf befriends her at Dogwood Creek.

Fern – Wife of the Muskogee trader Water Beetle. They adopted Running Fox into Muskogee tribe after buying him from the Yuchi.

Fire Arrow – The person who succeeded Standing Bear as Uku, or the principal chief of Birch Mountain.

Fish – Muskogee (Creek) older brother of the young girl, Red Stone.

Fishbone – Birch Trunk's wife, Frog and Fawn's mother. Lived in the village of Dogwood Creek.

Fox Claw – Deer Clan man who cons Green Rock (River Wolf) into making a pipe for him without paying for it.

Frog – Birch Trunk and Fishbone's son. Fawn's older brother. Lived in the village of Dogwood Creek.

Gar Scale – Chief of the Alabama Koasati village of Red Oak.

Goldfinch – Muskogee (Creek) maiden from the village of Leaning Oak. River Wolf and Goldfinch were fond of each other.

Grandma – Beaver Pelt's grandmother, whose name remains a mystery. Long Hair Clan.

Great Sun – The Chief or leader of Sun Village (known today as Cahokia).

Green Rock – River Wolf, as a child. Bird Clan.

Groundsquirrel – Payaya (Coahuiltecan) man who plotted to kill River Wolf over a love triangle with Laurel.

Jaguar – Mayan Shaman who lives among the Muskogee (Creeks) at the village of Good Medicine.

Jumping Deer – Snow Bear's war game chief – Wolf Clan.

Kicking Elk – The person who preceded Standing Bear as Uku, or the principal chief of Birch Mountain.

Kingfisher – Calusa trader that River Wolf and Bald Eagle met as they passed by in the river.

Large Fish – Calusa trader who helped navigate River Wolf back to familiar territory after River Wolf spent ten years with the Coahuiltecans.

Laurel – Payaya (Coahuiltecan) woman whom River Wolf befriends and develops a fondness for.

Limping Wolf – One of Snow Bear's playmates in the war games.

Linden – An elder who let Buck stay with him at his lodge in Eagle Peak after Birch Mountain was burned to the ground.

Loner – Muskogee (Creek) hermit who suffered from schizophrenia. He lived alone at a prime flint source, receiving trinkets by traders who visited to obtain flint.

Mallard – Chickasaw hunter from River Village.

Medicine Wolf – Retired Biloxi trader who helps River Wolf get back home. Medicine Wolf's daughter, Sand Dollar lives with him on their island.

Mole – A friendly Alabama Koasati woman who spent a night with River Wolf on a trading excursion.

Moon – Panther and Sand Dollar's daughter. Long Hair Clan.

Moonbeam – Arrowhead's wife. Tonkawa.

Mouse – Twisted Stick's wife. Wild Potato Clan.

Mouse Eyes – Chickasaw woman with whom River Wolf had feelings for, but circumstances didn't permit a relationship. Widow of Woodpecker.

Mushroom – River Wolf's only surviving child. Daughter of Redbird from Eagle Peak. She was born after River Wolf's death. Through her, River Wolf's seed survived.

Oyster – Catfish's Karankawa friend.

Paint Pot – Bird Clan leader.

Panther – Running Fox's adult name. River Wolf's long lost younger brother.

Pearl – Muskogee woman at Dead Hickory. Her deceased father had been a captive Cherokee warrior, captured, enslaved and then became a Muskogee.

Prancing Deer – The man, from Dogwood Creek, who replaced Fire Arrow as Uku, or the principal chief of the Cherokees.

Puppy – A wolf pup brought home by Broken Spear. Puppy was Raccoon's (another dog) grandmother.

Raccoon – Snow Bear's dog, granddaughter of Puppy.

Red Bone – Medicine Wolf's brother – Biloxi tribe.

Red Stone – Eleven-year-old Muskogee (Creek) girl who was very talkative. She was lost in the woods and rescued by River Wolf and Bald Eagle. She lived in the village of Wolf Creek.

Red Talon – The Shaman who preceded (and trained) Eagle Medicine.

Redbird – River Wolf's girlfriend, and mother of River Wolf's daughter, Mushroom.

River Wolf – Green Rock's adult name. Bird Clan artist and trader whose life story is the focus of this novel.

Running Fox – Green Rock's younger brother – Bird Clan. His adult name is Panther.

Runs Away Screaming – Chickasaw hunter from River Village.

Rutting Buck – Muskogee (Creek) Chief of Wolf Creek village.

Sand Dollar – The Biloxi, Medicine Wolf's daughter, Panther's second wife. She was very timid.

Seagull – Calusa trader that River Wolf and Bald Eagle meet and spend the day with on the beach.

Six-Lined Racer – Payaya (Coalhuiltecan) hunter that River Wolf met after leaving the Tonkawas and spending the winter in the canyon.

Snow Bear – River Wolf and White Feather's son.

Song of the Wind – Crooked Arrow's adult name. Cherokee warrior and ball player.

Sparrow – Turtle Shell's Long Hair Clan wife, a loving influence to the family, and later held the title of Honored Woman.

Squirrel Fur – Green Rock and Running Fox's Bird Clan mother.

Standing Bear – The Uku, or principal chief of the Cherokee capital, Birch Mountain, preceded by Kicking Elk, and succeeded by Fire Arrow.

Stomping Bison – Chickasaw hunter from River Village located on the Big Muddy River.

Stone Axe – Titmouse's husband.

Stone Spear – Drunken Blue Clan flintknapper who taught Wolf Tail his trade.

Tanager – Buck's wife, Titmouse's mother, Corn Leaf's daughter. She became the Honored Woman after Sparrow's death. Bird Clan.

The Duck Flies By – Beaver Pelt's mother, Long Hair Clan.

The Raven Calls – Muskogee (Creek) the father of the little girl, Red Stone.

Three Crows – Eagle Medicine's Shaman trainee (after Green Rock eloped from training).

Titmouse – Buck and Tanager's daughter, Bird Clan.

Tobacco Leaf – Alabama Koasati maiden from Red Oak village; rejected by River Wolf.

Turkey – Beaver Pelt's aunt, Long Hair Clan.

Turkey Caller – Muskogee (Creek) Shaman, Red Stone's uncle.

Turtle Shell – Green Rock and Running Fox's uncle (Squirrel Fur's little brother). Sparrow's first husband.

Turtle Shell Rattle – Chickasaw hunter from River Village.

Twisted Stick – Sparrow's younger brother. Long Hair Clan. A hunter who provided soapstone for young Green Rock.

Two Bears – Muskogee (Creek) one of Red Stone's boyfriends. Lives in the village of Wolf Creek.

Walking Thunder – Chickasaw hunter who leads River Wolf, Buck, Bone Flute, and Watersnake to the Chickasaw village.

Water Beetle – A Muskogee Trader from Good Medicine who bought Running Fox from the Yuchi. Water Beetle and wife Fern later adopted Running Fox into the Muskogee tribe.

Waterfowl – A man who let Panther stay in his lodge at Eagle Peak after destruction of Birch Mountain.

Watersnake – Bone Flute's Calusa companion who travels with River Wolf and Buck.

White Feather – The infant that ten-year-old Green Rock rescued from the burning lodge. She would eventually grow up and become his second wife and mother their son. Wolf Clan daughter of Eagle Medicine.

Wildflower – Beaver Pelt's older sister, Long Hair Clan.

Winged Rattlesnake Chief – Panther's Muskogee (Creek) nemesis. A sleazy character who lived in Good Medicine. Very formidable.

Wolf Tail – Orphaned Blue Clan friend who as a child, lived with Green Rock and his family. His adult name is The Buck Kicks the Drum, or Buck for short. River Wolf's (Green Rock's best friend).

Wood Duck – Muskogee (Creek) brother of Bald Eagle. Lives in the village of Good Medicine.

Woodcarver – Twisted Stick and Mouse's son.

Woodpecker – Deceased husband of Chickasaw woman, Mouse Eyes.

Conch Shell Cup for the White Drink.
Engraved with the Birdman Motif.
Redrawn from Reader's Digest 1986.

Prologue: The Arrival

"I am River Wolf. The end has come. I am here. My ego fading, I once again truly see the past, present and future, as it was always destined to be. In the early days, I can see our land was locked in perpetual icy winter. The very oceans receded, making dry land from what was seabed. The evaporated water from the sea fell as freezing rain and snow, forming ice, covering much of our land."

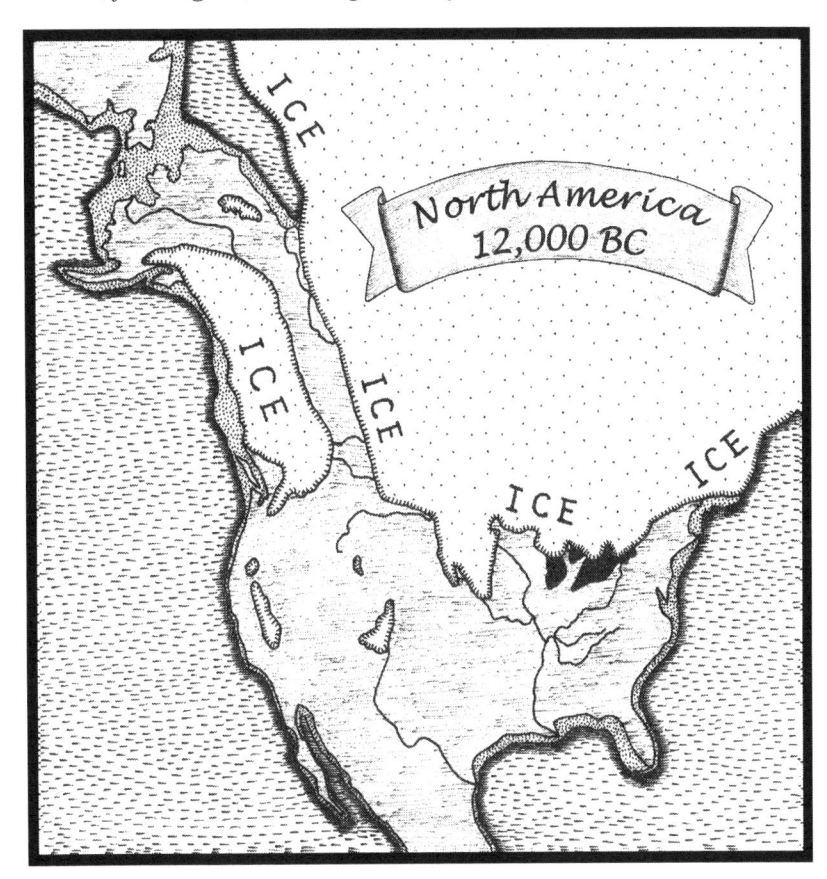

Redrawn from Lewis & Kneberg 1958.

"The Ancient Ones migrated over newly exposed dry land that brought together old and new worlds. Over thousands of cycles, our people came in waves from the other side of the circle of the Earth, and into this new world of plenty. They found an unexplored virgin realm where massive behemoths lived. Bravery and hunger as their companions, our people hunted monsters to live."

Animals of Ice Age North America

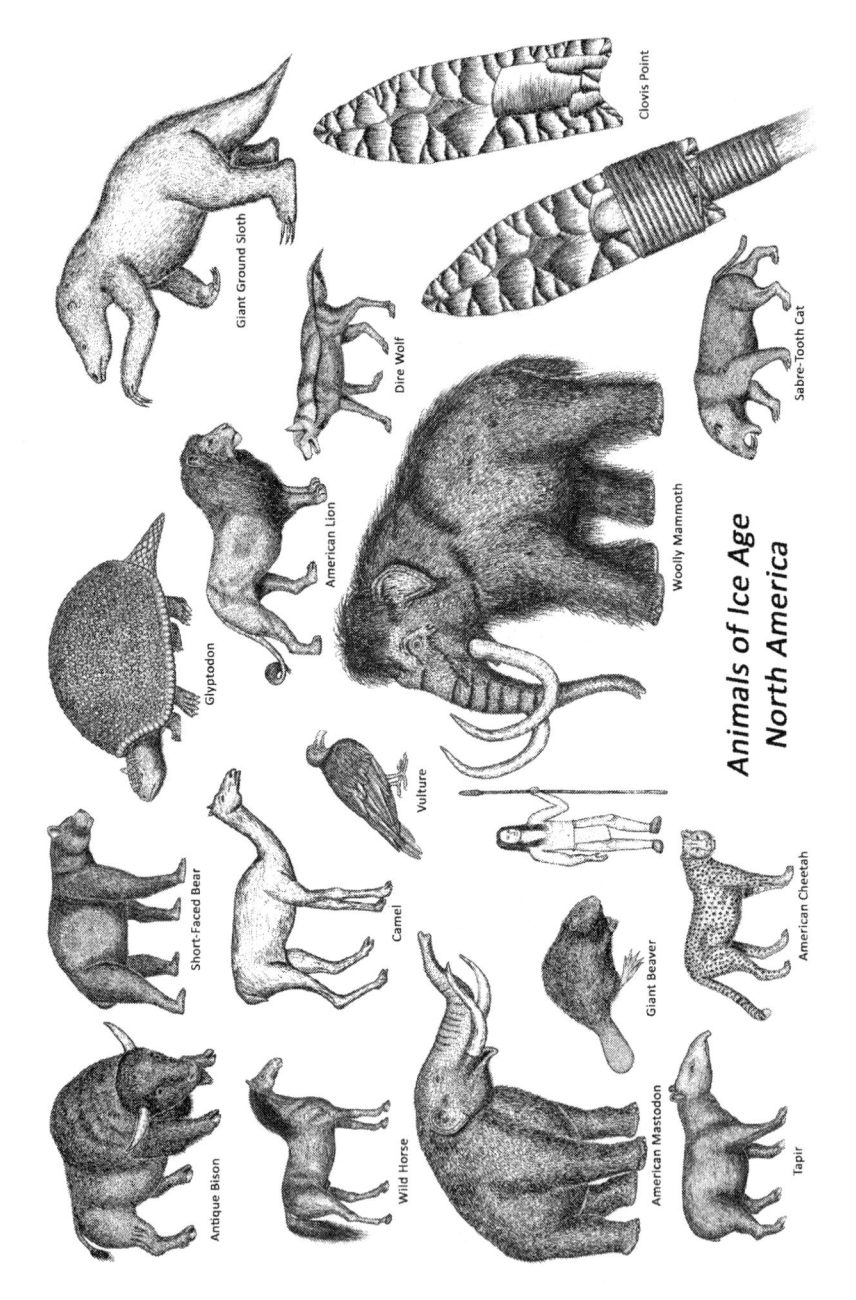

Redrawn from Various Sources.

Fluting a Clovis Point.

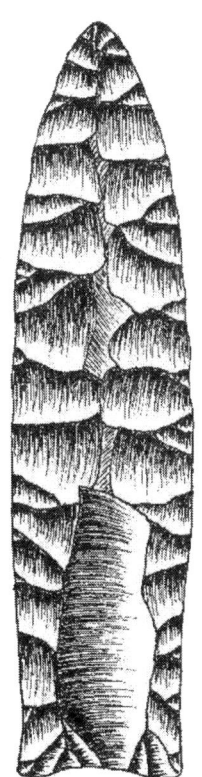

Redrawn from Van Buren 1974.

"The weapons of these hunters were lethal and effective, but took extraordinary skill to make. I see the most distinctive feature of these weapons as the unique thinning techniques applied to forming the bases of their spearheads. Known to our people as fluting, these long and wide channels were bloodletting grooves, also intended to facilitate mounting them into spears. Their skill in flint work was far better than ours.

"Because these flutes were the result of striking off just a single chip of flint, forming them was simple and quick, but still required much skill to accomplish without breaking the unfinished spearhead in half. The makers of these fluted points hunted the giant animals until they were no more. They spread across our land – into mountains, deserts and forests, swamps, seashores and prairies, but, as with the giants that had once roamed our land, even their memory would become obscured in time, until they became forgotten, even by us, their descendants. Until now...

"There followed their seed, the many nations or tribes of people over the next thousands of cycles. Finally there appeared the first of the Mound

Builders. *Their first mounds were conical and circular burial mounds and even ceremonial mounds in the forms of animal, reptile and bird effigies.*

Building an Earthen Mound.

"Centuries after, close to the time our people first used the bow and arrow, there began the practice of temple mound building. It was out of this group that my tribe, the Cherokee, sprang forth."

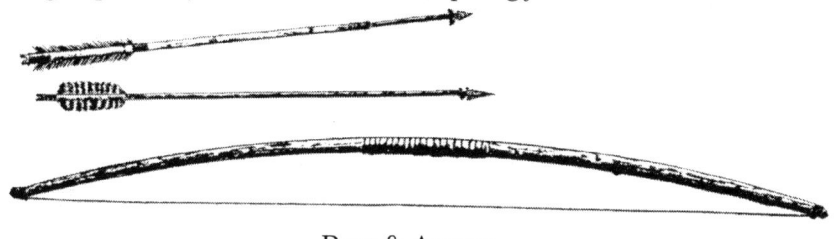

Bow & Arrows.

"I have arrived with a story to tell, for any soul whom it would interest. Now that I have told you of my people's proud past; I shall now tell you of the tragedy of mine. I began as a foolish youth named Green Rock, who later became River Wolf. My folly led to the demise of my family, the people I loved. Embarrassed as I am at my cowardice, I have to tell it all, so you might learn from my naivety. Out of shame, I must tell you this story as though from another person's view, although I cannot escape that this can never hide the truth about me. May it spare you of suffering. May you gain wisdom from these, my final words, and learn the lessons I couldn't. And so my story begins..."

Chapter 1: Green Rock

The Smoky Mountains – 1307 AD

The ominous thunderhead slowly moved towards the east over the rugged landscape. Elk Antler labored over the steep foothills, carrying the deer he had shot and gutted. "No chance of reaching Birch Mountain and staying dry," he muttered under his breath. Not long after, the cool rain began to beat down on him. After seeking shelter in a small cave he knew of in the side of a nearby cliff, he loosened the taught sinew string on his bow – the pitch coating would provide some protection from the rain, but the bowstring would soon break when damp and under pressure.

It was beginning to get dark. Now the rain grew intense, and brought heavy gusts of wind and frequent lightning. Mother Earth was replenishing herself, but Elk Antler was greatly annoyed about the delay this was causing him. He would have to spend the night here.

Meanwhile in Birch Mountain, the capital village of the Cherokee, Elk Antler's family was preparing for the coming storm, which obscured the setting Sun. After this was done, Green Rock, his younger brother Running Fox, and their best friend, Wolf Tail resumed working on repairing the small blunt-tipped arrows used in their childhood game of mock combat.

Green Rock and Running Fox's mother, Squirrel Fur, stood in the doorway of the lodge, watching the rain begin to fall. "It looks like Father won't be back tonight," she said as the rain fell harder. "Green Rock," she said. "How should you treat any weapon?"

"With great respect," he replied.

"Then why do you leave your bow, that Father made, in the rain?"

He immediately ran outside where the toy bow was leaning against the lodge wall, and brought it inside. It was only a toy, but all aspects of the war games were taken seriously because they honed the children's battle skills, and prepared them for adult situations. But Green Rock was ten cycles old, and children were allowed their mistakes so they could learn from them.

As he was sitting back down, he heard a thumping sound, announcing that his bowstring had broken. He had also forgotten to loosen it.

"Now you have to make another one if you are going to play tomorrow," Running Fox said.

"Why don't you fix your arrow?" Green Rock retorted.

Wolf Tail silently chuckled. He knew that Green Rock was not very interested in the war games. Green Rock was usually preoccupied with more artistic endeavors. Most of his free time was spent carving figures, and even small crude pipes, out of the local dark green soapstone – hence his name. Many of the villagers, including his brother, teased him because he was lacking somewhat in his skills as a warrior, and was "wasting time doodling with rocks."

Squirrel Fur's Namesake, the Red Squirrel.
Adapted & redrawn from a public domain image.

Squirrel Fur and her relatives thought he had extraordinary talent with stone, but Elk Antler had expectations of his son becoming a mighty warrior. In the tribe of the Cherokee, the clan of the mother's side of the family was the clan that the children belonged to, and Squirrel Fur was of the Bird Clan. Green Rock's fellow clansmen were supportive of his aspiration to be an artisan, but his father, Elk Antler, would not hear of it. Officially, he had no say in the matter, though he strongly but silently objected, and had ways of letting Green Rock know about it.

The rain poured down over Birch Mountain, and the gusts of wind rocked the walls of every lodge in the village. The lightning began to intensify and strike closer. The thunder made the children jump. Running Fox and Wolf Tail continued working on their toy weapons, while Green Rock started to fiddle with a small piece of black soapstone that he'd found earlier that morning.

Suddenly, a terrific bolt of lightning lit up the sky, startling everybody and striking a nearby tree. They screamed as the tree fell into the back corner of the lodge, and made a large hole in the side and roof. The deafening thunder shook the whole village.

Squirrel Fur and the children quickly moved the blankets and bedding from the exposed corner into a drier area. Her brother, Turtle Shell, and his wife appeared in the doorway and offered their help. "I don't think we can do anymore until the morning," replied Squirrel Fur. "It is a little crowded in here now though."

Turtle Shell's wife, Sparrow said, "We have room for Green Rock and Wolf Tail to spend the night in our lodge." Turtle Shell nodded in agreement.

"We'll get some of our clan together in the morning to help you repair your lodge," added Turtle Shell.

"Thank you so much," said Squirrel Fur with a smile.

"I want to help too," Wolf Tail volunteered. Wolf Tail was orphaned the previous summer when Birch Mountain was raided by a war party of the Yuchi, whose territory was two days journey towards the Southeast. They killed his father and his Blue Clan mother to prevent her screams from alerting the rest of the village. Then they shot fire arrows over the palisade, which burned down five lodges including Wolf Tail's home. Then the Yuchi warriors disappeared into the night. Elk Antler, and several other villagers who had lost loved ones or property during the attack on Birch Mountain, had later avenged the attack. Elk Antler was of the Blue Clan and, because of this and the strong friendship between Wolf Tail and Elk Antler's two sons, the family took in Wolf Tail. This was fitting, as they were like brothers.

Now, at the age of thirteen cycles, Wolf Tail felt a strong obligation to help the family when it was needed, but the family did not expect it from him anymore than they would have from any other family member.

After getting inside of Turtle Shell's lodge, Sparrow gave Green Rock and Wolf Tail each a large piece of cornbread and some dried meat. It was good, and the lodge was a warm and dry refuge from the pouring rain outside.

Turtle Shell got out his pipe and began to fill the bowl. This attracted Green Rock's attention. "Someday I will make a pipe like that," he said, "but I want to make effigy pipes."

"Why not now?" Turtle Shell asked.

"I don't know if I can."

"Well, you can't unless you try," and with that, Turtle Shell pulled out the most beautiful piece of dark green soapstone Green Rock had ever seen. It was very large – perfect for making more than one pipe like Turtle Shell's – and was of the finest quality.

"Where did you find that?" asked Green Rock.

"A half a day northeast of here, during yesterday's hunting trip. There is a whole mountain of it there."

"It sure is nice – you could make three pipes out of it."

"Take it."

"It's for me?"

"Make me a fine bird effigy pipe for hauling it home, and keep the rest of it. Make yourself two others for bartering when the next trader arrives." Turtle Shell then took a twig from the fire and lit his pipe.

Green Rock was speechless. This was partly because he did not think he had the skill to carve an effigy pipe of the quality of Turtle Shell's. He had also never even considered actually trading his work to a real live trader from a distant land. Not that he was opposed to the idea, but he simply felt inadequate.

Wolf Tail stared at the piece of soapstone with admiration. He smiled at Green Rock, knowing how this arrangement would please him.

However, after some thought, Green Rock finally said, "I don't think I can carve a pipe as nice as yours right now – especially an effigy pipe."

"Any pipe made by my nephew will be nice enough," replied Turtle Shell. "I just want you to try. If you can't carve the bird on it, try to engrave it on the pipe. I have seen your animal carvings, they are small, but I know you walk on the path of a fine artist," and he puffed some more on his pipe. The fragrant smoke filled the lodge.

The storm raged on, as they went to bed. Long after everybody else was asleep, Green Rock just lay there pondering over the day's events, particularly the conversation with his uncle. He didn't want to let him down, but he was still apprehensive about it. Eventually he drifted off to sleep.

Green Rock was awakened by a tap on the shoulder from Sparrow. There was nobody else inside the lodge. "I almost overslept," yawned Green Rock.

"You were up late," replied Sparrow. "I heard you – you had a restless night, didn't you?"

"Yes, I was thinking about what Turtle Shell said."

"You know he was right, don't you?"

"I don't know – but I will give it a try."

Sparrow smiled and hugged her nephew. They went outside, and joined the other villagers at the river for morning bathing and prayers to the rising Sun.

When they returned, Green Rock saw for the first time the extent of the damage to his family's lodge. He had never realized how large that tree was! Fortunately, the main trunk and the heaviest branches missed the lodge. They had all been very lucky – if that tree had fallen much more to the south, both of their lodges would have been smashed and the people inside might have been crushed.

As it was, the branches that did the damage were small enough to be cut with axes, or simply broken off. Turtle Shell was busy chopping the heavy branches with a stone axe, while Wolf Tail was breaking up the smaller ones. Green Rock joined Wolf Tail in breaking up the smaller branches. "Well, at least we will have plenty of firewood," Wolf Tail commented.

Sparrow left the immediate area to recruit some volunteers from other areas of the village to help lighten their workloads. As Green Rock worked, he noticed how the lightning had split the mighty trunk into tiny splinters. It amazed him. Three volunteers from the Bird and Blue Clans arrived with Sparrow, and then what seemed to be a rigorous chore turned out to be much fun as the volunteers were in great spirits. They told jokes and everybody was in a great mood and laughing. It made the work seem to go by much faster. The portions of the tree that would have interfered with the repairs on the lodge were completely out of the way by the time that Elk Antler arrived with the deer from his hunting trip. One of the volunteers went to help Elk Antler, Squirrel Fur, and Sparrow finish dressing the deer.

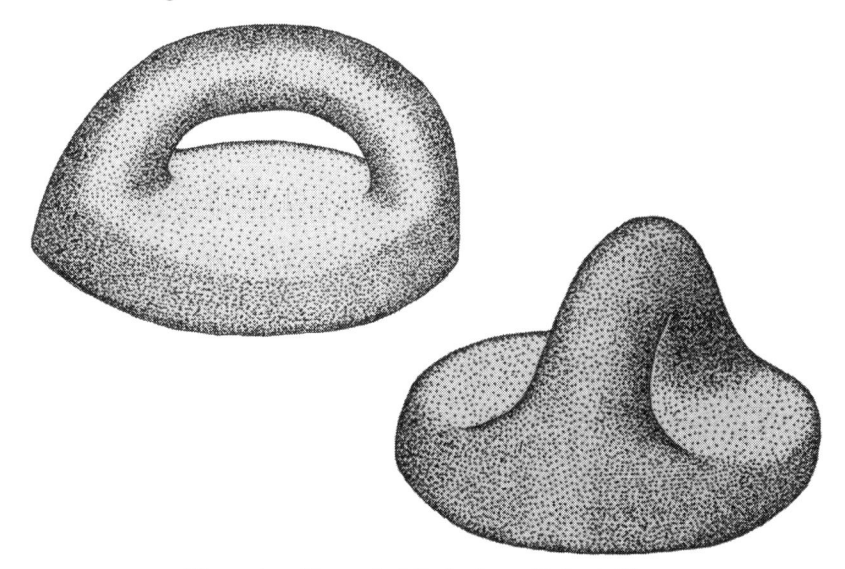

Plastering Trowels Made from Baked Clay.
Redrawn from Thruston 1897.

The other two assisted Turtle Shell and the children in repairing the lodge. They had to replace the corner post, and repair the cane wall and apply a new coating of clay over it, smoothing it out with plastering trowels made from baked clay.

Applying Clay Daub onto Cane Wattle to
Form Weatherproof Wall of Lodge.

    This clay, along with the clay for the wall came from a small manmade pond just outside the palisade that surrounded the village. It was beginning to get dark by the time this was done, and all they needed to do was patch the roof the next morning. They would not need the volunteers' help anymore, so they sent them on their ways – each with some firewood and venison.
    That night, Green Rock visited a flint knapper that Wolf Tail had told him about by the name of Stone Spear. He hoped that he could obtain some thin flakes of flint. These he could serrate and use for saws for cutting the large piece of soapstone that Turtle Shell had given him. The old flint knapper was not in a good mood, since he had just broken a five-inch knife that he was thinning right when Green Rock arrived.
    "What do you want?!" he gruffly said.
    "I am sorry to disturb…"
    "Disturb me? You made me waste a good piece of flint! Now, little boy, what *do* you *want*?"
    "Wolf Tail told me to come to you. He said you would have some…"
    "Wolf Tail? Who are you to him?"
    "He has lived with my family and me ever since last summer when his parents were killed."
    "Let me guess… Running Fox?"

"I am Running Fox's older brother."

"Green Rock."

"Yes."

Stone Spear's expression changed from angry to slightly embarrassed. "I think I've seen you around the village a few times, but I didn't know who you were. I am Wolf Tail's flint knapping mentor. He has told me about you – carving animals and things. What do you need?"

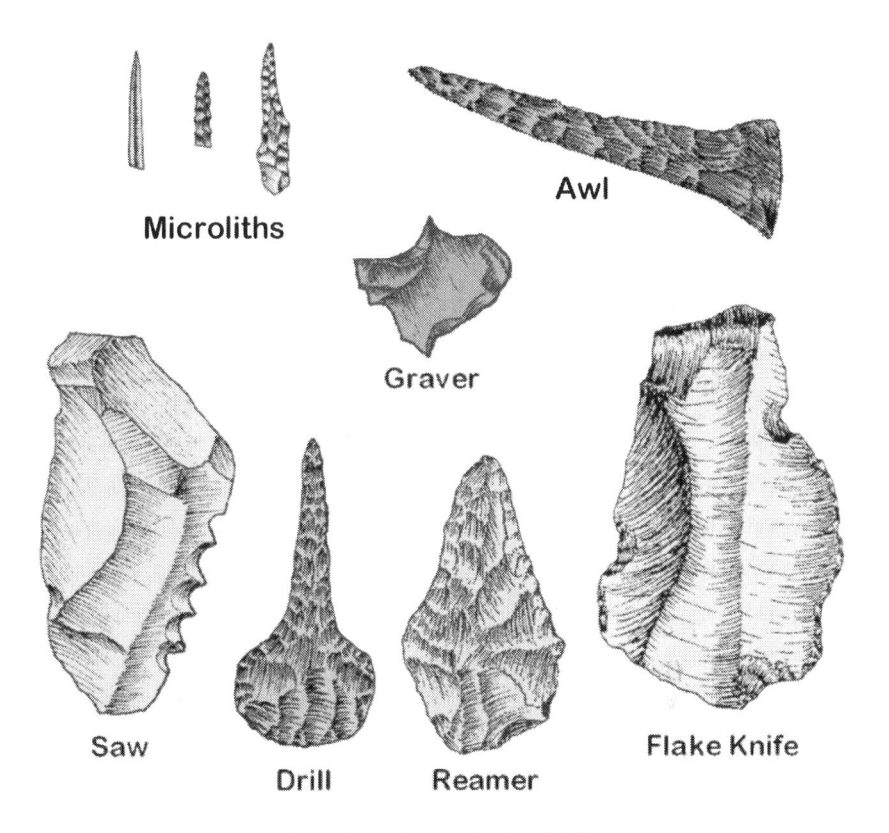

The Pipe Carver's Tool Kit.

"I need some thin flakes of flint so I can serrate them and use them for saws for my stone."

"You won't be able to saw *granite* very easily with *that!* Or with anything else," he said with a chuckle.

"I want to saw *soapstone*."

Now Stone Spear's demeanor was one of annoyance. This intimidated Green Rock. But Stone Spear was more bark than bite, and he simply said: "How many flakes do you need? What size?"

"Whatever you can spare that you think would be good for cutting a piece of soapstone this long, this wide and this thick," Green Rock replied while motioning with his hands. "I need around four."

Stone Spear pointed Green Rock towards the pile of debitage where he had been working. "Pick out what you want."

"Thank you," Green Rock said, as he began to search through the flakes. When he got close to Stone Spear, he noticed a peculiar odor on the old man's breath. "These four will do," he stated.

"You are going to need more than those," Stone Spear said, as he began to dig through the debitage flakes. He found four more and handed them to Green Rock. "Take these – and while you're at it, take *these* too!" he yelled as he handed Green Rock the two pieces of the knife he broke when Green Rock arrived.

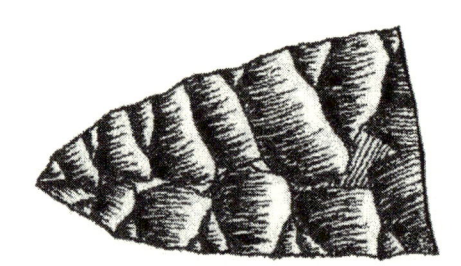

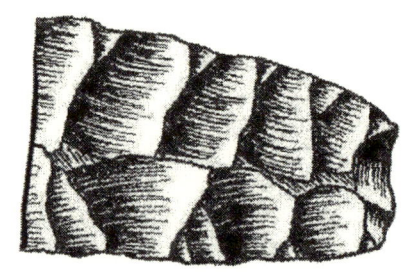

Stone Spear's Broken & Unfinished Flint Knife.

This startled Green Rock, and he did not know how to respond.

"Make drills out of them – you *do* know you need a *drill* to make a *hole*, don't you?" raved Stone Spear.

"Why, yes – I have made pipes before."

"If you need any help making those into drills, just ask Wolf Tail." And with that, Stone Spear reached to his side and picked up a pottery cup and took a drink from it. He gulped for such a long time that Green Rock wondered how he could hold his breath for that long. When Stone Spear emptied the cup, he put it down and let out a loud belch. "If you ever want to learn flint knapping, I'm your man," he said.

"Thank you very much," Green Rock replied politely. At that, Green Rock left and headed back home. On the way, he wondered about Stone Spear. He was mysterious in more than one way. What was that smell? Why was he so loud and bossy? Old men were often very opinionated, but this man took it to the extreme.

When Green Rock arrived home, his mother said that he and Wolf Tail would be spending the night at his uncle's lodge again, because of the mud that remained in the corner of the floor of the lodge from the night before. This was fine with Green Rock, because he wanted to ask

Wolf Tail some questions about the mysterious flint knapper – preferably away from his father.

Green Rock went to his uncle's lodge, and was greeted by his aunt Sparrow, who was grinding corn in the dark. She used a wooden mortar and pestle in a pounding motion. "I am catching up," she said, "Today's work put me behind and we need food tomorrow."

Wooden Mortar & Pestle.

"Do you need any help?" offered Green Rock.

"No, and you need to eat. Turtle Shell has cooked plenty of venison. It's been a long day. Go and get some food. I'll be in after a little while."

Green Rock was indeed extremely hungry. After eating his fill of the succulent deer meat, his thoughts returned to Stone Spear. "Wolf Tail," he said while pulling the flakes and the broken knife preform out of his deerskin pouch.

"I see you have met Stone Spear," Wolf Tail answered. "What did you think of him?"

"He seemed upset with me," replied Green Rock as he showed him the broken knife.

"I can see why!" laughed Wolf Tail.

"I didn't mean to distract him."

"Ah, he will forget all about it tomorrow."

"Why is he so... so *strange*? His breath smelled funny."

Wild Grapes.

"Did you see his unusual vines planted in the clay pots?" asked Turtle Shell after lighting his pipe.

"No, I didn't – I was too busy watching *him*."

At that both Turtle Shell and Wolf Tail burst out laughing.

"What's going on in there?" asked Sparrow from outside. "Are you all making fun of me grinding corn in the dark?"

"Green Rock met Stone Spear," answered Turtle Shell.

They heard Sparrow quietly chuckling outside.

"What about the vines – what are they?" Green Rock asked.

"One of the traders brings him those baby grapevines from very far to the southeast, by the Great Sea," answered Turtle Shell. "He special-orders them to be brought in clay pots once a cycle. He tries to grow them here, but they usually don't survive the winters up here."

"What are they for?"

"Many cycles ago, Stone Spear was a trader before his wife died. He used to go all the way to the Great Sea in the land of a tribe called the Calusa. He traded many different things for whelk shells and other items, which he later traded for flint and chert because flint knapping was his favorite trade. It was the Chief of the Calusa – called the Cacique, who introduced him to those grapes. They brew a strong drink from it that makes your head spin. Stone Spear liked it so much that he learned how to make the drink himself from the grapes.

"After evil spirits took his wife, he asked another trader to bring him those grapevines in clay pots from the land of the Calusa. He trades his spears and knives for them and flint. He invited me to drink some of it one day, but it made me very dizzy and I didn't feel like myself. I don't really remember a lot of things that day, but my head started to hurt very bad so I returned home. I could barely walk in a straight line. I went to sleep before the Sun had gone down. I woke up well after sunrise, and had a terrible headache. The headache eventually went away, but I felt pretty bad for a few days afterwards. I wouldn't advise you to try it. Not that Stone Spear is a bad man, he is rough around the edges, but he means well. It seems to be his way of dealing with life and losing his wife at such a young age. He loved her dearly."

"He knows a lot of interesting tales," Wolf Tail added. "He has been to a lot of places and seen many things that most folks here never see. He is also a good knapping instructor. He taught your father and my father how to pressure flake fine sharp arrow points cycles ago."

"We were not much older than you two," said Turtle Shell.

Sparrow entered the lodge with a skin full of cornmeal. "Are you all still up? I am ready to rest my bones."

"They were telling me the story about Stone Spear's drink," Green Rock said.

"I hope you don't want to try it, Turtle Shell was a mess the day he drank from Stone Spear's cup."

"It couldn't have been *that* bad," Turtle Shell argued.

"It was," she quietly replied, as she started eating some of the deer meat that was now cold. There was a long silence as she ate, and then she went to bed.

"How old is Stone Spear?" asked Green Rock.

"I don't know for sure," stated Wolf Tail. "I think maybe more than thirty-five cycles."

"Forty cycles," confirmed Turtle Shell after lighting his pipe. "Doe went to the Darkening Land fifteen cycles ago – that's a long time to be alone. A long time."

They sat there quiet for a long time, in the light of the coals that remained from the cook fire. It was so peaceful. Green Rock silently hoped that Doe was resting in a peace like tonight was for him.

The Repaired Lodge.

As they retired to their beds, Sparrow said to Turtle Shell, "It will be chilly tonight from last night's rain; you better give the children some extra blankets." Turtle Shell got two bearskins and gave one to each, then lay down in the bed with Sparrow.

The next morning they were all up early as usual. They went down to the river to bathe and say their prayers to the rising Sun. Elk Antler,

Squirrel Fur, and Running Fox gathered the cane leaves for the lodge roof. By the end of the day, the lodge was completely repaired.

That night, Green Rock and Wolf Tail brought their things back from Turtle Shell's lodge – including the large piece of soapstone. When they entered, the first thing Green Rock saw was his father looking over his damaged toy bow. Elk Antler glanced up, and his eyes fell on the piece of soapstone in Green Rock's hand. "I see you have once again neglected your duty as a warrior," Elk Antler said with look of contempt in his eye.

Green Rock's eyes shifted to the floor.

"You should *always* be ready for combat."

"I am sorry."

"It doesn't really matter now, but someday you will have a family to protect, and *you* must be ready. You'd better practice now while you are young, or else you won't amount to anything, and your family will *die!*"

Green Rock stood silent. Wolf Tail could sense that he was hurt by his father's words, but being a child himself, he couldn't do much about it. Running Fox was sitting on his bed with an amused look on his face, and that angered Green Rock.

"So what are you going to do now?" asked Elk Antler.

"I will fix the bow," Green Rock replied in a shameful manner.
"I want to see you with the rest of the children in tomorrow's war games," said Elk Antler. He then picked up a tiny container of sap from a milkweed plant. The roots of this plant were poisonous, but the sap was rubbed on the skin to treat warts, poison ivy, ringworm, and skin eruptions. With care, a decoction was even made for treating gonorrhea. But Elk Antler had a mild case of ringworm, and the Shaman, Red Talon had given him this sap for treating it.

After Elk Antler finished applying it to the affected areas of his arm, he grabbed his flint knapping tools and began pressure flaking a new tip on an arrowhead that a tip that had been nicked from hitting a rock. Since the arrowhead was still mounted on the arrow, it required special care to avoid making the arrowhead come loose in the arrow shaft.

Sometimes Green Rock hated the whole idea of the war games. It was partly because his father practically forced him to participate. Many times his best friend Wolf Tail was on the opposing team because he was of a different clan than Green Rock. Green Rock didn't like shooting arrows at his best friend, even though they were toys. It also kept him from doing what he liked to do, which was carving animals and things out of stone. Sometimes he would sneak off and do some carving but, when his father found out, he got lectured. Sometimes he just wished that he didn't exist.

Green Rock took his toy bow, and began to make the new bowstring. There was plenty of sinew from the deer that Elk Antler had killed the night of the storm. He started to make twine from it, and he was about halfway done when his mother and aunt walked into the lodge with some clay bottles full of some fresh water from the river. Then they began to talk about their plans for tomorrow.

Painted Southeastern Waterbottle.
Redrawn from Moorehead 1900.

Things seemed better then, because Elk Antler wouldn't speak harshly to him in front of his mother. His mood improved and soon he finished the new bowstring. This time he put a heavier coating of pine pitch on it, just in case he accidentally got it wet again. Elk Antler left the lodge to go see a friend of his who had helped in repairing the lodge.

Wolf Tail and Running Fox had been finishing making and repairing their blunt-tipped arrows, while Green Rock had been working on his bow. Wolf Tail gave Green Rock some arrows. He had made some for him. Green Rock smiled and thanked him. Wolf Tail was a good friend.

The next day, many of the children of Birch Mountain were engaged in their game of mock combat – Green Rock, Running Fox, and Wolf Tail included. As usual, Wolf Tail was on the opposite team than Green Rock and his little brother.

The two clans had started their game – each clan had twenty boys deep inside the woods with one clan on each side of the village, so they were about the distance of eight arrow-shot lengths apart.

Running Fox was very enthusiastic. He had emerged as a natural leader for the boys of the Bird Clan in previous games, and now he and Beaver Tooth were working on a scheme to ambush the Blue Clan's boys.

"Why don't we send three of our warriors along Bear River – and they can make plenty of noise. That will attract the enemies into that area," said Running Fox, "Meanwhile, the rest of us will be quietly making our way around the hill that the village is on, and ambush them from behind!"

Beaver Tooth was apprehensive. "Wolf Tail won't fall for it," he replied. "I think it would be too obvious."

"Then we will only send three around the hill to make noise from that direction to confuse them, while the rest of us cross the river and go around on the other side!"

"That sounds good."

"We need to pick the noisiest ones to go first," said Running Fox, as his eyes shifted to Green Rock. "You, and you two, follow the river – make plenty of noise, and keep out of sight. Retreat as they get closer."

An annoyed Green Rock left with the other two.

"You three go around the hill and stay quiet until you hear the other three," Running Fox commanded some others.

After they left, the remaining fourteen crossed the river and very quietly made their way in the thick woods until they were behind the Blue Clan boys. They could hear Green Rock's party making noise by stepping on dry leaves and twigs. They crossed back over and looked for the enemies' tracks. They were reasonably well hidden, but Beaver Tooth was a good tracker, and that enabled him to tell that the Blue Clan had also split up, each party investigating each source of the noise. It looked as though the majority had gone to investigate the three posted on the other side of the hill away from the river instead of Green Rock's party. Wolf Tail had grown suspicious and advised his war chief, Crooked Arrow to do this.

Running Fox decided that all fourteen members of his remaining party should follow the majority of the Blue Clan, and attack them from behind. Then there were war whoops ahead in the direction of the far side of the hill. The Blue Clan must have located the party that Running Fox had stationed there. No need for silence now, the fight was on! Running Fox's party began to run in that direction, and was soon shooting arrows at the Blue Clan boys from behind.

Green Rock and the other two members of his party had retreated as they were told. By the time the battle had started, they had joined the other three stationed on the other side of the hill.

The Blue Clan was caught by surprise and within a short time many of them (including Wolf Tail) had been hit by the Bird Clan's arrows, which came from behind. They scattered. But the remaining four boys of the Blue Clan, who had separated in order to investigate the noises made by Green Rock's party, had scattered also. The three parties of the Bird Clan were now reunited. None of them had been hit. Neither Running Fox nor Green Rock knew exactly how many enemies were left, or where they were located at this time.

Green Rock suddenly felt a powerful thump in his back. He had been hit! Four more enemy arrows were loosed, narrowly missing Running Fox and one of the other boys. The other two arrows hit two more, taking them out of the game. Running Fox shouted, "There they are! Get them!" There were loud war whoops as they all rushed the enemies except for Green Rock and the other two who were now "dead" according to the rules of the game. The remaining Blue Clan boys had regrouped and circled around and attacked the overconfident Bird Clan from behind.

Green Rock got up and started back to the village, while the eleven "dead" Blue Clan boys followed the battle to see what the outcome would be. He saw Wolf Tail, who had also been hit by an arrow. "I see that you died too!" laughed Wolf Tail, as he got back up. "How many on your team got hit?" he asked.

"Three including me," replied Green Rock. "Father won't be too happy."

"I got shot too," replied Wolf Tail, "and I represented his clan."

They later learned that the Bird Clan had won the game, losing a total of sixteen, while the Blue Clan lost all twenty of their boys. As it turned out, Green Rock had an important role in the Bird Clan's victory, as it was his decision for his party to join the three on the other side of the hill – alert for the four enemies who were following them. It was Green Rock who gave the first war whoop to alert their comrades before the majority of the Blue Clan arrived. He had heard them split up.

Because of this, Running Fox's main party had managed to catch up with the main body of the Blue Clan before they reached Green Rock and the other five. That was good, because Green Rock's party of six was preoccupied with the enemies that had followed him and the other two to that location.

Green Rock felt that he had been lucky in that respect, even though the arrow had hit him. He hoped Elk Antler would be pleased with the outcome.

After arriving home at midday, Green Rock, Wolf Tail and Running Fox ate a hearty meal of cornbread and venison that Squirrel Fur and Sparrow had prepared. They knew there would be three very hungry boys after the game was over. How right they were! All three of the boys wanted seconds, Green Rock and Wolf Tail each ate three helpings.

Squirrel Fur and Sparrow left to fetch more water from the river, taking their large clay pots with them.

When the children finished eating, Green Rock went straight towards the stone his uncle had given him. He grabbed his deerskin pouch and got the best flake of flint out, and borrowed Wolf Tail's antler tine and began serrating the flake along the edge. In a few minutes he had a saw for cutting the soapstone. Then he picked up the soapstone and began examining it, deciding where to begin sawing.

Elk Antler entered the lodge with a newly made cane blowgun that had several darts in one end. "I see you are back to carving stone again," he said. Green Rock's eyes met the floor. "You did good today," added Elk Antler. "If that had been real life, you would have died with honor."

Green Rock glanced back at his father who was smiling at him. "How did you find out?" asked Green Rock.

"I spoke with Crooked Arrow; he told me how you outsmarted him and the others. So I stopped by Eagle Tail Feather's lodge and traded some arrow points I knapped this morning for this blowgun. Take it. It's yours."

Green Rock was shocked. He took the blowgun and didn't know exactly what to say.

"I have to go," Elk Antler said. "I still have several arrow points that I need to trade for feathers and flint chips."

"Are you going to Stone Spear's for the flint?"

"Yes. How did you know?"

"I didn't, I just know that he has plenty. Do you drink his wild grape drink?"

"No, not anymore, and don't try it yourself. He may offer it to you, but do not take it. I have got to go. I am proud of you, Green Rock. I'll see you tonight."

This was so unusual for Green Rock's father to approve of his behavior. He decided to try making Elk Antler proud again by killing a rabbit for him and then presenting it to him. But he needed to practice first, as this would be his first kill. In the meantime, he had pipes to carve. This turned out to be one of the happiest days of his life.

* * *

Several days later, Green Rock was polishing his first effigy pipe, while Wolf Tail watched. All he had to do was ream out the bowl once he finished polishing the rest of the pipe. This was by far the best stone carving he had ever done, so much that he felt some reluctance to give it to his uncle, Turtle Shell. He had worked for so long on it! The fine-grained soapstone polished to a glossy finish, and had few if any impurities at all in it. He had worked extra hard to make it symmetrical.

The polishing was now finished, now he had to ream out the bowl. "Wolf Tail," he said. "Can you show me how to make the reamer?"

"I will make it for you," replied Wolf Tail.

"No, show me. I want to learn flint knapping myself."

"I will show you then, but don't be disappointed with your first try."

So, Wolf Tail gave Green Rock his first knapping lesson, and Green Rock made his first reamer out of the basal half of the knife that Stone Spear had broken the night Green Rock had met him. The reamer was crude, but it did the job. Green Rock, like most boys his age knew some very basic flint knapping, but had a lot to learn. He decided to take lessons from Stone Spear if he was willing to teach him.

Green Rock mounted the reamer in a shaft with pine pitch and sinew to hold it in place. Then he held it between his hands and rubbed his hands back and forth, the shaft in between, as if he were making a fire. He had used a bow drill before, but for him it was very awkward, and he wasn't taking any chances with *this* pipe.

In a short time the bowl was formed, and Green Rock was blowing the dust out of the bowl from the stem. To him, it looked as if he were smoking it as the dust blew upwards.

Now he took it outside the village to the river and washed it thoroughly to remove all of the dust. Then he went back to his family's lodge and rubbed it with bear grease while heating it over the fire. He did this repeatedly until the full color of the stone showed, and it had a glossy finish.

Green Rock wanted to surprise Turtle Shell, so he went to his lodge to make sure he was not home. Sparrow welcomed him in, and said that Turtle Shell had gone hunting. "Oh, good," said Green Rock.

"Don't you like your uncle?" asked Sparrow with a frown.

"Yes, but I have a surprise for him. I'll be right back."

He ran back home and got the pipe and returned to Sparrow with the pipe in his hand. "Here it is."

"Oh, that is so *beautiful*," she said, with a look of admiration. "Did you carve this?"

"Yes, it's for Turtle Shell."

"Green Rock, you should do this for a living! I know your father may object, but we will talk to him about it. You are just amazing!"

"Do you think Turtle Shell will like it?"

"I am sure he will *love* it! You really did a fine job, especially for a little boy your age! The Spirits have given you a gift with stone."

"I wanted to surprise him by putting it somewhere where he will find it, and not let him know about it.

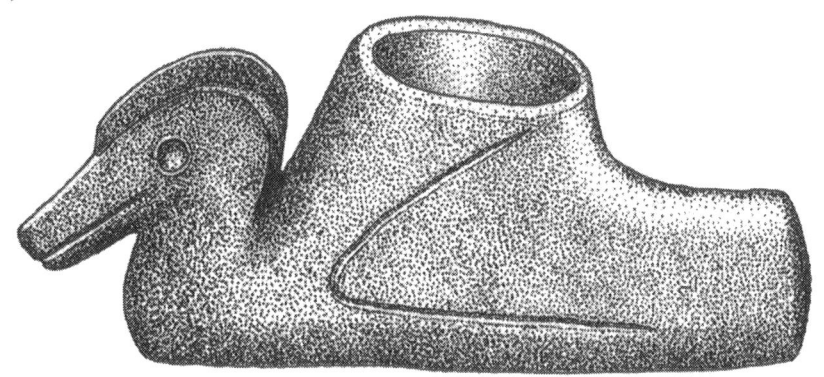

Turtle Shell's Bird Effigy Pipe – Carved by Green Rock.
Redrawn from Thruston 1897.

Sparrow smiled. "Let's hide his other pipe, and replace it with this one. He will then find it when he wants to smoke."

"Good idea," answered Green Rock with a look of anticipation. "I still have enough for two more for the trader – but tomorrow I want to kill a rabbit with my blowgun that father gave me."

"Carve the other two pipes first, or you may miss the trader next time he comes to Birch Mountain."

"Okay, I'll start now," said Green Rock, and then he returned home. When he got there, his mother was preparing dinner.

"Do you need any help?" asked Green Rock.

"No, but Wolf Tail told me you were just about finished with the bird effigy pipe. Show it to me," she said.

"I can't, I finished it and left it with Sparrow to surprise Turtle Shell."

"That was nice; I have dinner taken care of. Why don't you start on another pipe? The trader may be here before long," she said, echoing what Sparrow had said.

37

So Green Rock started sawing on the rest of the soapstone. His hands were still sore from making the last pipe, but he wanted to be ready for the next trader. He sawed on it until the serrations on the flint flake were dull, then he created new serrations and sawed some more until dinner was ready.

While he and his family were eating, they heard Sparrow's voice approaching the lodge. "No! He really carved it himself," she said.

"Well it's much better than I expected," answered Turtle Shell.

Squirrel Fur got up to show them in. They entered, and Turtle Shell said, "Look at this masterpiece your son made!" as he approached Elk Antler.

"That's a nice one," he replied, though to Green Rock he didn't seem as proud as he was on the day of the war game.

"Let me see it," said Squirrel Fur. After looking it over she said, "You are really getting better at this!"

"Thank you," said Green Rock shyly.

"Thank *you!*" said Turtle Shell, and he handed Green Rock another piece of soapstone. "Keep this one, you don't owe me anything for it. The bird pipe was much more than I had expected. Good job!"

"Oh, thank you. Did you get a deer?" asked Green Rock.

"No, I didn't even see any. I'll be going back out tomorrow. I think I will try going north this time."

"I'll go with you, if you would like some company," said Elk Antler.

"Can I go too?" asked Wolf Tail. "I have never taken a deer before. I *am* thirteen cycles old," he added hopefully.

"Do you think you can keep up with two grown men?" asked Turtle Shell.

"Sure! I will run if I need to."

"What do you think?" Turtle Shell asked Elk Antler.

"He needs to start sometime. Do you have an extra bow for him?"

"I have a bow!" Wolf Tail asserted.

"Yes, but I made it for you to use in the war games. It isn't powerful enough to kill a *deer*," replied Elk Antler.

"He can use my bow if need be," said Turtle Shell. "I am short, and so is my bow."

It was settled. The next morning when Green Rock woke up, Wolf Tail, Elk Antler and Turtle Shell were long gone. Green Rock only had one flint flake left, and he had already started using it the night before. So he went to see Stone Spear in hopes that he could get more.

"Well if it isn't Gray Rock," said Stone Spear. Green Rock thought it best not to correct him. In the morning light he noticed the pots with the grapes growing in them. There were too many to count! Some of the pottery was unfamiliar to him and he assumed it was of Calusa origin.

"Do you like my grapevines?" asked Stone Spear, noticing him spying them. "You should try the drink I make from them. But that may anger your father, and I need his business. Let me guess... you need more flakes of flint?"

"Yes," replied Green Rock.

"And what do you offer in return?" asked Stone Spear.

Green Rock was unprepared for this, though he realized that Stone Spear was right. He had nothing to trade. "I, uh... Right now I don't have anything. Can I do some work for you and pay you that way?"

"Take that large clay pot to the river and fetch me some water. I will get you what you need while you are doing that."

"Thanks," said Green Rock, and then he got the pot and left for the river. As he neared the first guardhouse at the entrance of the palisade the guard greeted him, and he noticed how high the wall of posts was. It was nearly twice the height of a grown man. It must have taken a lot of effort to build it. The entrance of the palisade was overlapped. That is, to go in or out, a person would walk between two walls of posts for about the length of five or six men lying down. The corridor was about the width of a man's height, and there were two guardhouses, one on each end of the corridor. There were guards stationed there all day and all night. It was a good means of protection from attack, but not for people on the outside of the wall.

Green Rock got to Bear River and filled the pot, and lugging it back proved to be much harder than he had anticipated, as the pot was rather large, and he was only ten cycles old. After a long walk up the hill, he entered the palisade, and the walk was a little easier. Fortunately Stone Spear's lodge was near the entrance.

After carefully setting the water pot down, he asked Stone Spear where he got his flint.

"An eagle brings it to me from distant places," replied Stone Spear with a smirk. Green Rock didn't believe him, although there were many types of flints and cherts that he knew weren't from the area.

Stone Spear handed him a large pouch that contained about twenty good flakes. "Thank you," said Green Rock.

"You earned it," replied Stone Spear. "I am a little old to be carrying that big thing up from the river."

"Can you teach me flint knapping like you are doing with Wolf Tail?" Green Rock asked. "You said you would."

Stone Spear frowned. "I don't remember *ever* saying *that*! Why don't you ask Wolf Tail? He knows enough so that he can now teach himself over time. He is new to the craft, but has some experience and he could relate to you better. By the time you are as good as Wolf Tail, he will have learned more. I am too old to be teaching anyway. Do you know how old I am?"

Green Rock didn't want to cause any difficulty between Stone Spear and Turtle Shell, so he simply replied, "No."

"Forty cycles!" Does that surprise you?"

The boy didn't know how to answer that question without offending Stone Spear. "Judging by your skill I would say you were older," he finally replied.

Stone Spear's Cup.
Redrawn from Thruston 1897.

"Honesty hidden by a compliment," laughed Stone Spear, and then he drank from his all familiar cup. "No, you get Wolf Tail to teach you. He already knows a lot. The only reason I took him under my wing was the fact that he was orphaned."

"Thank you for the flint," said Green Rock.

"And thank you for getting the water," returned Stone Spear. Green Rock then went back home and continued sawing his soapstone.

Green Rock's father, uncle and Wolf Tail, returned later that day with a six point buck deer that Wolf Tail had killed. Wolf Tail was ecstatic.

"He dropped him in his tracks!" said Elk Antler with a smile. After the butchering was done, Wolf Tail took some venison to his mentor's lodge, but he found the priest and his helpers there.

"Is something wrong?" asked Wolf Tail.

"An evil spirit has taken Stone Spear," answered one of the priest's helpers. "His last wish was that you have his lodge and possessions. Wolf Tail, I am sorry."

"No! No!" cried Wolf Tail, and he dropped the deer meat in the dirt and ran home in tears. Wolf Tail was devastated. He wouldn't eat, and he had disturbing dreams. It was as if he were reliving his parents' death all over again. Green Rock and his family did what they could to comfort him but he didn't respond to anything they said or did. Sparrow took him to Red Talon, the priest and he did a healing dance, blew smoke on him via a medicine tube, and gave him some herbs.

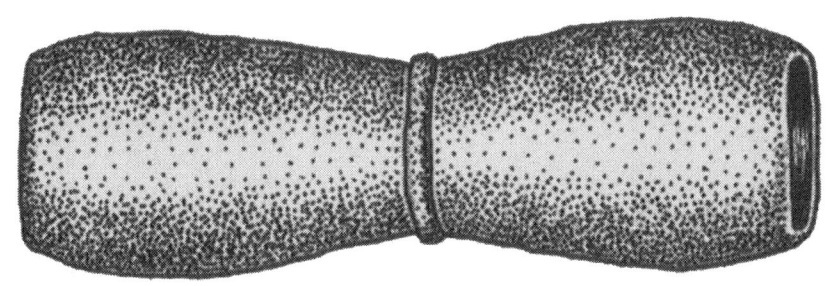

Soapstone Medicine Tube.
Redrawn from McGuire 1897.

Red Talon also gave Wolf Tail some tea made from Dogwood bark. This bark was from the same tree whose blooming of its white flowers each year indicated when it was time for the people to plant corn. The bark from this hardwood tree was usually boiled and drank for treating fever or it could be rubbed into aching muscles. But Red Talon now used it as an appetite stimulant for Wolf Tail because he really needed to eat if he was going to get better.

Meanwhile they moved Stone Spear's body to the charnel platform by the burial mound. Wolf Tail saw this and was in a quiet state of numbness. The priest continued his therapy and, after several days, Wolf Tail began to get better. One night, Stone Spear visited Wolf Tail in a dream. He said, *I have gone to a better place, Wolf Tail, my wife Doe is here, and your parents are too. One day you will be here with your forefathers and us. Until then, live your life, and take care of my lodge. Continue with what I have taught you, and I won't be completely gone.*

It was then that Wolf Tail finally accepted Stone Spear's death, and he vowed to not let him down. In essence, Wolf Tail was healed, though only time would return him to normalcy.

Wolf Tail began spending nights at Stone Spear's lodge, and continuing his heritage by teaching Green Rock and other children of

Birch Mountain the flint knapping trade. Green Rock also carved more effigy pipes there for trading, and Wolf Tail taught him how to drive a good bargain. He had learned that also from Stone Spear, who was a trader himself in his younger days. Squirrel Fur and Sparrow dropped in at least once a day to make sure Wolf Tail had what he needed, and so did Elk Antler and Turtle Shell.

One day Green Rock was at the river washing the dust out of a fine eagle effigy pipe – he now had four pipes to trade. As he washed it, a stranger came up in a dugout canoe. He obviously was of a different tribe, and Green Rock was afraid.

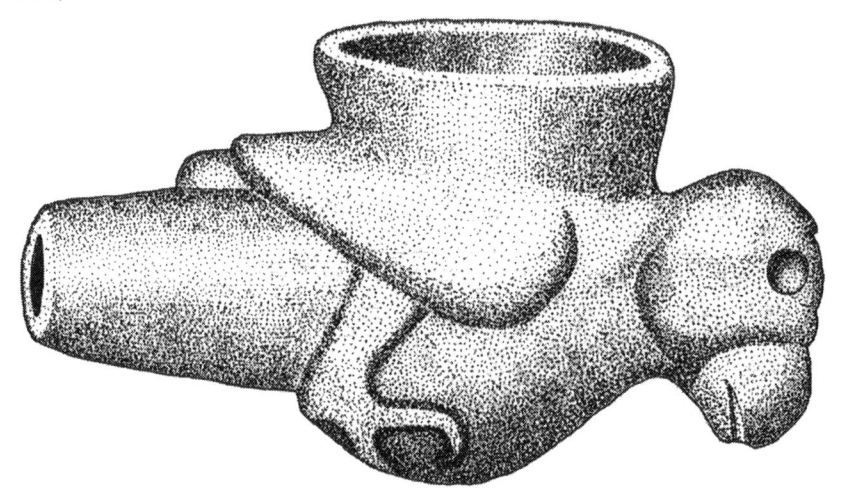

Eagle Effigy Pipe Carved by Green Rock.
Redrawn from Thruston 1897.

"What do you want for that eagle pipe?" the stranger asked in bad Cherokee.

"Are you the trader?" asked Green Rock.

"I don't know if I am *the* trader, but I am *a* trader," replied the stranger. "I am Bald Eagle."

Green Rock noticed that among this trader's wares there were pots full of grapevines – just like Stone Spear's. There were large nodules of flint in the canoe also, and he wondered if this was the "eagle" Stone Spear referred to on the day that he died. By then several warriors of Birch Mountain had made it to the shore, their bows ready. The guards stationed at the palisade entrance had seen the stranger and alerted them. They recognized him and relaxed. They ran back to the village and announced that the trader was there. The Uku, or Chief, Standing Bear arrived with many of his servants and wives. He welcomed the trader, invited him into the village, and assured him that the contents of his canoe would not be molested.

Because of the distraction, Green Rock had not finished his conversation with the trader, but this gave him the opportunity to rub bear grease into the eagle pipe. It had to look its best so it would bring a good price.

Bald Eagle enjoyed the hospitality of the village for the next three days, the Uku fed him the best Birch Mountain had to offer, and each night he had the company of one of the village women.

During the days, he bartered his wares to all the villagers who had things to offer in trade. When the village had no more trade items to offer, Bald Eagle asked, "Where is that little boy who had that eagle pipe?"

"I will go and get him," answered Turtle Shell, and he got up and left. Turtle Shell went to Stone Spear's old lodge, knowing Green Rock and Wolf Tail would be there. "It is time for you two to do some trading. He is ready for you."

Green Rock was very nervous, although he and Wolf Tail had rehearsed for this many times. He gathered his four pipes, and Wolf Tail got his preforms (unfinished knives and spear points) together.

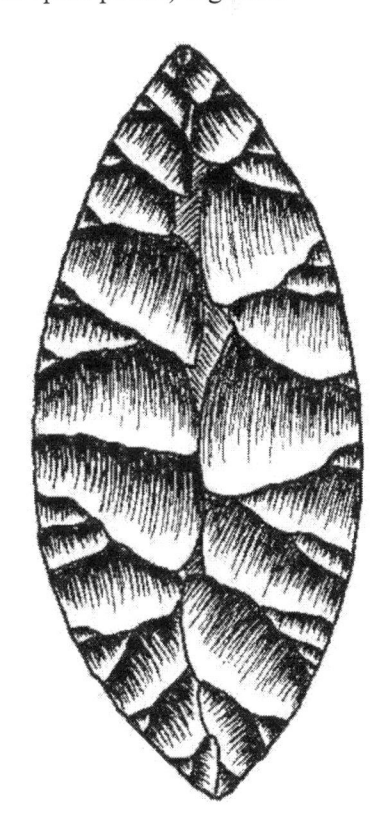

Wolf Tail's Flint Preforms.

When they arrived at Bald Eagle's canoe, the trader was trying desperately to find a home for the pots with the grapevines intended for Stone Spear, but nobody seemed to be interested. He was frustrated.

A skinny old woman smiled eagerly and in a screechy voice said, "If you don't want those pots, I'll be glad to give you these two bone awls for them, if you don't mind getting rid of the vines!"

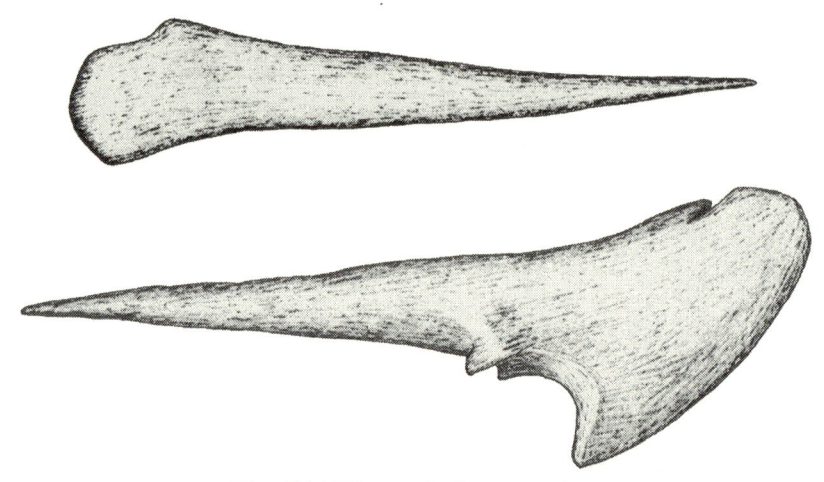

The Old Woman's Bone Awls.
Redrawn from Thruston 1897.

Bald Eagle, obviously angry and insulted, retorted, "I'm sure there are plenty of people in the next village who will pay much more than that for them!" and, under his breath, defiantly whispered, "So there, you stinky old witch!"

As much as Bald Eagle tried to hide his frustration, Green Rock saw it, and chuckled silently.

Bald Eagle's eyes shifted to Green Rock, and Green Rock quickly hid his smile. He still had to bargain with this trader, and the last thing to do right then would be to insult him in any way.

Wolf Tail saw that many of the large nodules of flint and chert were still in the trader's dugout canoe, but knew that he didn't have much to offer, in quality or quantity, but he showed what he did have. The trader said, "I will give you one tenth of the flint I have for them."

Wolf Tail looked insulted by the offer and said, "One fourth of the flint and they are yours." Green Rock was paying close attention. It was *his* turn next.

Bald Eagle laughed and said, "I can get twice as many preforms of better quality at the next village for one fourth! Come now, I will be nice and throw in this piece," he said while pointing to a larger nodule.

Wolf Tail considered. "Throw in that piece, and the largest one and we have a trade."

The trader made another counter offer. "I will trade one tenth and the biggest piece, but that's the best I can do."

Wolf Tail agreed and they removed the nodules he had traded for. Once they were out of the boat, it didn't look like very much flint at all.

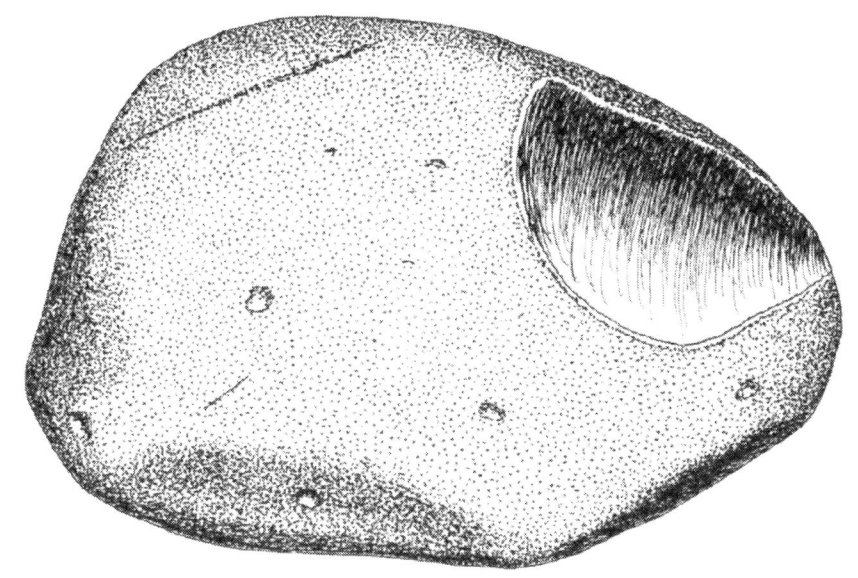

Raw Flint Nodule with Test Flake Removed as Test for Quality.

Green Rock observed this, and it was now his turn. He decided to help Wolf Tail out. He pulled out his four effigy pipes. Bald Eagle couldn't help staring at the eagle pipe. He wanted it, and Green Rock knew it. "I will trade the wolf pipe, and the two deer pipes for the rest of the flint. I don't want to trade the eagle pipe."

The trader refused. "I will trade one fourth of the flint for the eagle," he counter offered.

"I will trade all four pipes for all of the flint left," responded Green Rock.

Bald Eagle refused. Then Green Rock said, "That's fine, I sort of wanted to hang on to these anyway." Excitement pulsed in every one of his veins. He thought he'd ruined his chance. Every part of him wanted to retract those words, but you can't unsay something, once it has been said. Green Rock's rapid pulse threatened to give him away, but he made himself "keep it together." After all, in the worst case, he would still have his pipes. He reminded himself, *There is nothing to lose*. But he was still about to burst!

But the old trader looked surprised, though he tried to hide it. He'd never imagined a little boy being so skilled at driving a hard bargain! There was a long silence.

Green Rock, mostly out of panic and embarrassment, turned to go, but the trader asked for him to wait. "I will trade all the remaining flint except for this piece – you know? Just in case I need arrows."

Green Rock coolly nodded his head. The trading was done. Green Rock gave Bald Eagle the four pipes while Wolf Tail began to unload the rest of the flint. He smiled at Green Rock when the trader was not looking.

Bald Eagle was impressed with Green Rock's skills, both in stone carving, and at haggling. Ten cycle old Green Rock seemed to be a master at both! "Hey boy," Bald Eagle said, "I got something else for you." He reached into a pouch, and pulled out a mysterious item made from a material foreign to Green Rock.

"What is that?" asked Green Rock.

"If you are this good with stone, at your young age, you need to try your hand at carving whelk shell jewelry," replied Bald Eagle. "This is a copper rod, with a deer antler handle. Heat the tip in a fire, and you can burn your holes into shell gorgets and beads, instead of having to drill them. It'll never wear out. It will save you lots of flint that otherwise would be wasted in maintaining flint drills. Take it. It's yours!"

Copper Rod with Carved Antler Handle.
Redrawn from Thruston 1897.

Green Rock's jaw dropped, along with the rest of the villagers who were there present. It was extremely unusual generosity for a trader to part with something so rare and valuable, without receiving hefty compensation in return. Perhaps he was laying the groundwork for a future trade relationship with Green Rock. It was always good to have people owe you favors. Bald Eagle was definitely impressed with this young boy.

"Thank you!" smiled Green Rock. He and Wolf Tail just stood there in awe of such a fine gift from a man who could have easily traded it for five turkey feather cloaks.

"I can't help you with engraving them," said Bald Eagle, in a more gruff manner which made it obvious that he was hiding his real feelings of admiration.

The trader, Bald Eagle waved at the Uku, and began paddling away, with his canoe full of goods from Birch Mountain. This included turkey feather cloaks, pelts of various animals, and of course, the pots containing the grapevines that nobody but the stingy old lady wanted. He left behind several whelk shells from the Great Sea; three of them had been traded to Sparrow. Green Rock and Wolf Tail began hauling the flint up the hill to Stone Spear's old lodge.

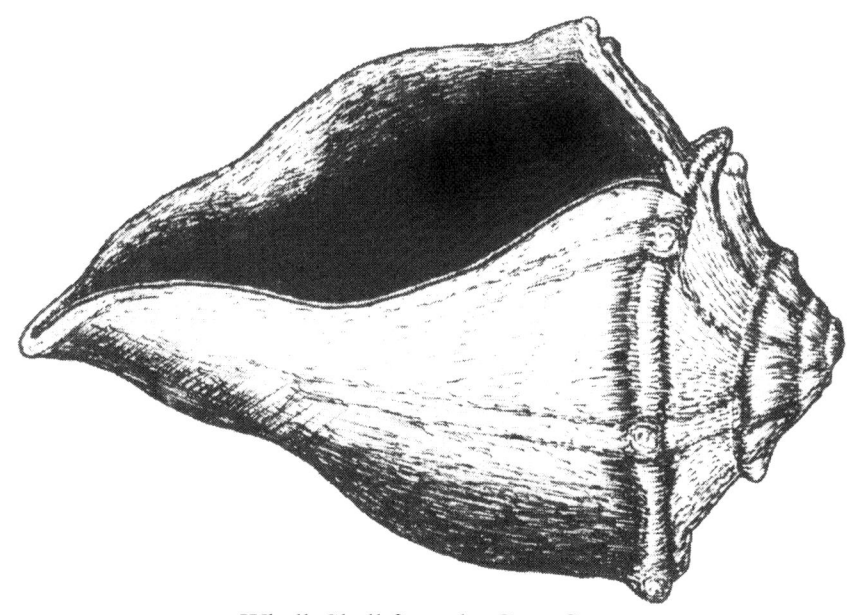

Whelk Shell from the Great Sea.
Adapted from Holmes 1880.

"I want to give you this flint," said Green Rock. "I know you need it to further your knapping skills."

Wolf Tail objected, "But this is worth a fortune! I can't take it from you."

Green Rock said, "I traded for it to help you out. Consider it as payment for teaching me flint knapping."

"Oh Green Rock, thank you," said Wolf Tail. "You have really helped me at a time when I needed it."

They finished moving the flint to Wolf Tail's lodge, and Turtle Shell showed up to visit. "Where did you learn to trade like that?" he asked.

"From Wolf Tail. He learned from the best," replied Green Rock.

"Yes, he did," replied Turtle Shell, remembering old Stone Spear.

"Can you get me some more soapstone?" I want to carve some more pipes before the next trader arrives."

"Yes, I certainly will," said Turtle Shell, and then he gave Green Rock the three large, beautiful whelk shells that Sparrow had just bartered from Bald Eagle earlier, in exchange for a turkey feather cloak that she had made. "Sparrow said to give you these. If you can learn to carve jewelry out of shells like these, you will one day be very wealthy. The locals love beads, gorgets and masks made out of whelk shells like these. The tribes to the south and west also greatly value shell jewelry."

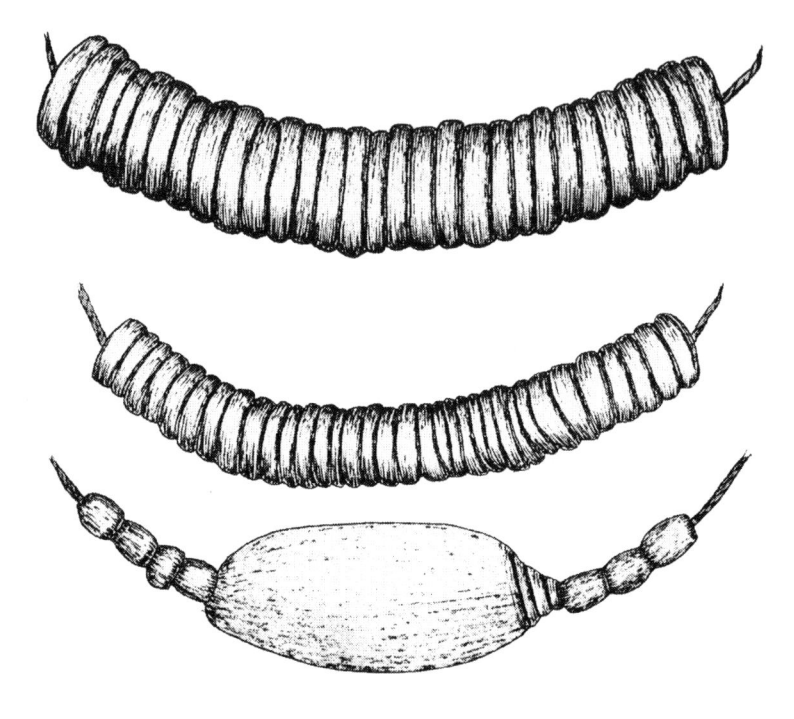

Shell Beads.
Redrawn from Thruston 1897.

"How would I trade with them? They would kill me as soon as they knew what tribe I was from!"

"A trader is always welcome – it doesn't matter what tribe he is from. Artists are also welcome, and are well paid for their work. When you get older, I would like to see you traveling with a trader."

Green Rock was apprehensive. "I am still nervous about being among an enemy tribe. What if they decide they don't want me around?"

"Bald Eagle is of the Muskogee tribe. They are enemies of the Cherokee – they are even friends with the Yuchi. You saw how well our villagers received him. Believe me, if he had not been a trader, he would have had arrows sticking out of his chest the moment the guards spotted him. If you travel with a trader like him, you will be safe."

"Why are they our enemies?"

"The land to the south has been in dispute for a long time."

"Oh. Well, tell Sparrow I said thank you for the shells!" said Green Rock, still uncertain about the idea of traveling among enemies.

"She will say you are welcome, I'm sure. We are still amazed at how you got all of Bald Eagle's flint off of him," said Turtle Shell. "And that copper awl too! You must have really impressed him! You did good, Green Rock. Really good."

And so it was that Green Rock became a professional artisan at the age of ten cycles. The seed that Turtle Shell had planted was now the sapling that would continue to grow and change Green Rock's life forever.

Chapter 2: Raid

Green Rock spent all of that night at Wolf Tail's lodge practicing flint knapping. He was beginning to get the basics of pressure flaking down. After some practice he managed to make a small crude triangular arrow point from one of Stone Spear's heat-treated flakes. "Hey, that is pretty good!" remarked Wolf Tail when he saw it.

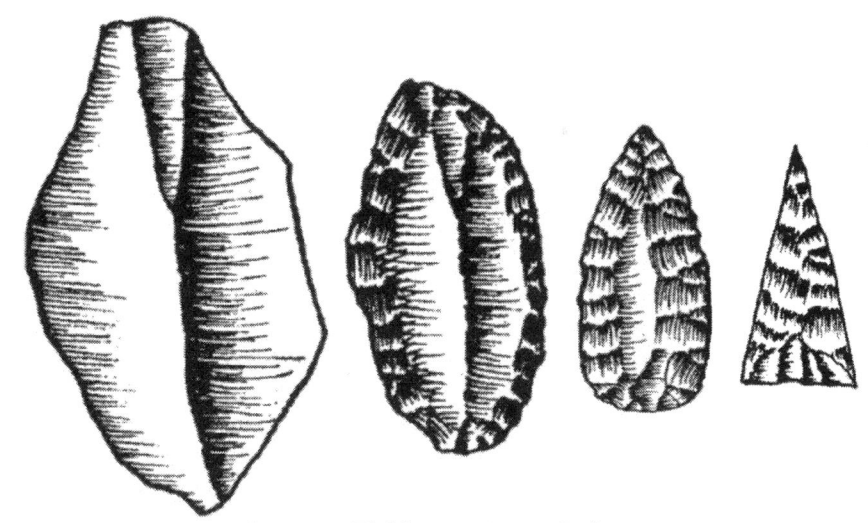

Pressure Flaking an Arrow Point.

The next morning before sunrise Green Rock returned to his family's lodge to get his blowgun. "Good morning," said Squirrel Fur; she was up early grinding corn in a wooden mortar and pestle just outside of the lodge.

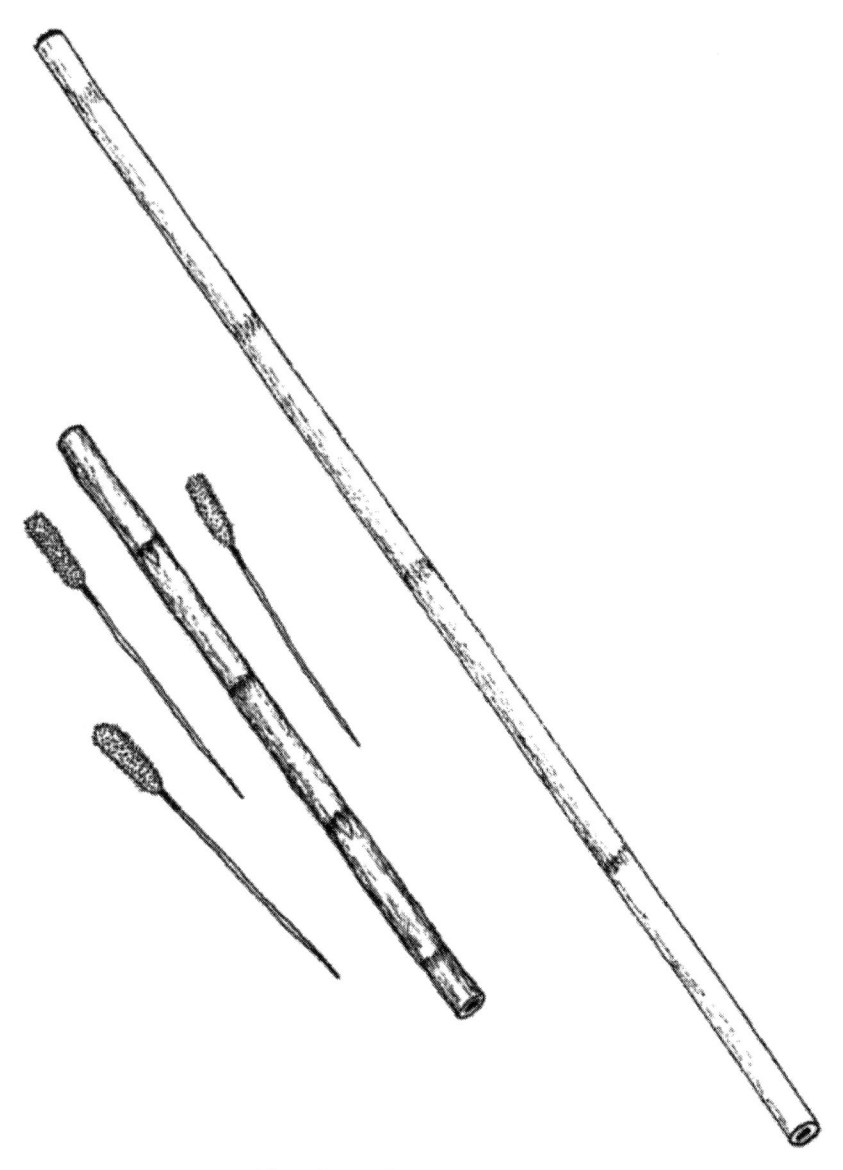

Cherokee Blowguns & Darts.

    "Good morning, Mother," returned Green Rock, and then he went inside and got the blowgun and darts. Running Fox was looking it over.
    "Give it to me," said Green Rock.
    "No," replied Running Fox.
    "Please let me have it."
    "No."

"It's my blowgun and you are going to break it!"

"I won't break it!"

"Mother, Running Fox won't give me my blowgun!"

"Running Fox, stop tormenting your brother!" shouted Squirrel Fur.

Running Fox let go of the blowgun with a smirk on his face. Green Rock just shook his head and walked out of the lodge. As he left, Squirrel Fur asked, "Where are you going off to now?"

"I am going to practice with the blowgun," he replied. "I want to kill a rabbit for Father."

"Well, be careful. Watch for snakes."

"I will," and then he left. Green Rock went outside the palisade and straight to the pond. He thought he might be able to target practice, aiming at a spot he made in the mud, if it was soft enough. It was. He made a shallow hole with his finger, and backed up to a distance he thought he could get to a rabbit. He removed the darts from the end of the tube. The small slender darts were made from locust wood, pointed on one end and had thistledown lashed to the other side. This served as wadding, but also created drag, and kept the tip pointing towards the target when the dart was in flight, similar in function to arrow fletching.

He put a dart into the blowgun, put it to his mouth, aimed and blew as hard as he could. The dart hit less than a finger's width from the hole. He couldn't believe how accurate it was! After building his confidence with more practice, he decided he was ready to shoot a rabbit.

Cottontail Rabbit.
Adapted & redrawn from a public domain image.

The Sun was rising by the time Green Rock arrived at a thicket where he had seen rabbits before. He quietly crept into the thicket and waited, listening. Nothing. He went deeper into the thicket, and accidentally stepped on a twig. It snapped, and then he heard some rustling in the bushes nearby. He turned to look and a rabbit hopped into view from behind a tree. He was very close. As he turned to take aim, the rabbit saw him moving and hopped to a safer place, but Green Rock didn't lose sight of it. He began to take aim again. The rabbit was watching him, but was evidently satisfied that it was in a safe place. Green Rock blew as hard as he could and the dart struck the rabbit in the side. The rabbit squealed and hopped away, but Green Rock knew it was injured severely. The rabbit was making a lot of noise in the bushes, and Green Rock was able to find it easily. When he got to the rabbit, it was laying on its side kicking, with the dart protruding up out of its side.

Green Rock got out a flint knife and cut the rabbit's throat. This was his first kill, and he felt bad about it. Then he remembered something very important. "Oh, Brother Rabbit," he said, "I am sorry to kill you, but my family needs meat. I do honor your speed and agility." It was always important to apologize to the animal's spirit; otherwise it would seek vengeance and make anybody who ate of its body very ill. Green Rock hoped he had apologized in an appropriate way.

He picked up the rabbit, removed the dart, and started back home. Elk Antler was eating breakfast with Squirrel Fur and Running Fox when Green Rock arrived home.

"I give this rabbit, my first kill to you, Father," said Green Rock, in an almost formal manner.

"Big rabbit hunter! Ha!" jeered Running Fox.

"Why don't you shut up?" Elk Antler shouted. Then he said, "I accept your gift, and I am proud of you."

Green Rock smiled, but noticed the jealous look on Running Fox's face. It wasn't his problem though, so he decided to just ignore him.

"Sit down and eat," said Squirrel Fur.

Green Rock did so, and when he was done, he went to help his father clean the rabbit. "Did you remember to apologize to the rabbit's spirit?" asked Elk Antler.

"Yes, I almost forgot, but I did do it," answered Green Rock. When they were done, Green Rock took it inside to his mother.

"I'll cook it for lunch," she said, with a proud smile.

"If you don't need any help, I will go to Wolf Tail's to practice flint knapping some more," said Green Rock.

"No, I'll be fine. Go on and enjoy yourself."

"I'll see you at lunch time," replied Green Rock as he left. Wolf Tail had started heat-treating some flint by the time Green Rock arrived. Sparrow was there and had given Wolf Tail some breakfast.

"Wolf Tail showed me your arrow point. It's nice!" said Sparrow. "You will be making some like your father's and Turtle Shell's before long."

"Where is Turtle Shell?" asked Wolf Tail.

"He is out chopping some wood to use for patching a gap they found in the palisade. They will probably be working on it for a couple of days. Green Rock, are you hungry?"

"No, thanks, I just ate," replied Green Rock.

"Okay, I'd better get home and start on lunch. Turtle Shell will be hungry when he returns," said Sparrow, and then she left.

After she was gone, Wolf Tail said, "She sure is a kind woman. She would never let me go hungry."

"I am lucky she is my aunt," replied Green Rock. "And also lucky to have an uncle like Turtle Shell. By the way, I got my first rabbit this morning. Father was happy, but Running Fox was jealous."

"That sounds like him, he seems to like trouble."

"Yeah, but I won't let him get to me."

"He's young," said Wolf Tail as he put more wood into the fire. "He'll outgrow it someday."

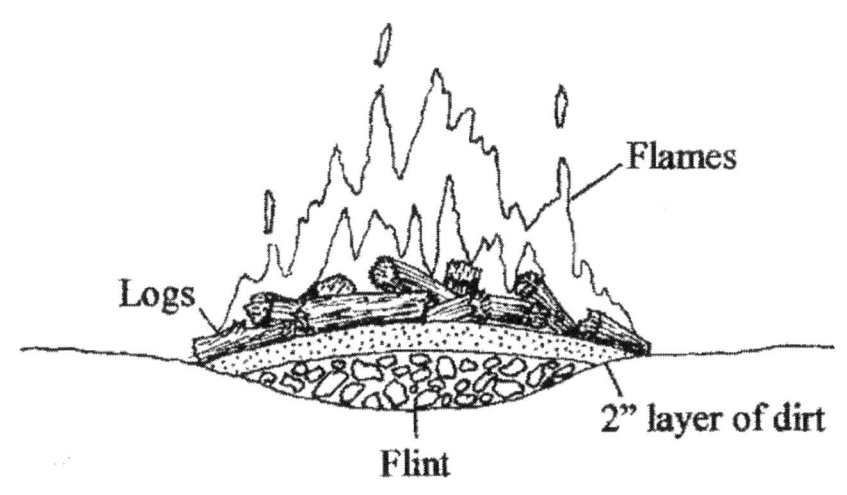

Heat-Treating Flint for Making Arrowheads.

"So, exactly how do you heat the flint, and why?" asked Green Rock.

"It makes the flint easier to knap; it makes it glossy and nice-looking. You can thin pieces easier, but they can break easier too. Stone Spear taught me how to do it. You dig a shallow pit and put the flakes and preforms in it, and then cover them with a layer of dirt that is about as thick as three fingers. Build a fire over it, and keep it burning strong for at least a day. Then let it cool off for two more days and then it is ready to dig up."

"Wow, I wonder how they discovered that," said Green Rock.

"Stone Spear never told me. I just remembered – I found a good piece of flint for you to practice pressure flaking on while you were gone. Here it is."

"I want to learn percussion flaking."

"One thing at a time. Once you have mastered pressure flaking, you will find that percussion flaking is easier to learn. Besides you would only waste good flint right now."

So, Green Rock practiced pressure flaking some more and by lunchtime he had a fairly well made arrow point. He took it home to show his family.

Turtle Shell, Sparrow, and the rest of his family, except for Running Fox, were there. They ate the rabbit that Green Rock had provided, along with some cornbread and dried meat. It was good. Green Rock felt satisfied that he had helped provide some of the food.

"Where is Running Fox?" asked Green Rock.

"He went off down the river – he saw your blowgun and now he wants to try to make one like it. He said he was going to the canebrake for materials."

Green Rock rolled his eyes.

"Your brother wants attention, and now he is seeking it in a positive way," said his mother, "so don't be angry with him."

Green Rock knew she was right, and offered no argument. Turtle Shell finished eating and got up to leave.

Turtle – Turtle Shell's Namesake.
Redrawn from Image by OpenClipart-Vectors from Pixabay.

"Be careful," said Sparrow. "I want you home tonight."

"I am just chopping wood!" argued Turtle Shell.

"Be careful," she repeated. It was as if she knew something was very wrong.

"I will," he assured her. "And when I return, I want plenty of deer meat and cornbread! You cook so very well."

That was the last thing he ever said to her. If he had known what was to happen, he probably would have said more. On the way back to the woods he thought about it some more, but disregarded it as nonsense. Women always worried. It was their nature. But still, he noticed that the birds were not singing like normal. It was unnaturally quiet.

Turtle Shell arrived at where he had been working, but nobody else had returned from lunch yet. So he began chopping the branches off of the post by himself. Suddenly an arrow struck him in the back of his left leg. He turned around and saw three warriors of a different tribe advancing. Another arrow struck him in the chest. He dropped his axe and fell over backwards. Before he could get up, fight, or even call out a warning, one of the warriors picked up Turtle Shell's axe and struck him on the head with a heavy blow, crushing his skull.

Then ten more warriors emerged from the woods and advanced on the village. They lit fire-tipped arrows with a small fire pot that they had brought with them.

Green Rock finished eating and, no sooner than he got up, there were confused cries coming from other areas of the village. He and Squirrel Fur ran to see what was wrong, while Elk Antler grabbed his bow and arrows. Sparrow ran up and joined Green Rock and Squirrel Fur.

As Elk Antler was emerging from the lodge with his bow and arrows, he shouted, "What do you see?"

"There are some lodges on fire!" said Squirrel Fur in a desperate tone.

"You stay here inside the palisade!" shouted Elk Antler.

"Running Fox – he is *not* in the village!" cried Squirrel Fur.

"Do not leave! I mean it!" he commanded. They could sense the urgency in his voice. Elk Antler was gone in a moment to meet with the other warriors. Whoever did this was going to pay.

Green Rock, Squirrel Fur and Sparrow ran to assist the families whose homes were burning. The whole village was in a panicked uproar. They did not have a way to put out the fires. All they could do was get their belongings away from the fire. Green Rock heard an infant crying and coughing inside one of the burning lodges. Without thinking, he ran inside and into the choking smoke. He listened and felt around until he found the baby, and then he grabbed her and ran back out.

Squirrel Fur and Sparrow were assisting others in moving their belongings out of harm's way. One of the priest's helpers came from the village circle with his wife. "White Feather, my daughter!" he cried when he saw his lodge burning.

"Is this your daughter?" asked Green Rock.

Immediately the man's wife recognized the infant, and burst into tears. Green Rock gave White Feather to the man and the man thanked him as he hugged his wife.

A total of eight lodges were burned down to the ground. Several more fire arrows had missed the lodges and burned out where they landed. There were not many men in the village – most had left to chase down the enemies. Wolf Tail had left his heat-treating fire that he had been tending, so he could help out.

Everybody in Birch Mountain was in a state of silent anger and fear. What if the men didn't return? Raids on Cherokee villages in the outlying territories were common, but Birch Mountain was the national capital, and had only been rarely attacked in the past. Why now? They all stayed inside the palisade, except to go to the river for water, and even then they were guarded by the village guards armed with bows and arrows. These were the same people whose job it was to man the guardhouses at the entrance of the palisade. They normally worked in shifts, but now they were all needed constantly.

* * *

Two days later, the men returned home. They had seen many tracks, but the enemies had left in canoes that they had beached on the banks of Thunder River, on the other side of the ridge. They were long gone. None had been seen, but they had left behind the arrows in Turtle Shell's body. The villagers were able to determine by their arrowheads and tribal markings that they were of Yuchi origin.

Yuchi Arrowheads (Flint).
Redrawn from Overstreet, Cox & Cooper 2015

In total, only two from Birch Mountain died: these were Turtle Shell, and an elderly woman who was the mother of the Uku, Standing Bear. She couldn't walk and perished in the flames. Running Fox never returned. They assumed he had been kidnapped and taken as a slave by the Yuchi. Now Green Rock felt very guilty for the way he had thought of his younger brother. He should have let him use the blowgun.

Squirrel Fur and Elk Antler were obviously very grieved. Squirrel Fur had lost a son and a brother. Elk Antler swore he would get retribution, and Squirrel Fur would object to him leaving on a war party, and they ended up fighting over it, over and over again. Green Rock hated to see them like this.

Sparrow had sunk into a deep depression. Her husband gone, she had the lodge to herself, and nobody to cook for. She was barren and thought nobody else would want her for marriage because she couldn't bear them children. She had also received a nasty burn on her left arm while assisting an unknown woman whose lodge had been hit with one of the fire arrows.

When he managed to get the time, the Shaman, Red Talon brought Sparrow some mucilage from the inner bark of the American linden tree. This type of tree was thought to be immune from lightning strikes, and its leaves and flowers were often used to treat coughs and sore throats. He instructed her on how to use the mucilage for treating her burns.

Green Rock and Wolf Tail visited Sparrow every day in the hopes that she would know she was loved. They also fetched water from the river each day and Green Rock brought her a rabbit or some squirrels when he was successful with his blowgun. Other people helped her also, mainly members of the Long Hair Clan to which she belonged.

The villagers got together and volunteered in rebuilding lodges for the families who lost in the raid. After one moon, they were finished. The Uku, Standing Bear then called a council meeting – and it was no ordinary meeting – this was a council of war.

All of the available men of the village went to the meeting, which was held in the heptagon council house located on the west side of the village square. The entrance was on the east side facing the square. This large building primarily functioned as a temple for religious ceremonies, but was also used for military and civil functions.

Birch Mountain's council house could seat three hundred people, and it was seven-sided; seven was the sacred number of the Cherokee. There were a total of seven clans of the Cherokee; the clan names were Bird, Blue, Deer, Paint, Long Hair, Wild Potato, and Wolf. The members of a particular clan sat in that clan's designated section of the council house.

Elk Antler entered the building and sat with his fellow Blue Clansmen. He saw the sacred seventh pillar located in the west corner of the building. The Uku, his speaker and right hand man were sitting there on carved wooden seats that were painted white – symbolic of purity. He noticed in front of these three seats there had been three new seats added, painted red, which symbolized war. This was where the war leaders sat. After everybody was situated, the War Chief said something to his speaker.

"A black cloud has rolled over Birch Mountain," said the speaker, "saddening our hearts, and blocking us from the light that comes from the Sun. We know who is responsible for this dishonor on our people." Then he held up the two Yuchi arrows that were found in Turtle Shell's body. "Do you see these arrows? They are Yuchi! They have drawn Cherokee blood – unprovoked! The Yuchis have attacked us for no reason! No reason at all! Well, now the Yuchi shall see *our* arrows!"

Cherokee Arrowheads (Flint).
Based on Mails 1992 & Allely & Hamm 1999.

Only the men attended this meeting. The council of war lasted into the night, and was followed by the warrior dance. Squirrel Fur was in a silent state of fear as she heard the drums beat faster. Then there were four loud war whoops at the end of the dance, and silence. Green Rock hugged his mother, who was crying.

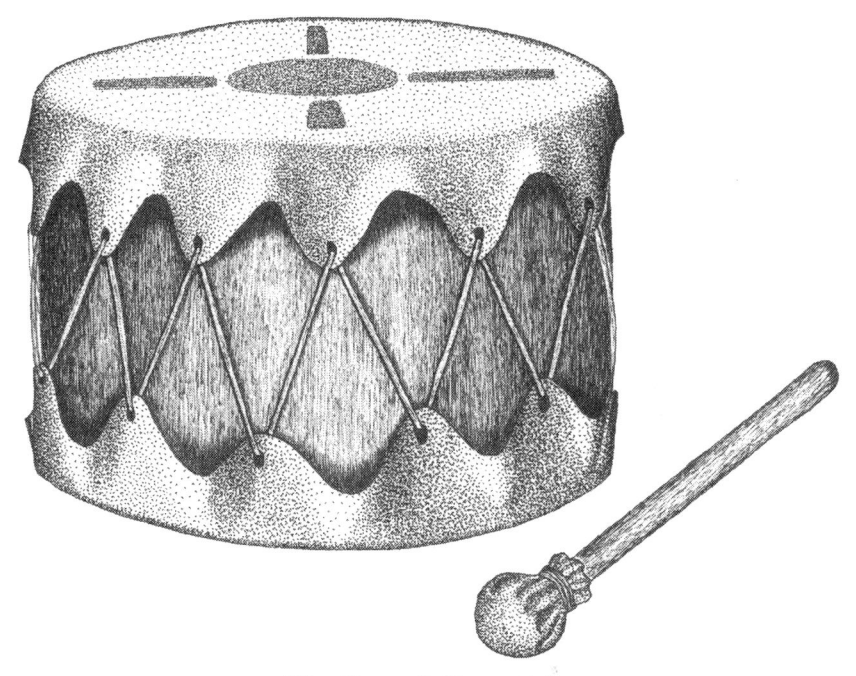

War Drum & Drumstick.

The next morning forty-nine warriors who were selected during the war council meeting prepared to leave. This included Elk Antler. Squirrel Fur was still in tears. She was fearful about her husband's safety, but also hoping there would be a way for him to rescue Running Fox.

"Green Rock," said Elk Antler, "you take care of your mother. I will be back in several days."

When the war party left, Green Rock then burst into tears and Squirrel Fur hugged him as they both wept.

"Will we ever see Father again?" cried Green Rock.

"He will be back soon," answered Squirrel Fur, trying to sound reassuring. "You go on to Wolf Tail's and make something nice," she said, in an attempt to build a confident front, "I'll be fine." She did not want to distress her son anymore than necessary.

So, Green Rock left, and as soon as he was out of sight, Squirrel Fur ran into the lodge and cried bitter tears.

Green Rock was full of disturbing thoughts about his little brother's fate, and what might happen to his father. He arrived at Wolf Tail's lodge but Wolf Tail was gone. He looked around for him, and eventually found him lugging a pot full of water. Green Rock went to help. He noticed that it was the same clay pot that he had used to fetch water in for Stone Spear the day he had died. "Thanks," said Wolf Tail after they set down the pot.

They spent the day trying to focus on being positive and productive. But there was an underlying gloominess in the atmosphere around all of Birch Mountain for several days.

The villagers had taken Turtle Shell's body and what was left of the Chief's mother's body to the charnel platform. The bird effigy pipe Green Rock had made for his uncle was now a grave offering. This hurt Green Rock deeply, and he remembered Turtle Shell giving him that first piece of soapstone not so many days before. They interred Turtle Shell with a carved shell death mask that was engraved with a weeping eye motif.

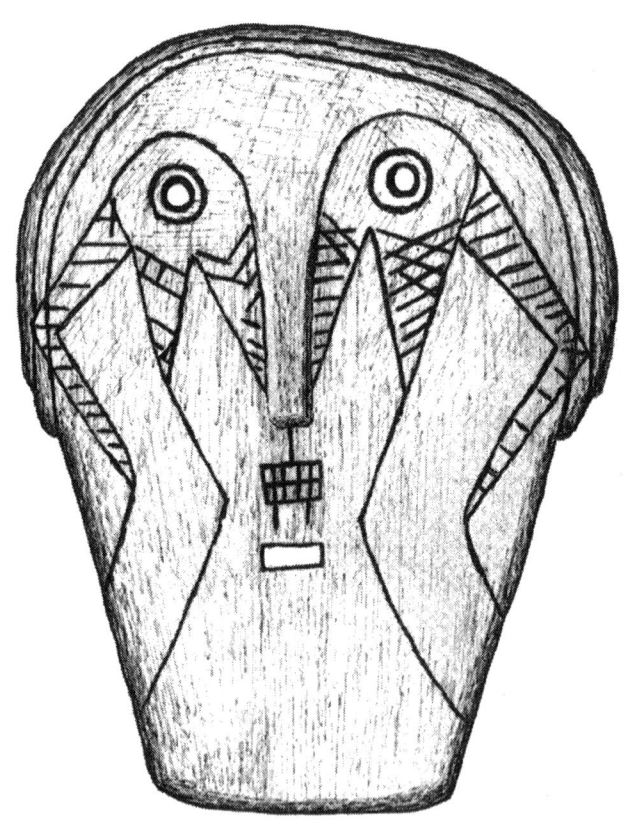

Turtle Shell's Death Mask.
Redrawn from Lewis & Kneberg 1958.

Turtle Shell had been so kind and now he was gone. It wasn't fair. Green Rock wanted to kill all the Yuchi himself for the pain they had caused his family and village. He had never felt that kind of hatred before. He went to bed sad, and without even eating dinner. Over the next couple of days, Green Rock spent his free time at Wolf Tail's lodge.

One morning, Sparrow finally appeared. "Good morning," she said. This was the first time she had visited Wolf Tail's lodge since Turtle Shell had been killed.

"Good morning, Sparrow!" said Wolf Tail.

Green Rock smiled at her. "It's good to see you out again," he said, feeling better with her company.

"Well, I made up my mind," she replied. "Turtle Shell would not want me to spend the rest of my life moping around feeling sorry for myself, so I am going to put it all behind me, and move on."

"Good for you!" said Wolf Tail.

"Are you two hungry?" she asked.

"Yes!" answered Green Rock and Wolf Tail together.

Sparrow laughed and said, "Well, I brought some cornbread and sunflower bread that I made last night."

The three ate a good breakfast and then Sparrow asked Green Rock, "Do you still like carving pipes?"

"Yes, but I haven't done much of it lately," replied Green Rock.

"All of our routines have been messed up for the last moon. Do you have any soapstone left?"

"Just enough for one pipe."

"You make that pipe. I will ask your uncle, my little brother, Twisted Stick if he can get you some more. He will be doing a lot of hunting for other families while the war party is gone. I don't want your stone carving to be set aside. It is a useful talent that will make you wealthy some day."

"Thank you," said Green Rock. "I'll start on it today."

Sparrow left and Green Rock found the piece of soapstone and began whittling on it with a flint flake. He really enjoyed making things with Wolf Tail at his lodge; Wolf Tail was his best friend, and he also liked getting away from home life. It made him feel "grown up."

For the rest of the morning Green Rock worked on his pipe, not sure of what type of animal to feature on it. As he roughed out the preform, he thought about it. He thought of carving another wolf pipe, and then he thought about making it into another eagle. He finally decided to make it a bear effigy pipe because it was so large.

After making that decision, he said to Wolf Tail, "Are you hungry? Let's go see what Mother and Sparrow have cooked."

"Good idea – I'm starving," replied Wolf Tail as he set down the spear point he had been working on.

On the way, Wolf Tail asked, "Do you know sign language? You will need to learn it if you are to be a traveling trader."

"I never really thought of it," answered Green Rock.

"It is the universal language of traders. It varies slightly from tribe to tribe, but most people will get the idea you are trying to convey. Stone Spear taught me what I know, and he said that you can learn the dialects of the different tribes by using sign language."

The next few days were spent doing stone carving, flint knapping, and hunting small game for Squirrel Fur and Sparrow, with the blowgun. When they were not busy with that, Wolf Tail taught Green Rock some sign language.

One afternoon a man approached the lodge and said, "Hello," to Green Rock.

Green Rock turned to see and he recognized him as the man whose baby daughter he had saved from the fire.

Wolf Tail recognized him as the priest's assistant who informed him of Stone Spear's death.

"How are you?" answered Green Rock.

"I am fine. I… We want to thank you for saving White Feather from our burning lodge, I have been asking around, trying to find out who you are and where you were living. I am Eagle Medicine."

"You are welcome, Eagle Medicine, I am Green Rock, and this is Wolf Tail."

"We have met. My wife and I would like you to join us for dinner tonight. Wolf Tail can come too."

"I should go and check up on my mother. My father, Elk Antler is gone with the war party."

"Take care of your mother, and let me know when you two can join us. You can go to the council house on the temple mound – they will know where to find me." And then Eagle Medicine left.

"You saved the *baby daughter* of the *assistant priest*?" asked Wolf Tail, amazed.

"Is that who he is?" Green Rock asked.

"He was the man who told me about Stone Spear's death."

"Wow, I had no idea," said Green Rock, as he was finishing carving on the bear pipe.

Sparrow visited them and said, "I spoke with Mouse, your aunt, and Twisted Stick is out hunting. She said he would get you plenty of soapstone, starting tomorrow."

"Oh, thank you!" replied Green Rock.

"You are welcome, and don't forget what I said about your stone carving."

"I won't," Green Rock assured her.

"I am going to check up on your mother and see if she needs any help with lunch," Sparrow said, and then she left.

At around noon Green Rock and Wolf Tail arrived at Green Rock's family's lodge, but nobody was there. So they went to Sparrow's lodge and found Sparrow and Squirrel Fur finishing up lunch. Sparrow had managed to get Squirrel Fur out of her lodge, which was good. Squirrel Fur's mood seemed to be a little better, which was evidently Sparrow's goal.

They ate a meal of dried deer meat, cornbread and sunflower seed bread, and mushrooms. Green Rock said, "Wolf Tail and I have been invited to eat dinner with Eagle Medicine and his family. He is the father of the baby I rescued from the fire. He wants to know when we can make it over."

"Why not tonight?" asked Squirrel Fur.

"I... I thought I should help you work around here. Especially since..."

Sparrow interrupted him. "You and Wolf Tail go on; I will help your mother." Sparrow was trying to comfort Squirrel Fur, and also not put a burden on the children, and she thought this was a good diversion.

"Yes, go on, eat with Eagle Medicine and his family," added Squirrel Fur, trying to be cheerful. They finished eating, and Green Rock and Wolf Tail returned to Wolf Tail's lodge. Green Rock started rubbing grease into the finished bear pipe he had been working on. Then he went to the council house and looked for Eagle Medicine. The High Priest, Red Talon, had one of his assistants show Green Rock to Eagle Medicine's new lodge. It was built on the same site where his old lodge stood but, in the confusion of the raid, Green Rock had forgotten exactly where it was. Eagle Medicine's wife, Dances Like the Deer, greeted him and showed him in.

"Eagle Medicine will be back shortly," Dances Like the Deer told him. "We are very grateful for you saving White Feather." Then she picked up the baby and let Green Rock hold her.

"She sure is a beautiful girl," said Green Rock, while smiling at the infant. He noticed a white feather tied to her hair. "How old is she?" he asked.

"Seventeen moons," replied Dances Like the Deer. "She is learning to walk. Let me show you," and she picked up White Feather and held her upright by her arms. The infant began walking with her mother's help.

Eagle Medicine entered the lodge. "Green Rock," he said, "I am glad to see you! When can you and Wolf Tail make it for dinner?"

"I spoke with Mother and she said we could come tonight," replied Green Rock.

"Then tonight it is. I will tell Standing Bear and Red Talon. They will be here. I hope you don't mind a crowd. They want to meet the boy who saved my daughter's life. We will be eating good."

"That sounds great. I will tell Wolf Tail."

"Have you ever thought of joining the priesthood?"

"I don't know, I am learning stone carving and flint knapping. My uncle wanted me to become an artisan."

"Are you the boy of ten cycles who made those effigy pipes and traded them to the trader, Bald Eagle?"

"Yes."

"It is obvious that you have a prodigiously divine talent with the stone! I think you may have what it takes to learn the art of healing also, if you think you'd want to become a Devoted Son and learn."

Green Rock was flattered.

"You saved White Feather from the burning lodge," said Eagle Medicine. "That's big Medicine. Just think about it for a while. What types of stone carvings are you doing now?"

"I just finished a bear effigy pipe; all I have to do is finish greasing it."

"I would like to see it when you are finished. You and Wolf Tail should be here before sunset. We eat at sunset. I will see you then."

"I'll bring it tonight," said Green Rock, and then he returned to Wolf Tail's lodge. Wolf Tail was finishing up a large spear point that he had started on earlier that morning.

"Hey, that's going to be a nice one," commented Green Rock.

"It's the largest one I have made," replied Wolf Tail. "Do you think it's thin enough?" he said while handing it to Green Rock.

"That's amazing! How did you keep from breaking it?"

"I held it firmly all around while I took off the thinning flakes. It worked very well."

"How did you hold it?"

"Like this," said Wolf Tail while demonstrating. "You spread out your fingers so that they are supporting the tip and base, giving it strength. Stone Spear never actually told me about it, but I remember how he held the preform while thinning it, and I decided to try it. Here, let me notch it."

Green Rock gave back the preform, and Wolf Tail began to notch it with a split piece of a hollow turkey leg bone. Before long, Wolf Tail had a large thin spear point with deep symmetrical notches. He was proud of it.

"I found Eagle Medicine," said Green Rock, "and he said we should be at his lodge just before sunset. The Uku, and the Shaman, Red Talon will be there too."

Sparrow arrived. "What are you two doing?"

"Look at Wolf Tail's new spear point," said Green Rock. "It is a very nice one."

"Wow! That *is* nice! Why don't we show it to Squirrel Fur," said Sparrow.

The three went to Sparrow's lodge where Squirrel Fur was grinding corn in the wooden mortar. "Take a look at what Wolf Tail just made!" said Sparrow.

Wolf Tail handed the spear point to Squirrel Fur.

"You made this?" asked Squirrel Fur.

"Yes," replied Wolf Tail.

"I think you're catching up with Stone Spear," said Squirrel Fur. "That is very nice."

Wolf Tail smiled proudly. He felt lucky to have Squirrel Fur as a godmother.

"Are you two going to Eagle Medicine's tonight?" asked Sparrow.

"Yes, I went to see him today," replied Green Rock, "He said we should be there just before sunset. The Uku and Red Talon will be there."

"You'd better get ready then," said Squirrel Fur.

Green Rock and Wolf Tail arrived at Eagle Medicine's lodge just before sunset. The sweet smell of cooking meats, bread and vegetables filled the air. Green Rock couldn't help looking forward to this treat.

Eagle Medicine greeted Green Rock and Wolf Tail. Then he said, "I am glad you two made it. This is the Uku Standing Bear, and this is Red Talon, the High Priest."

Green Rock and Wolf Tail greeted the Uku and High Priest. Green Rock was feeling very nervous, but he tried to hide it. He wondered if Wolf Tail was as anxious.

The Uku, Standing Bear spoke. "What is that you have with you?"

"It's a bear effigy pipe I just finished today," replied Green Rock, while handing it to the Uku.

Standing Bear looked it over and, at first, didn't believe that it was made by a boy of ten cycles. "Seriously, did you carve this?"

"Yes, he did," answered Eagle Medicine, "Remember the boy who traded the effigy pipes for the flint from Bald Eagle?"

"I heard about him, but never saw him. Green Rock, you have an enormous talent," said the Uku.

Green Rock was flattered and anxious at the same time. He didn't want to embarrass himself or be disrespectful. "Take it Uku, as my gift to you."

The Uku looked surprised. After some thought he said, "I will have something to give you and your family in return. I won't forget this." He smiled proudly at Green Rock.

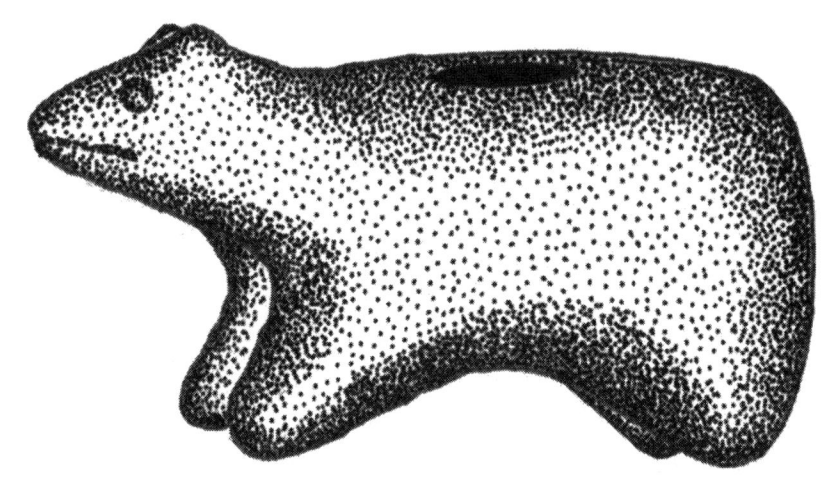

Bear Effigy Pipe Given to Standing Bear by Green Rock.
Based on Hothem 1994.

Eagle Medicine was talking to Red Talon at the other side of the lodge. He motioned for Green Rock to approach them. When Green Rock drew near, Eagle Medicine said to Red Talon, "This is the young man whom I've been telling you about. He is very bright, modest, and courageous, and I feel that he would qualify to become a Devoted Son, if he is willing." He turned to Green Rock and said, "If you decide to join the priesthood, Red Talon and I would be training you."

Red Talon spoke, "I have heard much about you. We will be visiting you in the future to answer any questions you may have. Remember, it is your decision. We both think you are an excellent candidate. But you must decide, take your time and listen to your inner self before you decide."

"I will be considering it," replied Green Rock, shyly. He was flattered and honored.

"Dinner is ready," said Dances Like the Deer.

They all sat down and ate their fill of the feast before them. When they were finished eating, Eagle Medicine gave Green Rock an engraved shell spider gorget as a gift of gratitude for saving his daughter's life. Both Green Rock and Wolf Tail left feeling like their stomachs were going to burst. They hadn't eaten that much in a long time.

Shell Spider Gorget Given to Green Rock by Eagle Medicine.
Redrawn from Holmes 1880.

On the way back home, Green Rock thought a lot about being a Devoted Son and becoming a Shaman. His ego was somewhat boosted by this opportunity, and he couldn't help but have grandiose ideas of what it would be like to have the status of a Priest.

They arrived at Wolf Tail's lodge, and talked about the evening's events. "What do you think I should do?" asked Green Rock.

"I don't want to tell you what to do, but you are good at carving stone, and you enjoy it," replied Wolf Tail.

This answer disappointed Green Rock. "But I could cure the sick! And drive away evil spirits! Isn't that good also?"

"I am not saying I would disapprove of you becoming a Shaman," asserted Wolf Tail, "but I know you better than Red Talon and Eagle Medicine do."

Green Rock was angry and Wolf Tail could see it. "I didn't mean to upset you, but you *did* ask for my opinion," said Wolf Tail, "You shouldn't be so defensive when I answer."

"Well then, I will just ask Mother and see what she thinks!" shouted Green Rock, and he got up and left.

Wolf Tail called out to Green Rock as he left, but Green Rock just ignored him. He arrogantly decided that Wolf Tail was no friend of his, and he never wanted to see him again.

Green Rock arrived home and Squirrel Fur could sense something was wrong. "How did it go at Eagle Medicine's?" she asked.

"It went well," answered Green Rock, "Eagle Medicine and Red Talon want me for a Devoted Son. What do you think?"

Squirrel Fur was surprised at the idea. "It is your decision," she answered. "Just make sure your heart is in whatever you do."

"Wolf Tail was angry with me for even considering it," lied Green Rock. "What do you think Father would say?"

"That doesn't matter. I think he would be proud, and I know I would be. But you need to really think about it before deciding. I know how much you like carving stone, and I hate to see you give it up, but the priesthood is a more noble profession. If you want, I will speak to Wolf Tail. I doubt he will be angry for long, he's your best friend."

"Don't worry about Wolf Tail," replied Green Rock. "I'm not."

This troubled Squirrel Fur, and she began to figure out that it was Green Rock who was angry with Wolf Tail and not vice versa.

Sparrow appeared in the doorway. "Hello, Green Rock," she said. "Did you and Wolf Tail have a good time?"

"Yes, and Eagle Medicine gave me this gorget," replied Green Rock, trying to sound cheerful. He felt uncomfortable and dreaded her finding out about the recent events.

"That's nice," said Sparrow, but she also could tell something was wrong.

Green Rock felt guilty because he was considering abandoning the ideas that were instilled in him by Turtle Shell and Sparrow. He decided to bury the emotion.

Sparrow visited for a while and, when she left, they went to bed.

* * *

Several days later, forty-one of the forty-nine men who had been sent out on the war party returned. Elk Antler was among them. Many of the warriors had Yuchi scalps on their belts, and had brought back one Yuchi prisoner who was tied up. They had gotten retribution, but saw no sign of Running Fox. It was noon when they came through the palisade gate. The villagers flocked to the gates to greet them. Squirrel Fur, Sparrow, Wolf Tail and Green Rock were among them. Many of the villagers shouted insults at the captive, spat on him, and beat him with sticks.

It was a bittersweet reunion – Elk Antler's family was overjoyed that he had returned home safely, but also saddened that Running Fox wasn't with him. When Elk Antler saw Sparrow, he gave her the scalp on his belt – she could hang it in her lodge so that Turtle Shell's spirit would know that they had avenged his murder. Another warrior presented a scalp to the Uku, Standing Bear for a similar purpose.

In total, twenty-nine scalps were taken, and the one prisoner. They had lost only eight, so the expedition was considered very victorious.

All of the villagers searched the war party for their loved ones. Many unfortunate people were obviously grieved when they discovered that their family members had not returned with the rest of the war party.

The enemy captive was stripped of his clothing and tied to a stake in the village square until the time came for the Honored Woman to decide his fate. Meanwhile, he was subject to public ridicule and torment from the villagers. He looked pitiful and haggard.

The warriors each returned to their families' lodges to eat and rest, Elk Antler included. Squirrel Fur and Sparrow hastily prepared a good meal for him; Green Rock and Wolf Tail helped. Green Rock didn't speak to Wolf Tail unless it was absolutely necessary.

"Why are you two not speaking?" asked Elk Antler.

"Green Rock wants to join the priesthood, and he thinks I am angry with him for it," answered Wolf Tail.

"No! *I* am angry with *you!*" shouted Green Rock, "You are just jealous because you didn't get invited yourself!"

"I think I am going to stay out of this," said Elk Antler. "I have no idea what's going on here."

"Green Rock saved Eagle Medicine's daughter from his burning lodge," explained Wolf Tail. "Now he wants him for a Devoted Son. I told him he should stay with what he's good at, and that's stone carving."

"Healing people is more important than making material things for them," said Green Rock in a self-righteous way.

Elk Antler rolled his eyes and said nothing. He still wanted Green Rock to be a warrior, but it was obvious *that* was not going to happen. He thought this situation was very silly and he didn't want any part in it.

Squirrel Fur said, "You two need to stop this petty bickering. All along you have been best friends. You shouldn't let something like this end your friendship. Besides, I think your father has seen enough fighting for now."

"Yes, I have," said Elk Antler.

"Well, if Wolf Tail wasn't so…"

"That's enough, Green Rock!" Squirrel Fur interrupted sternly.

"Why don't Green Rock and I go to get some water?" said Sparrow. She wanted to talk to Green Rock alone.

"Thank you; that would be good," replied Squirrel Fur.

Sparrow got the large water pot and said, "Come on, Green Rock."

On the way to the palisade gate, Sparrow asked Green Rock, "What is going on with you? Wolf Tail is your best friend."

Green Rock was tense. He loved his aunt, and didn't want her to be hurt by his decision to become a Shaman. "I just think that helping people is more important than carving stone," he replied, "Wolf Tail is being unreasonable with me."

"Think about what you just said. Do you really think that you are being totally reasonable with him?"

Green Rock's eyes shifted to the ground. "I don't know."

"I would like to see you become an artisan – but what you do is your decision – but *you* will have to live with your decision," she said.

The two got to the river and filled the water pot. They walked back up the hill in silence. Green Rock was thinking about what Sparrow had said to him.

When they arrived back at the lodge, the Uku, Standing Bear was there, talking to Elk Antler. Then his eyes shifted to Green Rock. "I have some gifts for you and your family," he said, pointing to four fine deer hides.

"Thank you, Uku," replied Green Rock.

"The Eagle Dance will be performed in eight days," the Uku said to Elk Antler. The Eagle Dance was performed to celebrate victories in combat, or to celebrate peace when welcoming guests into the village.

Copper Plate Embossed with Eagle Motif
Redrawn from Thruston 1897.

Only a trained eagle killer knew the protocol involved in killing an eagle without bringing calamity on the village. Eagle killers were selected at a young age and trained for this specific task, which became their trade. He went up into the mountains, to fast and pray for four days. Then he killed a deer and placed the carcass in an open area like the edge of a cliff. The eagle killer then hid nearby with his bow and arrows ready, while praying and singing songs and prayers that were kept secret. When an eagle landed on the deer carcass to eat, the eagle killer shot the eagle with an arrow.

When the eagle was dead, the eagle killer said prayers to its spirit, begging it to not inflict harm on the villagers, and saying that it was a Muskogee or a Yuchi who killed it, and not one of the Cherokee. This was to protect the village from the wrath of the eagle spirits because the golden eagle was the most sacred bird of the Cherokee, and killing it was necessary, but it was also sacrilegious.

Then the eagle killer left the eagle where it lay and returned to the village. When greeted by the first villagers, he simply said, "There is a dead snowbird on the mountain." This was the eagle killer's way of letting the village know that he had succeeded, without the Eagle Spirits knowing. A snowbird was considered insignificant and therefore the Eagle Spirits would not care. After saying this, his work was finished.

Meanwhile, Green Rock had visited several times with Eagle Medicine and Red Talon. He was asking numerous questions about the priesthood, and some couldn't be answered readily, because Shamans kept a lot of secrets. They told him that he would find out some of the answers later if he decided to become a Devoted Son and go through the training. This only made Green Rock more curious.

"I believe I am willing to commit to it," Green Rock said to Eagle Medicine.

"It's a big step," Eagle Medicine would reply. "Think about it thoroughly before making your decision. When you have no doubts whatsoever, I think you will be ready."

At another time, Green Rock spoke with Red Talon. "My friends want me to be an artisan, but I would like to join the priesthood. What should I do?"

"Your training will take up most of your time," answered Red Talon. "You will have few, if any, chances to ever do any stone carving. You will have to say goodbye to that life. You must decide. So, take your time with it."

Green Rock was avoiding Wolf Tail and Sparrow both. He really wanted to start the training, but he secretly wondered about his intentions.

* * *

Four days after the eagle was killed, when all of the parasites were thought to have left the eagle's body, warriors from the village found the eagle and removed its wing feathers and tail feathers. They wrapped the feathers in a fresh hide from another deer that they had just killed. They left the eagle's body where they found it. The skinned deer carcass was also left there as a sacrifice to appease the Eagle Spirits.

On the village square was a small round hut, which was built exclusively for the eagle feathers. The feathers were brought here, still wrapped in their fresh deer hide, and hung inside the hut. The feathers were thought to be hungry from the journey, and a dish of corn and deer meat was placed under it so the feathers could "eat." A dead scarlet tanager was also hung with the hide containing the eagle feathers – also intended to be food for them.

On the morning of the day of the Eagle Dance, the feathers were removed from the deer hide, and made into dance wands or fans for the dance. The mightiest warriors who could be trusted would wear some of the feathers during the dance. Elk Antler was one of these warriors.

They were, of course, warned of the strict protocol to adhere to when wearing the feathers. To drop the feather fans on the ground or to fall down while wearing the feathers would cause bad luck or even death.

Eagle Dance Wand.

While these ceremonial items were being made, a council meeting was called to decide the fate of the Yuchi captive. Honored Woman, or Beloved Woman was a title given to an older and wise woman of the village. It was her job to decide the fate of enemy captives. She had the power to order him killed, or have him spared and be a slave. After awhile, he could then be adopted into the tribe if they thought it was prudent. The Honored Woman's name was Corn Leaf.

The Yuchi warrior could not speak the Cherokee tongue, so they had a man translate for him in sign language. They asked him if he would be willing to adopt the lifestyle of the Cherokee. The captive screamed out a couple of sentences in the Yuchi tongue, and had a look of contempt in his eyes. Then, Corn Leaf approached him and implored him to cooperate and listen to reason. She wanted to show mercy to this man by giving him a second chance and offering the potential to earn the friendship of the village. No sooner had the translator finished signing, the captive spat in Corn Leaf's face.

"Burn him at the stake," she ordered, sadly.

The villagers were in better spirits than Corn Leaf was; their rage still burned hot against the Yuchi. They tied the captive back onto the stake and gathered brush from outside of the palisade. When they began to pile the brush around the bottom of the pole he was bound to, the captive began talking to himself in his own language. It seemed as though he was praying to whatever gods he worshipped.

The villagers set the brush on fire, and their war whoops covered up any cries that the captive may have made. Tears came to Corn Leaf's eyes, as the smell of burning flesh filled the air around the square.

Green Rock was also troubled at this incident, and when the Uku, Standing Bear saw the tears in his eyes he said, "That's how my mother felt! You are young, but foolish to weep at the death of an enemy. Don't doubt that he would do the same to you if given the opportunity."

Green Rock knew the Uku was right. It was the harsh reality of war that he had to accept – sooner or later.

By the time the Sun had set, the villagers were ready for the Eagle Dance. The men and women danced counterclockwise in a circle around a bonfire. The women carried eagle feather fans in their left hands, while the men carried the fans in their right hands, and in their left hands were gourd rattles.

During the dance, the villagers were expected to donate offerings to pay the eagle killer for his work. The dance concluded, most of the people went home, and the eagle killer collected his payment.

Green Rock saw Eagle Medicine on the way home, and stopped to speak with him. "I am ready," he said.

"Are you really sure?" asked Eagle Medicine.

"I have thought about it for many days now, and I can say there are no doubts in my mind," replied Green Rock, but inside he wondered if the latter was entirely true.

"Well then, can you meet me at the council house on the temple mound tomorrow morning?" asked Eagle Medicine.

"I will be there first thing," said Green Rock.

"Oh that's great. I will tell Red Talon. He will be there too."

"I will see you tomorrow then."

"Sleep good."

They parted and, when Green Rock arrived home, his family was getting ready for bed.

"Well, I've made up my mind," said Green Rock. "I am going to be a Devoted Son. I am joining the priesthood."

"That's very good," said Elk Antler.

Squirrel Fur smiled. This affirmation assured Green Rock that what he was doing was right. He went to bed with his head full of anticipation, and a little anxiety.

The next thing he knew it was morning.

Chapter 3: Shaman

After eating a hearty breakfast, Green Rock left for the council house that was in the center of the village. He was very excited about what the day would bring. He went up the steps in the front of the temple mound. The size of the mound amazed him. It must have taken a very long time to complete, especially since it was built one basketful at a time.

He got to the top of the steps, and was at the entrance of the council house. He didn't know whether to enter or wait outside, so he played it safe and remained outside. He looked around from the top of the mound – he could see the entire village from there, and over the palisade in the distance. He noticed the manmade pond just outside the palisade – this pond had been dug out for building the mounds in the village like the one on which he was standing. This mound was the largest by far. It was quite a sight.

Then he saw Eagle Medicine coming up the steps towards him. "Good morning," greeted Green Rock.

"You made it here," returned Eagle Medicine. "Good boy. Are you ready to get started?"

"Yes," replied Green Rock.

"Then come on in," said Eagle Medicine, as he showed Green Rock into the council house. Green Rock had no memory of being inside of this large heptagon-shaped building. He was awestruck at the wooden animal carvings in this sacred place. They sat on the benches on one of the seven sides.

"Do you have a good memory?" asked Eagle Medicine.

"I think so," replied Green Rock.

"I hope you do, because I am about to test it. I am going to recite an incantation – it is sort of long and, when I am finished, you must repeat it to me, word-for-word. You have only one chance to get it correctly. This incantation is used during childbirth to urge the child to come out with ease. Are you ready?"

"Yes," answered Green Rock.

Eagle Medicine began:

"Small boy child, small boy child, quickly, quickly, come on out, come on out! Small boy child, make haste, a bow, a bow; let us see who will get it, let us see who will get it!

"Small girl child, small girl child, quickly, quickly, come on out, come on out! Small girl child, make haste, a sifter, a sifter; let us see who will get it, let us see who will get it!"

Green Rock repeated the incantation. He did it so well that Eagle Medicine couldn't find any flaw in it, and that's what Eagle Medicine wanted.

"You have done well," said Eagle Medicine.

"So, I passed the test?" asked Green Rock.

"Yes, and congratulations."

"I noticed it calls both a boy and a girl."

"Yes, the boy child – or bow – is summoned first, and if he doesn't come, the Shaman tries to coax a girl child – or a sifter – to come out."

"I wonder where all of this knowledge began."

Eagle Medicine smiled and produced a small leather bag. "Now that you have made a commitment to join the Priesthood, I will show you some sacred items." Eagle Medicine sat down, and motioned Green Rock to do likewise. "Here are some items only to be seen and known about by Shamans."

He opened the leather bag, and showed Green Rock its contents. There were several items, such as leather amulets containing bones, teeth, various seeds and other mysterious things. But the most impressive item was a carved and polished stone bird with protruding snail-like eyes.

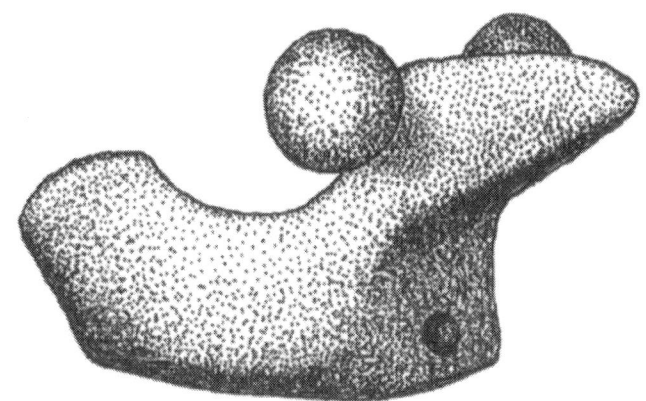

Pop Eyed Birdstone.

"This is an ancient birdstone, older than our tribe itself," said Eagle Medicine. "It is carved from the hardest of rocks."

"Where did it come from?" asked Green Rock.

"From a distant place northwest of here is what I was told. I don't know its original purpose or who even made it, and neither does Red Talon. But it has power. Ancient power. Hold it in your hand."

Green Rock took the birdstone and held it up to his chest. "I can feel it!" he said.

"You now know," smiled Eagle Medicine, and he took back the birdstone and carefully placed it back with the other items in the Medicine bundle. "Yes, you now know." He reverently returned the bundle to where it belonged.

How did we come to our understanding of Medicine?" asked Green Rock.

"It took many generations. Maybe even starting when that birdstone was made. Maybe even earlier. Have you ever heard the story of the origin of diseases and Medicine?"

"No, I haven't."

"Then I will tell you the story."

"When Mother Earth was young, animals, birds, fish, insects, plants, and men could all talk and lived in peace and harmony. But soon mankind multiplied and crowded Mother Earth, and the animals had little room. The animals soon got resentful at mankind, and forgot about their friendships with man. They were further alienated when man invented weapons and began killing animals, birds and fish for food and their skins. The animals were shocked at what mankind was now doing, and they opted to have a council meeting to decide what to do to save their own.

"This was initiated by the Bears, who held a meeting led by their chief, Old White Bear. The animals each testified about the terrible things done by man, and they all voted to wage war against mankind. They decided to make bows and arrows and fight man with his own type of weapons. One of the Bears obtained a fine piece of locust wood to make into a bow. Another Bear volunteered to sacrifice himself to provide gut for the bowstring.

"They finished the bow, but soon discovered that their claws got in the way, and the arrows missed their marks as a result. So the Bear trimmed his claws and had better results. But Old White Bear stated that he was opposed to the idea of trimming their claws, as this would interfere with hunting and climbing trees. The Bears resolved to keep their claws and teeth, and their council meeting was unfruitful.

"Then the Deer held a council meeting led by their chief, Little Deer. They decided to inflict any man with rheumatism if he slew a deer without asking for forgiveness from the Deer's spirit. They told the people at the nearest village of their decision, and instructed man how to render proper respect.

"To this day, when a man kills a Deer, Little Deer runs up to the kill site and asks the Deer's spirit if the hunter paid proper respect. If the answer is 'yes,' Little Deer runs away. If the answer is 'no,' Little Deer follows the hunter home and cripples him with rheumatism.

"Some hunters build a fire in the trail to block Little Deer's path if they are not knowledgeable of how to give proper respect.

"Now, the Reptiles and Fish held a joint council meeting. They decided to inflict man with terrifying dreams of snakes and of eating rotten fish, so that man would suffer from apathy.

"Then, the smaller animals, including the Birds and Insects, held their own meeting. Grub Worm led this meeting, and they each decided on a different disease with which to inflict man.

"The Plants were still friends with man. They heard the bad things that the animals, birds and fish were planning, and decided to help mankind. Every herb, bush, moss, and tree each decided on a specific disease that it would cure.

"Thus, Medicine was created. Any time a man is ill from the mischief of the Animal Spirits, and the Shaman does not know what to do, all he needs to do is look to the Plant Spirits. In them lies the cure for disease."

"I have heard about paying respect to animal spirits when you kill animals," said Green Rock, "but I never heard the complete story behind it."

Red Talon then entered the council house. "Good morning, Green Rock, Eagle Medicine," he said.

"Good morning," returned Green Rock.

"Green Rock passed the memory test," said Eagle Medicine, proudly.

"That's good to hear!" replied Red Talon. "I will leave you two alone so you can get started," he said, before leaving.

"Why doesn't Red Talon stay for my training?" asked Green Rock.

"He has left it up to me. He is getting up in age and is placing more responsibilities on me. He will be assisting me in training you – but he is my trainer, and I am your trainer. I will replace him, and you will eventually replace me."

"What do we do next?" asked Green Rock.

"There are several more tests that you must pass. First I would like to tell you about some of the things we will be studying. We might have time to start on some of these things today. Tell me, what do you already know about a Shaman's responsibilities?"

"A Shaman cures the sick and drives off evil spirits. He oversees ceremonies also."

"Yes, that is true," said Eagle Medicine with a smile, "but, above all, they also must be modest – humility is a very practical Medicine in itself."

This made Green Rock question his own intentions, but he said nothing.

Eagle Medicine continued, "Shamans must have a good memory – this is necessary for memorizing the protocols and incantations that they use. They must keep these formulas under strict secrecy, and not tell anybody about them – not even family members or friends. They must also memorize which herbs cure which diseases. They have to know how to identify these herbs, where to find them, and how to prepare teas, decoctions, ointments and pastes from them.

"They watch the stars and the phases of the moon to calculate the best days for ceremonies; and for giving newborn infants their natal names."

Green Rock listened throughout the morning to Eagle Medicine. After eating lunch, they went up into the mountains to a secluded spot. There they began the series of secret tests that proved to be physical ordeals that involved fasting and other rituals. These tests lasted for the next several days.

* * *

Green Rock passed the tests, and now the training started. Early that morning, Eagle Medicine began speaking of the sacred Medicine Wheel, "The Medicine Wheel represents the four cardinal directions. These go around in the same way as dancers go around a fire. They are the East, North, West, and South. The Medicine Wheel appears as a circle because of the four directions. But it actually represents a sphere because it also includes below, within, and above – these total seven directions. The numbers four and seven are held sacred to our people, especially the number seven. If you look around the village, you will see the number seven used in all aspects of our lives. There are seven clans, seven directions, and the council house is even seven-sided. Did you notice how many warriors left on the last war party?"

"Forty-something," replied Green Rock.

"Forty-nine, that is seven sevens. This number was chosen for a reason. There are six ceremonies in a cycle, and the Sacred Seventh ceremony is only held once every seven cycles."

"What do the seven directions mean?" asked Green Rock.

"Well, the East represents Spirit, Life, Success, Power, and Victory. The Element of the East is Fire, the Season the East represents is Spring, and the time represented is Morning. Red Spirit is the guardian of the East. You will learn more about Red Spirit and the other Honored Spirits later. Your first soul is represented in the East.

"I like the East!" said Green Rock.

"That's good, but we need to try to focus," replied Eagle Medicine.

Green Rock realized he should perhaps listen more and not talk as much.

Eagle Medicine continued, "North symbolizes Midnight, Winter, Surrender, Defeat, Modesty. The Element of the North is Air. The Guardian of the North is Blue Spirit. The second soul is represented in the North.

"West represents Death, Impermanence, Change, Ancestors, and Eternity. The Element of the West is Water. The Season represented is Autumn. The time represented by the West is Evening. Black Spirit is the guardian of the West. Your third soul is represented in the West.

"South symbolizes Healing, Peace, Harmony, Natural Space, Summer, and Noon, or Midday. The South represents your fourth soul. White Spirit is the guardian of the South."

"What do you mean by my fourth soul?" asked Green Rock, "Do people have more than one soul?"

"Each person has four souls," answered Eagle Medicine, "Your first soul lives in your head, and it is the thinking soul that seeks to learn more about and remember everything around you. When you die, this soul leaves your body first – leaving during the first day. It travels to a place where it can learn more.

"The second soul lives in your abdomen and oversees digestion of what you eat. Seven days after death, it leaves your body, and is passed on through the blood to future generations.

"Your third soul is in your heart, and it pumps blood through the rivers of circulation throughout your body. It leaves your body a moon after you die. It, like the second soul, is also recycled.

"The fourth soul is in your bones. It supports your whole body. A cycle after death, it leaves your body and moves underground and turns into Crystals."

"I never heard about that," said Green Rock. "What about the Honored Spirits?"

"Be patient, little boy. We will talk about them later." Eagle Medicine paused, as if he had heard something.

What's wrong?" asked Green Rock.

"Shhh!" Eagle Medicine squatted down, while motioning Green Rock to do likewise. "Over there," he whispered. "I heard something."

"Was it a deer?" whispered Green Rock.

"We can't take that chance with the Muskogee warriors out and about these days. It could very well be one of their war parties."

They sat there silently, listening. Something was definitely there, as they could hear twigs snapping and leaves crackling. Eagle Medicine made sure he still had his knife.

"Maybe it's one of our hunters," speculated Green Rock in a whisper.

Eagle Medicine whistled a bird call. There was no response. The two sat there motionless, listening.

Suddenly, they saw a black bear with two cubs walking into the clearing.

"Having cubs, she will be on the fight," warned Eagle Medicine in a whisper. "Stay out of sight, and keep quiet. Fortunately, we are downwind."

The mother bear was foraging for food, while the cubs were playing. Time passed slowly, but finally the bears wandered off into the woods, and disappeared.

After a few minutes, Eagle Medicine said, "I think they're gone."

The two got up, and caught two bullfrogs in a nearby stream, which they prepared for lunch. It had been a long morning.

"Do you like frogs?" Green Rock asked, as they cooked on the spit.

"Never knew any of them personally," replied Eagle Medicine.

"I meant for eating!" retorted Green Rock.

"They are alright," smiled Eagle Medicine.

"I love them," said Green Rock, and they began eating.

While they were eating, Eagle Medicine said, "Well, before this morning's little interruption, we were talking about the Medicine Wheel. These frog legs are hot! Anyway, We have covered the four cardinal directions and the Spirits who are the guardians of these directions. But there are three more directions, Above, Below and Within.

"So, Below represents Confusion, Turmoil, Suffering, and Birth. The time represented by below is the Past. The color represented is Orange or Brown.

"Within represents the Present – the Here and Now. Within is what we have the most control over. It is symbolized by the color Green.

"Above represents the Future, Divinity, Order, Wisdom, and Happiness. The symbolic color for Above is Yellow."

Green Rock asked Eagle numerous questions about the Medicine Wheel, which Eagle Medicine gladly answered. The lessons lasted all afternoon.

That evening, Eagle Medicine sent Green Rock out to fetch some firewood, while Eagle Medicine cleaned a muskrat he had killed. As Green Rock searched for some good dry sticks, a stone caught his eye. He picked it up to look at it. It was a piece of very high quality soapstone!

Muskrat.
Redrawn from Image by OpenClipart-Vectors from Pixabay.

Green Rock ran back to camp, carrying the firewood along with his soapstone. "Look at what I found!" he proudly announced.

Eagle Medicine looked at the soapstone. "This is nice," he said, "but you are not going to have much time for carving anymore."

Green Rock looked down, reluctant to accept this fact.

It crossed Eagle Medicine's mind that perhaps Green Rock becoming a Shaman was not meant to be. But he said nothing, but planned to think about it more. By now, Green Rock had learned so much, perhaps it was too late to change his mind, Eagle Medicine thought.

Green Rock sensed Eagle Medicine's misgivings. "Is everything okay? Green Rock asked.

"Yes, fine," replied Eagle Medicine. "Let's cook this muskrat."

They ate silently, and said little as the night progressed. Green Rock had always questioned his intentions secretly, hoping Eagle Medicine wouldn't ever notice. Eagle Medicine eventually forgot about his doubts, as he considered what he should be teaching Green Rock next.

* * *

Days went by unnoticed during the training. They spent most of their time talking and meditating in the mountains. Eagle Medicine began to talk about the Honored Spirits.

"As you grow older, you will develop strong relationships with some of the Honored Spirits – more so than with others. Not that the others are less important, but some will show you more favor, depending on your personality."

"Which of these Honored Spirits is the greatest?" asked Green Rock.

"The Creator is the supreme being who created all things in the Universe," replied Eagle Medicine. "The Creator *is* everything. Little is known about the Creator, though this being is the most-supreme deity.

"Mother Earth is the female spirit of the world we live on.

"Grandfather Rock is a very wise deity who is older than Mother Earth. He is the ancient keeper of records. He is the male form of Mother Earth.

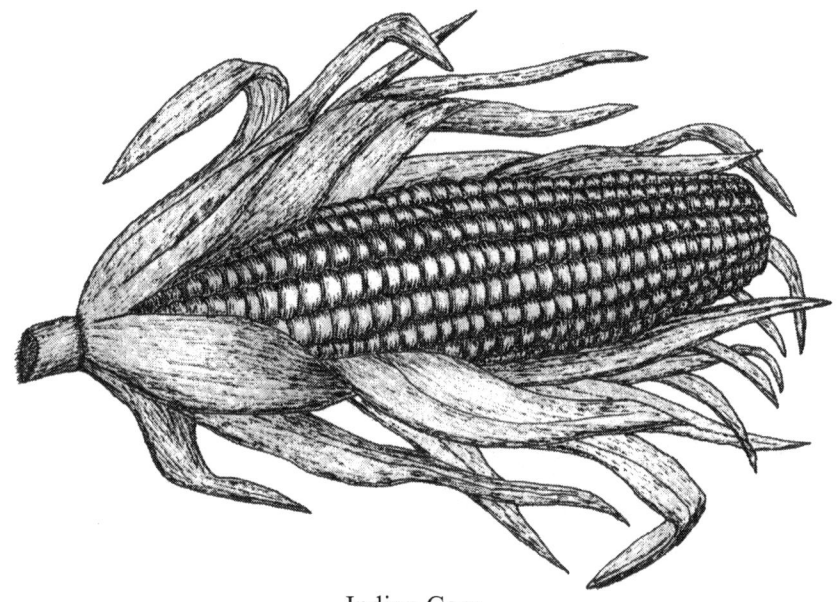

Indian Corn.
Redrawn from Harter 1988.

"Corn Mother is the spirit of the corn. In ancient days, she lived on the Earth in human form. When she was slain by her disobedient sons, corn grew from her blood and she became an Honored Spirit. Corn Mother teaches us kindness, generosity, and love. She and her husband, Great Hunter were the parents of the Little Red Men.

"Great Hunter is Corn Mother's husband. Warriors and hunters call on him to give them success in their hunting and battles. He is also called Great Thunder, and his two sons – who are the Little Red Men – live in the Darkening Land of the West. He, like Corn Mother, teaches generosity – but he also teaches us gratitude and respect. He may be the same being as the Red Spirit – the Guardian of the East. He is the ruler of the Thunder Beings.

"The Thunders are a group of spirits, who are led by Great Thunder or Great Hunter. Two of them are the sons of Great Thunder, the Little Red Men, while the others are his assistants. They live all around us, but particularly like caves that occur behind waterfalls, and some stay with Great Thunder in the West. The Thunders are the Storm Gods. The Honey Locust tree is sacred to them. The Rattlesnake is also associated with the Thunders.

"Long Being is the Spirit of the Water and, like Grandfather Rock, this deity has a vast archive of wisdom. Hunters and warriors who seek strength and wisdom often call upon Long Being. This deity is associated with Black Spirit – guardian of the West.

"Little Whirlwind is the Spirit of the Air. It is often called on by Shamans to carry away the evil spirits who cause illness, once they are removed from the sick person's body. This deity is associated with the Blue Spirit guardian of the North.

"Ancient Red is the Spirit of Fire, and is often called on by hunters. Ancient Red is associated with the guardian of the East and the Sun.

"And finally, Ancient White is the Spirit of Smoke, and it carries messages from us to the Spirits."

* * *

One day they sat by a mountain stream. They watched a doe drinking from the stream about twenty paces from them. Suddenly, a panther pounced on the doe from a short cliff above the stream. The panther's jaws locked down on her throat, and the doe's cries of terror were choked and abruptly silenced. Eagle Medicine and Green Rock remained at a safe distance.

"Will the panther come and eat us?" asked Green Rock, fearfully.

"He will leave us be. He has his meal for today," Eagle Medicine reassured him.

Green Rock was troubled by the sudden attack. Eagle Medicine noticed this and asked, "What are you thinking about?"

"That poor deer – the deer never have a chance against mountain lions," said Green Rock, almost with tears in his eyes.

"What about the mountain lion?" asked Eagle Medicine. "Doesn't he have to eat like the rest of Nature?"

"It's not fair," said Green Rock.

"Nobody ever said it would be. You should learn to trust and accept that Nature will look after all animals and plants. It is all a part of life's greater plan. It is the Creator's design. The strongest and smartest survive, so that the energy of life can be strong. Surrender to what is; don't be attached to anything. Bend but don't break. The less dependent you are on anything in life, the less suffering you will experience."

Next they began studying healing herbs and where to find them. "Why don't we walk around and study each herb as we see it?" suggested Eagle Medicine.

"Alright," returned Green Rock.

"You know what tree this is, don't you?" asked Eagle Medicine, while pointing up to it.

"It is a hickory tree," replied Green Rock. "Its green wood can be burned for smoking meats. It flavors the meat very good. My family uses it."

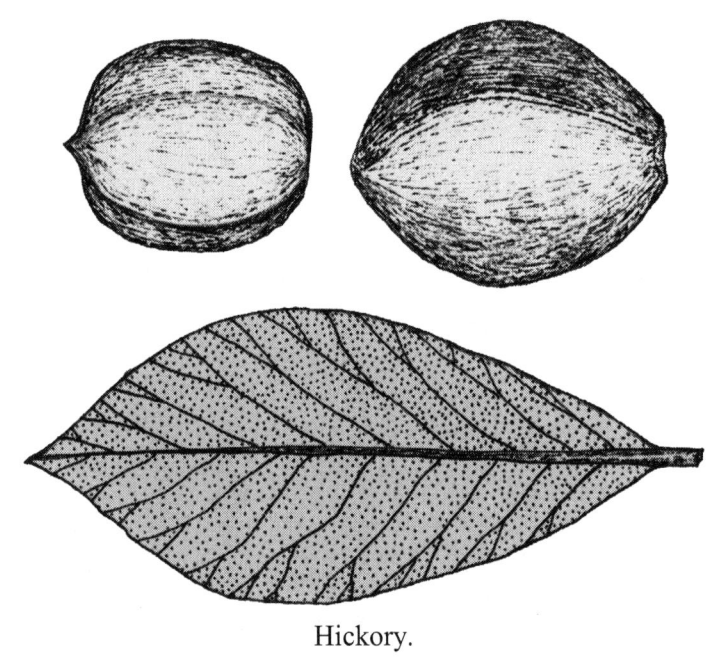

Hickory.

"Very good," said Eagle Medicine. "Let's go see what else we can find."

"This plant is called 'vetch', it is boiled and strained and then allowed to cool. Then you drink the decoction to treat indigestion and a sore back. It is also rubbed into the ritual scratches that are done on ball players. This is said to strengthen their muscles for the game. You can rub it on the stomach to relieve cramps. It is used with another herb, called 'life everlasting' in a decoction for rheumatism."

After walking a short distance, Eagle Medicine said, "This small plant is skullcap. It is made into a decoction that you drink. It is a sedative, diuretic, and a tonic. It's used for treating convulsions, spasms, and nervous disorders. There are four varieties; I will show you all of them as we see them. All four are mixed together in a decoction to drink for promoting menstruation – this is also used to wash impure people and things that were touched by a woman who is menstruating. A woman who is menstruating is required to stay in a hut built just for that purpose, and can reenter the village after she stops bleeding. Skullcap is also mixed with other herbs and used to treat breast pains."

"Why does a woman have to isolate herself during her moon time?" asked Green Rock.

"Women are separated, and not allowed to participate in ceremonies, because they possess a special power to create life. If they participate in ceremonies, their powers will interfere with the rituals. They are not rejected in any way. On the contrary, they are honored by this custom.

As they made their way through the woods, Eagle Medicine asked, "You do know what a pine tree looks like, don't you?"

"Yes," replied Green Rock, "it is an evergreen."

"That is correct. All evergreens, including the pine tree, should be shown great respect because they are sacred. You can make incense from the sap as an offering to the Honored Spirits. It sends forth a thick, white smoke. It is used in death rituals. It is also a diuretic and can be used internally on kidney and bladder infections, respiratory problems, and rheumatism. It can also be used externally for a poultice, or heated and mixed with tallow for an ointment. When taking pinesap, always show respect and leave something in return.

"Another herb that should receive great respect is ginseng – the Little Man. It is very rare, and I will point it out and tell you more when we find a ginseng plant.

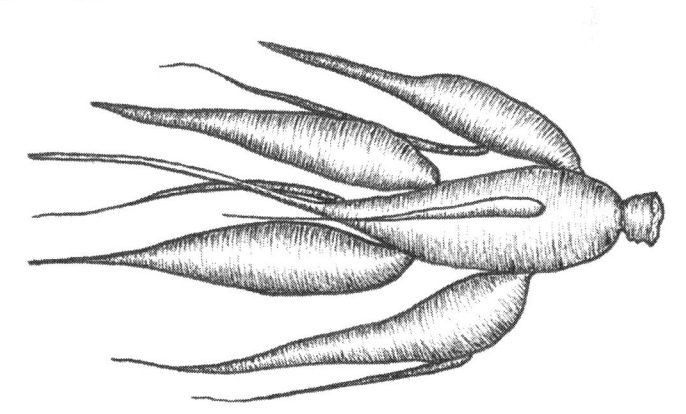

Ginseng Root (aka "Man Root" & "Little Man").

"This here is life everlasting – remember what this is mixed with?"
"Vetch," answered Green Rock, "for treating rheumatism."

"Very good," said Eagle Medicine. "This plant has great medical value. By itself, it is used as a tea for respiratory and intestinal ailments. It is used as well in sweat baths for many different diseases.

"Over here is sumpweed. You might recognize it – we grow it in our gardens for its edible seeds."

Sumpweed.

"Hey! There is a ginseng plant! I knew we would find one if we looked hard enough. This is also called the Man Root, and the Little Man. This plant is an evergreen, so it is sacred and requires respect. It is rare also. The dried root is made into a decoction that works well in treating headaches, cramps, and female conditions. It is good for colic. It is also an aphrodisiac, and a stimulant. Be sure to show respect and leave something behind when taking ginseng. Also be sure the root is completely dry before using it.

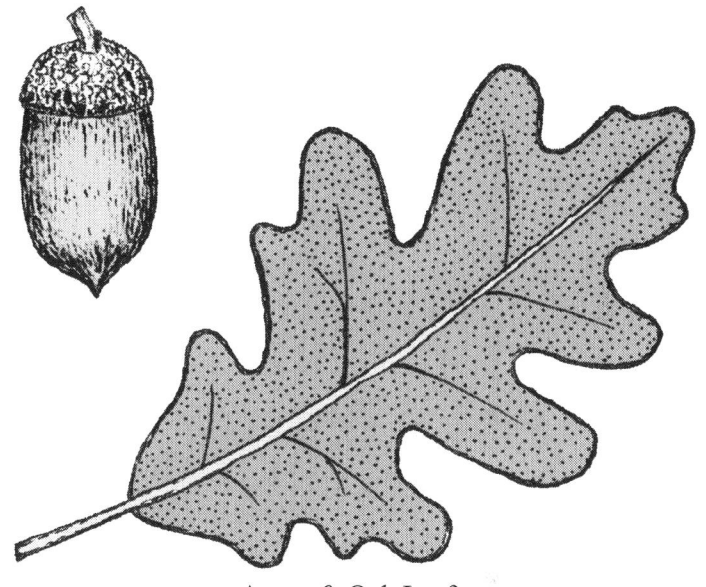

Acorn & Oak Leaf.

"This tree, as you probably know is an oak. What are oak trees used for?" asked Eagle Medicine.

"The acorns are boiled in at least two batches of water, and then ground into flour with a mortar and pestle," answered Green Rock. "The flour is used for acorn meal bread. The bark is used for tanning hides."

"Correct," said Eagle Medicine, "You can also make cooking oil out of the acorns. As for Medicine, it can be made into a decoction and used internally for blood in the urine, and externally for hemorrhoids. Occasionally it is made into a tea to treat fever also.

Something about this made Green Rock recall the things his father seemed to say to his mother all the time. Green Rock's father had always wanted him to be a mighty warrior, but instead, he had chosen the path of an artisan. Elk Antler had voiced his resentment repeatedly, although he had no say in the matter. In the Cherokee tribe, the fatherly roles were played by adult males of the child's clan. A child belonged to his mother's clan, which meant that his mother's brothers and other clansmen filled this responsibility. Although Elk Antler thought of Green Rock as a waste of time, he had absolutely no say in the matter.

The memory might have been triggered by the thought of tanning hides. Green Rock commonly had helped his father in doing that. Green Rock never felt like he had ever measured up. But now, he was in training for the Priesthood! That was far better than any warrior, or so Green Rock silently hoped. Suddenly, Green Rock realized Eagle Medicine was talking.

"Green Rock," said Eagle Medicine, "Are you listening?"

"Oh!" said Green Rock, "I'm sorry. I was thinking about something."

"What?" asked Eagle Medicine.

"Nothing," replied Green Rock, embarrassed.

"Well, as a Devoted Son who's going to be a Shaman, you need to outgrow that daydreaming."

"I'm sorry," said Green Rock.

Eagle Medicine said, "Perhaps we need to take a break anyway. See those buffalo up the hill over there?"

Green Rock looked where he was pointing, and spotted them, a good distance up the mountain.

"Let's have some!" smiled Eagle Medicine, as he pulled out some buffalo jerky. He handed a piece to Green Rock.

They ate in silence. Green Rock said, "I wish my father loved me."

Eagle Medicine didn't expect this comment. He knew the situation well. After some thought, he said, "I wish you could know how much he does love you." Even Eagle Medicine doubted this, but couldn't think of anything better to say. "There is nothing wrong with you. Never forget that. Your father can only do his best, as can you."

They ate in silence, and then resumed Green Rock's lessons.

"This is a wild tobacco plant," said Eagle Medicine. "This most sacred plant is also known as 'Old Tobacco'. As you know, we dry the leaves and smoke them during ceremonies, and we offer it to the Honored Spirits. You can chew the leaves and then spit on wasp stings to treat them. Tobacco smoke is used to purify. Witches strongly dislike the smell of tobacco smoke, and for this reason it is used to drive them away.

"Speaking of witches, this is a sapling of sourwood. It usually grows larger than this one. It grows in the moist bottomlands, and it can also be used to kill or drive away witches. It is an excellent wood for cooking spits; it gives flavor to the meat. It is not a good wood to use as fuel for cook fires, because it will make a person sick. It is good, however, for making eating utensils.

"Is this another ginseng plant?" asked Green Rock, while pointing to it.

"It sure is," replied Eagle Medicine. "You have good eyes!"

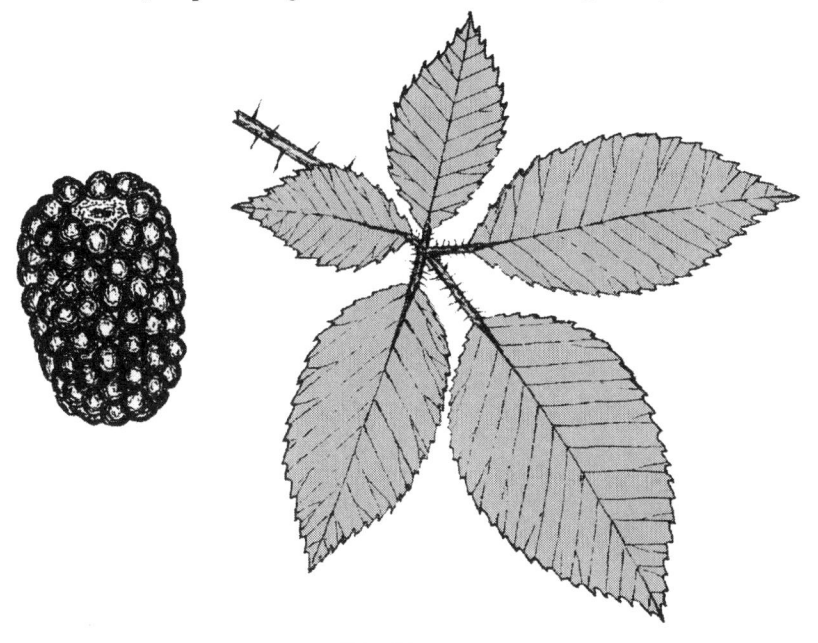

Blackberry.

It was getting dark, and they set up their camp and ate dried deer meat and blackberries they had picked earlier. Eagle Medicine told Green Rock some secret incantations and details about preparing some of the medicines Green Rock had learned about that day. Then they went to sleep.

They woke up and bathed in the stream and said prayers to the Sun. Eagle Medicine left for a while and returned with a rabbit he killed with his bow. Together they skinned and cooked it. It tasted great. Then they started walking through the woods again, Eagle Medicine teaching Green Rock more herbs.

They arrived back at the mountain stream, at a rock outcropping. "This small plant growing in the crack in the boulder is a maidenhair fern. A decoction of the leaves is good for fever, cough and congestion. It's also used for rheumatism."

"This is a sassafras tree. It is taboo to burn the wood from this tree.

"Up in this tree, where I am pointing is mistletoe. It is an evergreen, so it must always be treated with respect. The white berries are poisonous. The other parts of the plant are used as an ingredient in love potions. It is also used for abortions, but this is strongly discouraged, because it destroys the union symbolized by this plant.

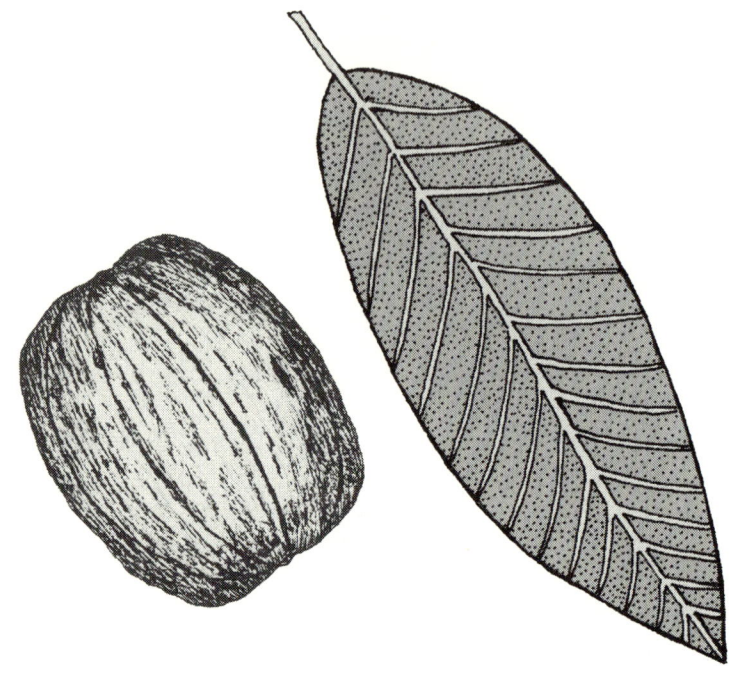

Black Walnut.

"This tree with the mistletoe is a black walnut tree. The leaves can be made into a wash that cleans the skin very well. The nut rind is pounded and tossed into a small creek. This puts fish in a stupor, and they are easy to pick out of the water. The nut rind is also made into a poultice that cures ringworm. The bark is made into a decoction that is used for a mouthwash, and to treat diarrhea. The nuts can be pounded into a powder and made into a tea that works as an anaphrodisiac for men."

Eagle Medicine smiled and said, "Many times when a father doesn't want a man to marry his daughter, he mixes it into the young man's drink and the man can't perform for the woman and she then decides she doesn't want anything to do with him." They both laughed.

"But back to fishing," said Eagle Medicine. "Other plant items can also be used for putting fish into a stupor too. There is turkey mullen, chestnuts, buckeye and soapweed."

"What do they look like?" asked Green Rock.

"I'll point them out when I spot them."

"I'm hungry."

"You are always hungry!" jeered Eagle Medicine. "Let's keep walking. We'll eat soon enough."

They continued walking, and after a while, Eagle Medicine said, "You know? I am getting hungry too."

"You are always hungry!" jabbed Green Rock. He immediately thought maybe he shouldn't have been disrespectful.

But Eagle Medicine chuckled and admitted, "You got me!"

I am sorry if I was disrespectful, you being a Shaman and my teacher."

"Relax. Even Shamans have to have a good laugh!" Eagle Medicine smiled with sincerity that reassured Green Rock. "Here's some jerky."

They ate and continued their walk through the woods.

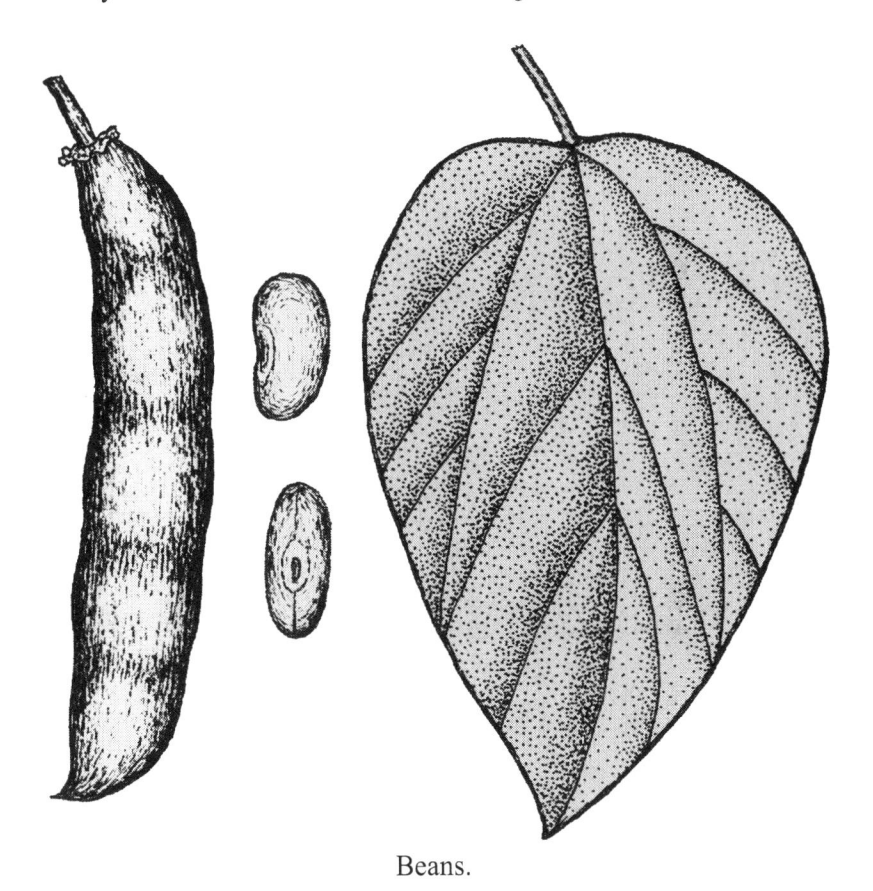

Beans.

As they walked, Eagle Medicine said, "Did you know that the green beans that we grow for food also have a medicinal value?"

"No, I didn't know," replied Green Rock.

"Well, they do. You can brew a tea from the pods that relieves rheumatism, swelling, and bladder and kidney problems. You can also treat acne by applying bean meal to the skin eruptions.

"The sunflowers that we grow in our gardens also have medicinal properties. The seeds that we eat are good for respiratory ailments and rheumatism also.

Sunflower.
Redrawn from photo by Unknown Artist from Pixabay.

"This is a wild plum tree. The inner bark can be made into a decoction that is gargled for treating mouth sores.

Wild Plum.

Just before sunset they arrived back at their camp by the stream. "Green Rock," said Eagle Medicine, "why don't you go and gather firewood while I shoot us another rabbit?"

"Okay," replied Green Rock, and they departed. As Green Rock gathered wood here and there, he saw many different herbs that they had discussed. Each time he saw one, he would quietly speak its name and what diseases it had power to cure.

Once his arms were full of firewood, he returned to camp and laid it on the ground. Then he returned to the woods to get more. He saw a good piece and walked over to get it. On his way, he noticed a beautiful white feather lying in the grass. He picked it up and examined it. It looked very much like the eagle feathers he had seen during the Eagle Dance. He looked around for a while and then said, "Little People, I want to take this if it is alright." He had heard about the Little People, but knew nothing about them, other than that they should be asked before taking something they might have left in the woods.

When Green Rock returned to the camp, Eagle Medicine had just started skinning a rabbit he had shot with an arrow.

"Eagle Medicine," said Green Rock, "I just found this. Is it an eagle feather?"

Eagle Medicine looked it over and said, "It sure is! Did you ask the Little People before taking it?"

"Yes, I did," replied Green Rock.

"This is a good omen," said Eagle Medicine. "Eagle feathers that are found are a gift and should be used in ceremonies and for healing. The eagle feather is sacred because of its healing energy. The Spirits were good to you today. I will teach you how to use it soon."

"Who are the Little People?" asked Green Rock. "I heard that you should ask them before taking something you find, but I don't know much about them."

"Why don't we make that our topic of discussion tomorrow?" suggested Eagle Medicine.

"Okay," answered Green Rock with a smile.

They skinned, cleaned and cooked the rabbit and ate well. They spent the rest of the evening going over the herbs and details on how to prepare them for Medicine. Then they went to sleep for the night.

At dawn, Green Rock awoke and joined Eagle Medicine in their baths in the cold stream, and prayers to the rising Sun. Then they went hunting and Green Rock killed two squirrels with his blowgun.

They returned to camp and as they prepared their breakfast Green Rock asked, "Can you tell me about the Little People now?"

"What would you like to know about them?" asked Eagle Medicine.

"I don't know anything about them – I have heard of them, but don't know much about them."

Eagle Medicine started, "The Little People are very short, usually about knee high to a grown man, but can be up to three feet high. Their hair is very long, often reaching the ground. They leave special things in places where a deserving person will find them, but sometimes the objects are left there by mistake. That is why you must ask their permission before taking something special that you have found.

"The Little People travel all over the circle of Mother Earth and bring back news from the far corners of the world.

"They are often heard singing, drumming, whistling, laughing, chanting, and whispering in the distance. Many people are curious and try to follow them, but they do not like uninvited guests, and sometimes wreak havoc on intruders. They do, however, care for lost children and adults, often taking them to their homes and caring for them. Then they see that they are returned home safely. Often women leave out cornbread in their lodge for the Little People. They sometimes like to visit our lodges, and they love cornbread. They take nothing unless they are hungry."

"Where do they live?" asked Green Rock.

"There are only a few clans of Little People. The Laurel Clan resides among the laurels. They endeavor to solve problems that arise in Nature. When hardship strikes the land in the forms of flood, drought, and forest fires, they help Nature and the environment to recover. They prevent plants and animals from becoming extinct, by moving them to better places if the area is damaged too badly. They teach us to be happy with what we have, and share with our fellow creatures.

"The Tree Clan lives in the trees, and they are welcomed by the trees. Their lodges are inside of hollow trees. These Little People and the snakes together protect all the animals and birds. When an intruder approaches, the trees drop their dead branches to warn the Little People. They can cause mischief on people who do not show proper respect to Nature. Usually they will hide things from a person who has been disrespectful, to show him what it's like to be without. They teach us not to kill anything unless it is absolutely necessary for our survival.

"The Dogwood Clan lives among the dogwood trees. They are seen only when they want to be, and the flowers of the dogwood trees are their tears. They are very emotionally and physically sensitive, and spend their time visualizing only good things for all animals, plants, fish, birds, and people. Some seasons their tears last longer than other seasons, indicating that we have been inconsiderate to each other and other living things. They cause no mischief; they only want the best for every living thing.

"The Rock Cave Little People live in caves in the mountainsides. They are known to harvest corn for us in the middle of the night if we are behind on these chores. They watch after our children, and bring healing herbs to the sick. They care about how we treat each other, and are sometimes mischievous by playing tricks on people. This is to remind people that a person is treated the same way he treats another.

"The Thunder Beings come down to the ground in the form of lightning bolts. It is said that for their wings to grow their largest it took thousands of cycles. During that time, they lived in the clouds and were fed by rain. It was similar to butterflies in cocoons. The Thunder Beings are the subjects of Great Thunder, also known as Great Hunter. The Little Red Men are his sons. They all are a source of wisdom and power.

"The Cherokee seem to have favor in the Little People's eyes, because the Little People only show themselves to our tribe.

"You should always respect the Little People and never mock them. People who sing along with their songs, or dance to the beat of their drums have unfortunate things happen to them. Many times people who do not believe in them are made to believe by the Little People. They have ways of making you believe because they wish for you to believe in them."

Eagle Medicine then told Green Rock about some of the forbidden places where the Little People were known to live. He instructed him to stay away from these places. The Little People did not want to be disturbed at their homes.

"Can you tell me about the ceremonies that Shamans preside over?" asked Green Rock.

"Yes," answered Eagle Medicine, and he began describing the ceremonies, along with the duties of Shamans during the ceremonies.

* * *

They returned to Birch Mountain after about one moon of training. They carried fresh herbs that they had gathered. On the way, Eagle Medicine said, "Now we will assist Red Talon with his work, so you can gain some experience. But first, go see your parents – I am sure they must miss you greatly! I will come and get you when the time comes for you to help."

They entered the palisade gate and Eagle Medicine headed for the council house on top of the temple mound, while Green Rock went to his family's lodge. He noticed Wolf Tail knapping a spear point at his lodge. Their eyes met, and Green Rock looked away.

He continued to his home, and when he saw it, he felt as though he had been gone for several cycles.

"Green Rock!" exclaimed Squirrel Fur and Sparrow simultaneously. They dropped their pestles and ran to greet him. The three collided and embraced for a long time.

"How is your training going?" asked Sparrow.

"I have learned a lot about herbs and the Honored Spirits, the Little People and much more," replied Green Rock. "I have missed you two so much!"

"It's so good to have you back home!" said Squirrel Fur. "Your father is at Twisted Stick's lodge – they killed a bear and are dressing it. We will have a feast tonight. Why don't you go and invite Wolf Tail?"

This disturbed Green Rock. Inside, he felt ashamed to face Wolf Tail. Sparrow sensed this and said, "I will go with you."

They left together. On the way, Sparrow said, "I hope you are not still angry at Wolf Tail."

Green Rock was silent.

"If the priesthood doesn't work out for you, you can still be an artisan," added Sparrow.

"I am doing very well with the training," said Green Rock, trying to put up a front.

They walked in silence. Sparrow's intuition told her not to believe Green Rock, but she opted to say nothing. They arrived at Wolf Tail's lodge and Green Rock saw a pile of soapstone on the ground.

"It's good to see you again," said Wolf Tail.

"Ask him, Green Rock," said Sparrow.

"Would... We would like you to eat dinner with us," said Green Rock, embarrassed.

Wolf Tail embraced Green Rock. He could tell that Green Rock was tense. It made Wolf Tail feel a little sadness and pity for him.

"It's nice to see you also," returned Green Rock, half-heartedly.

"Why don't you two stay here and catch up while I help prepare dinner with your parents?" said Sparrow.

"Good idea," said Wolf Tail, "It's been awhile."

Sparrow left, and Green Rock felt very awkward. Wolf Tail showed Green Rock all of the spear points he had made during Green Rock's absence. Green Rock could clearly see that Wolf Tail had gained a lot of skill in flint knapping.

Wolf Tail said, "I tried to carve this wolf pipe, but broke it while drilling it. I guess I need somebody good to teach me."

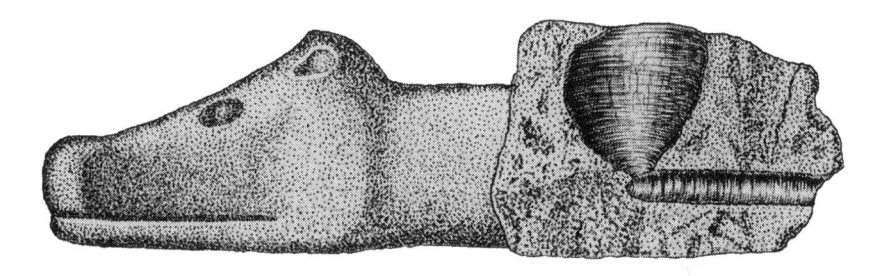

Wolf Tail's Broken Pipe.
Redrawn from Squier & Davis 1847.

Green Rock felt awkward at Wolf Tail's little hint, and even a little sad upon seeing Wolf Tail's ruined pipe. He began to miss working with his hands – carving pipes and learning flint knapping – but he tried to tell himself that he had chosen a more noble profession as a Shaman.

The day seemed to drag on for Green Rock and, just before sundown, Sparrow came up and said, "Dinner is ready." He welcomed the distraction.

They ate the best meal that Green Rock had eaten in a long time. There was bear meat, cornbread and acorn bread, sunflower seeds, and green beans. It was good but, still, Green Rock's gut bothered him.

They finished, and Wolf Tail returned home, much to Green Rock's relief. Then they went to bed.

Chapter 4: Crystal Vision

Green Rock had disturbing dreams that night, and didn't sleep well at all. In one dream Wolf Tail and Sparrow were laughing at him and saying bad things about him behind his back. He woke up shouting, "Why don't you just mind your own business?"

This woke up Squirrel Fur. "Are you alright?" she asked.

"Yes, I just had a bad dream," replied Green Rock, wishing to avoid the topic. Then he drifted back to sleep, and had another nightmare. He dreamed that he was at the crossroads of life, at the center of the Medicine Wheel. He walked to the South, but he heard White Spirit saying, "You are going the wrong way."

So he turned around, and started walking North, and then he heard Blue Spirit say, "You shouldn't be going in this direction."

He went East until Red Spirit spoke, "Don't go this way."

So he tried walking West but the Black Spirit said, "This is not the right direction."

Green Rock woke up saying, "Nothing is right! Where am I supposed to go?"

Squirrel Fur heard this and became worried. "You need to get some sleep," she said. "You are keeping us awake!"

"I just had a bad dream."

"Why don't I make some skullcap tea for you to drink so you can get to sleep?" offered Squirrel Fur.

"I will be fine," replied Green Rock.

"What is wrong?" asked his mother. "You are disturbed by something if you are having nightmares like this."

"Nothing is wrong; I just have a lot on my mind."

"Well, if you wake up your father and me again, you're going to have some skullcap, like it or not!"

They returned to bed, and Green Rock had another dream. Once again, he stood at the center of the Medicine Wheel. The center represented within, and the here and now. An unknown voice told him to remain there and analyze his intentions before deciding which direction he should go. Was it his intuition?

* * *

Two days later, Eagle Medicine visited and said, "There is a woman with rheumatism across the village. Red Talon has asked me to come and get you so you can be present while we treat her."

They left together, and when they arrived at the woman's lodge, Green Rock recognized her as Corn Leaf, the Honored Woman. Red Talon arrived shortly afterwards.

"Now pay attention," whispered Eagle Medicine to Green Rock.

Red Talon inquired of Corn Leaf about recent dreams, omens, and all other things that could be causing her ailment. His goal was to find the source of the illness and drive it away, and to treat the symptoms.

After much conversation and investigation, it was decided that she was under attack by the spirit of the Yuchi prisoner who she had ordered to be burned at the stake.

Red Talon, Eagle Medicine, and Green Rock left to get some fleabane, dried blackberry roots, blue cohosh root powder, vetch, life everlasting, a healing Crystal and other herbs and paraphernalia to use for healing rituals.

They returned and Red Talon led them in prayers, and healing rituals with a gourd rattle and the healing Crystal. He then recited a formula for rheumatism:

"Oh Red Man, you are the cause of this. You have placed the trespasser under her. Ha! Now you come from the Sun Land. You have brought the little red footstools, your feet relaxed on them. Ha! Now they have quickly retreated from you. Relief has happened. Let it not be for this day alone. Let the relief come immediately."

Then they made a tea from the leaves of the maidenhair fern, fleabane, and blackberry roots, and gave it to Corn Leaf to drink. Next they made the decoction of vetch and life everlasting for her to drink.

Then Red Talon said, "Use some green bean tea, and eat sunflower seeds. Also, here is some powdered blue cohosh root. You can mix it with water and drink it."

They were finished. Corn Leaf paid Red Talon and Eagle Medicine each with deerskins, and promised to make Green Rock a new pair of moccasins.

As they walked back to the council house, Eagle Medicine said to Green Rock, "What do you think? Do you think you will one day be able to perform a healing ritual like that?"

"Maybe after I grow up and learn more," replied Green Rock. "What do we do next?"

"We will be checking up on Corn Leaf periodically, to see how she is doing. Today was her second visit from Red Talon; he saw her first three days ago, on the morning of the day we returned to the village. But in the meantime, I should teach you about the Calendar.

"It's used to calculate the appropriate days for ceremonies to take place. It is also used to provide newborn infants with their natal names. When a baby is born, he or she must be immediately named and baptized in his or her mother's milk. If the infant dies before these events take place, its souls are lost forever. Natal names are sacred and are to always be kept secret."

"How do you know what to name the babies?" asked Green Rock.

"There are twenty day signs, and thirteen numbers – when you multiply these numbers, you get two hundred and sixty days. This is approximately how many days Venus appears as the morning star. It is also around the same number of days of the gestation period for humans.

"These are the twenty day signs: Terrapin, Whirlwind, Hearth, Dragon, Snake, Twin, Deer, Rabbit, River, Wolf, Raccoon, Rattlesnake Fang, Reed, Cougar, Eagle, Owl, Heron, Flint, Redbird, and Flower.

"The natal names consist of a number between one and thirteen, and a sign. They are calculated by using a system that goes by the date of the infant's birth."

Green Rock now understood the meaning of his natal name, which was Six Reeds.

"The new cycle begins when the Pleiades star cluster sets near the Sun," said Eagle Medicine. "The Great New Moon Ceremony (which commemorates the new cycle) occurs the first new moon after the new cycle begins."

They talked about the constellations and the legends associated with them. They also went over the twenty day signs and what traits associated with the names and numbers applied to the people.

The next day, they visited Corn Leaf, who showed improvement. She was very cheerful and thanked them for their assistance.

Green Rock spent one more night with his family, and then he and Eagle Medicine left the village again to continue his training. Later that day, Green Rock found himself alone, looking for a special Crystal that Eagle Medicine said would be waiting especially for Green Rock.

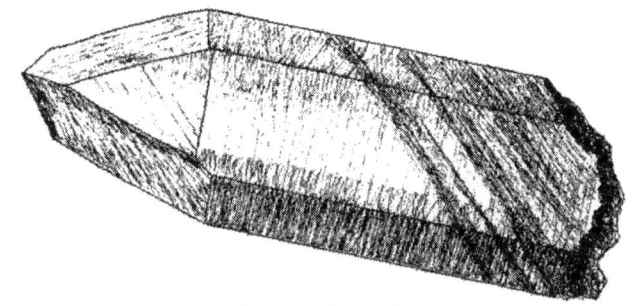

Quartz Crystal.

After searching alone for a good while, he found a pretty quartz Crystal that was very clear. It was about the length and thickness of a grown man's thumb. He said, "Little People, I want to take this if it's okay." He picked it up and spoke to it as instructed by Eagle Medicine. He said, "Hello Crystal, you are very beautiful. Would you care to work with me for a little while?"

As instructed, he held the Crystal in his left hand at arm's length and then slowly brought it close to his chest. He felt a warm energy from the Crystal. Green Rock thought that this would be his special Crystal.

He returned to where Eagle Medicine was and said, "The Little People left me a nice Crystal."

"I knew they would," answered Eagle Medicine. "Now let me tell you more about Crystals. Each Crystal has a spirit. Remember what I told you about your fourth soul?"

"It is the skeleton. It leaves the body one cycle after death and goes underground to form Crystals," replied Green Rock.

"That is correct," said Eagle Medicine. "A Crystal is a spirit that has power to heal. You can also see into the future with the help of a Crystal.

"When the Crystal gets weak and loses clarity, we put it in a stream for at least seven days to purify it and 'recharge' it. It must be 'grounded' with Mother Earth. When you receive a Crystal, you take on the duty of protecting and keeping it until it is time to give it away. Crystals can be 'trained' for specific tasks, such as healing, and other tasks.

"I am going to return back to Birch Mountain, and leave you here to seek your Crystal Vision. You may see the past, the future, faraway places, or other things. Most important, you will see your life's purpose."

"How do I start?" asked Green Rock.

"Walk around until you find a place that is peaceful and comfortable, and focus on the Crystal. You will receive your own Crystal Vision, do not doubt it; everybody's vision is different. Just accept what you see and feel. When you are finished, return to Birch Mountain with your Crystal, and find me."

Eagle Medicine departed, leaving him with his Crystal and blowgun. Green Rock began looking for a good place for his Crystal Vision. It was late in the afternoon when he came up on a mountain stream. On the other side was a shady area with some short, but thick, grass – and it looked very comfortable. He crossed the stream and sat down in the cool grass.

Green Rock took out the beautiful Crystal and gazed into it, trying to focus. He heard a faint drumming sound in the distance. It was getting closer, and he began to hear singing with the drums. He assumed it was the Little People. It was an intoxicating sound. He continued to gaze into the Crystal and suddenly saw some very unusual sights, and his intuition was that he was seeing into a vastly distant past. There were great dragon-like monsters and mountains that blew smoke out of their peaks.

Great Dragon-Like Monsters from a Vastly Distant Past.

Green Rock was led through all parts of time, and faraway places - everywhere. He saw other worlds with terrifying people who were not people. His intuition told him they had always been present in different places in the night sky.

Person from Another World Somewhere in the Night Sky.

He saw primitive people living on distant islands far across the great seas. This was far away, in a different part of the world, but somehow Green Rock knew it was happening in a time similar to that of his own life. There were great statues that were being carved by the natives of these islands.

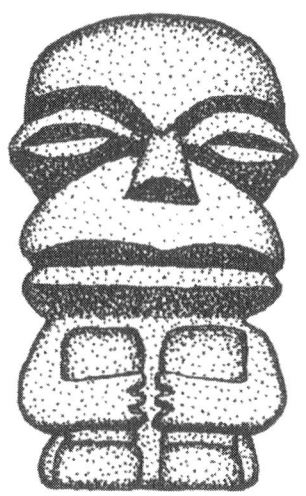

Statue from a Distant Island.

There was a vast desert, with numerous boulders, many of which had petroglyphs – images of Shamans carved by people far away to the west. Something told Green Rock these images were being carved into the boulders that very same instant as he had this Vision.

Petroglyphs of Shamans at McKee Springs, Utah.
Redrawn from Welsh 1995.

Then, he began seeing frightening things. Something told him that he was seeing into the future – what was to come.

"Enormous Canoe with Wings."
Redrawn from a public domain image.

There were pale-skinned people with hair on their faces coming in enormous canoes with wings. These canoes arrived from the Great Sea to the east. They had unfamiliar but beautiful clothing, and very long knives made from an unknown shiny stone. They also carried abnormally shaped sticks that had blowgun-like tubes, also made from the peculiar stone. They aimed them at an animal, and there was a loud thunderclap, instantly killing the animal, leaving only a tiny wound.

These people were strange and magical, but were also very evil. They took without asking, and showed no honor in battle. They also had terrifying animals like Green Rock had never seen before.

As the Vision progressed, Green Rock could hear the Little People's drumming, singing, and chanting getting closer and closer, becoming faster and faster. His pulse kept perfect time with the drumming.

The white men also carried evil spirits with them that wiped out entire native villages. They even traded blankets with the evil spirits to the natives. They did this with the intent of killing off the natives, so they could acquire their land.

Tears came to Green Rock's eyes. The Little People were very near at this point, chanting and drumming louder and louder, faster and faster.

Next he saw wide stone paths with painted yellow stripes running down the center. On these paths were monsters made of the shiny stone. They had round legs, and glowing eyes. The white men could climb inside of the monsters. They somehow controlled the monsters from within and made them take them where they wanted to go at high speeds, and then climbed out of them. There were also enormous shiny, stone birds in which the white men could ride.

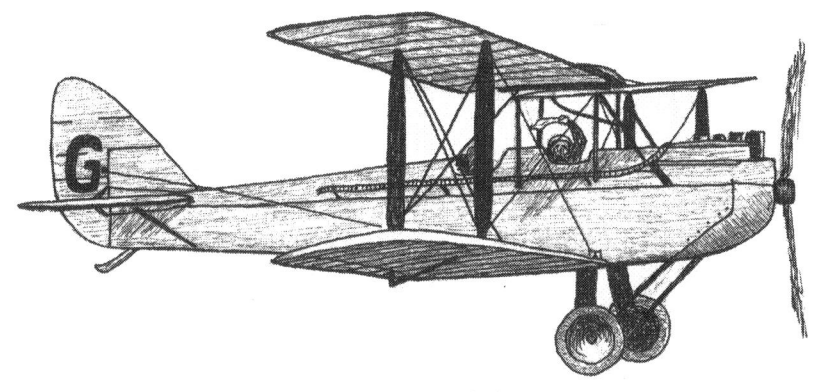

"Shiny Stone Bird."
Adapted & redrawn from a public domain image.

These stone birds could fly all over Mother Earth, taking the people along inside of them. The people built lodges that were as tall as the mountains. Some of their villages were so large that it would have taken three days to walk across them. The white men outnumbered the stars in the sky. These people neglected Mother Earth, and the balance and harmony that once existed between all living things had disappeared.

This horrified Green Rock. These people sought to gain every bit of wealth and glory that they could get, and even desecrated the ancient burial mounds of the natives for personal gain. They were not sincere and they were destroying Mother Earth with their greed, selfishness and false humility as a result.

Now Green Rock saw with absolute lucidity the consequences of living with false humility. But it wasn't at all like how he was living. Not at all. Or was it?

I am doing the right thing! Green Rock thought. *I have good intentions! I really do! I know I do!* His heart rate matched the increasing tempo of the Little People's rapid drumming.

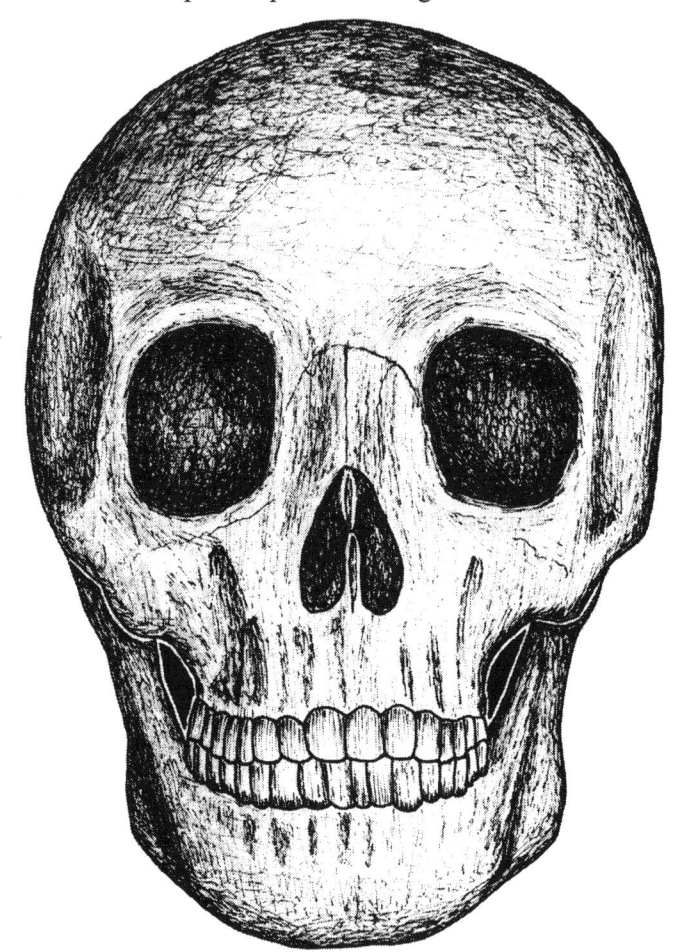

"The Skull of the Vain Person."
Redrawn from Garrigue 1851.

Suddenly, he came face-to-face with a terrifying skull. A voice said, "This is the Skull of the Vain Person. Somehow he knew it was his skull. *It can't really be me! This can't be the direction I am going!* It was. He couldn't escape from what he knew.

The drumming and singing suddenly stopped, and Green Rock came out of his trance. It was morning. As he looked around he felt stinging sensations in the skin on his back. He was not by the stream anymore. He realized that he was lying down on a briar bush – the thorns were sticking him in the back.

He carefully got up – the thorns sticking him all the while. "Ouch!" he cried several times while trying to get free of the briar bush. Once he had gotten free, he sat under a dogwood tree and pondered the unusual event. The Crystal was gone – the Little People must have taken it back. He thought of the strange white men's greed and false humility. He remembered the dreams that he'd had at home and was doing some soul-searching. *Why did I join the priesthood?* He thought. *I have not been honest with myself or with anybody else lately. It was all about foolish pride. But how can I change things? Red Talon and Eagle Medicine will be angry with me if I quit my training. The last person I want to be angry with me is a Shaman!*

Green Rock felt like he was in serious trouble. He wanted to set things right, but was deathly afraid to return to Birch Mountain. He didn't know where else to go. He decided to go to the neighboring village of Eagle Peak, which was about a day's walk from Birch Mountain. His mother's sister, Acorn lived there. Maybe she would let him hide at her lodge until he determined what he should do.

So, Green Rock started his journey. The first half of the trip was the hardest, because he was crossing over the ridge. Once at the top, the view was spectacular. The village of Eagle Peak was visible from here. He stopped and rested for a while. He became hungry and thirsty, and started down the ridge and stopped at a stream for a drink. It was a little past noon, and Green Rock killed a squirrel with his blowgun and ate.

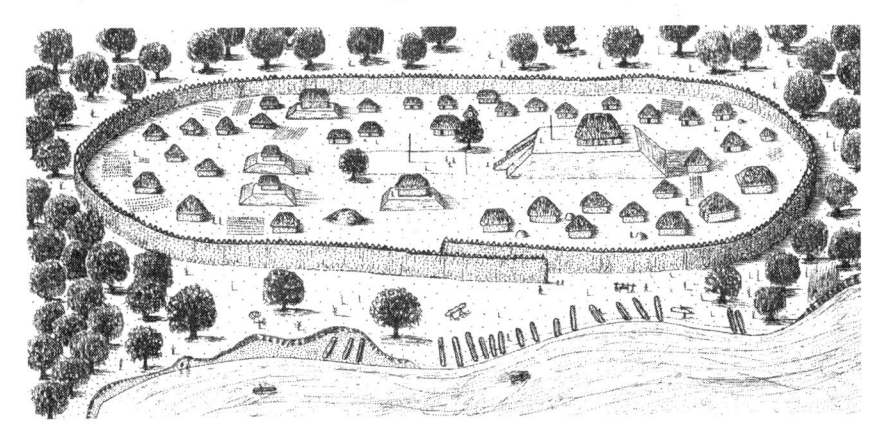

The Village of Eagle Peak.

On his way down the ridge, towards Eagle Peak, he saw a nice piece of soapstone. He took it with him in the hopes that he could make a pipe or two out of it. These he would trade for goods that would help him earn his keep at his aunt's lodge.

Just before sunset, he spotted through the woods the palisade that surrounded the village of Eagle Peak. He found the entrance, and the alert guards made sure that he didn't have mischievous intentions. "Who are you?" asked one of them.

"I am Green Rock, from Birch Mountain. I came to visit my aunt, Acorn. Can you tell me where her lodge is?"

"Come on in," said the guard. "It's the fourth lodge – over there." The guard was pointing to it.

"Thank you very much," said Green Rock.

"You are welcome," replied the guard. "Enjoy your visit."

Green Rock was fearful that his aunt would reject him, especially if she knew why he had come to Eagle Peak. As he approached her lodge, he noticed a thunderhead forming in the direction of Birch Mountain.

He saw a woman standing in the doorway. "Aunt Acorn, is that you?" he asked.

Her eyes shifted to him but, in the gathering darkness, she did not immediately recognize him. "Who are you?" she asked.

"I am your nephew, Green Rock."

"Green Rock! It is so good to see you! Where are your parents?"

"I came alone, and I need a place to stay for a few days. I have some soapstone and will make some pipes to trade and I will hunt for you and…"

"You are welcome to stay here, Green Rock. Come on inside and eat."

Acorn gave Green Rock some dried meat and cornbread. While he ate, she asked him, "Now, what brings you here alone? What has happened?" She had an expression of profound concern and pity.

"I had to get away from Birch Mountain."

"Why? What happened?"

"I can't tell you. I just had to leave."

"Why do you have sores all over you? Is it your father? Is he hurting you?" Acorn never liked Elk Antler; she had always thought he was too forceful and inappropriately involved in Green Rock's life. After all, that was the responsibility of Green Rock's clansmen, and not Elk Antler.

"No, it's not him," replied Green Rock.

"What is it then, Green Rock?"

"I guess I can tell you if you promise not to tell anybody."

Acorn had a very concerned look on her face. "I won't tell anyone, but I have to know. It is not usual for a ten-cycle-old child to just run away from home! Tell me!"

Green Rock burst into tears. "I became a Devoted Son, and started training to be a Shaman, and it did not work out. I am afraid of what Red Talon and Eagle Medicine will do to me! I deserve anything that happens though. But I don't know what I should do!"

Acorn hugged him and said, "It's okay, and I won't let anything happen to you. You can stay as long as you need to. So, a Devoted Son! You really went into training to be a Shaman? So, tell me, what would be good for this poison ivy rash I have on my leg?"

"Witch hazel," replied Green Rock in a matter of fact tone. "You boil the leaves, bark and twigs. It is used externally to stop bleeding, and as a gargle for a sore throat. You can make an ointment from the extract that is good for poison ivy, stings and bites, and minor burns. The inner bark can be used as a poultice for swelling of the eye, and hemorrhoids. It is used internally for treating diarrhea, and for its sedative qualities."

"Hemorrhoids and diarrhea, huh?" laughed Acorn. "I think I will just have to deal with the poison ivy!"

"I probably shouldn't be recommending any treatments for illness or anything. I am far from qualified – I had to get away from my training and all."

"Why didn't the training work out?"

"I did it for the wrong reasons. It was out of arrogance that I chose that path. I had a Crystal Vision and it was more than I could handle, and I then realized that I had been so wrong. I am an artisan and not a Shaman. I cannot pretend anymore."

"It is very mature of you to admit that you made a mistake," said Acorn.

"I was made to see my errors. My admitting it was hardly out of maturity. But I can't go home – I am afraid to. I have my blowgun – I will hunt game for you. I also have this soapstone that I found today. I will make things to trade so I can earn my keep."

"How did you get all of those sores on your back?" asked Acorn.

"The Little People left me in a briar bush during my Crystal Vision. They also took my Crystal. I feel so guilty for the way I've acted. I now see I am nothing but selfish and worthless."

"You just said you are an artisan – that is not worthless, so don't be full of self pity."

The storm was getting closer, and they began to hear the distant thunder. Green Rock helped Acorn prepare for the coming rain. Then they went to bed. It rained all night, and Green Rock slept soundly. He was exhausted.

The next day Green Rock went into the woods to hunt. He located a large oak tree and observed that it had a lot of squirrel traffic. He got a log about his height and leaned it at a forty-five degree angle against the thick trunk. He got some cord and made five nooses and hung them from the branch that he had placed the log under. Each noose was shorter than the last, so that each loop was an equal distance from the leaning log. Then he went back to Acorn's lodge to eat. When he returned to the oak tree, there were five squirrels hanging from the nooses. The squirrels used the leaning log as a ramp, and each got their neck caught in the noose. They were not at all bothered by the previously trapped squirrels dangling from the nooses. They just passed them by and walked right into the next waiting noose.

Green Rock got out his flint knife and cut their throats, one at a time. He smiled in satisfaction that his trap had worked. When he presented the cleaned squirrels to Acorn, she smiled proudly and began cooking them.

The next few days were spent carving pipes and hunting small game for Acorn. When he traded the pipes for goods, he offered them to Acorn, but his aunt told him to keep the goods for himself. So, he carved a small frog effigy pipe out of green soapstone and gave it to her as a gift. She smiled and hugged him. It was a pleasant life in Eagle Peak.

Frog Effigy Pipe Given by Green Rock to Acorn.
Redrawn from McGuire 1897.

* * *

One night, Green Rock had a dream of his mother weeping for him. He woke up very sad and full of guilt. She had now lost both of her sons. He was still afraid to return home though. He tried to hide it, but Acorn could sense that he was depressed.

Every night he had a similar dream, and during the days it weighed heavy on his mind.

Then one night, Eagle Medicine used a divining Crystal to visit Green Rock in a dream. Green Rock was fearful, but Eagle Medicine said, "Do not be afraid, Devoted Son. Red Talon and I are not angry. We know that you must have left for a good reason, but your family needs you. For your mother's sake, come back home."

Green Rock awoke saying, "I promise! I will go back home." It was morning.

Acorn was preparing breakfast when she heard Green Rock's words. "So you are going home?"

"Eagle Medicine spoke to me in a dream. He isn't angry with me. Neither is Red Talon!"

"Well, you'd better get on your way, I know your mother must miss you," said Acorn.

"Thank you for letting me stay here; I really enjoyed it. You have been very good to me."

Acorn gave Green Rock some dried meat and acorn meal bread for his journey home. She hugged him and then he departed. Green Rock was very excited that his life would soon be back to normal again.

After dark, Green Rock arrived at his parents' lodge. Squirrel Fur burst into tears when she saw him. As she hugged him tightly she said, "Where were you? I thought you were gone forever! Do not ever run away like that again!"

"Where is Father?" asked Green Rock.

"He is out looking for *you!*" she answered in an angry tone.

"I was at Eagle Peak, at Acorn's lodge. I am so sorry I did what I did – but I was very afraid to come back."

"Why? What happened to make you so afraid to come home?"

Green Rock told her about the Crystal Vision and the Little People. He explained that the vision made him realize it was a mistake to join the priesthood but was afraid of the consequences of not completing the training.

Squirrel Fur's expression softened. "I understand that you were afraid – I forgive you. But please do not do this to your father and me again! Promise me!"

"I promise," said Green Rock, and he meant it.

"Good boy," said Squirrel Fur as she hugged Green Rock tightly.

"Can I go to see Wolf Tail?" asked Green Rock, "I owe him an apology also."

"Certainly," answered Squirrel Fur, "It's about time you two settled your differences."

Sparrow appeared in the doorway. "Green Rock!" she exclaimed.

"Hello, Sparrow," he greeted.

"Where *have* you *been?*" asked Sparrow.

"Go on to see Wolf Tail before it gets too late," said Squirrel Fur. "I will explain it all to Sparrow."

"I've been alright," said Green Rock to Sparrow. "I am sorry if I worried you."

Sparrow smiled and said, "That's okay, now you go on and see Wolf Tail. Set things right with him."

Green Rock left as Squirrel Fur began to tell Sparrow his story. He approached Wolf Tail's lodge and saw Wolf Tail tending his fire.

"Wolf Tail," called Green Rock.

"Green Rock!" returned Wolf Tail, "Come sit down!"

Green Rock sat next to Wolf Tail by the warm fire. "Are you heating flint?" he asked.

"Yes."

"Wolf Tail, I am really sorry for the way I have acted the last couple of moons. I have treated you in a most shameful way. If you don't want us to be friends anymore…"

"I will always be your friend!" interrupted Wolf Tail. "And it is good to have you back."

"Thank you," said Green Rock with a bowed head. He had once been proud of his humility, but now he experienced real humility. He truly had remorse for his actions.

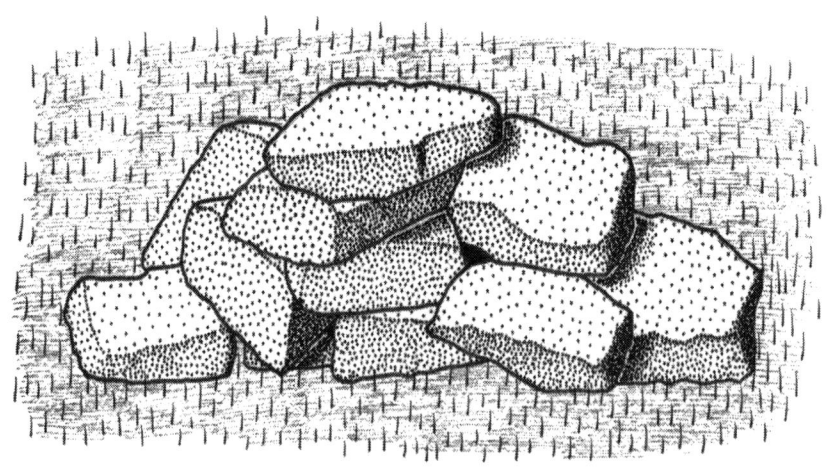

The Pile of Soapstone from Twisted Stick.

"I have something to show you," said Wolf Tail, and he pointed at something.

Green Rock looked where he was pointing, and saw a very large pile of soapstone there on the ground near the lodge.

"Twisted Stick has been bringing back one or two pieces each time he returns from a hunting trip," said Wolf Tail. "I've been keeping them for you."

Green Rock was touched. "Thank you," he said. He knew very well that Wolf Tail was his best friend – even through the recent trials that had occurred due to his selfishness..

It was getting late and Green Rock returned home and went to bed. He was awakened by his father's voice. "I am going to tan your hide!" shouted Elk Antler. He grabbed Green Rock's arm and yanked him out of bed. Squirrel Fur and Sparrow were gone. Green Rock was terrified.

Elk Antler slapped Green Rock in the face and shouted, "Who do you think you are? You made us worry for days!" Then he threw Green Rock onto the floor and began beating him across the back with his bow.

"You really have a lot of nerve!" Elk Antler shouted as he continued beating him. "I have been looking for you for *seven days!* And where do I find you? At home in bed! You are lazy! You disgust me!" When his bow broke, Elk Antler stopped and said, "Now I guess I will have to go and get a deer to feed my *lazy* son," and then he grabbed his other bow and left to go hunting.

Green Rock sat on the floor weeping for a long time. He had welts and bruises all over his back, and a swollen lip from being slapped. He wanted to tell somebody, but it would get his father into a lot of trouble, and he did not want to do that. He had to stay quiet about this incident. He had to think of a lie to tell people to explain the marks on his body.

Just then, Sparrow walked in. "What happened to you?" she asked with a shocked expression.

He had severe bruises all over, and the sores left from the briar bush only added to his dreadful appearance.

"I… I was climbing a tree and I fell to the ground," lied Green Rock.

Sparrow knew he was lying, and her suspicions were validated to some degree when she saw the broken bow on the floor.

"My goodness! How did this bow get broken?" she asked.

"I don't know!" cried Green Rock, and then he got up and left the lodge running.

Sparrow watched him as he disappeared behind the lodges in the direction of Wolf Tail's lodge. She intended to tell Squirrel Fur about this incident.

Eagle Medicine arrived and began talking to Sparrow. Sparrow showed him the broken bow and told of the marks on Green Rock's body. Eagle Medicine was angry with Elk Antler. He immediately went to Wolf Tail's lodge to visit with Green Rock. When he got there he saw the severity of the beating.

"What happened to you?" asked Eagle Medicine.

"I had my Crystal Vision and…"

"No, I mean what happened to you today?"

Green Rock bowed his head and said, "I was climbing a tree and fell out."

Eagle Medicine also knew he was lying, but he said nothing more about it. "I will be seeing you soon – we will talk about your Vision then." And then he left as if he had something very important that needed to be done immediately.

Squirrel Fur returned to her lodge, where Sparrow was kneading cornbread dough. Sparrow paused and showed her the broken bow. "Green Rock has welts all over his back," she said. "I asked him what happened and he lied and said that he fell out of a tree. I am sure Elk Antler broke this bow while beating Green Rock with it. I know he did it! He has no right to lay a hand on Green Rock!"

"I *know* you are right – but what can we do?" asked Squirrel Fur. "He never does these things when we are around, and we cannot be here constantly."

Squirrel Fur was very angry when she saw the marks on Green Rock for herself. Sparrow was right. She couldn't believe he'd actually broken his bow, hitting the boy with it! He had no right to do what he had done to Green Rock. It was not Elk Antler's place because he was his father, and not of Green Rock's clan. For the first time, Squirrel Fur actually wished for Elk Antler to move out of the lodge permanently.

Elk Antler did not return that night. He did not return the next night either. After he was gone for three days, some of the men went looking for him. They found his corpse not too far from Birch Mountain – he had been mauled by a grizzly bear.

His body was taken to the charnel platform by the burial mound. It was an awkward situation for the family. They had mixed feelings of anger with Elk Antler over his actions, and grief over his death.

Long afterwards, Green Rock wondered if Eagle Medicine had anything to do with the death – he had left so abruptly when he saw the welts on Green Rock's back. Did he use sorcery to punish Elk Antler? When he was in training, Green Rock had told Eagle Medicine of the abuse he had endured when the women were not around. Green Rock never asked, and Eagle Medicine never brought it up. It would forever remain a mystery.

Green Rock and Eagle Medicine were on good terms. They had a heart-to-heart conversation about why Green Rock quit the training. Eagle Medicine fully understood why Green Rock had eloped from the priesthood. They were still close friends.

Red Talon also carried no grudge against Green Rock; after all, nobody could be a good Shaman if they had entered that profession for the wrong reasons.

Green Rock returned to carving stone pipes, and his connections with the priesthood now began to provide him with business. He was now carving ceremonial items for Red Talon and Eagle Medicine.

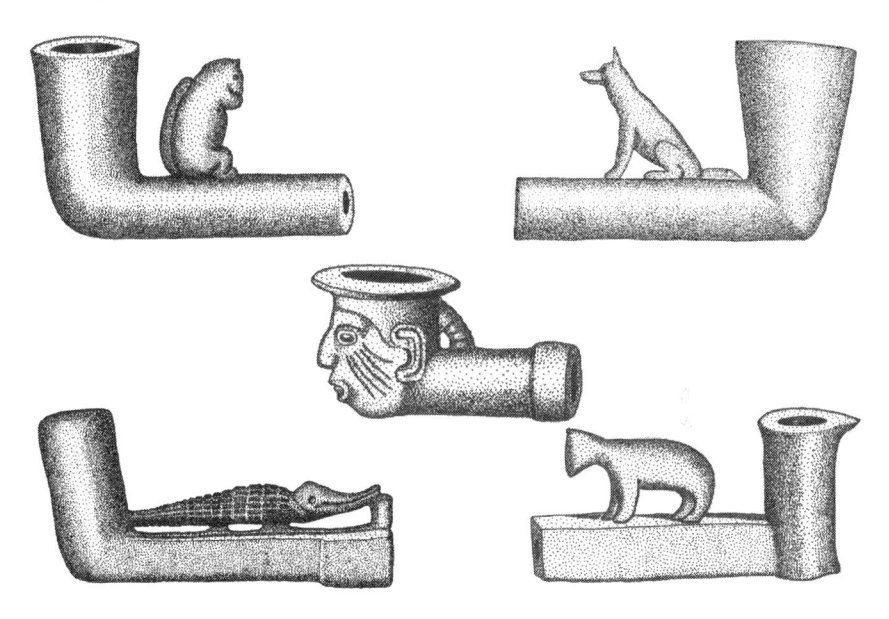

Soapstone Effigy Pipes Carved by Green Rock.
Redrawn from Thruston 1897 & McGuire 1897.

Before long, Eagle Medicine had recruited another trainee, named Three Crows. This made Green Rock very happy; he wanted badly for somebody to fill his void, because he still felt so much regret about leaving. Sadly, five days after Three Crows was initiated, Red Talon passed into the Darkening Land.

Now was the time to remove all the bodies from the charnel platform and give them a proper burial in the mound. It was the custom that the bodies of the common folk were not buried in the mound until somebody of status died. Until that time, they remained on the charnel platform. The last time the mound was added to was eight cycles before, when the last Uku, Kicking Elk died.

The villagers carried dirt from the pond by the basketful to the mound, under the close supervision of Eagle Medicine, who was now the High Priest. When they were finished, the burial mound was half again larger than before.

One day, Green Rock was visiting Wolf Tail. Green Rock said, "I want to try a fishing technique that I learned from Eagle Medicine."

"Tell me about it," said Wolf Tail.

"We can take Father's dugout canoe. When he died, Mother said it now belongs to us. We'll go to the small creek upstream from the village. There are some black walnuts there. Eagle Medicine told me that you could remove the rinds from the unripe nuts, pound them into a pulp, and throw a large amount of the pulp into a small stream. It makes the fish stupid and we can pick them out of the water with our hands!"

"I don't believe you," laughed Wolf Tail.

"I will bet you!" said Green Rock.

"What will we bet for?"

Green Rock said, "If I win, you make me my own flint knapping tool kit, so I can make arrowheads and knives. If you win, I will carve you two pipes that you can trade."

"It's a deal!" agreed Wolf Tail.

They immediately went to the river and took the canoe upstream to the small creek Green Rock spoke of. They saw several large fish in the water in the stream. After landing a good way upstream from the river, they found several black walnut trees. It was the right time of the cycle – the nuts were still green. The two peeled the rinds off of them and filled a medium-sized basket with the pounded rinds.

They put the full basket into the canoe and shoved off. Once in the middle of the calm creek, they emptied the contents of the basket into the water. Green Rock made sure that it was distributed over a large area around the canoe. They drifted downstream along with the nut rinds.

After a period of time, they noticed the fish were not moving around too much, and were drifting near the surface. Green Rock slowly dipped his hand into the water and picked a large catfish out.

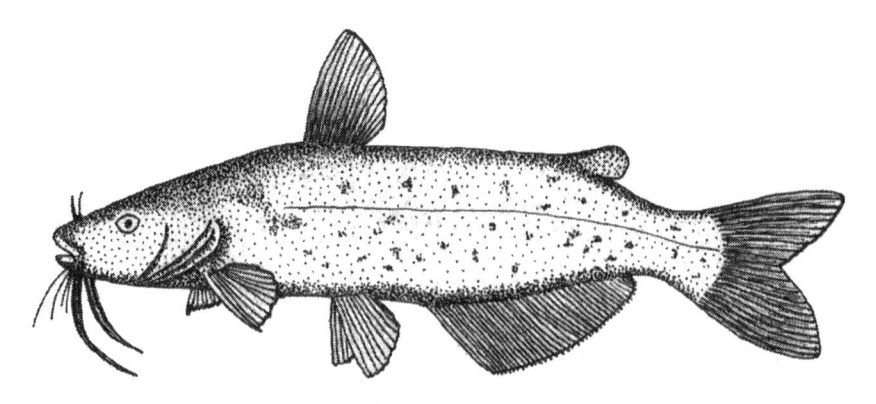

Catfish.
Redrawn from Clker-Free-Vector-Images from Pixabay.

Wolf Tail was awestruck. "I don't believe it!" he said. "I just don't believe it!"

"I just won a flint knapping tool kit!" shouted Green Rock. "Let's get some more fish! Mother will be so surprised!"

In total, they caught seventeen large fish, which they placed in the bottom of the canoe. The trip back to Birch Mountain was easy, as they just drifted downstream to the river, and then down the river to the village. On the way, they put all the fish into the basket. It was too heavy for the boys, so a man offered to carry the basket for them on his back.

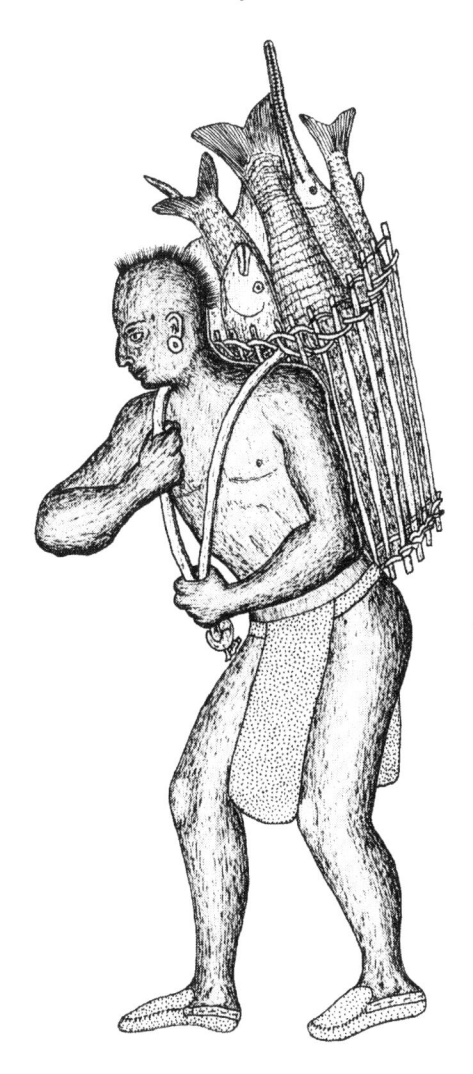

A Man Carries Home the Catch.
Adapted from Holmes 1891.

Sparrow was at the riverbank filling a water pot when they arrived. "What are you two up to?" she asked.

"Fishing!" said Green Rock. "And I just won a bet!"

Sparrow saw all the fish in the basket and said, "Oh my! How did you get so many?"

Green Rock and Wolf Tail described how they caught the fish, and Sparrow smiled in amazement, along with the helpful stranger.

Cleaning all of those fish took the rest of the day, and they gave some to that stranger, and to Squirrel Fur, Sparrow, Eagle Medicine, Twisted Stick, and Corn Leaf. They all ate well that night.

When Corn Leaf received her fish, she pointed and said, "There are the moccasins I promised you."

"But I am no longer Eagle Medicine's apprentice," replied Green Rock.

"Then take them for the fish," said Corn Leaf with a smile.

"Thank you," said Green Rock before leaving.

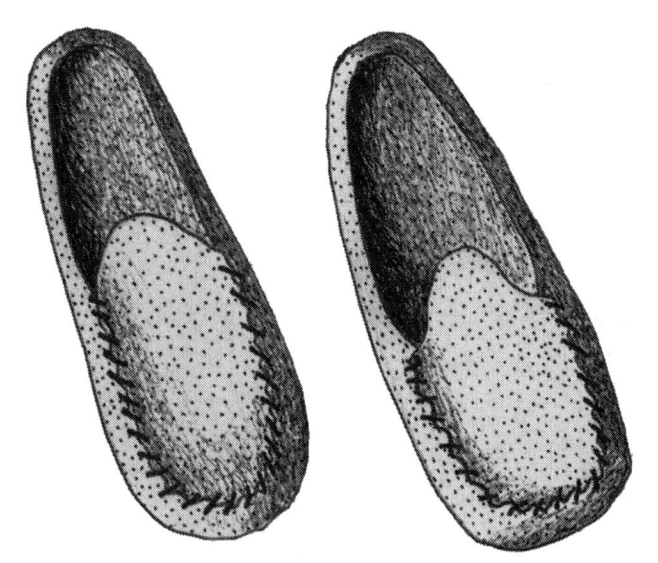

Green Rock's Moccasins Made by Corn Leaf.

The moccasins were very comfortable, but Green Rock still had misgivings about taking them from Corn Leaf. He couldn't seem to shake feeling like he was just a big fraud. It only reinforced the idea in him that he should make sure that selfishness and vanity ought never be the motivation for doing anything. Maybe this guilty feeling, and every one of his actions that led to it were all just Spirit's way of teaching him this valuable lesson. In true humility and gratitude, he chose to heed this warning, but it never really did completely put his mind at ease.

Hammerstone

Abrading Stone

Antler Billet

Antler Punches

Split Bone Notching Tool

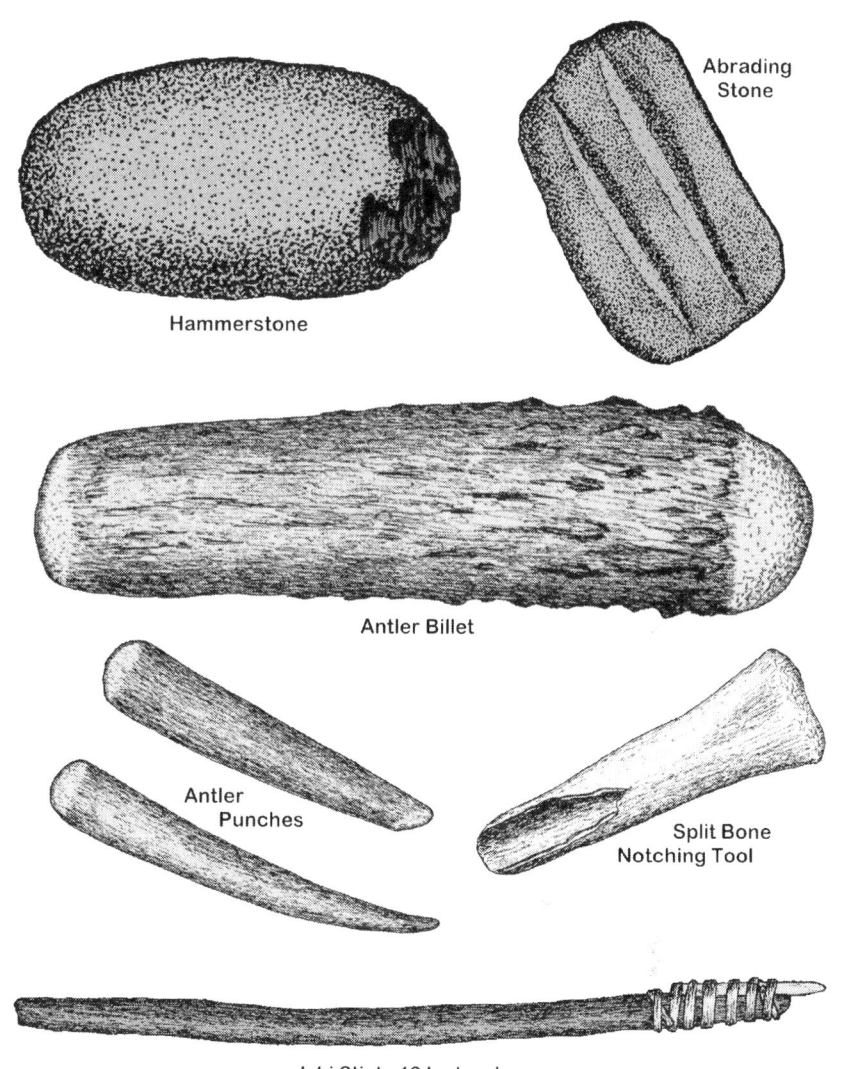

Ishi Stick. 18 Inches Long.

Green Rock's New Flint Knapping Tool Kit.

After a few days, Wolf Tail presented Green Rock with the newly-made flint knapping tool kit. Included were a granite river pebble hammerstone and an antler billet – both for percussion flaking, antler punches for pressure flakers, an Ishi stick for heavy duty pressure flaking, a sandstone abrading stone, and an arrowhead notching tool made from a split turkey leg bone. Wolf Tail had even made an elk skin bag to store the tools in. Green Rock was proud of the kit.

* * *

The warm growing season of summer had ended, and the village had celebrated the Green Corn and Ripe Corn Ceremonies. Now the weather was colder, and the red and brown leaves had begun to fall from the trees. On the next new moon would be the Great New Moon Ceremony, which marked the beginning of the new cycle. Runners were sent to all villages to inform them of the date of the ceremony.

Woman Tending a Hill of Corn with Flint Hoe.

Throughout the growing season, the women and children had tirelessly tended the corn and other crops. Now, the whole village of Birch Mountain was in a bustle gathering the corn, and other crops from the harvest, to donate for the ceremony. Some of these contributions were to be consumed during the feast that was to be held. The rest was stored in the treasury building located behind the council house on the ceremonial mound. This surplus was distributed to families who were less fortunate.

The night of the new moon, the ceremony began with the women doing a religious dance. Everybody in the village stayed up all night with the exception of infants.

The next morning, Eagle Medicine had everybody (including infants) in a long line leading to the river. He then placed a large clear quartz Crystal on top of a stand on the riverbank. One at a time, everybody submerged themselves and their babies in the cold water seven times. When each person finished, they stopped and gazed into the Crystal looking for the death sign. The death omen was a reflection of the person lying down instead of standing upright. When somebody saw the death sign, it indicated that they would perish before the spring.

The people who had not seen the death omen put on dry clothing and returned to the heptagon council house. Green Rock, Wolf Tail, and Squirrel Fur fortunately were among them. Sparrow had not been as lucky. She and the others who saw the death sign separated from the rest and fasted until later in the day.

"Mother," said Green Rock, "Sparrow stayed behind! Is she going to die?"

"I don't know," replied Squirrel Fur. "She has two more chances. I am sure she will be safe."

Meanwhile, Eagle Medicine sacrificed a deer tongue, which was the custom. Then they had the feast from the donated produce.

Green Rock had lost his appetite, worrying about Sparrow's fate. He prayed to Long Being – the River, that Sparrow would be cleared and could go on and continue with the ceremony.

Later, in the evening, Eagle Medicine returned to the river, and to the doomed people who were still fasting. Once again, they lined up and one-by-one gazed into the Crystal. Those who didn't see the death omen the second time around repeated the submerging in the river seven times and were then safe. Sparrow was very relieved that she was one of these. She returned and prepared for the women's dance.

Green Rock saw her return and was also relieved. He loved his aunt – she was always kind to him, and she did not deserve to die. Green Rock thanked Long Being for answering his prayer.

Those who still saw the death omen would have the final chance to repeat this ritual during the next new moon.

Once again, nobody except for infants slept, and the women performed another religious dance – Sparrow among them. The next morning, the Great New Moon Ceremony was finished. The new cycle had begun.

Everybody was exhausted and most of them went home to catch up on their sleep. During the following days, preparations were under way for the Friends-Making Ceremony, which was to take place ten days after the Great New Moon Ceremony. The Friends-Making Ceremony was the most deeply religious of all ceremonies. Differences between friends and spouses from the previous cycle were settled. Green Rock felt the importance of righting things between him and Wolf Tail.

During these ten days, seven men were sent out to gather seven types of evergreens. These were mistletoe, ginseng, cedar, greenbrier, heartleaf, white pine, and hemlock. Seven women fasted with the Uku

Standing Bear, Eagle Medicine, and Three Crows. In addition to that, seven hunters were sent out to kill game.

Hunter Shooting a Deer with a Bow & Arrow.
Adapted from OpenClipart-Vectors & Clkr-Free-Vector-Images from Pixabay.

Meanwhile, Green Rock was back to his flint knapping lessons at Wolf Tail's lodge. He percussion flaked a very nice medium-sized spear point, while Wolf Tail watched and offered advice when needed. When it was finished, Green Rock went to show it to Eagle Medicine. He was proud of it. It was his best knapped piece.

The next day, Wolf Tail was at the riverbank, mounting a large torch on the bow of the dugout. Green Rock had been sent down to fetch water.

"Wolf Tail," said Green Rock. "What are you doing?"

"I am going to show you an easy way I heard about for getting a deer. It's called 'jack-lighting'. Twisted Stick told me about it."

"How does it work?" asked Green Rock.

"After dark, animals are attracted to the flames," replied Wolf Tail. "They are curious and want to know what causes light in the darkness. When a deer approaches and looks at the fire, you can see its eyes. It is easy to throw an axe and hit the deer right between the eyes."

"I have got to see this," said Green Rock.

"Meet me here at sunset; it's a lot easier with two people anyhow."

"I will be here," promised Green Rock. He then filled the water bottle and carried it back home.

At sunset, Green Rock met Wolf Tail at the riverbank, as agreed. Wolf Tail had a knapped axe he had made about a moon ago. He was finished with the torch and had a fire pot to light it with. They departed and paddled upstream in silence. Then Wolf Tail lit the torch on the bow of the canoe. The flames grew bright and they silently drifted with the current. After awhile, they heard animals stirring in the leaves.

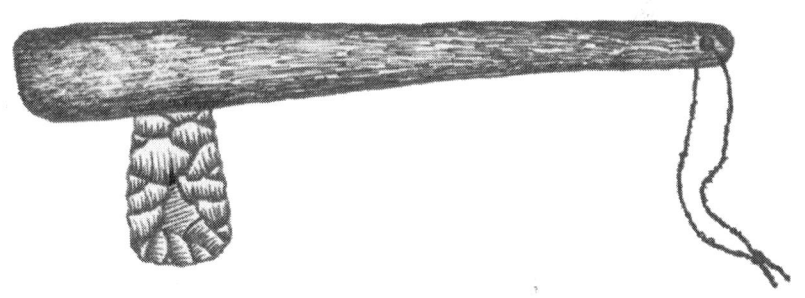

Wolf Tail's Axe for Jack Lighting.

Wolf Tail picked up his axe and whispered, "Be very quiet. When I whistle like a whippoorwill, keep the canoe steady, but be *very* quiet about it."

Not long afterwards, Green Rock could see deer eyes reflecting the light of the torch. Wolf Tail motioned Green Rock to move closer to the bank. Then came the whistle. Green Rock steadied the dugout canoe as quietly as possible. Suddenly Wolf Tail forcefully rocked the canoe as he threw the axe. Green Rock saw the axe disappear into the darkness, as he tightly gripped the gunwales with both his hands. There was a dull thud and the deer's eyes disappeared. There was a thrashing noise in the leaves where the deer had fallen.

"Help me get us to the shore!" cried Wolf Tail.

They landed, and Wolf Tail removed the torch from the canoe. There was a dead seven-point buck about three paces from the bank. It had worked!

"That was great!" cheered Green Rock.

After apologizing to the buck's spirit, they carried the buck back to the canoe and returned home. Inside the village, they hung it from a tree and gutted it and left it there overnight.

The next day they finished butchering the deer. That night they all ate well.

Just before sunrise, on the day of the ceremony, the Chief and his assistants' seats in the council house were painted white. White symbolized purity and peace. White deerskins were also draped over the officials' seats, and in front of them.

At dawn, all the villagers gathered inside of the council house to watch the ceremonial rekindling of the sacred fire. Seven types of wood were used in this fire. These were locust, redbud, post oak, blackjack oak, red oak, plum, and sycamore. Sometimes the fire was started by twirling a hardwood sapling between the hands, its bottom in a depression in a hearth stick, while other times, a fire bow was also used with a bow drill armature and the hearth stick. The top of the bow drill armature was held in place with a bow drill hand piece made from a pebble with a hole that was formed for this purpose.

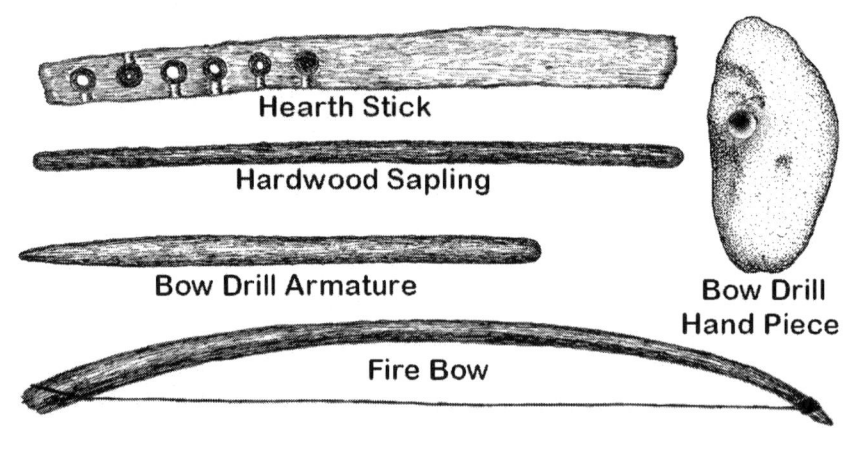

Assorted Fire-Making Tools.

After lighting the sacred fire, Eagle Medicine put some powdered tobacco into the fire and waved the smoke in the four directions with a white heron wing fan.

A white-painted clay pot full of water was put over the sacred fire, and then a basket full of the seven evergreens, gathered by the seven men, was placed into the pot. This brew would be used in purification rituals during five days of the ceremony.

Next, seven men went about the village chanting an incantation while striking the walls of every lodge with sycamore rods. Eagle Medicine's assistants dressed him in white clothing. Then the seven men with the rods returned to the council heptagon, and Eagle Medicine went outside of the heptagon, and climbed onto the roof, while singing a sacred hymn to the Creator. There were seven verses; each sung four times, and in a different progression of notes. When Eagle Medicine finished the sacred hymn, he climbed back down, and returned to the inside of the council house.

The seven men with the sycamore rods now got seven white gourds and filled each one with the brew, and handed them to the leaders of each of the seven clans. The leaders of the clans each took a swallow of the brew, and rubbed some on their chest, and passed it on down until everybody had partaken. Afterwards, Eagle Medicine sang the sacred hymn again.

Now, everybody did a ritual bath in the river. Eagle Medicine sacrificed a deer tongue, and repeated the hymn. It was now sunset, and everybody feasted, and afterwards, the women had a Friendship Dance.

On the second and third days the rituals were repeated – the only difference was the absence of the singing of the sacred hymn.

On the fourth day, everything was repeated again, including the singing of the hymn. On the last day the basket with the brew was removed from the clay pot and hidden in a secret location. Then Eagle Medicine and his helpers departed while saying "Now I go." The villagers followed them out and the ceremony was then over.

Green Rock and Wolf Tail had now truly reconciled their differences. This particularly meaningful ceremony assured them both that they would be best friends forever.

* * *

On the day of the next new moon, the villagers who had seen the death sign in the Crystal, during the last new moon, gathered at the river once again. The ritual of Crystal gazing was repeated for the last time before winter, and nobody saw the death omen. Apparently the Honored Spirits were pleased that all the conflicts of the previous cycle were settled adequately.

The next day brought a very cold rain. Green Rock disliked the winter. The warmth of the Sun was blocked by an overcast sky. It would be at least four moons before the next trader arrived. He was glad to have the warm moccasins that Corn Leaf had made for him.

It was now time for the Bounding Bush Ceremony, and that lifted his spirits. This ceremony was not a religious one; it was more of a festival.

It was also the last major ceremony before spring. There were several dances during this four-day event. The main dance involved men and women dancing together around in a circle. In the middle was a man who sang and danced inside the circle of dancers. He carried a little box in which bits of tobacco were dropped by the circling dancers. The dance concluded at midnight, and was repeated for the next two nights. On the fourth night there was a feast, followed by a dance that started after midnight. Now the dancers dropped pine needles into the box.

Just before the dance ended at sunrise, the dancers formed a circle around the fire on the altar. They approached the altar one-by-one, three times each, and on the third advance, they threw tobacco and pine needles into the fire.

Each family had a cozy hothouse that was built over a pit in the ground, and covered with clay or mud. During the summer, these hothouses were often used for storage. They were also used as sweat lodges in ceremonies, and the Myth Keepers met in the hothouses, passing down the secret stories of the Shamans to the selected children.

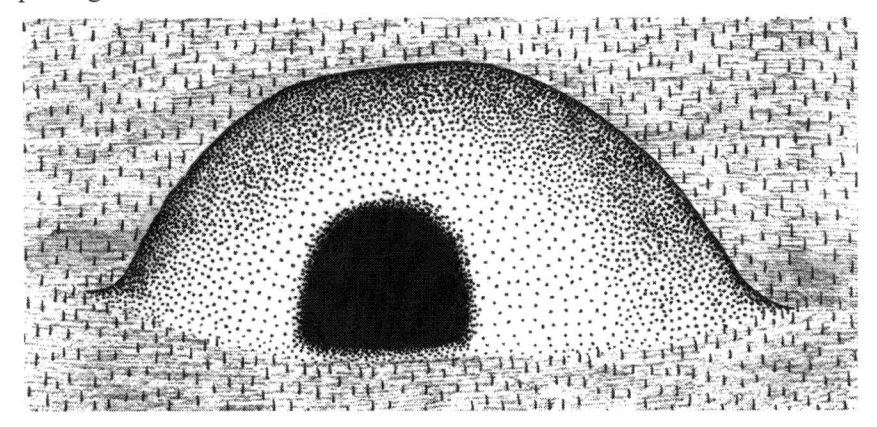

Winter Hothouse – Covered with Layer of Clay.

As the winter got colder, the families moved into their hothouses to escape the cold. Fires were kept burning all day in the hothouse, and extra fuel was added to the fire so that it would burn hot all night.

The summer lodge was now used for storage, and was loaded with corn, dried meats, sunflower seeds, and other items from the harvest. The families spent a great deal of time gathering firewood, from outside of the village, which was also stored in the lodges with the rest of the items.

Green Rock and Wolf Tail had plenty of time now to discuss their plans for the next summer. Green Rock carved on another piece of soapstone, while Wolf Tail discussed his dream to make a dugout canoe all by himself.

* * *

Chapter 5: Rites of Passage

Seven cycles later…

White Feather ran barefooted across the village hoping she had not missed Green Rock. Now eight cycles old, her long hair waved in the wind behind her back as she ran. She was shirtless, but wore a skirt woven from moss and other plant fibers.

Girl's Skirt Made from Plant Fibers.
Redrawn from Holmes 1891.

White Feather reached the palisade gate and saw Green Rock just before he disappeared into the woods.

When she caught up with him, she called out to him, "Green Rock! Green Rock! Wait!"

Green Rock stopped and said, "Good Morning, White Feather, what do you need?"

"My father asked me to tell you to come and see him when you return from hunting. He wants you to make something for him."

"Tell Eagle Medicine that I will be there tonight," said Green Rock. "Sooner if I can."

White Feather smiled at Green Rock. Green Rock returned the smile, and they each went on their separate ways.

As Green Rock walked deeper into the woods, he was frustrated. Wolf Tail had been initiated into manhood five cycles ago, at the age of fifteen cycles. His adulthood name was The Buck Kicks the Drum, but most people just called him Buck. He had earned that name and his adulthood title from a successful attack on the Yuchi. His Guardian Spirit, the Buck Deer had also appeared to him while he was on a Vision Quest. During the naming ceremony, he had accidentally kicked one of the drums while walking past it, which is how he got this name.

He had since been married to a young and beautiful woman named Tanager of the Bird Clan. She was the youngest daughter of Corn Leaf – the Honored Woman. Tanager was now pregnant, and Buck had a new family to provide for.

Being that Green Rock was the only male left in his mother's lodge, he was kept extra busy providing for the lodge. Green Rock was now seventeen cycles old and had never had the time to go on a raid with a war party, and had not had an encounter with any Guardian Spirits either. Every time he thought about it, he was reminded of his dissatisfaction.

Many of the young women of the village had dropped hints that they were interested in him. Green Rock particularly liked a sixteen-cycle-old maiden he had gotten to know, over the years, named Beaver Pelt. She also liked him, but she was frustrated with the situation. No woman of the village would be allowed to touch him until he had achieved adult status.

Cycles before, when Eagle Medicine was training Green Rock to be a Shaman, he had said that a person would develop a closeness with certain spirits, more so than with others. This held true with Green Rock, and he indeed felt a stronger closeness with Long Being – the Spirit of the River.

Sometimes Green Rock would pray to Long Being that he would reach adulthood soon. He was tired of this rut he was stuck in. He still had to dress and wear his hair like a child, but was compelled to do the duties of a man. This grieved and humiliated him.

Buck would help Green Rock and Squirrel Fur when he could, but he was currently away on one of his trade routes in the dugout canoe that he had made six cycles before. Green Rock hoped that someday he could join Buck on his trading circuit.

But, right now, he had to focus on hunting food for his mother. He arrived at a place where a deer trail crossed a stream, and waited silently. He thought to himself, *What if no deer comes along? I need a backup plan.*

So he backtracked for a while and set up his leaning-log squirrel trap, with four nooses – just in case he failed in getting a deer. Then he returned to the stream and waited again. The morning went by and he neither saw nor heard anything. He grew hungry, and ate some cornbread packed by Squirrel Fur. Then he heard a rustling in the woods.

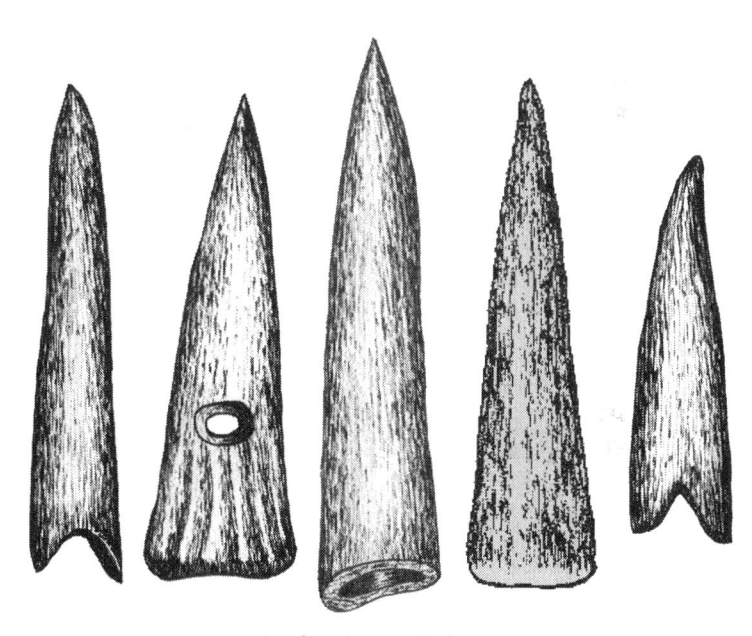

Antler Arrow Points.
Redrawn from Beauchamp 1902.

Green Rock got his bow and some antler tipped arrows ready as a nine-point buck appeared and began drinking from the stream. He aimed, and loosed his arrow. It struck the buck in the side. It was not a good shot. The buck staggered off, and Green Rock got another arrow ready. He followed the blood trail, and saw the buck at the same time it saw him. The infuriated buck charged after him. Green Rock dropped his bow and arrow just in time to protect himself by grabbing the buck by the antlers. The buck pushed him backwards; he caught his foot on a root, and fell on his back, with the angry buck on top of him.

Green Rock was terrified. The only thing he knew to do was to keep his firm grip on the buck's menacing antlers to protect his belly from them. The buck was stomping him in the belly and groin, and the pain was excruciating. He moved his legs around in an effort to protect himself from another blow from the buck's hooves. Suddenly an arrow struck the buck in the neck and it fell dead. Green Rock got out from under it and looked around. Where did that arrow come from?

"Are you okay?" said a familiar voice.

Green Rock turned to look and saw Twisted Stick in a dugout canoe in the stream. "No!" he replied in agony. Twisted Stick beached his canoe and helped Green Rock up. "You came along at a good time," said Green Rock, still in considerable pain. "Thank you."

"You are welcome. You looked like you needed some help there," Twisted Stick said with a chuckle.

"I would have had it under control shortly," defended Green Rock.

Green Rock noticed a dead deer in Twisted Stick's canoe.

"I am on my way back home," said Twisted Stick, "I have been gone for two days! I couldn't find any game around here. You got lucky. I will see you later. Oh, I got you some soapstone! See it?"

Green Rock looked in the dugout where Twisted Stick pointed and saw two large pieces. "Thanks," he said, still in pain.

Twisted Stick then shoved off and drifted back downstream towards the river, and home.

Green Rock cut the buck's throat with a flint knife, and paid proper respects to its spirit. After removing the antler tipped arrows and washing them in the stream, Green Rock sat down for a while to recover. Then he carried the buck on his shoulders back to the village.

When he arrived at his mother's lodge, he told her about the fight between him and the buck.

Squirrel Fur said, "I will skin it and dress it. Sparrow will be back soon. She can help. You certainly have done enough for one day."

"Thank you," replied Green Rock. "I need to go and see what Eagle Medicine wants for me to make."

Green Rock left. When he arrived at Eagle Medicine's lodge, Dances Like the Deer showed him in.

"Hello, Green Rock," said Eagle Medicine.

Green Rock was just about to greet him, and he suddenly remembered the squirrel trap. "I am very sorry, but I have to go. I promise I will be back later."

"What happened?" asked Eagle Medicine.

"I forgot to check my squirrel trap – the fight with the buck distracted me. I don't want to leave those squirrels there, suffering."

"Go on then, I will wait for you here."

Green Rock ran home and grabbed his flint knife. As he began to run off, Squirrel Fur said, "What is happening? I thought you were going to Eagle Medicine's."

"I forgot that I set some squirrel traps!" replied Green Rock as he ran off.

He arrived at the traps just before sunset. There were four squirrels hanging from the nooses. He cut their throats, apologized to each of their spirits, and took them back to Birch Mountain and gave them to Sparrow. He would have given two of them to Tanager, but it was taboo for a pregnant woman to eat meat, particularly squirrel, rabbit or speckled trout.

He returned to Eagle Medicine's lodge. "I don't think I am meant to be a hunter," he said.

"What happened?" asked Eagle Medicine, "You mentioned something about a fight with a buck."

Green Rock described the fight with the buck and they laughed at the story. Green Rock, now feeling better, was also able to laugh about it.

"You should learn to shoot arrows faster," suggested Eagle Medicine. "With practice, I have seen people accurately shoot up to four arrows before the first one hits its mark."

"I will have to work on that," replied Green Rock. "What did you want to see me about?"

"Have you ever carved anything out of granite?" asked Eagle Medicine.

"No, I have not," Green Rock answered.

"Have you seen how it is done?"

"One time, I saw a man pecking out an axe head with another piece of a hard stone, like flint."

"That's how it is done. The Uku wants a large chunkey stone made for the next game. There is plenty of granite in the river, a lot of it is rounded and will save you labor. Do you think you can do it?"

"It will take a while, but I am sure I can."

"You go on and start on it tomorrow; we will provide your mother with plenty of meat while you work on it. We will also give you two bearskins for you to keep for yourself. Are you interested?"

"Yes, I would rather be carving stone than fighting with some angry animal for food!"

At that everybody in the lodge laughed.

"I will go down to the river tomorrow and find the right piece of granite tomorrow. Do you have a color preference?"

"If you can find a dark gray or black piece that will be fine."

"What size do you want it?"

Eagle Medicine got out a game stone and said, "Larger than this one. We want it to be concave on each side, and drilled in the center."

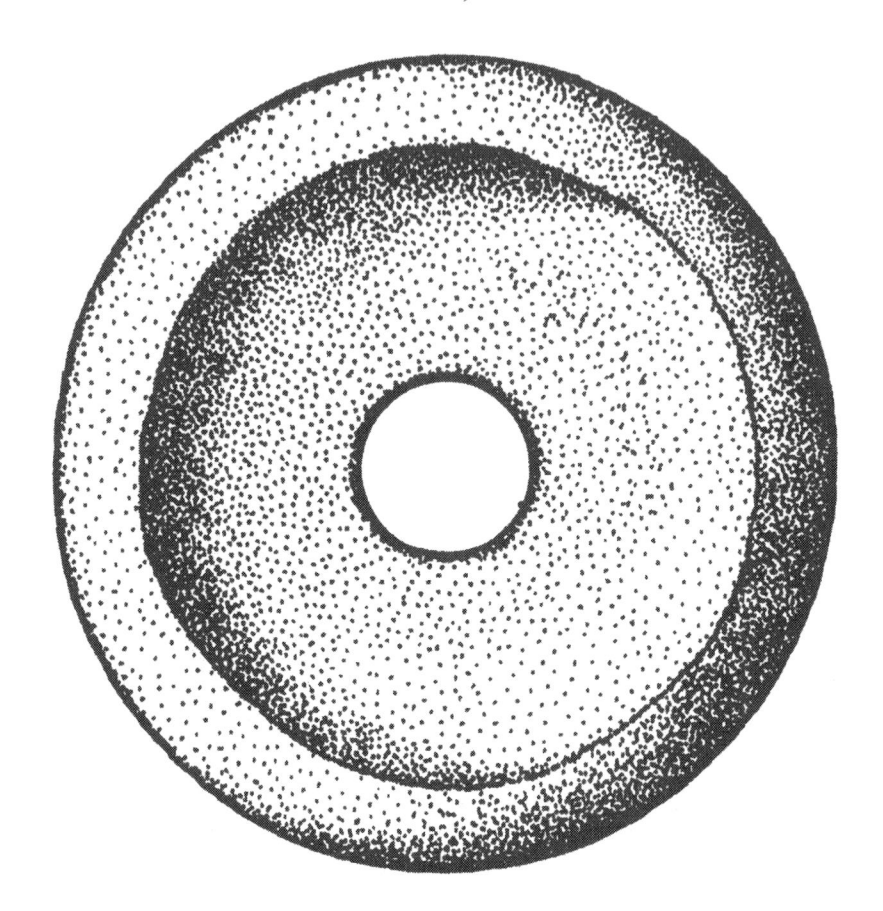

Discoidal Chunkey Stone.

"Okay, it's a deal!" said Green Rock.

"Very good," said Eagle Medicine.

Green Rock returned home and told Squirrel Fur and Sparrow the news. "You will have plenty of meat while I am working on this project."

The two women smiled. They were happy that Green Rock could help provide for them in a way he truly enjoyed.

Green Rock ate a good meal of venison from the buck he had fought with earlier that day. When they finished, Sparrow noticed that Green Rock was quiet.

"Is something wrong?" she asked.

"No," Green Rock replied.

Sparrow knew better.

"Yes!" Green Rock corrected. "I am tired of fighting with deer and never having time to pursue *my* dreams. I want to build my own lodge and have my own family! It's not fair! I do a man's work, but I am considered a child! I am seventeen cycles old! I am not angry with you or Mother; I just think I should be entitled to have my own life. But I never get the chance for whatever reason. I am really frustrated."

Sparrow's and Squirrel Fur's eyes met. They didn't expect this sudden outburst of emotions. Now that it happened, they both could understand Green Rock's reasoning. He had matured without them noticing. But he couldn't become an adult officially until he had gone through the rites of passage, and they had no control over that. They sat silently and listened.

"I am sorry – I didn't mean to lose my temper," he added. "I love you both and I don't mind hunting for you two; I just wish I could begin my own life. Sometimes it seems like the spirits have forsaken me." He had tears in his eyes. "I mean really – I am seventeen cycles old! Buck became an adult when he was fifteen! I wish I were out on a trading circuit like he is. It's not fair. I am sorry for bringing it up."

After some silence and thought, Squirrel Fur said, "Let us speak with our fellow clansmen. Maybe we can help in ways that we hadn't previously thought of."

"Don't worry about it, I'll manage," said Green Rock. "I want to help you two."

"And we should treat you like a seventeen-cycle-old," replied Squirrel Fur, "regardless of whether you have gone through initiation."

"I agree," said Sparrow. "You have done a lot for us in the past few cycles; it's time we did something for you."

Green Rock had no idea of what they could possibly do, but didn't say anything. He regretted saying what he had said. He went to bed in a bad mood.

Next morning, he went to the river and gathered there with the rest of the village for the daily bathing and prayers to the rising Sun. When that was finished, he noticed Squirrel Fur speaking to the Bird Clan's leader, Paint Pot. Green Rock had no idea what they could be talking about, and decided not to get his hopes up. He concluded that it would be better to be carving the hardest stone to provide for his family, than to hunt and wrestle with an angry buck for them.

Green Rock went back into the water to search for a good piece of granite. He picked up one piece, but it was too small. Then he spied a better piece, and went to pick it up. He was startled by the distant familiar voice of his best friend.

"What are you doing in the river?" the voice called.

Green Rock jumped, and looked in the direction of the voice. There was The Buck Kicks the Drum approaching in his dugout canoe.

"Buck!" greeted Green Rock, and he ran along the shore to meet him. "You are back early!"

"Yes, I decided to cut my circuit short," said Buck. "Tanager's time is getting near, and I thought I should be here for her. Besides, I have acquired a bunch of flint and I can get more trade value from it if I make preforms and knives out of it."

"It's so good to see you!" said Green Rock, as he got into the canoe.

"Have you been initiated into adulthood yet?"

Green Rock looked down, "No," he said.

"Too bad. You probably will not have to wait much longer. When it finally does happen, you will be with every lady in the village! A different one each night!" Buck said with a chuckle.

Green Rock couldn't help laughing also.

"It's good to have you back," Green Rock said after a short pause.

They beached the canoe near the village, and the guards in the guardhouses approached them for a closer look. They of course knew Buck, and they ran back inside the palisade to announce that he had returned. The whole village came out to greet him, as they would for any trader. But nobody was more eager to see him than Tanager was.

Buck announced to all of them that he would be staying until his unborn baby was old enough to take care of him or herself. That would be at least four cycles.

Now Tanager moved into the women's hut. She would remain there until a week after the baby was born. Meanwhile, Green Rock helped Buck with the enormous task of moving his wares from the canoe back to his lodge. They swapped stories in the process. Green Rock told Buck about his "deer fight" and Buck told stories of the places he had visited. He also talked about a temple mound he had heard about very far to the west that reached the sky. He had also heard about the enormous village named Cahokia, where this mound was located. "Someday I am going to visit Cahokia," said Buck, "I bet they have a lot of trading going on there."

"I want to travel with you when you go there," said Green Rock.

When the canoe was unloaded, Green Rock went back to the river to continue his search for a piece of granite. He finally found one that looked like it would work well. He began pecking on it. It took a few weeks of constant pecking to shape it. His hands were extremely sore, but at last it was roughed-out and ready to grind and polish.

Meanwhile, Squirrel Fur and Sparrow secretly met with Buck and members of the Bird Clan. They were negotiating for a lodge to be built for Green Rock. Buck owed a debt to Green Rock for the pipes he had sent with him during his trading route.

Green Rock was so caught up in grinding the chunkey stone smooth that he had completely forgotten the debt that Buck owed him. Buck began building the lodge; it was near to his own lodge. When Green Rock asked him whom the lodge was for, Buck simply said he owed a friend the labor.

Building Green Rock's Lodge.

Green Rock continued polishing on the game stone, which proved to take much longer than he had anticipated. He missed carving soapstone; it was so soft compared to this. But after a half a moon, he had it polished to a beautiful shine. It was now ready to drill. He got a piece of cane and some sand, and core drilled it, which was quite a chore in itself. Drilling it took another few days. When he was finished drilling it, he polished the inside of the hole. When it was completed, he presented it to Eagle Medicine. It was a very dark mottled gray and black with a white stripe through one side. It was beautiful and symmetrical.

Eagle Medicine said, "This is far better than I expected. We will give you three bearskins instead of two. Or, if you are willing, I can make you another offer."

"And what is that?" asked Green Rock.

"Come with me," said Eagle Medicine.

"Can I come too?" asked White Feather.

"Yes, you may," answered Eagle Medicine.

They stopped at the lodge that Buck had worked on. Squirrel Fur and Sparrow were there and so was Paint Pot. They were all smiling.

"What is going on?" asked Green Rock. "Is this a joke?"

"This is your new lodge," said Eagle Medicine.

"But how will I pay for it?"

"It is paid for," said Squirrel Fur.

"How?" asked Green Rock.

"You have done so much for us in the past few cycles," replied Squirrel Fur, "that we helped Buck build this lodge for you."

"But how did you pay Buck?"

"We didn't – *you* did."

"I never…" Green Rock now remembered all the stone carvings he had sent with Buck when he went on his last route.

"The pipes!" exclaimed Green Rock. "The pipes! I forgot all about the pipes!"

"What pipes?" asked Buck, jokingly.

Everybody burst into laughter, and Buck smiled.

Eagle Medicine asked, "Is this worth the three bearskins?"

"It certainly is!" said Green Rock, "I don't believe this!"

"Go on, look inside," said Squirrel Fur, with a smile.

Green Rock entered the lodge and found that it was completely ready to move into. There was even a pile of soapstone and flint that had been moved from Buck's lodge. He was speechless. As he emerged from the lodge, tears came to his eyes as he said, "Thank you all, Thank you."

Green Rock still was not an adult yet, but he was now ready for adulthood, whenever the spirits were ready. His wait was not to be much longer. Buck was going to make sure that an opportunity would soon present itself.

Eagle Medicine and White Feather left to return home.

"Why did Green Rock have tears in his eyes?" asked White Feather.

"He is happy," answered Eagle Medicine. "Sometimes people cry when they are happy."

"But he is old to be crying."

"That may be, but I think it is appropriate in his situation. Please do not tell any of your friends about it. It would embarrass him. Can you understand that?"

"Yes," she replied, "I promise not to tell anybody."

"Good girl," said Eagle Medicine while patting her on the back.

Buck walked with Squirrel Fur and Sparrow back to their lodges. He said, "Green Rock needs to go with me on a war party. He needs to prove himself."

"I know," returned Squirrel Fur, "but he hasn't had much practice. He has never pursued war."

"I know, but I will see to it that he is ready when the time comes. We will go together, and I will make sure nothing happens to him."

"I spoke to Paint Pot about it; he says he will see to it that some of the other clan members hunt food for us so Green Rock will have more time for himself."

"That's good. I will work with Green Rock to get him ready. It won't take long. Thank you both for your understanding."

Squirrel Fur and Sparrow both thanked Buck for offering to help Green Rock, and then they parted.

Buck went to Green Rock's lodge and found him there – still in a state of disbelief.

When Green Rock saw Buck, he said, "Thank you so much for what you did for me."

"You paid for it," replied Buck. "There is no need to thank me. We are now going to work together on honing your battle skills! I know this is not something you favor, but we only have to practice for one raid. After that, you can carve a whole mountain of stone. But for now, we need to focus on you being a fierce warrior."

"I am ready to start," said Green Rock.

Just then, they heard Tanager's voice calling from the women's hut nearby. Buck and Green Rock ran to see what was happening.

"Tanager," said Buck from outside, "What's wrong?"

"My time has come!" came the reply.

"I will run get Mother," offered Green Rock, and he ran off.

"Mother! Mother!" he called. She was not in her lodge. So Green Rock ran to Sparrow's lodge and found her there.

"Come quick, Mother," he said. "Tanager is having her baby!"

Squirrel Fur lost no time getting to the women's hut.

Out of respect, Buck waited nervously outside while Tanager gave birth to a baby girl. Green Rock had been sent to get Corn Leaf. Green Rock and Corn Leaf arrived and Corn Leaf entered the hut.

Green Rock and Buck were asked by Corn Leaf to fetch water. They left with the waterbottles and went to the river. Buck's legs were trembling. He felt faint and was slightly pale.

On their way back, Green Rock said, "Are you going to be okay?"

"Yes," replied Buck, "I'll be fine."

Woman Effigy Hooded Pottery Waterbottle.
Redrawn from Thruston 1897.

    They returned to the hut, with the clay bottles of water. They gave the bottles to Corn Leaf, and the baby was washed and then baptized in Tanager's milk. Corn Leaf, who was expecting this day to come, had consulted with Eagle Medicine as to what natal name should be given to the infant. It was calculated that the baby's name would be Four Raccoons. This was a temporary name, which was needed. If an infant dies before it is named and baptized in her mother's milk, her spirit would be lost in the cosmos for eternity. Buck now had the opportunity to see the baby and hold her. He was overjoyed.

The next day, Corn Leaf returned and said, "I saw a titmouse on the way home yesterday, it followed me for a while. I think we should call her Titmouse."

Tanager liked the name. So the name "Titmouse" was decided.

When Titmouse was about a week old, Eagle Medicine visited them, and picked up Titmouse and waved her in a circular motion seven times over the fire, while blessing the infant.

Buck began to stay with Green Rock in his new lodge. It was taboo for a man to eat food prepared by a woman until three moons after she gave birth. Sex was also taboo during this period, and he was to even avoid touching her in any way, anymore than necessary.

It was much easier to just stay with a friend. Green Rock needed help anyway. Buck began helping Green Rock practice with his bow. Green Rock wanted to learn to shoot arrows faster.

"Eagle Medicine told me that a person could shoot four arrows accurately before the first one hits its mark," he said.

"If you could shoot two arrows," replied Buck, "that would be an improvement."

They worked on it for several days, and Green Rock refined his technique. Buck also taught him how to throw an axe after some practice.

Eagle Medicine was also busy with his own project. Squirrel Fur had gone to him to seek his help concerning Green Rock. He also felt that the time was overdue for Green Rock to have his Vision Quest. He resolved to use sorcery to bring on the Vision when the time was right. They said nothing to Green Rock about it.

One day, Buck decided that Green Rock was ready to go on a raid. They went to the Uku, Standing Bear, with a plan to attack the Yuchi to get retribution for an attack on Eagle Peak the previous summer. The Uku approved – he also wanted to see Green Rock become an adult.

It was decided. Before sunrise, Buck and Green Rock set out over the ridge towards Eagle Peak. As they walked, Green Rock asked numerous questions about Buck's travels.

"Have you traded with the Yuchi?" asked Green Rock.

"No! And I probably never will." answered Buck, "I hear that all they have are a few pearls, and some crude totem effigies. There are plenty of other sources for pearls."

"Where else can you trade for pearls?"

"The closest freshwater pearls would be from the Muskogee to the south and west."

"Trading with the Yuchi would not be prudent after this trip, I suppose."

"I don't plan to find out either. They killed my parents. I have no intentions of being their friend."

"Where do you get your copper?"

"It is hard to come by. I trade it from the northeastern parts of our territory. They trade for it from farther to the northeast. I have also heard of some coming from many days travel to the northwest."

"Where do you get your flint from?"

"There are several places to the south and southwest that have flint and chert."

"What do they usually want in return?"

"Mica, turkey feather cloaks, salt, and other items. You have to see what they don't have much of. That is done with experience. When you are on a trading route, you have to be observant of what natural resources are in a particular area, and provide what they are lacking. Pottery and pottery clay are in demand at home because it doesn't occur there much."

They decided to hunt for some food and take it to Eagle Peak. There they planned to stay with Green Rock's aunt Acorn.

They heard a rustling noise in a nearby thicket. Buck got his bow ready, while Green Rock got Buck's axe. They cautiously entered the thicket, and saw a small black bear. Green Rock threw the axe at its head. The axe hit its mark. They ran up to it, picked up the axe and continued clubbing the bear in the head until it stopped kicking.

"That was a good throw, Green Rock," said Buck, as he cut the bear's throat.

They both paused to catch their breath. Then they apologized to the bear's spirit.

"That was my first bear," said Green Rock, "Have you ever killed a bear?"

"No, I have not," answered Buck.

Green Rock started chopping a long thick pole so they could carry the bear into Eagle Peak. When they arrived at Acorn's lodge, she was so surprised to have two guests and a feast walking right up to her door!

"How are you doing, Green Rock, and Buck?" she asked. "And how is Squirrel Fur?"

"We are fine," answered Green Rock, "Mother is doing well also."

"How is your trading going?" she asked Buck.

"Very well. I came back early because Tanager was due. We now have a daughter; her name is Titmouse."

"Congratulations! How is Tanager? She is such a sweet girl."

"She is doing well; she was glad I came back early, but she is worried about me leaving again. We are going into Yuchi territory on a war mission."

"You two better be careful; they are vicious fighters."

"We'd better start on this bear," said Buck.

They hung it from a tree and began skinning it.

"Green Rock," said Acorn, "I met a man who has heard of you and wants a pipe made. Would you like to meet him?"

"Yes," replied Green Rock, "Where is he?"

"I will go and get him – his name is Fox Claw," she answered before leaving.

As they continued skinning the bear, Green Rock asked Buck numerous additional questions about trading.

"So, you can actually be welcomed into an enemy village?" he inquired.

"As long as they don't recognize you from a recent raid, that is true. They are every bit as hospitable as our village is to traders. The Muskogee have different customs. Some are quite exotic."

"Can you tell me more about them?"

"Have you ever heard about the white drink?"

"Is it like the grape drink that Stone Spear used to make?"

"No, this is used during Muskogee ceremonies for purification. They brew a tea from yaupon holly. Then they drink very large amounts of it and it makes them sweat and vomit."

"Why would they want to vomit?"

"They believe it purifies a person."

"Why is it called the white drink?"

"White is symbolic of purity. You know that."

"Tell me more about the Muskogee."

"What do you want to know about them?"

"I don't know. Do they hate each other as much as they hate us?"

"No, they live together in harmony just like we do."

"Why is there the need for them to fight with us, if we are so much like them?"

"You definitely have the heart of a trader!" smiled Wolf Tail. "Traders are generally immune from tribal conflicts. It allows us the opportunity to see the best in each other from the ideal point of view."

"I wish that were true for everybody else."

"Me too, Green Rock, me too."

"What about the rest of the tribes? Are they just as dedicated to each other?"

"They are, as much as we are."

"What are the most impressive things you've seen that they make?"

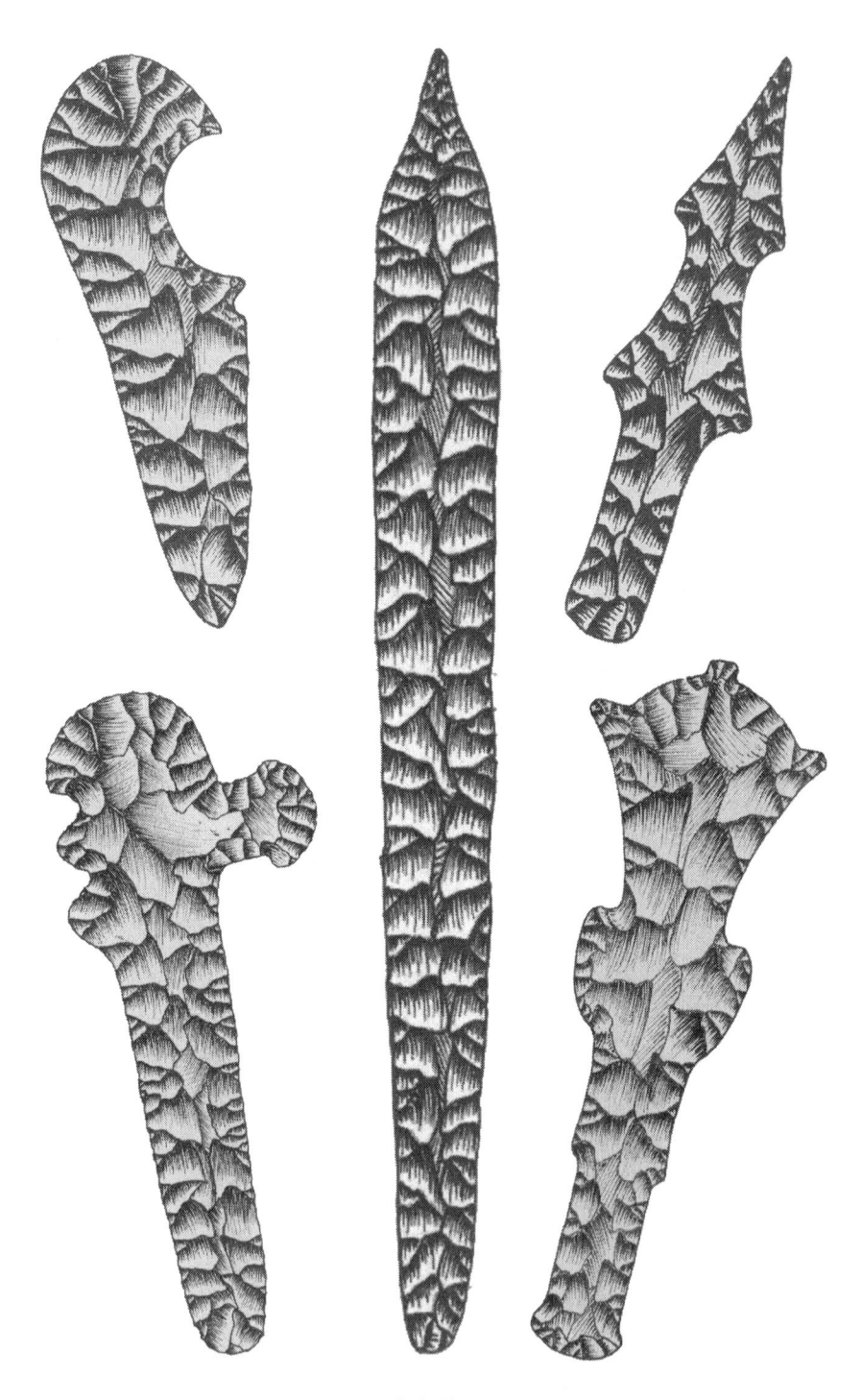

Ceremonial Chert Items.

"Some of them have very long ceremonial knives, daggers, monolithic axes, maces and other things made from chert. The knives are two to three feet long, less than three fingers wide, and very thin. They use them in dances. I've never personally met a person who makes them, or seen how they make them. I'll tell you what though, I sure would love to know where they get flint in pieces that large!"

They finished skinning and gutting the bear. As they began to cut it up, Acorn arrived with a stranger.

"Here is Fox Claw," she said. "And here is Green Rock."

"Hello," said Green Rock. "Acorn tells me you want me to carve something for you."

"Yes," replied Fox Claw. "I have heard about you carving effigy pipes. A friend of mine got one from Buck last summer. Very good work."

"What type of pipe do you want?" asked Green Rock.

"I have always wanted a regular elbow pipe with a standing deer facing the bowl. I am a member of the Deer Clan."

"What color do you want it?"

"I know where to get some very high grade dark gray soapstone. I would like it made from some of that."

"You don't already have the stone?"

"I can get it by tomorrow evening."

"We will be gone by then, but we can stop by here on our way back from the raid."

"I'll leave it with Acorn then."

"What will you trade for my services?" Green Rock asked.

"I will trade enough of this dark gray stone for making twenty pipes."

Green Rock was surprised at this man's generosity. "That will be fine," he said, trying to hide his excitement.

Fox Claw smiled and said, "Be careful on your raid, and good luck," and then he left.

Buck was skeptical. "You better be wary of him," he said.

"Why?" asked Green Rock, "He made me a good deal."

"It was too good of a deal. And I know him too."

"Have you dealt with him before?"

"No, but I have been told that he can be pretty cunning."

"Do you mean that he won't pay me?"

"I don't know. But his 'friend' Badger told me not to trust him; he didn't go into detail about it though."

"He will pay me," said Green Rock, "He seems like a likable person to me."

Buck was unconvinced, but offered no more argument.

"Why don't you two wash your hands in the river?" suggested Acorn. "And when you get back, I'll have some dinner for you. I will finish cutting up the bear tomorrow."

"That sounds good," said Buck, "I am hungry!"

"Me too!" added Green Rock.

They left for the river, and when they returned, they had a hearty meal of green beans, cornbread, and dried meat.

Then they went to bed. It would be a long day tomorrow.

The next morning, they were up early. They joined the rest of the village at the river to bathe and pray to the morning Sun. Then they returned to Acorn's lodge to eat breakfast. Acorn packed plenty of dried meat and cornbread for them to take on their trip.

They set out and resumed their journey, now heading down the banks of Thunder River, towards Yuchi territory. The closer they got, the more apprehensive Green Rock became.

"Are you as nervous as I am?" he asked.

"In war, being nervous can get you killed," Buck answered.

Green Rock didn't feel much like a warrior. In fact, he hated war.

"Maybe we will find Running Fox," he said after a long pause.

"Not likely," replied Buck. "He is grown up now, and we probably wouldn't recognize him. Besides, he could be in any Yuchi town. He could also have been traded to the Muskogee, or another tribe. Captives that live are made into slaves."

"Do you really think they killed him? He was only eight cycles old."

"By all probability, he was enslaved. But he could be anywhere. That is if he survived being a slave."

"But don't the Yuchi and Muskogee eventually adopt slaves into the tribe, like we do?"

"It is very possible."

"Do you think if we did locate him, he would come back with us?"

"If he is still a slave he would. But not after he is adopted into the tribe and has gained status there. I am hungry. Let's stop for lunch."

"Good idea," agreed Green Rock.

The two ate some of the dried meat and cornbread packed for them by Acorn that morning. They drank from the clear water of the river.

"How much farther do we have to go?" asked Green Rock.

"Just a little bit, and then the journey will be easier. There should be a canoe waiting for us."

Green Rock wondered why there would be a canoe in the middle of nowhere, but he didn't ask. They finished eating and resumed their journey down the riverbank.

"Keep your eyes open for Yuchis," said Buck. "We are getting near to their territory."

Green Rock nervously hoped that no curious buzzards would circle around them, making their presence known.

They finally arrived at a place on the river, near the outskirts of the Cherokees' territory. Buck explained that he had previously learned the whereabouts of some abandoned Yuchi canoes during his travels. Some Yuchi warriors who had done a raid on Eagle Peak had left them behind for a quick getaway. But the warriors had all been killed during the raid, which happened two cycles before. When the canoes were later discovered, they were kept hidden here, for use in future raids against the Yuchi. After Buck located these canoes, they took one of them downstream.

"Why do they call this river "Thunder River?" he asked. "It seems calm to me."

"I hear it gets pretty rough downstream," answered Buck, "I've heard there might even be a waterfall, although I am unfamiliar with it. I have never been that far into the territory of the Yuchi."

They went through rapids that got more intense the farther downstream they went. It was a scary and exhilarating experience for Green Rock. The rough terrain was breathtaking. Green Rock was staring at it in awe.

He was abruptly brought back to the here and now when Buck shouted, "We need to quickly get to the left!"

Green Rock saw the protruding rocks on the right. He paddled hard and fast. He was truly afraid while they went around the bend in the river.

"I now see why they call it Thunder River!" said Green Rock.

"It only gets worse from what I have heard," replied Buck. "Keep your voice down, it can easily be heard from the shore."

Their bows had gotten water splashed on them during the fury of the river. Green Rock picked them out of the puddle on the bottom of the canoe.

"Buck," he said, showing Buck the wet bows.

"Oh no!" whispered Buck, "We are going to have to dry them before we can attack. Try to keep them dry."

"We must be very close," said Green Rock.

"Yes we are."

They continued downstream as the day came to an end.

At sundown, Buck finally said, "Let's beach here."

They landed on the shore, and Buck looked around. "We are well inside of Yuchi territory now," he said in a whisper. "Let's carry the canoe well away from the shore and hide it. We won't be having a campfire tonight."

"But how will we dry the bowstrings?" asked Green Rock.

"You are right. We need to find a cave, but it's getting dark. I hope that a fire won't get us discovered."

Green Rock could tell that Buck was worried. They searched in the gathering darkness for a cave that could conceal their campfire. They were completely defenseless and vulnerable without their bows in working order.

"Take this axe. I should have made you your own axe before we left Birch Mountain," said Buck, angry with himself for his neglect.

Flint Double-Bitted Axe.

"We are never going to find a cave in the dark," said Green Rock.

"And if we do, who knows what kinds of animals will be inside waiting for us," added Buck. "At least it is not raining."

As the night progressed, they continued searching for a cave in the darkness. They couldn't find one.

"We are just going to have to risk it," said Buck. "It's getting too late to keep looking. We will never succeed in the dark. We will have to risk building a fire. It will have to be a small one, and we have to put it out once the bowstrings are dried."

So, Green Rock got some firewood together, while Buck found some fleabane to use as tinder. They got a little fire going, and both held the bowstrings simultaneously over the rising heat to dry them out. It seemed to take forever. They were very alert for the faintest sound of the approaching enemy. All they heard was the roaring river in the distance, and the crackling of the fire.

Once the bowstrings were dry, they tested them by stringing the bows and pulling on them. If either string broke, the attack would be called off. They held strong.

Now, they put out the small fire, and went a considerable distance from it to make their camp. If the fire was discovered, they wanted to be far away from it.

"How far is the nearest village?" asked Green Rock.

"I'm not sure," replied Buck, "but we won't be taking on a village. That would be suicide with only two of us. I planned on waiting for some hunters to come down a hunting trail, and ambushing them there."

"When do you think I will have my Vision Quest?" asked Green Rock.

"I don't know," answered Buck. "Just wait and see. It won't be long, I am sure. Don't worry about it. Everything will fall into place when the time is right."

They ate some more dried meat for dinner and went to sleep. Some rustling noises in the leaves in their camp soon awakened them. Both Green Rock and Buck feared the worst. Buck grabbed his axe, ready to kill a Yuchi warrior. But it was only several raccoons bent on stealing their cornbread and dried meat.

Raccoon.
Drawn from photo by ariesa66 from Pixabay.

"Get out of here! Get!" said Green Rock in a whispered shout.

The raccoons scattered as they threw sticks at them. They made quite a commotion in the leaves as they scrambled to get away.

"We need to do something with the food," said Buck, "or they will be back and we will never get any sleep."

"I have some twine," replied Green Rock. "Let's hang the food from a tree branch out of their reach."

"Hang it out of the reach of any raccoons that climb the tree also."

Green Rock tied the plant fiber cord to a branch, while Buck held the branch down. Then Green Rock tied the other end to the bag of food, so that it hung there.

"That looks good," said Buck. "It is high enough to be out of their reach, and long enough so that they won't reach it from up in the tree."

They lay back down to sleep. By the sound of his breathing, Green Rock could tell that Buck had gone back to sleep. Green Rock was still very excited about the attack they had planned. He couldn't sleep.

What if something went wrong? They were a long way from home. They both were unfamiliar with the territory. This was no childhood war game.

Green Rock lay there trying to sleep. All that he heard was the distant roaring of Thunder River. He knew it was getting very late, and they had to be up early.

Buck began to snore gently. Green Rock just lay there, his eyes open, looking into the night sky. He saw the Milky Way – Long Being – the Spirit of the River.

He had always felt a closeness with Long Being. Now, he began to silently pray to this Honored Spirit. *Oh Long Being, you have always been my friend. Look after Buck and me during tomorrow's raid. Bring us safely home.* Green Rock then drifted off to sleep.

Meanwhile, at Birch Mountain, Eagle Medicine recited an incantation, his divining Crystal in his hand...

As Green Rock slept, a dream began to crystallize. In this dream, he heard a voice – *Follow me.* He looked in the direction of the voice and he thought he saw a wolf running down to the river.

He woke up and listened. In the night, he heard the distant howling of a wolf. He thought it could be an omen, but decided it was not. He drifted back to sleep.

The dream continued, and he saw the wolf swimming in the river. *Follow me*, the voice repeated.

Once again, he woke up. He thought about it for a while. *Spirit of the Wolf, what are you saying to me?*

He fell back asleep. This time he slept for a long time. He was then awakened by a wolf howling nearby, up on a cliff by the river.

"This can't be a coincidence," he whispered. He got up and looked in the direction of the wolf. He couldn't see in the dark. Buck was still snoring peacefully on the ground.

Green Rock knew he needed the sleep that he was missing. He lay back down and fell asleep shortly afterwards. Now, in his dream, he saw a wolf's face staring him in the eyes.

Suddenly he felt a sensation all over his body. He was falling with water all around him. It was like a fleeting glimpse. His body jerked in his sleep. He saw the wolf's face again, and once again the voice said, *Follow me.* Then he had the falling sensation again, more vivid than the first time. He woke up screaming.

"Be quiet!" whispered Buck, "You will alert the Yuchis!"

"I had a dream about a wolf and the river," said Green Rock. "I think the wolf wants me to follow him down the river."

"Well, tell him you need to sleep!" said Buck, still irritated. "And *I* need to sleep."

Buck was soon snoring again. Green Rock saw that the sky to the east was beginning to get light. He tried to piece together the message in his dream. *The Wolf said, "Follow me." He swam in the river. He must want me to follow him in the river! This must be my Vision Quest.*

Green Rock got up and made his way towards the canoe. He saw the river in the early morning light. It was fierce and raging. He decided to pursue his Spirit Dream by taking the canoe down Thunder River. He had no idea what to expect from this – and he was afraid – but he knew he had to listen to the Spirits.

Green Rock labored to uncover the hidden canoe and dragged it to the riverbank. Then he grabbed one of the paddles, climbed into the dugout and shoved off, taking nothing else with him. He knew he was now truly at the mercy of Long Being.

Chapter 6: Thunder River

The raging river pushed Green Rock's frail canoe rapidly downstream and he now began to wonder if he had made a mistake. *The spirits were clear*, he reasoned, *I think…* But he knew he couldn't turn back now. He worried about leaving Buck behind.

His thoughts were soon cut short when he realized that he was headed for some exposed rocks. He paddled desperately to avoid them. He managed to steer clear of the majority of the rocks, but the bottom of the dugout struck a rock on one side. It hung there, and the swift current turned the canoe around.

More rocks were approaching. He tried his best to turn the canoe around. He couldn't make it work! Green Rock was terrified. The rear of the canoe crashed full force into the rocks, violently jarring Green Rock towards the stern.

Now, the current rotated the bow of the canoe back around while Green Rock repositioned himself. The stern was lodged on the rock bottom. He pushed the dugout free with his paddle. He was glad to be where he was when he saw the boulders with logs lodged in them on the opposite side of the river.

The river grew even fiercer than before. The dugout was moving sideways. Green Rock saw that he was rapidly approaching some standing waves. He fought hard to turn the canoe around. It worked.

As he passed through the standing waves, cold water poured over him, leaving a puddle in the bottom of the canoe. Now, he saw a log wedged between two rocks. He had no time to maneuver around it. He held onto the sides of the canoe as it hit the log. The current swept the dugout alongside and against the log. His fingers were caught between the canoe and the log. He grimaced in pain as he pulled his hand away. The undertow nearly capsized the canoe. Green Rock was too busy trying to free the canoe from the log, and never noticed the mountain lion spying him from the cliff above.

Once he cleared the log, he was faced with another problem. The river was now split in several places by large outcroppings of granite. He couldn't reach the widest branch of the river in time. The dugout was sideways again, and Green Rock paddled desperately to correct it. It was too late. The bow was stopped on the side of the boulder. The stern was quickly whipped around and he went through the narrow channel backwards. Before he knew it, the stern struck another boulder. He was jolted backwards, then almost went overboard as the racing current instantly brought the bow back around.

Now the dugout was turning sideways again. Green Rock managed to straighten it up just in time for the next series of standing waves. Water poured into the canoe. Green Rock began thinking he wouldn't last much longer.

The river widened as Green Rock passed by a smaller tributary that merged with Thunder River. It was now calmer – for the moment. He wondered if he might be near a Yuchi village. Villages were very common near where two streams joined.

When Green Rock went around the bend, the river got rougher than ever. There were large projecting rocks scattered throughout the riverbed. Green Rock worked quickly with the paddle, and avoided most of them.

He found himself headed straight for a boulder and, when he tried to steer away from it, the canoe only turned to its side. Fear played in his spirit as the wind played in his hair. Green Rock raised the paddle to cushion the sideways impact and the paddle broke! He had left the other one behind! He now had no control over the dugout canoe.

He now firmly held on to the sides of the canoe. He was headed for another large stone. When he struck it, it made a split in the canoe. He was taking on water. He looked ahead, and noticed a very distant horizon – far beyond the river. Then he noticed a rainbow just above the river ahead. *How... What could be causing... Waterfall!*

Green Rock was truly afraid. Every part of his seventeen-cycle-old body screamed out loud with terror. He was too close and had no time to get to shore. As he neared the waterfall, he raised his arms. *Oh, Long Being, I am in your care.*

It was like everything was happening very slowly. The canoe tipped forward as it crossed over the edge of the waterfall. Green Rock, now free of the canoe, plummeted towards the center of the earth – water all around him. The canoe struck a boulder and broke in two.

Green Rock plunged into a deep pool of water, and the extreme force of the falling liquid mass pushed him straight to the bottom. The angry Thunder River continued to rage as it had done since the beginning of time.

* * *

Sparrow arose early in the morning, and was the first person at the river for morning devotions. She was soon joined by Squirrel Fur and the rest of Birch Mountain. After they finished their prayers to the rising Sun and bathing, Sparrow greeted Squirrel Fur.

"Good Morning," answered Squirrel Fur. Her eyes then shifted to the ground.

"Are you alright?" asked Sparrow.

"I'm fine."

Sparrow could tell by her demeanor that she was worried about Green Rock and Buck.

"They will be okay," Sparrow said. "I am sure."

Tears came to Squirrel Fur's eyes as she said, "I just wish I could stop thinking about it! He's not a warrior. He never was! Last night I dreamed that Buck came back alone and Green Rock had drowned!"

"I know they are both alright," said Sparrow, "and they will both be back home in a few days. Why don't we check up on Tanager and the baby?"

The visit cheered up Squirrel Fur, which is what Sparrow was trying to do. Squirrel Fur spoke with Tanager while Sparrow went to fetch water at the river for her.

Corn Leaf appeared in the doorway. "Good morning," she said.

"Hello, Corn Leaf," returned Squirrel Fur.

"Hi, Mother," greeted Tanager, while nursing the baby.

"How is my beautiful granddaughter?" asked Corn Leaf.

"She is doing well," answered Tanager, "Would you like to hold her?"

"Yes, I would!" replied Corn Leaf.

"She has your eyes," said Tanager as she gave the baby to Corn Leaf.

"And your smile," added Corn Leaf.

"You picked a good name for her," said Squirrel Fur.

Sparrow returned with the water. "Good morning, Corn Leaf," she said. "How are you doing?"

"Actually, I have not been feeling well lately," returned Corn Leaf.

"What is wrong?" asked Tanager.

"I keep getting headaches," answered Corn Leaf, "They come and go. I guess I need to see Eagle Medicine one of these days."

"Tanager," said Sparrow, "do you have plenty of food?"

"Oh!" replied Tanager, "Thanks for reminding me! I only have dried meat left. I ate the last of the acorn and cornbread last night."

"Why don't Squirrel Fur and I go and make you some right now?" suggested Sparrow, "That way you and your mother can visit."

"Thank you," replied Tanager with a smile.

Squirrel Fur and Sparrow returned to Squirrel Fur's lodge and began preparing cornbread from cornmeal that they had ground the night before.

"Titmouse is such a cute baby, isn't she?" said Squirrel Fur.

"She sure is," replied Sparrow, "I wish I could bear a baby."

"Would you like for me to fetch the water?" offered Squirrel Fur.

"Let's go together," replied Sparrow.

They each took a large clay pot with them as they left. One of the guards at the palisade entrance smiled at Sparrow when she passed by. She was not expecting it, and she did not smile back. He hadn't been there earlier. They arrived at the river and filled their pots.

"You should get that man's name," suggested Squirrel Fur. "He likes you. I can tell."

"I seriously doubt it," replied Sparrow. "He was probably just being friendly. He won't want to talk to me anyway. I was rude to him."

"Well," said Squirrel Fur, "you never know unless you try. The worst thing that could happen is him saying no. You're lonely! You need somebody in your life."

"You are right," returned Sparrow. "I think I will talk to him."

The two reached the palisade gate and Squirrel Fur went on while Sparrow remained behind, talking to the guard.

A short time later, Sparrow returned to Squirrel fur's lodge, with a happy look on her face.

"So, what's his name?" asked Squirrel Fur with a smile.

"He is thirty-two cycles old, his name is Broken Spear," replied Sparrow, "he is of the Wild Potato Clan, and he is not married!"

"Did the two of you make any plans?" asked Squirrel Fur.

"He will be visiting me at my lodge tonight."

"Well, congratulations, Sparrow!" said Squirrel Fur. "You need a man in your life. I am happy for you."

* * *

A good friend's safety was all that concerned Buck as he followed the river downstream, searching for Green Rock. He was out of breath, but still he ran as fast as his legs would carry him. He kept a watchful eye on the river, hoping to find his missing comrade.

Buck carried the two quivers and bows, and his axe. Every moment, he prayed that he would spot his friend, but he didn't see him anywhere. *I hope the Yuchi didn't capture him. Why would he leave without me?*

He tried to look for tracks and signs, but that obviously was futile while he ran. He saw the terrible rapids with the treacherous granite boulders amongst them.

Buck reached the place where the smaller branch joined the river. He crossed the tributary and continued downstream for a little while longer. *I bet he was taken captive to a village near the tributary.*

He was about to turn back to conduct a better search for tracks, but he heard a deep roaring sound just downstream. He decided to investigate it. He ran through the woods on the bank, and saw a thirty foot waterfall. He spotted the dugout, broken in two, resting over a protruding boulder of granite. His worst fears had been realized. He fell to his knees and wept. Through his tears, he saw something.

* * *

Green Rock lay in the water at the river's edge, in a semiconscious, dreamy state. Even with closed eyes, he was aware of a Wolf's face above his. The Wolf stood with his front legs on Green Rock's shoulder, and Green Rock could feel a strong power being transmitted from the Wolf, through his paws, and into Green Rock's shoulders. It was exciting, yet serene, euphoric, yet sobering. The energy slowly seemed to radiate into Green Rock's torso, and spread into his arms, legs, neck and head. It rejuvenated him, spiritually and physically, in a profound way he had never before experienced.

His faith in the Wolf had earned him the Wolf Spirit's blessing. His bravery as he took on the River had resulted in Long Being's eternal protection. As Green Rock lay there, the wolf licked his cheek, and then ran away and disappeared into the woods. Absolute peace enveloped Green Rock as he drifted far away into nothingness.

* * *

"Green Rock! Green Rock! Are you okay? Green Rock!"

Green Rock slowly awakened and realized Buck was shaking him and talking to him excitedly.

"I am alright," Green Rock finally answered.

"Come on!" said Buck. "Get up! Why did you leave? You scared me halfway to the Darkening Land! Why did you leave without me?"

"I tried to tell you."

"Tell me what? I don't remember you telling me anything!"

"You were asleep. I tried to tell you."

"What did you try to tell me?"

The Wolf's Blessing & the River's Protection.

"The Wolf told me to follow him."

"Do you mean the wolf that I just chased off?"

"You saw it?" asked Green Rock.

"Yes, he looked like he was going to bite a piece out of your face! I just now scared him away!"

"He wouldn't have done that. The Wolf spoke to me in a dream last night. He said to follow him. I did."

Buck was awestruck. "You had your Spirit Vision!"

"I guess I did!" said Green Rock, feeling more alert.

"Do you think you can walk for a while?" asked Buck. "We need to get out of here before we are discovered. I am glad you didn't ruin one of *our* canoes!"

Green Rock stood up and said, "What happened to the canoe?"

"It's on the top of that rock," said Buck, while pointing, "in two pieces. You are lucky to be alive. Take your bow and arrows. I have a feeling we will need them soon."

Buck was looking into the sky. Green Rock looked and saw buzzards circling them, revealing their presence. The two climbed up the cliff and Green Rock saw the demolished canoe.

"I *am* lucky," he said.

They reached the tributary and crossed it in silence. They were in the woods when they noticed that no birds were singing. Buck pulled an arrow out of his quiver and nocked it. Green Rock saw him and did likewise.

They heard a twig snap nearby. Both of them ducked silently behind a yaupon holly bush. A Yuchi warrior appeared, gazing intently in the other direction, probably hoping to find what had attracted the buzzards' attention. Another warrior joined him, and said something in the Yuchi tongue. This one carried a war club with a stone head in his hand.

Yuchi War Club with Stone Head.

Both Buck and Green Rock knew to wait a while and see if there were any more enemies. They needed to know the situation before going on the attack. They waited quietly while the second warrior looked in their direction.

Green Rock's heart was racing. The first warrior spoke a short sentence to the second, and the second started running back. The Yuchis knew something was up. Buck and Green Rock knew the warrior was returning to the village to get reinforcements.

Buck leapt up and threw his axe at the running warrior's head. The axe struck him in the head, and he fell without uttering a sound. The first warrior heard him fall, and went to investigate. Green Rock put two arrows in the warrior's back. The man fell with a gasp.

Green Rock couldn't believe what he had done. It was automatic, as if he had no control over it. Now, he felt remorse. He had never killed a man.

Buck said, "We have drawn enemy blood. Our goal has been accomplished. Let's get out of here before they discover them."

Green Rock just stood there in a daze, looking at the fallen warrior he had killed.

"Come *on!*" whispered Buck impatiently, while pulling Green Rock's arm.

Green Rock was quickly jolted back into the reality of their situation. He took the Yuchi man's war club, and Wolf Tail retrieved his axe. Together, they began silently running back upstream, leaving behind the two Cherokee arrows in the Yuchi warrior's back.

They were about two hundred paces away when they heard war whoops coming from the area of the fallen warriors. Their presence was now known, and every available warrior in the village would now be looking for them.

Green Rock and Buck ran as fast as they could. The confusion would now work to their advantage for a little while. After their enemies were more organized, time would be against them. They endeavored to put as much distance as possible between them and the enemy war party. The two came upon a creek.

"We need to run in the water, up this creek a little way," said Buck, "to help hide our tracks."

Green Rock offered no argument. They proceeded up the creek, splashing the water with each step. The Yuchi warriors were still too far away to hear the splashing. Then Green Rock thought of a plan.

"Why don't we go straight to Birch Mountain, instead of Eagle Peak?" he asked. "They will assume we came from Eagle Peak because that is our nearest village."

"Good idea," answered Buck. "We will cross the ridge here instead of upstream! See, Green Rock, you *are* a warrior!"

Green Rock didn't really agree, but he had no time to start a debate. The plan worked. They stopped high up on the ridge, and they saw about fifty Yuchi warriors following the river, passing by their detour site.

Buck said, "Let's go. They might still figure out where we went after a while. We need to keep moving."

The ridge was steep, and they were both very tired, but they kept moving. Green Rock became hungry. Buck had left the bundle of food packed by Acorn hanging from the tree. They continued walking up the ridge. The view would have been very good, except for the thick trees overhead.

As he climbed, Buck said, "I am hungry. I wish we had our food we left behind."

They both continued climbing. The good in the situation was they were nearing the peak of the ridge. The bad news was the higher they climbed, the steeper it became.

Green Rock stopped suddenly. "Look," he said, "here are some raspberries!"

Raspberry.

They quickly picked all they could hold and then resumed their journey, while eating. It gave them both some much-needed energy.

At sunset, they reached the top of the ridge. Ahead of them was the Bear River valley, and behind them was the Thunder River valley. The view was breathtaking from here. They kept on the move, even after dark. They were now out of Yuchi territory, but that didn't rule out the possibility that they were being followed. They walked all night, using the North Star to navigate.

They heard a noise that sounded like a woman screaming.

"Who was that?" asked Green Rock. "She sounds like she is in trouble."

"That was our 'friend' the mountain lion," replied Buck. "There must be a den in a cave nearby. We'd better keep going – quietly."

Fortunately, they never had any encounters with the cougar. They stayed on the move all night long. Finally, at sunrise, they reached a stream.

"I am worn out," said Green Rock.

"So am I," replied Buck. "Let's walk down this stream for several hundred paces to hide our tracks. Then we can find a place to sleep for awhile."

Green Rock was ready to hear this. After they got away from the stream they found a grassy place, where deer had bedded down, and took a nap. The afternoon Sun woke Buck. He got up and gently kicked Green Rock.

"Time to go home, Wolf Man," he said when Green Rock stirred.

Green Rock got up, and they were back on their way. They now felt comfortable enough to talk normally.

"Well, have I earned an adult name?" asked Green Rock.

"I guess so," answered Buck. "But Eagle Medicine is the one to decide that. You really did do well in combat though. I will testify to that for you. You will have to tell him about your Vision."

This relieved Green Rock, because it was over. He had drawn blood, and had proven himself a man. He decided to never kill another man again.

"Thank you," he said.

"I won't be lying either, you did better than I thought. Two arrows in his back before he fell! That was great."

Green Rock still felt bad for killing a man, but he looked at it as being over with. And he was glad it was all over.

"That was one big bear," said Buck, pointing to a pine tree. There were claw marks high up on the trunk – marking the bear's territory.

"I hope we don't run into him!" said Green Rock in awe.

They arrived at Bear River at sunset. They followed it until they reached Birch Mountain. The guards greeted them and asked numerous questions about their little attack on the Yuchi. Green Rock was very glad when the conversation was done; he just wanted to go to bed!

But he had to see his mother, to let her know he had returned safely. She was very understanding.

"Go and get some sleep," she said, "You look exhausted. I will tell Sparrow you made it back okay. You can tell us your story in the morning."

Meanwhile, Buck visited Tanager and his newborn daughter. Tanager had tears of joy in her eyes, and Buck really wanted to hug her. But it was still taboo to touch her until after the baby was three moons old.

He simply said, "I love you."

"I am glad you are home safe," Tanager replied.

Buck left to find Green Rock. He found him walking towards his lodge, and Green Rock looked every bit as tired as Buck felt.

They both went to Green Rock's lodge, lay down on their sleep mats, and fell asleep immediately. It was so good to finally be back home. Green Rock was so exhausted, he didn't even dream. It was good to be home! They slept there on their sleep mats all night and half of the next day. When Green Rock and Buck awakened, they were extremely hungry.

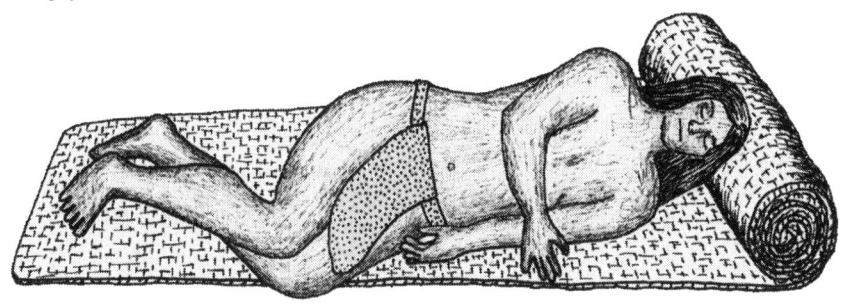

Green Rock Sleeps on a Sleep Mat.
Adapted from Holmes 1891.

They found some dried meat and acorn bread that Squirrel Fur and Sparrow had left in the lodge for them while they had been sleeping. They ate their fill, and went to visit Squirrel Fur and Sparrow to thank them for their thoughtfulness. Eagle Medicine was there.

"You two are finally awake!" said Sparrow with a smile.

"Yes, we are," answered Buck.

"Thanks for the food you left for us," said Green Rock. "That was you, who left us food while we slept, wasn't it?"

"Yes," replied Squirrel Fur. "Sparrow and I left it for you two. You are welcome."

Sparrow smiled at them.

"I believe that Green Rock has something to tell you, Eagle Medicine," said Buck.

"And what is that?" Eagle Medicine asked Green Rock.

"I think I had my Vision Quest," replied Green Rock.

"He also has definitely proven himself in battle!" added Buck.

"Tell me the story," said Eagle Medicine.

"Green Rock went down Thunder River," said Buck, "and when I found him, he was passed out on the riverbank. We then started back towards Eagle Peak, and then two Yuchi warriors appeared. When they were on to us, one of them ran to get reinforcements. I threw an axe at him and killed him. The other heard him fall, and Green Rock shot him *twice* with arrows before the warrior went down. It was a clean and quiet kill, and we were able to get away before they were discovered. After the chase began, he had the idea of crossing the ridge there instead of taking the obvious way back to Eagle Peak. I was proud to be with him."

"Is this all true?" Eagle Medicine asked Green Rock.

"Well, yes," answered Green Rock, modestly while shrugging.

"Why did you go down the river alone?"

"The Wolf I dreamed about told me to."

"Green Rock," said Eagle Medicine, "let's take a walk."

Together they left. Green Rock followed Eagle Medicine to the river outside of the palisade. They were now alone and could talk privately.

"Tell me about your Wolf Dream," said Eagle Medicine.

"I dreamed of a Wolf running down to the river. As he ran, he said for me to follow him. I woke up, and heard him howling far away. I fell asleep and woke up several times, each time the Wolf said to follow him. One time he was swimming in the river. The last time I woke up, I felt that the Wolf wanted me to follow him down the river. I took the dugout downstream, and it was very scary. I felt that I should trust in Long Being though. Then I saw a waterfall but my paddle was broken, and I couldn't avoid it. I went down the waterfall and landed in a deep pool at the bottom. I don't remember much after that, except for the Wolf licking me in the face before it ran off. Buck said he chased the Wolf away."

"That is amazing," said Eagle Medicine.

"It's amazing that I survived. I saw the broken canoe on top of a boulder just above the pool. Do you think it was a divine Vision?"

"I certainly do. And you have proven yourself in battle. That's good. Very good. We need to plan a naming ceremony. You will be hearing from me."

They returned to Birch Mountain and parted ways. Green Rock returned to his mother's lodge in great spirits.

"Well," said Squirrel Fur, "is my son an adult now?"

"Eagle Medicine said he will be organizing a naming ceremony!" answered Green Rock, with a smile.

Sparrow and Squirrel Fur hugged Green Rock joyfully.

"Congratulations, my son," said Squirrel Fur proudly.

The day of the naming ceremony came and Squirrel Fur was busy dressing Green Rock in the fashion of an adult. Now she tied his hair in a scalp knot on top of his head. He wore Turtle Shell's engraved cross motif shell gorget necklace that Sparrow had given her for him, along with ear pins carved from shell. His face was painted with black paint, in the weeping eye pattern. She had worked tirelessly on his appearance, and now she was proud to see her son looking as any other adult.

Green Rock was proud to wear an adult hairstyle, and now he would no longer be humiliated by his partial nakedness and childlike long hair. Children went naked, and in cases like his, where adulthood wasn't reached until well after puberty, a breechclout was the only item worn.

The ceremony was held and Green Rock was named River Wolf, after the Wolf he had followed down Thunder River. The Spirit of the Wolf was recognized as his Guardian Spirit.

River Wolf as a Young Adult.

After the ceremony, Beaver Pelt approached River Wolf. "I've been waiting for you," she said with a smile.

River Wolf shyly returned the smile. Beaver Pelt had been absent during the ceremony, and River Wolf didn't know why.

"I have cooked dinner for you," said Beaver Pelt. "Why don't you wait for me at your lodge?"

River Wolf returned to his lodge and found Buck there.

"Hello there, River Wolf," said Buck, with a proud smile. This was the first time he had used the adult name, and as he spoke, he put special emphasis on the new name.

"How are you doing, Buck?" returned River Wolf.

"I have a gift for you," said Buck. "I traded for it somewhere far to the west of here. Here it is."

Buck had a double-pointed bone with a groove in the center. River Wolf took it and asked, "What is it?"

"You can pierce your nose and wear it there," answered Buck. "It's a nose plug. It will drive the women crazy!"

"Thank you," said River Wolf.

Bone Nose Plug Given by Buck to River Wolf.

"Well, have any women shown any interest in you yet?"

"Beaver Pelt will be visiting me here tonight. She says she is cooking me dinner."

"I'd better go spend the night at your mother's lodge so you two can have some privacy."

"Thanks," said River Wolf.

Buck congratulated River Wolf and then left for Squirrel Fur's lodge. River Wolf grew more apprehensive as the evening wore on. What if he disappointed Beaver Pelt?

Beaver Pelt appeared in the doorway. River Wolf helped her serve the food. This was the easy part. River Wolf's nervousness grew as the night progressed. Beaver Pelt's cooking was very good. There was squirrel and deer meat, cornbread, green beans, and mushrooms. River Wolf tried awkwardly to carry on a conversation as they ate.

"What do you like doing most?" asked River Wolf.

Beaver Pelt was also nervous. "I enjoy walking outside of the village, foraging for food. I like being out in the woods."

"I do too," said River Wolf, "but I like to look for stones to carve. Do you like traveling?"

"Yes. I go now and then with my mother to visit my grandmother in Pine Bend. We have fun."

"Where is Pine Bend?" asked River Wolf.

"It is a tiny village upstream from Eagle Peak. I do enjoy traveling."

"Someday soon I want to make my own large dugout canoe and be a traveling trader. But first, I need to travel with one of the traders and learn more about the other tribes and the trade routes."

Beaver Pelt smiled. "That sounds like fun. I… I would like traveling with you. I like *you* – a lot."

River Wolf was startled. "I like you also."

They finished eating. Beaver Pelt was so beautiful. Before River Wolf knew it, he found himself locked in a passionate kiss with her. He became very self-conscious.

She had experience, but he didn't. Once puberty was reached, women were free to be with any man they wanted to prior to marriage. They drank a tea from boiled roots of the wild yam, which they believed was a form of birth control. Men however had to abstain from sex until they had proven themselves in battle, and had their Vision Quest.

Beaver Pelt was understanding, and was eager to complete his initiation. The two joined in a love that was passionately sweet. Three times River Wolf awakened in the night, and they joined each time. River Wolf wondered if she was trying to get him to marry her. He thought about it, the idea excited him, but he was uncertain about whether or not he was ready to be married.

The next morning, River Wolf gave Beaver Pelt the shell spider necklace that Eagle Medicine had given him cycles ago. She knew how much he had treasured it, and was touched by his gift. Now, *she* wondered if *he* might be hinting that he wanted to eventually marry her. He did not mention it, but she now decided to wait for him anyway.

Beaver Pelt left, and River Wolf went to his mother's lodge to find Buck. He had a lot on his mind – mostly he thought about Beaver Pelt. He arrived there just as they were preparing for their morning visit to the river.

"Good morning," said River Wolf.

"Hello," returned Squirrel Fur.

"You look like you didn't sleep much last night!" Buck said with a chuckle.

Squirrel Fur also had a grin on her face, but said nothing.

"So how was it?" asked Buck.

"She is a very beautiful woman," answered River Wolf, with a thoughtful expression, "I gave her the shell spider necklace that Eagle Medicine gave me when I was a child."

"You *are* in love!" laughed Buck.

River Wolf was blushing. "I think she is very nice," he said, "but I am not going to marry her yet."

Buck and Squirrel Fur's eyes met. They couldn't believe that he said what he'd just said. They smiled at each other.

After returning from the river, River Wolf decided to travel to Eagle Peak to pick up the soapstone for Fox Claw's pipe at Acorn's lodge. He located Beaver Pelt in the hopes that she would want to travel with him. He found her passing the area of his lodge, with a water pot.

"I have to go to Eagle Peak," he said, "and I was wondering if you would like to come with me."

"Sure! I will go," she replied. "Just let me tell Mother I am leaving."

"I will wait for you here," said River Wolf.

"No, I would like you to meet Mother."

"Okay, I will go with you then. Would you like me to carry your pot of water for you?"

"Yes, thank you," she answered, while giving him the water pot.

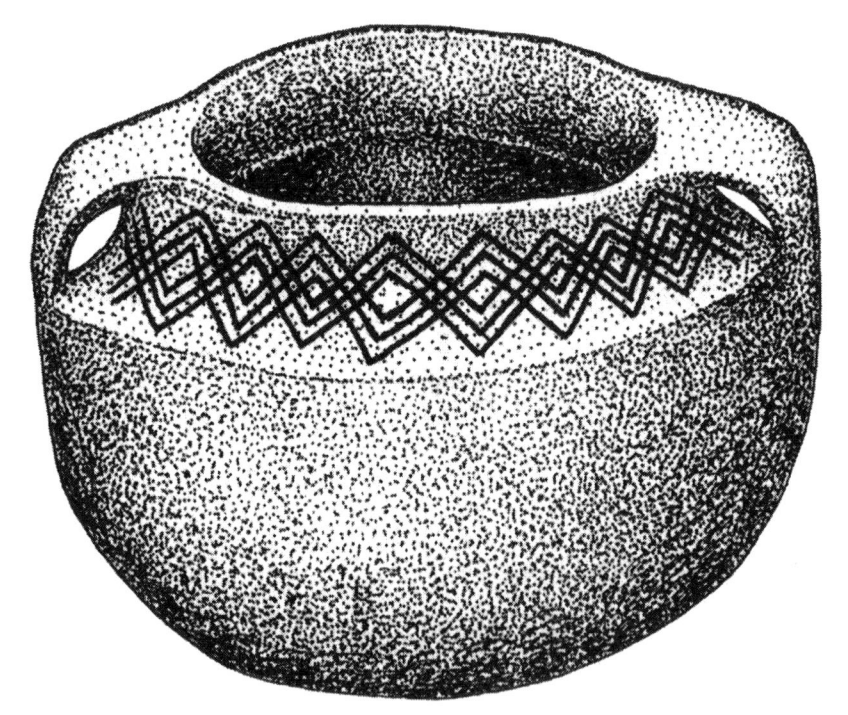

Beaver Pelt's Water Pot.
Redrawn from Thruston 1897.

The two went to the back of the village, near the cornfield. Here was where Beaver Pelt and her family lived. River Wolf had never been to this part of the village.

Her mother greeted them. "Is this the River Wolf I have heard so much about?" she asked.

"Yes," replied Beaver Pelt. "This is my mother, The Duck Flies By."

"It's nice to meet you," said River Wolf. "Here is your water."

"Thank you," said The Duck Flies By.

A flint knapper that River Wolf did not know showed up with several flint hoes, intending to trade them in this part of town where the cornfields were. As he spoke with the people gathering to see, River Wolf looked at his wares.

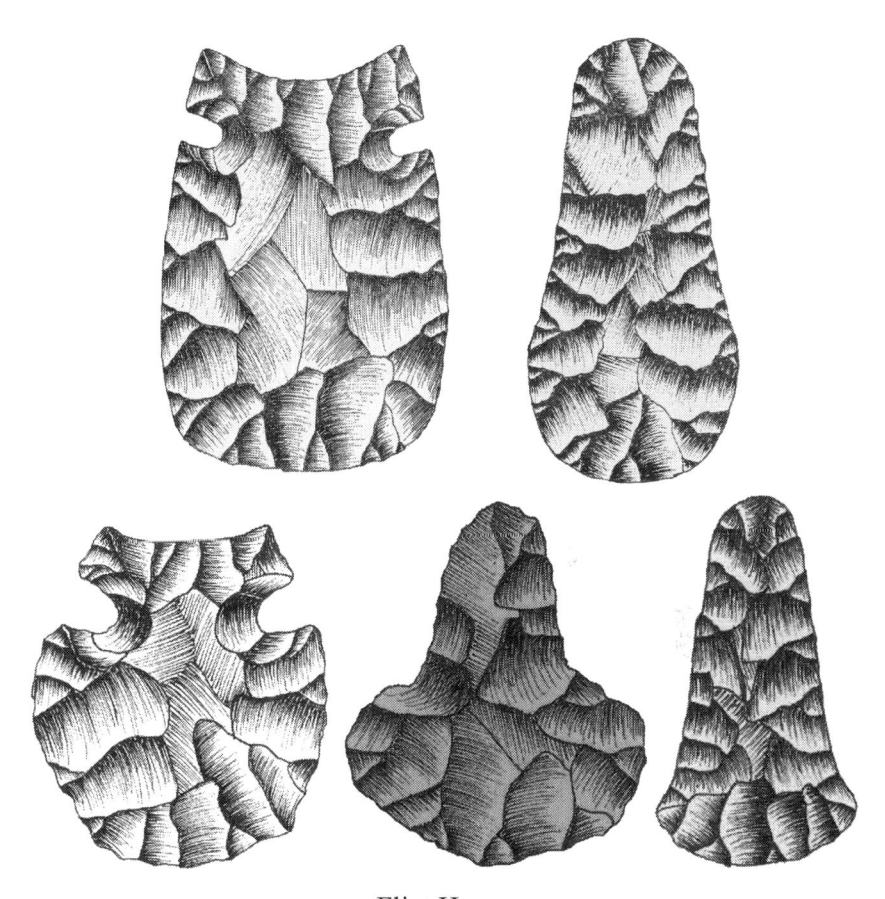

Flint Hoes.

After taking careful mental notes, River Wolf turned to Beaver Pelt and said, "I'm ready to go when you are."

"We are going to Eagle Peak," announced Beaver Pelt to her mother. "We will be back tomorrow."

"Be careful," said her mother, "and enjoy yourselves."

"I will see you tomorrow," promised Beaver Pelt.

"It was nice meeting you," said River Wolf.

They went to River Wolf's lodge to pick up supplies for the trip. They were traveling lightly, but they needed some cornbread to eat during the journey.

They left the village and started for Eagle Peak. As they walked, they began talking to each other.

"Would you really like traveling in a canoe?" asked River Wolf. "What I mean is, would you enjoy traveling to faraway places with me in the distant future?"

"Are you saying you want to marry me?" asked Beaver Pelt hopefully.

This caught River Wolf off guard. He was considering the idea, but he didn't really want to answer that question yet.

"I love you a lot," he said. "I like your company just as much. I feel like it's too soon though for either of us make any serious commitments."

"Why is it too soon? We love each other."

"I would like to travel with an experienced trader and learn more before I take a wife along. I don't think it's fair to you to marry you and then leave you by yourself for moons at a time."

"Shouldn't I decide what's alright for my life? I do not mind waiting."

"I do not want to restrict your freedom with other men by making you wait constantly for a long time. I really do not know how long at a time I will be gone."

"Then why don't we marry and then when you leave, we can have the understanding that while you are gone, I have freedom to be with another man?"

River Wolf was surprised to hear this idea. He knew that men of the Cherokee shared their wives with other men occasionally, but it was not very common. He thought about it for a while, and finally said, "And what if you find another man you like better than me?"

"I don't think I ever will," she replied, though she was not too sure she could accurately say that at that point.

"Beaver Pelt, I should respect you enough to let you wait for what's best for you. There is nothing wrong with waiting. We can get married later, if you still love me in this way. You are young, and have plenty of time. Can you understand that?"

"I guess so," she replied in a disappointed manner, "But someday you will see that I still love *you*. And I will wait for you as long as I have to."

River Wolf was flattered at this remark. He felt the same. He gazed into her beautiful brown eyes and then kissed her. Before long, they were making love next to a clear mountain stream. It was an intoxicating and romantic experience.

They reached the top of the ridge around noon, and stopped to take in the view. Then they proceeded into the Thunder River valley, where Eagle Peak was located.

River Wolf set one of his leaning-log squirrel snares, and while they waited to catch them, they made love again. This was surely better than traveling alone!

At sunset, they arrived at Acorn's lodge in Eagle Peak. River Wolf dressed the four squirrels he had caught, while Acorn got ready to cook them. Beaver Pelt helped her, and they got to know each other.

After they finished eating, Acorn showed River Wolf the piece of soapstone left by Fox Claw.

"He said he would get enough stone for twenty pipes!" said River Wolf, disappointed.

"He promises to bring the rest later," explained Acorn.

"Well, tell him I should have this pipe finished and brought here within a moon."

"I will tell him," promised Acorn.

Beaver Pelt went to the river for some water.

"She is the sweetest girl," whispered Acorn with a smile.

"I think I love her," returned River Wolf.

"Are you going to marry her?"

"We have talked about it, but I think it best to wait."

"Don't let her get away from you. When you find a good girl like her, try to hang on to her."

River Wolf agreed that she was a nice girl, but opted not to talk about the conversation between himself and Beaver Pelt during the journey. Beaver Pelt returned.

"River Wolf," she said, "why don't we go and see Grandmother in Pine Bend tomorrow? I want for you to meet her."

"How far upstream is it from here?" asked River Wolf.

"It won't even take a half-day to get there," she answered. "It is the same distance from Birch Mountain as Eagle Peak. We will get back late, but that's okay with me if it is with you."

At first, River Wolf worried about his mother being concerned if he didn't show up back home on time, but then he remembered – he was an adult now, and could take care of himself.

"Okay, we will go then!" he answered, with a satisfied smile.

The next morning they started for Pine Bend. They followed Thunder River upstream for most of the morning and, as Beaver Pelt promised, they arrived at Pine Bend before noon.

This tiny village was all that was left of a once thriving community. Most of the old palisade still stood, but had been neglected for a very long time. No guards manned the heavily weathered huts at the entrance anymore, and the clay daub that once covered the palisade's posts was obviously not maintained anymore.

They came through the entrance, and River Wolf saw that there were only ten lodges that were occupied. But the ceremonial mound in the center of the village was surprisingly large.

"Pine Bend used to be the largest trade center in the valley," said Beaver Pelt. "This village used to be the home of over two hundred people. My grandmother told me."

River Wolf was fascinated. "What happened to make all of the people leave?"

"The crops began to fail," explained Beaver Pelt, "The cornfields were moved farther away several times, and eventually they were too far away. Then everybody, one-by-one, moved to Eagle Peak and other villages. My parents came to Birch Mountain right before I was born."

They arrived at her grandmother's lodge. She was standing in her doorway.

"Grandma!" greeted Beaver Pelt.

"Who are you?" said her grandmother. "I can't see well anymore."

"I am Beaver Pelt."

"Beaver Pelt! It's been so long! How are you doing?"

"I am fine," said Beaver Pelt. "This is my friend, River Wolf."

"I didn't know you had somebody with you!" said Grandma, surprised.

Beaver Pelt and River Wolf glanced at each other. The old woman's vision was pretty bad – she had been looking right at them.

"Come on in," said Grandma.

They entered the lodge, and Grandma offered them some cornbread. River Wolf never heard what "Grandma's" name was.

"How is my daughter?" asked Grandma.

"Mother is doing fine," answered Beaver Pelt.

Beaver Pelt and her grandmother visited while they ate.

"Do you have somebody to take care of you?" asked Beaver Pelt when they finished eating.

"Your aunt, Turkey, visits me everyday," answered Grandma. "She is young and lonely. I keep telling her she should go down to Eagle Peak and find a husband, but she refuses to leave me by myself."

"That's good that you have her," said Beaver Pelt.

"Yes, it is, but she needs to think of herself for once," returned Grandma.

"Well, we'd better leave," said Beaver Pelt, "so we can get back home before it gets too late."

"It was so good to see you!" said Grandma. "Come back soon."

"Take care," Beaver Pelt replied.

"It was nice to meet you," said River Wolf.

River Wolf and Beaver Pelt started their journey back to Birch Mountain. They had no time for anymore love adventures; the hour was late and they had a long way to go. River Wolf had a plan to help them get back home sooner.

"Why don't we take turns and run for ten paces, and then walk for ten paces?" he asked. "We will cover more territory without wearing ourselves out."

It worked. They reached Birch Mountain at around midnight that night. River Wolf and Beaver Pelt were both exhausted. They went to River Wolf's lodge and shared a bed.

The next morning, Beaver Pelt left to help her mother, and tell her about the visit with Grandma. Meanwhile, River Wolf began working on Fox Claw's pipe. The black soapstone was a little more difficult to work but, in a week's time, he was rubbing bear grease into the finished pipe. The high-grade soapstone had polished into a beautiful shine. River Wolf couldn't wait until he got the rest of this nice stone from Fox Claw.

When River Wolf went to visit his mother, she told him some surprising news. Sparrow had married Broken Spear! River Wolf was surprised – he didn't know she was even seeing a man. He was very happy for his aunt.

Now, River Wolf began digging a large hole near his lodge. He wanted to build a hothouse for spending the winter in. Buck, who was still off limits from his wife, helped River Wolf in exchange for room and board. Beaver Pelt made sure that they did not go hungry.

One day, Fox Claw came to Birch Mountain. He found River Wolf, and Buck working on the hothouse.

"Did you carve my pipe?" he asked River Wolf.

"Yes," answered River Wolf, "Here it is. Did you bring the rest of my stone?"

"No, I have been pretty busy lately."

"Do you feel like helping us finish this hothouse in trade instead of the soapstone?" asked River Wolf.

"I can't," said Fox Claw, "I promise I will have your stone very soon though."

Fox Claw left, and Buck shook his head. "You know he won't be paying you," he said.

"Ah," returned River Wolf, "He will. You need to trust people more."

Buck disagreed, but said nothing. He had much experience as a trader, and he had learned to read people. River Wolf would learn – eventually.

"Let's go hunting," suggested River Wolf. "I am tired of eating nothing but cornbread."

"Sure, let's go," said Buck.

They each got their bows and arrows and left the village. They passed the place where River Wolf had fought the deer not so long ago. They walked down the deer trail for a while, and then they heard a disturbance in the woods nearby.

River Wolf got his bow ready and nocked an arrow. Buck did likewise. They heard a low growling noise that was not far away. Suddenly, a black bear appeared. The bear looked at them for awhile before turning around and walking off.

They followed the bear, and eventually the bear stopped and turned to face them again. River Wolf shot three arrows into the bear's side. Buck began shooting arrows also.

The infuriated bear roared in pain, but quickly had numerous arrows in him. He fell over and was kicking. After he had stopped kicking for a while, they thought it was safe to approach the bear and cut his throat.

Black Bear.
Redrawn from Clker-Free-Vector-Images from Pixabay.

They apologized to the bear's spirit, and Buck got an axe and began chopping a long pole for them to use for carrying the bear home.

When they arrived back at the village, they began skinning and dressing the bear. Beaver Pelt came over to visit, and River Wolf gave her the skin.

"You can have this," he said. "Tan it and sew up the arrow holes and it will make a great blanket."

Beaver Pelt smiled and took the bearskin back to her lodge. River Wolf and Buck shared the meat with Squirrel Fur, Sparrow, and Beaver Pelt's family. They all ate heartily that night.

The next day, River Wolf and Buck resumed work on the hothouse. While they worked, River Wolf said, "I need to get my nose pierced so I can wear your gift."

"I can do it!" offered Buck.

"When?"

"Now, if you want."

"What do we need?"

"Just a bone needle."

The two found a needle and took it down to the river and washed their hands. Buck pierced River Wolf's nose and the pain made him sneeze repeatedly. Blood was all over his face before it was all over with.

"Keep the nose plug in your nose till it heals," said Buck, "or else the hole will heal shut and we'll have to do it again."

"Okay, I will definitely be doing that!" said River Wolf, glad that it was over with. "Thanks."

Later, when Beaver Pelt saw River Wolf with the bone in his bloody nose, she had a somewhat startled expression on her face.

River Wolf noticed her unexpected reaction and said, "What?!"

Beaver Pelt wanted to laugh, but didn't. River Wolf had wanted to impress her with the bone in his newly-pierced nose, so she decided to just "be impressed."

They resumed working on the hothouse. It was hard work, but they managed to finish it in time for winter. The usual ceremonies were observed, and River Wolf and Buck stopped work on the hothouse in order to attend them.

It was now getting cold. River Wolf was glad the hothouse was finished. The three months passed, and Buck could now return to his own lodge. Beaver Pelt presented River Wolf with a bearskin blanket made from the bear he had shot. She spent most of that winter with River Wolf in his new hothouse, making him winter clothes and keeping him company. This proved to be the most pleasant winter of River Wolf's life.

Chapter 7: Bald Eagle

Corn Leaf's headaches grew dramatically worse through the winter. Eagle Medicine had visited her and treated her vigilantly, having her drink a tea he brewed from the bark powder of the redbud tree. While its leaves were poisonous, redbud flowers could sometimes be eaten raw, and could be made into a diluted tea that is good for sinus congestion, kidney and bladder infections, and for preventing scurvy. Sometimes they could cook the young bean pods and buds and eat them. They used dried root powder to stop bleeding in deep wounds, and dry bark powder was applied to swelled areas and skin irritations. The tea brewed from the bark powder was good for dysentery, diarrhea, bone and joint discomfort, muscle spasms and fever. This tea brewed from redbud bark was also good for headaches, which was why Eagle Medicine was preparing it for Corn Leaf.

Eagle Medicine also had Corn Leaf smoking coneflower in a tobacco pipe because it was good for relieving headaches. It was also thought to be good for sore throats and an upset stomach. The coneflower root was also sometimes made into a decoction that was used for washing snakebites and swelled eyes, and they thought you could drink the decoction to help in curing diarrhea. This plant was used for purifying in sweat lodges as well.

But, in spite of Eagle Medicine's efforts and these remedies, Corn Leaf's condition grew worse and she went blind. She passed away at the end of the winter. Her body was moved to the charnel platform near the burial mound. Sparrow was then chosen by the village leaders to be the next Honored Woman, because of her generosity and caring heart.

River Wolf spent the winter carving pipes from the pile of soapstone that Twisted Stick had given him during the last cycle. He now had twenty-seven fine effigy pipes to take along when he left with the next trader who visited the village.

One day during a hunting trip, he walked down a snow-covered deer trail hoping to find some meat. The icy wind blew constant and hard. It chilled River Wolf to the bones. He looked forward to returning to the hothouse and Beaver Pelt.

He saw a buck through the trees. After nocking an arrow, he began stalking the deer. As he took aim, he heard a crackling noise. He turned to look, and saw a hickory tree falling towards him. He scrambled to get out of the way. The tree barely missed him as it came crashing down.

The deer was, of course, nowhere in sight. River Wolf was frustrated and returned home empty-handed. The next day, he ventured out again. It was now warmer than the day before, and the snow was melting. River Wolf was glad the winter was nearly over.

He found some deer tracks and followed them. After walking for what seemed like a half a day, he spied a rabbit. He nocked his arrow, took aim, and released. The arrow flew true and hit the rabbit in the heart.

River Wolf was glad to finally have some meat to take home. He cut the rabbit's throat, and apologized to the rabbit's spirit. Then he carried it back to Birch Mountain.

As he butchered the rabbit his wet hands were extremely cold. His finger bones were aching. While Beaver Pelt cooked the rabbit, River Wolf covered up under a bearskin blanket.

The winter was ending, and the weather gradually became warmer. Now, preparations were being made for the First New Moon of Spring Ceremony. The new leaves of spring had appeared, and the Uku and seven other high-ranking people met in the council house. Several honored women did the Friendship Dance – this included Sparrow and Squirrel Fur.

Runners were sent out to all of the villages, with news pertaining to the day of the ceremony. Meanwhile, hunters from Birch Mountain were recruited to hunt meat for the ceremony. Seven men were appointed to be in charge of the feast, and seven women were appointed for cooking.

The travelers arrived at Birch Mountain, and soon there were more people than could be counted. There was a festive atmosphere all around. The First New Moon of Spring Ceremony was always River Wolf's favorite event of the cycle, because it marked the beginning of the warmer days of summer that were just around the corner. He and Beaver Pelt milled around together and spoke with old friends from other towns. They ran into Acorn, and many other friends and family members.

River Wolf even saw Fox Claw. He went to talk to him. Fox Claw saw River Wolf and had a startled expression on his face.

"River Wolf," he said, "I am sorry to have kept you waiting on that soapstone. I *promise* I will deliver it *immediately* as soon as I get back home."

By now, River Wolf had learned not to believe him. He was angry and disappointed about not receiving payment for the pipe he made for Fox Claw, but didn't want to make an issue of it.

"Okay, Fox Claw," he said, cynically.

Fox Claw bowed his head shamefully. River Wolf turned to leave.

"He will never pay me," he said to Beaver Pelt. "Buck warned me not to trust him, but I didn't believe him."

"Look!" said Beaver Pelt, "There is my sister! I want you to meet her."

The two approached the woman. "Wildflower!" called Beaver Pelt, "Wildflower! Here!"

Wildflower turned to look. "Beaver Pelt!" she said, surprised, "How are you doing?"

"I am fine," answered Beaver Pelt. "This is River Wolf. River Wolf, this is my sister, she moved to Crow Foot Canyon several cycles ago when she married a warrior from there. River Wolf and I have been together for a while now."

"That's so nice!" exclaimed Wildflower.

Buck, Tanager, and the baby appeared out of the crowd.

"I ran into Fox Claw," said Buck to River Wolf.

"Yes," returned River Wolf, "I saw him too."

"I'll bet he promised to bring you your soapstone," said Buck.

"I am not going to hold my breath," answered River Wolf.

Bonfires were started, and all the people ate. After the feast, selected women did the Friendship Dance. Then the people went to sleep.

The next morning, the entire population congregated around the giant heptagon on top of the massive ceremonial mound. In the center of the building was a small cone-shaped mound that was flat on the top. This was the altar where the sacred fire was burning. Three deerskins – one from a buck, one from a doe, and one from a fawn were made white with clay. These lay flat on the floor with their heads facing the altar. The bark from seven types of trees was placed on the altar for fuel. The trees used were the basswood, blackjack oak, black oak, chestnut, water oak, white oak, and white pine.

The principal assistant picked up a clay pot that contained the blood of some type of animal. He dipped a small weed brush into it, and sprinkled the blood on the deer hides. Then he painted a stripe down the center, from head to tail with blood on all three hides. Next, he placed a large Crystal on the buckskin, and sprinkled dried tobacco flower buds on the hides.

Now, the Uku, acting as the High Priest, had everybody assemble at the river. There were seven tables placed at the riverbank. There were also benches on the bank that were parallel to the water. This is where the Uku and the other leaders sat.

Everybody was required to look ahead, and not to the side until they reached the river. The reason for this is it symbolized focus on the ceremony. The Uku was the last to arrive.

The chief speaker brought some small flags, and seven appointed councilors carried seven boxes full of roots of various herbs. The Uku's principal assistant carried the sacred Crystals wrapped inside of seven deerskins.

The deerskins were placed one on each table. Now, the principal assistant removed the flags from the containers. He dipped the ends of the tiny flagpoles in the river, and then stuck them in the sand along the riverbank in a line. The people intently watched for any bugs that crawled out of the water and fought; the person nearest to that flag would become ill or die.

Next, everybody submerged themselves seven times in the water, facing east, with their clothing on. Meanwhile, the Uku unwrapped the Crystals from the seven deerskins, and covered the tables with the herb roots.

The people waded out of the river, one-by-one, and they circled one of the tables four times and wet their right forefingers. They ran their forefingers down the length of the Crystals, and then touched their foreheads, nose, lips, chin, and their stomachs. The older citizens and common folk went first, while the younger people and people of status went last.

Once each person finished, they picked up some of the herb roots off the table, and returned back to the village. When they returned, they put on dry clothes and began fasting. Babies fasted until afternoon, and the rest of the citizens fasted until after sunset. At sunset, the citizens gathered at the council house.

When the Uku arrived, he and his assistants sat on the west side of the altar, and they picked up the tobacco flowers that were still on the deer hides. They sprinkled it on the fire, and sacrificed a deer tongue. The people watched the fire to see which direction the bits of the tongue went. If it went towards the east, it was a sign of life. If it went west, it meant that somebody would soon perish. Fortunately, it was carried eastward.

Now, the buck was cooked, cut up into tiny pieces, and served along with some mush, to all of the citizens. It was late at night by the time all of the people were served.

Ritual scratching was done on people who chose to participate. Some of the herb roots were chewed, and rubbed over the body.

The women performed the Friendship Dance again, and nobody except for babies slept. At sunrise, the ceremony ended, and people began to return to their home villages.

The Sacred Night Dance was held seven days later. The people of Birch Mountain were joined at the heptagon with representatives from all of the other villages.

The next morning, all fires in the village were extinguished. Seven appointed men rekindled the sacred fire, which was fed with goldenrod, and then transferred to all parts of the village.

Twisted Stick needed to do some hunting. His friends all had plenty of food, and he didn't like hunting alone. So, he visited Sparrow, hoping that Broken Spear would go with him.

"He is already out hunting," said Sparrow. "Why don't you go with River Wolf?"

"I was hoping for somebody my age," said Twisted Stick. "Oh, it doesn't really matter. I will ask him. Thank you, Sparrow."

Twisted Stick arrived at River Wolf's lodge and found him carving on a pipe.

"Hello, River Wolf," he greeted.

"How are you?" returned River Wolf.

"I am alright, I came to ask you if you wanted to go hunting with me."

"Sure, I will go with you. I am out of venison."

It was decided. River Wolf got his bow and arrows and, together, they left. They walked in the direction of Eagle Peak for half of the day and saw nothing. They stopped to eat some cornbread that Twisted Stick's wife, Mouse had packed for them.

They found a place where the deer had bedded down, but there were no other signs of them. Twisted Stick was frustrated. They moved on. At sunset, they started back towards home.

River Wolf now remembered when he and Buck had gone jack-lighting when they were young.

"Have you considered jack-lighting?" he asked.

"That's a good idea!" said Twisted Stick, "Why don't we eat dinner and then take the canoe up the creek to the place where the deer bedded down?"

They returned home and prepared the torch and put it on the bow of the canoe. Then they went to Twisted Stick's lodge and ate dinner cooked by Mouse. When they finished eating, they went to the canoe and set out.

When they arrived at the spot where the deer bedded down, River Wolf lit the torch with a fire pot. They could hear the deer stirring. The flames began to burn stronger, and River Wolf paddled quietly to keep the canoe stationary.

Pretty soon, several pairs of eyes appeared. The deer were curious about what caused light in the darkness, and came for a closer look. Twisted Stick threw his axe and struck one of the deer between the eyes, killing it.

They beached the canoe, and Twisted Stick cut the deer's throat. After they paid their respects, River Wolf helped him load it into the dugout.

"Can you get the axe?" asked Twisted Stick.

"Sure," replied River Wolf.

He stepped out and looked around in the dark for the axe. He felt around with his hands for a while. Then he found it. He began walking back to the canoe. Suddenly he heard the distinct sound of a rattlesnake. Before he could stop, he felt a piercing blow on his right foot.

"Ouch!" he said.

"River Wolf," called Twisted Stick. "What happened? Are you alright?"

"A rattlesnake just bit me!" said River Wolf, while groaning.

Twisted Stick helped River Wolf into the canoe. Then he removed a leather strap from his bag so he could use it as a tourniquet. Then he began trying to suck the venom out of the wound.

"I sure hope you don't have any sores in your mouth," said River Wolf.

"You are awfully young to be dying," returned Twisted Stick, "I don't mind taking a risk for you."

He continued sucking on the wound as the canoe drifted downstream. They got to the river and followed it to Birch Mountain. By now, River Wolf's right leg was swollen very large.

Twisted Stick helped him up the hill and back to River Wolf's lodge. Beaver Pelt was there. When she saw them, she asked, "Oh no! What has happened?"

"River Wolf got a rattlesnake bite," said Twisted Stick. "Can you go and get Eagle Medicine?"

Beaver Pelt left, and River Wolf sat down. They loosed the tourniquet for a short period of time, and then retightened it again. When Eagle Medicine arrived, Twisted Stick left to haul the deer from the canoe back to the village. Eagle Medicine had some skullcap, coneflower roots, tobacco, and Virginia snakeroot.

He made decoctions from skullcap, and coneflower roots. He made River Wolf drink a large dose of skullcap for its sedative qualities. Then he washed the bite thoroughly with the coneflower root decoction. Now, he sang and recited an incantation:

"It has penetrated, it has penetrated, it has penetrated, it has penetrated, it has penetrated, it has penetrated. Listen! Ha! It was just a frog that passed by and put the trespasser in you. You small reptile! You small reptile! You small reptile! You small reptile! You small reptile! You small reptile! Listen! Ha! It was just a lizard that passed by and put the trespasser in you."

While he sang and repeated the incantation four times, he rubbed tobacco juice, and blew in circles around the snakebite four times. As he did this, he circled to the left – to symbolize uncoiling the snake, which always coils to the right. Then he mashed some roots of Virginia snakeroot and applied it to the snakebite.

"You will need to stay active as much as you can," instructed the Shaman. "The swelling will last for a long time. Carve some pipes or do something else to keep busy."

"I don't have any skins to give you right now," said River Wolf, "but when I can, I will give you a deer hide."

"Don't worry about it," replied Eagle Medicine, "I will be checking up on you every day. We'll get you through this."

Eagle Medicine left, and River Wolf now noticed just how swollen his foot and lower leg were. Beaver Pelt came for a visit.

"Oh, River Wolf," she said when she saw his foot, "It looks bad, but I know you will make it."

"It will take a lot more than a snake to kill me," agreed River Wolf with a smile that was partly a grimace.

"It's nice to see you in good spirits," said Beaver Pelt.

The hour was now very late, and they went to bed. Beaver Pelt kept River Wolf warm, and they talked until they went to sleep.

Next morning, Beaver Pelt helped River Wolf down to the river for the morning devotions. When that was finished, they returned to the lodge. River Wolf began carving on another pipe, while Beaver Pelt made breakfast.

Twisted Stick then appeared in the doorway with the skin of the deer he had killed with River Wolf's help.

"Good morning, River Wolf, Beaver Pelt," he greeted.

"Good morning," said Beaver Pelt, "What is the deerskin for?"

"I brought it for you and River Wolf to tan. You can use it to pay Eagle Medicine for his services."

"Thank you," said River Wolf.

"How is your leg?" asked Twisted Stick.

"It's swelled up pretty bad," answered River Wolf. "Thank you for helping me when I was bitten."

"Don't mention it. I felt at least partly responsible because I'm the one who asked you to go along on that hunting trip. You two take care, I will see you later."

"Goodbye," said River Wolf.

River Wolf got nauseated. Next thing he knew, he was vomiting. The swelling went down, and River Wolf thought he was getting better now. Then the swelling and nausea returned. But he followed Eagle Medicine's advice, and worked on carving pipes when he could.

Beaver Pelt was tanning the deer hide that Twisted Stick had given them, and Eagle Medicine continued treating River Wolf.

For two and-a-half moons River Wolf's lower leg would swell and return to normal, only to swell up again. The nausea would come and go.

During this time, the Yuchi had attacked. War parties had been sent out, and after being away for a moon, they returned with two captives. Now, the eagle killer went to work. A few days later, the Eagle Dance was performed to celebrate the victory.

Embossed Copper Plate with Depiction of a Mississippian Culture Falcon Dancer. Found at Etowah Mounds, Georgia.
Redrawn from Thruston 1897.

The captives were publicly ridiculed and tied to stakes by the villagers. Now for the first time Sparrow, the new Honored Woman had to decide their fate. She went with Buck to speak to them. Buck functioned as a translator because he knew sign language, which he used on his trade route.

Sparrow spoke. "Do you wish to be spared?" she asked.

Buck translated in signs.

The two captives were silent.

"You will have to adopt our customs," said Sparrow, "and you will be slaves. If you do well and show loyalty, you will be given an opportunity to become adopted into the tribe."

Buck translated, and the two captives glanced at each other. One of them uttered a sentence in their language. The other nodded in agreement.

They both nodded at Sparrow.

"Spare them," said Sparrow, "but keep a close eye on them."

They now became slaves. As Sparrow had ordered, they were watched closely and, at first, they were kept tied up. The Uku and other people of rank had them assist the workers with repairing holes in the clay daub on the palisade surrounding the village, among other tasks. They were never given a chance to escape. Slaves held no honor, so they were likely to try to escape at their earliest opportunity.

The slaves began to learn the local language and, when they weren't busy with the Uku, they helped the women with their tasks. The women were happy to have their assistance.

When River Wolf was completely recovered from the snakebite, he gave the tanned deer hide to Eagle Medicine to pay him for his services. He went to see his mother.

"River Wolf," she said, "why don't you take this cornbread to the slaves and ask them if they know the whereabouts of Running Fox?"

"I will ask them," replied River Wolf.

He ate dinner at his mother's lodge, and then went to where the slaves were working. They looked up at him, curious about why he was there.

"I am River Wolf. I came to you to ask if you knew the whereabouts of my little brother, Running Fox. He was taken from outside of this town by your people."

The captives didn't understand all of the words, so he repeated it accompanied with sign language.

The slaves looked at each other and spoke in their dialect. One of them then looked at River Wolf and asked in signs how long ago was Running Fox taken prisoner.

"Eight cycles ago, he was kidnapped in a raid on this very village," signed River Wolf. "He was caught outside of the village."

"I remember a boy," signed the slave, "perhaps eight cycles old, who was taken captive by our war party about that time."

"Where is he now?" asked River Wolf in signs.

"He was very obstinate, and would not cooperate. They traded the boy to a Muskhogean-speaking trader from the west. That was the last we saw of him."

"Thank you very much," signed River Wolf before giving the prisoners the cornbread. River Wolf returned to his mother's lodge and told her the news.

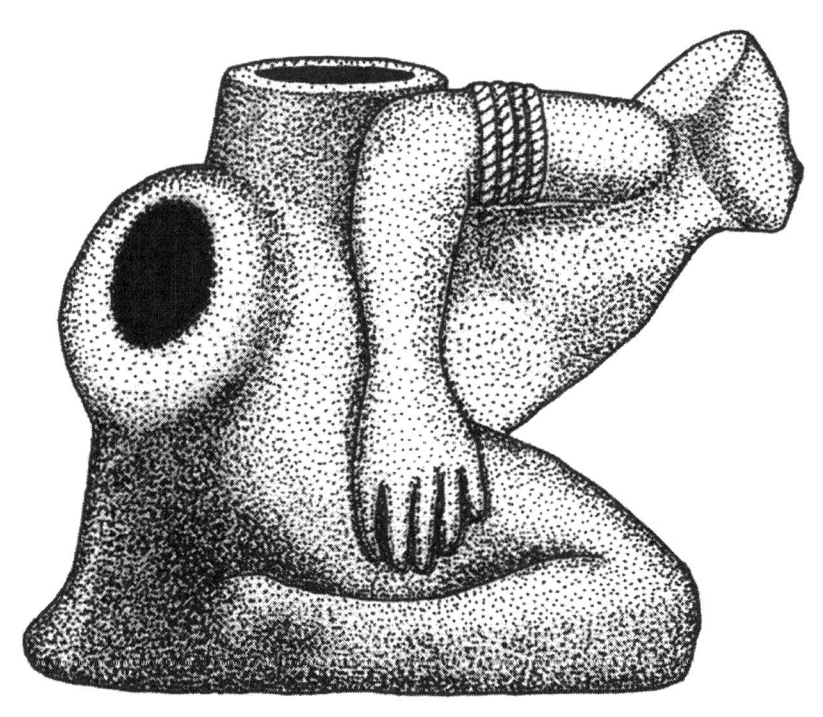

Effigy Pipe Depicting a Prisoner.
Redrawn from Moorehead 1900.

"They think they remember him," said River Wolf. "They say he was sold to a trader from the west."

Squirrel Fur had an empty and disappointed expression. River Wolf hugged her.

"This is the first we have heard about him since he was missing. Maybe I will be able to find him on a trading route," he said hopefully.

"I hope so," replied Squirrel Fur.

River Wolf returned to his lodge and began carving another pipe. Buck stopped by for a visit.

"How many pipes do you have now?" he asked.

"Thirty-one," answered River Wolf.

"Would you like to go hunting?" asked Buck.

"As long as I don't have to fight with any deer," replied River Wolf with a chuckle.

"We won't be hunting deer," said Buck, "You know it is taboo for me to kill a deer – the Buck Deer is my Guardian Spirit."

"What do you want to hunt then?"

"Rabbits, squirrels, maybe we can even do your black walnut fishing trick."

"I vote for the latter. I haven't had fish in a long time."

"Let's go, then."

They went to the river and took Buck's canoe upstream until they arrived at the creek. They went up the creek to the place where the black walnut grew in abundance. They beached the dugout, and began peeling the rinds off of the nuts.

"Did you know that these have anaphrodisiac qualities in men?" River Wolf asked.

"You never told me that," replied Buck.

"Eagle Medicine told me cycles ago that when a father doesn't want a man to marry his daughter, he mixes it in his drink. Then the man can't perform and the daughter loses interest in him."

"Well, I will have to keep that in mind when Titmouse gets older!"

They both laughed as they sat there peeling the rinds off of the nuts.

"The squirrels will love us for doing some of their work for them," said River Wolf. "Hey, that gives me an idea! Why don't we return here after getting the fish, and see if I can get some squirrels with my blowgun?"

"That sounds good to me," replied Buck.

They filled the basket with the pounded nut rinds while observing the curious squirrels already watching them. They put the full basket into the canoe and shoved off. After awhile, they had plenty of fish, and they returned to the black walnuts. They found several squirrels collecting the peeled nuts that they left behind.

River Wolf got out his blowgun, aimed at one and blew as hard as he could. The dart hit the squirrel in the neck, and soon it was dead. He fired at another one, but the dart missed and hit the squirrel in the abdomen. The squirrel struggled violently, but managed to get up the tree.

River Wolf had to shoot the squirrel four more times to kill it. He was sad for it. This incident frightened the rest of the squirrels away.

After apologizing to the spirits of the squirrels and fish, they loaded them into the dugout and returned home.

River Wolf resolved to use his leaning-log squirrel trap from now on, whenever he hunted squirrels. He was disturbed about making the squirrels suffer anymore than necessary.

They returned home with the two squirrels, and fifteen large fish. They spent the rest of the day butchering, and talking.

They reminisced about things that happened cycles ago, when they were children.

"Remember the time we sought shelter under the canoe during the thunderstorm?" asked Buck.

"Yes," replied River Wolf. "The wind blew the canoe off of us, and we both got soaked anyway!"

They both laughed at the memory.

"Remember when you told Running Fox that if he put a bean in his nose, it would sprout?" asked Buck.

"Oh boy, yes I do!" answered River Wolf with a chuckle. "It swelled up so bad, and Red Talon had the hardest time removing it. And then Dad had to pay him two badger skins for that. He wasn't too thrilled about it either! By the way, I asked the two slaves about Running Fox."

"What did they say?" asked Buck, very curious.

"They seemed to remember him. They say he was traded to a Muskhogean-speaking trader who came from the west. Do you know much about the people who speak Muskhogean?"

"We call them the Muskogee," replied Buck. "Some of them call themselves the People of One Fire, but there are several other groups also. I have done trading with many of them. They are very hospitable."

"Did you see anybody who looked like they could be Running Fox?"

"No, I haven't. But I wasn't looking for him. I assumed he was still with the Yuchi, or dead."

"I will be looking for him when I travel with the next trader that visits here. By the way, would you like for me to take any of your items and do some trading for you?"

"No, but I will trade you knives, and spear points for you to do some hunting for me before you leave. I can't eat deer meat, but my wife and daughter would love some that is dried. I can furnish fresh rabbit and squirrel for them."

"I will hunt in trade. I should get started now – I do not know when the next trader will arrive, but it will be soon."

Sparrow arrived at the river with a large water pot.

"How is the married life, Sparrow?" asked Buck.

"It's great. It is so nice to share a lodge again," replied Sparrow. "How is your beautiful daughter doing?"

"She is well."

"And how are you, River Wolf?" asked Sparrow.

"I am fine. Beaver Pelt is doing well also."

"You'd better marry her soon," she said. "She is a very good young lady. Don't let her get away." Sparrow filled up the water pot and returned to the palisade, stopping at the entrance for a few words with her husband, the guard.

"You really should marry Beaver Pelt," said Buck. "It worked well for Tanager and me."

Beaver Pelt appeared with a water pot as they spoke. River Wolf wondered how much she had overheard.

"I see you two have been busy!" she exclaimed after seeing all the fish they had caught.

"Would you like to cook these for dinner?" asked River Wolf, while pointing to the fish that was prepared.

"Yes," she replied. "I will make a meal you will never forget!"

River Wolf wondered if she truly meant what might happen after the meal. He knew that she really wanted to marry him now, but was being passive about it to please him.

She picked up some of the fish, and River Wolf started to give her one of the squirrels. She had a lot to carry, so River Wolf offered to carry the fish and the squirrel back with her.

"Thank you," she said with a smile.

"I will be doing some deer hunting for Buck's family before I leave," he said while they walked.

"I guess it could be any day now," she said reluctantly.

"I will return," reassured River Wolf, "Before you know it, I will come home to you. Then maybe, we will get married."

They arrived at the lodge and Beaver Pelt began cooking. River Wolf returned to the river to help Buck finish butchering the fish.

The Sun had set and they finished soon after. They returned to their lodges, and Beaver Pelt had River Wolf's dinner ready by the time he arrived. There was fresh squirrel and fish, in addition to many vegetables and cornbread. It was a tasty meal.

After they finished eating, they made love that was savagely sweet. This was the first time since the rattlesnake bit him. He wondered if she was trying to tell him something with this gesture.

The next day, Turkey arrived with some sad news. Beaver Pelt's grandmother in Pine Bend had died. Beaver Pelt was shattered by the news. Her mother, her aunt, and River Wolf accompanied her on the trip to Pine Bend. It was a sad time, and River Wolf tried to be helpful to the small group as they traveled. After about a day of walking, they arrived at the top of the ridge.

River Wolf caught and butchered several squirrels to feed the group. The sunset was breathtaking, but River Wolf seemed to be the only one to notice. They went to sleep and were awakened, in the middle of the night, by the sound of a bear fight at the nearest stream. River Wolf stood by with his bow and axe ready for trouble.

The bears never molested them, and they resumed their journey at sunrise. The party arrived at Pine Bend at around noon. The burial mound was overgrown and unkept, and they voted to bury the old woman under her bed inside of the lodge. Once that was finished, they began to divide up her possessions that were not buried with her.

Turkey wanted to move to Eagle Peak, where there would be more people around. She had been extremely lonely while taking care of Grandma. Even though she was shy, she wanted to break out of her isolated lifestyle.

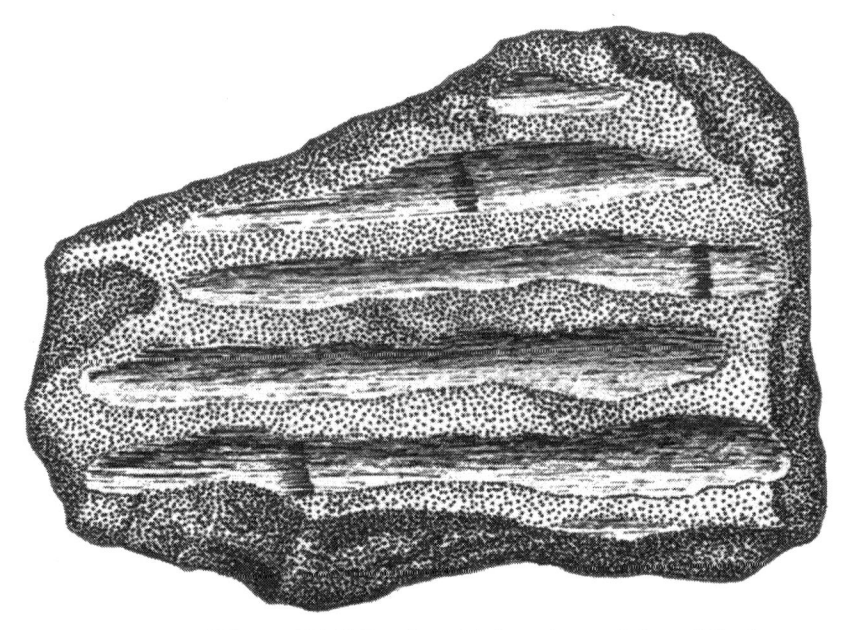

Fragment of House Wall Daub, with Imprints of Cane Wattle.

River Wolf, and the rest of them, helped her build a lodge in Eagle Peak. While they were plastering clay daub for the wall of the new lodge, Fox Claw visited. Turkey was attracted to him immediately.

"River Wolf," Fox Claw said, "I am sorry I still haven't paid you for that pipe. I *promise...*"

"Why don't you leave me alone and *stop lying to me?*" interrupted River Wolf. "You know where I live, and you can bring my soapstone anytime. Stop making promises, and start delivering. Otherwise, leave me alone!"

"He's right!" added Beaver Pelt.

Fox Claw was ashamed and embarrassed. He quickly left in silence.

"What was that all about?" asked Turkey.

"He got River Wolf to make him a pipe," replied Beaver Pelt, "but he never paid him the soapstone that he promised him."

"Well," said Turkey, "I'll be sure to warn everybody I know about him if he's that way!"

Acorn appeared. "River Wolf!" she greeted. "How are you?"

"Hello, Acorn," returned River Wolf. "I am fine."

"I had no idea you were in Eagle Peak. You didn't forget about your aunt, did you?"

"No, I planned to come and see you tonight. How are you doing?"

"I am fine, and how are you, Beaver Pelt?"

"I am doing well," answered Beaver Pelt.

"Have you two gotten married yet?"

"No, we haven't," answered River Wolf.

"Well, you should."

Beaver Pelt smiled in agreement, her eyes fixed on River Wolf, glad to have Acorn's support.

"Do you need any food?" asked Acorn. "I just made some cornbread. I also have a *lot* of sunflower seeds. *Please* take some of them!"

"We are getting hungry," replied Turkey.

They all went to Acorn's lodge and ate lunch.

"We won't finish the lodge for at least two days," said River Wolf as they ate. "I should go and get some squirrels for us to eat."

"That sounds good," asserted Beaver Pelt.

They finished eating, and they resumed working on the lodge, except for River Wolf, who left to set his squirrel trap. He returned and helped on the lodge for a while, and then went to check his trap. He found five squirrels hanging from the nooses.

They ate a good dinner that night. In three days, they finished the major work on the lodge and Turkey said she could do the finishing touches.

They started their journey back to Birch Mountain, taking with them a large bag of Acorn's sunflower seeds. Just before sunset, they crossed the top of the ridge. They arrived home at noon the following day.

River Wolf visited his mother and Sparrow, who were cutting up a deer killed by Broken Spear. They gave him some venison, which he took back to his lodge. Beaver Pelt cooked it and some vegetables. It was a tasty dinner.

The next morning, the Uku announced plans for a chunkey game, to be played by the young men of Birch Mountain. Chunkey was both a game of skill and luck. Usually, only males played this game, and the public often gambled on the outcome.

The chunkey court was located in the front of the ceremonial mound, and covered with a layer of sand. The people made sure that the sand was even and had no lumps or dips anywhere. The disc-shaped or spherical game stones were all made by River Wolf over the years, and were the property of the community, and not any particular player.

Chunkey Game & Discoidal Chunkey Stones.

Two teams were organized, with two male youths on each team. A neutral young man sent the discoidal game stone rolling down the court and, while it was still rolling, the teammates threw poles at the place where they thought it would stop. The team that got closest scored a point. All types of people wagered jewelry, weapons, and even clothing, except for breechclouts. The game lasted all day, and by the time it concluded, everybody was very tired.

Eagle Medicine approached River Wolf. "You did a good job on those discoidals," he said, "We get a lot of compliments on them."

"Thank you," replied River Wolf.

"You should do more carvings from harder stones. Axes, effigies, there are many things in demand."

"I am sure I could make a nice axe. I've just never tried it."

So, River Wolf decided to start carving granite axes to accompany the rest of his trade items. Before too long, he had finished carving a granite celt. He made another, and another. After he had completed six of them, Eagle Medicine dropped by for a visit.

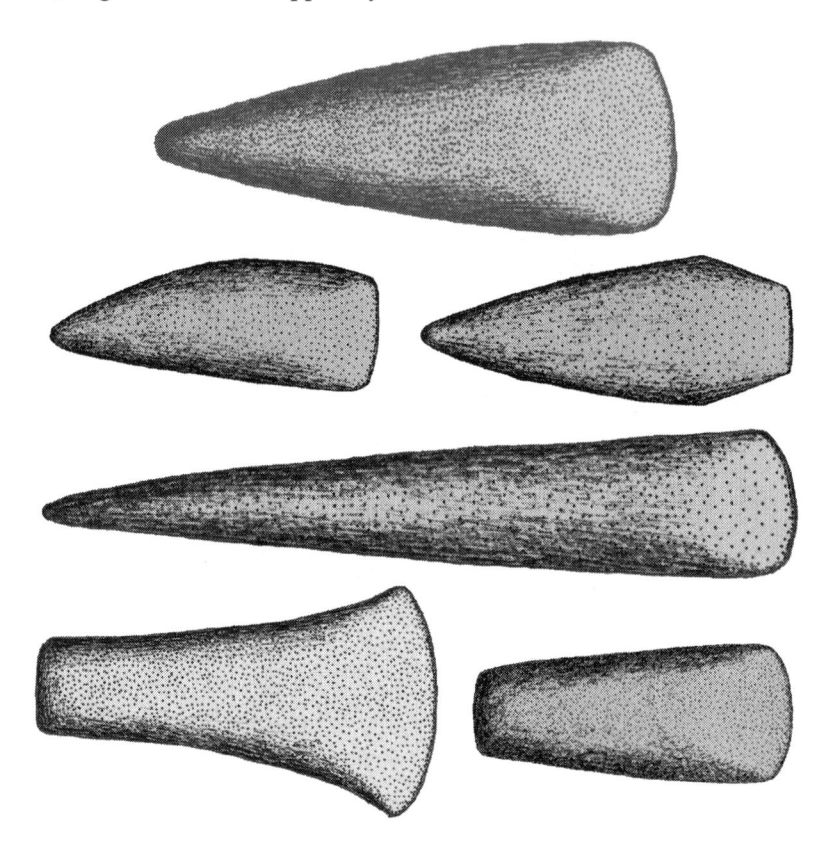

Six Celts (Axe Heads) Made by River Wolf.

Eagle Medicine was impressed with the celts River Wolf had carved. "You should try to carve a monolithic axe. Do you know what that is?"

"No," answered River Wolf.

"It's an axe head and handle – both carved out of one piece of stone. They are usually made out of greenstone."

"Wow, that is amazing. But wouldn't it break if you tried to chop down a tree with it?"

"They are used for ceremonial purposes by the Muskogee. When a chieftain dies, they kill his or her relatives and slaves with them so they can bury them all together. They have strange customs, but you could profit from it."

This made River Wolf worry about Running Fox. He resolved to not tell his mother the story.

"Is everything okay?" asked Eagle Medicine.

River Wolf was so worried that he had forgotten to respond. "Yes, I am fine," he said, trying to be cheerful. "The Muskogees sure have some strange customs – their white drink, and killing their slaves and all."

"Well, you will soon be traveling amongst them. Do not laugh at them for being different. If you offend them, they may not be as friendly or as eager to trade with you. There are all kinds of people in the world. I had better go now. I have to take some mulberry sap to a person across the village who has ringworm."

River Wolf remembered learning about mulberry while he was training to be a Shaman. He recalled that the milk from an unripe fruit could bring on hallucinations and upset your stomach. But the milky sap from the leaves was good for treating ringworm on the scalp.

River Wolf took breaks from stone carving so he could hunt deer for Buck's family, using a bow and arrow. But his favorite way of hunting was his leaning-log squirrel trap. He was rigging eight nooses a day and, while he waited to catch squirrels, he would either be hunting deer or carving stone.

One day, he remembered the conch shells given to him by Turtle Shell so many cycles before. They had not been touched for several cycles now. He found them and, with a hammerstone, he broke them up into usable fragments. Breaking up these beautiful shells was difficult, both because they were so hard and tough, but River Wolf also hated to destroy shells that were so pretty. He hoped his end results could justify such a "heinous" act.

First, he made a rattlesnake gorget. Shell was very hard and tedious to carve, but he still enjoyed making it, so next, he made a spider gorget. Then a gorget with woodpeckers, followed by more gorgets with other designs.

He remembered to use the copper rod Bald Eagle had given him so many cycles ago for burning the holes into shell gorgets and beads. Bald Eagle was right – it did not ever wear out, and River Wolf didn't have to waste time or flint in the process of resharpening flint drills. River Wolf even used the heated copper rod to form fenestrations (shaped holes) on the rattlesnake gorget. It worked beautifully.

He wanted to put them on shell bead necklaces, so he carved shell disc beads. They took a long time, and he wanted to get to something else. So he decided to use tube beads made from turkey wing bones, with shell discs separating each tube. He finished the necklace sooner by doing that, and now he could get on with other things.

River Wolf's Shell Gorgets.
Redrawn from Holmes 1880 & Thruston 1897.

The trader was expected to arrive any day now, and he worked extra hard to make anything he thought he might be able to trade. On one

190

hunting trip, he happened on some mica, and took home as much as he could carry.

One day he was in the woods, near Birch Mountain, and he walked up on a grizzly bear. The bear charged him, but River Wolf quickly had five arrows in the bear. He cut the bear's throat, paid his respects and went home to get Buck's help hauling it back.

He traded the meat, hide, and his labor butchering the bear to Buck in exchange for ten large flint preforms, but kept the bear teeth. In addition to the preforms, Buck gave him some more teeth and claws. River Wolf drilled some of the bear teeth, grooved others and strung all of them on turkey-bone tube-bead necklaces.

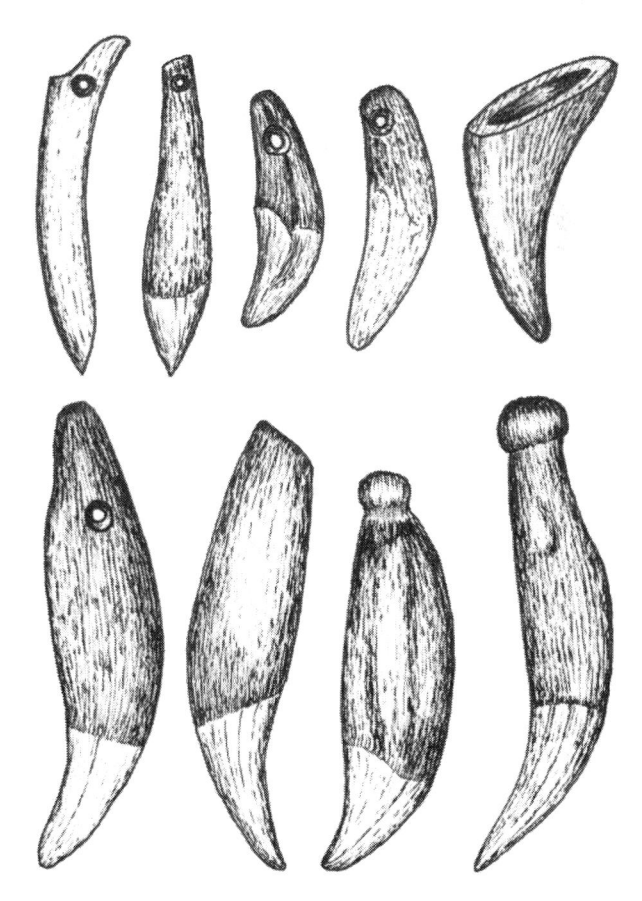

Pendants Made from Animal Teeth.
Redrawn from Beauchamp 1902.

River Wolf was setting one of his leaning-log squirrel traps when he heard a noise. He turned to look, and saw a mountain lion stalking him. He slowly backed away, but the cougar began running after him. He ran straight for the river and jumped in. The cougar jumped in behind him, but cougars do not like being in the water, so it swam back to shore and kept a watchful eye on him.

River Wolf's bow had gotten wet, but he decided to risk using it anyway. Maybe the water hadn't penetrated the pitch coating on the bowstring yet. It worked. River Wolf shot the cougar three times before the bowstring broke. The cougar hissed and screamed in a threatening manner, before falling dead.

River Wolf waited in the water for a considerable length of time before returning to shore and cutting its throat. He then paid his respects. Some of the villagers came running up to investigate the cougar's cries. They helped him haul the carcass back to the village.

River Wolf saved the fangs, and put them on necklaces. Beaver Pelt tanned the hide and they kept it as a souvenir. He traded the cougar meat to Sparrow for two turkey feather cloaks that she had made.

River Wolf's pile of trade goods was growing larger every day. He now had forty-five fine effigy pipes, twenty large flint preforms, two axe heads, the two turkey feather cloaks, a good quantity of mica, and twenty-one assorted necklaces. He thought that he might actually have more than he would be able to take along.

One night, he was visiting Buck, and told him of this dilemma.

"Why don't you borrow my canoe?" offered Buck.

"What if something happens to me while I am gone?" asked River Wolf.

"Then I will make another one," said Buck. "That one is old anyway."

"Thank you, Buck," River Wolf said. "I will pay you back for letting me borrow it."

"Don't worry about it. I won't have any use for it while you are gone."

River Wolf went back home. When he arrived, Beaver Pelt was waiting for him. She had a wonderful dinner cooked for him.

"Any day now," he said.

"I will miss you," she replied sadly.

The two went to bed and made love all night. Beaver Pelt knew the day was coming that she would be alone, and she wanted to make up for the time he would be gone.

The next morning, they joined the rest of the village for morning devotions at the river. Then they returned to the village and had breakfast.

When they finished eating, there was a commotion throughout the village. The old trader, Bald Eagle, had arrived! Everybody flocked to the riverbank, eager to see what items he had brought to trade.

When River Wolf saw Bald Eagle, he noticed that he had aged considerably, but still looked as mentally sharp as ever. The Uku welcomed him to the village and invited him to his lodge to talk.

Bald Eagle left with the Uku, and the villagers looked over the contents of his canoe. Nobody touched anything, for it was a serious dishonor to steal anything from a trader.

Buck saw in the trader's canoe some large quality nodules of flint, and wanted them. He also saw a pair of pretty copper earspools that he knew Tanager would love. He returned to his lodge and gathered flint preforms he had made, and furs of many different animals that he had hunted recently.

River Wolf spied some copper sheets in the trader's dugout and wondered where they came from. He speculated that it might be easy to work them into gorgets or plates. He had never worked with copper before, other than with the copper rod Bald Eagle had given him.

The village was in a bustle to get things together for trading. River Wolf began hauling his pile of trade goods down to Buck's canoe, with the help of Buck and young White Feather. River Wolf hoped that Bald Eagle would be willing to have his company on the trip. He also wondered what his fee would be, if there would be a fee.

That night, the trader enjoyed a feast, and the Eagle Dance was performed to welcome him. The next day, he was at his canoe bargaining with the villagers. Buck managed to trade preforms for most of Bald Eagle's flint nodules, and the pair of copper earspools, which he almost didn't trade for, due to how expensive they were.

Copper Earspools.
Redrawn from Thruston 1897.

The trading ended at sunset. Now, River Wolf approached the trader.

"I don't have much left to trade," said Bald Eagle in sign language.

"I do not wish to trade for any objects," replied River Wolf. "I would like to trade for a service."

"And what service is that?" asked Bald Eagle.

"I want to travel with you and learn your trade."

"What do you offer in return?"

"I can assist you by hunting food for you on the trade route."

"You will only slow me down. I can't be taking along a baby. And besides, how do I know that I can trust you?"

"I am eighteen cycles old. I know sign language, and I can keep watch while you sleep. I am good with a bow and arrows, and a blowgun. And I have never stolen anything from anybody. I am not a thief."

"What else do you offer in trade?" asked Bald Eagle, eyeing the pile of goods in Buck's canoe.

"I will give you two effigy pipes."

"I will let you tag along for four pipes."

River Wolf was at a disadvantage, and he knew it. He made no counter offer, he was glad enough that the trader was even considering letting him travel with him.

"It's a deal," said River Wolf.

"We take only my canoe so you can help me paddle. I will see that you get back home. Load your items in the bow end. That's where you will be sitting. We leave at dawn."

River Wolf was so excited! He immediately began transferring his goods to Bald Eagle's large canoe, while Bald Eagle ate dinner with the Uku. While River Wolf was doing this, he noticed a beautiful copper pendant with an embossed cross on it. He had to get this for Beaver Pelt!

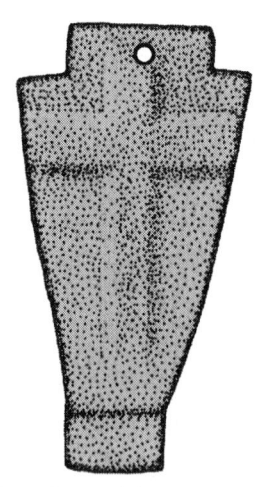

Copper Pendant with Embossed Cross.
Redrawn from Thruston 1897.

River Wolf found Bald Eagle and offered two shell necklaces to Bald Eagle for the copper pendant. Bald Eagle accepted, and River Wolf took it home with him. He wanted to spend time with Beaver Pelt one last time.

"Are you leaving me?" asked Beaver Pelt.

"Yes," replied River Wolf, "first thing in the morning."

Tears came to her eyes, but she tried to hide them. She had cooked an excellent meal of bear, venison, and assorted vegetables. River Wolf was sad to leave her.

"I have something for you," he said, and he gave her the copper pendant. She normally would have gasped at such a fine gift, but she fought the tears instead.

"I will be back before you know it," he said, "and then, if you are still available, we will get married."

"You know I will wait for you."

River Wolf knew she was sincere. Beaver Pelt knew he wanted what was best for her, but she also believed he was who was best for her. The uncertainty and the long wait would be unbearable.

He could sense that she was worried, and they ate in silence. Then they went to bed, and he held her all night long, and they talked.

The next morning, they got up early and River Wolf prepared to leave. He hugged and kissed Beaver Pelt who was still fighting the tears. She didn't want him to leave, but didn't want to distress him with her worrying.

"Goodbye," she said.

"I will be back before the fall," he reassured her.

They parted ways, and River Wolf said his good-byes to his mother, Sparrow, Buck, and Tanager.

He climbed into the trader's canoe and they shoved off. River Wolf waved goodbye to his mother and his probable bride-to-be. He swallowed hard and held back the tears. The journey had begun. It would be a long time before he would see his home again.

Chapter 8: Journey

River Wolf paddled in silence. Bald Eagle observed this, and began speaking the best he could in the Cherokee tongue.

"You are going to miss her," he spoke.

"Yes, I will," responded River Wolf.

"You are going to have to learn the language of my people," said Bald Eagle to change the subject, "I have seen that you already know sign language; that will be a big help. But if you learn different languages, you can understand what people are saying to each other. You don't have to let them know you understand their language. It will give you an edge on the situation."

River Wolf pointed to the water and said, "What is the word for river?"

Bald Eagle uttered a Muskhogean word, and River Wolf repeated it several times.

Then River Wolf asked, "What is wolf?"

The trader told him the word. He repeated it, and Bald Eagle coached him until he got the pronunciation correct.

Then River Wolf pointed to himself and said, "River Wolf" in the Muskhogean language. While they traveled, he learned words this way. He pointed to different types of trees, animals, and types of stone. Before long, he was composing short sentences in this new language.

They reached a point in the river, and Bald Eagle said, "Now we go up this creek. Then we have a long portage that'll take all day, dragging the dugout uphill, before we get over the divide. Then it's downhill. There is a creek on the other side that will lead to another river."

They paddled upstream, the paddling was more laborious, and the traveling was slower.

Now, River Wolf thought of his little brother. "What is your word for the people who call themselves the Children of the Sun from Far Away? They are the tribe to the southeast of our territory. They are our enemies."

Bald Eagle answered. "You mean the Yuchi."

"Do you know anything about an eight-cycle-old boy from Birch Mountain who was traded to your people from the Yuchi around eight cycles ago?"

"There are lots of people traded or sold back and forth among different tribes. Why would I remember one from that long ago?"

"I was told that a Muskhogean speaking trader bought my little brother from the Yuchi eight cycles ago."

"Well, it wasn't me!" defended Bald Eagle, "I do not deal in slaves!"

"I am not saying you do; I was only hoping you might have known of his whereabouts."

"How did he get into the hands of the Yuchi?"

"He was outside of the palisade when they attacked. He never came back home."

"Well," said Bald Eagle, "we will be visiting plenty of Muskogee villages; you can look around for him, but I wouldn't ask anybody about him. People might get the impression that you are there for reasons other than trading. Seriously, it could turn real bad for you."

"Yes, I guess so," conceded River Wolf, sad for his brother, yet very aware there was not much he could do about it.

They paddled in silence for a while. Then Bald Eagle joked, "To the east is where your 'friends' are."

"Do you mean the Yuchi?" asked River Wolf.

"Yes, but we are going west," said the trader.

River Wolf was relieved. He hated them with a passion. They continued upstream until just before sunset. They reached the headwaters of the creek. Then they beached the giant dugout and set up camp. The next morning they began dragging the dugout up the divide.

"This will be my last trading excursion," stated Bald Eagle, "We will be going over most of the circuit, and I will see you back home as I promised. I am getting too old to be traveling. Dragging this dugout uphill is hard on an old man."

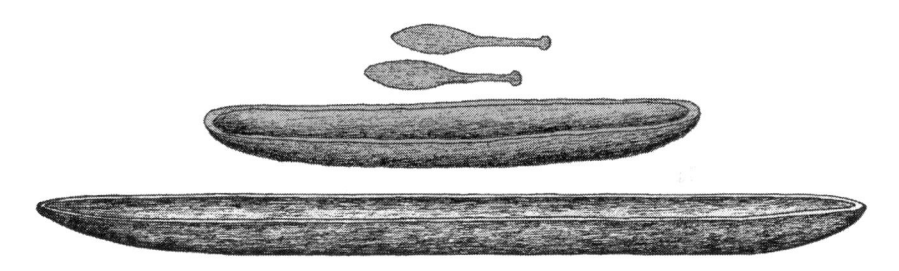

Two Dugout Canoes and Two Paddles.

"I am worn out also from paddling upstream," said River Wolf, "Can you show me the places where you get your flint?"

"Normally, I would not. But since I am retiring, it makes little difference to me anymore. I will show you."

"Do you quarry it yourself, or trade for it?"

"I do both. I will take you to a secret place that few people know about. I have found my best flint right there. But don't tell anybody about it. That way, you can offer better flint than what most folks have."

River Wolf set a leaning-log squirrel trap and caught three squirrels. They dressed them, cooked them over the campfire, and ate. Then they went to sleep.

Early the next morning, they continued the journey. The next day, they arrived at a small stream that Bald Eagle said led to the river he had spoken of. They went down this creek, and after a half a day of paddling, they arrived at a small village. The people spoke a dialect of the Muskhogean language, and Bald Eagle said they were of the Alabama Koasati tribe.

The locals flocked to the stream, eager to greet the trader and his companion. Their Chief appeared out of the crowd. River Wolf couldn't understand what he said, but he picked up the word 'oak'. The Chief said something and motioned for them to follow him. He led them to a building on the west side of the town square. River Wolf noticed on the support poles of the building were carvings of garfishes.

Garfish.
Adapted from OpenClipart-Vectors from Pixabay.

The Chief and Bald Eagle talked and laughed for a long time. Then Bald Eagle motioned to River Wolf to approach them.

"River Wolf, this is Chief Gar Scale," and then he said something to the Chief. River Wolf guessed that Bald Eagle was introducing him to Chief Gar Scale, since the only words he understood were River Wolf. River Wolf knew that in some places the scales of garfish were often fashioned into arrow points and, because of this, the Chief's name likely had a far more powerful meaning than it may have sounded.

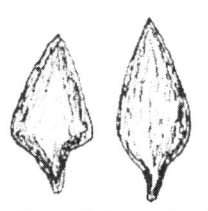

Arrowheads Carved from Garfish Scales.
Based on Davis 1991.

The Alabama Koasatis held a feast in their honor, and they each ate their fill. Then a single lady approached River Wolf. She smiled at him, and began talking in sign language. She signed, "I am Tobacco Leaf. I will be accompanying you in the guest lodge tonight. This way."

River Wolf didn't quite know what the protocol was, so he followed her to the guest lodge. Bald Eagle was already inside, and was enjoying the company of another woman of the village.

Now River Wolf knew what was happening, but he felt like he should be faithful to Beaver Pelt back home. As Tobacco Leaf was going to kiss him, River Wolf motioned for her to stop.

"I can't do this," he said in sign language.

"Am I unattractive?" she gestured, obviously hurt by his rejection.

"No, you are very beautiful. I just can't do this."

Tobacco Leaf was embarrassed and humiliated, and she left River Wolf with Bald Eagle and his woman.

River Wolf felt terrible. He was only trying to be faithful to Beaver Pelt, but now he had insulted his hosts. *Why didn't I tell her I am going to get married?* he thought to himself. The next day, after the trading was done, they left.

As soon as they got out of earshot, Bald Eagle said, "Turn around and talk to me."

River Wolf faced him and said, "I know I made a mistake last night, but I didn't know what to do."

"Why on Earth did you turn down that beautiful woman? Are you in your time of the moon, or what?"

River Wolf was offended at this insult to his manhood.

"I shouldn't have said that." apologized Bald Eagle, "I'm sorry. But please tell me – what happened?"

"I plan to get married when I return home. I was trying to be faithful to Beaver Pelt."

"You are not married yet. Do you see how your actions are bad for business?"

"But what if I was married?"

"If you take your wife along, they won't expect for you to have one of their women. That woman had good intentions, and you insulted her! Next time, accept what is offered without asking questions. Beaver Pelt will understand. Did you make some kind of deal with her restricting you from other women, or what?"

"She wanted to marry me. I told her that we should wait until I return."

"Why did you want to wait?"

"I don't know. So she could have freedom."

"Then she should understand that you have that same freedom. Next time don't turn down hospitality. Or else you will be very rude and leave them with a really bad impression."

"I can't do that. It would really bother me."

Bald Eagle rolled his eyes and that worried River Wolf. "Why would you…" began Bald Eagle, but he stopped. Then he said, "I don't know what to tell you. I can see you feel like you should do what you think is right, and that is not flawed thinking. But I don't know what to tell you."

"If I was married," began River Wolf, "would they understand and not require things of me? Would my wife necessarily have to be traveling with me?"

Bald Eagle stroked his chin, deep in thought. "Well, I guess not. Either way, they don't know every custom of every tribe, so that might be a good way to address the situation. At least you would have a reason that they might feel is believable or, at least, makes sense to them. I see what you are concerned about. I wouldn't make the same choice as you, but that's me. But it is an indicator of your good character, you choosing this path. I'll tell you what: if anybody asks me why you don't participate in village hospitality, I will back you up and tell them your reasons for not doing so."

"Thank you for understanding, Bald Eagle." River Wolf was greatly relieved that they had found a good way to deal with it.

They continued downstream in silence, and finally arrived at the river, which Bald Eagle called the Mud River. They followed it downstream until the evening. As they traveled, River Wolf learned more of the Muskhogean language.

"What was the name of the village we just left?" asked River Wolf.

"Red Oak," replied Bald Eagle.

They began telling stories to each other. River Wolf started by telling the story of the origin of Medicine. Bald Eagle liked it so much he requested another. River Wolf began:

"Long ago, there were seven hungry wolves. They managed to catch a Groundhog, and said to him, 'Now we'll kill you. You'll taste so very good!'

"Groundhog spoke, 'You must always give thanks for good food, like humans do in the Green Corn Ceremony. I know you are just going to kill me, and there is nothing I can do about it, so I will sing so you can have a dance. But this is a new dance, like you have never danced before. I will stand with my back against seven trees, one at a time, while you go back and forth, as I call it, and when the dance is over, then you can eat me.'

"The hungry wolves decided to see what this new dance was all about. So in spite of their hunger, they said, 'Proceed.'

"So the Groundhog stood with his back against a tree, and began singing a lively tune. The wolves began dancing, away from the Groundhog, until the Groundhog gave the signal, at which time they turned around and approached him.

"'You are doing great!' cheered the Groundhog. Now the Groundhog moved to the second tree and began another song. The same dance was repeated by the wolves.

"Again, the Groundhog cheered them on, and then moved to the third tree and began another song. This went on until the Groundhog finally reached the seventh tree, which was very near to his hole.

"'Okay!' said the Groundhog, 'Now when I give you the signal, all of you can try to get me, and whomever succeeds will get to eat me!'

"He began his song, and waited till the wolves were away, and gave the signal. The wolves turned around and made a dash for the

Groundhog, but he dove into his hole. One of the wolves managed to nip off his tail, which is why the Groundhog's tail is short to this day."

"Tell me another Cherokee story," said Bald Eagle.
"Have you heard the Cherokee story about how the world was created?" asked River Wolf.
"Tell me," said Bald Eagle.
So River Wolf began:

"All the earth was covered with water, and all animals dwelt in the sky vault. But it was getting crowded, and the animals wanted more room. They were curious about what lay under the water, and Water Beetle volunteered to go down and investigate.

"He strode all over the water, but was unsuccessful at finding a solid place to support anything. Then he dove under the water, and brought some mud to the surface. The soft mud increased in size until it was a small island. It was called the earth, and attached to the sky by four cords. Who suspended the island by these cords remains a mystery.

"The earth was soft, damp, and flat. The animals, tired of being crowded, sent various birds down to see if the earth had dried enough for them to live there, but it hadn't. Then Grandfather Buzzard was sent down, and he was gone for a while. When he flew over Cherokee country, he was so tired that his wings struck the mud, causing the mountains and valleys. The animals didn't want there to be mountains over the rest of the earth, so they summoned Grandfather Buzzard to return to the sky vault.

"Finally, the earth was dry enough, and the animals began to come down and populate the earth. It was dark, and the animals had difficulty seeing, so they created a path for the Sun to follow. This path ran from the east to the west. However, the Sun was much too close to the earth, and it was very hot. It even singed the shell of the Red Crawfish, which is how it became bright red. Its meat also went bad and the people refused to eat it.

"They placed the Sun a little higher, and the situation improved slightly, but it was still too hot. They raised it a total of seven times before it was comfortable for everybody. By this time, the Sun was just under the sky vault. Every morning, the bowl-like sky vault is lifted, so that the Sun can pass through. The Sun follows its path to the west and at dusk, the sky vault opens back up, allowing the Sun to exit. Then the Sun travels east above the sky vault, and this daily cycle is repeated.

"The underworld is similar to this world; there are animals, plants and people. The rivers and streams are paths to the underworld. The springs are the doorways to the underworld. The seasons differ down there from our seasons. This is proved by the warmth of spring water in the winter, and its coolness in the summer.

"All of the animals and plants were ordered to stay awake for seven nights. They tried vigilantly to stay awake during this period, but by the time the seven nights were over, only a few animals and plants remained awake. This included the Mountain Lion, and the Owl. They were awarded the ability to see and hunt in the dark.

"The plants that remained awake included the pine, laurel, cedar, holly, and spruce. They were awarded the ability to stay green throughout the winter.

"Men and women were created last. There were only a brother and a sister, and the brother jabbed the sister with a fish and said, 'Multiply," and she bore a child every seven days. Soon the world had plenty of people, and the animals feared being crowded again. They made it so that a woman could only bear one child a cycle. And it remains this way today."

"That was great," said Bald Eagle, "Tell me another one. But try to use Muskhogean words as much as possible. If you don't know a word, use the Cherokee word, and I will teach you the words as they come."

"Alright," agreed River Wolf. "Here is the story about Selu – the Corn Mother, and the hunter." River Wolf started:

"After walking up and down the mountains all day, a hunter failed to find any game. At sunset, he built a campfire in a hollow stump. He drank a little bit of corn gruel, and went to sleep in despair. After sleeping for a while, he began to have a dream. He heard the sound of a lovely song that lasted until dawn, and then disappeared into the sky.

"He got up, and spent the whole day hunting again and, again, had no luck. He returned to his campsite, went to sleep, and had the same dream. This time it was more vivid, and seemed very real. He got up before dawn, and still heard the beautiful music. He was sure now that it was real, and began walking in the direction that the song came from. He saw a single stalk of corn. The corn plant began to speak to him. It said, "Cut off some of my roots, and take them back to your village. The next morning, before anybody is awake, chew the roots and take them to the water. Your hunting will then be prosperous." The corn plant told him many hunting secrets, but also that he must share what he killed with others. The Sun was at its highest, and the corn plant assumed the form of Selu, the Corn Mother. She soon disappeared and was out of sight, and he was alone.

"The hunter returned to his village, doing what Selu had ordered, and telling the story to the village. The following cycles were the most plentiful and successful in hunting ever."

"I have always been interested in the myths and beliefs of different tribes," commented Bald Eagle. "Tell me another one."

So, River Wolf told another story about Ataga'hi, the Enchanted Lake:

"In the deepest and most isolated part of the mountains of the Cherokee territory, there is a beautiful lake known as Ataga'hi. It is known to exist, though nobody except for the animals have seen it because it is so difficult to reach. It is said that if a wandering hunter gets near the area of the lake, he would know by the sounds of the wings of thousands of ducks flapping. These ducks live in the lake, and move about it. But if the hunter got to the site of the lake, he would only see a flat desert, void of plant or animal life. It is possible to see the lake, after he honed his spiritual vision by fasting and praying throughout the night.

"Most people believe the lake is long since dried up, but that is untrue. If the steps mentioned are done correctly, the lake's water will appear at sunrise, as a wide but shallow body of purple water, with springs in the towering cliffs that surround the lake. The lake is the home of ducks, pigeons, all types of fish, and reptiles.

"Bear tracks are often seen all over the shores of the lake. It is said that when a bear is wounded by a hunter, it heads for the lake, and dives into the water. When the bear emerges out of the opposite shore, his wounds are healed. This Medicine lake of the animals and birds is kept invisible so that hunters can't see it."

"That was a charming tale," said Bald Eagle. "Let's hear another."
River Wolf began:

"There was once a hunter who had hunted for a very long time, but failed to find any deer. Finally, out of despair, he sat down on a log to think of what he should do next.

"A buzzard who was passing overhead saw him and went down to investigate. The buzzard asked 'What seems to be the trouble?'

"'I have been hunting all day and have seen no deer to shoot and take home to my wife.'

"There are lots of deer over the ridge. If you could see it from above, you would be able to bring home all the deer you could want! Why don't we trade places?'

"So the buzzard and the hunter traded places, and the hunter flew over the ridge, while the buzzard went to the hunter's lodge and wife. All the while, the wife thought the buzzard was her husband. Finally, the buzzard said he would go hunting again.

"He met the hunter, in the same place where they'd parted ways, and they changed forms again. After the buzzard departed, the hunter killed several deer. His hunting was always successful after that."

"Tell me another one," said Bald Eagle.

"This is a long story," River Wolf told him, "about the origin of corn and game." River Wolf started:

"Many cycles ago, not long after the world was made, a great hunter named Kanati lived with his wife, Selu. They had one son who also lived with them. Kanati was a very successful hunter, never returning empty-handed. Selu would always prepare the meat, and wash the blood off of it in the nearby river.

"Their son spent his time playing in the river. One day they heard the sounds of more than one child playing, talking and laughing at the river. When the boy returned home that night, they asked him with whom he was playing. The boy said, 'He emerges from the river and says he is my older brother.'

"Now they knew their son's new companion had sprung forth from the blood in the meat that Selu had washed in the river. Their son played with the mysterious boy every day, but neither Kanati nor Selu ever saw the boy. One evening, they instructed their son to challenge the boy to a wrestling match the next morning. They told him to call for them while the two boys wrestled, so they could see this boy.

"The boy from the river agreed to the match, and as soon as they gripped each other, Kanati's and Selu's son called for them. His parents came down quickly to see. The Wild Boy saw them and shouted, 'Let me go now! You cast me aside!' The boy kept a tight grip on the Wild Boy until his parents could help drag him home with them. They locked him in the lodge until he was tame, but he never totally lost his mischievous disposition. He usually was the instigator when the boys got into trouble. They soon learned that he possessed magical powers, and they named him He Who Grew Up Wild.

"Every time Kanati returned from hunting in the mountains, he always brought back a plump deer, or some turkeys. Wild Boy observed this, and said, 'Why don't we follow Father next time he leaves, and then we can see where he gets all of his game.' Soon after, Kanati left, taking his bow and some feathers. He went westward, and the two brothers followed him from a distance so their presence would not be known.

"Kanati arrived at a swamp that was abounding in reeds that were good for making arrow shafts out of. Wild Boy used his magic to transform himself into a piece of bird's down. The wind carried him towards Kanati, and he landed on Kanati's shoulder undetected. Kanati cut pieces of cane, and attached feathers to the shafts to make arrows.

"The Wild Boy, still in the form of a piece of down, wondered what the arrows were for. Kanati finished the arrows, and resumed his journey. Wild Boy was blown off of Kanati's shoulder, and then he returned to his usual shape. He then told his brother what he saw, while giving Kanati a head start. Once again, they followed him at a distance.

"Kanati arrived at a certain place up the mountain, and removed a large rock, exposing a hole. A large buck immediately ran out of the hole, and Kanati shot it with one of the arrows. He then carried the buck on his shoulders back towards home.

"The boys were surprised and amazed that he kept the game in the hole, and killed it with the arrows. They ran home as fast as they could, and arrived there before their father got back. Kanati was totally unaware that he had been followed.

"Several days later, the boys went to the same swamp, and made seven arrows. Then they went to the hole in the mountain where Kanati was keeping the game. They lifted the rock, and a deer ran out of the hole. They got ready to shoot it with one of the arrows, but another deer ran out. It was followed by more and more deer. The boys were perplexed, and forgot why they were there.

"Wild Boy began shooting arrows at the deer, and struck them in the tails, forcing them to point up. Deer tails point upwards to this day. All of the deer escaped from the hole, and were followed by rabbits, raccoons, and other four-footed animals, except the bear, which did not exist yet. Finally, the fowls and birds came out of the hole. All the commotion raised a cloud of dust that darkened the sky, and it made a sound like thunder.

"Kanati heard this and said, 'My disobedient boys have gotten into mischief. I better go and find out what they have done.' He went to the hole in the mountainside, and found the two boys there next to the rock. All the animals had escaped, and Kanati was very angry. He entered the cave, and removed the lids off of four jars that were inside. Out came a multitude of gnats, bedbugs, lice and fleas. They covered the boys, and the boys screamed and attempted to brush them off. But they got stung and bit all over, and fell down almost dead.

"Kanati decided that they had been punished enough, so he brushed the bugs off of them and got them to talk to him. 'Now, you scoundrels,' he said, 'all your lives you have had plenty to eat without having to earn it. When we needed food, I just had to come up here and get some meat to take home. But from now on, we will have to hunt meat, without always being successful. Go home and I will try to get us some dinner.'

"The boys returned home, and were very hungry. They asked Selu for some food, but she said, 'There is no meat to eat. Wait here and I will find something.' She got a basket and went to the small storehouse that was raised off the ground, on poles. This kept the animals out. She climbed up the ladder to the door of the storehouse, which was the only opening in the building.

"Before cooking each meal, Selu would go into this storehouse with the basket, and return with it full of corn and beans. The children had never seen the inside of the building, and were curious about where the corn and beans came from. 'Let's find out what she does in there,' said Wild Boy. They went to the back of the storehouse and climbed up between the poles and made a hole in the clay daubing in the wall. They looked in and saw Selu standing in the center of the storehouse with the basket on the floor in front of her. She rubbed her stomach, and corn appeared in the basket. Then she rubbed her armpits, and beans appeared in the basket.

"The boys decided that she was a witch and that the food she prepared would poison them. 'We better kill her,' they agreed. They returned to the lodge, and Selu was waiting inside, and she apparently could read their thoughts. 'Are you going to kill me?' she asked. 'Yes, you're a witch,' they replied. 'Well then,' she said, 'after you kill me, clean up a large area in front of the lodge, and drag my dead body around in a circle, seven times. Then drag my body around seven times inside of the first circle. Stay up until dawn and keep watch, and at sunrise, you will have lots of corn.'

"They beat her to death with clubs, then cut off her head. Then they placed the severed head on the lodge roof, facing westward, and told the head to look for Kanati. They cleared the ground in front of the lodge, but only cleared seven small places instead of the whole area. For this reason, corn only grows in certain places instead of growing wild throughout the world. They drug her body around the circle twice, instead of the seven times that she had instructed. This is why corn is worked twice a cycle to this day. Now, the brothers watched the corn all night, the corn grew in the ground where Selu's blood had dripped. At dawn, the corn was ready to harvest.

"Kanati returned home and asked, 'Where is Selu?' They said that she was a witch and that they had killed her. 'Her head is on the roof of the lodge,' they said, while pointing. Kanati was full of rage and said, 'I am leaving you two, and I will now go to the Wolf People.' He left, and Wild Boy once again assumed the shape of a piece of down. He rode on Kanati's shoulder again, without being detected. Kanati arrived at the

Wolf People's village, and they were holding a meeting in their council house. He sat down, the piece of down still on his shoulder. Wolf Chief inquired of Kanati's business there, and he answered, 'There are two bad boys at my home. Can you go there in seven days, and play a ball game against them?' The Wolf People knew he really wanted them to kill the two brothers. The Wolf People promised to go.

"The piece of down that was Wild Boy was swept off of his shoulder, and the smoke from the fire blew it outside via the smoke hole in the roof. After landing on the ground, Wild Boy assumed his normal shape, and ran home. When he arrived, he told his brother the news. Kanati left the Wolf People, but instead of returning home, he went farther away.

"The two brothers started getting ready for the Wolf People's arrival. Wild Boy, being a magician, gave the orders. They made a trail that formed a wide circle around the lodge, leaving a small opening on the side the Wolf People were expected to enter. They made four bundles of arrows, and put them at four places along the outside of the circular path. Then they concealed themselves nearby in the woods and waited for the Wolf People. Within a day or two, a party of Wolf People appeared, and surrounded the lodge, intent on killing the boys. They failed to notice the trail, because they had entered the circle at the opening they had left. The moment they had entered the circle, the trail changed to a tall brush fence that trapped them. The brothers took the arrows they had made, and began shooting the Wolf People from outside of the brush fence. The Wolf People could not jump the brush fence, and soon most of them were killed. Some escaped out of the opening, and ran into a large nearby swamp. The brothers ran, circling the swamp, and fires were started in their tracks. The fire spread, and burned up almost all of the remaining Wolf People. Only two or three wolves escaped, and they were the ancestors of all wolves in the world today.

"Not long after, strangers appeared from a distance. They had heard about the wonderful grain that could be made into bread, and wanted to ask for some. At that time, only Selu's family had corn. The brothers gave them seven kernels of corn, and told them to plant them on their way home, the next night. The boys told them to stay awake, and watch all night long, and at sunrise they would have seven ears of corn. Then they were to plant all seven ears of kernels, and stay up watching. The strangers were seven days from their home village, and the boys told them to repeat this every night until they were at home. But after a few days, they were exhausted and fell asleep. When they awoke, the corn they had planted did not even sprout. They took what was left, and returned home with it. After vigilant care and time, they managed to get a crop from the last of the corn. To this day, corn must grow half of a cycle and be tended with care to be fruitful, instead of growing in a single night, as before.

"When Kanati failed to return, the brothers resolved to go and find him. Wild Boy got a chunkey stone and rolled it towards the Darkening Land of the West. After it rolled back, they knew he was not there. So they rolled it to the south, and it returned. They rolled it to the north and, once again, it came back. When they rolled it to the Sun Land to the East, it did not return, and they knew that Kanati was in that direction. They started their journey and, after a long while, they found him walking with a dog beside him. 'Are you bad boys here now?' asked Kanati. 'Yes,' answered the brothers, 'We are men and always reach the goals we set.' Kanati said, 'This dog started walking with me four days ago.' The brothers knew the dog was the chunkey stone they had sent rolling after him. Kanati continued, 'Well, now that you have found me, we might as well walk together, but I will lead.'

"They soon arrived at a swamp, and Kanati said, 'Stay away from the swamp, there is something dangerous there.' He walked ahead, and was soon out of sight. Immediately, Wild Boy said, 'Let's go and see what's in the swamp.' In the swamp, they found a giant mountain lion sleeping. Wild Boy shot an arrow into the side of the mountain lion's head. The mountain lion turned his head, and the other boy shot him in the other side of his head. The mountain lion turned his head again, and both brothers loosed several more arrows. But the mountain lion was never injured, and ignored them. They caught up with Kanati, and he said, 'Did you find the danger?' 'Yes,' they replied, 'but we are men, and we did not get hurt.' This surprised Kanati, but he said nothing, and they all started walking again.

"After they had gone a distance, and Kanati said, 'Watch out, we are passing through cannibal territory. If they catch you, they will roast and eat you.' Kanati continued walking. The brothers got to a tree that had been splintered by a lightning strike. Wild Boy said, 'Gather some of the splinters.' He told his brother what to do with them. Soon, they got to the cannibals' village and were spotted. The cannibals were hungry and said, 'Here are two fat boys that we can eat!' They captured the two brothers, took them to their council house, and put out the word that everybody in the village should attend the feast. They built a grand bonfire, and put a giant pot of water over it to boil. Then they threw Wild Boy into the boiling pot, but the other boy was not afraid, and didn't try to escape. He put his splinters into the fire like he was feeding it. After a while, the cannibals decided their meal was cooked, and removed the pot from the flames. Suddenly, blinding light filled the council house, and lightning bolts went from side to side, striking and killing all of the cannibals. The lightning then went out of the smoke hole above, and the two brothers appeared outside of the council house, unharmed. Again, they caught up with Kanati, and he was surprised to see them. 'Wow!' Are you back again?' he asked. 'Certainly, we do not give up! We are great men!' they replied. 'What did they do with you two?' asked Kanati. 'They brought us to the council house, but they failed to hurt us,' they answered. Kanati didn't say anymore, and they resumed walking.

"The two brothers lost sight of Kanati, and they continued walking until they reached the end of the world. They saw the giant inverted bowl of the sky vault coming down at the edge. They waited until the Sun pushed it up at sunrise the next morning, and passed under it before it shut behind them. As they climbed up the other side, they saw Kanati and Selu sitting next to each other. Their parents were kind, and welcomed the two brothers. They said that they could stay for a while, but then they would go to the Darkening Land to the West, and live there. The two brothers are still there, they are known to us as 'The Little Men,' or the 'Thunder Boys,' and we hear them speaking to each other in the form of thunder coming from the west.

"When the two brothers had let all of the game out of the hole in the mountain, hunters had great difficulty succeeding in getting food for a long time. The people began to starve. Then they heard that the Thunder Boys now resided in the Darkening Land to the West, behind the Sun's exit in the sky vault. They sent messengers to the Thunder Boys, as they knew the brothers could make the game return. The Thunder Boys visited, and told them to stand ready with bows and arrows. Then the Thunder Boys sat down in the center of the council house and sang. There came a noise like a strong wind in the northwest, and it became louder as the song progressed. When they sang their seventh song, a herd of deer appeared, led by a majestic buck. The hunters shot all of the deer they needed before the deer reached the woods.

"The Thunder Boys returned to the Darkening Land, after teaching the people the seven songs that would call the deer. Most of these songs have been long since forgotten, though some of them are still sung by hunters who are going after deer."

"That was a great story!" remarked Bald Eagle, "I want to hear another."

River Wolf started:

"The messenger of the birds is known as the little Wren. Early in the morning, each day, she flies through the village, checking every lodge, seeking news, and returns to the bird council to tell them what she was able to find out.

Little Wren.
Redrawn from a public domain image.

"After hearing of any baby's birth, the Wren flies up to see the gender of the child, which she reports to the bird council. If the child is a boy, the birds sing lamentations about how he will grow up and shoot them with his blowgun, cook them in a fire, and eat them.

"But if the child is a girl, the birds celebrate, singing of how she will someday grind corn and how they will get to feast off of the grains of corn left over from her sweeping.

"The Cricket also prefers girls to boys. When a boy is born, the Cricket wails, 'He will shoot us with his tiny arrows!'

"But when a girl child is born, the Cricket rejoices and gratefully offers to sing in the house of the baby."

"I liked that one," commented Bald Eagle, "You know so many stories. I never could remember them that well. Tell me another."

The tales made the days go by almost unnoticed. During this time, they paddled, camped and hunted. Now, Bald Eagle said they were approaching another Alabama Koasati village. They received a warm welcome from the locals. After the Sun went down, and they finished feasting, a single lady approached River Wolf. Now, he signed to the woman, "I am to be married."

The woman looked surprised, but said she understood. She signed, "Alright. Would you prefer to be alone?"

"Not at all," he signed. "I would love to pass the night in conversation with you, if that is okay."

She smiled cheerfully. "Okay, Follow me!" She led him to a guest lodge. When they entered, she asked, "What do you want to talk about?"

"Well, what is your name?"

"Mole," she signed. She seemed self-conscious about it.

"I like that name. I am River Wolf. Tell me about your people."

Mole signed, "Well, my father is the village Shaman."

"Really?"

"Yes. He has healed a lot of people too. My grandma had kidney issues and he gave her beggar lice of all things! But it worked, at least for her, it did."

River Wolf smiled and signed, "That's the plant with the tiny sticker burrs that cling to your legs when you walk through them! It's used in love potions and can improve your memory. A decoction, that you drink, is made from the root. This is the treatment for kidney problems."

"How did you know?"

"I started training for the priesthood when I was little, but I never finished the training."

"What do your people use for nervousness?"

"We use wild cherry. It calms the stomach, and is good for sore throats. It can also be used for sores and lung conditions. The bark can be made into a tonic that is good for digestion and has some sedative properties. Do you have anxiety?"

Mole looked away and signed, "Yes, I guess."

"It is nothing to be embarrassed about. If you want to talk about it, you can, but I won't be upset if you prefer not to." River Wolf seemed very sincere to her.

Mole's Namesake, a Mole.
Redrawn from Clker-Free-Vector-Images from Pixabay.

"I prefer not to. Well, I don't know. My mother and I were once at the river getting water, and an enemy warrior tried to kidnap us. I really don't like being away from the village at all."

"Was it a Yuchi warrior?"

"No, a Cherokee."

"How old were you?"

"Six cycles old."

"I am Cherokee."

Mole quickly looked down. "Sorry."

"It's okay. I'm not going to hurt you."

"Yes, I know. I'm sorry."

"I am no warrior though. I wish we could all just somehow…"

"Get along?" smiled Mole after a lengthy pause.

"Exactly. When you look at the people of different tribes, the people all care about each other. What I mean is, we have so much more in common than we do differences."

"You are right! You know? You have shown me that not all Cherokees are bad."

"We are all just people."

This time, Bald Eagle was in a separate lodge. It was just River Wolf and Mole. It gave River Wolf and Mole the chance to talk deep into the night, uninterrupted. River Wolf enjoyed talking with her, and learned much about her, her family, and her people. It occurred to him that these nights with village women had a real potential in that he could become better informed about the places he visited, which could have endless advantages. If nothing else, it was a chance to make friends. It also presented the opportunity to learn more of their languages.

The next morning, River Wolf gave Mole a bone bead necklace. It was common practice for a man to give a woman some sort of payment for hospitality but, there were no rules specifying what kinds of hospitality were to be shown. And even if there were, who would find out? River Wolf's gesture helped create whatever appearances she might need to be created. It was discreet, and raised no awkward questions from her fellow villagers. It was the perfect solution to the problem. Mole smiled and hugged him, and they parted ways.

River Wolf walked to the canoe and saw that Bald Eagle was already up and was negotiating a deal in Muskhogean with one of the villagers.

"Good morning, Bald Eagle," said River Wolf.

Bald Eagle ignored him, as the heat of bartering intensified. River Wolf now understood more of what was said between the two. He picked up the words "That's an insulting offer! Give me three of them and it's a deal," from the villager.

"Two is the best I can do," replied Bald Eagle, "if you throw in that conch shell."

"That's my best one!" exclaimed the villager, "I will give you the small conch shell, and two strings of freshwater pearls for the large copper nugget. That's my final offer."

Bald Eagle said, "This is not to my advantage, but I will go ahead and do it for you." and they made the exchange.

River Wolf silently laughed at Bald Eagle's style of negotiating. Bald Eagle would almost never agree to something not to his advantage, but it was important for people to think you are giving them a good deal, and Bald Eagle was a grandmaster at it.

Another villager had his eyes fixed on one of River Wolf's larger pieces of mica. He asked River Wolf in Muskhogean what he wanted in trade for it. River Wolf was about to answer him in the new language, but Bald Eagle quickly moved in and translated the man's words for River Wolf in signs. He thought it best that they think he couldn't understand Muskhogean.

River Wolf signed, "What do you offer?"

The man now believed that River Wolf could not understand the language, and turned to his wife and said, "Go and get the axe."

"The polished red one?" asked the wife.

River Wolf was curious to see this "polished red one."

"No, stupid!" replied the villager. "Get that old, ugly one."

River Wolf now saw the advantage of the locals not knowing that he understood their language. He waited for the woman to return, while conversing in signs with the villager.

The woman returned with the axe, and showed it to River Wolf. After inspecting it, River Wolf thought to himself that mica of this quality and size was not common in this area. He signed, "Do you have an axe that's made any better than this one? Do you have something that has a good polished finish?"

The villager had a reluctant look on his face. After thinking about it for a while, he turned to his wife and said, "Go get the polished one."

Then he signed, "Wait for a little bit, she is getting a better axe. It's polished smooth. You will love it!"

The woman left with the axe, and the villager continued his conversation with River Wolf.

She returned with the polished red axe, and it was a beauty. They made the trade. Bald Eagle and River Wolf remained at that village for another day and, the morning after, they resumed their journey down the river.

Bald Eagle said, "You did well. I thought you might blunder and speak to that man. Do you see how a trader can profit by being mysterious?"

"Yes," replied River Wolf, "thank you for stopping me."

"Tell me another story," said Bald Eagle.

"Let me think," said River Wolf. "Oh! I know a good one, this is about the Stone Man," and he began:

"One time all of the men of a certain village were on a great hunt. One man who volunteered to scout on ahead climbed to the top of a tall ridge, and discovered a large wide river flowing on the other side. He looked across the river and saw an older man moving around on the opposite ridge. He carried a cane made from a shiny, and glowing, type of stone. The scout watched him for a while and he observed the old man pointing the cane here and there, and smelling the bottom end of the cane every time he pointed it at something. Then he pointed the cane in the direction of the scout, and then smelled it repeatedly, as if it smelled very good. Then the old man began walking down the ridge, very slowly, towards the hunters' camp. He reached the river, and tossed the cane into the air in front of him, and the cane turned into a shiny stone bridge that crossed the river. When he finished crossing the river, the bridge changed back to the cane. The old man grabbed it, and continued towards the hunters' camp.

"The scout feared trouble, and decided to return to the camp to warn his people before the old man arrived there. The scout lost no time in telling the Shaman about what he had seen, and the Shaman said the old man was an evil cannibal named 'Dressed in Stone.' He said the cannibal dwelt in the area, looking for stray hunters that he could eat. He was difficult to avoid, because his cane could lead him to food, like a dog. He couldn't be killed easily because his skin was made of the hardest stone.

"The Shaman warned that if the old man found them, he would eat all of them, but there was a way for them to save themselves. The old man was afraid of women in their moon time and, if they could locate seven women in their moon time and place them between him and them, he would die when he saw them.

"They found the seven women who were menstruating, one of whom had just started. The Shaman instructed them to remove their clothing and stand in the trail that the old man would be taking. Soon, Dressed in Stone was upon the first woman. He saw her, and said, 'Oh! Grandchild! You don't look too good!' and he made haste to pass her by. Then he saw the second woman, and his reaction was, 'Oh! Daughter! You look terrible!' and as he walked past her, he began vomiting blood. Each woman that he passed by made him sicker and sicker and, when he saw the seventh woman – the one who had just begun menstruating – blood poured out from his mouth and he fell over onto the ground.

"The Shaman pinned his body to the ground with sourwood spikes. After dark, the people piled large logs over the old man's body and built a great fire there. Dressed in Stone was a magician and knew many great secrets. He began telling the people all the cures for diseases. Then at midnight, he started singing songs that called game near. His voice grew deeper and deeper as he burned. By morning, his voice couldn't be heard, and all that was left was a pile of white ashes.

"The Shaman instructed them to clean the ashes off of where the old man lay. All they found was some red paint, and a magic Crystal. The Shaman kept the Crystal, and painted the hunters on the face and chest with the red paint. The people prayed as they were being painted, for hunting success, or a long life. They got all they asked for in their prayers."

"Let's go up this tributary," said Bald Eagle. "There is a good source of flint east of here, three days upstream. It's the best flint source I know about. Afterwards we will return to the river and go upstream for a day and-a-half. But we will worry about that when we have to."

They began the arduous task of paddling up the stream. River Wolf was now thinking about how difficult the trip back home would be. It would be upstream for a long distance. After three days, River Wolf's muscles ached terribly. They beached the canoe and walked uphill from the riverbank. They each carried a large bag to load with flint.

"There is an eccentric old recluse who lives in this area," said Bald Eagle. "He is very nice, but a little strange."

"What is his name?" asked River Wolf.

"I don't really know," answered Bald Eagle. "Most people just call him Loner."

"Why doesn't he live in a village with other people?"

"You will just have to meet him. Then you will understand. If we do run into him – and I am sure we will – try to be tolerant of his strange behavior. He lives where the flint outcroppings are, and we should each give him a little trinket for the flint we take from the area. Then he will welcome us here in the future."

They walked up the hill in silence. River Wolf noticed that the birds were silent also.

"We are getting close," said Bald Eagle. "Loner! Loner!"

"What do you want?" asked a stranger from behind.

Both River Wolf and Bald Eagle were startled, and quickly turned to look.

"Loner!" greeted Bald Eagle. "How are you doing, old friend?"

"Hello Bald Eagle," said Loner. "Who is this? He isn't going to start any trouble, is he?"

"No," replied Bald Eagle, "he is a friend. He won't hurt you. He is traveling with me."

"You are not a cannibal, are you?" Loner asked River Wolf, as he circled him, eyeing him up and down, suspiciously.

"No! I am River Wolf. I am here to pick up some flint."

"Flint!" exclaimed Loner with a thoughtful smile, "Flint, flint, flint. Flint! Come on, we will eat. I just killed a big rabbit. Let's eat. Let's eat! Let's eat! I'm no flying snail, so there! Why don't we eat? Follow me."

Bald Eagle motioned River Wolf to follow Loner. They arrived at Loner's small, and crude, shelter. Loner whistled a skilled bird call, and a chickadee immediately flew out of the shelter and landed on his head. Loner reached over and picked up the chickadee and placed it on his shoulder. Then he put the gutted rabbit on the spit, and then over the fire. He rotated it slowly.

"What's your chickadee's name?" asked Bald Eagle.

"Chickadee!" replied Loner. "What else?"

Loner's Bird, "Chickadee."
Redrawn from a public domain image.

"So, have you been to a village lately?" asked Bald Eagle.

"Those people just want to control my mind," replied Loner. "All they ever do is try to think me into all kinds of trouble."

Suddenly, Loner reached over and slapped River Wolf very hard. River Wolf was shocked and angry. He was about to start yelling at Loner, but Bald Eagle spoke before he could.

"Was it a spider?" asked Bald Eagle.

"Yes!" replied Loner, "It was one of those big hairy ones too! I didn't want it to bite your friend."

River Wolf began speaking, "But there was no spider on…"

Bald Eagle interrupted him again, "River Wolf, you should thank Loner for stopping that spider from biting you."

"But…"

"He saved your life. Thank him."

River Wolf realized that Bald Eagle was dropping him a hint. "Thank you, Loner," he said.

"Don't mention it," said Loner with a satisfied smile. "Last night there were hundreds of them crawling all over me. I was really scared they would bite me, but I asked my bird to tell them to leave."

"Did they leave?" asked Bald Eagle.

"Chickadee said, 'Get out of here, you bad hairy spiders!' and they left," replied Loner. "I'm glad I rescued her, last cycle, when she fell out of her nest. You know something? She's my only true friend."

They ate dinner with Loner, and then went to sleep outside on the ground. Loner only had one bed, for himself. It was an uncomfortable night on the rock ground. River Wolf had a hard time sleeping.

When he did doze off, he was quickly awakened by the sound of Loner slapping Bald Eagle on the chest.

Bald Eagle woke up saying, "What!" he groaned out of annoyance and said, "Thanks Loner!" He sounded slightly irritated about being awakened.

"You are welcome," came the reply.

They both went back to sleep, but River Wolf had trouble getting back to sleep. He turned over on the hard ground, and he was glad that they would be leaving the next day. He hoped that Loner would not have anymore spider hallucinations again. Eventually he fell asleep.

The next morning, Bald Eagle and River Wolf were awakened by Loner's shouting.

He said, "Chickadee, tell those crickets to go away, and leave me alone! I'm tired of it! Tell them to go and bother the spiders!"

River Wolf yawned, and got up. Loner had caught a fish and was cooking it. Bald Eagle got up slowly, and in pain from sleeping on the hard ground.

After eating, Loner led them to a place that was very abundant with large pieces of flint. River Wolf had never seen so much of it, and he was very impressed. They loaded their bags, and Loner carried some more with them back to the canoe.

Bald Eagle then gave Loner a turkey-bone necklace, and River Wolf gave him a carved bone human effigy he had traded for. Loner smiled like a child.

"You and River Wolf come back soon," he said.

"Goodbye, Loner," said Bald Eagle.

River Wolf waved at him and they shoved off.

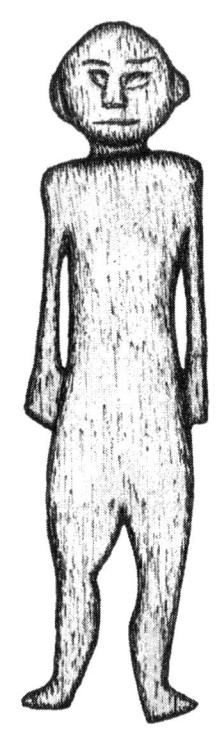

River Wolf's Gift to Loner.
Redrawn from Beauchamp 1902.

Chapter 9: Good Medicine

The trip back to the river was an easy one – all they had to do was steer the canoe. When they arrived at the river, it became extremely difficult. They had to paddle constantly to keep ahead of the current. River Wolf was already sore from the trip up the stream.

"How far did you say we had to go?" he asked.

"A day and-a-half," replied Bald Eagle. "It's good for you. It makes your arms *strong!* You will definitely need *that* when we make the trip back to your village."

"Where are we going?"

"To *my* village – eventually."

"What is the name of your village?"

"Good Medicine. We will be going up another creek to the west again. Then we will have to drag the dugout over another ridge. But this one's not as far. A half-day on the other side is another creek that flows into the Black Warrior River. Good Medicine is several days downstream. We will be staying there for a couple of weeks. But there are several settlements between here and there."

They continued paddling for the rest of the day and, that evening, they stopped to hunt some food. Bald Eagle managed to shoot a wild turkey with an arrow. The first thing he did was pull out all of the wing feathers and tail feathers so he could save them. He might be able to trade them for a favor someday. They ate the turkey and fell asleep.

Wild Turkey.
Redrawn from a public domain image.

Next morning they were back in the canoe early. River Wolf's arms were terribly sore, but he continued paddling. Just before sunset, they reached a creek that joined the river on the west side.

"Here is where we turn," said Bald Eagle.

They went up the creek until sunset, and set up camp. Lightning was lighting up the western sky, and Bald Eagle became nervous.

"That rain is headed in this direction," he said, "We'd better turn the dugout over and put all the wares underneath. Let's drag it well away from the river in case it floods. Don't forget to get some water."

River Wolf filled several clay bottles. They turned the canoe upside down, and under it they placed the turkey feather cloaks, furs and other items that would be ruined if they got wet. They also put some firewood under the canoe to protect it from the rain. River Wolf's effigy pipes and stone carvings were placed outside; the water would not harm them. Soon the rain arrived, and it lasted all night. River Wolf and Bald Eagle slept in the rain, and the next morning the stream was flooded.

"The creek is really up high," Bald Eagle said as River Wolf was getting up. "Why don't you make one of your squirrel traps?"

"Alright," returned River Wolf.

Then he went to the canoe to get some twine to use for the nooses. By noon, he returned with four squirrels. Bald Eagle built a fire with some of the firewood they had stored beneath the canoe, while River Wolf finished cleaning the squirrels.

"You sure are good with that leaning-log squirrel trap," complimented Bald Eagle, while he put the first squirrel on a spit.

"How far is it to the portage?" asked River Wolf.

"About two days," answered Bald Eagle.

"I didn't think it would be that far," said River Wolf, disappointed.

"The creek is high and therefore the current is faster," explained Bald Eagle, "but we will camp here until it goes down a little."

"Well, I am going to make some arrowheads."

River Wolf then went to the swollen creek to get a hammerstone to use. When he got to the bank, he slipped in the mud and fell in.

He returned soaked, but with the hammerstone. He spent the rest of the day making arrow points and swapping stories with Bald Eagle.

"Do you have a turkey leg bone that I can split and use for notching?" asked River Wolf. "Or a deer rib?"

"I have a deer rib that I use for that, in the leather bag in the back of the canoe," replied Bald Eagle.

River Wolf found it and notched five arrow points. Then he went and cut some hardwood saplings to use as arrow shafts. He stripped the bark off of them with a spokeshave crafted from a chip of flint with a manmade notch on its side. Then he straightened them over the fire, and Bald Eagle gave him some of the turkey feathers to use for fletching. After fastening the flint tips, he had five new arrows for hunting.

River Wolf went out hunting for a deer to feed them for several days. After a half a day he returned, carrying a doe over his shoulders.

"Hey!" said Bald Eagle. "Good work!"

"I dropped it in its tracks with one arrow too!" bragged River Wolf.

They dressed and cleaned the deer, which had been shot directly in the heart. The eating was good. They camped by the creek for three days, until the water returned almost to normal. Then they loaded up the dugout, and resumed paddling upstream. River Wolf had an easier time propelling the dugout upstream, as his muscles had begun to get stronger from the constant rowing.

They continued paddling constantly against the current, and stopped just before sunset. They ate and went to sleep. River Wolf dreamed of Beaver Pelt, and his mother and aunt. He woke up downhearted. It had now been two moons since he had left them.

Bald Eagle returned with two rabbits and said, "Tonight we will not have to hunt our food. There is a Muskogee village a half a day's journey upstream. We can trade for some *cornbread!*"

River Wolf said nothing and had a sad expression on his face.

"Miss your girl, huh?" asked Bald Eagle.

"It's been a little while now," replied River Wolf. "And it will be even longer until I see my family again."

"Yes, I remember my first trading trip," related Bald Eagle, "but you will get used to being away from home eventually. But then, you start to realize you are free! You get to do what you want, and go where you want, and there is nobody to argue about it with you."

"I plan on taking Beaver Pelt along on my next trip."

"Well, it can be very pleasant with a woman traveling with you also. I packed me a wife along for a little while. It wasn't too bad."

They ate and resumed their journey upstream. The Sun was getting low in the sky when the trader announced that they were almost to the village.

"What is this village called?" asked River Wolf.

"Rattlesnake Creek," came the reply.

They made it around the bend, and River Wolf saw the palisade and buildings of the village. The guards at the palisade entrance ran to the shore to see who the approaching strangers were. But they had bad news.

"Traders, you may as well continue upstream," said one of the guards, keeping his distance.

"What is the matter?" asked Bald Eagle.

"There are evil spirits in the village. Leave before they attack you."

"You will be in our prayers," said Bald Eagle, "We will see you next cycle."

The guard nodded and returned to the village. Bald Eagle and River Wolf continued upstream. River Wolf wondered what these villagers had done to provoke the rogue spirits.

"Well, it looks like we won't have cornbread after all," said Bald Eagle, disappointed.

"How far is the next village?" asked River Wolf.

"On the other side of the ridge."

River Wolf's heart sank. He had so much been looking forward to a woman's cooking. They paddled on, and swapped more tales. Well after sunset, Bald Eagle deemed that they were far away enough to not be affected by the evil spirits, so they stopped there and set up camp.

The next morning they started out early. By late afternoon, the waterway was becoming more shallow and narrower. They were nearly at the headwaters of the creek.

"Well, here comes the fun part," said Bald Eagle, sarcastically. "Now, we drag the canoe up the ridge to the creek on the other side. It will only take half a day if we move fast. But we will camp here and start across tomorrow morning."

"I will try to get some game," offered River Wolf.

He had no luck getting a raccoon or a rabbit, but managed to shoot a small young buck with an arrow. He returned back to camp late at night.

Young Whitetail Buck.
Drawn from photo by J. R. Anderson.

"I was wondering when you would bring dinner," said Bald Eagle, tending the fire he had started.

Together they dressed the deer and cooked it over the fire. River Wolf saved the hide for trading. The next morning they began carrying and dragging the dugout uphill over the low ridge. They reached the creek on the other side in the late afternoon, and set off downstream.

River Wolf noticed his foot was wet, and he looked down to see why. It was then that River Wolf noticed a crack in the canoe. There was a small puddle on the bottom. He pointed it out to Bald Eagle.

"Oh, toe jam!" lamented Bald Eagle. "We're going to have to somehow manage. Do you know how old this canoe is?"

River Wolf said, "I couldn't even guess."

"Too old! We will make do, and bail out water, I guess."

Fortunately, the journey was so much faster and easier now that they were drifting downstream. Instead of rowing, they bailed. Just before dark, they arrived at a Muskogee village where the creek joined the Black Warrior River. The village guards approached them with their bows ready and, when they identified the canoe's occupants, they rushed back to the village to announce their arrival. The welcome was warm, and River Wolf was looking forward to the feast they would soon enjoy.

"What is the name of this village?" asked River Wolf.

"Dead Hickory," replied Bald Eagle.

The village chieftain appeared and said, "I am Chief Copperhead. Welcome to Dead Hickory."

Bald Eagle replied by introducing himself and River Wolf. They ate an excellent meal of cornbread, venison, mushrooms, and many other delicacies, including crawfish, which River Wolf found especially tasty.

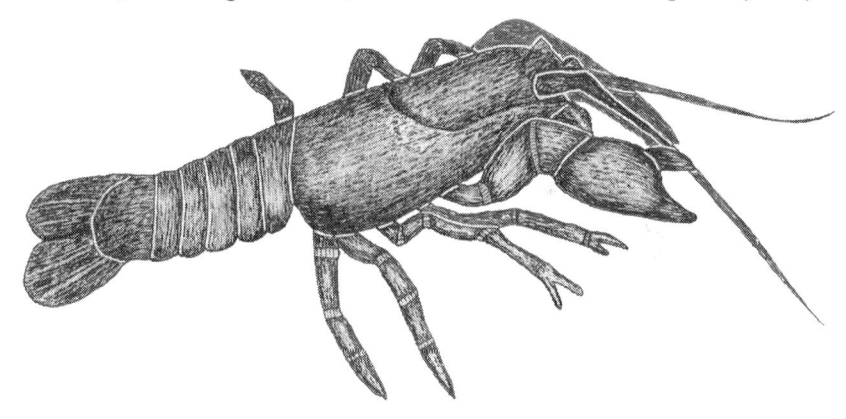

Crawfish.
Drawn from photo by Perkons from Pixabay.

While they feasted, Bald Eagle mentioned to Copperhead the evil spirits that were ravaging Rattlesnake Creek.

Copperhead said, "They just attacked us here at Dead Hickory two moons ago! They killed many of our residents, but our Shaman successfully drove them away."

"Do you mind me asking how he did it?" asked Bald Eagle.

"By using a plant called 'rattlesnake's master.'"

River Wolf had learned about this herb while in training for the priesthood. He remembered Eagle Medicine saying it was good for impotence, inflammation of the genitals, laryngitis, and bronchitis. River Wolf thought it curious and even amazing that it had apparently successfully driven away evil spirits attacking an entire village!

Now, Chief Copperhead slyly asked, "Do you like games?"

Bald Eagle replied, "Only if there is lots of wagering involved."

Copperhead laughed and said, "We can do that! Red Wolf! Go and get the gaming pieces!"

A younger servant man left the lodge and returned a short while later with some bone sticks that were each incised on one side. They apparently were used in a sort of dice game. River Wolf wanted to see how this game was played. What he didn't realize was that Copperhead was a clever old fox, who had intended to take advantage of Bald Eagle.

Before the night was over, Copperhead owned Bald Eagle's dugout canoe. River Wolf was terribly upset at the foolishness of Bald Eagle! He wondered how Bald Eagle could be so badly beaten at his own game!

But before River Wolf could confront him, two village women came, to provide companionship for the two guests. River Wolf would have to wait. But he was feeling quite irate.

One of the women showed River Wolf to her lodge and, as before, River Wolf and his female companion talked till late that night. Although he was angry, he knew better than to talk about it with anybody but Bald Eagle himself. He couldn't do that till the next day, so he had to wait.

So, he just had to ignore his anger and try to somehow enjoy his visit with this woman. Her name was Pearl, he found out, and her father had, in his youth, been a captive Cherokee warrior who was enslaved. Eventually, she said he had earned his freedom and the trust of the village, and started a family and lived the rest of his days there at Dead Hickory. River Wolf thought it was nice to have met a woman who was possibly kin to him, in such a faraway place.

The next morning, they were trading their wares to the villagers. There was a great demand for River Wolf's effigy pipes. He traded for numerous items, including shell necklaces and freshwater pearls. He also traded some of his flint that he had picked up at Loner's place. But how would they leave here with all of this stuff? There was no canoe!

After the trading was finished, they had a little time alone. "Why did you lose your only canoe to Chief Copperhead so easily and carelessly?" asked River Wolf. "You had to play the fool, and now, you lost!"

Bald Eagle smiled and said, "It had a leak." He turned around, and grabbed three turkey feather cloaks. "Please unload all of our things out of my... I mean out of *Copperhead's* canoe. I'll be back," he said with a smile, and he walked into the village.

River Wolf was furious! With great resentment, he began unloading the canoe.

Shortly after, Copperhead and Bald Eagle walked up, and Copperhead said, "There it is." He was pointing at a larger canoe.

Bald Eagle looked it over carefully, and said, "It's a trade!"

Copperhead smiled, shook Bald Eagle's hand, and returned to the village.

"River Wolf," said Bald Eagle, "could you help load our wares into this larger, better, newer canoe?"

River Wolf didn't believe his eyes or ears! But he did what Bald Eagle had asked. When they finished loading everything aboard, they said their farewells to the villagers.

They started down the Black Warrior River in the brand new, recently-made dugout. Bald Eagle's mood was noticeably improved, as they would be arriving at his home village in two weeks.

"Do you mind explaining to me exactly what happened back there?" asked River Wolf.

Bald Eagle smiled cleverly, and said, "I meant to lose the leaky canoe in the game because, although it seemed like a big prize to the Chief, it was worthless. Copperhead won it, as is, sight unseen. It was too dark for them to inspect it, but they wouldn't have looked it over anyhow! They thought they would win it, and I hoped they would! If I had wagered something else, I would have been out of that something else, and nobody would have wanted my canoe after inspecting it, and I would have had to leave it behind anyway. So I wagered it, as is, and I knew they'd be content with that. It was an old leaky canoe, and I don't need it. But Copperhead won it, and thought he had gotten the best of me. That's what I wanted – for him to believe he'd outsmarted me. And the three turkey feather cloaks, well, I traded them to his wife for this bigger canoe, instead of losing them in the game. Copperhead was more willing to give me a better deal on this new bigger canoe, because of my apparent "bad luck" last night. Basically, it was all just my surefire way to lose a game without really losing at all."

River Wolf's jaw was gaping. "You old swindler!"

"I never told a single lie! If Copperhead had asked me if there was a leak, I would have surely told him there *was* a leak. But, he was trying so hard to take advantage of me, he made himself fair game for me!"

River Wolf just shook his head with a chuckle.

Bald Eagle laughed. Copperhead had thought he had outsmarted Bald Eagle, but Bald Eagle was far more clever than anybody had thought, even River Wolf.

They traveled downstream until just before sunset. Then they set up camp. Bald Eagle said they were near a Muskogee village – but he thought it would be better to arrive in the morning, lest the villagers suspect mischief. River Wolf was sent to hunt some food to accompany the cornbread they had bartered for at Dead Hickory.

He walked silently through the woods, with his bow ready, in search of a rabbit or a deer. He had wandered far from the camp, without any luck. Suddenly he felt a powerful blow to his abdomen. He cried out as he saw the Muskogee arrow protruding from his belly. He sank to the ground and soon was surrounded by three young Muskogee hunters. He knew that he looked like a Cherokee and, without Bald Eagle, he would be treated like an enemy captive.

One of the hunters pulled out the arrow, and the pain almost made River Wolf faint. The three hunters smiled at his suffering, and began dragging their prisoner back to their village. River Wolf could understand most of their words.

One said, "We will be regarded as great warriors now!"

River Wolf tried to tell them that he was a traveling trader, but they didn't believe him, and would punch him in the stomach every time he spoke. The blood was running freely down his breechclout, and he felt weaker by the minute.

Well after dark, they arrived at a Muskogee village downstream from where Bald Eagle camped. River Wolf hoped he would not be killed before Bald Eagle arrived in the morning. He began to worry that Bald Eagle would not know where to find him.

The villagers crowded around him, beating and slapping him. Many of the village women spat in his face. They tied him to a stake and left him there all night long. He could not sit down, let alone sleep. The pain was unbearable. He tried to relax his legs, but the binding dug into his wrists, and hurt badly.

He began to pray. *Oh Long Being, rescue me or let me die quickly.* Then he passed out. He saw Beaver Pelt crying over him. Then he saw the Wolf at Thunder River, watching over him. He woke up with his hands asleep and stood to allow blood to flow to his hands. His consciousness faded and returned several times throughout the night.

Just after dawn, the villagers began a naming ceremony for the three young braves who had brought him to the village. Once that was done, they began piling brush around the pole that River Wolf was tied to. They were going to burn him at the stake! There was no Honored Woman here to save him.

The excited villagers began setting fire to the brush, and River Wolf was sure this was the end. The flames reached his feet and the pain was excruciating. But River Wolf had decided not to give them the satisfaction of his crying out, though every part of him wanted to.

He closed his eyes, and surrendered himself to his death. Suddenly there was a commotion on the edge of the village square, and soon after the villagers were hastily moving away the burning brush. River Wolf opened his eyes and saw Bald Eagle working quickly with them.

Then a man of status ordered one of the young warriors to cut River Wolf free of the stake. This was the same hunter who had shot him with the arrow. He had a shameful expression on his face. He now knew he had really messed up. Bald Eagle and the young warrior helped River Wolf to a guest lodge, and a Shaman immediately treated him. The Shaman's treatment was different than what he was accustomed to, and he secretly wondered if it would be very effective.

The Cherokees would have treated his wounds with a plant with lavender flowers known as woundwort. There were two varieties, the hedge variety, which grew in the woods. The marsh variety grew in moister areas. They both were used for treating worms. But the tea made from woundwort was good for internal wounds, or for washing external wounds. It helped stop bleeding, and promoted healing. That was what Eagle Medicine would have likely used in this situation, but this Muskogee Shaman instead used another plant, unknown to River Wolf. River Wolf just hoped he would heal quickly, no matter the means.

Then the village Chief entered and apologized profusely to River Wolf and Bald Eagle for the misconduct of the young warriors. He gave River Wolf an exquisite duck effigy pottery bowl.

Duck Effigy Pottery Bowl.
Redrawn from Moorehead 1900.

It was skillfully crafted and stunningly beautiful. The duck's head was gracefully and artistically made, by a woman or man who was obviously very experienced in pottery making. The Chief must have felt enormous guilt about what had happened to give him a gift like this.

River Wolf thanked him, and the Chief left. River Wolf was in terrible pain and had fever for several weeks. During this time, several nice women visited him to keep him company and ease his suffering. They brought flowers and placed them in the pottery bowl in hopes that it would lift his spirits.

River Wolf really enjoyed their visits, though he wished he could be in better health. There was one in particular who he liked, named Goldfinch. Although she looked completely different, her personality and mannerisms reminded River Wolf of Beaver Pelt.

The Chief visited River Wolf every day and was constantly apologizing to him. He ordered the young hunters who had injured River Wolf to provide food for him while he recovered.

One day, Bald Eagle visited him and asked how he was doing.

"I feel terrible," replied River Wolf, "but I will manage."

"I took the liberty of trading some of your pipes and mica for you," said Bald Eagle.

"What did you get for them?"

"Some engraved shell jewelry. I know how much demand there is for these items at your home."

Shell Spider Gorget with Fenestrations.
Adapted from Holmes 1880.

Bald Eagle pulled out a beautiful engraved spider gorget necklace and showed it to River Wolf. It was exquisite. The outline of the spider was cut out, and there were crescent-shaped fenestrations, or shaped holes that formed a circle around the gorget.

"What is the name of this village?" asked River Wolf.

"Leaning Oak," answered Bald Eagle.

"Well, I am sorry to delay your visit to your home."

"It was not your fault; I am the one who sent you out hunting alone so close to an unfamiliar village. I feel bad for my neglect."

Eventually, the burns on River Wolf's feet were mostly healed, and the time came for him to try to walk. It was painful, and his legs had become weak. But he was determined to get back to normal, the sooner the better. He wanted to return home to Beaver Pelt as soon as possible. All the attention from the single women of this village had made him very homesick.

His gut still grieved him from the arrow, but he sat and did some flint knapping. He made a large knife and gave it to the young warrior, who had shot him, as a peace offering. There could be no hard feelings; that would only jeopardize business on later trading visits.

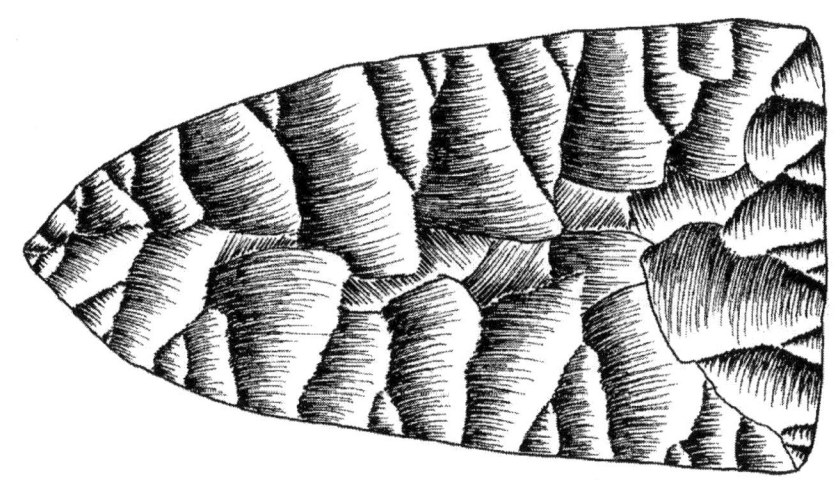

River Wolf's Peace Offering to the Young Warrior.

Finally the day came when River Wolf felt well enough to travel again. Bald Eagle visited him and he told him he was ready. That night the Chief held a feast in their honor.

The next morning, they left the village of Leaning Oak with plenty of cornbread and dried meat given to them by the village Chief. River Wolf's gut was still a little sore, and he was very glad they would be traveling downstream.

They traveled all day and, at sunset, they beached the dugout and set up camp. Just as they began eating, they heard a rustling noise from the woods nearby. Bald Eagle and River Wolf stood up to look, and immediately a cougar appeared. They ran to the water, knowing that cats did not like getting wet. They stood and watched the cougar as he ate up all of their dried meat and cornbread.

"Why didn't I get my bow and arrows?" lamented Bald Eagle. "Now we will have to cross the river and sleep on the other side."

They began crossing the river, and the water was very cold. Once they reached the opposite bank, they pulled up grass to make bedding. They lay down, and worried about the safety of their merchandise on the other bank.

The next morning, they quietly crossed back over and gathered their things that had been scattered by the cougar. There was no food left. They were cold, hungry, and angry. The cougar had even chewed up their sinew bowstrings. They loaded up the dugout and shoved off. About two hundred paces downstream they heard the scream of the cougar. It sounded just like a woman's scream. They looked and saw him up in a tree overlooking the river. The cougar screamed again, looking at them as they passed by.

"Shut up you thief!" shouted Bald Eagle.

"I am so hungry," said River Wolf.

"So am I," replied Bald Eagle. "Let's go to the other bank and maybe you can find something to make into twine, so you can set one of your squirrel traps. We will get new bowstrings at the next village."

They beached the canoe, and River Wolf found a fibrous plant and made his cord nooses for the squirrel trap. By noon, the trap was set. Then he left the trap and returned to the dugout canoe and they took a nap. When they awoke, River Wolf went to check the traps, and found five squirrels dangling from the nooses.

"Well, it looks like we have lost another day," said Bald Eagle while they dressed the squirrels.

"Can you throw an axe?" asked River Wolf.

"It's been awhile."

"My best friend taught me how. If we have more troubles with animals bent on thieving, I am a good aim with an axe."

"That's good to hear. I would say we should get a deer with your axe, so we could make bowstrings, but then the squirrel meat would go to waste. You'd better make a fire so we can cook these."

The fire pot had gone out because they could not tend it while they were away the previous night. River Wolf had to start the fire from scratch. He found a sapling and cut it to use as an armature. Then he split a dry piece of wood for a hearth stick. He made a depression in the hearth stick and put one end of the armature in the depression. Then he twirled the armature back and forth between his palms. It began smoking, and he fed the coals with tinder. He blew on the coals and soon had a small fire going. He added more and more wood and finally had a good strong fire.

They put the squirrels on spits and cooked them over the fire. Then River Wolf put some of the new coals into his fire pot. They ate, and went to sleep early – they planned to resume their journey early the next morning.

River Wolf was awakened by Bald Eagle gently tapping him on the shoulder.

"It's time to go," Bald Eagle said.

River Wolf yawned and got up. The eastern sky was beginning to brighten, but the Sun had not risen yet. They got into the dugout and started downstream.

"What did you say is the name of your home village?" asked River Wolf.

"Good Medicine," replied Bald Eagle, "It is the largest Muskogee village."

"Is it as large as Cahokia?"

"No, but I don't know of any village other than Cahokia that is larger than Good Medicine."

"What is our next stop?"

"Wolf Creek. There is a small settlement there."

"How far?"

"Two days."

They continued down the river. This was an easy and enjoyable existence, floating downstream. All they had to do was steer the dugout. That night, as they cooked some squirrels, there were footsteps in the woods. Their bows, still not in service, were useless. River Wolf picked up a ball head wooden war club, ready for trouble.

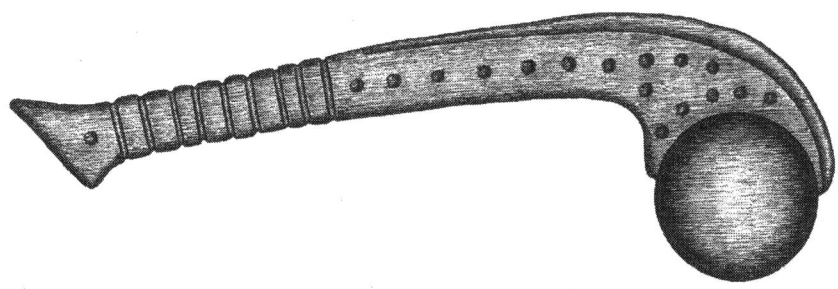

Ball Head Wooden War Club.

There was a whimpering sound in the direction of the footsteps. River Wolf and Bald Eagle glanced at each other. Whoever or whatever was making the noise either was not very good at stalking, or else not trying at all to be stealthy.

The whimpers sounded almost like a child weeping. The sound drew closer and closer and then abruptly stopped. River Wolf and Bald Eagle listened silently, but heard nothing.

"Who's there?" called Bald Eagle. "Hello! Hello!"

"Maybe they left," suggested River Wolf.

"Well I am not going to sleep until we find out for sure."

The Sun had gone down, and it was dark. They each took a stick out of the fire to use for torches. Then they went in the direction of where they had heard the last noise. Soon they found tiny tracks in the dirt. River Wolf immediately suspected the Little People were playing tricks on them. He was afraid of irritating them.

River Wolf reluctantly followed the tracks with Bald Eagle. The tracks led to a thicket. They stood there searching all around the thicket. Suddenly River Wolf realized that he was looking directly at a little girl who was anxiously watching him.

"Bald Eagle," he said.

Bald Eagle looked where River Wolf was pointing, and saw the girl. Suddenly she sprang up and began running away. The two gave chase, and the girl tripped on a log. They grabbed her, and kept her from getting away. The girl let out piercing screams and tried to bite both of them.

"We will not hurt you!" said Bald Eagle to her.

The girl calmed down and stopped struggling.

"Who are you?" asked Bald Eagle. "Where are you from?"

"My name is Red Stone," answered the girl. "I am lost. I came from Wolf Creek."

"Why were you sneaking around?" asked River Wolf.

"I was afraid of you," replied the girl. "I am so hungry!"

"Do you like squirrel?" asked River Wolf.

"I'll eat anything! Can you please take me home in your canoe?"

"We will take you back to Wolf Creek," offered Bald Eagle.

"Oh thank you!" said Red Stone.

"How long have you been lost?" asked River Wolf.

"Two days," answered Red Stone. "I was looking for the river and found it, but I didn't know whether to follow it upstream or downstream. It has been cloudy and I couldn't tell which way I had gone. I have not spent much time out of the village."

"How did you find the river?" asked Bald Eagle.

"I just went downhill and found a creek," replied Red Stone, "then I followed it to the river. Then I went upstream, looking for my village."

"Wolf Creek is downstream," said Bald Eagle.

The squirrels were now ready to eat, and Red Stone ate like she hadn't eaten in a moon. Then they lay down to sleep.

"I am so glad that I found you two instead of some Cherokee, or somebody else that bad," said Red Stone.

River Wolf didn't comment, other than to say, "I am glad you found us also. How old are you?"

"Eleven cycles," answered Red Stone. "I hope my parents are not angry with me when I get back. My mother is probably worrying about me terribly."

Bald Eagle began snoring. River Wolf was very tired.

"How far is Wolf Creek?" asked Red Stone.

"We will get there the day after tomorrow," answered River Wolf.

"Thank you so much for taking me back home," said Red Stone.

"You don't have to thank us," replied River Wolf.

"You cook good squirrel," commented Red stone.

"Can't you two be quiet?" mouthed Bald Eagle, "I am trying to sleep!"

Red Stone had an embarrassed expression on her face.

"Why don't we go to sleep?" whispered River Wolf. "We can talk tomorrow."

"Alright," whispered Red Stone, "Good night."

"Good night!" mouthed Bald Eagle, in an annoyed tone.

When Bald Eagle began snoring again, Red Stone whispered, "I hope he isn't mad at me."

"We need to get some sleep," whispered River Wolf sternly.

The next morning, Red Stone was up very early. She shook River Wolf to wake him.

"What's going on?" asked River Wolf while wiping the sleep from his eyes.

"I am ready to go home now," replied Red Stone.

Bald Eagle stirred. "Are you two *still* talking?"

"Red Stone just now woke me," answered River Wolf.

"Along with the rest of the world!" said Bald Eagle as he got up.

They ate and set off downstream. As they traveled, Red Stone talked constantly.

"My father is a mighty warrior," she said. "I have two brothers, one is younger than me; the other is older. Do you have any siblings?"

"I have a younger brother who was kidnapped in a raid on my home village when I was young," replied River Wolf.

"Where is your home village?" asked Red Stone, "What tribe are you?"

"I am from the capital village of the Cherokee."

Red Stone became uneasy, because Cherokees were enemies of the Muskogee. "You aren't going to start a war with my village, are you?"

"No!" answered River Wolf, somewhat offended, "I am a traveling trader!"

"What happened to your feet?"

"Before we arrived at the last village, I was sent out to hunt dinner and some of the hunters from the village thought I was an enemy warrior. They shot me with an arrow and began to burn me at the stake. But Bald Eagle arrived in time to save me."

"What is the name of the village you are from?"

"Birch Mountain."

"What mountain? I don't know what 'birch' means."

"It's a kind of tree that grows in the mountains where I live."

"My mother is teaching me how to make cornbread," said Red Stone, "Her name is Deer Skin. My father's name is The Raven Calls. My younger brother's name is Bent Stick, and my older brother's name is Fish.

"Bent Stick is five cycles old, and he makes bows and arrows for their war games. Fish is thirteen cycles old, and he is always catching fish from the river. My mother cooks his fish and what Father brings home also. They grow corn and other vegetables – we eat them too.

"My uncle is a Shaman, his name is Turkey Caller. He heals anybody in the village when they get afflicted by evil spirits."

"Did Wolf Creek get attacked by rogue spirits?" asked River Wolf.

"Yes!" answered Red Stone, "About three moons ago. How did you know?"

"Dead Hickory and Rattlesnake Creek were affected," answered River Wolf.

"Turkey Caller drove them away," said Red Stone, "He really knows what he is doing. One time my mother fell ill and Turkey Caller gave her some herbs and she was better the next day!"

"What was wrong with her? How did Turkey Caller treat her?"

"She had real bad cramps. My uncle gave her lady's slipper herb."

River Wolf remembered learning about lady's slipper when he was young. Eagle Medicine had told him not to touch it more than necessary because the live plant could irritate your skin. The roots were acquired in the autumn, and had sedative qualities. They were made into a tea that was good for nervousness, headaches, spasms, and cramps. Eagle Medicine had warned that large amounts could bring on dreadful hallucinations. Lady's slipper was sometimes also made into a decoction to treat worms in children.

Red Stone continued talking. "My favorite thing to do is look around the woods foraging for mushrooms. I am getting good at finding my way through the woods."

River Wolf opted not to ask her how she had gotten lost if she was so good at navigating.

Red Stone continued, "Are you a Cherokee warrior?"

"No, I said I am a trader. I was never good at being a warrior," answered River Wolf.

"My father could teach you. He is a fine warrior. He would be glad to teach you. He knows many tricks. You will like him."

"I do not want to become a warrior. I just want to be an artisan," said River Wolf.

"*You* don't want to be a *warrior*?"

"No, I don't! I take no joy out of killing people."

Red Stone changed the subject. "I have a boyfriend who lives in Wolf Creek. His name is Two Bears. But the boy I really love lives in Good Medicine. His name is Buck Horn. I never get to see him, except for during ceremonies when we travel there. It makes me sad. Two Bears says he will be my boyfriend, but I love Buck Horn. What should I do?"

"You are only eleven cycles old! Don't you think you should just have friends right now?" asked River Wolf.

Again, Red Stone changed the subject. "My parents will be glad to see me return safely. But my brothers are always getting on my nerves. They constantly tease me. Sometimes I hit my little brother, but my big brother hurts me a lot. But I am good at getting him into trouble."

Bald Eagle spoke in Cherokee to River Wolf. "I really, really wish she would shut up."

"I know," replied River Wolf, hoping to somehow sooth the situation.

"What did he say?" asked Red Stone.

"He said we would get to Wolf Creek this evening," lied River Wolf.

"What did you say back to him?"

"I said that I was looking forward to getting there."

Bald Eagle rolled his eyes.

"You two weren't talking about me were you?" asked Red Stone.

"It's none of your business what we were talking about!" retorted Bald Eagle.

Red Stone was chagrinned and became silent for a while. But soon she began her constant talking again.

"Have you ever been to Good Medicine?"

"No," answered River Wolf, "but Bald Eagle is from there."

"Are you two going there after Wolf Creek?" she asked.

"Yes, we are," replied River Wolf.

"Oh! Can I go with you?"

"Your parents will not allow it," said Bald Eagle.

"Oh, I will ask them," returned Red Stone optimistically. "They will! They will – I *know* they will!"

"You can't go with us!" stated Bald Eagle.

"But Buck Horn lives there! I want to see him."

"We are not coming back upstream. You have no other way to get back home. You cannot go with us!" Bald Eagle said sternly.

Red Stone's eyes shifted hopefully to River Wolf.

"You can't come along with us," said River Wolf softly.

Red Stone was disappointed, and River Wolf could tell. But he was almost as tired of her company as Bald Eagle was. They stopped to eat lunch and Red Stone continued her constant chattering with River Wolf. Soon Bald Eagle returned with a rabbit and the three dressed and cooked it. A dog had followed him back to the camp. They tried to chase the dog away, but he kept returning, wagging his tail.

"What are we going to do with this dog?" asked River Wolf.

"I suppose he will be traveling downstream with us also," replied Bald Eagle in a frustrated tone. "Along with the rest of the world!"

"He is so cute," said Red Stone, "and friendly too!"

"Well, you will be in charge of keeping the dog still in the dugout," ordered Bald Eagle, "and I don't want him getting in our way or ruining any of our goods."

"Oh, I will keep him on my lap," offered Red Stone. "I promise!"

"We will arrive at Wolf Creek late tonight," said Bald Eagle.

River Wolf wondered why he didn't want to wait until morning, but eventually he realized that Bald Eagle was anxious to be rid of Red Stone and the dog.

During the trip downstream, Red Stone was playing with the dog. The dog got excited and began playing rough. He got away from Red Stone and she nearly tipped over the canoe while trying to catch him. His claws scratched two of River Wolf's effigy pipes.

"I said to watch the dog!" shouted Bald Eagle, "Not play with him! You almost capsized us and ruined our wares!"

"Either control the dog, or we throw him out," said River Wolf. "He scratched my pipes. Now I have to polish them again!"

"I'm sorry!" cried Red Stone. She was angry.

The overloaded dugout arrived at Wolf Creek just before sunset. As usual, the guards made haste to identify these strangers. Then they returned into the village and told their Chief that the traders had arrived. The Chief and his assistants went to the riverbank to greet the occupants of the canoe.

"Welcome to Wolf Creek," said the Chief, "I am Rutting Buck."

Chief Rutting Buck invited them for a feast, while Red Stone returned with the dog to her parent's lodge. After the feast, they were accompanied by women in the guest lodges. River Wolf's companion's name was Rabbit Fur. When River Wolf mentioned beginning training for the priesthood as a child, Rabbit Fur seemed to become extremely interested. She said she wanted to hear more.

So, River Wolf began. "Well, the wild senna plant is used to clean out the system. It is a very good laxative. It's used as a treatment for the 'black' disease in which your eye sockets and hands turn black. The bruised roots make excellent poultices to help sores heal.

"Catgut herb is used as a hair wash because it is said to strengthen the hair. It is also rubbed into the ritual scratches on ball players to strengthen their muscles.

"We sometimes play double ball here," said Rabbit Fur, "at least us women here do."

River Wolf was familiar with this women's game, which was similar to the men's ball game. The goal was approximately six feet wide, with a cross bar that was about six feet above the ground. There were two sewn leather balls, tied together by a short cord. The slender sticks used in this game had handles that were around an inch thick, and the remainder of the stick was narrower. The sticks were used to snag the cord between the balls, and hurl them towards the goal. For a team to score a point, the balls were to be caught and hanging, from the cross bar of the goal, by the cord that connected them.

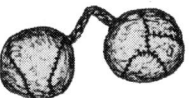

Double Ball Stick & Tethered Balls.
Adapted from Salomon 1928.

"Tell me about more medicinal plants," requested Rabbit Fur.

"Well, sharp-lobed hepatica is made into a tea that is good for stomach bleeding," continued River Wolf. "It is also good for ailments of kidneys, bladder, liver, and gallbladder. It is often used for bronchitis. Use only small amounts – large doses can poison a person.

"Are you sure you're not getting bored?" River Wolf asked her.

"No! Not at all! I really want to hear this!"

So, River Wolf continued. "Curly dock is gathered in the spring, and makes a good tonic for getting out of the winter sluggishness. The ground root is boiled into a tea that's good for scurvy. Crushed leaves can help stop itching in sores. It is also a good source for yellow dye.

Rabbit Fur seemed to be getting sleepy. River Wolf felt awkward. It seemed to him that she wanted him to talk so he would feel more welcome there. He felt awkward, and wanted her to talk more also. But she didn't seem to be near as interested as she said she was. She seemed to be a very selfless woman, whose primary goal was for River Wolf to feel listened to, and comfortable. If there was a term for the most opposite of narcissism, River Wolf didn't know the term. But he thought, if he did know a word for it, it would definitely describe her personality.

"Tell me more," said Rabbit Fur.

So, River Wolf began again. "Blackberries, as you know, are good to eat, but their leaves and roots also have medicinal value. They are good for chronic appendicitis, and diarrhea. A tea can be brewed from the dried root that works for treating edema, calming the stomach, and for rheumatism. Chewing the leaves helps stop the gums from bleeding.

"Another berry, the wild raspberry, is good for suppressing vomiting, and a tea can be made from the leaves. This tea works well for treating diarrhea.

"And then there are wild strawberries. Their leaves and roots are made into a tea for blood in the urine, diarrhea, and dysentery, and love potions."

Rabbit Fur began snoring.

River Wolf smiled and said, "And that, I think, pretty much covers everything." He yawned, and settled into his bed, and soon was fast asleep himself.

The next morning, the business of trading was at hand. River Wolf traded mica and effigy pipes for more shell jewelry and freshwater pearls. These were in great demand back at Birch Mountain.

Red Stone's parents arrived and thanked them repeatedly for bringing their daughter back home.

Bald Eagle smiled and said, "She is such a sweet little girl. I wish I could have traveled with her longer."

River Wolf heard this and stifled his laughter. It was important for a trader to be on good relations with potential customers because it was good business. And Bald Eagle was a well-seasoned professional at this.

Her parents gave each of them a deer hide for taking care of the girl. The two traders spent another night at Wolf Creek, and River Wolf stayed with Rabbit Fur again.

This time, she wanted him to describe the seven major ceremonies of the Cherokee. While he would have preferred to hear more about her, she completely lacked the inclination to do anything but listen. So, he told her about the Sacred Seven – at least until she finally feel asleep.

The next morning, Bald Eagle and River Wolf departed from Wolf Creek.

When they were out of earshot, Bald Eagle said, "I am sure glad to be rid of that little noisy brat!"

They both laughed.

"So, where is our next stop?" asked River Wolf.

"Burnt Bluff," answered Bald Eagle. "It is three days downstream. Here is some dried meat."

"Thank you," said River Wolf as he took a piece from him.

"I traded for a bunch of it," added Bald Eagle.

"Where are we going after Good Medicine?"

"All the way to the Great Sea at the mouth of the river, then east and up the Copperhead River. That will take us very near to your home. But we will be stopping at most of the villages on the way."

"I sure miss home."

"You will get used to it after awhile. And next time, you can take your wife-to-be along. That will be pleasant."

"Yes, it will. Very much so. Very much so."

They traveled for the rest of the day and, at sunset, they beached the canoe and ate their fill of dried meat and cornbread. Early the next morning they were back on the river.

They spotted a canoe approaching from downstream. They got their bows and arrows ready, but it was only another trader who was headed upstream. They came alongside and held the two dugouts together so they could visit.

The trader knew a slightly different dialect of the Muskhogean language that only Bald Eagle was familiar with. This trader's name was Kingfisher, and he was from the land of the Calusa to the southeast. His dugout was filled with conch and whelk shells from the Great Sea. Now River Wolf knew where the shell came from that was used for making the shell necklaces he had been trading for. Bald Eagle and Kingfisher conversed for a very long time, while River Wolf held the two canoes together. His arms were getting very tired by the time they parted ways.

"He was very nice," said Bald Eagle, "This is his first trading trip alone. He has never been north of Good Medicine. I told him there were a few settlements upstream with people who would like his shells."

"Someday I will go to the land of the Calusas," said River Wolf.

They paddled downstream in silence, and then River Wolf pointed to the shore.

"My totem," he said.

Bald Eagle looked where he pointed and saw a wolf watching them as they passed. The wolf drank from the river, then disappeared into the woods.

"Good omen," asserted Bald Eagle, "I do believe something good is going to happen to you in the next few days."

River Wolf believed it might be true, but soon forgot about it. They stopped and set up camp in the late afternoon. River Wolf set a leaning-log squirrel trap and then repolished the pipes that Red Stone's dog had scratched. Then he checked the trap and found that he caught three squirrels. They ate well that night.

* * *

Three days later they arrived at Burnt Bluff. They had the usual reception, and a feast of mussels and other items. They had the company of women from the village. The next day they traded with the locals. One man approached them with some conch shells like what the trader they met on the river was carrying. The shells were of no value to Bald Eagle and River Wolf, as they would soon be at the Great Sea where they were very common. The man wanted to trade the shells for some mica. River Wolf asked him what else he had to offer.

The man pulled out a large piece of tabular flint unlike any River Wolf had seen. It was a translucent brown color. River Wolf traded the mica for the flint, and asked where the flint came from.

"Very, very far to the southwest, in the land of the people who call themselves the Tickanwatic," the man replied.

River Wolf had never heard of the Tickanwatic, and asked the man to tell him more about them.

"They are a people who live far to the southwest, beyond the territory of the Caddo."

River Wolf had heard of the Caddo to the west, and was satisfied enough with the explanation. He was thinking he would like to go there and get more of this flint one day.

They finished their trading at sunset, and spent another night at Burnt Bluff. They each shared the night with different women from the previous night. The next morning they resumed their journey.

"Is our next stop Good Medicine?" asked River Wolf.

"No," replied Bald Eagle, "Cypress Bend, then Good Medicine."

They continued paddling downstream, and in the afternoon, they saw a thunderstorm forming in the west.

"That is headed right for us," warned Bald Eagle.

They made it to the shore and pulled the dugout well away from the riverbank. Then they emptied the contents and placed them under the upside-down canoe, and filled their water bottles. Soon the cool rain came down in torrents. The river swelled, and the two were soaked. But the goods were dry, and that was what was important.

When the rain stopped, Bald Eagle said, "We will be staying here until the river goes back down. Why don't we go and get a deer so we can have food for a few days?"

Their bows were useless because the bowstrings were damp, so they set out with axes. The constant dripping of the water from the trees covered the sounds of their footsteps, but it also camouflaged the noises of their quarry.

Eventually they walked up on a herd of deer by a small waterfall. River Wolf threw his axe and killed a large buck. Each apologized in his own way to the buck's spirit. Then River Wolf carried it over his shoulders back to their camp. They skinned and gutted it and had enough food to last them until the river went down enough for them to resume their journey.

Three days later, Bald Eagle said, "I am tired of sitting around. Let's get out of here."

They loaded the dugout and shoved off. The river was still high, and the water was moving fairly fast. Because of this, they made excellent time and arrived at Cypress Bend in two days.

They traded at Cypress Bend, stayed for one night, and left the next morning. Bald Eagle's mood was improving – he was almost to his home. River Wolf was looking forward to seeing this large village.

The river had gone down some, but was still moving faster than normal. In two days, Bald Eagle pointed to a bluff up ahead on the left.

"There is Good Medicine," he said.

River Wolf was excited and nervous. He now realized that he was in the very heart of enemy territory. He was glad he was a trader and not a Cherokee warrior! They saw part of the enormous palisade that surrounded the village. Then around fifteen guards ran up with their bows ready.

"I am Bald Eagle!" he loudly announced.

The guards signaled to more guards at the palisade, and soon there were too many people to count flocking around the canoe. River Wolf grew more nervous – he had never seen so many people in his life. A person of rank appeared out of the crowd and escorted them into the village. River Wolf counted sixteen large mounds before he stopped counting. There was an exciting, bustling commotion all around him.

They were led to a high-ranking person's lodge atop of one of the large mounds. River Wolf looked around the enormous village from this vantage point. Now he thought of Cahokia – how could it be any larger than this?

A man appeared out of the crowd and said, "Bald Eagle! How are you doing?"

"Hey, Wood Duck!" shouted Bald Eagle. "River Wolf, this is my brother, Wood Duck."

"It's nice to meet you, Wood Duck," greeted River Wolf. "I am traveling with Bald Eagle."

Wood Duck's Namesake, the Wood Duck.
Drawn from photo by wam17 from Pixabay.

They ate a grand feast with all kinds of meats, vegetables, and mushrooms. River Wolf noticed the designs incised on the pottery. One design he saw often was a motif of a hand with an eye in the palm. There were also bone and skull designs.

Bald Eagle showed River Wolf his lodge, which was kept by his daughter. Then River Wolf was led to a guest lodge.

The next morning the trading took place. Bald Eagle traded away all of his copper, and River Wolf's mica was also in great demand. In return, they received elaborately engraved shell gorgets and masks.

One man showed a particular interest in River Wolf's pottery duck effigy bowl. When he asked about it, River Wolf said that it was a gift and it was not for trade.

Then River Wolf saw a man who looked strangely familiar. He looked again, but the man disappeared in the crowd. *Who was that?* He thought.

"Did you see that man?" he asked Bald Eagle.

"There are a lot of people here," came the reply, "Who are you talking about?"

"Never mind. He is gone now."

River Wolf traded an effigy pipe to a man for a shell death mask. When the deal was made, River Wolf saw the familiar man again. The man looked at him, and did a double-take. He seemed to recognize him also. The man approached him.

"Do I know you?" asked the man. "I think I do. You make effigy pipes."

"Yes, I do," replied River Wolf. "Were you at one of the settlements upstream? I know I have seen you before."

"Your name is Green Rock," said the man.

River Wolf was startled. Who could know this about him? Suddenly it came to him.

"Running Fox!" he exclaimed.

* * *

Chapter 10: Panther

Beaver Pelt woke up abruptly after having another nightmare. She worried about River Wolf's safety as he traveled amongst the many enemies of the Cherokee. He had been away for so long that she wondered if he was even still alive. In her recurring dreams he would always bid her farewell and she would never see him again.

She would fetch water and do other things to help her mother, but The Duck Flies By knew that her daughter was troubled. She would introduce Beaver Pelt to many young men of the village, hoping that she would be distracted from her worries. But Beaver Pelt could not stop thinking about River Wolf.

One day, after Crooked Arrow had proven himself in battle, and had a Vision Quest, he was awarded the status of adulthood. His new name was Song of the Wind. Beaver Pelt had a crush on him, and she found herself torn between Song of the Wind and River Wolf. She had promised to herself to wait for River Wolf's return, but now she thought, *What if he never returns?* She often consulted Eagle Medicine and his divining Crystal to find out if River Wolf was still alive.

Song of the Wind wanted to marry her, but now *she* wanted to wait. She was uncertain of her feelings and her intentions. If she married Song of the Wind, River Wolf would be hurt if, and when, he returned. She couldn't do that to him. But if she waited and never saw River Wolf again, Song of the Wind might move on. She resolved to wait for River Wolf until the Great New Moon Ceremony. She told Song of the Wind her decision, and three weeks later, he married another woman from across the village. Beaver Pelt was hurt and angry when she heard the news. To add insult to injury, the woman had been a friend of hers since childhood. Beaver Pelt felt betrayed by both of them. She went in tears to see Buck and Tanager.

"River Wolf will be back," reassured Buck. "I know the trading circuit and I know that he is being treated with respect and courtesy. Traders are never considered enemies, no matter what tribe they are from."

"I felt the same way waiting for Buck to return," related Tanager. "I was carrying his child, and I worried that Titmouse would not have a father."

"Bald Eagle is trustworthy," added Buck. "He is dependable and knowledgeable and will not lead River Wolf into trouble."

Often Beaver Pelt visited them seeking reassurance. She continued to sometimes consider being with other men, but felt guilty about it. As time went on, she began to avoid all single men her age, altogether. This worried her mother deeply.

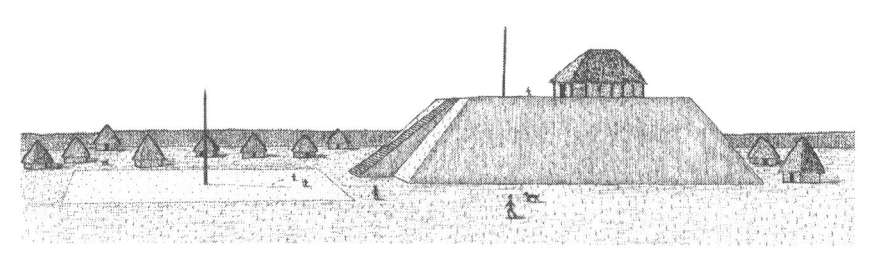

* * *

The Village of Good Medicine.

"Yes, I am your little brother!" said Running Fox, "My name is now Panther."

"It's so good to see you!" exclaimed River Wolf, "My adult name is River Wolf."

"Why don't we meet at my lodge and catch up after the trading is done for the day?" said Panther.

"Where is your lodge?" asked River Wolf.

"I will meet you here at sunset and show you," replied Panther. "I will have some of my men kill a deer for us to eat. But please don't tell anybody we are brothers."

Panther left and River Wolf continued his trading. All the while he was very preoccupied with seeing his brother. He wondered why Panther wanted to keep it secret. It seemed that Panther was now a man of some status. River Wolf wanted to give him a gift. He couldn't decide on what. As he returned to the dugout to get some more pipes to trade, he saw the pottery duck effigy bowl. That would make a marvelous gift for his long-lost brother.

The trading came to an end for the day, and Bald Eagle approached River Wolf. "Who was that man?" he asked, "You two seemed to know each other."

"That was my little brother I was asking you about," replied River Wolf, "but do not mention it to anybody."

Bald Eagle seemed to understand why and said, "Do not worry, I won't."

At sunset, Panther appeared as he had promised. River Wolf gave him the duck effigy bowl. Panther was caught off-guard because it was such a fine gift. They went to Panther's lodge and ate a fine meal.

"This is my wife, Autumn Leaf," introduced Panther.

"It's nice to meet you," greeted River Wolf.

"We have a lot to talk about," said Panther.

"Can we go for a walk – alone?" asked River Wolf.

"Sure," came the reply from Panther.

They left together and headed for the river, outside of the palisade. On the way, River Wolf saw people hauling dirt by the basketful to add to the largest mound. This was a very large village with at least a thousand residents. When River Wolf and Panther got outside of the palisade, River Wolf saw the trail to a pond where the dirt had come from.

They found a secluded rock to sit on and talk. River Wolf started the conversation in Cherokee so the wrong people would not overhear him.

"Would you like to return home with me?" he asked. "We could sneak away and be at Birch Mountain in less than a moon. I would not mind leaving all my wares behind if it meant getting you back home."

"I really couldn't," answered Panther. "I appreciate the offer, but I have the status of a war leader here. All of my friends are here."

"How did you get here? I heard from some Yuchi captives that you were sold to a trader who spoke Muskhogean. Tell me what happened."

"I went to get some cane," Panther began, "to make myself a blowgun like the one that Father made for you. I was cutting a piece, and suddenly Yuchi warrior grabbed me and covered my mouth. I fought with him, but he was very strong, and much bigger than me.

"They took me to their village, and made me a slave. They kept me tied up unless they were making me work for them. The warrior who owned me was very mean and he beat me every day. I never cooperated with him unless I had to.

"Several moons later, a trader from the west arrived and I was sold to him. His name was Water Beetle was nice to me and I gradually became compliant and helped him. Water Beetle and I traveled for two cycles, trading and such, and then he retired. He adopted me into the Muskogee tribe, and I became a regular citizen. He died three cycles after that, and his wife, Fern died one cycle after he died. I inherited their lodge and have lived here ever since."

"How did you get the name, 'Panther?'" asked River Wolf.

"Three cycles ago, when I went on my first war party, I found myself alone in the woods with an enemy warrior tracking me. I climbed a tree with my knife. When he tracked me to the tree, I jumped out of the tree and stabbed him to death. They thought I was like a panther so they gave me that name."

"How did you get the name, 'River Wolf?'" asked Panther.

River Wolf told the story of his Vision Quest and the trip down Thunder River.

"How are Mother and Father doing?" asked Panther.

"Mother is doing fine, but Father was killed by a bear not long after you were kidnapped."

River Wolf did not mention the beating and Eagle Medicine's possible hand in their father's death.

"How are Turtle Shell and Sparrow?"

"Turtle Shell was killed during the same raid in which you were kidnapped. Sparrow has recently remarried to a man named Broken Spear. She is very happy."

"Are you married?"

"I have a girlfriend who I plan to marry when I return home. Her name is Beaver Pelt. This is my first trading trip, and I felt it prudent to gain some experience on the trade route before taking along a wife."

"You didn't marry her?"

"No. I thought I should wait so that both of us could think about it first."

"Do you love her?"

"Yes, very much."

"You should have married her! What if she marries another man while you are gone?"

"I love her enough to give her that freedom." By now, River Wolf was getting tired of having to explain this to everybody. He wished he *had* married Beaver Pelt. Even more, he wished she had come with him.

"Do not let on that we are brothers," said Panther, changing the subject. "I have gained much status here, and I don't want people thinking I might be a traitor."

"I will say nothing," assured River Wolf, "except to Bald Eagle."

They returned to Panther's lodge and went to sleep. The next morning, Panther left and returned with a stranger who had features that were unfamiliar to River Wolf. Panther carried a large piece of greenstone.

"This is Jaguar, the priest's assistant," introduced Panther.

"What does that name mean?" asked River Wolf. "I have never heard that word before."

"He is a Mayan from a land far across the Great Sea to the south. A jaguar is a large cat native to that land, similar to one of our cougars. Do you know what a monolithic axe is?"

"It is an axe with the head and handle carved from one piece of stone, isn't it?"

"Yes. Jaguar has one to show you. We have seen your stone carvings and we want you to try to carve one. This stone is harder than soapstone, and we obviously do not expect you to finish it on this trip. Bring it next summer when you visit Good Medicine again."

"I will try my best to make it as nice as I can," said River Wolf.

"You will do well," assured Panther. "You always have."

River Wolf noticed a large stone disk with two rattlesnakes and a motif consisting of a hand with an open eye in the palm. It seemed to be a popular icon in this area, but River Wolf never found out what it represented. This disk was about a foot in diameter. It was beautiful.

Panther's Rattlesnake Disk with Hand with Eye Motif.
Redrawn from Hodge 1910.

They left Panther's lodge and went to the dugout to start the day's trading. Bald Eagle was there, and he greeted them. River Wolf placed the piece of greenstone in the dugout among his things. Then he began bartering with the villagers.

One taller villager approached River Wolf and said, "I was thinking about trading with you, but you being Cherokee, I don't know whether to barter with you or fight with you." He wore a buffalo horn headdress.

River Wolf was shocked at the man's rudeness. "I do not want to fight with anybody," he replied with a nervous smile.

Then a shorter, stout man joined the tall man and they whispered words to each other. They laughed, and River Wolf was intimidated.

"Do you know who I am?" asked the tall man, "I am Winged Rattlesnake Chief. I am a war chief. And this brave war leader is Dead Buzzard Warrior. If you are looking for trouble, you will find more than you can handle here."

"I want no trouble," replied River Wolf, anxiously.

"Why are you and Panther such close friends all of a sudden?" asked Dead Buzzard Warrior.

Bald Eagle overheard all of what was said and came to River Wolf's rescue.

He said, "This young man is peaceful, and a very talented artist. I am proud to be traveling with him."

The two warriors suddenly were polite in the presence of Bald Eagle. Nothing more was said, but River Wolf could not forget the blatant violation of the normal trading customs by these men. It worried him. He never wanted any trouble.

They stayed at Good Medicine for two more weeks, bartering and visiting with relatives. Then Bald Eagle decided it was time to move on. They loaded their wares back into the dugout and stocked it with plenty of dried meat and cornbread. They had just finished loading the dugout when it started raining.

"Oh great," lamented Bald Eagle, with a worried expression.

"It is only a rainstorm," returned River Wolf.

"We are closer to the Great Sea than your village is," said Bald Eagle. "Tremendous storms sometimes come up from out of the sea. They bring a lot of rain and wind like you probably have never seen. Get all of the perishables inside quickly."

"How do you know it is a great storm?" asked River Wolf.

"I have lived here many cycles. It is the wind direction that makes me nervous. See how it is coming from the east?"

"Yes," answered River Wolf. "It usually comes from the west."

"Leave the stone pieces there in the dugout," ordered Bald Eagle. "First we need to move the cloaks and other things that will ruin in the rain. Don't forget to fill up the water bottles."

Bald Eagle was right. There were light showers coming from the east. Gradually during the next day the rain intensified. Now it was clear that this was a hurricane, and the villagers scrambled down to the river to drag their canoes up the bluff to keep them from washing away. River Wolf and Bald Eagle had a harder time because their dugout canoe was loaded with stone carvings and flint. River Wolf saw Winged Rattlesnake Chief and Dead Buzzard Warrior watching them, apparently amused at their difficulty.

They dragged the dugout to a high place and turned it upside down, with the stone pieces under it. They tied it to the ground with stakes. After securing the dugout and their wares, Bald Eagle returned to his lodge, and River Wolf stayed with Panther.

"Why don't you start pecking on that monolithic axe?" asked Panther.

"Good idea," replied River Wolf. "There isn't much else to do."

River Wolf went to the dugout and got the piece of greenstone and his pecking stone. He returned to Panther's lodge and began pecking on it. He could tell it was going to take some time to complete.

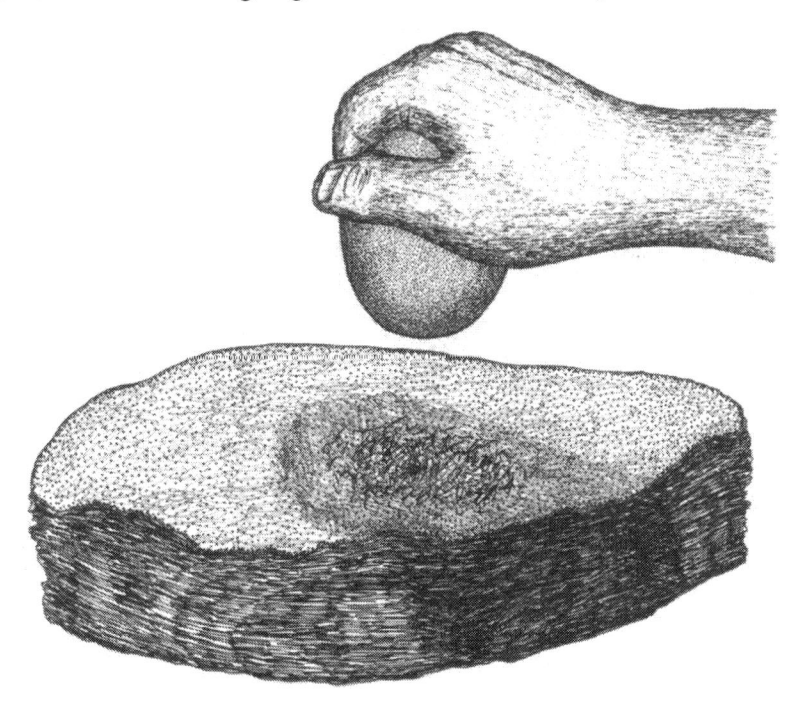

River Wolf Begins Making a Monolithic Axe.

The wind blew harder and more constant. For five days it rained like River Wolf had never seen before. Water seeped through the bottom of the lodge and most of the mud floor was wet and mushy.

"Do you know Winged Rattlesnake Chief and Dead Buzzard Warrior?" asked River Wolf.

"Yes, answered Panther. "Winged Rattlesnake Chief is the highest-ranking war chief. Nice person if you get to know him."

River Wolf was very uneasy at this remark. He said nothing.

"Have you met him?" asked Panther.

"Yes, but he seemed to want to start a fight with me," answered River Wolf in Cherokee.

"Really?" asked Panther, now speaking in Cherokee.

"Yes."

"You're joking! What did he say?"

"He said he didn't know whether to fight me or trade with me because I am Cherokee."

"I don't believe it! That arrogant piece of rat dung!"

Autumn Leaf asked, "Why do you two speak in a foreign tongue? Are you planning something behind my back?"

"Be quiet!" retorted Panther. "We are trying to discuss something and it's none of your business!"

Autumn Leaf let them talk without further interruption.

"What did Dead Buzzard Warrior say to you?" asked Panther in Cherokee.

"He asked me why I was so friendly with you, and they whispered things to each other and were laughing at me."

Just then a swift gust of wind ripped a hole in the roof of the lodge. The heavy rain came through the hole and onto the muddy floor.

"I hope you still have a lodge when this storm passes," commented River Wolf.

"These hurricanes always tear up the village," returned Panther. "We will rebuild soon enough." He continued in Cherokee, "You didn't tell them we are brothers, did you?" asked Panther.

"No, I didn't. Bald Eagle came to my rescue."

"I can't believe the arrogance of those two. You know, when Winged Rattlesnake Chief dies, he will be replaced by Dead Buzzard Warrior, and then me. Then I will have the title of Great Warrior, and my name will be Panther Chief."

River Wolf wondered what Panther might be suggesting, but didn't make any comment about that. "You now have some status, then," he said, "to be third in line to be the war chief of a large village."

"I guess I do."

"What do you use a monolithic axe for?" asked River Wolf, in Muskhogean.

"To kill slaves and relatives of a deceased person during the burial ceremony. That is only done with high-ranking people though. The slaves and relatives are buried with the aristocrats so that they might accompany them in the afterlife."

"That is dreadful!" remarked River Wolf.

"They volunteer to be killed. They are drugged and unconscious when they are killed. They don't suffer. It's not cruel, or anything."

"So that means that if, and when, you become a war chief, and die, your wife will be killed and buried with you?"

"Yes."

River Wolf looked at Autumn Leaf. She smiled and eagerly nodded in agreement. She seemed to be satisfied with the arrangement. River Wolf saw the need to show respect, even though they were different.

Panther continued, "The person's lodge is burned, and his successor builds a new lodge at the site of the old lodge. The old lodge is burned down so that it will also accompany them in the afterlife."

"I like your rattlesnake disk," complimented River Wolf.

Panther said, "I have another one. Let me get it." He arose and dug through a basket of items and pulled it out. He handed it to River Wolf.

Panther's Smaller Engraved Disk.
Redrawn from Reilly & Garber 2007.

This disk was smaller, and had a more complex design. On the upper right there were two hand and eye motifs and, on the lower right, was a bi-lobed arrow motif. Down the center was a pillar with two skulls. On the left side was a motif Panther said was a moth representation. It was an extraordinary work of art.

Most of the lodges in Good Medicine were damaged to different degrees by the relentless wind. The Black Warrior River swelled over its banks and when the storm finally ended, the river reminded River Wolf of Thunder River, except that it was very muddy. The ground was saturated with water.

"You were right," River Wolf said to Bald Eagle a few days later.

"I am just glad we weren't on the coast when that storm passed through," replied Bald Eagle, while puffing on his pipe. "We would have lost everything, and maybe even gotten killed."

They stayed another week, waiting for the river to go down, and many of the villagers – including River Wolf – became ill from drinking the muddy water. River Wolf had a bad bellyache that lasted for days. On top of that, he got a sinus infection from breathing the dust of the greenstone he had been carving. The Shaman and his assistants were very busy treating everybody, so their visits with River Wolf were brief.

Then River Wolf got diarrhea. He raced down to the ditch where people went for natural functions, but did not get there in time. River Wolf at least could laugh about it, even though he was miserable.

After cleaning up in the swollen river, River Wolf decided to look in the nearby woods for a cranesbill plant. He knew that you could eat the young leaves for food. While he was in training for the priesthood, he learned that, when boiled and allowed to cool, it made a good type of eyewash. It could be used for dysentery, diarrhea, and the root could be made into a powder and applied to swollen feet. It was also a good mouthwash for treating thrush in children.

On his way, he was lucky enough to spot an American elm tree. He remembered that the bark was used as a poultice for swelling in the skin and minor wounds. But it was also used internally for dysentery, sore throats, diarrhea, and urinary problems. He knew to use care when removing the bark from these trees, because they were rare, and you could make the tree susceptible to diseases by removing bark.

He harvested some of its bark, and located some cranesbill growing nearby. He harvested some. Then he spotted a meadow rue plant. For treating diarrhea with vomiting, he knew you could make a decoction from the root of this plant, and have the sick one drink it. Next, he noticed a tall fleabane plant. This tall weed, he knew was made into a decoction for treating dysentery, internal bleeding, diarrhea, and hemorrhoids. When made into a tea, it was good for rheumatism, and irregular menstruation. It was also commonly used for starting fires.

With the meadow rue, fleabane, cranesbill and American elm bark, he planned to prepare what he thought would be the ultimate treatment for his diarrhea that, hopefully, would be effective and fast acting. He was hoping to avoid it turning into dysentery.

As he walked back up the hill, he saw many of the villagers repairing their wind-damaged lodges. Most of the Muskogee he had been bartering with seemed like nice people, and he wondered why they and the Cherokee had to be enemies. He had always been told that the land between Cherokee territory and Muskogee Territory was in dispute. River Wolf hated war.

River Wolf made his cranesbill, fleabane, meadow rue and American elm bark preparations and he shared it with Bald Eagle, Panther and Autumn Leaf. The whole world seemed to be a soggy mess. River Wolf thought of Beaver Pelt. He wondered what she was doing, whether she was thinking of him. Just then the Sun came out. It made him feel better. He wondered if Beaver Pelt could see the Sun.

* * *

Squirrel Fur and Beaver Pelt returned from gathering mushrooms that had grown from the last night's rain. Birch Mountain had gotten a little rain from the storm, and now the clouds were clearing.

"I sure hope that River Wolf is alright," said Beaver Pelt. "I wonder where he is right now."

"I am sure he is safe," replied Squirrel Fur, trying to hide her worry.

They entered the palisade gate and were greeted by White Feather and Dances Like the Deer, who were fetching water.

"Why don't you two join us for dinner this evening?" asked Dances Like the Deer.

"Alright," replied Squirrel Fur.

"Be there just before sunset," said Dances Like the Deer. "You will have a meal you won't forget."

"We will be there," promised Beaver Pelt.

They returned to Squirrel Fur's lodge and stored the mushrooms. After finishing the day's chores, they went to Eagle Medicine and Dances Like the Deer's lodge and feasted with them.

"Are you going to marry River Wolf?" asked White Feather.

"Yes, I will," replied Beaver Pelt with a smile.

"But what if he never comes back?" said White Feather.

"White Feather," said Eagle Medicine, "It is time for you to go to bed. Go and lay down."

"Yes, Father," submitted White Feather.

"Thank you for inviting us for dinner," said Squirrel Fur.

"You are welcome," replied Dances Like the Deer.

"River Wolf will be back home soon," Eagle Medicine reassured Beaver Pelt, "and then you two will marry and be very prosperous."

"Thank you, Eagle Medicine," returned Beaver Pelt.

Beaver Pelt and Squirrel Fur returned to Squirrel Fur's lodge. On the way, Sparrow, who was returning with a pot of water from the river, saw them and greeted them as they passed each other. They entered Squirrel Fur's lodge and tidied up the place. Beaver Pelt returned to River Wolf's lodge, where she was staying. The next day, she visited Squirrel Fur and helped prepare some acorn meal bread. When that was finished, Beaver Pelt started to leave.

"Take these," said Squirrel Fur, pointing to some dried meat and acorn bread.

"No, I couldn't," objected Beaver Pelt.

"Go on and take it. And soon you will have a husband to provide for you. You will be my daughter-in-law and then I will be truly happy," said Squirrel Fur with a proud smile.

Tears came to Beaver Pelt's eyes and she hugged Squirrel Fur. Then she left for River Wolf's lodge. On the way, she noticed how brightly the Sun was shining down on her.

* * *

The day finally came for Bald Eagle and River Wolf to depart from Good Medicine. They loaded the perishables back into the dugout, and dragged it back to the muddy riverbank. Bald Eagle bade farewell to his tearful daughter, and River Wolf did likewise with Panther. Their secret was safe with Bald Eagle; most of the villagers just thought they had quickly become good friends.

They shoved off and resumed their journey downstream. It was bittersweet – River Wolf hated to leave his brother, but he was also relieved to be away from Winged Rattlesnake Chief and Dead Buzzard Warrior.

"You will miss your brother, won't you?" asked Bald Eagle, noting River Wolf's silence.

"Yes," replied River Wolf.

There was a period of quiet reflection.

"Do not worry about those two ruffians," said Bald Eagle.

"Why did they want trouble?"

"Some people just like trouble. It's their nature."

"People like that start wars. I *hate* war."

"I know you do, River Wolf."

"People would get along better without troublemakers – they just stir things up. It is not fair to the innocent folks."

"Well, River Wolf, every tribe and every village has troublemakers – that *is* how wars are started. I have found that most people are good-natured and peace-loving. But many warriors seek glory at the expense of others. Sometimes at the expense of their own village. That's just the way it is."

Later that day, they arrived at a small village. The people were still recovering from the storm.

"What is the name of this village?" asked River Wolf.

"Snake Town," replied Bald Eagle.

Not much trading took place at Snake Town, since many of the villagers were still sick from the water.

The next morning, they left with a little bit of food bartered from Snake Town. By the evening, the food was gone. They beached the canoe and set up camp.

"Why don't you start pecking away on that monolithic axe," said Bald Eagle, "while I hunt for a deer?"

"That's a good idea!" said River Wolf. "The banging noise will attract deer!"

At sunset, they were cooking a small doe over the campfire.

"Business will get worse the farther downstream we go," said Bald Eagle.

"Why?" asked River Wolf.

"There will be much more storm damage the closer we get to the Great Sea," came the reply. "I vote we should hurry along, and not spend much time at villages for the following week or so. They won't be up to dealing with traders anyhow. We should just get to the coast as soon as we can. We have already lost enough time with delays."

"Sounds good to me," said River Wolf.

The two ate their fill and retired to their bearskins. In the middle of the night, River Wolf felt something touch his leg. He was startled, and kicked it. Then came an awful odor. He had been sprayed by a skunk! River Wolf was very angry, but Bald Eagle thought it was funny.

The next day, as they headed downstream, Bald Eagle was unusually quiet. Finally he said, "Head for the shore over there."

"But there is plenty of daylight and we are not near any village!" protested River Wolf.

"You are going to sit in the stern," said Bald Eagle, "and I will be in front so I won't have to smell you anymore!"

River Wolf was chagrined, but offered no argument. They traded places and continued downstream.

"Don't expect to have any village maidens approach you for several weeks!" scoffed Bald Eagle. He was having a grand time making jokes at

River Wolf's expense. River Wolf endured his continued taunting with good nature, but he was getting tired of the strong smell.

A week and-a-half later, the river merged with a larger river.

"Go up this river and you will get to the place where Loner lives," said Bald Eagle. "Remember when we portaged between Rattlesnake Creek and Dead Hickory?"

"Yes."

"If we had continued down the river, instead of portaging, we would have ended up here."

"Can we go on back to Birch Mountain now?" asked River Wolf. "You said there would not be much business anyway."

"We are going all the way to the coast," replied Bald Eagle. "There are free conch shells there. Pretty ones that will bring a good price. After we get a load of them we will return to your home."

River Wolf's heart sank.

"You miss your woman," said Bald Eagle. "We will get there soon enough. I want to show you where to get conch and whelk shells. You will become very wealthy if you know where to get them."

The days went by and they passed many villages that were heavily damaged during the storm. But many people were ill and, as Bald Eagle had predicted, there was not much trading. So, they continued downstream. River Wolf saw giant lizard-like animals on the banks and in the water.

"What are those?" he asked.

"Alligators," answered Bald Eagle. "Do not get out of the canoe unless you want to be their dinner. By the way, to the west is the territory of the Biloxi. Their language is totally different from the Muskhogean language."

Two nights later, they arrived at an enormous island in the river. They camped there for the night. River Wolf killed a duck with an arrow and, together, they dressed and cooked it.

"What is the name of this island?" asked River Wolf.

"I don't know," said Bald Eagle, "How about Copperhead Island?" He was pointing towards some dried leaves.

"What is it?" asked River Wolf.

"Don't you see it?"

"No! What is it?"

Just then a copperhead moved, catching River Wolf's eye.

"I see it!" said River Wolf.

"Get a stick and chase it away."

River Wolf picked up the snake with a stick and carried it a good distance from the camp. It fell several times, and was getting agitated and was striking at the stick.

"I would have never seen that snake if he had not moved," said River Wolf when he returned.

"Yes, they have really good camouflage," added Bald Eagle. "You have to watch for them. They are pretty docile, but poisonous. Cottonmouths are more hot-tempered, and they are really good swimmers too."

River Wolf thought he should have brought along some Virginia snakeroot that Eagle Medicine had taught him about. The root was mashed and then applied to snakebites. You could also put a piece of the bruised root in a cavity to treat a toothache. It could be made into a decoction that can be gargled for sore throats. But Eagle Medicine also warned that you should never swallow any of it though because it is poisonous. But River Wolf wished he had some in case of snakebites.

Bald Eagle was soon asleep, and River Wolf lay there awake. He saw a shooting star through the trees, and heard wolves howling in the distance, across the water. He took it as a good omen. He fell asleep dreaming of home.

They set out early the next morning and, late that afternoon, they came to another large island. They camped on the south end of the island. Bald Eagle left and returned with a rabbit. They cooked it over the fire that River Wolf had started.

As they ate, River Wolf said, "I remember the first time I heard of you."

"Tell me about it," returned Bald Eagle.

"Do you remember old Stone Spear?"

"Yes, how could I forget him?"

"I asked him where he got his flint, and he said 'An eagle brings it to me from a distant land.'"

Bald Eagle chuckled, "That's not all I brought that old drunk."

"Yes! The wild grapevines!"

"Did you try the drink?"

"No, I didn't."

"Boy, that stuff was pretty crazy, but I'm too old to be having that much fun."

"What did you do with those grapevines you left with after he died?"

"I threw them in the river to make room in the dugout, yawned Bald Eagle. "We need to get to sleep. There is another large island immediately downstream. It is larger than the last two. We will camp there tomorrow. The south end of the island is the mouth of the river."

The next evening, they finally reached the mouth of the river. They camped on the large island, and filled their water bottles in the river. The next morning they entered a large bay. It took all day and all night to paddle across this bay. They took turns paddling and sleeping. The next morning, they arrived at the tip of a narrow peninsula that pointed westward.

After they went around the peninsula, they paddled east along the beach. River Wolf had never seen so much water! This was the Great Sea he had heard so much about. It was overwhelming. There were unusual birds that Bald Eagle said were called seagulls. The two spent the night on the beach. The roaring of the waves crashing on the shore was a spectacular sound.

The next morning, they continued eastwards along the coast and set up camp on the beach, near the mouth of a small freshwater stream. River Wolf walked along the beach with Bald Eagle.

"These little critters are crabs," said Bald Eagle.

"What is this?" asked River Wolf, holding a white round and flat object with five holes in it.

"Oh, that's a sand dollar."

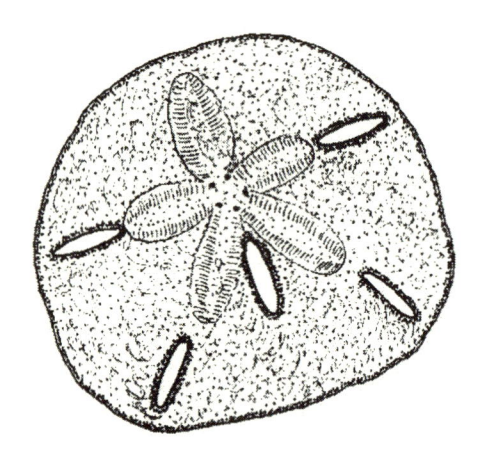

Sand Dollar.

This was a whole new world for River Wolf. There were so many things he had never seen before! The water seemed to go to the end of the earth.

"So, what direction across the sea is the land of the Maya?" asked River Wolf.

"That way," said Bald Eagle, pointing to the south-southwest.

"How far?"

"I don't know. Many weeks. If you were to follow the beach to the west, it would eventually go south and to their territory, or so I've heard."

River Wolf picked up a shell and examined it, but was startled when he saw several legs move inside the shell. River Wolf dropped it, and Bald Eagle laughed.

"What was that?" asked River Wolf.

"That was a hermit crab. They find abandoned shells and live in them."

They walked along the beach and suddenly Bald Eagle stopped River Wolf abruptly.

"Watch out!" Bald Eagle shouted. "That is a jellyfish. You don't want to step on one of them, or even touch them. They will sting you. It hurts badly and sometimes they can kill you. Always watch for them, on the beach and in the water, when we are getting shells. Do you know what a shark is?"

"No," replied River Wolf.

"They are large fish with teeth that are as sharp as a fine flint arrow point. They are usually quite harmless, but can attack and kill people. If I see one while we are diving for conch shells, I will point it out and we will have to get to shore quickly. Why don't you look around while I set up camp?"

River Wolf walked alone in the shallow water for a long distance, looking around at the sights. The waves were crashing on the shore. He saw a giant crab. He cautiously backed off and the crab chased him. Startled, he jumped and the crab rapidly retreated. He backed up again, and the crab ran out after him again. River Wolf didn't trust that crab with his large claws, and just stood still for a long time watching it.

Crab.
Redrawn from Garrigue 1851.

Suddenly he heard a man shouting something in a foreign language. River Wolf saw a man to the east in an unusual double canoe with a wing. He was afraid that the man might be an enemy, and he was alone. River Wolf tried to communicate to the stranger in signs.

"I am a trader," he signed.

"So am I," signed the stranger.

River Wolf was relieved, but kept an eye on the stranger.

"Where is your boat?" signed the stranger.

"I am with a friend. He is down the beach," signed River Wolf, while pointing.

The man signed his name, but River Wolf didn't recognize the sign.

"I do not understand," signed River Wolf.

So the man signed, "Water Bird." Then he signed, "Go to your friend, I will be there shortly."

River Wolf ran back to the camp that Bald Eagle had set up.

"There is another trader coming, I think his name is Water Bird," he said to Bald Eagle.

Bald Eagle stood up to see the stranger and recognized him, even though he was still far off.

He said to Water Bird, "Hello, old friend, it's Bald Eagle!"

"You know him?"

"Yes," replied Bald Eagle, "His name is Seagull, not Water Bird. He is a Calusa trader."

"I didn't know the sign for Seagull," said River Wolf.

Seagull arrived at the campsite and beached his double canoe. He and Bald Eagle began talking in that Muskhogean dialect that River Wolf still had difficulty understanding completely. He assumed it was the Calusa tongue. Then Seagull got a bunch of large crabs out of his canoe. They were the same kind as the one that River Wolf had encountered. River Wolf looked in Seagull's canoe and it was overloaded with all kinds of seashells.

Seagull and Bald Eagle began cooking the crabs over the fire, and talking in the strange dialect. Earlier, River Wolf thought that crab was going to eat him, but now they would eat these crabs. He sat there, listening to their words to try to pick up on some of what was said.

The crabs were an unusual meal, but they tasted very good. Bald Eagle and Seagull talked all night long while River Wolf slept. When River Wolf awakened, Seagull was gone and Bald Eagle was asleep.

River Wolf got the piece of greenstone out of the dugout. He took it and a pecking stone out of earshot, down the beach, and continued working on the monolithic axe. He did not want to wake up Bald Eagle. It was a lovely atmosphere for stone carving – the noise of the ocean. He vowed to bring Beaver Pelt to visit this place someday. As he pecked away on the stone, Bald Eagle appeared.

"Are you ready to get some shells?" asked Bald Eagle.

"Sure!"

"Let's go then."

"Where did Seagull go?" asked River Wolf.

"He went west. He will be going up a river to trade his shells."

"Why did his two canoes have a wing?"

"That 'wing' is called a 'sail.' It catches the wind and propels the boat. You can even sail into the wind by going back and forth. That type of canoe with the two dugouts and sail is called a 'catamaran.'

"Let's get the dugout and head out. Remember to watch out for jellyfish. We will be in the water, holding on to the dugout. We will take turns diving for shells. Don't drink water from the ocean – it is salt water and will kill you."

They swam, holding the canoe until their feet didn't touch the bottom. Then both of them dove together and Bald Eagle showed him how to find the shells. They gathered shells most of the day, putting them in the dugout. As the Sun began to set, they returned to camp. When they were beaching the dugout, River Wolf stepped on a jellyfish, but didn't get stung.

"I'm telling you, watch out for them," warned Bald Eagle. "They can hurt you badly – even kill you."

They ate a meal of raw oysters. Bald Eagle said that oysters had aphrodisiac qualities.

"That's just what I need," replied River Wolf, "being away from my woman."

"Well, you are going to be staying away from me too!" Bald Eagle laughed.

They retired to their bearskins and slept well. The next morning, they found a small dead fish, pierced it with Bald Eagle's bone fishhook, and tied it with some twine to a pole stuck in the sand. They caught many crabs with this device. The crabs would grip the fish with their claw and would not let go, even while they were being pulled upwards. Bald Eagle used a net to capture the crab. It was very easy.

After eating crabs, they relaxed for a while. Then they returned to the water and dove for more seashells. Late that afternoon, they saw a small storm approaching.

"We better cover up the perishables," suggested River Wolf.

"You are right."

They guided the dugout to shore and emptied the seashells, flint and stone carvings on the beach. Then they covered the cloaks and other perishable items with the canoe. It started raining, and they went swimming in the rain.

Then River Wolf saw something he had never seen before. It was a narrow cylinder-shaped cloud that was vertical. It went from the water to the sky, and it was spinning.

"Bald Eagle, look!" he said while pointing. "What is that?"

"That's a waterspout. They are common on the ocean. If it gets within a couple arrow shot lengths to us, I would be worried. Otherwise, they are harmless."

They watched as the waterspout passed them by, missing them by about three hundred paces. It was only about twenty-five paces wide. After it passed them, it went onto the beach and blew down some trees before dissipating.

"That was neat!" shouted River Wolf, awestruck.

"Let's get some more oysters," suggested Bald Eagle.

"I will check to see if we caught another crab," offered River Wolf.

There was the biggest crab he had seen yet holding the bait in its claw. River Wolf used the net to pull it out of the water. They ate well that night. The next morning found them diving for shells again. The dugout was getting full of them.

Suddenly, Bald Eagle pointed to a large fish rapidly circling nearby. They went up to the surface.

Bald Eagle shouted, "That is the biggest shark I've ever seen! Let's get out of here!"

They could not swim very fast. River Wolf was panicking.

"If he attacks me, leave me!" said Bald Eagle urgently. "If he attacks you, I will try to fight him off. Either way, try to take the dugout back to shore as fast as you can."

"I won't leave you!" cried River Wolf, petrified.

"Do it! You are too young…"

Bald Eagle was interrupted by the shark nudging him.

"Take the dugout back to… Ah!"

Bald Eagle was instantly pulled under the water, his cries cut short. River Wolf felt his skin crawl. Bald Eagle surfaced again crying in agony. The water was red with his blood. Suddenly Bald Eagle was propelled swiftly away from the dugout, and then back under water.

"Bald Eagle!!!" cried River Wolf.

There was nothing he could do to save him. Bald Eagle surfaced one more time with a choked cry, and then disappeared forever. River Wolf just held onto the dugout motionless. He was in a state of disbelief as he drifted.

Then the sea bottom touching his foot startled him. This brought him back to his senses and he walked the canoe back to the shore in tears. He was now all by himself in an unfamiliar land with dangers that he knew he was completely oblivious to. He had no idea how he would ever get back home again.

* * *

Chapter 11: Medicine Wolf

Winged Rattlesnake Chief went to Panther's lodge for a visit. Panther was out hunting, and Winged Rattlesnake Chief took advantage of his absence to question Autumn Leaf.

"How are you doing, today?" he started.

"I am fine," she replied, "I am tidying up for Panther's return."

"That trader, I believe his name was something Wolf. Or was it Bear?" he asked slyly.

"River Wolf," she answered.

"What tribe was he – Yuchi?"

"He was Cherokee."

Winged Rattlesnake Chief rubbed his hand over the pottery duck effigy bowl that River Wolf had given to Panther. "Panther was a Cherokee also."

"He was adopted into our tribe," added Autumn Leaf.

"They seemed to be good friends. Why did River Wolf give Panther such a nice gift? It's as if they know each other. River Wolf stayed here, while he was in Good Medicine, didn't he?"

"Yes, he did," answered Autumn Leaf.

"Did you see anything that was suspicious between them?"

Autumn Leaf remembered the two conversing in the Cherokee language, but decided not to tell. She did not want to jeopardize her husband's reputation.

"No, I didn't," she said and she looked away.

Her body language made Winged Rattlesnake Chief even more suspicious. "But he gave him such a nice gift. What did he get in return?"

"I don't know. Lodging. Is it a crime to be friends with a trader?" she asked, irritated.

Winged Rattlesnake Chief got defensive. "Oh no! I can even see how that could be an advantage, maybe, if the trader got something in return – after giving away such a nice bowl. But Panther and Jaguar commissioned him to make a monolithic axe, did they not? How is he getting paid?"

"We will see when the axe is delivered. Now I think you should leave."

Panther walked into the lodge in the middle of her sentence. "What's going on?" he asked.

"I was just visiting with Autumn Leaf," responded Winged Rattlesnake Chief. "I'd better go now. 'Bye."

He left, and Autumn Leaf had a disturbed expression on her face.

"What was that all about?" asked Panther.

"When River Wolf was here, why were you so friendly to him?" asked Autumn Leaf, "I demand to know. What were you two talking about in that foreign language? You'd better tell me! That's what Winged Rattlesnake Chief was asking me about."

"He is my brother," replied Panther. "We wanted to keep it secret from the villagers."

Autumn Leaf was stunned. "Why didn't you tell me? Didn't you trust me?"

"I didn't want to get you involved. I was trying to protect you. We need to think of a story to tell them, or else they will think we are traitors."

"I told him that he traded the duck bowl for lodging," said Autumn Leaf. "I didn't know what else to say."

Panther was frustrated as he went outside to dress the deer he had returned with. He had an advantage; he was just as sly as Winged Rattlesnake Chief. He decided to use politics against him, and tell of how this Great Chief had treated the visiting traders. A rivalry would result from this, but Panther saw no other alternative. The two warriors had been friends, but he had no choice in the matter. He had to look after himself and his wife.

* * *

River Wolf thought of returning to Good Medicine, where his brother might be able to help him. But Winged Rattlesnake Chief and Dead Buzzard Warrior might convince the rest of the village that River Wolf was an enemy spy. It might also look like he had murdered Bald Eagle for his canoe and trade goods. That would be dangerous for both him and Panther.

He did not know how to get food in this strange land, and was afraid to go into the water for oysters because of sharks. He didn't want to travel inland back into Muskogee territory either. He found the creek and drank water from it, but did without food. After three days without food, he became delirious.

He knew he had to eat, or else die. He found the bone fishhook and twine amongst Bald Eagle's things, but he had neglected to learn how to prepare crabs to eat; he had been too busy thinking about other things. He managed to catch a fish out of the stream with the fishhook.

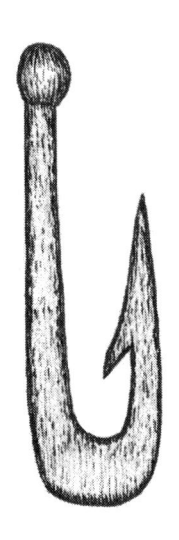

Bone Fishhook.
Redrawn from Beauchamp 1902.

After eating it raw, he went to sleep. He dreamed of Bald Eagle. When he woke up, it was noon the next day, and he was back in this horrible reality. Bald Eagle was dead.

River Wolf didn't have the luxury of time for self-pity. He knew that Bald Eagle would want him to return to Birch Mountain, so he decided to overcome his obstacles and figure out a way to find his way back home. Traveling upstream alone would not work. He needed a partner and friend. River Wolf decided to go west to try to find a Biloxi village and take his chances there.

He paddled the dugout back down the peninsula to the large bay at the mouth of the big river. Then he beached the dugout on the west shore of the bay. When he turned around, he saw an old man, his bow ready, and aiming an arrow at him.

River Wolf quickly signed, "Trader."

The man relaxed and walked up to see the contents of the canoe. Then the man signed, "I trader, long ago."

River Wolf couldn't believe this turn of luck.

The man continued signing, "Nice canoe."

"Would you like it?" signed River Wolf.

The man was surprised. "Why would a trader give away the most valuable tool of his trade?" he signed.

River Wolf signed, "My friend's canoe. We were traveling together – my first trading trip. He was training me. We were diving for seashells and he was attacked and killed by a large sea fish. I am alone and afraid people will think I killed Bald Eagle. I loved him like a father." Tears came to River Wolf's eyes as he signed, "I am afraid nobody will believe me."

The man gestured his condolences. "I believe you," he signed. "What was your friend's name?"

"Bald Eagle of the Muskogee. His home was in Good Medicine."

The man told River Wolf about himself. His name was Medicine Wolf, and he was Biloxi, but was a hermit who lived nearby with his daughter. They seemed to bond when he found out River Wolf's name. They were both Wolves, and Wolves stuck together.

The man told River Wolf that his dugout canoe had been washed away during the storm. River Wolf told Medicine Wolf of Birch Mountain, and he seemed to know the general area that the village was in.

"Is it near the Cherokee village, Pine Bend?" Medicine Wolf signed.

"Yes, Birch Mountain is the new Cherokee capital," replied River Wolf, "It is a day's journey from Pine Bend. Help me get there, and the dugout is yours."

"And the contents?"

"No, I must keep my wares," replied River Wolf.

The man picked out a wolf effigy tubular pipe and signed, "This and the dugout, I take you home."

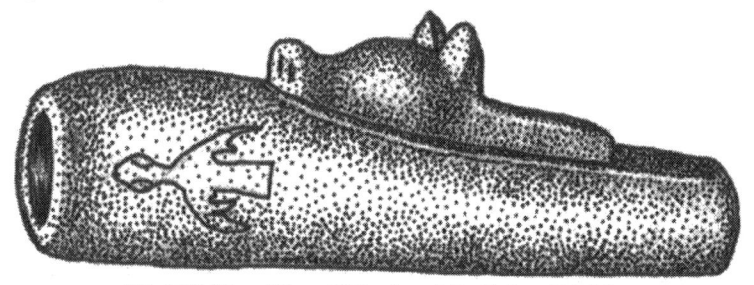

Wolf Effigy Pipe Gifted to Medicine Wolf.
Redrawn from McGuire 1897.

"Yes," signed River Wolf, "Good."

"Do you have tobacco?" signed Medicine Wolf.

"Yes, I will give Bald Eagle's tobacco to you."

"Let's go to my lodge and eat," signed Medicine Wolf. "I knew Bald Eagle when he was your age. He was honest and fair. Excellent at driving a hard bargain."

They arrived at Medicine Wolf's newly repaired lodge and River Wolf saw a beautiful woman doing chores. She had a strong resemblance to Beaver Pelt. River Wolf wondered if he still smelled like a skunk.

"This is my daughter, Sand Dollar," signed Medicine Wolf and he introduced her to River Wolf in the Biloxi tongue.

They ate a fine meal of fish from the sea and took a nap. When River Wolf woke up the next morning, they prepared their provisions for the journey. Before sunrise the next morning, Medicine Wolf and River Wolf bade farewell to Sand Dollar and began their trip up the river. It was then that River Wolf realized that he had not landed on the west shore of the bay; rather, it was an island south of the shore.

"Are we just going to leave Sand Dollar alone on that little island?" signed River Wolf.

"My brother visits frequently," answered Medicine Wolf. "I told her to return to the village with him in a couple of days when he shows up. Don't worry, she's a tough girl, and she has plenty to eat."

Then Medicine Wolf spoke words in a language that River Wolf understood, "Do you know Muskhogean?"

"Yes, I do!" replied River Wolf. "Bald Eagle taught me."

"Good! I was wondering how we would be able to talk and paddle, at the same time."

River Wolf was also very relieved that they could now talk and understand each other's words. He decided that this would be a good opportunity to start learning the Biloxi dialect.

The constant paddling was very strenuous and River Wolf knew that it would be upstream all the way back to Birch Mountain. But he was glad to finally be headed for home again. Medicine Wolf however was old and the constant paddling made his shoulders hurt him badly.

When they arrived at the west shore of the bay, they followed it north until just before sunset. They caught and cooked crabs. This time, River Wolf paid attention to how to prepare them.

After they ate, Medicine Wolf told River Wolf about all the damage the hurricane had done to his island home. He said that his younger brother from the Biloxi village came to visit immediately after the storm. He brought food and helped him and Sand Dollar repair their lodge.

"What is your brother's name?" asked River Wolf.

"Red Bone," came the reply. "We used to travel together on trading excursions. He and Sand Dollar are about the only people who understand me now that my wife is gone."

They were silent after that, and before River Wolf knew it, the morning Sun awakened him. Medicine Wolf was still asleep, so he went into the woods and set some squirrel traps. He returned to camp and started a fire.

Medicine Wolf woke up and said, "I will get breakfast."

"Don't worry about it," replied River Wolf. "I have already set some squirrel traps."

He left to check the traps, and returned shortly with three squirrels. They ate and were back on their way. By the next evening, they were at the mouth of the river and the large island.

They set up camp and Medicine Wolf went into the woods empty-handed. River Wolf wondered how the man intended to get any food without a weapon. Medicine Wolf soon returned with six doves.

"How did you get those?" asked River Wolf.

"I threw rocks and hit their heads."

River Wolf was amazed. He decided to learn how to do that when he got the time.

The next morning they were on their way again. As they traveled, River Wolf continued learning Biloxi a little at a time.

* * *

One moon had passed, and River Wolf began to recognize the scenery. They were at the creek where Loner lived.

"Do you need any flint?" asked Medicine Wolf, "There is plenty of it up this creek."

River Wolf was surprised that Medicine Wolf knew the territory so well. He was also relieved. "Buck will be needing some," he replied.

"Who is Buck?"

"He is my best friend. His name is The Buck Kicks the Drum, but we just call him Buck. He is a very good flint knapper."

They started paddling up the creek towards Loner's place.

"Do you know Loner?" asked River Wolf.

"Who?"

"Loner. He is a recluse that lives where the flint outcroppings are."

"I never met him."

"He is nice, but he is very strange. I think he is touched in the head a little. He sees spiders, crickets and things that aren't really there."

They beached the dugout and walked up the hill looking for Loner. They looked and called his name for a long time, but could not find him. Finally, River Wolf spotted Loner's tiny shelter through the woods. "Loner!" he called. "Loner!"

They arrived at Loner's shelter and found that it was abandoned and falling apart. They saw no signs of Loner. River Wolf wondered what could have happened to him.

The two gathered flint, and soon found a skeleton with a flint knife next to it. There was little flesh left as buzzards had devoured most of it. River Wolf wondered if Loner had committed suicide, or if he had been killed. The presence of the fine knife did not suggest robbery. Either way, Loner would not be frightened by imaginary spiders anymore.

They built a charnel platform and placed what was left of Loner's body on it. River Wolf had started training to be a priest when he was young. But Loner was Muskogee, so neither River Wolf nor Medicine Wolf felt like they could perform an adequate burial ceremony. Each of them said prayers in his own way and departed. It was all they could do for him.

They filled their bags with flint and returned to the canoe to set up camp. It was a very hot and humid afternoon. River Wolf set some squirrel traps. Then he joined Medicine Wolf for a swim in the creek. They started a fire, and then River Wolf checked his traps. He returned with six squirrels and found Medicine Wolf making a fish arrow.

Harpoon-Like Tip for a Fish Arrow.

"Look what I got," said River Wolf, holding up the squirrels.

"Oh good!" replied Medicine Wolf. "I was just getting hungry too. Let's skin them."

They dressed the squirrels and began cooking them over the fire. The heat of the fire added to the hot afternoon.

"Man, it is so hot!" complained Medicine Wolf, "Look up there – not a single cloud in the sky."

"I will be glad when we get back to the mountains of home," added River Wolf.

"This is such a comfortable shady place for a day like today," said Medicine Wolf, "I like it here. Why don't we take a break and camp here for a couple of days?"

River Wolf hated to hear that. He wanted to get back home to Beaver Pelt as soon as possible, but he decided to give the old man a break.

"I want to get home as soon as possible," he said, "but you are sore. Why don't we just pass villages we would normally stop and trade at? That way, we can stop and relax when we want to. I have plenty of good things that are in demand at home. They would love these shells and the flint. Why don't we just save it all for them?"

"That sounds good to me," answered Medicine Wolf. "I now remember why I retired. This constant paddling is wearing me out. I have some advice for you – don't get old."

They ate squirrel meat and Medicine Wolf saved some of the guts for wrapping his fish arrow with. River Wolf wanted to resume the journey now, but he had to wait. He tried to enjoy himself, even though he was still away from home.

Then he thought of the piece of greenstone. He looked around in the dugout and found it and his pecking stone. He resumed work on the monolithic axe. That helped to relax him. He pecked on it until dark.

They ate more squirrel meat and smoked their pipes. The two talked until Medicine Wolf fell asleep. River Wolf lay there thinking about Beaver Pelt. Then his thoughts shifted to memories of Bald Eagle. He missed him and wondered if it would ever be safe to return to Good Medicine again. Then he had an idea – after he got to Birch Mountain, he should send Medicine Wolf with some trade goods for Bald Eagle's daughter. That was the least he could do. He owed it to Bald Eagle.

Early the next morning, River Wolf heard a distant chuckling sound. He stirred in his bearskin, but went back to sleep. Suddenly, there was a loud thud right next to his head. He jumped up and saw an enormous catfish right next to where his head had been. He looked up and saw Medicine Wolf smiling at him.

"Good morning," he greeted reluctantly.

"Let's cook it up!" laughed Medicine Wolf. "I will clean it, and you start the fire."

River Wolf wiped the sleep out of his eyes and began rekindling the campfire. After he was wide-awake, he helped Medicine Wolf finish cleaning the fish, and they cooked it. There was no breeze, heavy fog, and it was already pretty warm. River Wolf could tell it was going to be another hot day.

They stayed at that place on the creek for one more night, and left early the next morning. River Wolf was glad to be on the move again. They passed many villages, but only after dark. There was no sense in alerting the people when they had no intentions of stopping to trade.

"I want to ask you a favor," River Wolf said to Medicine Wolf.

"What do you need me to do?"

"This dugout belonged to Bald Eagle, along with around half the cargo. He would have wanted me to keep the dugout, but I can't keep all his things. He has a daughter in Good Medicine who will be wondering what happened to him. She needs to know. I trust you. Do you think you could find a way to tell her and give her back her father's things? That way, she will have at least some of her father's wealth."

"I will not be able to do it myself," answered Medicine Wolf, "but I have a lot of friends who are traders. Many of them visit me on their way to Good Medicine. I can send his things with one of them."

"I would appreciate it if you could arrange that for me," said River Wolf.

"I would be glad to do it. You are very thoughtful. Most people would just keep everything."

"He was very good to me," River Wolf said after a period of silence. "He saved my life. Twice. He stopped the Muskogee from burning me at the stake, and then he died protecting me from the shark." River Wolf chose to look at the shark attack like that, even though he didn't know for certain that it would have been Bald Eagle's intention to be attacked instead of him.

* * *

Gourd Rattle.

The heat of the summer had passed. Preparations were being made in Birch Mountain for the Ripe Corn Ceremony. Runners were sent out to notify the nation of the date to gather at Birch Mountain.

Beaver Pelt knew that the Great New Moon Ceremony was less than three weeks away. She tried to be confident that River Wolf would soon be back, but her hope was now fading as time went by.

All the citizens of the nation arrived a few days later, and the Ripe Corn Ceremony began. There was the usual feasting, and the men performed a dance, carrying green tree limbs in their right hands. They did this dance on each of the four days of the ceremony. The women were forbidden to enter the village square while these dances took place.

Beaver Pelt and Squirrel Fur visited with their relatives during the ceremony, but they could sense that Beaver Pelt was preoccupied with something. The ceremony ended, and everybody returned to his or her home village.

The residents of Birch Mountain now began harvesting their crops. Beaver Pelt helped Squirrel Fur and Sparrow gather the crops from the field they shared. Things should have been joyful. The harvest was plentiful, but they were all silent in their work. River Wolf's return was definitely overdue now.

Now the date was set for the Great New Moon Ceremony, and preparations were being made. The harvesting was finished in a week. Beaver Pelt was exhausted from worry and the harvest. She went back to River Wolf's lodge and began weeping bitter tears until she slept. She was awakened by a commotion in the village. She raised her head and listened. She heard the word, 'Trader!' being shouted repeatedly.

She immediately leaped out of the bed and ran as fast as she could towards the river. As she exited the palisade gate, she saw the crowd of villagers gathered around a dugout canoe. As she made her way through the crowd, she saw an elderly man she had never seen before. It wasn't Bald Eagle. Her heart sank, and she fought the tears as she headed back towards the palisade.

She heard a woman's voice calling, "Beaver Pelt!"

She turned around and saw Sparrow.

"Did he find you?" asked Sparrow.

"Who?"

"River Wolf! He is back! He and his mother went back inside the village looking for you!"

Beaver Pelt raced as fast as possible back into the palisade. First she went to Squirrel Fur's lodge. They were not there. So, she ran to Buck and Tanager's lodge and nobody was there either. Finally she ran back to River Wolf's lodge and there he was, exiting the lodge, talking to his mother. Beaver Pelt couldn't believe her eyes. She just stood there staring at him.

River Wolf's eyes shifted to her and he smiled at her. She ran to him and embraced him tightly for what seemed like an eternity.

"I will leave you two alone," said Squirrel Fur, and then she left, unnoticed by both River Wolf and Beaver Pelt.

"I missed you so much," whispered Beaver Pelt.

"I missed you too. I forgot to tell Mother about Panther!"

"Who?"

"I found Running Fox! His name is now Panther. I should tell Mother about it today."

"Then you'd better go," said Beaver Pelt. "Tonight I will cook you a meal you will never forget! I know you have a lot of things to do. I will see you tonight."

They kissed and then River Wolf went looking for his mother. She was not at her lodge, so he went back to the canoe. He saw Buck among the crowd, looking at all of the flint and conch shells.

"Hello, Buck," greeted River Wolf.

"River Wolf!" exclaimed Buck, and the two hugged each other tightly.

"How have you been?" asked River Wolf with a smile.

"We have been fine," replied Buck, "We were beginning to worry about you. Who is this new person? Where is Bald Eagle?"

"This is Medicine Wolf. Bald Eagle got killed by a large sea fish while we were diving for conch shells. Medicine Wolf guided me back home. A lot has happened. I ran into some hardships that delayed my return."

Medicine Wolf looked as though he was feeling awkward. River Wolf observed this and spoke to him in Muskhogean.

"This is my best friend Buck," he introduced. Then he spoke to Buck in Cherokee, "Meet Medicine Wolf."

"You know Muskhogean?" asked Buck, amazed.

"Bald Eagle taught me," answered River Wolf.

Buck and Medicine Wolf began a conversation in Muskhogean. River Wolf had so much to do, and he did not know where to start. He wanted to tell his mother about Panther.

"Buck, excuse me for interrupting," he said. "I really have to go. I have some news for you and Mother. I will tell you later, but I must tell Mother right away."

"I will see you later then," said Buck. He continued his conversation with Medicine Wolf as River Wolf left.

River Wolf ran back inside the palisade and to Sparrow's lodge. He found his mother and Sparrow inside.

"Hello, River Wolf," greeted Aunt Sparrow.

"Hello, Sparrow," he greeted as they hugged each other again.

Then River Wolf said, "I need to speak with you, Mother."

"I will leave you two alone," offered Sparrow.

"No, Sparrow, you need to hear this too. You two will never guess who I ran into during the trip."

Squirrel Fur and Sparrow looked at each other and then at River Wolf.

"Who?" asked Squirrel Fur.

"Running Fox!"

"You shouldn't play jokes like that on your poor mother, River Wolf," said Sparrow sternly.

"It is no joke! I am serious! The Yuchis traded him into the Muskogee tribe. He was a slave, but was later adopted. He is now a war chief, and lives in a village that's twice the size of Birch Mountain. His name is now Panther. I stayed with him while we visited the village."

"Are you sure it was really him?" asked Squirrel Fur.

"Absolutely! He knew plenty of details about the kidnapping. He told me his story; he said he was getting cane for making a blowgun when he was captured."

Tears came to Squirrel Fur's eyes, and both River Wolf and Sparrow hugged her.

"I asked him to return with me," continued River Wolf, "but he didn't want to give up his position in Good Medicine. He also has a wife there, named Autumn Leaf."

"Who has a wife?" asked Beaver Pelt as she walked in.

"Running Fox," answered River Wolf.

"And soon you will too!" smiled Beaver Pelt.

"Yes, I will," he replied and he hugged her.

"I did not mean to interrupt your visit with your mother and aunt," apologized Beaver Pelt. "I was just going to ask them if they had some venison left from Broken Spear's hunting trip last night."

"You didn't interrupt us," said River Wolf. "I was just finished."

"I have some left, and some cornbread," offered Sparrow.

Beaver Pelt took the deer meat and cornbread, and thanked her as she turned to leave.

"Wait!" said River Wolf. "I just remembered – I brought you a gift!"

"What did you bring me?"

"This." River Wolf gave her a beautifully engraved antler comb.

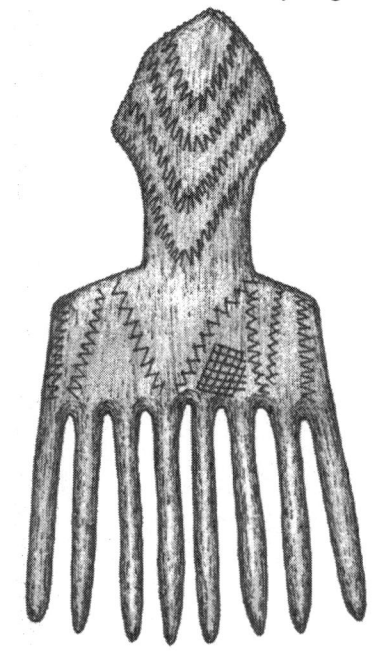

Engraved Antler Comb.
Redrawn from Lewis & Kneberg 1958.

Beaver Pelt gasped when she saw it, and kissed him. "Thank you!"

"You are welcome! I'd better go and help Medicine Wolf," said River Wolf, then he departed for the river. On the way, he saw the Uku and Eagle Medicine returning from the river.

"River Wolf!" greeted Eagle Medicine. "It's so good to see you! Your family was very worried. But you are back home safe again."

"Hello, Eagle Medicine, Standing Bear," replied River Wolf. "It's good to see you two."

He returned back to the river and saw Medicine Wolf unloading the goods from the dugout.

"I took the liberty of starting to unload your things," said Medicine Wolf. "I want to start out early in the morning. I figured you didn't want the cloaks since your people make them."

"I hate to see you leave so soon," replied River Wolf.

"I have to. I don't like the cold, and it will take a moon to get back to my island. My daughter is waiting."

"I understand," said River Wolf. "I know what it is like to be homesick too."

They continued unloading and deciding what to send back to Bald Eagle's daughter. As it turned out, River Wolf was left with most of the shells and flint.

"These are more valuable here than at Good Medicine," suggested Medicine Wolf.

The Sun had gone down, and Medicine Wolf found lodging with a single woman in the village. There was only one thing left for River Wolf to do. He went to Sparrow's lodge with a pretty conch shell to do some bartering with Broken Spear.

"I will trade you this conch shell for a large full bag of tobacco," he offered.

"Alright," agreed Broken Spear.

River Wolf put the tobacco in the stern of the dugout, where Medicine Wolf would surely find it. Then he returned to his lodge and Beaver Pelt.

He walked inside and ate the best meal he had ever had in his life. He noticed her drinking wild yam tea. Beaver Pelt noticed the burn scars on his feet.

"What happened to your feet?" she asked.

"Bald Eagle and I camped just upstream from a village. He did not think we should show up there after dark. He sent me hunting, and some young men of the village shot me, thinking I was an enemy. They took me home and started burning me at the stake. But Bald Eagle appeared out of the crowd and stopped them. See where I got shot with the arrow?"

River Wolf showed her the scar. He smiled at her curiosity. Then they went to bed together. They shared the most passionate night that either one of them had experienced. It was so good to be back home again! They held each other tightly all night long.

The next morning, River Wolf went to bid farewell to Medicine Wolf. River Wolf found him alone, loading provisions into the dugout.

"Good morning!" greeted River Wolf.

"What's this?" Medicine Wolf said, pointing to the deerskin bag.

"That is my thank-you gift to you. It is full of tobacco."

"Thank you! I almost forgot to get some."

"You take care of yourself, and have a safe trip home. I will probably see you next summer."

"It has been good traveling with you."

"Thank you for navigating me back home," said River Wolf. "Goodbye."

"Goodbye, River Wolf."

Medicine Wolf shoved off and began his journey back to his daughter and their island home. River Wolf would miss his friend. He sought the company of his other friend, Buck. When he arrived at Buck's lodge, only Tanager was there.

"Where is Buck?" asked River Wolf.

"He left early this morning to hunt for a bear," replied Tanager. "I hear you found Running Fox. Is that true?"

"Yes," answered River Wolf, "He is a war chief at the Muskogee capital. He is married to a beautiful Muskogee woman.

"I thought the Yuchi had him," said Tanager.

"They captured him, but he was traded to the Muskogee, and then adopted into the tribe."

"Is he happy there?"

"He seemed to be. I offered to help him escape, but he refused. How is Titmouse doing?"

"She is asleep. She is learning to talk now."

Buck walked in.

"Oh, River Wolf," said Buck. "I need your help in bringing a bear home."

"You've already killed a bear?" asked Tanager, surprised.

"Yes, I did. Can you help me, River Wolf?"

"Sure, I will help."

The two found some rope, and then they exited the palisade and headed west towards the place where the dead bear lay.

"How far away is he?" asked River Wolf.

"Not too far," replied Buck, "I got lucky today. Let's find a thicket and cut a pole to carry the bear with."

After cutting the pole, they got to the bear and tied its front and rear legs to the pole. Then they lifted the pole and carried the bear back to the village. Butchering the bear was a joyful experience, because many relatives came and helped. Sparrow and Broken Spear came, along with Squirrel Fur and Twisted Stick. Beaver Pelt couldn't come because it was her moon time and she had gone to the women's hut.

The bear was very large, and it took two days working on it before they were finished. Everybody had plenty of bear meat and grease. Buck saved the enormous claws and teeth to use for trading, whenever he went on his next trading excursion.

River Wolf was bored while Beaver Pelt was away, so Buck and Tanager invited him over to eat and visit with them and Titmouse. One day, Beaver Pelt appeared in the doorway of Buck and Tanager's lodge. She was back.

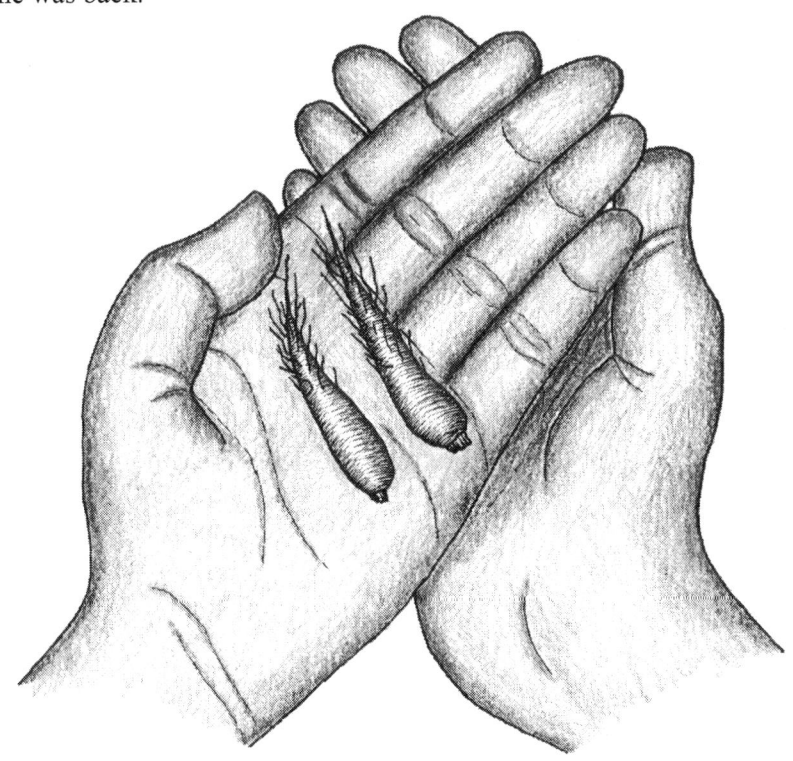

An Omen for a Wedding.

Now River Wolf had something important and meaningful to do. He told his mother about his desire to marry Beaver Pelt. She spoke with the leaders of the Long Hair Clan to which Beaver Pelt belonged. After getting their consent, they set a date with Eagle Medicine for the ceremony.

On the morning of the day of the wedding, Eagle Medicine gathered two roots of a small plant and placed them in his hand, side-by-side. He faced the east and said a prayer, asking Spirit if the couple was compatible. If the roots moved closer together without wilting, it was thought to be a sign that the couple would enjoy a long and happy marriage. If they didn't move, or if either root wilted, it was considered a bad omen and the wedding would be called off. The omen was good.

So, late that afternoon, many members of the Bird Clan and the Long Hair Clan gathered in the heptagon for the ceremony. River Wolf was on one side of the heptagon, being escorted by Eagle Medicine.

Beaver Pelt was on the other side, being escorted by Three Crows. River Wolf carried a blanket and a deer leg, given to him by Squirrel Fur. They both approached the center of the heptagon.

"Beaver Pelt," said River Wolf, "I bring you this venison to show that I am committed to provide for you as your husband."

"I accept your venison," replied Beaver Pelt in the same formal manner, and then she held up another blanket she'd had, along with an ear of corn. "Here is some food which is a token that I shall grow and cook food for you like a wife should do," she said.

"I accept your corn," replied River Wolf.

The two blankets were brought together, symbolizing the new union being formed.

"You are welcome in my lodge," said Beaver Pelt, motioning him to leave with her. The lodge was originally River Wolf's but, by tradition, a woman was the lodge keeper, and therefore the owner.

They were now married. The Great New Moon Ceremony would be in a few days, during which they had time to reconsider their vows. After the ceremony, their marriage would be official.

The nation gathered at Birch Mountain for the Great New Moon Ceremony. The Ceremony lasted for two days and nights. During the ceremony, River Wolf and Beaver Pelt sealed their marriage.

"River Wolf, of the Bird Clan, do you promise to fulfill your duties providing meat as a husband," asked Eagle Medicine, "and not speak unkindly to her, no matter how angry you are with her?"

"Yes, I do," replied River Wolf.

"And do you, Beaver Pelt, of the Long Hair Clan, promise to keep the lodge and be tolerant of him speaking unkindly to you?"

"Yes," answered Beaver Pelt.

They were now officially husband and wife. But something disturbing happened during the Great New Moon Ceremony that is worthy of mention. The people gathered at the river to gaze into the Crystal and submerge themselves.

As Beaver Pelt gazed into the sacred Crystal, she saw the death omen, meaning she would perish that winter. She isolated herself and fasted. River Wolf heard the news from his mother and silently prayed for his wife.

The next morning, Beaver Pelt repeated the Crystal gazing and once again, she saw the death omen. She was terrified, and angry. *Why me? I have just begun my life. I have a husband who needs me!* she thought. She had one more chance, but that wouldn't be until the next moon. The time between was filled with worry.

She realized that her time with River Wolf was limited, and she wanted to make the most of it. They spent many long hours in the woods together, walking, sitting on rocks and talking to each other.

Beaver Pelt tried to be cheerful but, inside, River Wolf was very worried. He wondered what could happen to take her away at such a young age. *Why? She can't die! She is too young!* He thought to himself. He put on a front and reminded her that she had another chance.

The next moon came, and now was the time for the unfortunates who saw the death omen to gaze into the Crystal again. When it was Beaver Pelt's turn, she saw no death sign. It seemed she was cleared of this early fate. She rejoiced and submerged herself in the river seven times, keeping with the tradition. River Wolf was also overjoyed to hear the news.

One cool morning, River Wolf and Beaver Pelt moved into their hothouse. After they got settled in, River Wolf resumed carving on the monolithic axe.

"We are almost out of meat," reminded Beaver Pelt.

"I will go and get some," returned River Wolf, and then he went to the summer lodge and got a conch shell. Then he had a better idea. He got a piece of flint and took it to Buck's lodge and traded for bear meat. He returned to the hothouse with the meat.

"Where did you get that?" asked Beaver Pelt, surprised.

"I traded for it," he answered, with a smile.

"You trade for everything, don't you?"

"It's better than freezing out in the woods, waiting for some animal to appear," he laughed.

"But the bears will be hibernating soon," said Beaver Pelt, as she began cooking the meat.

River Wolf started carving on the monolithic axe again. Its basic form was now beginning to show. But there were still many weeks of work left to do. He thought of Bald Eagle and Medicine Wolf while he carved. Before he knew it, it was time to eat.

They ate their fill of bear meat, cornbread and acorn meal bread. Then they cuddled on a bearskin in front of the fire.

"Tell me about the Great Sea," said Beaver Pelt.

"It goes as far as the eye can see. There are all kinds of strange animals. Some of them are dangerous. A large sea fish killed Bald Eagle. But it is also very beautiful – almost as beautiful as you."

Beaver Pelt smiled shyly and kissed him. He continued talking about the ocean.

"There are strange little critters called crabs. They are like giant spiders but they have claws. They are easy to catch; all you need to do is tie a dead fish to a piece of twine. Tie the other end of the twine to a pole that is anchored in the sand. They grab the fish with their claw and do not let go, until you pull them out of the water with a net. It is such a wonderful place. I swore I would take you there someday so you could see it for yourself. But when Bald Eagle died, I had second thoughts."

"You grew close to him," observed Beaver Pelt.

"Yes, he was like a father to me," he said. "I learned so much from him."

"You are close to Medicine Wolf also," she said.

"I was left all alone in unfamiliar territory. I was really in trouble, but I happened upon Medicine Wolf and he helped me to get back home. He is very old, and he tired easily. He had to rest, so we didn't trade at many villages on the way back. Instead, we stopped, and camped between villages, so he could rest."

"How are we going to travel next cycle?" asked Beaver Pelt. "We have no canoe."

"Next spring I will make a dugout," he replied. "Then we will leave in the following spring."

"Can you make a canoe all by yourself?"

"I will trade for help if I need to while doing the more difficult parts. That reminds me – I need to make some adzes to hollow it out with."

The weather was getting colder by the week. One morning Beaver Pelt woke River Wolf.

"Take a look outside!" she said.

River Wolf wrapped himself in a bearskin blanket and ventured outside the hothouse. The ground and the trees were white with snow. It was a beautiful sight, but the cold made him wish it were summer. River Wolf could not stand being out in the cold.

"We need more meat," she said, when he got back inside the hothouse.

"Well, I am sure that there are no bears out and about in this weather," he replied, "and Buck can't kill a deer because of his totem."

River Wolf went to the summer lodge and got two conch shells. He took them to Broken Spear and Sparrow's lodge. Broken Spear had just returned from a hunting trip, and was skinning a large deer.

"Hello, Broken Spear," greeted River Wolf.

"How are you doing?" returned Broken Spear.

"We are fine, but we need meat. Will you trade some of that deer for these conch shells?"

Broken Spear paused his work to look the shells over. Finally, he said, "I will tell you what I need more than pretty shells. I dropped my pipe on a rock and broke it. Do you have any pipes left?"

"Not many," answered River Wolf. "What did you have in mind?"

"Anything. A plain one. I just want to smoke!"

"I have a duck effigy tubular pipe that is good."

Duck Effigy Tubular Pipe.
Redrawn from Thruston 1897.

"I will give you half of this deer for that pipe," offered Broken Spear, "and your help in preparing the deer. But I keep the skin and antlers."

"That sounds fair," agreed River Wolf.

"Go get the pipe. I want to smoke!"

River Wolf went to his summer lodge, where he was keeping his trade goods. He found the duck effigy pipe and returned to Broken Spear's lodge.

"Here you are," he said.

"Come inside," said Broken Spear, motioning him inside of their hothouse. Broken Spear loaded the pipe, and had a smoke. When he finished smoking, they went outside to finish butchering the deer. Later that evening, River Wolf carried home his half of the meat.

"Where did you get that?" asked Beaver Pelt.

"I traded Broken Spear a pipe for it." He replied.

They cooked up some of it, and started making jerky from the rest. River Wolf took some cooked venison to his mother. Then he returned home and put more logs on the fire. He crawled under the bearskin blanket next to Beaver Pelt. They kept each other warm throughout that long, and cold night.

Chapter 12: Canoe

The warm south winds of spring found River Wolf polishing the monolithic axe he had been working on for so long. It had taken the entire winter of almost constant work to get to this point, and now his hands were very sore.

The First New Moon of Spring Ceremony had ended the previous day. The sacred fire had been rekindled throughout Birch Mountain, and the visitors from all reaches of the Cherokee nation had returned home with coals from the new fire.

"Why don't I move us into the summer lodge?" asked Beaver Pelt. "That hothouse is too dark and crowded for this pretty weather."

"Let me help you," offered River Wolf.

"No, you are almost finished with that axe," said Beaver Pelt. "I don't want to interrupt you."

"Are you sure?" asked River Wolf.

"Yes, this warm day has me feeling energetic. Polish your axe. I will have it taken care of in no time."

Now they would live in the lodge, and use the hothouse for storage. There was some flint and about half of the conch shells left. Beaver Pelt was amazed that River Wolf provided meat the entire winter, solely by bartering for it. He was good at bartering, to still have that many shells left.

As River Wolf polished, he thought of hunting. It had been a long time, and the weather was very good. He wanted to set some squirrel traps. He decided to finish the monolithic axe first. He spent two weeks polishing it alone. Now that the polishing was finished, he just had to drill the hole at the bottom of the handle.

River Wolf got out his flint drill and, by the end of the next day, the hole was drilled. Now he polished around the hole to clean up minor nicks and scratches from drilling. He heated it and rubbed bear grease into it for another day. It was finally finished.

"Beaver Pelt," he called, as he entered the lodge. "Look. I am finally done with it."

"Wow!" exclaimed Beaver Pelt, "That is beautiful! What did you say they use those for?"

"For killing relatives and slaves of a dead person so they can all be buried together."

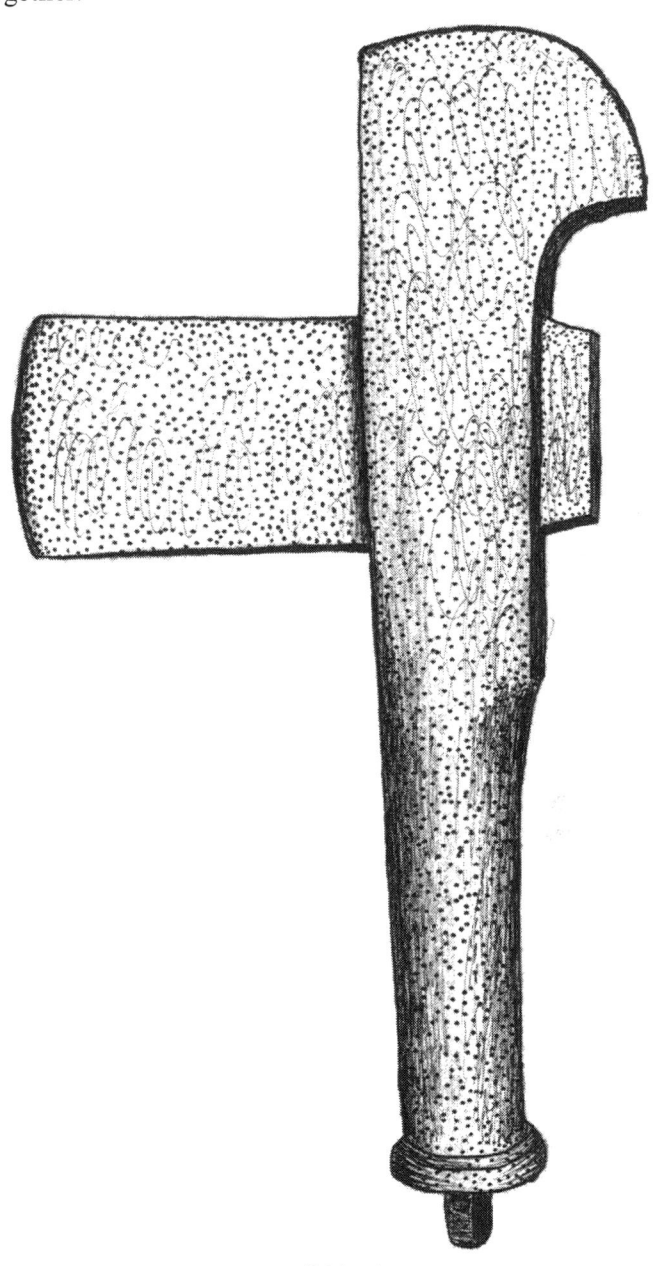

Monolithic Axe.
Redrawn from Saville 1916.

It now didn't seem as pretty to Beaver Pelt as it did before she knew what it was used for. She had a disappointed expression that made River Wolf laugh out loud.

"You didn't think they put all that work into it just so they could chop down a tree, did you?" asked River Wolf with a smile.

"Of course not!" returned Beaver Pelt, "I knew it was ceremonial. You did a good job on it."

"Thank you," said River Wolf. "By the way, how does squirrel meat sound for dinner?"

"You are going to set traps?" asked Beaver Pelt.

"Yes, right now, unless you want something else."

"That sounds fine, it's been a long time since we had squirrel."

River Wolf got some twine he had traded for, a moon ago, and left for the woods outside the palisade. He set up seven nooses and the leaning log and then went to visit his mother. After a half a day, he checked the traps and found that he had caught five squirrels. As River Wolf and Beaver Pelt ate dinner, he was silent.

"What are you thinking about?" asked Beaver Pelt.

"I need to start making a dugout canoe," he replied, "but first, I need to make a good large axe and an adze. I think I will make them from flint. It will be faster than pecking them from granite. Do you still want to come with me on trading trips?"

"Yes," answered Beaver Pelt, "of course."

"Then I will make the dugout large enough for both of us. It will be pretty small when compared to the average dugout, but it will serve its purpose."

River Wolf and Beaver Pelt cuddled in front of the fire. They kissed and whispered sweet words in each other's ear. Then they retired and went to bed for the night.

They rose early the next morning, and joined the village for morning devotions and bathing in the river. They returned home and ate breakfast. Then River Wolf knapped a large flint axe head and an adze.

After eating lunch, River Wolf went outside the palisade and into the woods to find handles for the axe and adze. He was walking down a path when he heard something up ahead. He crept silently closer and saw a turkey hen and around twenty chicks scratching around in the dirt for food. Suddenly the chicks scattered and the hen flew up and collided with a hawk! The hawk was bent on taking one of the chicks for a meal. River Wolf was awestruck at this motherly act of protection. The turkey hen had risked her own safety to protect her young. The hawk flew away, without her meal, and the mother turkey landed. The twenty chicks stood there looking up into the sky. Meanwhile the mother turkey just scratched around as if nothing had happened. River Wolf watched them for a long time. The chicks never stopped looking into the sky. They appeared sort of stupid to River Wolf and he smiled at the unusual sight. Finally he decided he had wasted enough time and he continued looking for wood. After a few days of woodworking, he completed the handles for the axe and adze.

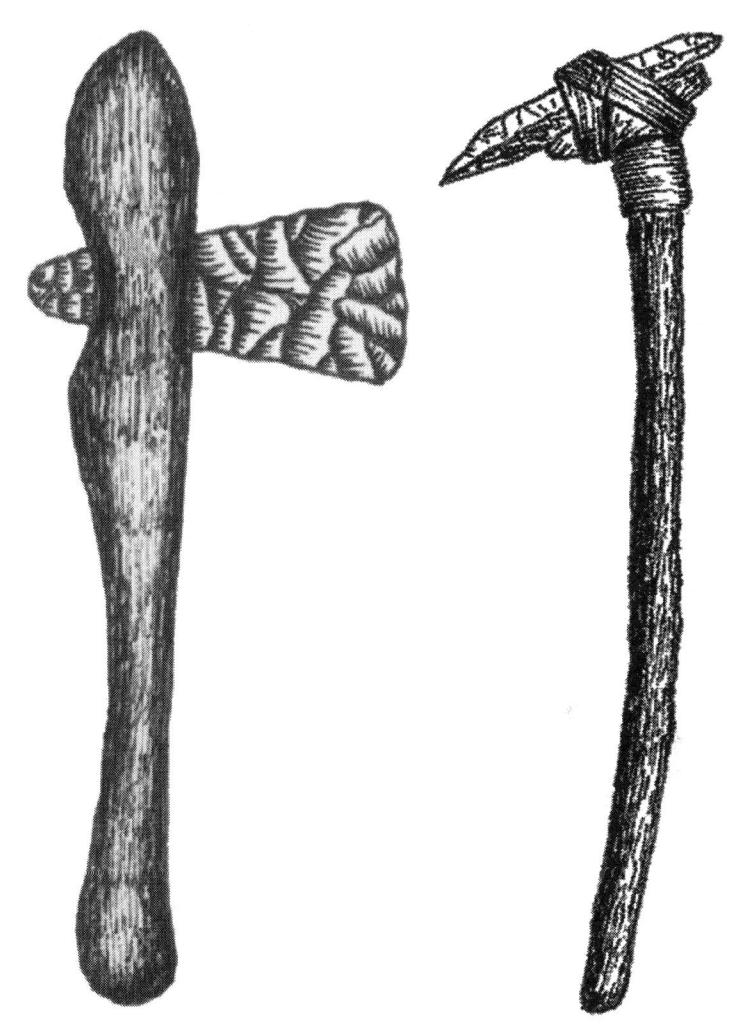

Flint Axe & Adze.

The next morning, he took the axe and hunted for a good poplar tree. After searching for most of the morning, he selected a good tree. He took the axe and chopped away the bark in a circle around the base of the tree, exposing the wood. This would kill the tree, by cutting off the circulation from the roots.

On his way home, he heard war whoops. He began running towards the village, fearful for his family's safety. When he reached the palisade, there were warriors running out to intercept the enemies. He managed to get inside of the palisade, and saw three lodges burning. He ran towards his lodge, as fast as his legs would carry him.

"Beaver Pelt!" he called. "Beaver Pelt!"

She was not at home. He ran to his mother's lodge and found Beaver Pelt and his mother looking after Sparrow, who had been struck by a fire arrow. River Wolf looked the arrow over. It was Muskogee. They had not attacked in many cycles! Why now?

Sparrow lay there moaning in pain. River Wolf ran inside his mother's lodge and got the water bottle. He gently poured the water on Sparrow's burn to soothe it.

He knew that a war would result from this incident, and now he feared for his brother's safety. There was the usual Warrior Dance, and the next morning the warriors departed to the southwest, seeking retribution.

Things calmed down in Birch Mountain, but many wives and children worried about their husbands and fathers who were away from home.

After a few days, River Wolf returned to the dead poplar tree, which had dried out some. He built a fire all around the base. The next day he began chopping away the charcoal where the fire had burned. When the wood was exposed, he built another fire. He repeated this process of burning and chopping for a week, until the tree fell down. Then he chopped and burned the branches off until he had a log about eighteen feet long, and three feet in diameter.

All the while, his father's words echoed in his mind - *You should always be ready for combat... It doesn't really matter now, but someday you will have a family to protect, and you must be ready. You'd better practice now while you are young, or else you won't amount to anything, and your family will die!*

He tried not to think about it as he began making the rough shape of the dugout by burning and chopping with the adze.

When he returned home that night, Beaver Pelt noticed that something was troubling him.

"What's wrong?" she asked.

"Sometimes I feel like I should be out there risking my life fighting the Muskogee, with the rest of the warriors," he replied. "But I have always hated war. My father often lectured me about why I should be a warrior. He forced me to participate in the war games. Now, it seems that my own brother is an enemy. I just don't feel cut out for it."

"Maybe you *aren't* cut out for it," said Beaver Pelt. "You are an artist and trader."

"It doesn't sound very noble or heroic," he continued, "doodling with shells and rocks, instead of defending the village."

"You are *my* hero," she said, "and I love you just the way you are. I don't want you to get killed doing something you were not meant to do. Your mother feels the same way. Don't let your father's words ruin your life."

"You are right," agreed River Wolf, "Every village has warriors, and every village has craftsmen. I shouldn't try to be something I am not."

The next morning, he was back to work on the canoe. He made the top flat, and began hollowing it out. He built a fire over the area to be removed, and then afterwards, chopped away the charcoal with the adze. River Wolf saw how slow the process was, and began to wonder if he would finish it this cycle.

Meanwhile, Buck was loading his dugout to go on a trading trip. River Wolf heard about this, and went to visit Buck.

"Hello, Buck," he greeted.

"River Wolf," responded Buck.

Which direction were you planning to go on this trip?" asked River Wolf.

"Southwest to Good Medicine, and to the coast."

"Isn't it a little risky traveling among the Muskogee, now that they have attacked us?"

"I am a trader, not a warrior. They won't mess with me. I can't let this stop me from my work."

"Well, can you deliver something for me?" asked River Wolf.

"What do you need delivered, and where to?"

"The monolithic axe I carved needs to go to Panther and Jaguar at Good Medicine. Jaguar is the Shaman there. They are expecting me to deliver it this summer."

"What did you want in trade for it?"

"Whatever you can get. Don't try to drive a hard bargain, I don't want them to become angry with you."

"I will deliver it for you," said Buck.

"Thank you a lot. When are you leaving?"

"Tomorrow morning."

"Well, be careful, and say hello to Panther for me, if you see him. I will provide meat for your family while you are gone. What do you want in return for delivering the monolithic axe?"

"Meat for Tanager and Titmouse would be fine," answered Buck.

River Wolf headed back to the village. On his way, he passed Tanager, who was walking towards Buck at the river. He saw tears in her eyes. It grieved River Wolf. He, too, was worried about his friend.

He arrived home and ate the dinner that Beaver Pelt had cooked for them. Buck's leaving under these circumstances troubled River Wolf.

"I will be hunting both for us and for Buck's family," he said, "so it looks like the canoe will take even longer to finish. I might have to work on it all summer. I am not going to trade shells for meat next winter. I need them for the next trading trip."

The next morning, they bade farewell to Buck, and River Wolf gave him the monolithic axe. Tanager hugged Buck tightly and whispered in his ear.

"You come back home safe," she said.

"I will be back before you know it," replied Buck.

He shoved off, and Tanager held back the tears. Little Titmouse started crying. It was too much for River Wolf, and he returned to the village. He went to his lodge and got his bow and arrows. He had an obligation to fulfill.

That afternoon, he returned with a doe he had shot. Beaver Pelt and Tanager both helped him skin and dress the deer. After sunset they all ate together.

River Wolf Hollowing Out His Dugout Canoe

The next morning River Wolf returned to work on the canoe. The young grass was replacing the last cycle's dead blades, and the trees were returning to their beautiful green. This was River Wolf's favorite time of the cycle. He set some squirrel traps.

Once again, he gathered firewood and started a fire up and down the log, where he was hollowing it out. After tending the fire until the late afternoon, he left it and checked his traps. There were five squirrels, which he took home.

Beaver Pelt and River Wolf shared them with Tanager and Titmouse. Tanager had baked up plenty of cornbread, and they all ate that with squirrel and venison. It was a delicious meal.

The next day, River Wolf took the adze and cleared out the charcoal from the previous day's burning. It was beginning to look like a canoe. But there was still plenty of work to do. He started the fire again and, when it had died down, he returned home.

On his way back to the village, he saw Broken Spear carrying home a wolf puppy he had found.

"What have you got there?" asked River Wolf.

"I found her up the mountain," explained Broken Spear. "I don't know where her mother is. Do you think Titmouse is old enough to have her?"

"I don't know," replied River Wolf. "We should ask Tanager. I don't think she would mind."

They entered the palisade and went straight to Tanager's lodge. Many of the children of the village were flocking around them to see the puppy. Beaver Pelt and Tanager were preparing acorn meal bread. They looked up and saw the puppy in Broken Spear's arms.

"Do you think Titmouse would like a little friend?" asked Broken Spear.

"Ah! Look at the puppy!" said Beaver Pelt. "It's so cute!"

"Titmouse," called Tanager. "Come here."

Titmouse came running out of the lodge and, when she saw the puppy, she was afraid.

"She won't hurt you," reassured Tanager, and she gently put Titmouse's hand on the wolf puppy's fur.

"What is it?" asked young Titmouse.

"It is a wolf pup," said Tanager, "Broken Spear brought it back for you. Are you going to thank him?"

"Thank you," said Titmouse, while Broken Spear put the pup on the ground by her. She hugged it and smiled.

"What are you going to name her?" asked Tanager.

"Puppy," said Titmouse with a giggle.

Broken Spear smiled at her.

"I think that Puppy must be hungry after the long journey," said Tanager, and she got some deer meat and gave it to Titmouse to feed the wolf pup.

Puppy devoured it all very quickly.

"I'd better get home to Sparrow now," said Broken Spear. "I have to eat, and then man the guardhouse tonight."

"Thank you, Broken Spear," smiled Tanager, as she hugged him.

River Wolf, Beaver Pelt, and Tanager cooked up some more deer meat and they all ate, including Puppy. Tanager gave Titmouse the bone she had been eating off of.

"Give it to Puppy," suggested Tanager.

Puppy eagerly took the bone from Titmouse and went to the corner of the lodge to chew on it. Titmouse followed Puppy and started petting her.

"Titmouse," said Tanager. "Leave her alone while she chews on it, or else you will get bit."

Titmouse smiled innocently and backed off. But soon she was back to petting Puppy again.

"Titmouse! No!"

Titmouse gave up and came back to sit in her mother's lap. All the while, she watched the wolf pup, while her mother visited with River Wolf and Beaver Pelt.

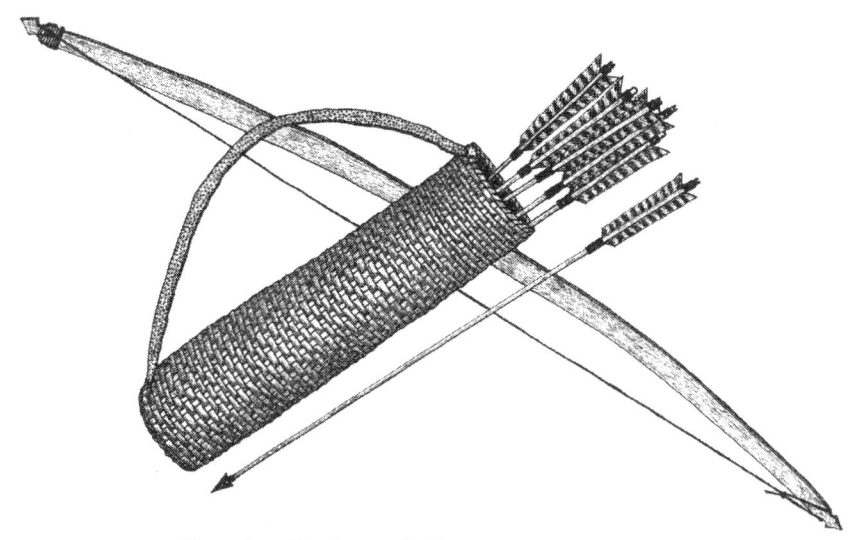

Cherokee Basketry Quiver, Bow & Arrows.
Based on Allely & Hamm 1999.

Early in the morning, River Wolf left with his bow and quiver of arrows. He had walked a good distance up the ridge towards Eagle Peak, when he was stopped by a grunting noise in the woods. He stood there and listened. The noise continued and River Wolf followed it into a thicket by a stream. A small black bear appeared in front of him. It took five arrows to kill the bear.

River Wolf was happy at his good fortune. Now there was enough meat to feed everybody for a few days. He would have time to get back to working on his canoe for a while. He paid respects to the bear's spirit, as he cut its throat with his flint knife.

The next day found him chopping away, hollowing out more of the canoe. The weather was very warm, and sweat got in his eyes. But he kept chopping with the adze until late afternoon. His whole body was dark with soot and charcoal.

He decided to bathe in the river before returning to the lodge. At the river, he met Beaver Pelt, who was carrying a water bottle.

"You are filthy!" laughed Beaver Pelt. "I am going to fill this upstream from you. How is the dugout coming along?"

"It's beginning to look like a canoe," replied River Wolf, "but there is plenty of work to do yet."

"Tanager has made some sunflower seed bread for you," said Beaver Pelt, "and I have been gathering mushrooms all morning. I just got back. I hope you are hungry."

"Very much so. I will be there as soon as I wash off."

River Wolf returned to the lodge and ate one of the best meals of his life. Squirrel Fur and Sparrow visited them after the meal.

"How is your burn, Sparrow?" asked River Wolf.

"It is healing up," replied Sparrow. "I won't let any fire-tipped arrow ruin my day. Are you making any progress on your canoe?"

"It is coming along – slowly."

* * *

Two weeks later, the warriors returned. They had taken no prisoners, but had many scalps on their belts. Song of the Wind had nine scalps, and he was feeling quite proud of himself. The Eagle Dance was performed, along with the rituals associated with it.

Song of the Wind decided he wanted a ball game. This fiercely competitive game was often referred to as "The Little Brother of War" because of its violent nature.

Song of the Wind went to the Uku and requested that a game be organized between Birch Mountain and Eagle Peak. They sent two messengers to Eagle Peak to meet with the village leaders and deliver the challenge.

It was decided. Because of its large size, the courtyard of Birch Mountain was to be the place the game would be held. Each town leader recruited players that had honorable character, who could be trusted not to cheat during the ball game.

When the players were selected, each town held separate ritual dances at their own secret locations. The Shaman of a town used sorcery to weaken the opponents, and to strengthen the players of his town. The Ballgame Dance lasted for seven days. Seven men were appointed to assist the Shaman. These men could be married, but their wives could not be in their moon time or pregnant.

One of these men was an elder, and he was assigned to be the leader of the preparation ritual. There was also a man who did war whoops, and one who sang for the players. Seven women were chosen along with a musician to accompany the women's dance held on the seventh night. Another seven women were appointed to cook for the feast that was held on the seventh evening. No woman was allowed at the secret location, or to even cross the path to that location until the seventh night. Women were thought of as the more delicate sex, and their presence would weaken the players.

A fire was started at the secret place, and the players gathered and sat away from the fire with their ball sticks. The elder called them to approach the fire, carrying their sticks. The whooper did war whoops, which were answered by whoops from the players.

The singer would shake a rattle and sing while the players danced and sang a song. The players danced around the fire four times, waving their racquet-like ball sticks in the same manner as they would during the game.

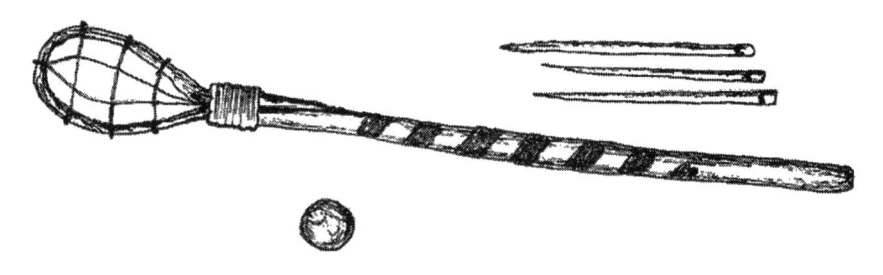

Ball, Racquet & Tally Sticks for Ball Game.
Based on Taylor & Sturtevant 1991.

Then the whooper raised a loud whoop while running away for a short distance. The players walked east to a designated place where they hooked their sticks together and hung them on a rack located there. They rested for a short period before repeating the dance. This dance was performed four times, then the players submerged in the river seven times and went to bed.

At sunrise, the players went back to the river and submerged themselves seven times, while the Shaman used his conjury on them. He gazed at a red bead while saying elaborate prayers for the success of his players. In these prayers he elevated them to the status of gods, saying they were swift, like hawks and other birds of prey.

The Shaman's attention then shifted to a black bead while he lowered the opposing players underground, saying they were confused like scared rabbits, or slow like turtles.

On the second day of the ritual, young boys were appointed to kill a squirrel with clubs and their hands. The skin of this squirrel would be used for making the ball.

River Wolf was of the Bird Clan and, because of this and his talent with his hands, he was selected to make the ball. He prepared the squirrel skin, and stuffed it with deer hair and sewed it into a ball. He wrapped the ball in a deer hide given to him by Eagle Medicine for this purpose. River Wolf was now required to fast until the end of the ball game.

During the remainder of the seven days and nights of the preparation ceremony, the players repeated the same dances. Finally on the seventh night, Eagle Medicine hid near the river and his seven assistants tended to him while he prayed. He prayed for strength for the players of Birch Mountain, and disaster for the opposing players of Eagle Peak.

The ball players danced seven times, counterclockwise around a fire, raising loud whoops against the opponents. They ran in the direction of Eagle Peak, brandishing their ball sticks in a show of defiance. This was also done seven times.

The players were purified by smoke from pinewood that had been tossed into the fire, and then they submerged in the river again. Meanwhile, the seven women (one from each clan) performed their dance, accompanied by any other women who wanted to. They faced the direction of Eagle Peak and acted as if they were stomping on Eagle Peak's ball players.

When the players returned from the river, the women were led to the river by Eagle Medicine, where they washed their hands and faces. On their way to the water, they mimicked the actions of a ball player, while the musician sang a song.

On the last night before the game took place, the players endured ritual scratching of their bodies. They received deep scratches on their upper and lower arms and legs, and their chests and backs. If the blood that was drawn was dark, they were scratched until it ran bright red. A decoction of vetch and catgut was rubbed into the scratches. This was believed to strengthen and purify them. The ball players were not to go near any women, not even their wives, for twenty-four days after they had undergone the scratching ritual.

Early the morning of the ball game, the alert players were ready for the game. They chewed slippery elm and rubbed the spit all over their bodies, causing them to be slippery when they sweated. They were painted with good luck symbols, and Birch Mountain's players' bodies were painted white, and Eagle Peak's team red.

The players now ate cornbread made by the women, but served by boys of the village. A deerskin was spread on the ground, for conjury items. The players placed items they were wagering next to the skin.

There were loud whoops as the Sun came up, and the players marched, single file, to Birch Mountain's courtyard for the game. They were naked except for their breechclouts.

Song of the Wind got the ball from Eagle Medicine and held it while a speaker addressed the ball players, telling them to not give up, to get up when they fell down, and other words of encouragement. There was another loud whoop, and the opposing players met each other in the center of the courtyard.

On each end of the courtyard were two stakes in the ground, about three feet apart. These functioned as goals, and the first team to score twelve points, would win the game.

Two scorekeepers from each village were appointed to see that the rules of the game were observed. They each had twelve tally sticks that were stuck in the ground, one at a time, each time a team scored.

Spectators from each village stood on each side of the court dressed in their finest clothing. They were eager to wager on the outcome.

An elder took the ball from Song of the Wind, threw it into the air – and ran for his life! Instantly there was pandemonium – the game had begun! The players piled over each other, trying to get the ball, while the crowd cheered.

Eagle Peak scored the first two points. Then Song of the Wind managed to pass the ball to another teammate, who scored a point for Birch Mountain.

Song of the Wind scored the final point, and Birch Mountain won the game. Eagle Medicine's conjury had prevailed. Song of the Wind was at his proudest moment as he led the team marching out of the courtyard and back home. The excited villagers listened over and over to the storytellers' accounts of the game, but River Wolf was just glad his period of fasting was all over with, so he could finally eat!

* * *

It was late summer, and River Wolf was getting close to finishing the dugout. It was now lightweight enough for him to move by himself. This was the time he should be extremely careful. The finished canoe would be between two and three fingers thick. If River Wolf hollowed too much out in one area, the dugout would be weak in that area. There was also the possibility of accidentally making a hole in the hull.

The hot afternoon made River Wolf sweat profusely. It was interfering with his concentration, so he decided to quit for the day. On the way home, he checked his leaning log squirrel traps and found five squirrels dangling from the nooses hanging from the tree branch. Upon returning home, he greeted Broken Spear at the guardhouse.

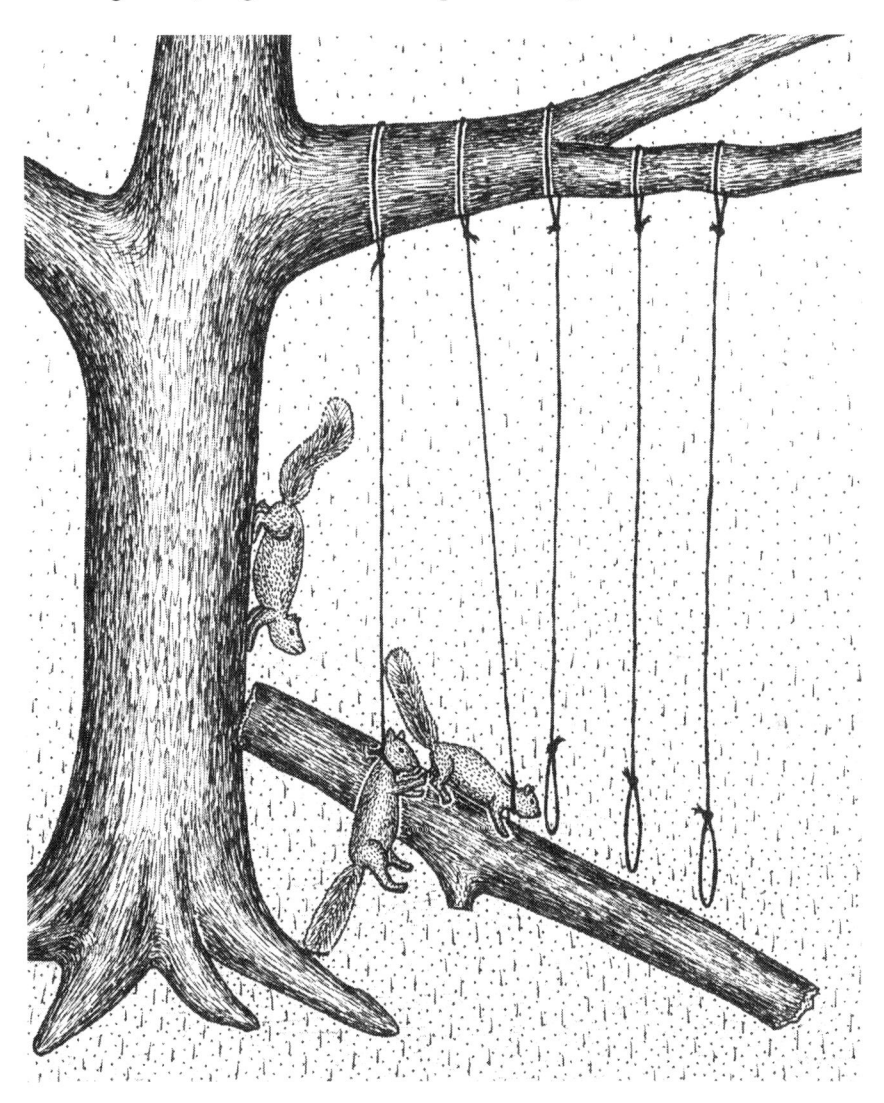

River Wolf's Leaning Log Squirrel Trap.

The corn crop was getting ripe enough to eat, and the date was set for the Green Corn Ceremony. Nobody was to eat of the new corn until the ceremony took place. Runners were sent out to all the towns of the nation, and people gathered ears of corn from the fields of each of the seven clans. The Uku and his seven helpers began to fast for six days.

The citizens arrived at the capital, and relatives visited with their family members. On the night of the seventh day, the ceremony commenced with a men's dance. Eagle Medicine, being the Shaman of the nation's capital, led the dance. He shook a small gourd rattle while singing.

Eagle Medicine led the dancers across the courtyard in a zigzag path until all the dancers had gone around the courtyard.

Then the sacred fire was doused and the new fire was kindled in the traditional way. The Uku, Standing Bear prepared a sacrifice of a deer's tongue, and kernels of corn that were produced by each of the seven clans. The Uku blessed the corn, and put it and the deer tongue into the new fire. Then he sprinkled tobacco powder into the fire.

Cornbread and other foods made from the new corn crop were now served to the citizens. The Uku and his seven assistants had to wait for seven more days before eating of the new corn, and in the meantime they ate of the last cycle's corn crop. The Green Corn Ceremony concluded a few days later.

River Wolf left early in the morning to work on the canoe. Now that the new crop was in, he would not have to hunt for meat for a few days. He walked up the ridge where the unfinished dugout was. He began chopping with the adze.

Suddenly he heard the sound of a cougar screaming nearby. It sent chills up his spine. There was a loud rustling in the woods, and several deer ran right by him without even noticing he was there.

River Wolf made ready his bow and arrows and waited. He didn't want to ignore the cougar, but he had to get back to work. He nocked an arrow and cautiously made his way towards the direction from where he had heard the cougar's scream. River Wolf kept an eye above in the trees, alert for the cougar to be anywhere. Then he saw the cougar feasting on a small deer.

Now he knew the deer would keep the cougar occupied. He decided to not try to kill the cougar, considering he had little experience in doing that. River Wolf returned to the dugout and resumed his work on it, but he remained alert and watchful for the cougar.

The Sun was getting low in the western sky, and River Wolf decided to return home. When he arrived, he saw that Beaver Pelt had made a lot of cornbread.

"That sure smells good!" complimented River Wolf.

"Let's take some to Tanager," said Beaver Pelt.

They went to Tanager's lodge and they all ate their fill. It was delicious.

"I will see if I can get a deer tomorrow," offered River Wolf, "that is, if a cougar doesn't scare them away again."

"You saw a cougar?" asked Beaver Pelt, surprised.

"I heard it scream this morning," River Wolf replied. "I went looking for it and found it eating a deer. When the cougar screamed, the deer were frightened and they ran right past me. We should warn the rest of the villagers that the cougar was so close. "I would hate for it to kill a child from the village. Maybe we could get a hunting party together to kill it."

That evening, River Wolf went to see Eagle Medicine at his lodge.

"Hi, River Wolf!" greeted White Feather.

"How are you, White Feather?" returned River Wolf. "Where is your father?"

"He is at the council house," said Dances Like the Deer, as she walked out of the lodge.

"Thank you very much," said River Wolf as he turned to leave.

"Mother," said White Feather, "can I go with River Wolf?"

"Yes," replied Dances Like the Deer, "if he will let you."

"Can I?" White Feather asked River Wolf.

"Sure you can," answered River Wolf and they left for the council house.

"Why are you going to see Father?" asked White Feather. "Are you sick?"

"No, nobody is sick. I just have to tell him something."

"Father says you are building a canoe," said White Feather.

"Yes, I am," returned River Wolf. "I am nearly finished with it too. I will be taking Beaver Pelt on trading trips in the canoe."

"I wish I could go with you and see all those places," commented White Feather, "but I am stuck here in this village."

They found Eagle Medicine just as he was leaving the council house door. The Sun had set, and it was getting dark.

"Eagle Medicine," called River Wolf.

"Hello, River Wolf," greeted Eagle Medicine.

"I need to talk to you about something."

"White Feather," called Eagle Medicine. "Go back home and see if your mother needs anything."

White Feather had a disappointed look on her face as she left.

"Now," said Eagle Medicine, "what did you need?"

"I was working on the dugout today, not far from the village, and I saw a cougar. I am worried that one of the children will get hurt or killed by the cougar. Do you think we should organize a hunting party to kill it? I had a chance, but I thought it would be foolish to try to kill it all by myself.

Cougar.
Redrawn & adapted from Kate 1999.

"I don't think it would be necessary," replied Eagle Medicine. "Those cougars come and go. If we sent out a party, they would probably not find any sign of it."

After a few days, Song of the Wind went out to hunt deer. The cougar leapt from a tree and killed him. When he didn't return, his worried wife went around the village asking about him. Several people were sent out to find him, and they returned with the grim news. Now the whole village was determined to find the cougar.

Two days later, a hunting party left Birch Mountain early in the morning, led by Twisted Stick because of his excellent tracking skills. River Wolf accompanied them. They went to the place where fresh tracks were reported to be. They all followed Twisted Stick silently through the woods until late afternoon. They were stopped short when they heard the scream of the cougar. The noise made River Wolf's skin crawl. They located the cougar in a tree and shot it dead with many arrows.

The next day found River Wolf hunting for deer again. He returned that evening with a dead buck. He had killed it by striking it in the head with an axe he had thrown. Beaver Pelt was fetching water at the river when he appeared with the deer over his shoulders.

"River Wolf!" she exclaimed. "Tanager will be happy. Your mother will be eating with us too. She has made plenty of cornbread to go with the venison. We all will help you clean it."

"Good!" said River Wolf with a smile. "I had to carry this deer a long way."

That night they each ate their fill of venison and cornbread. They talked and told jokes while they ate. The next afternoon, River Wolf finished working on the dugout canoe. He dragged it down the ridge to the river. When he arrived at the river, he tried it out by getting in it and drifting downstream to the village. River Wolf was proud. All he needed to do was carve two paddles.

When he arrived at the village, he stepped out of the dugout and walked it to shore. He went inside the palisade and to the lodge.

"You are home early," said Beaver Pelt.

"I think I am home late," joked River Wolf.

"It is only just past noon," argued Beaver Pelt.

"Don't you need to fetch water?" River Wolf said.

"How dare you tell me what to do?!" shouted Beaver Pelt.

River Wolf smiled and said, "I have something to show you."

"What?" asked Beaver Pelt. "Where?"

"Come with me to fetch water," said River Wolf. "I will even carry it back."

Beaver Pelt's expression changed from angry to curious. They left together for the river. Beaver Pelt's jaw dropped open when she saw the freshly-made dugout.

"You finished it!" she exclaimed. "I can't wait for next summer when we can travel together!"

They hugged each other and kissed. River Wolf had a satisfied smile.

"I just need to carve two paddles," he said. "One for you and one for me."

"Are you hungry?" asked Beaver Pelt.

"Starving!" answered River Wolf.

"Let's go and eat," said Beaver Pelt.

After lunch, River Wolf took his axe to chop the logs from which to make the paddles.

The corn crop had matured, and plans were now being made for the Ripe Corn Ceremony. The village square was prepared by building a tree with green tree branches, and a large pavilion was made that had many seats in rows.

A religious dance was performed, and the feast would be held in twenty days. As usual, runners were sent out to all the villages in the nation with news of the date on which the ceremony would take place. Hunters were sent out to procure meat for the festival.

River Wolf carved the paddles during these twenty days. He finished two nights before the festival. Next he found a large round rock, and pecked a full groove that completely encircled the rock. He tied a rope around the groove, and attached the other end of the rope to the canoe. It would function as a canoe anchor.

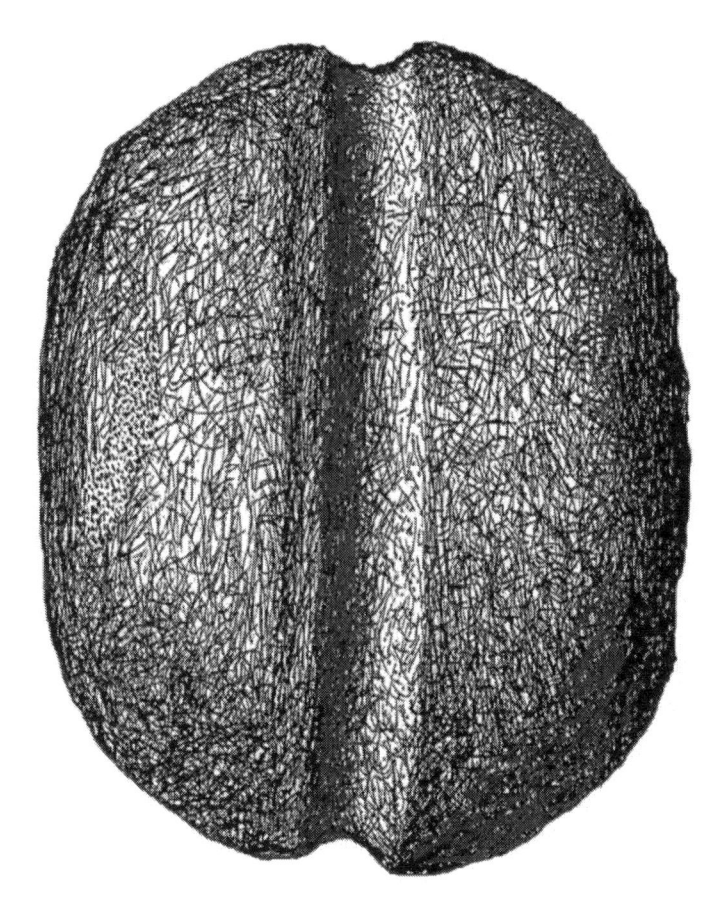

Canoe Anchor.
Based on Miles 1963.

He was now ready for the next summer's trip, and was very excited about taking his wife along. Beaver Pelt was proud of her husband, and they looked forward to the many trips they would be taking in the dugout.

The people of the nation filed in for the ceremony, and stored the food they brought with them in the storehouse behind the heptagon. The next day the victory dance was performed, followed by four days of seven other dances representing the fields with corn growing. While the men performed these seven dances, they circled the tree in the center of the courtyard. The shade from the branches of this tree represented the eternal protecting arms of the Creator.

The Uku, his assistants, and other ranking people sat in the seats of the pavilion that had been erected. The Great War Chief sat in a chair that was carried by six men. At night there were social dances where women were allowed in the courtyard.

For four days, this was repeated. On the last evening, after sunset, the great feast took place. Then the ceremony concluded and the citizens returned home.

River Wolf got up early and set some squirrel traps, then he and Beaver Pelt went canoeing to hone her skills. It was so relaxing, paddling up and down the river with each other. Both looked forward to the trip next summer.

After lunch, River Wolf checked his traps and found that he had caught eight squirrels. He took them home and butchered them. They took some squirrel to Tanager's lodge.

"Do I have a father?" asked little Titmouse.

"You sure do," replied Tanager. "He has gone far away, but will be back soon."

"What is his name?" asked Titmouse.

"His name is The Buck Kicks the Drum. We call him Buck."

"When will he be back?"

"I don't know for sure, but it is your bedtime."

"Ah, Mother," objected Titmouse.

"Go on to bed," said Tanager.

Titmouse obeyed, and Tanager, Beaver Pelt and River Wolf went outside to talk. Beaver Pelt observed the sad expression on Tanager's face. She hugged her.

"Don't worry," she said. "He will be back before you know it."

Just then, there was a quiet commotion at the palisade gate. They turned to look, but whatever the disturbance was, it seemed to have ended.

"I need to get to bed," said Beaver Pelt. "My stomach hurts a little."

They now heard excited talking in the direction of the gate. They turned to look, and Buck appeared, talking to the guards.

"Buck!" shouted Tanager, as she ran to greet him. They embraced for a long time and returned to the lodge.

"Hello, River Wolf," greeted Buck. "It's been a long time."

River Wolf hugged his best friend tightly.

"Let's leave them alone," Beaver Pelt said to River Wolf. "It's very late."

They returned to their lodge and went to bed. Beaver Pelt had difficulty sleeping from a pain in her belly. Her tossing and turning kept River Wolf awake.

"Are you okay?" asked River Wolf.

"My stomach hurts low down in the side," replied Beaver Pelt.

"I will get Eagle Medicine to see you tomorrow morning," offered River Wolf.

"Oh, it's not bad. I am sure it will go away."

The pain gradually got worse as the night progressed. The next morning River Wolf went to see Eagle Medicine. He found him on the way to the heptagon.

"Eagle Medicine," called River Wolf.

"Good morning, River Wolf," greeted Eagle Medicine.

"Beaver Pelt needs to see you," said River Wolf. "Something is wrong. She told me she did not need you to visit her, but I am afraid for her."

"I will be there shortly," promised Eagle Medicine.

River Wolf returned home worried. Beaver Pelt was clearly in pain, though she tried to hide it.

"Eagle Medicine will be here to see you today," he told her.

"I told you I am alright!" objected Beaver Pelt.

"I am certain you are," he said, "but I want to make sure."

Beaver Pelt sighed in pain and frustration. She began to have cramps in her neck and shoulders. River Wolf was silent with worry. He made her some breakfast and she ate. He could tell she was hurting. He wanted to do something to help her.

When Eagle Medicine came to see her she tried to make light of her symptoms.

"It's nothing big," she said, "I just have a stomachache."

Eagle Medicine could tell she was hiding her pain.

"She is having pain in her lower belly on one side," asserted River Wolf. "Just a while ago she started having cramps in her neck and shoulders."

Eagle Medicine left and returned with some lady's slipper, skullcap, Solomon's seal, and passionflower. He performed a healing dance and recited incantations.

Over time Beaver Pelt got worse. The pain was getting more and more severe. Eagle Medicine continued his visits, and River Wolf stayed by her side. Squirrel Fur and Sparrow frequently brought cornbread for them to eat.

River Wolf was hurt inside, watching Beaver Pelt in pain and not being able to do anything for her. He prayed constantly for her. *Oh, Long Being, please do not let her die. Please save her.*

She sank as the days went by. Her pain was excruciating. The Great New Moon Ceremony took place, but River Wolf didn't attend any of the activities. He feared that bad luck would come from his being absent.

The Duck Flies By came to visit her daughter every day. Eagle Medicine continued his visits, but they did no good. River Wolf couldn't bear to see her suffer. He knew she was going to die. He had been praying to Long Being to save her, but he had little hope left. Now he prayed, *Long Being, end her suffering.*

"River Wolf," called Beaver Pelt weakly.

"Yes, Beaver Pelt," he replied.

"I want to be buried under the lodge, then I will always be near to the man I love."

River Wolf broke down in tears.

Beaver Pelt continued, weakly.

"Go on with your life. Oh!" A sharp pain made her gasp.

She reached up and touched him on his wet cheek. She smiled at him.

Her final words were a weak, "I love you."

"I love you too."

Her hand fell to the floor, limp.

"Beaver Pelt? Beaver Pelt!"

He wept bitterly as he closed her eyelids. It was not good for a grown man to weep, and he fought the tears. After he regained his composure, he went to tell Eagle Medicine and The Duck Flies By. Eagle Medicine called for Three Crows, who would perform the burial.

The Duck Flies By and all of the women in River Wolf's family wept loudly and chanted Beaver Pelt's name over and over in a lamented and sorrowful way.

River Wolf couldn't bear to be around them. He and Buck both wore worn-out clothes and put ashes in their hair. The period of mourning lasted for seven days. River Wolf stayed at his mother's lodge during this time.

When he returned to his lodge, he saw the freshly replaced dirt under their bed. She would always be near. River Wolf was not sure what to do next. He would sit in the opposite bed, staring at his wife's grave for long periods of time. Buck stopped by each day to make sure he had food and a friend to talk to. Buck felt like he needed to distract him some way.

The chill of winter came upon the village, and Squirrel Fur helped River Wolf move into his hothouse, and River Wolf did likewise with her. It was a very cold and lonely winter.

* * *

River Wolf had been too caught up with Beaver Pelt's illness and death to even think about his trade goods which Buck had been keeping for him. So, one spring morning, Buck came over for a visit, as River Wolf was moving into the summer lodge.

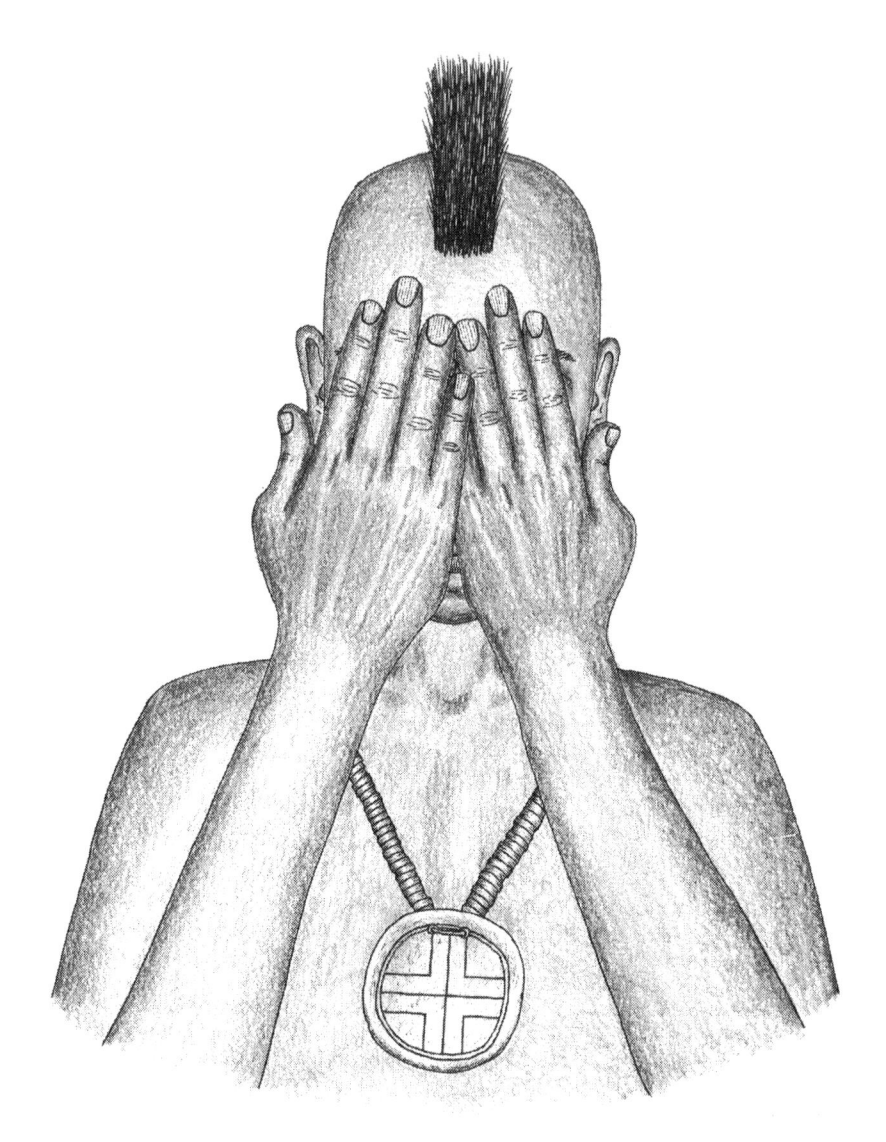

It Was Not Good for a Grown Man to Weep.

"River Wolf," said Buck, "I have something to show you."
"What is it?" asked River Wolf.
"Come and see."
The two went to Buck's lodge and buck showed him all of the shells he had gotten in exchange for the monolithic axe.

"All of this is yours," said Buck. "You were preoccupied with things, and we never had a chance to move your things to your lodge. So, let's go see Cahokia! We have plenty to take along."

"How will we get there?" asked River Wolf.

"We will just follow Bear River downstream. Then we'll join another river. Eventually, it will take us to a river that will lead to an enormous river. Cahokia is upstream on that river. We will get home by taking that river to the Great Sea and then follow the coast until we get to the river that leads to the portage to Bear River. What do you think?"

"Alright," replied River Wolf, "I have always wanted to see Cahokia!"

"Well, now is your chance. We will see it together."

River Wolf had planned to take Beaver Pelt along on his next trading trip, but she was dead. He tried not to think of her. Squirrel Fur and Sparrow promised to maintain his lodge during his absence.

Buck and River Wolf traded for a large bag of tobacco and dried meat, and made their preparations. River Wolf bade farewell to his mother and relatives, and Buck did likewise.

River Wolf went inside his lodge for a silent visit at Beaver Pelt's grave. As he sat there, he thought he heard Beaver Pelt say, *I will be with you on your journey. I love you.*

"I love you too, Beaver Pelt," he whispered. Then he went to Buck's dugout and helped him load it. They hugged their relatives one last time, climbed in, and began paddling the dugout downstream on Bear River, heading west. River Wolf had no idea that it would be ten cycles before he would see his home again.

Chapter 13: Cahokia

Panther was losing trust amongst the Muskogee. He was increasingly becoming suspected as being a traitor to the tribe. Winged Rattlesnake Chief had managed to turn the villagers of Good Medicine against him. Panther tried to use politics against the war chief, but Bald Eagle's death had caused suspicions against him because of his unusual friendship with River Wolf. River Wolf had not returned but, instead, had sent Bald Eagle's possessions back with Medicine Wolf. He had also sent the monolithic axe with Buck instead of delivering it himself.

Bald Eagle's daughter had been plotting with Winged Rattlesnake Chief against Panther. "His friend killed my father!" she wailed constantly.

Eventually, Winged Rattlesnake Chief and Dead Buzzard Warrior figured out that Panther was the brother of Bald Eagle's alleged murderer. The villagers began to cast sidelong glances at Panther, and even Autumn Leaf had all but abandoned him to avoid becoming an outcast. Eventually, she threw him out of the lodge and Dead Buzzard Warrior began courting her.

A dual resulted between Panther and Dead Buzzard Warrior, in which Panther won. But since he had killed a war leader, he was now considered a murderer.

Panther fled to another town. In the Muskogee tribe, there were red towns, like Good Medicine, which were war towns. Then there were white towns, which were peaceful towns where outlaws could seek refuge if they could keep a low profile.

Panther took his dugout down the Black Warrior River to a white town at a place near the Great Sea, and settled there. He had no friends left, and hoped nobody would treat him badly.

* * *

River Wolf and Buck continued paddling with the current. It was early in the spring, but already it was hot. River Wolf tried not to think about Beaver Pelt. The memories of their much-too-short life together haunted him. As he paddled, he fought the tears. Buck noticed his silence, but did not know what to say.

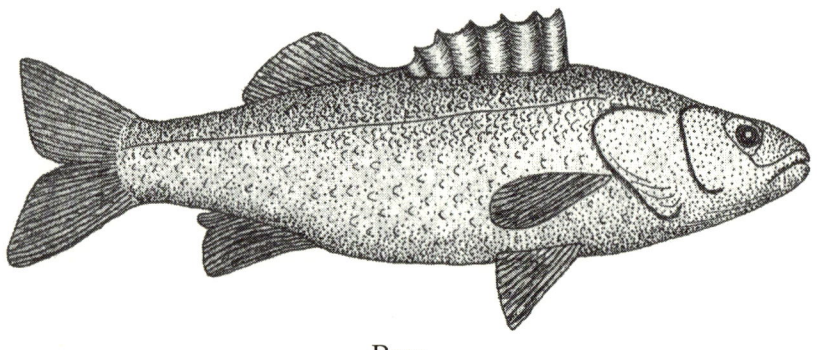

Bass.
Redrawn from camisetasFD from Pixabay.

They camped at a creek and ate a bass that Buck caught. Late the next evening, they reached the place where the river merged with another. They followed it northwest with little effort, stopping at night at some of the Cherokee villages. River Wolf had never been in this part of their territory. They enjoyed the usual hospitality that traders received.

They stopped at many villages throughout the following few weeks, mostly trading turkey feather cloaks for freshwater pearls that were common in this area. River Wolf had never seen so many pearls in his life.

The river took them westward into Chickasaw territory for about a week, before abruptly turning north. After a moon, the river merged into a large river that was wider than in River Wolf's wildest fantasies.

"Now we follow this river southwest to the Mississippi River," said Buck. "I am not sure which language the name, 'Mississippi' is from, but it means "Big Muddy.""

In three days they arrived at the Mississippi River. It was wider than River Wolf could have ever imagined. He wondered if anybody could possibly swim across it.

They traveled upstream for three days, and saw four hunters on the shore. Buck motioned, "Traders" to them. The hunters signed for them to approach. They conversed in signs. The hunters were from a village up a nearby creek on the eastern shoreline.

Buck and River Wolf learned their names – the leader was named Stomping Bison, and he had a hooked nose and thin lips. There was also Runs Away Screaming, which didn't sound like a name for a very brave person. The shortest in the hunting party was Mallard and, finally, there was Turtle Shell Rattle. He was heavily-built, and looked like he would be formidable in a fight.

The four hunters led them to their village, which seemed to be named River Village. River Wolf and Buck stayed there for two days, trading. Stomping Bison asked them if they were headed for Cahokia.

"Yes," replied Buck, "we are."

"Well, you should trade for plenty of corn. It will bring a good price there because their crops have been failing for several cycles. It is as though the Great Sun has angered Mother Earth. The village has plenty of mouths to feed, but their ears of corn don't grow any longer than your little finger nowadays. Many of the surrounding villages are paying tribute to Cahokia, but now their crops are failing too. They have to travel greater and greater distances just to hunt food and firewood."

Buck and River Wolf heeded Stomping Bison's advice and traded for as much corn as they could get. They left River Village and continued up the Mississippi River. After five days, they were in the territory dominated by Cahokia. They stopped at the first village subject to Cahokia's rule. The villagers eyed their cargo of corn with more envy than they did the pearls.

The next morning, they continued upstream. Just across the wide river was another large village, but they passed it by, anxious to see the splendor of Cahokia. In a few days, they arrived at a large village at the mouth of Sun Creek. Cahokia was only a day up this creek.

They spent the night at this village, which they learned was named Moon Village. When they made ready to leave the next morning, Buck noticed that about one third of their corn had been stolen. "What happened to our corn?" he demanded in signs.

The locals played dumb. Buck became angry and started to reach for his axe. River Wolf stopped him as the villagers brought out their weapons. "No, Buck," urged River Wolf. "We will not win this one."

Buck stopped, but had a look of disgust in his eyes. "That's fine, but we won't be trading with *these* people anymore."

Incised Pottery Ramey Pot from Cahokia.

"Just remember that we have to pass this village when we return from Cahokia," added River Wolf.

The villagers were watching them closely, their weapons still ready. Buck and River Wolf could not believe these people's lack of morals.

"Well, one day they will get what's coming to them," said Buck, frustrated but helpless. "Let's go."

They shoved off and made their way up Sun Creek. Most of the latter part of that day they passed by dwellings and canoes on the shores – the outskirts of this great metropolis. The closer they got, the fewer the trees they saw along the way. They saw many different sizes of temple and burial mounds, and then suddenly Buck pointed ahead to the right. "Look at that!"

River Wolf saw an enormous mound that reached into the sky. He was awestruck. "Wow!" was all he could say.

"It looks like the Great Sun wants to be as close to the Sun as he can get!" said Buck with a smile.

On the highest terrace of the mound stood a very large temple, the largest building that either of them had ever seen before. There was a tall palisade surrounding the large mound and it's courtyard of smaller mounds. This was where the highest-ranking people lived.

River Wolf and Buck beached the dugout and an enormous crowd gathered, eager to see what these traders had brought. When the locals saw the corn, they hastily left to get trade items and returned as fast as they could. Many of the locals' ribs showed, making their desperation obvious. How could such a large city have formed if there was no food here?

Within a short time, all the corn was traded to the locals. River Wolf and Buck acquired many copper items, and several very sharp knives made of a shiny black stone called "obsidian."

One item that River Wolf saw that he thought was interesting was a war club, with knapped flint shark teeth mounted into the handle. It looked formidable, and River Wolf didn't savor the idea of fighting with a person armed with one of these!

Cahokia Knapped Flint Shark Tooth War Club.
Modeled after photos by Gilcrease Institute, Tulsa, Oklahoma, and ancient Polynesian designs.

They stayed in a guest lodge and had the company of some friendly village women. River Wolf conversed in signs with one of them.

"Why are so many people starving here?" asked River Wolf.

"Cahokia used to have plenty of trees and fertile soil, many cycles ago, but our Great Sun has angered Mother Earth and she has abandoned us. Would you like some goosefoot?"

"Only if it won't cause you hardship." River Wolf was well aware that these people were hungry.

"Not at all. My father is a wealthy trader." She brought the goosefoot and some jerky for River Wolf to eat.

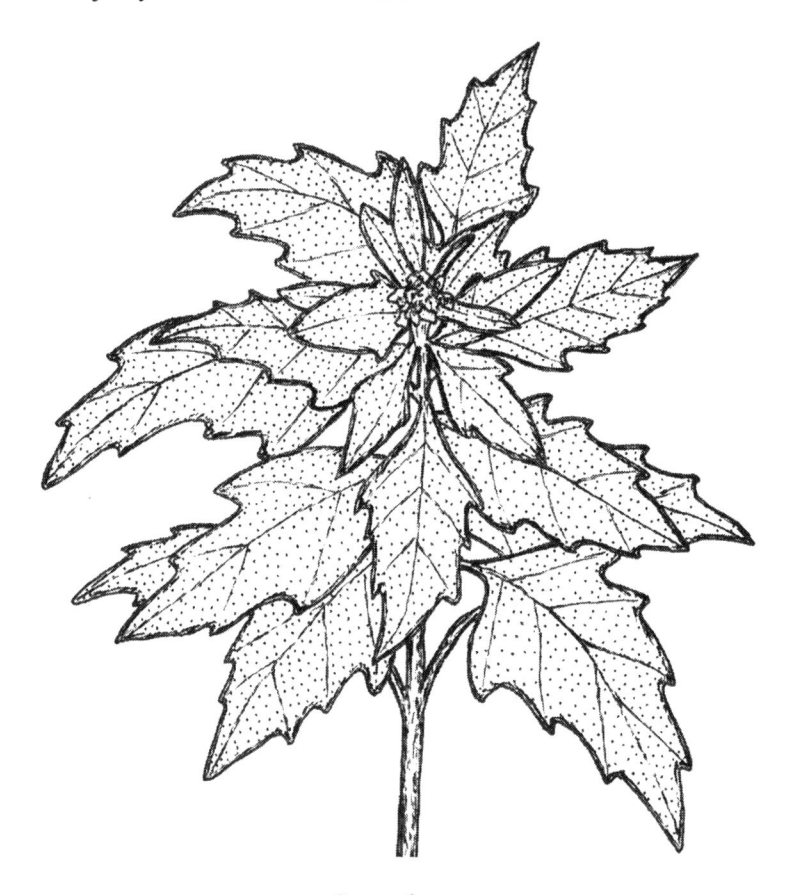

Goosefoot.

"What did the Great Sun do?" asked River Wolf as he ate.

"Nobody knows, maybe not even the Great Sun himself. Cycles ago, all of the villages in this area formed an alliance with Cahokia. Tributes of food were given to stock the granaries in Cahokia. This was distributed to the needy. But with the drought, and the crops failing, there are more and more people who are needy. The outlying villages are now producing less food also. But the Great Sun is still demanding tribute from them, and they either give up all their food, or face attack from the warriors of Cahokia. It is really sad. My aunt and uncle live in Moon Village. My brother is a warrior here, and he has to live with the fact that he fights his own family for the Great Sun. The whole world has gone insane." She seemed so sad.

River Wolf hugged her. He wanted to take her from this place and give her a new life. "Would you like to leave this area and go with us?"

"No!" she retorted. "My family is here and I cannot leave them."

River Wolf was embarrassed at her rejection. "I didn't mean to offend you; I was just offering my help."

"Thank you, but I really can't."

"What kinds of things does your father trade?"

"Mostly pottery."

Madonna & Child Pottery Water Bottle.

They talked all night long, and the next morning as he left, he gave her two necklaces of freshwater pearls. Maybe she could trade them for food. It was all he could do.

That day, River Wolf and Buck spent trading the rest of the pearls with the wealthy elite inside the large courtyard. It was an extraordinary sight. River Wolf learned that the immediate village was the home of fifteen thousand people, and that did not count the outlying villages that surrounded the metropolis.

Birdman Tablet.

They spent the night at a different guest lodge with different women. The next morning, as they prepared to leave, there was a large bustle at the creek. Warriors were leaving in canoes towards the Mississippi River. River Wolf counted over one hundred canoes leaving. "They must be going to collect the tribute."

"What tribute?" asked Buck.

River Wolf shared the details of the conversation he'd had with the woman two nights before. Buck became very nervous. "Let's wait for awhile before we leave. We don't want to get mixed up in the local conflicts."

They ate breakfast while the Sun rose, and then they shoved off. That afternoon, they passed all of the war canoes that were returning to

Cahokia, their mission accomplished. They were loaded with stores of grain, and many scalps.

That night, they passed Moon Village in the dark. There was a mournful wailing of women and many lodges still smoldered from the battle. Buck was right, they got what was coming to them for stealing the corn, but River Wolf felt badly for them anyway. They were desperately hungry and, if he were in their situation, he might have stolen a little corn also.

Cahokia Arrowheads.

They reached the Mississippi River, and silently went downstream. Rather than simply drifting with the current, they paddled, because they wanted to quickly get a good distance from this bad situation, for their own safety. The visit to Cahokia had been a major disappointment for them both. They had heard the popular rumors of a giant thriving city, but found out that the people were victims of their own wealth. They had used up the land around them, and now they were paying the price. It reminded him of what Beaver Pelt had told him about the fate of Pine Bend.

River Wolf thought that the whole metropolis would be abandoned in a matter of time – that is, if they didn't kill each other off while fighting for food. Copper earspools and shell beads are worthless when there is no food for which to trade them.

Both River Wolf and Buck were hungry. They couldn't trade for food, in fact, they had traded away all of *their* food. They beached the canoe, and River Wolf began working on making a fishhook from the toe bone of a deer. As the Sun lowered into the sky, he carved on it.

Buck fell asleep early and, by the light of their campfire, River Wolf carved away. As he worked, his thoughts returned to Beaver Pelt. With Buck being asleep, River Wolf had nobody to talk to. He felt sad and lonesome, and finally went to sleep without dinner.

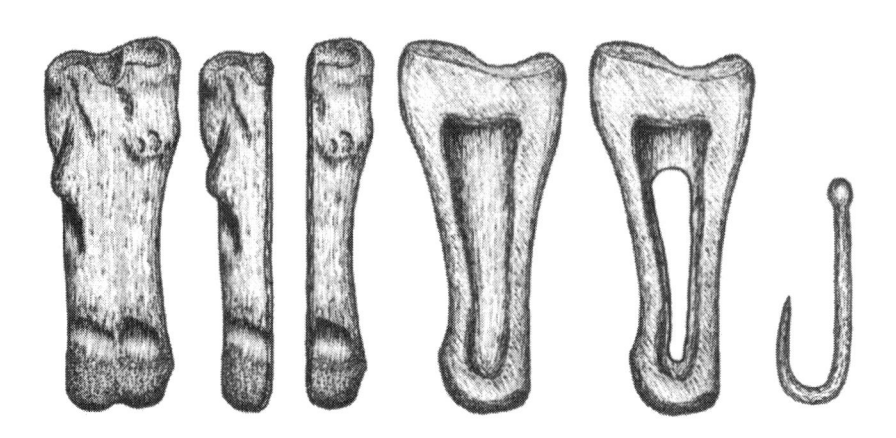

Making a Bone Fishhook from a Toe Bone of a Deer.
Based on Lewis & Kneberg 1958.

The next morning, Buck harvested some mussels, and managed to catch a fish while River Wolf trapped two squirrels. They ate and resumed their journey. River Wolf thought of the woman at Cahokia. Then he thought of Beaver Pelt. She was so young to die. All of the memories saddened him.

Mussel.

They shoved off and in two days they were well out of the territory of Cahokia, and they were both relieved. The two stopped to camp and relax for a couple of days. The weather was hot, but there were plenty of squirrels to trap.

Finally they continued their journey and stopped at River Village two days later. Stomping Bison greeted them. "Did you get a good price for your corn?"

"We got robbed of some of the corn before we even got to Cahokia," replied Buck, "but we got plenty of goods for the rest of it. We have copper earspools and hair ornaments. We also have obsidian knives."

"Do you have any cornbread?" asked River Wolf, "It has been a while since we had any."

Stomping Bison smiled. "My wife has plenty that we can part with."

They stayed at River Village for three days, bartering and enjoying the hospitality. After trading for tobacco and food, they continued down the Mississippi River. They passed the place where the two giant rivers met, and continued down the Mississippi River.

They stopped to camp for the night, and River Wolf began pressure-flaking a new arrowhead to replace one that had broken after striking a tree. Meanwhile, Buck went into the woods and returned, with a rabbit, by the time River Wolf finished the arrow point.

"Rabbit!" exclaimed River Wolf, as he got out his knife.

They both cleaned the rabbit, and then put it over the fire. River Wolf got some of the gut to haft the point on the arrow.

"Who is that?" asked Buck, pointing towards the river.

River Wolf turned to see and saw, in the fading light, two canoes tied together with two people heading upstream. "Are they traders?"

Buck went for a closer look. River Wolf was reminded of the catamaran with the sail, even though this one had no sail. He heard Buck calling to them. They turned the canoes about and began paddling towards the shore. As they approached, they slowed down to be cautious. Buck signed, "Traders."

They signed back that they were also traders. In their dugouts, they had all kinds of seashells. When they arrived at the shore, Buck and River Wolf helped them beach their double dugout.

"I am Buck, and this is River Wolf," Buck introduced in signs. Then he verbally asked, "Do you speak Muskhogean?"

"Yes, we do!" the stranger replied in a strange, but vaguely familiar, accent of Muskhogean, "I am Bone Flute, and my friend here is Watersnake. We are on our way to Cahokia."

"We just came from there," said Buck. "It is not a really good situation there."

"What happened?" asked Bone Flute.

"They are starving and desperate. They even stole from us. Then, on the morning we were to leave, the warriors of Cahokia attacked one of their subject villages."

Bone Flute and Watersnake glanced at each other. Finally, Bone Flute suggested, "Maybe we shouldn't continue any farther. I have heard of the large city with the temple that reaches the Sun. I heard they drink the White Drink from pottery beakers that have their Woodhenge motif on them. I even have one! It was traded to us several cycles ago."

"What is Woodhenge?"

"A giant circle of posts that indicates the time of year by where the shadows fall from the poles."

"We didn't see that while we were there."

Cahokia Woodhenge Pottery Beaker.

"Well I had no idea the situation there was that bad. I was going to take my friend to Cahokia to cheer him up. His wife just died three moons ago."

River Wolf immediately felt compassion for Watersnake. He said, "I know what you are going through. My Beaver Pelt died young two moons ago. I loved her dearly."

"What tribe are you two?" asked Buck.

"We are Calusa, from the peninsula very far to the southeast," replied Bone Flute. "We were going to take our cargo of shells to Cahokia, but I think we've just changed our minds."

"Would you like to go back to the coast with us?" asked River Wolf.

"Well," answered Bone Flute, "it beats going to Cahokia if it's as bad as you say it is. Where will you be going after you reach the coast?"

"Our home is up a river to the east of the Mississippi River," answered Buck. "We were going to head east and gather shells to take back northward."

"Would you two like to go southwest and gather shells there? We have a mast and sail that we hid at the coast. We can tow your dugout and you won't even have to paddle."

"How long will it take? We need to get back home by winter."

"With a sail, we can travel very fast. Come on, it will be fun! We can get you back to your river quickly."

"What do you think, River Wolf?" asked Buck.

"It sounds like fun!" answered River Wolf. "Why not? I have never been that far west."

Buck told the Calusas their decision. They nodded, satisfied with the new arrangement. Buck looked at the little rabbit that was on the fire. "We will need more than that to feed the four of us."

They unloaded Buck's canoe and went jack-lighting for deer. Buck stayed behind, because of the conflict with his totem. He would eat the rabbit, and the others could eat the deer they killed.

River Wolf had his axe ready while the two Calusas paddled the dugout up a creek. The torch burned brightly while River Wolf watched intently for curious deer eyes. After some time, some eyes appeared. The canoe rocked as River Wolf threw the axe, aiming between the deer eyes. He hit his mark, and they went to shore to find the deer.

The vegetation on the banks was very thick, and they made a lot of noise while locating the deer. Finally, River Wolf stepped on it. "Here it is," he said before cutting its throat and paying his respects.

They hauled it aboard the dugout and shoved off. It was getting very late by the time they returned to the river and the camp. They skinned and gutted the deer in the light of the campfire. Then they all ate deer meat – with the exception of Buck, who ate the rabbit.

"What tribe are you two?" Watersnake asked.

"We are of the Cherokee," replied River Wolf. "Our territory is in the mountains east of here."

"We have had traders from your tribe visit our village. They always bring turkey feather cloaks. We trade lots of shells for them."

"Do you ever have any traders arrive from across the Great Sea?"

"Yes, we do. They are the Arawaks, who come from islands to the south and southeast."

"I never knew there were islands out there. Are they large islands?"

"Some of them are. The nearest island is the largest – or so I have heard. I was going to travel there with Clam, but then she died. I really miss her."

"I miss my Beaver Pelt also. I had just finished a canoe that we were both to travel in. But then she died. Buck took me away with him so I would not think about it so much."

"Is Buck your friend or is he related to you?"

"He lived with my family after he was orphaned during an enemy attack. We have been best friends since we were very young."

"Bone Flute is a good friend to me also." Watersnake searched the starry sky for the moon. Then he realized it was in its dark phase. He saw many constellations. "Tell me about the constellations of the Cherokee," he requested.

River Wolf pointed to the Milky Way and said, "Long Being – the Spirit of the River. He is my protector. On Earth he is the River of Life, and up there in the sky vault, he is the River of Death. When a man dies, his spirit walks that path to the afterlife." Then he pointed to the Northern Cross and said, "That is the Tree of Life, growing beside the River of Death."

Then River Wolf pointed to the Pleiades star cluster. "Those stars are the center of the universe. The brightest star there is where all of mankind originated."

"Where did you learn all these things? You seem to be very knowledgeable about the beliefs of your culture."

"When I was a child, I began training to be a Shaman. But my intentions were not pure, and the Spirits rebuked me. Then I went back to stone carving and flint knapping."

"Tell me about some of the herbal preparations the Cherokee use," requested Watersnake.

"Well, wild onions, as you may know, are often cooked with other foods, but have medicinal qualities as well. They can be put on wounds to help them heal. When eaten, they are good for the heart, and can prevent heartburn and gas pains.

"Solomon's seal can be made into a wash out of it that can help a rash from poison ivy. It also makes a good poultice. You can make a tea from the root that is good for female ailments.

"Passionflower has sedative and painkilling powers, and can help painful menstruation. It can also be used as a poultice for bruises. It works well for treating muscle spasms and heart conditions.

"Blue cohosh root is dried and ground into a powder and then infused with water. This is good for menstrual cramps, colic, bronchitis, and rheumatism. It is also given to pregnant women during the last ten or so days to ease the pain of childbirth. It is said to cause a miscarriage if consumed too early in pregnancy. It is harvested in the late autumn. But you shouldn't eat the blue berries – they are poisonous.

"Black willow bark is made into a tea that has a calming effect. The tea is also used for fever, and internal bleeding. I personally wash wounds with it.

"Really?" asked Watersnake.

"Yes," replied River Wolf. "It works very well."

"Tell me more of what you learned."

While River Wolf told Watersnake more of the different herbs, Buck and Bone Flute shared a conversation of their own. The four talked until they fell asleep. They slept late; it had been a long night. Finally, they all woke up and ate. Then they loaded up their things and shoved off at around noon.

Buck and Bone Flute were in the double canoe, while River Wolf and Watersnake manned Buck's canoe.

"I am already hungry!" said Watersnake. "I wish we had the time to build a fishing weir. My people build them and catch a lot of fish with them."

Fishing Weir.
Redrawn from Holmes 1891.

"Yes!" replied River Wolf. "We sometimes fish that way also!" Then River Wolf explained how the Cherokees used black walnut to put fish in a stupor.

"I had no idea you could do that!" marveled Watersnake.

"Did you know Bald Eagle?" asked River Wolf. "He was a trader who visited the Calusas regularly."

"Yes, we both knew him!" answered Watersnake. "We have not seen him for a long time. Did he retire?"

"I went with him on my first trading trip two cycles ago. When we arrived at the coast, we were diving for shells and a large sea fish attacked him. He disappeared into the water and I was left there alone."

Watersnake was saddened by the news. "He was a good trader," he said. "He drove a hard bargain. He stretched the truth like traders do, but he never told a direct lie."

"Yes, he was," replied River Wolf with a smile. "He was a good friend. He saved my life."

"Tell me about that."

River Wolf told his story about how he had almost been burned at the stake, and how Bald Eagle had rescued him in the nick of time.

"Are the scars on your legs from that incident?"

"Yes, and here is where I got shot with the arrow." He pointed to the scar on his belly.

After a day's traveling, they were in the western portion of Chickasaw territory. They stopped at the first Chickasaw town that evening. The villagers flocked to the shore, eager to see what fabulous things the four traders had brought. These people spoke a dialect of the Muskhogean language, most of which the four traders understood.

One pretty lady caught River Wolf's eye. She smiled at him. He immediately felt apprehensive. Then he remembered that his wife was gone. His eyes shifted to the ground in sadness. He missed being bound to Beaver Pelt. River Wolf decided to put the past behind him and live his life. When he looked at the lady again, she had already started a conversation with Bone Flute.

River Wolf was discouraged and frustrated. He returned to the dugout to get out some of his merchandise. Watersnake saw that he was upset. "I know how you feel. It just isn't right when your mate is gone forever."

River Wolf said nothing in response. He just dug through the trade items in the canoe, as if he were searching for something – even though he had no idea what he was looking for. He felt the tears swelling in his eyes. He fought to keep his composure.

River Wolf walked away to a secluded spot. He just wanted to get away for a while. Now alone, he wept bitterly. *Why did Beaver Pelt have to go and not me? She was a good person. She didn't deserve it. If anybody did, it was I.*

He heard footsteps behind him. When he turned to look, the lady who had smiled at him was there. She saw that he had been weeping, but pretended not to notice. He left her there and returned to the canoe.

River Wolf pulled out some effigy pipes that he had made and began bargaining with the villagers. Later that night, the four traders were invited to the Chief's lodge. Several women were there, including the woman River Wolf had encountered earlier.

When they all finished eating, the woman approached River Wolf and said, "You can come with me, if you want to."

They left together and went to the woman's lodge. The woman said, "I am Mouse Eyes. I live here alone, so nobody will disturb us."

River Wolf asked, "Why do you choose to live alone?"

Mouse Eyes looked down. "It is not a choice. My husband was killed two cycles in battle."

"Oh, I am sorry to hear that," replied River Wolf sadly. "My wife also recently died."

Mouse Eyes said, "I am sorry for you too. My husband's name was Woodpecker. Now, every time I see a woodpecker, I feel as though he is checking up on me."

Woodpecker's Namesake, a Woodpecker.
Redrawn from a public domain image.

They talked deep into the night. River Wolf and Mouse Eyes had something significant in common, and he actually thought of staying here with her. But his heart had not completely healed from Beaver

Pelt's death, and he decided to keep these thoughts to himself. If he did not fall in love, he could not be hurt again.

The next morning, he gave her three shell necklaces and a freshwater pearl bracelet. He felt bad about leaving her, and she could see it in the way he acted. It frustrated her because she could sense his true feelings.

The other three gave gifts to the women they shared the night with. Then they all loaded up their canoes and resumed their journey down the Mississippi River. River Wolf hurt inside from leaving her. Several times he almost changed his mind, but he never said a word about it.

He didn't say much about anything else either. Watersnake was also unusually quiet, and River Wolf wondered if he was feeling the same way. The more distance they got from that village, the more absurd the idea of turning back became. It was a good enough excuse for River Wolf to just forget it.

They continued downstream for many days. As they traveled, River Wolf learned more of the Calusa tongue, and it's variations from the Muskhogean language. He also taught Watersnake some of the Cherokee language.

One afternoon, they arrived in Quapaw territory. They had no contact with any of the Quapaw. Three days later they were back in the southern reaches of the Chickasaw territory. They camped at another island in the river. They saw smoke rising from the other side of the island, and went to investigate – leaving Bone Flute behind to watch their canoes.

Bone Flute's Namesake, a Bone Flute.

The woods on this island were thick, and moving quietly was difficult. They arrived at the south end of the island, and saw two strangers cooking over a fire. Their canoe was beached nearby.

Buck called out to them in Muskhogean. "Hello the camp," he said.

The two strangers lost no time in grabbing their bows and arrows. In an instant, they were ready for battle. "Who are you?" asked one in Muskhogean.

"We are traders," answered Buck. "We are headed for the Great Sea."

The two strangers relaxed somewhat. The older one who had spoken set down his bow, but the younger one seemed less trusting. "They will not hurt us," said the older one.

The youth finally lay down his bow, but kept a vigilant watch on the three traders.

The older one said, "We are on a hunting trip. We come from a village downstream. My name is Walking Thunder, and this is my little brother, Bear Claw Necklace, but we all just call him Bear Claw."

River Wolf noticed the bear claw necklace around Bear Claw's neck. "Are you two Chickasaw?" he asked.

"Yes," came the reply.

Buck decided to introduce them. "I am Buck, this is River Wolf, and we are Cherokee. This is Watersnake; he is Calusa. We also have another Calusa traveling with us. He stayed with our canoes on the north end of this island."

"Why don't you four bring your canoes here and eat deer with us?" offered Walking Thunder, "We will take you to our village tomorrow."

"Thank you," said Buck. "You are very kind. We will go back and get our canoes."

They left, and arrived back at their canoes quickly, because they didn't have to worry now about making noise. Bone Flute asked, "Who was there?"

"Friends," answered Watersnake. "They have invited us to eat with them. Tomorrow they'll take us to their village."

The three loaded up their things, and they arrived at Walking Thunder and Bear Claw's camp a little after dark. They ate their fill of venison, except for Buck, who ate cornbread to avoid any conflict with his totem.

The next morning, the two canoes and the catamaran arrived at the Chickasaw village, and they spent the day trading with the locals. They left the next morning, after giving gifts to the two hunters who showed them to the village. In two days they were in Tunica territory. After three more days they arrived in the territory of the Natchez. They stopped at the first village, but were turned away because the villagers were involved in a burial of a chieftain.

"How close are we to the coast?" asked River Wolf.

Buck paused to hear the answer.

"About a week," replied Watersnake. "We will be seeing alligators in three days or so."

"What tribes live there?" asked Buck.

"Chitimachas. They are fishermen. I sure hope they haven't found our mast and sail."

They had no contact with any of the Chitimachas and, in a few days, they finally reached the coast. Bone Flute and Watersnake searched for most of the day before finding the mast and sail for their catamaran. The four caught crabs and cooked them. They camped overnight and, early the next morning, they made ready for their sea adventure.

River Wolf had difficulty hiding his excitement about the trip. He and Buck helped the two Calusas erect the mast and sail. Next, they tied Buck's dugout to the catamaran with a hemp rope. Then they filled four old water bottles with fresh water. They were ready!

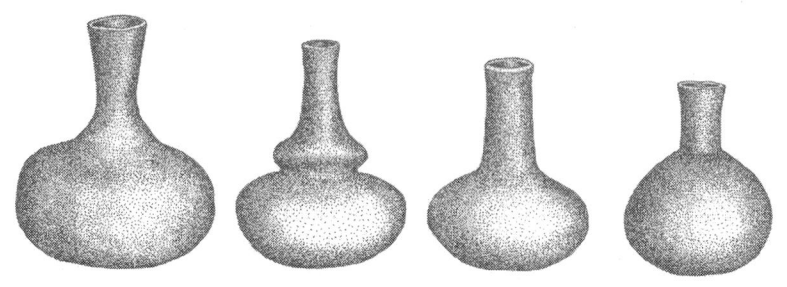

Four Old Water Bottles.
Redrawn from Moorehead 1900.

The four embarked on their trip, immediately heading southwest over the vastness of the sea. River Wolf was amazed at how they glided effortlessly over the water. After half a day, no land was visible anywhere. River Wolf hoped these Calusas knew what they were doing, and that they would not accidentally sail right off the end of the Earth. He had no idea where the world ended and the sky vault began. He didn't care to see the Underworld firsthand. Then he began to get sick in the stomach. Soon, he was followed by Buck. The two Calusas were amused at their vomiting, and told them that they would get used to the motion of the sea in time.

The Calusas slept in shifts. On the next morning, the rising Sun was hidden by a storm. The sea gradually got rough, and the storm moved closer. Now River Wolf really worried. He remembered the giant sea storm that had hit while he was at Good Medicine two cycles before. Bald Eagle had warned him about being near the ocean during one of these storms.

"We need to get to the shore," said Bone Flute, also uneasy.

But they were very far from any land and the storm overtook them. Soon the towering waves rocked them violently. The wind became very strong. Bone Flute and Watersnake argued about whether or not to lower the sail. Bone Flute was certain they could reach land before the main part of the storm capsized them. But Watersnake disagreed.

Clouds covered their only means of navigation. They might already have sailed the wrong direction without knowing. Also, the wind could have been blowing them even farther off course.

River Wolf heard through the wind the sounds of the Calusas shouting to each other. Apparently they were still in a heated argument. The wind got much stronger. Suddenly a tremendous blast of wind capsized the catamaran; all of its contents sank to the bottom of the sea. Buck frantically cut the rope to separate the two boats. The two Calusas disappeared into the towering waves, never to be seen by their comrades again.

River Wolf and Buck were alone in the violent sea, with no clue of their whereabouts. Rain filled their dugout, and now they used the water bottles to bail water out of the canoe. River Wolf began to pray. *Oh, Long Being, get us out of this one, and I will never leave my home again.* Then it occurred to him – *Maybe we are falling off the end of the world into the Underworld.* It was a frightening thought.

Their cargo of stone carvings, flint knives, pottery, and copper jewelry had long since washed over the side, and now both River Wolf and Buck were in the water, gripping the flooded canoe with all their might.

The towering waves jerked them around fiercely, and then River Wolf realized that Buck had disappeared. Another wave wrenched loose River Wolf's hold on the dugout. All was lost. He knew this was the end. But he kept fighting to stay afloat. Night came, but the storm raged on.

River Wolf had swallowed a lot of seawater and he was vomiting, choking, and delirious. He thought of Beaver Pelt. How he loved her. He would be joining her soon. He wanted it to end…

Chapter 14: Lost & Exiled

River Wolf woke up coughing. He had sand in his mouth and nose. He felt things crawling over his body. His sand-encrusted eyelids opened and, through the sand, he saw crabs all around him. *Is this some cruel joke the Spirits are playing on me?*

He lay there in a semiconscious state for what seemed like an eternity. A gentle rain fell on him. He had to sneeze. That brought him to his senses. He went to wash the sand out of his eyes, and then looked around. The treeless coast stretched as far as he could see in the rain. *Where am I?* He walked a distance down the beach, and soon realized that he was on an island. He was very thirsty. He noticed that he still had the flute that Bone Flute gave him; it was still hanging around his neck on the leather thong. It was the only thing he had left of the world he had been so violently taken away from.

Luck was on his side, and on the west shore of the island he found an unusual dugout canoe half-buried in the sand. The dugout still had bark on the outside, and had blunted ends. River Wolf spent some time digging it out. There was no paddle. He scanned the horizon and, through the light rain, he could see land. He was hopeful as he dragged the heavy and crude dugout into the water and washed it clean. Then he got in on the front and paddled with his hands. It was a long slow task, but he managed to get to the land on the other side. He continued into the bay and found the mouth of a flooded and muddy river. Fresh water!

River Wolf drank plenty, though he knew it could make him sick like it had at Good Medicine. He decided to follow this river inland to see if he could find a village. Then he found a dead fish floating in the water. He didn't have his fire pot, and there was no dry wood or tinder, so he ate the fish raw.

His energy somewhat replenished, he continued. He walked up the river, trying to avoid the mud. Suddenly he saw two very tall men through the woods. "Hello!"

The two strangers quickly turned to see who had spoken that word they couldn't understand. They only had fish spears for weapons, and they approached River Wolf, curiously, but cautiously.

River Wolf signed, "Trader."

They spoke in a dialect unlike any that he had ever heard. They could tell by his expression that he didn't understand. One of them signed, "Friend."

River Wolf repeated the word in signs. Then he said, "I am lost. I came from the sea."

"We have a campsite nearby," signed the stranger, "Follow me."

"What tribe are you two?"

They made a gesture that seemed to mean "dog lovers" to River Wolf, but he thought this was a strange name for a tribe. "What was that?" he signed.

The man spoke, "Karankawa." Then he signed that his name was Catfish. Catfish introduced his friend as Oyster.

River Wolf had never heard of this tribe, and now he really knew he was lost. The man signed, "What tribe are you?"

"I am of the Cherokee," replied River Wolf in signs, "From the mountains. My name is River Wolf."

"From the what?"

River Wolf realized that these people had never seen mountains, so he signed "Large hills."

"Across the sea?"

"Yes. My friends and I were traveling southwest from my land and we were caught in the storm. I have no idea where I am."

They arrived at the campsite. There were nine very crude shelters, each about ten feet in diameter. They were only covered on one side with animal skins – more like windbreaks than lodges. Near the swollen river were dugouts identical to the one River Wolf had used to get to the mainland. The people were all unusually tall.

There was a large mound of mussel shells – a trash pile. River Wolf was introduced to the leader, whose name was Alligator. There were only around twenty-five people total in this campsite. They lived on the coast, but were nomads. They were staying on the island River Wolf had landed on, but were driven here by the storm.

The Karankawas were very friendly with River Wolf, and he was glad to have happened upon them. They fed him some venison from a deer that had perished in the storm. The meat was spoiled, but River Wolf pretended not to notice. The Karankawas seemed to really enjoy this meal. It made him curious. Another strange thing he noticed about these people was their unusual practice of crying at all sorts things and occasions. It was almost comical to see, but River Wolf had the manners not to laugh at them.

The next day, the Sun came out and after a few days the river returned to its normal level. The locals decided to break camp and head inland. River Wolf helped as much as he could.

After three days of following the river inland, they set up their camp at the site of another shell midden on the river. They were there for several days when they noticed buzzards circling over an area a short distance away. Catfish and Oyster went to investigate, and soon returned with an old carcass of a buck deer. The smelly carcass had spots that were obviously eaten away by the vultures. The Karankawas showed excitement as they cut it up. They not only ate the spoiled meat, they seemed to savor it. River Wolf decided to take his chances catching squirrels.

So, River Wolf lived with these friendly but somewhat strange people for two moons. During this time, he trapped his own food while traveling with them.

One dark night, they were attacked. The Karankawa warriors chased the enemies, which River Wolf learned were several bands of the people who called themselves the Tickanwatic. River Wolf remembered that name. The man from Burnt Bluff had traded the piece of tabular flint to River Wolf. He had mentioned that it came from the land of the Tickanwatics far to the southwest. Now River Wolf had a rough idea of where he was. He remained behind so he wouldn't be involved in the local battles.

"Tell me about your tribe," signed River Wolf to a woman named Cottontail. "What territory belongs to your people?"

"To the south, along the coast, are the Kopanos. They are one of our bands. Their territory runs to about two days' walk south.

"To the northeast is the territory of the Kohani, Capoque, and Han – also Karankawa bands. The Kohanis are the nearest, and the Capoques' and Hans' land ends about a week's walk from here."

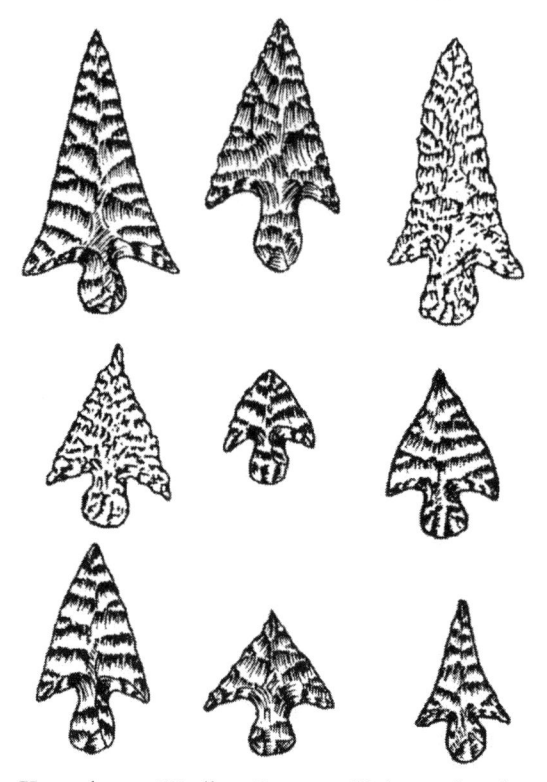

Karankawa "Bulbar Stemmed" Arrowheads.
Based on Turner & Hester 1993.

"How far inland does your territory cover?" signed River Wolf.

"About four days inland. Then you get into Tonkawa territory. They are the ones who call themselves the Tickanwatics."

The next night, the warriors returned with a dead Tonkawa warrior. After a lengthy crying ritual, they cut him up, roasted him over a fire, and ate him, much to River Wolf's horror. When Alligator offered a leg to him, River Wolf signed, "I am sick."

He hadn't lied to him. He went into the woods and vomited. He decided to wait until these people were asleep and leave them. Better to risk it alone than to stay with these cannibals.

So, the next night, after everybody was sound asleep, River Wolf began following the river upstream. He walked all night, and crossed the river two times to hide his tracks. When daybreak came, he found a comfortable place to sleep.

He was awakened by a noise in the woods that sounded like footsteps in the dried leaves. He quietly went to investigate and saw three warriors. He guessed by their resemblance to the Tonkawa captive that they were Tonkawas. River Wolf was afraid – these people had attacked the Karankawas and he wondered how they would treat him if he were discovered.

The Tonkawas were headed towards Karankawa territory, possibly to avenge their lost warrior. River Wolf could still see the leg of that warrior that had been offered to him as food.

They disappeared into the woods. River Wolf silently continued northwest, keeping the river nearby. He stopped at noontime at the river to get a drink. Then he smelled smoke from a cook fire, and he knew there was a village nearby. Just then he heard a voice speaking in an unfamiliar tongue. River Wolf turned around and saw a hunter with an arrow nocked and pointed at him.

"Trader," signed River Wolf. The hunter looked like a Tonkawa.

"If you are a trader, where are your wares?" signed the hunter, skeptically.

"I was lost at sea, and I escaped from the Karankawas."

The hunter relaxed. "Are you hungry?" he signed.

"Very," came the reply.

"We will go to the camp across the river."

They crossed the river to the camp. There were about thirty small round lodges that were crudely constructed out of brush and skins.

"Are you Tonkawas?" signed River Wolf, speaking the word, Tonkawas.

"We are The Most Human of People," signed the hunter. "What tribe are you?"

"I am of the Cherokee. My name is River Wolf. Why are you the most human of people?"

"Tickanwatic," spoke the hunter, and then he signed, "That is what we call ourselves. It means The Most Human of People. We are the Cavas band of the Tickanwatic. My name is Arrowhead."

As they entered the camp, River Wolf saw that the majority of the citizens were women – the men were probably gone to attack the Karankawas once again. The women had black stripes painted on their bare bodies, and concentric circles on their breasts around the nipples.

They arrived at Arrowhead's lodge and River Wolf waited while Arrowhead got him something to eat. A woman entered the lodge with Arrowhead. Arrowhead signed, "This is Moonbeam, my wife."

Moonbeam presented River Wolf with some unknown meat. River Wolf ate it eagerly, though he didn't know what it was. He hoped it wasn't a piece of Karankawa warrior. His worries were laid to rest when Arrowhead signed, "It is rattlesnake."

"It is really very good," signed River Wolf.

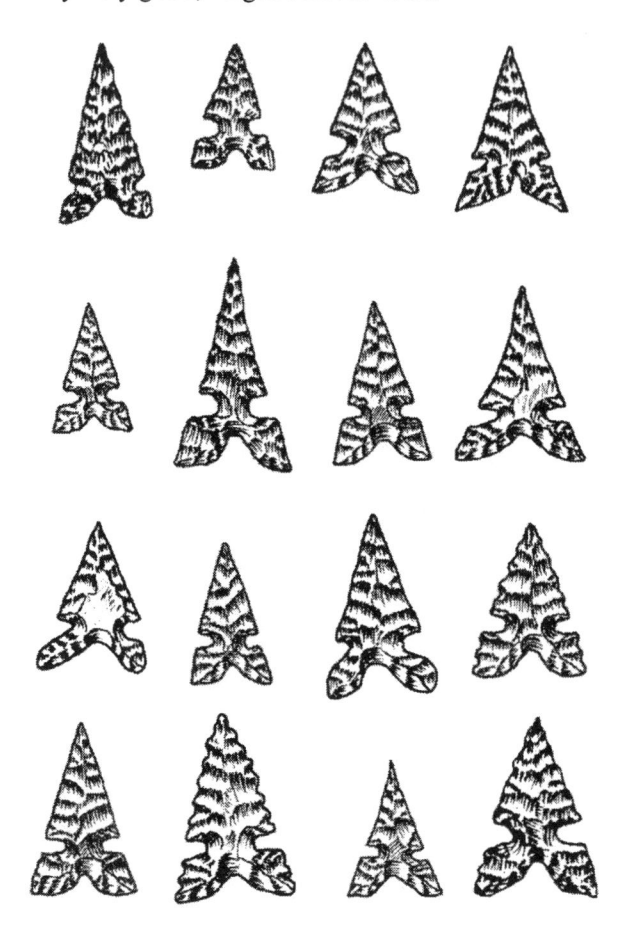

Tonkawa "Toyah" Tri-Notched Arrowheads.

River Wolf looked around the small lodge and saw some crude pottery and river-cobble flint. He noticed a pile of unusual tri-notched arrowheads that somebody had made, and had yet to haft onto arrows. His thoughts were interrupted by Arrowhead signing, "So where is the land of the Cherokee?"

"We are in the large hills far away, I think to the northeast, across the great sea. I would like to return there, but I am not sure I can find my way back. We traveled a long distance on the water before the storm overtook us."

"Well, you can stay with us as long as you need to," offered Arrowhead.

"Thank you, but I won't be here too long. If I can find a trader who can take me back home, I will go with him."

River Wolf stayed there for a week, learning their language from Arrowhead and Moonbeam. Then the warriors returned with Karankawa captives, including Catfish. Catfish recognized River Wolf, and that made River Wolf nervous.

The Cavas killed the captives, including Catfish. Then they began roasting them over a fire. River Wolf was once again horrified as the Cavas ate them. He waited for them to be distracted, and slipped away in the dark. This was a terrible land he was in. Everybody was eating each other!

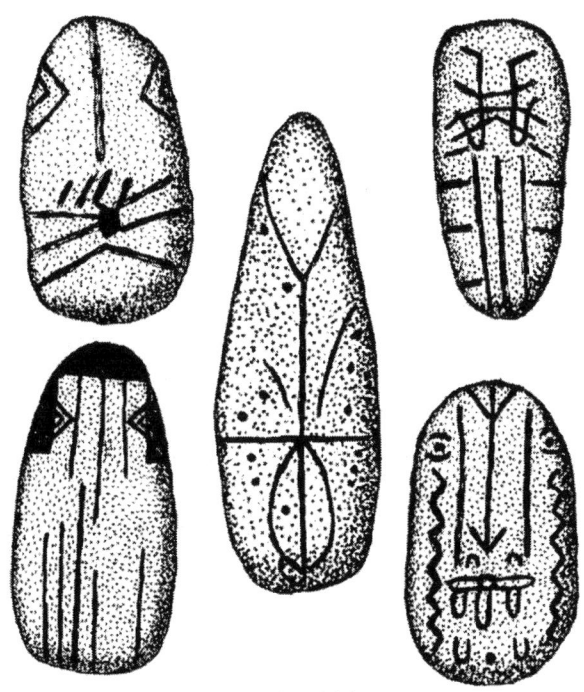

Painted Pebbles.
Based on Shafer & Zintgraff 1986.

He continued following the river at a distance. He trapped squirrels during the day, and slept in thickets at night. In a week, he encountered some more people, whom he found out were the Sana – another band of the Tonkawa. He didn't stay with them long, and continued upstream until he reached a large and beautiful canyon. He followed the canyon until he reached a place where there were many caves. There was evidence that people had occupied these caves, in the form of five curiously painted river pebbles. But the caves were currently vacant.

River Wolf guessed that these people spent the winters here. It got dark rapidly in the bottom of the canyon, and River Wolf spent the night in one of the caves. It was very uncomfortable on the rock floor. Finally he fell asleep, but was quickly awakened by a stinging sensation in his back.

He jumped up and got stung in the foot. In the darkness he saw something small running around on the floor of the cave. He picked up a rock and crushed it. The pain was not bad, but bad enough, and lasted for a long time, keeping him awake.

At first light, he finally had a good look at the strange bug that had stung him. It had eight legs and claws, like a crab's. At the end of its long tail was a nasty little hook-like stinger. How he missed his home!

He was hungry. The places he had gotten stung were reddish. He found two river pebbles with natural holes and took them with him. He discovered a plant with tough, fibrous leaves and made twine from the leaves. This he used with the rocks with holes to make a bola.

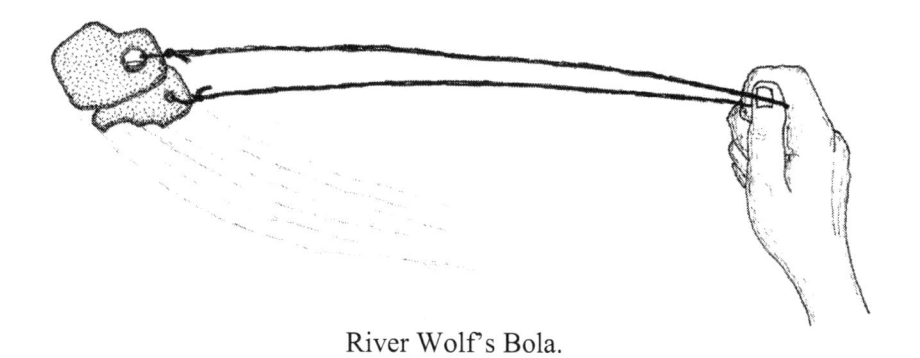

River Wolf's Bola.

He found some flint in the river and made some crude flake knives. He hunted jackrabbits with the bola he had made. He planned to kill some deer, if he could figure out how soon enough. Winter was coming, and he needed skins to keep warm.

* * *

Beaver Pelt entered the lodge carrying a full water bottle. River Wolf awakened and was shocked to see her. Beaver Pelt noticed the surprised expression on his face.

"You act as if you haven't seen me for a long time!" she commented with a smile.

"Wow!" exclaimed River Wolf. "You are alive! I had dreamed you died. I was so sad! Then Buck took me to see the Cahokia to keep my mind off of things. After that we were caught in a storm at sea and Buck went overboard. I was stranded in a strange place among cannibals."

"Well, Buck is out hunting meat for Tanager, I am here, and so are you," assured Beaver Pelt, with a smile.

River Wolf got up and embraced her. They kissed and made love for what seemed like an eternity.

"I love you," whispered Beaver Pelt, "and I will always be with you."

They clung to each other tightly until they drifted off to sleep…

* * *

River Wolf woke up on the hard floor of the cave he was sleeping in. He realized that it was only a dream and he wept bitterly. Life was so cruel. He got up and left with an axe he had finished the night before. He followed the canyon downstream a short distance to where a dry creek intersected with the river. He followed the creek quietly until he saw a buck. He stalked the deer until he was in range, and then threw the axe. It hit the buck in the head. The deer dropped in its tracks and River Wolf cut its throat with his flake knife.

He apologized to the buck's spirit, and he wondered if it was his best friend reincarnated. He missed Buck and his home. Maybe he would join them soon in the afterlife. River Wolf dressed the deer, and was glad to have a skin; it was a cold morning, and he knew it would only get colder.

After staying in the area for two moons, River Wolf went into a thicket hoping to bag a rabbit. He stepped on something and it snapped. Out of curiosity, he looked down and saw that he had stepped on a fresh arrow. He quietly picked it up to inspect it. It had the unique tri-notched style of arrowhead that was used by the Tonkawas! He was very uneasy. He had thought he had gotten well away from those cannibals. He dropped the broken arrow and made his way upstream. He crossed the icy cold shallow river to the shore opposite from the caves.

He saw smoke through the cypress trees, indicating there were people camping in his cave. He was sure they knew a stranger was in the area because he had neglected to clean up the trash he had left there. He hoped they would just think it was a local who camped there on a hunting trip. River Wolf continued upstream, staying away from the water for a day. He stopped to rest and hunt for some food.

Through the mountain laurel and cedar, he saw a deer. The deer was looking in the other direction. He threw his axe, but the deer ran away and he missed. Something else seemed to frighten the deer from the opposite direction.

River Wolf froze and listened. He heard talking in an unfamiliar language. It sounded vaguely like the Tonkawa language, but something about it seemed different. He decided to play it safe and retreat. He didn't bother to spend the time looking for his axe. The mountain laurel and cedar were thick, and River Wolf was glad to be concealed by the brush.

The voices disappeared in the direction of the river. River Wolf continued silently, following the river upstream at a safe distance. By sunset, he arrived at a small creek flowing with clear water.

He camped there, and made himself a spear. He would have made arrows, but did not have the time to make a good bow. The spear was very simple; it was a hardwood sapling with a point he carved with his flake knife.

He found a yucca plant with a dry stalk. The Tonkawas had shown him how to split the dry stalk and use it for a hearth stick for fire-making. He made a fire, and hardened the point of his crude spear. The heat of the fire felt good on this cold night. When the fire died down, he covered it with dirt and slept over it with the deerskin covering him. This kept him warm until it started raining.

He wandered the canyon all winter and through the spring, avoiding contact with any of the locals. He frequently saw signs and tracks they had left. One hot day, he was hunting jackrabbits with the bola he had made. Suddenly he found himself face to face with another person. Terrified, he signed, "Lost trader."

The stranger signed, "Friend."

River Wolf repeated the sign to the stranger and then signed, "I am River Wolf, of the Cherokee," speaking the words Cherokee.

The stranger introduced himself in signs. It appeared that his name was Lizard. He signed that he was a member of a certain band, and said the word "Payaya," when referring to the name of the group. Then he signed that his people were camped at the rockshelters downstream – the very place that River Wolf had camped the previous autumn.

River Wolf followed Lizard to the rockshelters while they conversed in signs. He hoped that the Payayas weren't cannibals also. Lizard introduced him to the twenty-two others there. They seemed to be good people, and River Wolf began to relax after a few days. He helped in the daily chores, and made an effort to learn their language. Soon he learned that Lizard was actually "Six-Lined Racer," named after a large striped lizard that was common in this region. A friendly, older Payaya woman named Laurel showed River Wolf how to make sandals out of yucca leaves. He was grateful to her, and gave her a rabbit he had snared.

River Wolf traded his bone flute, and help with certain tasks around the campsite, for a small bow and arrows. He began hunting deer for these poorly equipped people. Soon the Payayas and River Wolf left the rockshelters and headed southwest over the hilly terrain. They stopped at a river where there were clear springs.

Being the nomads they were, they covered lots of territory. After traveling with them for several days, they arrived at the biggest rockshelter River Wolf had ever seen. They stayed there during the spring, and the hotter part of the summer.

Overlooking a Dry Creek Below a Giant Rockshelter.

After about a cycle with these people, River Wolf was speaking their language fairly well. He learned that they were a band of the Coahuiltecan tribe, and in the distant past they had been separated from their relatives, far to the west, by invaders from the north. These invaders, called the Aztecs, had now created a large empire far to the south. The Payayas' description of the Aztecs civilization reminded River Wolf of life at Cahokia.

The Payayas did remarkably well living off the land, in spite of the fact that food was scarce. They migrated over a large area, camping here and there in rockshelters and small crude huts. They ate bugs, lizards, and almost anything that moved or grew. They even ate rotten wood and deer dung.

Digging Sticks.
Based on Shafer & Zintgraff 1986.

They used pointed digging sticks to uproot yucca and lechuguilla bulbs. These they buried in baking pits and then dug up to prepare them for eating after they had finished baking.

The Payayas made large nets and erected them over an area that had no trees. Then they formed a line and began yelling, banging sticks together to make noise while approaching the net. This would scare jackrabbits away from them and right into the net.

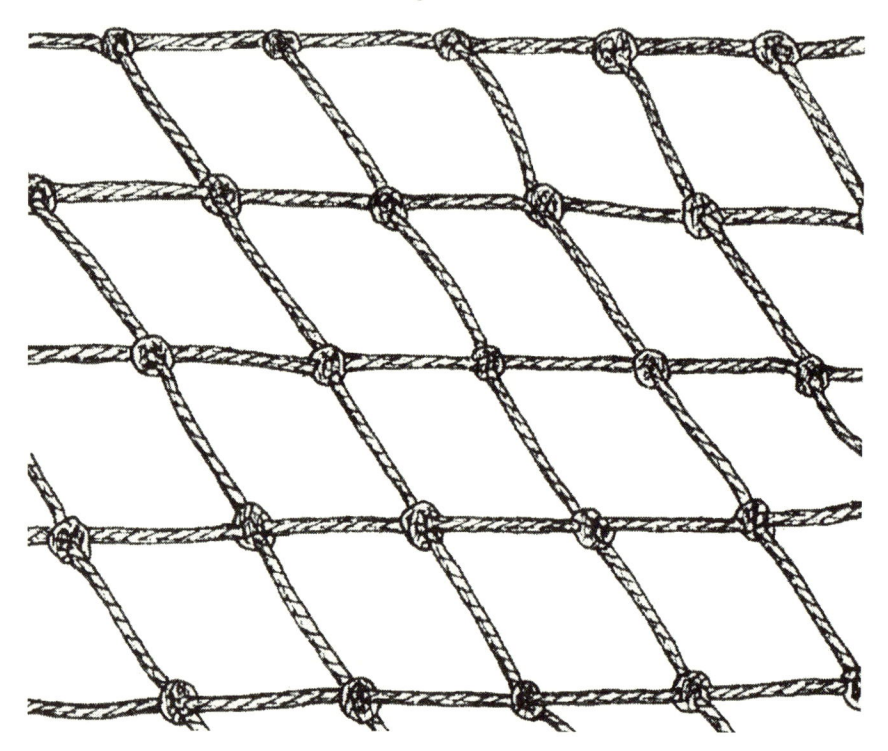

Yucca Netting Used for Catching Jackrabbits.
Redrawn from Holmes 1891.

One thing that River Wolf found very revolting was a custom referred to as the "second harvest." This was a practice that involved looking through human feces for seeds and things to eat again. River Wolf did not participate in this activity, but he did hide his true feelings about it for the sake of courtesy.

One night the Shaman died. The people cooked him and the women ate him. They ground his bones into powder, using a mortar and pestle and sprinkled it on peyote and all the Payayas ate it. They believed that this would let his magic powers remain with the people. It seemed to have some type of magic, because of the bizarre behavior that it created in the people who ate it. They just lay around, talking about love, howling like wolves, jumping like frogs, and trying to fly like birds. It vaguely reminded River Wolf of old Stone Spear's wild grape drink. River Wolf was horrified because of the bone powder, but accepted it and stayed with them. He was tired of running in an unfamiliar land. He didn't participate in this ritual either.

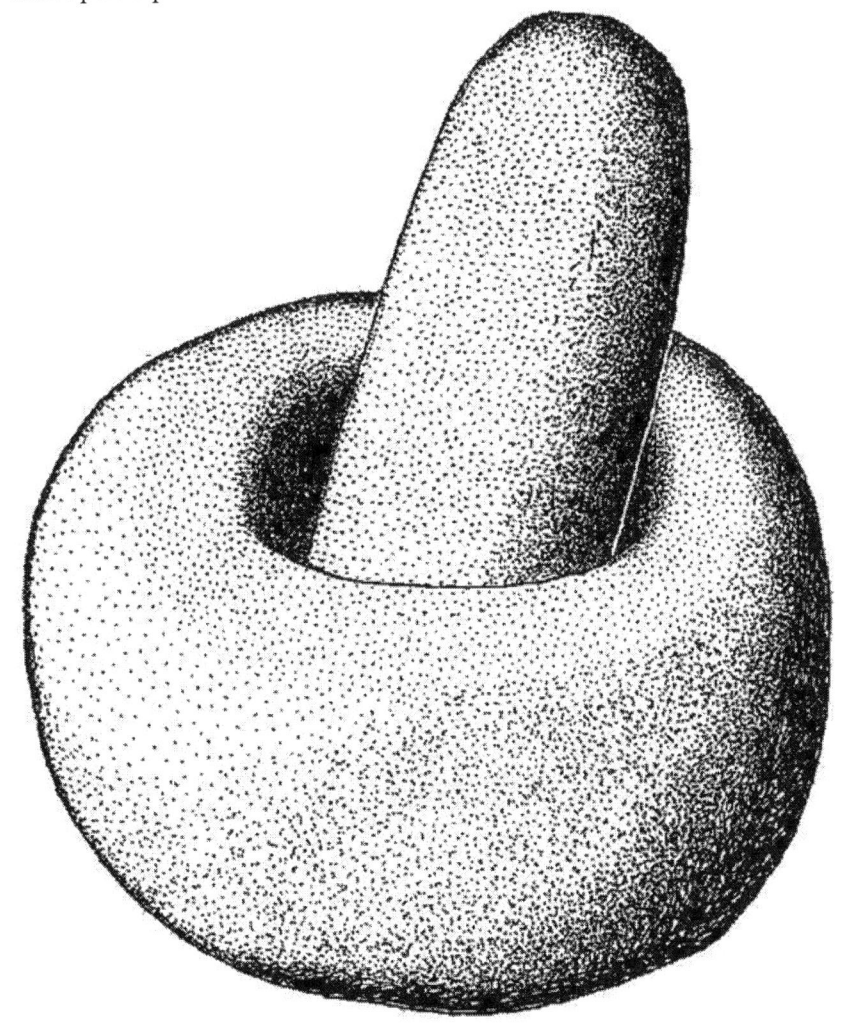

Stone Mortar & Pestle.

Another intoxicant was made during the wintertime by grinding the seeds of a certain bush into a powder and mixing it with agave leaf juice. They called this drink 'mescal.' River Wolf was talked into trying it, only because it didn't have any human ingredients in it.

The mescal made him see bugs crawling over everybody. He decided not to drink anymore when he felt these bugs crawling over his body. Now he knew how Loner must have felt.

The Payayas made a food called "mesquitamal" out of mesquite beans. When they were plentiful, the Payayas gathered and dried the beans and ground them, with a mano and metate, into a type of flour. They stored the coarse flour, and mixed it with other ingredients and dirt. Then they mixed in water and ate it.

Mano & Metate.

There were often feuds between clan members, which resulted in killings. These disputes were often over women or possessions, and River Wolf accidentally became involved in a conflict over a woman.

Laurel had feelings for River Wolf, but a man named Groundsquirrel had feelings for her. River Wolf was at the springs swimming one summer, and Laurel joined him. Groundsquirrel took notice of her spending more time with River Wolf and less time with him.

One afternoon, Six-Lined Racer approached River Wolf. "You need to get away from here."

"Why?" asked River Wolf.

"Groundsquirrel plans to kill you tonight in your sleep."

"Are you serious? Why?"

"He wants to marry Laurel. You are not one of us. If don't leave tonight, you will be tomorrow's dinner. I am your friend. Please heed my advice and leave this area now!"

River Wolf went and got his things and pretended to go on a hunting trip. Groundsquirrel smiled at him, thinking River Wolf was unaware of his plans. River Wolf returned the smile, though he really wanted to punch him in the stomach.

That evening he left his friends, and his supposed enemy. His heart was bitter as he followed the creek downstream until late in the night. The next morning he continued downstream, and later arrived at a river.

River Wolf followed the river downstream for four days and stopped at a creek to hunt for food. The place seemed deserted, so he built a small shelter, using yucca stalks as poles, and he wove bundles of dried bluestemmed grass between the poles.

River Wolf's Small Hut.

He was satisfied with his new home; it was warm and a good windbreak. When it rained, he put deer hides over the conical top to prevent the rain from soaking through the grass. River Wolf stayed here through the summer, fall, and winter, hunting deer and squirrel for food.

In the autumn, he found pecans, a local type of nut that he had heard of but never tried. He found them very tasty and, while gathering them, he was also given many opportunities to observe squirrel traffic. With this information, he could make better decisions about where to set his squirrel traps.

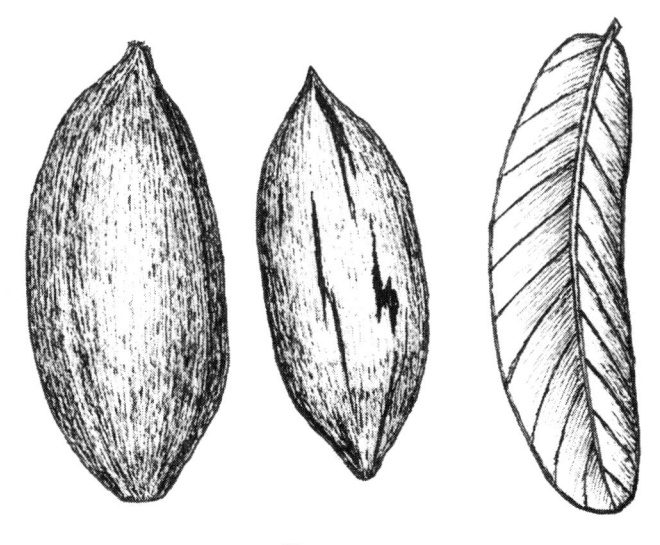

Pecans.

When spring came around, River Wolf began to think of home. He wanted to see his mother before she died. She was getting pretty old by now. All the lost time... He was sad. It occurred to him that he should make every effort to get back to Birch Mountain, even if he had to travel through Tonkawa and Karankawa territory again. He wished he had a canoe. Then he got an idea.

There was an abundance of cane growing near the creek, and there were plenty of yucca plants in the area. He cut cane stalks and tied them together with yucca twine. It took a long time, but he worked diligently until he had a raft that he could stand up on.

River Wolf kept the raft dry, as he went to cut plenty of yucca leaves so he could make repairs during the trip to the sea. He loaded the raft with all the supplies he could fit on it, and shoved off. His plan was to travel only after dark, and when he arrived at the sea, maybe he could ride with a northbound trader back to his home. As he guided the raft with a long pole, he felt an excitement that made him glad to be alive. He was on his way home!

He lost a lot of sleep during the trip to the sea, because maintaining the raft proved to be more work than he had anticipated. This he did during the day, in addition to hunting and fishing. Every day, at sunrise, he found a thicket in which to hide himself and his raft.

River Wolf was not certain of which tribe's land he was on, but he played it safe. He passed the place where another river to the southwest merged into the river he was on. After two week's traveling, he had stopped for the day and went hunting. He killed a rabbit, using a boomerang-like rabbit stick. This type of weapon was made for throwing, and/or by using as a club. It was widely used by the Coahuiltecans, from whom he learned on how to throw them with accuracy. When he returned to the place where he had concealed his raft, there were three hunters looking at it.

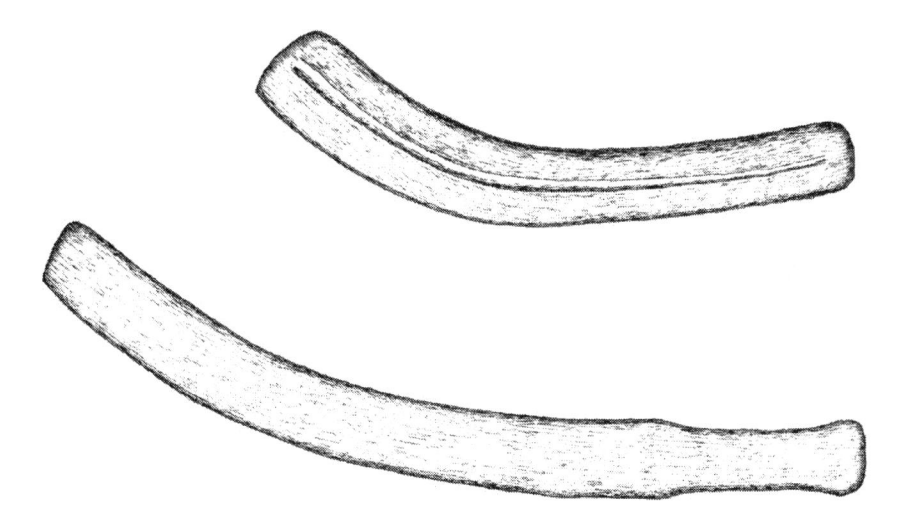

Boomerang-Like Rabbit Sticks.
Based on Shafer & Zintgraff 1986.

"Traveler," he said in Coahuiltecan.

The startled hunters turned to look at him. One of them said, "What band are you?"

"I was staying with the Payayas. I was a trader who got lost. What band are you?"

"Aranamas – of the Coahuiltecan tribe. We have killed a Tonkawa warrior. Come and join us for the feast."

River Wolf was annoyed. "I would love to, but I am in a hurry to return to my home before winter sets in. I still have a very long distance to travel."

"Our camp is just downstream. If you can't feast with us, we will give you a leg or an arm to take along with you."

Out of courtesy, River Wolf said, "Thank you. You are very generous."

They went to the Aranama camp, and they gave River Wolf the lower left leg of the Tonkawa warrior, roasted and ready to eat. River Wolf thanked them profusely and left. As soon as he was out of sight of the village, he threw the leg overboard. *If I ever make it back home, I will NEVER travel again!* he thought as he washed his hands in the river.

The next morning he encountered more Coahuiltecans. He was going around a bend at sunrise, looking for a thicket to hide in, but suddenly came up on a campsite. The people were friendly, and River Wolf learned that these were of the Tamique band. They gave him some mesquitamal to take with him. River Wolf felt he should give them something in return, so he gave them one of his deer hides, and continued his journey.

A few days afterward he was out hunting and when he returned to his raft, he heard numerous voices coming from the raft's hiding place. They didn't speak Coahuiltecan – or at least the dialect he was accustomed to. He feared they were Karankawa. His suspicions were confirmed when he saw them through the woods. They were tall, like Karankawas.

River Wolf decided to just leave the raft and get out of the area before they began tracking him. They might have been friendly, but he didn't take any chances. The Karankawas were usually at war with the neighboring tribes, and River Wolf did now look like a Coahuiltecan. After a day's walking, the river merged with another, and he recognized this place. This was the bay where he had arrived at cycles ago, after paddling that crude dugout from the island. The river to the north was the one he had followed inland. He was at the same place!

Now he drank as much water as he could hold and swam to the island. When he arrived there, he began walking northeast along the eastern shore, eating oysters and dead fish he found.

He walked for most of the day and then saw smoke from a campfire ahead of him. He cautiously approached, and saw a catamaran with the sail down. A trader! He ran up to the camp. The startled trader grabbed a spear and got ready for combat.

River Wolf signed "Trader. Lost trader."

The man laughed and said something in a foreign language.

River Wolf smiled and signed, "Friend."

The man lay down his spear and offered him some water. As River Wolf drank, the stranger signed, "You certainly look like you are lost."

River Wolf laughed out loud. He now realized how haggard he must have looked to the stranger. He signed, "I am River Wolf – of the Cherokee. I haven't had a good night's sleep for more than a moon."

The stranger signed, "I am Large Fish, of the Calusa tribe," speaking the word 'Calusa.'

"Then you know Muskhogean?" asked River Wolf in that language.

Large Fish was surprised. "Yes, I do," he said.

"I need a ride home, but I have nothing to trade."

"I have heard of the Cherokee, but not good things. I heard those things from the Yuchi. But they don't know everything, so I will give you the benefit of the doubt. Is it true you have soapstone at your home?"

"Plenty of it."

"I would like some. I will take you home in trade in exchange for some. I know a good pipe carver. I will trade him some for pipes."

"I can carve animal pipes," offered River Wolf. "I can carve all of the pipes you could ever want! Even effigy pipes!"

"Agreed. I will take you home and return the next cycle for the pipes. Eat some fish."

"Thank you. I promise I will not cheat you."

They ate and then went to sleep on the beach. River Wolf was tired and slept very soundly. He had a strange dream that night, in which he drank some of old Stone Spear's grape drink. Large Fish had a difficult time waking him the next morning.

"Come on, let's go!" Large Fish demanded, while shaking River Wolf. "You can sleep after we set sail."

River Wolf was still half asleep as he climbed into the catamaran.

"Hey!" scolded Large Fish. "Aren't you going to help me shove off?"

"I'm sorry," replied River Wolf and he helped as much as he could. They pulled the catamaran into the deeper water together. They climbed aboard and raised the sail.

"*Now* you can sleep," said Large Fish.

Large Fish woke River Wolf just before sunset so he could help beach the catamaran. They caught crabs and roasted them. They ate and talked late into the night.

"Did you know Bone Flute and Watersnake?" asked River Wolf.

"Where were they from?"

"They were Calusa traders. My best friend and I were traveling with them in their catamaran ten cycles ago. A violent storm overtook us and they were lost. I guess they drowned. They were nice people. That is how I ended up here."

"I think I remember meeting a man named Bone Flute once, but I don't recall anybody named Watersnake. I need to get some sleep. Good night."

"Good night," replied River Wolf. He was wide-awake. He tried to sleep, but couldn't. He was glad to be on his way home. Finally he did fall asleep, and the next thing he knew it was morning.

Large Fish was gone, but the catamaran was still there. There were tracks leading inland. He must have gone hunting. River Wolf decided to be productive and catch some crabs. He found a small dead fish, and got some twine and a stick out of the catamaran. While he waited for a crab to take the bait, he started a fire with Large Fish's fire pot.

He checked to see if he had caught a crab and found a large one gripping the bait. River Wolf removed it and waited for another one. By the time Large Fish returned, River Wolf had five crabs roasted and ready to eat.

"You have been busy!" commented Large Fish, pleased. They ate the crabs and Large Fish said, "Now let's go and get that fat buck that I killed."

They carried the buck to their camp, its legs tied to a stick, with Large Fish in front and River Wolf behind. After butchering it and cutting it up, they had enough supplies for a long journey in the sea. Butchering it took most of the day, and the next morning they set sail.

For three days and nights they sailed northeast and then made for the shore. River Wolf noticed that they never ventured as far from the coast as Bone Flute and Watersnake had. As they set up camp, River Wolf asked Large Fish why.

"We need to be nearby in case of a storm," came the answer.

River Wolf could see the reasoning behind this idea – Large Fish was older, and more experienced, than Bone Flute had been. He was glad to be traveling with him. They set up camp and River Wolf caught more crabs for their dinner while Large Fish started the fire.

While the crabs were roasting, Large Fish made ready his bow and arrows for the next morning's hunt. They ate and Large Fish lit his pipe. Shortly after, they went to sleep. At sunrise, Large Fish started heading inland to hunt.

"Can I go with you?" offered River Wolf.

"No, you need to stay and watch the camp." Large Fish left. He returned a little while afterwards with three rabbits and a wild turkey. They set sail and traveled for two more days and one night. The second night they camped in a bay near the coast.

"What area are we in?" asked River Wolf.

"Atakapan territory. There are not many of them, but they have a large area that they occupy. We probably will not encounter any of them."

The next day they went hunting together and killed a large alligator and dragged it back to their camp. After butchering it they resumed the journey eastward.

After three days, Large Fish said, "The land along the coast is the Chitimachas' land. After that is the mouth of the Big Muddy River."

"You mean the Mississippi?"

"Yes."

"When we get there, we will be almost to the river that leads to my village!" exclaimed River Wolf, excited. The whole time, he was a mixture of excitement and intense boredom. He played with three clay marbles that had been rolling around the catamaran since who knew when. There was little else to do, except wait.

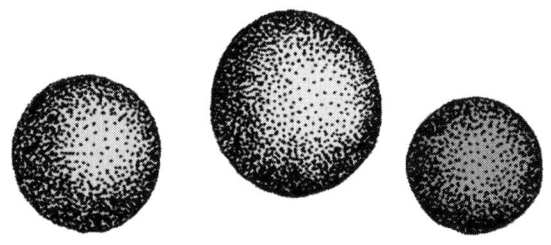

Three Clay Marbles.

"You're going to get really bored just playing with marbles," observed Large Fish.

"What else is there to do?" asked River Wolf.

"Well, you could sit and do nothing, or play a little bit of ring and pin!" Large Fish handed him the game. "It's still mine, but you can borrow it. It beats playing with marbles, doesn't it?"

River Wolf smiled as he took the ring and pin. But rather than playing the game, he studied it.

"I guess you're going to do nothing then?" said Large Fish with a chuckle.

"I was thinking about making one like it someday."

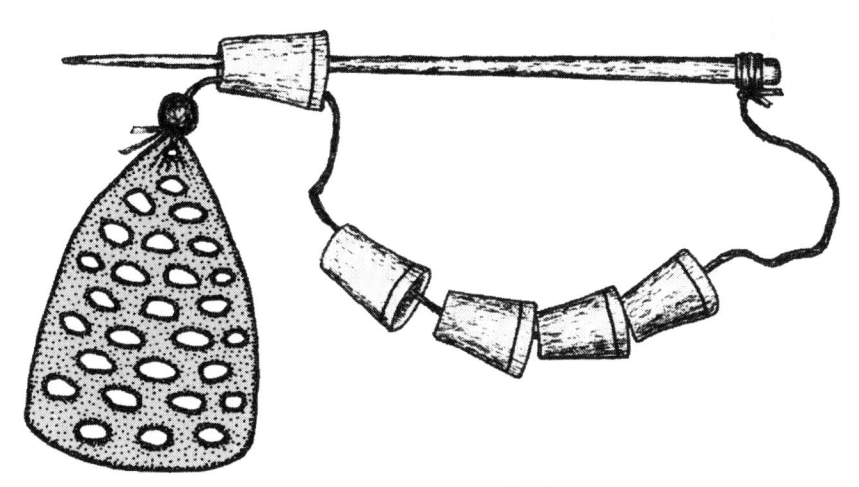

Large Fish's Ring & Pin Game.
Based on Hothem 2006.

"I should have known!" laughed Large Fish. "Study it then!"

They finally arrived at the Mississippi River two days later. After going upstream to get fresh water, they caught three large catfish and returned to the shore. Now they sailed northeast, passing the Biloxi land, and they landed on the island that Medicine Wolf had lived on with his daughter, Sand Dollar.

River Wolf said, "After a while, I am going to look for some old friends of mine. But I will be back later. Please don't leave without me."

They set up camp, and River Wolf went looking for them. He saw in the distance a familiar-looking man, but it was not Medicine Wolf. He said, "Trader," to the man, in Muskhogean.

The man got closer and, in Cherokee, he said, "Brother."

Chapter 15: White Feather

River Wolf looked him over. *Who is this?* He thought. Suddenly it came to him. "Panther!" The two ran up to each other and embraced.

"How did you get here?" asked River Wolf.

"The Muskogee were plotting against me. Even Autumn Leaf. I knew they would kill me eventually, so I fled from town to town, and ended up hiding out on this island. I married a sweet woman named Sand Dollar."

"I knew her! Is she still here?"

"Yes, she is. Let's go to my lodge and you can see her."

They arrived at Panther and Sand Dollar's lodge and River Wolf visited with them. Medicine Wolf had gone to the Darkening Land several cycles before, right after Panther happened on them. Panther had taught Sand Dollar the Muskhogean language.

"I have to introduce you to the friend who is taking me back to Birch Mountain," said River Wolf to them.

"Let us talk alone for a minute," requested Panther. He called Sand Dollar aside. "Would you like to leave this island and go with me to my home village?"

Sand Dollar was apprehensive. "I don't like living in villages. Crowds scare me."

"But these are good people. I am sure you will like them."

"I can't live in a village."

"We won't have to. We can build a lodge outside the village. The land there is green and very fertile. We can grow corn and I can bring you plenty of meat every night. My family is there. Come on, let's try it."

Sand Dollar considered it and said, "Alright, but only if we can live outside of the village."

Panther hugged her and then asked River Wolf, "Can we go with you to Birch Mountain? I have no more status here, and I miss home so much! Man, it's so good to see you!"

They embraced each other again while Sand Dollar smiled. "I have a dugout that we can travel in," offered Panther, "if your friend can't fit all of us in his canoe."

Then the three went to Large Fish's camp. Large Fish saw them approaching and asked, "So these are your friends?"

"They are my brother and sister-in-law. This is Panther, and this is Sand Dollar."

"It's nice to meet you," said Large Fish, cordially. "Would you like some crabs?"

They all ate, but there wasn't really quite enough to go around.

River Wolf spoke, "My brother and his wife would like to return to Birch Mountain with me. They have a large dugout they can ride in."

"Well, River Wolf, I would just as soon just go east back to my home. You could ride with your brother, and you owe me nothing. I have enjoyed your company immensely. In fact, here is a gift for you." Large Fish gave River Wolf a shell gorget engraved with depictions of two turkeys.

River Wolf gasped and replied, "I cannot repay you for this!"

"Don't worry about it, River Wolf. Take it. You are welcome."

Shell Gorget with Two Turkeys Given by Large Fish to River Wolf.
Redrawn from Lewis & Kneberg 1958.

"I will miss you, Large Fish, and I'll always be grateful to you for showing me the way back to this river. We will go to Panther and Sand Dollar's lodge to make ready for the journey."

"I will be leaving early in the morning, so I guess this is goodbye."

"It was good knowing you, Large Fish, and thank you again." Then they left Large Fish and returned to the lodge.

The next morning they started packing all their possessions into the dugout. It looked like Bald Eagle's canoe, but it seemed to have a few more cycles of wear on it. They went diving for conch shells – they might need them for trading during the journey.

Then Panther and Sand Dollar loaded as many of their personal items as they could fit in the dugout. They were forced to leave behind many things. Sand Dollar repeatedly swapped items from the dugout to the lodge; it was obvious that she couldn't make up her mind what to take and what to leave. Many of her effects had sentimental value.

It appeared by her expression that the whole island was dear to her – it had been where she had lived all of her life. Finally she decided that she had wasted enough time dilly-dallying and had to end it. Reluctantly, she said she was ready to go.

As they shoved off and paddled into the bay, she looked back at her island, and suppressed tears. She knew she had to let go of her father and her home. She clearly loved Panther and wanted to help him better his life. Hiding out on that island held no future for him, so she supported his decision to leave.

* * *

Sparrow returned from the river with a full water bottle. As she entered Squirrel Fur's lodge, she noticed that the roof had a small hole in it. "Your roof has a leak," she said to Squirrel Fur. "I will have Broken Spear take a look at it."

"You are so kind," replied Squirrel Fur as she took the water bottle. Squirrel Fur was now forty-nine cycles old and she had no more family. She often spoke about her two sons who were far away, hopeful that she might soon see them again.

Sparrow had totally given up hope. She believed that River Wolf was dead, and Panther was an enemy warrior. It was unlikely that they would ever come back. But she didn't have the heart to tell Squirrel Fur. Why tell her something that would only upset her?

Squirrel Fur's health was failing, and she would likely pass into the Darkening Land before the next spring. She could barely walk, or even stand, for any length of time. In a way, she longed for death, for she believed that then she would be with her loved ones.

Eagle Medicine was also growing old; Three Crows now took care of most of the Shaman's responsibilities. Dances Like the Deer had been killed two cycles ago during a Muskogee attack that had occurred while she was out foraging for food.

White Feather tended her father, Eagle Medicine. His Paint Clan relatives hunted meat for the two. White Feather, still traumatized by her mother's death, worried constantly for her father. She had never left his side. Eagle Medicine tried to encourage her to have relations with men, but she always refused.

She was now twenty-one cycles old, and had grown up into a very attractive woman. She caught the eye of every young man in Birch Mountain. Often a man would show interest in her, but she would simply turn around and run home to her father without saying another word to them. She was afraid to love, because she had lost so many of the people she had loved. Some people even suspected there was an incestuous relationship between her and her father.

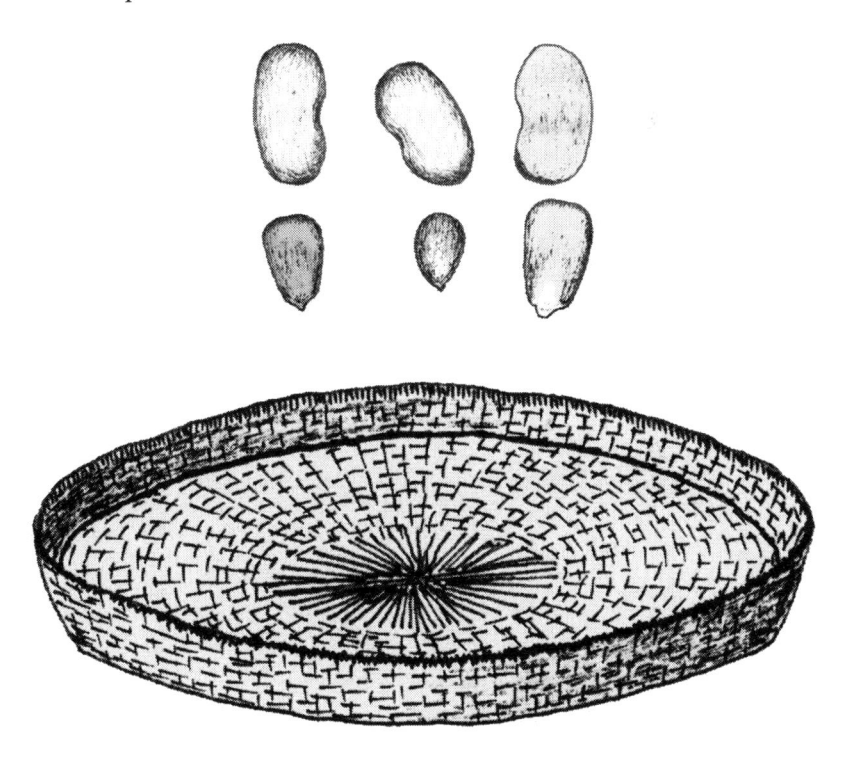

Butterbean Game.

In his old age, Eagle Medicine enjoyed playing games with his daughter, White Feather. One of his favorites was the game of butterbean. The Cherokee butterbean game was played using three butterbeans, each split into two halves (totaling six halves). Corn kernels were used for keeping score. A basketry tray or lid was needed for the game, as well as a bowl for the corn kernels. The six butterbean halves were placed in the basketry tray, and when it was a team or player's turn, that person/team would lightly flip the tray, and catch the butterbean halves in the tray. Different numbers of points scored by a player or team depended on certain different combinations of how the butterbean halves landed in the tray. Whichever side first scored twenty-four points won the game.

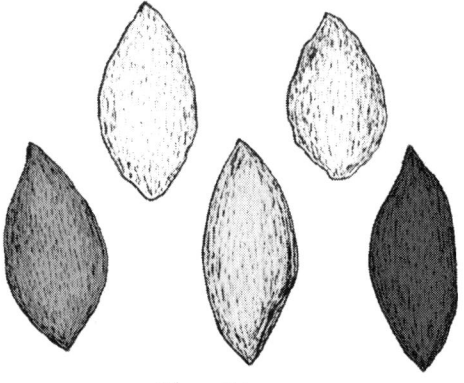

Plum Stones.

    Another game was the plum stone game. Eagle Medicine had learned of this game from a trader from the northeast. It was similar to the Cherokee butterbean game, but plum seeds (plum stones) colored on one or both sides were instead used. Twigs were used for keeping score. The first player/team to win a hundred points won the game. The plum stone game was primarily a women's game, but Eagle Medicine had no issue with that, as long as he could spend more time with his daughter.

    White Feather was also a talented basket weaver and potter. Her baskets were beautiful works of art, but were also sturdy, and could be used for storing and carrying many different items. In fact, some were even woven tightly enough, they could actually hold water without leaking. Not only were her woven basketry items used throughout the village for containers, they were also used by many households for serving food, as mats spread over benches that functioned as seats, and even in the frameworks of the village council house, along with many other uses. Eagle Medicine's work as Shaman had its advantages when it came to providing business for his daughter.

    Bamboo-like river cane was what White Feather mostly used for her basketry. Her baskets were often decorated with designs, by coloring some of the cane to be woven, with plant dyes. The dyes that she utilized were made from the roots of bloodroot for red dye, and black walnut bark for black dye. The river cane was soaked or boiled in the dye for several hours, before being woven into a basket. When it was woven and allowed to dry fully, it became rigid and sturdy again.

White Feather Weaves a Basket.
Redrawn from Holmes 1891.

White Feather could make both singleweave, or doubleweave baskets. Doubleweave baskets were unique to the Cherokees, and were very durable and strong. They are essentially two baskets in one. Singleweave baskets were woven from the bottom up. But when the top was completed, the weaver could make it into a doubleweave basket by continuing the process, from the top, back down to the bottom. The result was a very beautiful, extremely sturdy and water-resistant basket.

Often, she would visit a special place, just outside the palisade, where she would suspend an unfinished basket from a tree branch. She could sit comfortably on a rock, and do her weaving with ease.

Doubleweave Basket Made by White Feather.
Based on Fariello 2009.

As a skilled potter, White Feather's work with clay was also popular in Birch Mountain. She dug for clay at a nearby secret source, using a pointed digging stick, or a hoe and even her hands. Ideally, clay that had the fewest impurities possible was used. She avoided clay with too many foreign items, such as the debris of leaves, roots, twigs and bark.

Her mother taught her at a young age to pound the clay thoroughly with a wooden pestle, or a hammerstone. This was to both, make sure it was mixed well, but also to eliminate any air pockets that could cause breakage while firing the vessel.

Amongst the different tribes, different substances were added for tempering the clay. These included crushed potsherds (called "grog"), bone, sand, charcoal, and even stone – such as limestone or mica.

Without a tempering agent, most clay would shrink unevenly while drying, and this caused cracks to form in the vessel, ruining it. So, a ground up tempering agent was mixed into the wet clay, which helped prevent such problems.

For this purpose, White Feather mostly used ground-up clam shells that were crushed and then cooked. These shells were widely available in the nearby river, so they were seldom in short supply. The amount of grinding she did to the tempering agent varied – finer pottery had finer ground clam shells, while the more utilitarian pieces had rougher ground shell.

Once the clay was prepared, it was molded into snake-like or rope-like shapes. These "ropes" were coiled around in a circle (sort of like a large "spring"). The coils were then mashed together, creating the walls of the pottery vessel.

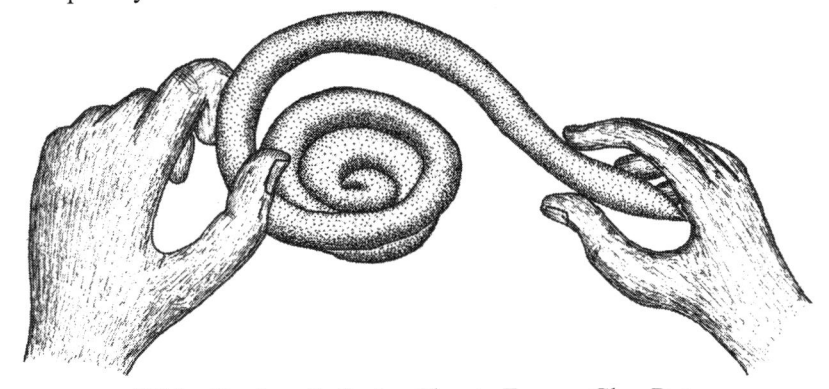

White Feather Coils the Clay to Form a Clay Pot.

Pottery trowels were handheld, baked clay, mushroom-shaped tools used for rounding out the insides of pottery vessels. They also functioned as "anvils" which firmly pressed the clay from the inside while mashing the vessel from the outside to thin down the walls of the vessel. Bare hands could do the same, but perhaps not quite as neatly as these trowels could do. The handles of the trowels were irregularly shaped, each being designed by its maker to be comfortable in her/his hand.

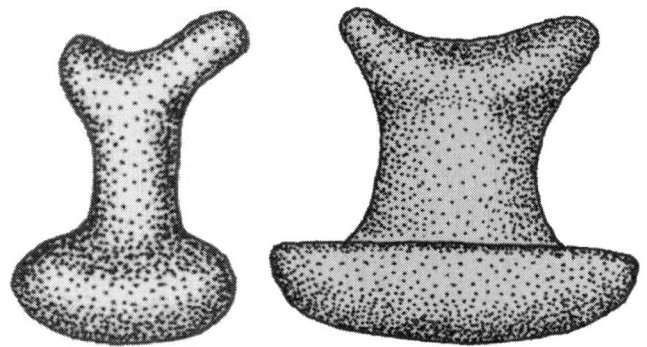

White Feather's Pottery Making Trowels.
Redrawn from Thruston 1897.

Once the clay vessel took shape, White Feather often finished it by decorating it in various ways. She used textured wooden paddles to stamp designs into many of her vessels, and sometimes corncobs and even crude cloth from worn-out garments were used for impressing designs and textures in the vessel's outer walls.

White Feather's Textured Pottery Paddles.
Based on Fariello 2011.

Another tool that was handed down through White Feather's family was a shiny polished burnishing stone, used for burnishing the walls of a pottery vessel, making it smooth and more watertight.

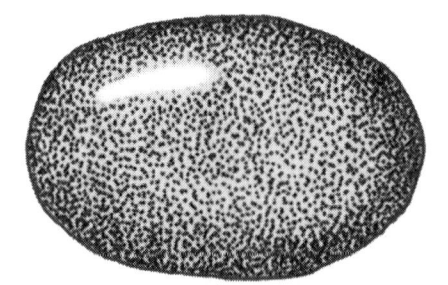

White Feather's Shiny Pottery Burnishing Stone.

Many of White Feather's nicer pieces of pottery were painted, occasionally using different kinds of plant items, by making dyes from berries, barks or roots. But, more frequently, she used powdered mineral substances as paint. Graphite produced a black paint. Ground-up ochres could produce a red, brown, or orange-yellow color. Galena lead made white, and hematite created a red or even purplish paint, depending on how she prepared it.

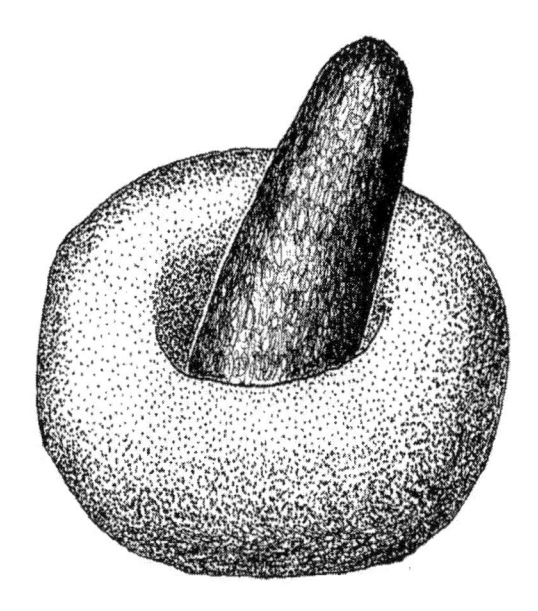

White Feather's Paint Grinder.

She used a small stone mortar and pestle for grinding such items in the manufacture of her different pigments. She applied the paint to the unbaked pottery via finger painting, or with brushes made from different kinds of plant items. Fibrous plants could have their pulp removed by chewing them or pounding them between two rocks. With the pulp gone, the fibers remained, and formed the working ends of her paintbrushes.

She also knew how to do negative painted pottery by coating the design areas with bear grease or beeswax. Once this was done, she painted the colored design all over the entire vessel. The bear grease or beeswax would burn away during firing, leaving behind only the finished painted designs.

When she finished a vessel, she allowed it to dry. Drying it slowly helped prevent it from cracking. This could be done by wrapping it in a deer skin, or something that will contain the moisture, and keep it from escaping too rapidly.

Once the vessel was dry enough, it was ready for baking. Although the different kinds of paints were usually water-based, they would bond with the clay during firing and, like the clay, they became waterproof.

Baking, or firing the pottery would transform water-soluble clay into baked waterproof clay. To do this, White Feather built a big fire, and preheated the vessel, by placing it close to the fire. This was to make sure it was absolutely dry. Next, she put the vessel, upside down, into the fire, and covered it with small burning fragments of tree bark, etc. After being baked there for sufficient time, she let the fire die. It was allowed to cool down slowly and, when it was cool enough to touch, it was finished.

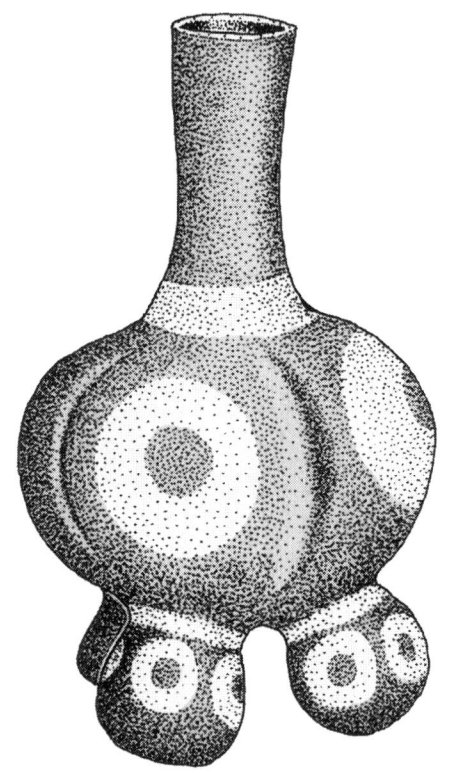

Painted Water Bottle Made by White Feather.
Redrawn from Thruston 1897.

One evening, White Feather was filling one of her water bottles at the river, when she saw something terrifying. A canoe was approaching, with three people of a foreign tribe. She ran to the guardhouse to alert the village.

The guards and some warriors lost no time in getting to the shore with their bows and arrows. When the canoe got closer, they could see that it contained two men and one woman.

One of the men said, "Traders," in Cherokee, out of habit to end the warriors' suspicions. It worked, and they lowered their weapons. Just then, Sparrow came down to fill another water bottle.

She saw the three in the dugout. One of them seemed to look familiar. She studied this man, and recognized him. "River Wolf!"

"Sparrow!" returned River Wolf as he jumped out of the dugout to hug her.

"Where on this earth have you been for ten cycles?" asked Sparrow.

"It's a long story, Aunt," he replied. "Here is Panther and his wife, Sand Dollar."

Sparrow didn't recall the new name and had a perplexed expression.

"My brother, Running Fox," added River Wolf, sensing her confusion.

"Running Fox! How are you doing? Oh! We missed you terribly!"

"His name is now 'Panther,'" River Wolf corrected, as politely as he could.

Panther hugged Sparrow tightly.

"We need to tell Buck that you are alive," said Sparrow. "He has felt tremendous guilt for many, many cycles – he thought you had drowned."

"I thought *he* had drowned!" returned River Wolf. "Where is he?"

"At his lodge. Go with your brother to your mother's lodge. This will do wonders for her! I will see that Buck meets you there."

They went to Squirrel Fur's lodge. Sand Dollar was anxious about being around so many people – especially since she didn't understand their language.

"It will all be alright," Panther reassured her in Muskhogean.

Sand Dollar smiled nervously at him. They entered Squirrel Fur's lodge. Squirrel Fur's jaw dropped open as she gasped in disbelief. "River Wolf! Panther!"

Panther hugged her frail body, then River Wolf did likewise. Squirrel Fur trembled all over as she burst into tears of joy. Then Buck entered the lodge. Panther and River Wolf hugged him tightly. Squirrel Fur grasped River Wolf's hand and motioned for Buck and Panther to come to her. When they did, she placed all of their hands in her fist. "Let us *never* be far from each other from now on!" she said, tearfully.

"I will never travel again," said River Wolf. "I have had enough of it."

Sparrow entered the lodge and hugged them all. She immediately felt a compassion for timid Sand Dollar. They all talked through the night; River Wolf told of his adventures amongst the cannibals, Panther told his stories about the Muskogees and how he ended up at the island with Sand Dollar, while Sparrow spoke in signs with Sand Dollar, making her feel at home.

That evening, River Wolf went to his old lodge. He could feel Beaver Pelt's presence there. *I am back, and I won't leave you anymore,* he promised her. Panther and Sand Dollar spent the night at Squirrel Fur's lodge.

The next day, River Wolf went to see Eagle Medicine. He beheld the most beautiful young woman he had ever seen in his life. She seemed vaguely familiar to him. He could tell by her body language that she seemed to recognize him also.

"Does Eagle Medicine still live here?" he asked her.

"Yes, he does," she replied. "I am his daughter. You look familiar. Who are you?"

"River Wolf."

She immediately ran to hug him. Then she showed him in to see Eagle Medicine. The old Shaman immediately recognized him. "Come in and sit down, River Wolf!"

River Wolf told his stories to them. White Feather had a look of admiration in her eyes. To her, River Wolf was family. He had saved her from the burning lodge when she was an infant. Eagle Medicine could see that she liked River Wolf.

Eagle Medicine told River Wolf of all the events that had taken place during his absence. The Uku, Standing Bear had passed into the Darkening Land one cycle after River Wolf left. An elder named Fire Arrow succeeded Standing Bear as Uku.

That night, Beaver Pelt visited River Wolf in a dream. *Marry again,* she said.

But there is nobody here that I know anymore, he replied.

There is a woman who will soon need you more than ever. You already have met her.

River Wolf woke up and it was morning. He thought about his dream. Who was Beaver Pelt referring to? Then Sparrow came to his lodge. "River Wolf," she said grimly, "I don't know how to tell you this. Your mother has passed away. Sometime last night."

Chapter 16: Wedding

River Wolf had an expression of disbelief. "No! That can't be!" he shouted in anguish.

Sparrow hugged him tightly. "She has been in poor health for a long time now. I think that somehow she knew you and Panther were returning to her. She hung on for you two, you know?"

Squirrel Fur was buried in the same fashion as Beaver Pelt had been, that is, inside the lodge under her bed. Three Crows performed the burial ceremony while Sparrow and the other women wept out loud. River Wolf had to leave, so he went to the river.

There was Medicine Wolf's dugout, full of shells and other trade goods. Nobody had unloaded it yet. River Wolf heard a voice. "I know it hurts," she said.

River Wolf turned to look and saw White Feather. She hugged him and he wept. She never told a soul about him weeping; she remembered what her father had said the first time she saw River Wolf weep. She also knew firsthand how it was to lose a mother. His secret was safe with her. She would never tell, never judge and never laugh.

Panther and Sand Dollar lived in Squirrel Fur's lodge, and old Sparrow visited them every day. She spent numerous hours with Sand Dollar, teaching her the Cherokee language, and making her feel more comfortable. Sand Dollar began to come out of her shyness and enjoyed Sparrow's company.

One day, while Sparrow was teaching her how to cook some of the local vegetables, Sand Dollar tried some green beans. "These are very good!" she said in bad Cherokee, emphasizing with signs.

"Wait until you try the squash!" answered Sparrow.

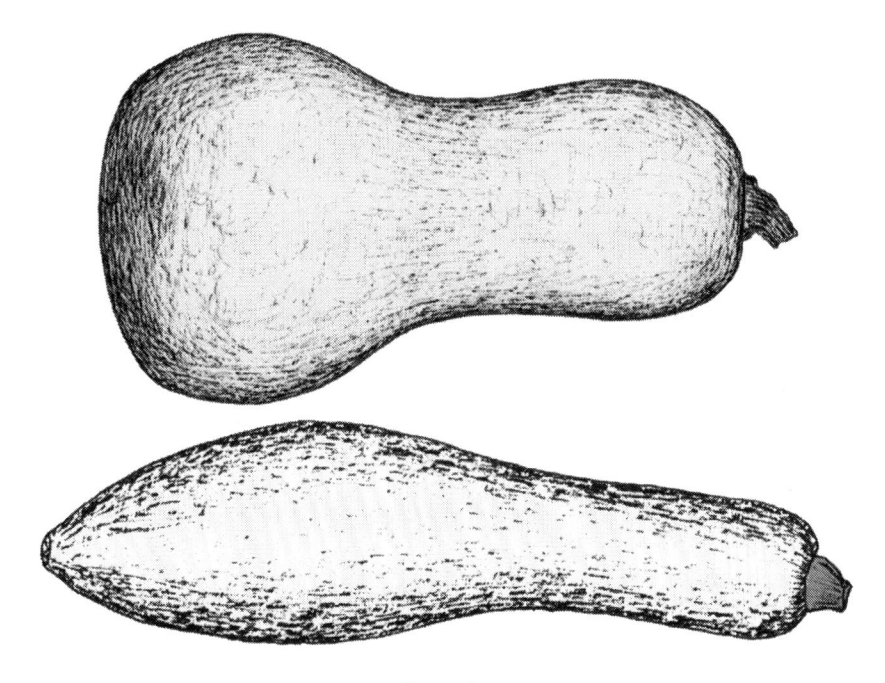

Squash.

"I have eaten fish and crabs all of my life," continued Sand Dollar. "I had no idea that there were so many other tasty things to eat!"

River Wolf and White Feather spent a lot of time together. She was in love with him, though he was slow to realize it. He hunted food for her and Eagle Medicine.

White Feather spoke to Eagle Medicine alone. "I have been thinking about River Wolf."

"What have you been thinking about him?" he asked, very interested.

"He is so sweet, and he has a good heart. I like him a lot."

Eagle Medicine was surprised, but also relieved. "It's about time you paid attention to a man. I was beginning to worry about you. Most young ladies fall in love at an age much younger than twenty-one."

White Feather was disbelieving both his and her own words. She began to blush. "I don't want to leave you."

"You won't be leaving me if you have a boyfriend or husband. That is what is normal! I have hoped for cycles that you would find a man you would be happy with; it would be selfish of me if I didn't."

River Wolf arrived with a deer over his shoulders. White Feather helped him dress the deer in silence. Finally, River Wolf commented, "You sure are quiet."

White Feather just smiled at him.

"What's funny?" he asked.

"Oh, nothing," she said, but her face flushed red.

River Wolf shook his head at her.

They finished the deer after dark and River Wolf went home. Buck came to visit, and they swapped stories of how they made it back home. River Wolf told of the cannibals, and Buck talked about going overboard and landing on an island. He was there for a week before an Aztec trader rescued him. Then he went with another trader up the river and back home.

"I heard of the Aztecs while I lived with the Payayas," commented River Wolf. "They have a large empire far to the south of where I was."

"Yes, they do."

"Where was that island you landed on?" asked River Wolf.

"The trader said it was very far from any of the mainland. I never knew there were little islands out there. I was lucky that he arrived. There was not much food on the island. There was no water either, only coconut milk."

"Do you still have that dog that Broken Spear found?" asked River Wolf.

"No, she died last cycle. We do have one of her pups; she is two cycles old." Buck left and River Wolf got ready to go to bed. White Feather appeared in his doorway.

"Hello, White Feather," greeted River Wolf, "What do you need?"

"I came to spend the night with you, if you are comfortable with it."

River Wolf was surprised. "Is your father alright?" he asked.

"He is fine. He knows where I am."

Well, let me clean off the other bed for you," offered River Wolf nervously.

"I want to stay with you tonight," she said.

"But you are... We can't do that! Your father would cast a terrible spell on me!"

"He knows why I am here, and I am no longer a child."

River Wolf said nothing as she walked to him and took his hand. His hand was cold and sweaty, revealing his anxiousness.

"Why don't we just talk," she suggested.

River Wolf relaxed a little when he heard that. He wanted to be certain to have Eagle Medicine's approval before being intimate with the man's daughter. He was Eagle Medicine's friend, but didn't care to provoke such a powerful man. He remembered what had happened to his father.

So, White Feather and River Wolf lay in the bed together talking for most of the night. River Wolf was trying not to look at her as a child anymore. This child had blossomed into a beautiful woman.

The next morning, they went to check on Eagle Medicine. When White Feather went to fetch water, the old Shaman asked River Wolf, "Well, how was she?" he had a naughty grin on his face.

River Wolf was embarrassed. White Feather had not lied! Eagle Medicine *wanted* something to happen between them. "We talked all night," said River Wolf.

Eagle Medicine was disappointed. "You two didn't *do* anything?"

"I... I was afraid of offending you."

"Offending me?! That girl needs a boyfriend like a fish needs water. Besides, I am tired of her hanging around the lodge constantly. I never get to be alone! Do you realize she is twenty-one cycles old? She desperately needs a husband. Why not someone I like?"

"I had no idea you would feel that way," explained River Wolf, "I guess she grew up while I was gone. She is very pretty and sweet. You should be proud of her."

"I am," said Eagle Medicine. "I truly am. I didn't mean what I said about her being here constantly. I love her, but she needs to marry somebody someday. She needs someone to take care of when I am gone. She is going to need someone to take care of her too!"

White Feather returned with the full water bottle. She and River Wolf exchanged smiles. Then River Wolf went to visit his brother.

Sand Dollar greeted him in Cherokee.

"Hello, Sand Dollar," he returned. "I see Sparrow has been teaching you our language."

Just then Sparrow walked out of the lodge saying, "Who is talking about me? River Wolf! How are you doing?"

"I am fine. How are you all doing?"

"Sand Dollar is learning Cherokee very well," replied Sparrow, with her arm around Sand Dollar, who smiled shyly. "Sand Dollar, what do you call that?" Sparrow pointed at an orange pumpkin.

"Pumpkin!" said Sand Dollar proudly.

Pumpkin.
Redrawn from OpenClipart-Vectors from Pixabay.

"Where is Panther?" asked River Wolf.

"He went hunting early this morning," replied Sparrow, "He will be back tonight."

"Do you need anything?" asked River Wolf.

"No, we don't. Thanks for asking. Go and spend some quality time with White Feather."

River Wolf was surprised. The word had gotten around quickly! "Do you think she is too young for me?"

"Of course not! If you truly love somebody, age is not an issue. Don't ask silly questions."

He smiled at her. Turtle Shell was long since dead, but Sparrow would always be his aunt. Sparrow returned the smile and began grinding corn.

River Wolf went to look for White Feather. He found her, at her father's lodge, grinding corn.

Eagle Medicine saw River Wolf and said, "White Feather, we have plenty of food. You are always working! Go and have some fun for a change. Take along some of your cornbread."

"Why don't we go for a walk outside the palisade?" suggested River Wolf. White Feather smiled and grabbed his hand.

After they left, Eagle Medicine consulted his divining Crystal…

Sparrow looked up from grinding corn with Sand Dollar. She saw River Wolf and White Feather approaching the palisade gate, holding hands. "Love is in the air," said Sparrow, shaking her head and smiling.

Sand Dollar didn't understand her words, but got the meaning of them when she looked where Sparrow was looking. They looked at each other and giggled before returning to their work.

River Wolf and White Feather arrived at the river. White Feather said, "Your canoe that you made long ago is still here." She pointed it out. It was weathered, but it was still a good useable canoe.

"Why don't we take it upstream?" suggested River Wolf.

"Alright," smiled White Feather.

Her beauty was mesmerizing. She was innocent and delicate, as her name suggested. River Wolf was falling in love. She smiled and he realized that he had been staring at her for a length of time. They moved closer to each other and kissed passionately.

"Are we going upstream?" she asked.

"Oh! Yes," he replied, somewhat embarrassed.

They shoved off and began paddling. As they paddled, they talked. They stopped at noon and ate the cornbread they had brought with them. River Wolf picked some flowers and gave them to her. Then they made love in the soft grass until sunset. The fireflies were out, and the moon was full. They went swimming in the dark. It was a lovely time.

"We'd better start back to the village," suggested River Wolf.

They shoved off and drifted with the current downstream.

"Are you going to travel as a trader anymore?" asked White Feather. "If so, I will go with you."

"I have had enough of traveling," answered River Wolf. "It is too dangerous. I want to settle down and have my own family. I hope you aren't disappointed. I wouldn't put you in that kind of danger. Does that bother you?"

"No, I just want to be with you."

River Wolf felt the same. He thought to himself, *I am not going to put off marrying her like I did Beaver Pelt. I want to spend as much time with her as I can.* He was startled by this thought. *Marrying her?* It felt right inside. He knew that the Spirits could take her away at any time, so he decided not to delay.

They arrived at the village and beached the dugout. River Wolf asked, "Will you spend the night with me at my lodge?"

"Yes, I hoped you would ask me. But let me check on my father. I will be there soon."

They kissed and parted at the palisade gate. River Wolf was so happy to be alive. He returned to his lodge and started a fire. Soon, White Feather arrived, and they made passionate love all night long.

River Wolf got up early the next morning and went to see Eagle Medicine. He brought with him some conch shells. He was very nervous as he blurted out, "May I have your daughter's hand in marriage?"

"I would be honored to have you as a son-in-law. You more than anybody else. Of course you may. I'll talk to her clansmen about it since your mother is gone."

Eagle Medicine made arrangements with Three Crows for the date of the ceremony. As was tradition, on the morning of the wedding, Eagle Medicine performed the ritual involving using the roots to predict the fate of this marriage, and all the omens were good.

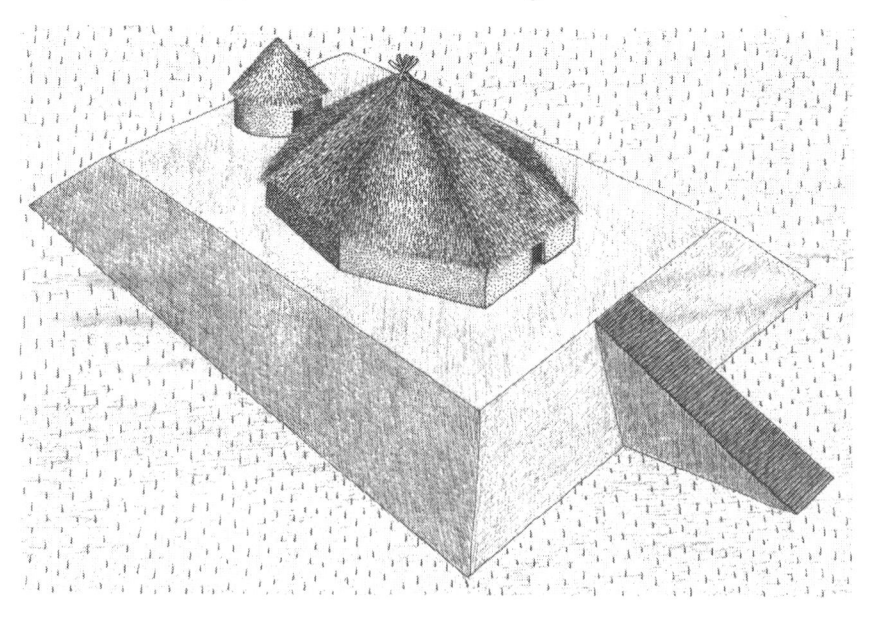

The National Heptagon on a Mound, with Grain Treasury in Rear.
Adapted from Mails 1992.

As before, the groom and his escort were at one end of the heptagon, while the bride and her escort were at the other end. This time, Eagle Medicine accompanied White Feather, while Three Crows was with River Wolf.

River Wolf, once again, carried a deer leg and a blanket. White Feather carried a blanket and an ear of corn. When both parties met in the center of the council house, River Wolf started, "I... I... bring you this venison to show my... my..." He was obviously very nervous. He glanced at Eagle Medicine.

Eagle Medicine had a warm and understanding expression that calmed him.

He looked back at White Feather and continued, "...m... my commitment to provide for you like a good husband should do."

"I accept your venison," said White Feather with a smile. "I bring you this corn to show my commitment to grow and cook food as a wife should do."

"I accept your corn," said River Wolf. They put their blankets together, symbolizing the new union between them.

"You may come to my lodge," said White Feather. As before, the lodge was originally River Wolf's, but the wife was traditionally the lodge keeper and owner.

Later, during the Great New Moon Ceremony, their marriage was sealed.

"River Wolf, of the Bird Clan, do you promise to fulfill your duties providing meat as a husband for White Feather," asked Three Crows, "and not speak unkindly to her, no matter how angry you are with her?"

"Yes, I do," replied River Wolf.

"And do you, White Feather, of the Wolf Clan, promise to keep the lodge and be tolerant of River Wolf speaking unkindly to you?"

"Yes, I do," answered White Feather, while smiling at River Wolf.

It was finished. River Wolf and White Feather were now officially married. The Great New Moon Ceremony ended, and the citizens returned to their home villages.

Buck and Tanager gave River Wolf and White Feather a large bearskin blanket as a wedding gift. Panther and Sand Dollar gave them a basket full of cornbread, and Sparrow gave them some seed corn.

* * *

It was an unusually cold winter. River Wolf spent the winter in the hothouse with White Feather. He had plenty of pipes that he had carved during the cold season. White Feather spent her time making turkey feather cloaks, and checking on her father. His health had deteriorated considerably. Now the young green leaves of spring were appearing.

River Wolf took his old dugout on a hunting trip with Buck. After two days, they returned with a bear. They were gutting it when White Feather walked up and called River Wolf aside so they could talk alone.

"I missed my moon time," she said, "I am pregnant."

River Wolf's jaw dropped open. "Are you sure?"

"I should have gone to the women's hut over two weeks ago. I wasn't sure, but now I am."

"Do you need me to do anything?"

"No, not now. I just wanted to tell you. I love you."

"I love you too," said River Wolf as he hugged her tightly.

White Feather left and River Wolf resumed working on butchering the bear. Buck noticed River Wolf was quiet. "Alright, what's the matter?"

"I am going to be a father."

"Are you serious?"

"That's what White Feather wanted to tell me."

"Well, I would hug you, if my hands weren't such a mess."

"I wonder what to name him or her. I wonder if it will be a boy or a girl. I hope I will be a good father."

"I felt the same when Tanager told me she was pregnant. Don't worry; the answers will come to you when you need them."

* * *

One and-a-half moons later, White Feather went to check on Eagle Medicine when he suddenly had chest pains and collapsed. White Feather lost no time in finding Three Crows, but when they returned, it was too late. White Feather was distraught. She had no more blood relatives left.

River Wolf was at home carving a pipe when White Feather ran to him in tears. "What's wrong?"

"My father is dead!" she sobbed.

"Dead?" asked River Wolf, stunned.

"Yes!"

River Wolf hugged her tightly. This was a serious loss for River Wolf, but even greater for White Feather.

Now the villagers removed all the bodies from the charnel platform and gave them a proper burial in the mound. River Wolf helped in the grim and laborious task. Three Crows supervised, as he was now the highest-ranking Shaman in the village. Eagle Medicine was buried with the remains of his wife. The mound was slightly more massive than before, and the pond was also larger. Eagle Medicine's lodge was burned to the ground.

White Feather sank into a depression. She constantly wept for her father and River Wolf was worried about her. Sparrow and Sand Dollar visited her frequently to try to cheer her up.

One day, about two moons after Eagle Medicine's death, River Wolf came home from hunting. He had no luck on his trip, and he was hungry. White Feather was laying in bed weeping. River Wolf looked for some cornbread to eat. He found nothing at all to eat. He became angry. "White Feather! There is no food left! I have been hunting all day and you haven't done a thing! Even the water bottle is empty!"

White Feather turned over in bed and sobbed harder.

"I am serious, White Feather. You need to pull out of this. Life goes on. We have a baby on the way."

"*I* am going to have a baby!" retorted White Feather, "You can just leave!"

River Wolf was shocked and hurt. He silently gathered his things and went to Panther and Sand Dollar's lodge. Sand Dollar and Sparrow were making cornbread.

"What happened?" asked Sparrow.

"White Feather threw me out of the lodge," replied River Wolf.

"Why?"

He threw up his hands and said, "I confronted her for not doing anything. There wasn't even any water there!"

"You can stay here as long as you need to," offered Panther.

"She didn't mean it, I am sure," consoled Sparrow. "If you want, I will try to talk to her."

"Whatever," resigned River Wolf.

Sparrow left with some food for White Feather while River Wolf, Panther and Sand Dollar ate. Sand Dollar had overcome her shyness considerably. Sparrow had spent endless hours working with her, and she now could speak very good Cherokee. River Wolf hoped she could help White Feather. He loved her, but couldn't live with her this way anymore. He prayed that she would come out of this – if for not their sake, for the sake of their unborn child.

Sparrow arrived at White Feather's lodge with the food. White Feather sat up but would not eat. Sparrow sat beside her and put her arm around her. "Try to eat – for the baby."

White Feather was deep in thought. After a period of silence she whispered, "I want some mistletoe."

"No! White Feather, you can't abort this baby! It would break River Wolf's heart."

"I want some mistletoe."

"I think you just want attention."

"I don't care what you…"

"I am forty-nine cycles old! You should respect your elders! And not talk back to them! I don't think your father would approve of you feeling sorry for yourself and ending your relationship with River Wolf. He is all you have left! You two have your lives ahead of you. You have a baby in your womb! A new life that is depending on you! Do you know what it is like to want children and not be able to have them?"

"No."

"Well, I do. We tried constantly, and now I am long past the age. Now who will take care of Broken Spear and me when we are urinating all over ourselves because we can't make it to the ditch? I am not pitying myself, I am glad for what I do have. Everybody loves and loses, and you are no exception. I know it hurts, but you need to accept the pain. Feel your feelings and experience life! Stop running! Can't you see what I am saying?"

White Feather's eyes teared up and Sparrow hugged her tightly. "It's okay to feel sad," said Sparrow. "Accept it. Then you can move on."

They sat for a long time holding each other. Sparrow repeatedly whispered, "It's going to be alright." Then she asked, "Now, are you going to eat?"

White Feather ate while they talked some more. Finally Sparrow said, "Well, I have to return home. What shall I tell River Wolf?"

"Tell him I love him, and that I am sorry. Please do not tell him about the mistletoe. I want him to return to the lodge."

Sparrow smiled. "You should tell him. And I won't say a word about the abortion." So they both walked to Panther's lodge to find River Wolf. When they arrived, Sparrow went into her lodge to give them some space.

River Wolf was outside and White Feather motioned him to an isolated area. "I am sorry for not having any dinner for you."

"I am more concerned about *you* than food," said River Wolf.

"Let's go home," suggested White Feather.

"I am sorry for shouting at you. I love you."

They returned and ate the rest of the food Sparrow had brought. Then they went to bed and talked all night.

"I am sorry for telling you to leave," said White Feather, "I...I guess I was afraid of losing you also. It was a stupid thing for me to do."

"It's okay. I love you, and I always will."

"Hold me."

They held each other close and now River Wolf remembered what Beaver Pelt had said in the dream. She rested under the very bed that he and White Feather slept on. River Wolf's wife did need him, and he planned to be there for her.

* * *

White Feather went to the river with Three Crows, River Wolf, and Sparrow for a ritual purification and prayers. This occurred every new moon of her pregnancy. Three Crows put water on her face, the top of her head, and chest. He also used red and white beads in a ritual to predict the baby's future.

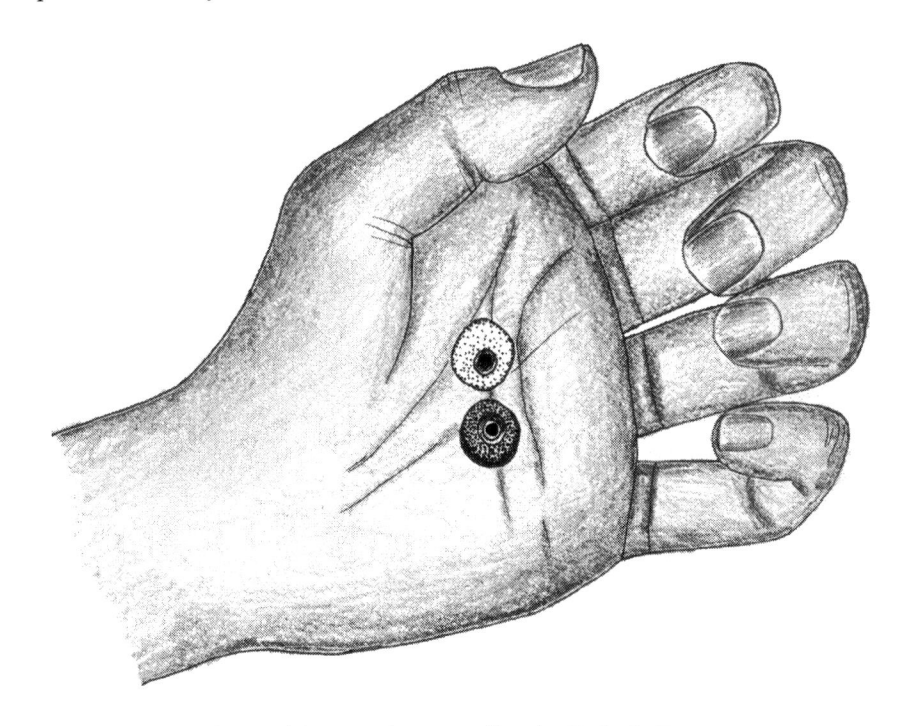

Red & White Beads to Predict the Baby's Future.

Now it was wintertime, and White Feather was beginning her final three moons carrying the child. River Wolf and Sparrow helped move her into the women's hut, where she would stay until the baby came.

River Wolf had the lodge to himself, and was not allowed to touch his wife. He decided to make use of his time and make things to trade with. He took an old deer hide and left for the woods. After setting a squirrel trap, he went looking for soapstone. He carried the stones, in the hide, over his shoulder, back to the village. Then he went back out to check his traps. He found three squirrels and killed them and ate them that night.

Sparrow came by that evening and left plenty of cornbread. "I had plenty delivered to White Feather also," she said.

Pregnant women rarely ate any kinds of meats, so River Wolf didn't need to hunt any game for White Feather. He carved many pipes that winter. He had just finished polishing a large beautiful duck effigy pipe, and before he knew it, he got a surprise visit from old Sparrow. She ran up to the hothouse he was in and said, "The time has come."

Duck Effigy Pipe.
Redrawn from Thruston 1897.

River Wolf waited outside the women's hut nervously. It was the custom for a woman to kneel over a hide with her legs wide open during childbirth. If the baby landed on its back, it was a good omen. If not, they would wrap the baby in a hide and dip it in the river. When the hide separated from the baby, and had floated away, the bad luck was thought to float away with the hide.

The omen was good; the baby landed on its back. River Wolf heard it crying from outside. He was a father! Sparrow shouted, "It's a boy!"

The newborn was bathed and baptized in White Feather's milk. They gave the baby boy a temporary name, which was "Six Whirlwinds." The baby had to have a name immediately. If he died without a name, his spirit would be lost forever.

Now River Wolf took away the placenta and buried it away from the village. On his way back, he was full of happy thoughts about his new son. What would his name be? What did he look like?

Two days later, it began to snow. Three Crows waved Six Whirlwinds over a fire four times while praying and blessing him, bestowing a long and happy life. On the baby's seventh day, the snow was deep. Three Crows took the infant to the river and immersed him seven times in the icy water.

The naming ceremony took place, in which a prominent elder woman of the village gave a permanent name to the baby. The choice was Sparrow, because she was the Honored Woman and also a relative who was well liked by the family.

Sparrow observed that Six Whirlwinds was an unusually large newborn, so she named him "Snow Bear." White Feather bathed in the frigid water and put on clean clothes. Everything that she had touched during her pregnancy was purified with smoke. She could now return home with the baby.

River Wolf had made the hothouse ready for her return, and had plenty of dried meat for his new family. He then stayed at Buck and Tanager's hothouse for the rest of the winter, because it was taboo to eat food prepared by White Feather for three moons after the baby was born.

Panther and Sand Dollar walked together to see White Feather and the infant.

"I am a mother!" said White Feather proudly.

Sand Dollar was delighted when White Feather gave her the baby to hold. "We need to have a baby of our own," she said to Panther on their way home.

* * *

Springtime found River Wolf hunting deer. He crept up, with his bow ready, into range of a buck. He was taking aim when suddenly he was struck hard by something falling on him. The buck ran off and River Wolf heard the call of an eagle.

He looked up but didn't see anything in the sky. Then he looked down and saw a fish on the ground. The eagle had dropped the fish on him as it flew by. River Wolf was frustrated about losing the deer, but he took the fish home so he would have something to show for his efforts.

White Feather was there, grinding corn in a wooden mortar and pestle. "I thought you were going to hunt, not fish," she said.

"I was. I was about to shoot a nice fat buck, when an eagle dropped this fish. It just happened to land on me. The buck ran off, so it looks like we will be having fish tonight. How is Snow Bear?"

"He is asleep. He has been crying all day. Be quiet so we won't wake him."

River Wolf cleaned the fish, and they cooked it. River Wolf was surprised that an eagle would have caught such a large fish. Maybe that was why the eagle dropped it.

They were eating, when they heard people of the village shouting "Trader!"

River Wolf went to see, and sure enough, there was a trader in a large dugout. He was glad. Now he could trade the pipes he had carved during the winter. He returned to the lodge.

"Is there a trader here?" asked White Feather.

"There sure is. I will wait and talk with him tomorrow."

"You aren't going with him, are you?"

"No! I told you, I have had enough of traveling. I will stay with you and Snow Bear."

White Feather seemed to relax now. She didn't feel like traveling with such a young baby, and was also worried that River Wolf would be restless by now and want to leave without her. They finished their meal of fish and cornbread, and then Snow Bear woke up. White Feather fed him and put him back to bed.

River Wolf gathered all of his pipes for tomorrow's trading. "Is there anything in particular that you need me to trade for?"

"I would like another large bearskin," replied White Feather.

Buck appeared in the doorway. "How are you three doing?"

"We are fine," answered River Wolf.

"You know there is a trader here, don't you?"

"Yes, we do, thanks. Are you going to trade for flint?"

"If he has any. Do you want some?"

"I could use some for arrow points."

"I will give you some of my flakes. You don't owe me anything for them."

"Thank you, Buck."

The next morning, bright and early, River Wolf was trading his pipes, and other stone carvings, to the trader. He traded for two bearskins, conch shells, and a necklace of freshwater pearls. At the end of the day, Buck brought the flint flakes as he had promised.

"I sure appreciate it, Buck," thanked River Wolf. "Can you make me a good knife in exchange for these three conch shells?"

"Sure! I will make you a nice one for those." Buck took the shells and left.

"You got two nice bearskins!" said White Feather as she looked through the items River Wolf had traded for.

"Yes, I did. And I have a surprise for you." River Wolf pulled out the freshwater pearl necklace and put it around her neck.

"It's very beautiful," said White Feather, and she kissed him. They spent the night making passionate love and got little sleep.

* * *

Snow Bear was now four cycles old as he ran across the village towards Sparrow's lodge. "Aunt Sparrow! Aunt Sparrow!"

"Hello, Snow Bear," greeted Sparrow, "What have you got there?"

"It's a bear that Father carved for me! Isn't it nice?"

"Yes, it is! You must be a very special boy to have your father carve you that!"

Snow Bear smiled shyly as Sparrow hugged him. Sparrow was now fifty-three cycles old. Broken Spear had passed into the Darkening Land two cycles before. She was alone, but her aged body was still full of energy. "Didn't your father go hunting today with Panther?"

"Yes, they went away early this morning. He left this bear as a surprise for me."

"It sure is a nice one. He loves you. You know that, don't you?"

"Yes."

"Take care of that bear, and don't lose it in the forest."

* * *

Elk.
Redrawn from Kate 1999.

River Wolf heard the call of an elk in the woods. "Did you hear that?" he whispered.

"Yes," came the whispered reply from Panther.

They quietly moved through the forest, stalking the elk. They heard the noise again. They were getting closer, and they were downwind of the elk. They made ready their bows and arrows as they crept through the thick woods. Then River Wolf stopped. "There it is," he whispered while pointing.

They moved in closer so they would have a clear shot. When they were satisfied that they were in shooting distance, they stopped. The elk was near a mountain stream, and seemed to be unaware of the hunters.

River Wolf released an arrow. Before the first arrow hit the elk, both River Wolf and Panther had shot three more arrows into it. Each arrow hit its mark, and the elk collapsed. They lost no time in cutting its throat with a flint knife. Then they paid their respects."We are going to need help carrying this elk in," said Panther, "He is huge!"

"Let's return to the village and get some help then," replied River Wolf.

* * *

"Father says you are the wisest woman in the whole village," said Snow Bear to Sparrow.

"Well, I am wise enough to tell that you would like some cornbread! Would you?"

"Sure!"

Sparrow gave Snow Bear some cornbread to eat. He giggled with his mouth full when she pinched him on the cheek. Right then, Sand Dollar appeared in the doorway.

"Hello, Sand Dollar!" greeted Sparrow.

"Hello, Sparrow. How are you, Snow Bear?"

"Fine," answered Snow Bear, with his mouth still full.

Sand Dollar had a preoccupied demeanor about her. "Do you know where Panther is?"

"He went out hunting with his brother. Didn't he tell you he was leaving?"

"Yes, he did. I just thought he would be back by now. I have something important to tell him."

Sparrow suspected she was pregnant, but it wasn't her business, so she didn't ask. "Well, you are welcome to wait here for him. Would you like some cornbread?"

"No, thanks," replied Sand Dollar.

"But it is Aunt Sparrow's *special* cornbread!" said Snow Bear with a grin.

Sparrow laughed out loud. Sand Dollar smiled at them both and said, "Okay, I guess I should have some then."

As they ate, Sparrow continued to notice something was on Sand Dollar's mind. When they finished eating, Panther returned. "River Wolf and I just killed an elk. A big one! We returned so we could get help hauling it in. I'd better go."

"Wait," said Sand Dollar, "I need to talk to you alone."

"I really have to go," urged Panther.

"It's important."

"Alright, we will talk on the way to River Wolf's lodge."

"I will go with you!" shouted Snow Bear.

Sand Dollar didn't want to be rude, but she didn't know exactly what to say. She needed to be alone with Panther.

"No, no. You stay here and talk to me," Sparrow suggested to Snow Bear, sensing her distress.

"Alright," answered Snow Bear as Panther and Sand Dollar left. "What do you suppose they need to talk about?" asked Snow Bear.

"Something private," replied Sparrow. "You should not meddle in people's personal affairs."

"I'm sorry. I just thought something might be wrong. She seemed like she was upset. I didn't mean to meddle."

Sparrow picked up two empty pottery water bottles and said, "Why don't we take these and go down to the river and fetch some water? You could go swimming."

Snow Bear replied, "Sure!"

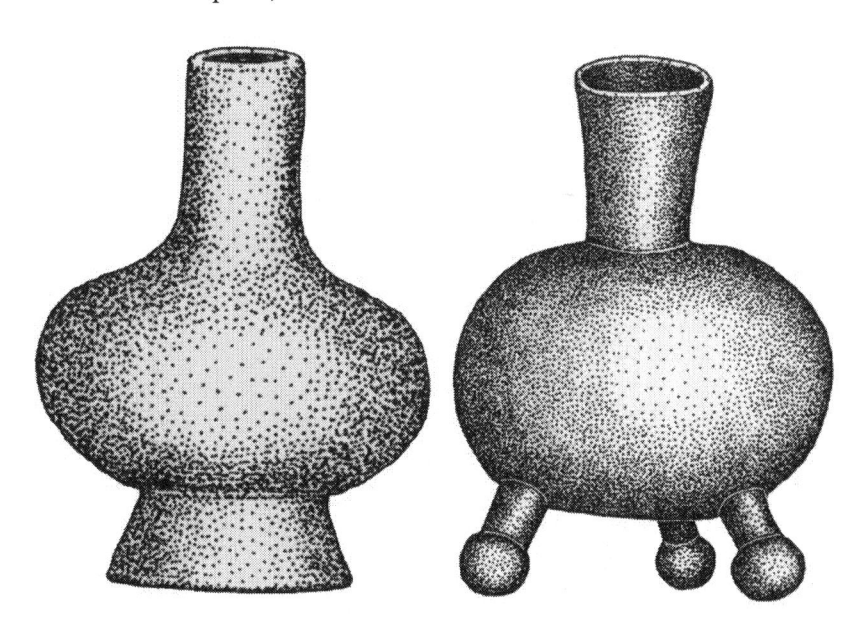

Two Water Bottles.
Redrawn from Moorehead 1900.

They left for the river together, Sparrow carrying the two water bottles. The young guard at the palisade gate greeted them – reminding Sparrow of her last husband on the day she had met him.

* * *

"What did you want to tell me?" Panther asked Sand Dollar.

"I am pregnant."

"Are you sure?"

"Yes, I am."

"That's great! I will tell everybody."

It was the custom for a woman to tell her husband immediately when she discovered she was pregnant, and then the husband would inform the village.

Sand Dollar returned home, while Panther and River Wolf left with Twisted Stick and his son, Woodcarver. The four cut a thick pole and tied the elk's feet and its head to it. Then they carried it in, two on each end of the pole. Panther told them the news he'd heard from his wife.

"Congratulations!" exclaimed River Wolf.

"We are happy for you both," said Twisted Stick.

"Yes, we are," added Woodcarver.

"Thank you very much," said Panther.

They arrived back at the village with the large elk. When they passed Buck's lodge, Buck saw the antlers on the elk. Immediately he gathered some things to trade for the antlers. They would work great for flint knapping! Then he realized – their dog had four puppies that spring, and they were trying to find a home for them. Maybe he could trade the puppies for the elk antlers.

Buck followed them to Panther's lodge. Sparrow helped all of them butcher the elk. Buck helped also. "Would you all like to trade the antlers?" asked Buck.

"It's Panther and River Wolf's elk," said Twisted Stick. "You should ask them."

"What do you offer in trade?" asked Panther.

"I have four puppies that need a home. I will give you, River Wolf, Twisted Stick, and Woodcarver each one of them."

"I don't want a dog around the lodge!" retorted Twisted Stick.

"I do!" said Woodcarver.

Panther and River Wolf looked at each other.

"I think that Snow Bear would enjoy a puppy," River Wolf said.

"I don't want one," said Panther, "He will only make a mess of the lodge. But River Wolf shot the elk first, so it's his more than mine."

"Well, I will go and get two puppies then," said Buck, and he left. He returned a short while later with the two puppies.

Sand Dollar saw them and said, "Oh! How cute! Panther, can we get one?"

Panther rolled his eyes and said, "Okay, I guess we will have one of those puppies after all."

"I will go and get it then," answered Buck, satisfied with the trade. He returned promptly with Sand Dollar's puppy.

They finished processing the elk and divided up the meat. River Wolf and White Feather hung theirs outside to dry. The puppy was hyper and she kept Snow Bear busy. It was comical to see Snow Bear hanging on to that puppy, and being dragged around the lodge.

"What are you going to name her?" asked River Wolf.

"I don't know," replied Snow Bear.

"What would you like for dinner?" asked White Feather.

"Elk sounds good to me," replied River Wolf, "and some of that cornbread Sparrow made."

"I know!" exclaimed Snow Bear, "Why don't we name her Raccoon!"

"That sounds like a good name," replied River Wolf. "Look, she is already stealing like a raccoon."

Snow Bear turned around and saw Raccoon making off with some elk meat. "Oh no!"

"We are going to have to train that dog!" shouted White Feather when she saw him running out with the elk meat that she was going to cook. She ran out after Raccoon and retrieved the meat. She slapped the puppy on the rump and returned to the lodge with the meat. She wiped the dirt off of it and began cooking it.

After eating, White Feather said, "Snow Bear, it's time for you to go to bed."

"Ah, Mother," he pleaded.

"Go to bed," she repeated sternly.

"Oh, all right," he conceded and went to bed.

River Wolf and White Feather went to bed not long afterwards. Early the next morning, Sparrow arrived at the lodge with some of her cornbread for them.

"Did you hear that Sand Dollar is pregnant?" asked River Wolf.

"I suspected it," replied Sparrow.

"How did you know?"

"She came by and said she had something to tell Panther. I guessed that was it by her body language."

"Is that what the secret was?" asked Snow Bear, while playing with Raccoon.

"Yes, it is," replied Sparrow. "I'd better go and tend the crops."

"Do you need any help?" asked White Feather.

"It's just pulling weeds," returned Sparrow. "Sand Dollar can help me if I need it. Besides, you have your own garden to tend. But thanks for offering."

Sparrow left and River Wolf said, "I need to go hunting, or fishing, or something."

"But you killed a large elk just yesterday!" reminded White Feather.

"But we are drying that meat for the winter," he said. "We need food for the present. I think I will wait until tonight and go jack-lighting."

"Oh can I come with you?" asked Snow Bear, "I can help you paddle the canoe."

"But can you be very quiet?"

"Yes!" answered Snow Bear.

"Why don't we go out in the canoe today and I will instruct you – then you will know what to do tonight."

"Oh boy! I am going hunting with Father!"

"Only if you can learn to maneuver the dugout *quietly*." River Wolf whispered the word "quietly." "You can't be bumping the oar on the side of the dugout."

"Oh, I can learn! I can learn!" Snow Bear said eagerly.

"Alright then, let's go."

"Are you sure about this?" asked White Feather. "He is only four cycles old!"

"He has to learn sometime. I won't let him out of the dugout or do anything else that will get him snake bit."

"Alright, I will see you when you return," said White Feather, before kissing him. Then she said, "Snow Bear, do exactly what he tells you to do."

"I will, I promise."

River Wolf and his son left for the river. When they exited the lodge, they saw Raccoon jumping up, trying to reach the meat that was on the rack drying.

"Will he reach it?" asked Snow Bear.

"No, he won't. We built that rack high enough to keep any animal from reaching the meat. Other people have adult dogs, and they are just as bad about thieving."

They arrived at the river and River Wolf said, "Now, we are paddling upstream, and then we will drift downstream. When we are drifting, you keep the dugout stable. Don't let it turn in either direction."

"I won't," replied Snow Bear.

They paddled a good distance up the river, and Snow Bear spotted a raccoon. He nudged his father and pointed. River Wolf looked and saw it. River Wolf was impressed that Snow Bear had the self-control to not speak while pointing out the raccoon.

They arrived at the place River Wolf had intended, then began slowly drifting downstream. Snow Bear honed his skill at keeping the dugout pointed in one direction. At first, he made some noises by bumping the side of the dugout, but improved with practice.

"We will be doing this after dark," said River Wolf, quietly, as he prepared the torch, "So make sure you can do it without seeing very well."

"I will," whispered Snow Bear.

By the time they arrived at the village, the Sun was setting. River Wolf completed the torch. They returned to the lodge to get the fire pot, a bow and a quiver of arrows, an axe, and some cornbread to eat.

After eating a small meal of cornbread, they left. It was completely dark now, and the time was perfect for jack-lighting. River Wolf placed the torch in the holder on the bow of the canoe. They silently paddled upstream – a greater distance than before. Then River Wolf used the fire pot to light the torch, and they began drifting.

"No noise," whispered River Wolf.

Snow Bear didn't even reply. He wanted to obey his father. He did a wonderful job steadying the canoe, and only bumped it once with the paddle. Before long, they saw deer eyes glowing – reflecting the light from the torch.

River Wolf stood up, his axe ready. Snow Bear silently kept the dugout steady. Suddenly, the canoe rocked as River Wolf threw the axe – aiming right between the eyes. There was a dull thud and the eyes disappeared. They heard a thrashing in the woods.

"Take us over there!" shouted River Wolf.

"Did we get it?" asked Snow Bear.

"We got it. Stay in the canoe while I cut its throat."

River Wolf carefully got out of the dugout and cut the doe's throat. Then he saw the torch going downstream.

"Snow Bear! Keep the canoe here! Don't worry about making noise now."

"I'm trying!"

River Wolf waded after him in the water. He caught up and grabbed the bow of the dugout and walked it back to the deer. Then he remembered to apologize to its spirit.

"I'm sorry," said Snow Bear.

"That's alright, you are only a boy. Stay in the dugout while I put the deer in it. You did very well!"

River Wolf put the deer into the dugout, and they began paddling downstream for home. Snow Bear was excited. It was the first time he had helped in bringing food to the family.

Chapter 17: Booger Dance

Four cycles later…

Sparrow had aged considerably. Now fifty-nine cycles old, she could not get around as well as she did before. She was well-loved by the whole village, and many people brought her meat, vegetables and cornbread. Tanager brought her water every day, and helped her to the river for morning devotions.

Sand Dollar also helped her by cooking all kinds of meals for her; it was Sparrow who had taught her to cook so many cycles before. Sparrow had taught Sand Dollar everything she knew about the ways of the Cherokee.

Sand Dollar was at Sparrow's lodge, cooking up some mushrooms she had gathered earlier that morning. She was snapping beans while some cornbread was baking.

Panther and Sand Dollar's three-cycle-old daughter, Moon, entered the lodge. "Mother!" she said. "They are going to have a game!"

"What kind of game?" asked Sand Dollar, "A ball game?"

"No! Chunkey!" answered Moon, "I can't wait to watch it."

"When?"

"Tomorrow morning."

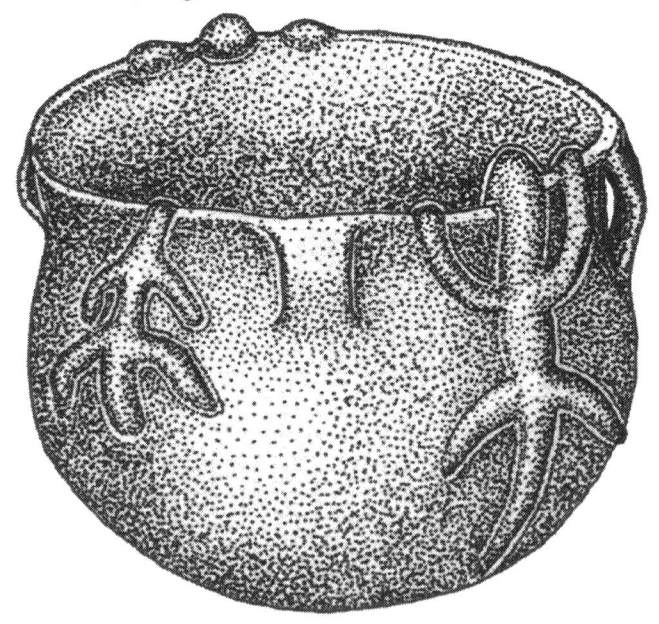

Lizard Effigy Pot.
Redrawn from Thruston 1897.

"Moon, can you take this pot and fetch water for Sparrow?" asked Sand Dollar.

"Ah, Mother, can't you do it?"

"I am cooking for Sparrow. Do what I tell you to."

"Okay," and Moon grabbed the lizard effigy pot and left to fill it with water. On her way back to the palisade gate, Snow Bear appeared out of the bushes and said, "Get out of here! You are going to give away our location!"

Snow Bear was now eight cycles old, and was currently involved in a war game with the other boys of Birch Mountain. "Get! Go home!" he exclaimed in a whisper.

Moon ran up the hill towards the palisade entrance, hurt by his rebuke. As she ran, she heard war whoops behind her from the boys' game of mock combat. She hoped she hadn't betrayed her cousin by blowing his cover.

Blunt-Tipped Arrows for Childhood Mock Combat Games.

She returned to Sparrow's lodge and set the water pot down where it belonged. Her mother was finishing up Sparrow's lunch. "Did you bring the water?"

"Yes, I did," replied Moon. "Why was I named Moon?"

"You were born during the First New Moon of Spring Ceremony," said Sparrow. "I named you. You couldn't have a temporary natal name forever."

"Why do we have natal names?" asked Moon, "What do they mean?"

"A natal name is a name given to an infant immediately when he or she is born," answered Sand Dollar. "If a child is not named, and he or she dies, the child's soul becomes lost in the cosmos."

"What was your natal name, Mother?"

"I didn't have one. I am Biloxi, from a far away land. Your Aunt Sparrow adopted me into the Long Hair Clan. But natal names are supposed to be kept secret."

"How do they decide a child's natal name?" asked Moon.

"The Shaman keeps track of the days and the name depends on the day you were born. Let's eat."

* * *

River Wolf returned from his hunting trip with a buck over his shoulders. White Feather was grinding corn and acorns to make into bread. "The Spirits were good to us!" she said after seeing the buck.

"Yes, they were," replied River Wolf. He lay the buck down and embraced her.

Raccoon went to the buck and smelled it. She didn't try to take any meat though; this dog was now four cycles old and well-trained. She no longer made messes in the lodge and, now that the puppy was out of her, she had mellowed out and wasn't hyper anymore.

"Is Snow Bear still out in a war game?" asked River Wolf.

"Yes, I have been hearing their war whoops. They have been at it all day."

River Wolf was glad that his son was so devoted to the war games; it made it easier for him. Elk Antler had forced River Wolf to participate when he was young, and he was grateful that he didn't have to do the same with his son. He wondered if he could even handle it if it were otherwise. He didn't want to be cruel like his father had been. Either way, discipline was the responsibility of the mother's side of the family, so it wasn't his job to punish the boy anyway. He was glad, because his father had left him confused about what was appropriate.

Now, River Wolf hung the deer in a tree and began butchering it. Raccoon hung around, staring at him constantly. Every so often, River Wolf threw some meat to Raccoon for her to eat. The dog would take the meat and run to her favorite place and eat it. Sometimes she would bury the bones and then return to beg for more.

"You have had enough, I think," said River Wolf to the dog.

Then Raccoon would squeal and whine, lie down, and rest her head on her paws in front of her. She never took her eyes off of River Wolf as he cut up the meat.

Snow Bear returned just as River Wolf finished hanging the deer meat out to dry.

"How was the game?" asked River Wolf.

"It was great!" replied Snow Bear. "We licked them good. There were thirty of us on each team; we lost ten, but they lost twenty-seven. The last three surrendered, and we made them slaves. We beat up Limping Wolf too!"

"You shouldn't be so cruel to the other kids," said River Wolf. "You wouldn't want them to treat you that way, would you?"

"No," answered Snow Bear, "but they would have done it to us if they had won!"

"Your father is right," stated White Feather, reinforcing what River Wolf had said.

River Wolf was glad to have her support. She and her relatives were in charge of disciplining the boy. River Wolf could only state his opinions. "Just because they might misbehave doesn't give you the right to treat them badly."

"Well, Jumping Deer was our chief, and he ordered it."

"I will talk to his mother then," said River Wolf.

The Sun went down, and River Wolf made five arrow points by the light of the fire. Then he went inside the lodge and found White Feather lying in the bed. She had that look in her eyes.

"We don't want to make any noise," whispered River Wolf.

"You make more noise than I do," said White Feather with a naughty smile.

River Wolf laughed quietly. Snow Bear was asleep in his bed on the opposite side of the room. River Wolf climbed into the bed with White Feather and they held each other deep into the night.

The next morning there was excitement in the village. The chunkey game was to happen today! Everybody who was interested gathered at the village courtyard, below the large mound on which the national heptagon stood.

Three Crows gave the chunkey stone to River Wolf. He would be the person to send it rolling down the court. River Wolf recognized it as the same one he had carved out of granite so many cycles ago for Eagle Medicine.

Several pairs of players were ready. They were all to play each other, then the finalists would play each other. Many villagers wagered with great enthusiasm on the outcome.

River Wolf sent the disc rolling down the court, and the pair of players threw poles at where they thought it would stop. The one who got closest scored. The game lasted most of the day, and the two finalists were Panther and Woodcarver.

The disc was sent rolling, and they threw their sticks at it while the crowds cheered. Panther's stick was closest, and he was the winner. Three Crows presented him with a shell gorget necklace that River Wolf had carved during the last winter for this event. On the gorget was an engraving depicting a person with a chunkey stone, prepared to send it rolling down the courtyard.

Shell Gorget with Engraved Depiction of Chunkey Player.
Adapted from Fundaburk & Foreman 1957.

They held a celebration to congratulate Panther, and Sand Dollar went to tell Sparrow the news. She arrived to find Sparrow dead in her bed. Sand Dollar ran to her lodge, where the feast was taking place, and told them the sad news.

It ruined the festive occasion. Everybody was downhearted, but none were as sad as Sand Dollar, Panther, and River Wolf. Sparrow was buried in the burial mound, as she had the title of Honored Woman. She had definitely been a wise and good-hearted woman – and most deserving of that title.

When the burial was completed, Sand Dollar clung tightly to Panther. "She was so good to me. She taught me everything I know about your people, your land. She taught me how not to be so shy. She gave me courage to look people in the eyes. I could never repay her for what she has done."

"Sparrow was good to everybody she knew," said River Wolf to White Feather.

"She is in a better place now," consoled White Feather.

"What do you mean?" asked River Wolf.

"My father always told me that when you die, you go to a better place and you are reunited with your loved ones."

"So, Sparrow is with Turtle Shell, and Broken Spear?"

"Yes, she is with your parents too."

River Wolf found this hard to believe, but said nothing. He made himself accept it. It was a comforting thought.

Tanager was chosen to be the next Honored Woman. Buck was surprised at the village leaders' decision. Their daughter, Titmouse was now nineteen cycles old and she was looking for a husband. She had been spending nights away from her parents' lodge, and she was particularly interested in a young man named Stone Axe.

Buck and Tanager built her a lodge near the lodge that had been owned by Beaver Pelt's mother. The Duck Flies By had passed into the Darkening Land during the ten cycles that River Wolf was gone. Now her niece, Dove, and her family occupied her old lodge.

Titmouse was excited when her parents finished her lodge and, soon after, she married Stone Axe. Buck and Tanager were both proud, and glad to have their lodge to themselves again.

River Wolf and Snow Bear left early in the morning in their dugout. On their way out, they saw Woodcarver, who was leaving on a hunting trip. They paddled downstream to a place where soapstone was common. They landed, and River Wolf showed his son how to set the leaning-log squirrel trap. Then they spent the day collecting the stone. When the dugout was full, they checked the trap and found that they had caught four squirrels.

They cut their throats, paid their respects and put them in the dugout. Then they began paddling upstream towards home. As they paddled, they talked.

"That squirrel trap was a good idea," said Snow Bear.

"I have used that type of trap for many cycles," replied River Wolf. "I was especially glad to know about it when I was living amongst the cannibals to the southwest."

"Tell me about them."

River Wolf recounted all his experiences among the Payayas. Snow Bear listened with interest.

"What is that?" River Wolf was pointing at something, in the dugout, that looked like a bloody piece of hide.

"I don't know," answered Snow Bear as he picked it up.

"Oh no," said River Wolf. "It looks like a scalp! Somebody was here! Look! My bow and arrows are gone!"

A Scalp!

When they came around a bend in the river, Snow Bear pointed at some dugouts upstream. "Who are they?"

There were five canoes; each was manned by at least six people. "Quickly!" ordered River Wolf, "Get to shore!"

"Who are they?"

"Be quiet! And hide the dugout in this thicket." River Wolf knew that they were not Cherokee; he would have known beforehand if they were.

They hid silently in the bushes, and the five canoes passed them by. The Muskogee occupants were paddling vigorously to get away. When they were out of earshot, River Wolf said, "They raided Birch Mountain."

They waited until the enemies were out of sight. When they were sure they were safe, they moved their dugout out of its hiding place and paddled back to the village as fast as they could. On the way, they saw warriors from Birch Mountain running through the woods to intercept the enemies.

"Hello!" called River Wolf.

The warriors stopped and one of them asked, "Did you see them?"

"Yes, they left in a hurry in five canoes. You won't be able to catch up with them. There's no way."

The warriors headed back home, while River Wolf and Snow Bear paddled upstream to the village. When they arrived, they saw the damage from the attack. Twelve lodges were burned and there was chaos everywhere.

River Wolf and Snow Bear were lucky. The Muskogees had scalped somebody and left the scalp in the dugout while River Wolf and Snow Bear were gathering soapstone away from the shore. Then they went to Birch Mountain and shot fire arrows into the village, setting some of the lodges ablaze.

Woodcarver returned to the village; it was he that had gotten scalped. He was lucky to be alive. Everybody was very angry. A war large party was organized and sent out to seek retribution.

* * *

Five days later, the warriors returned with twenty-three scalps and two captives. It was the best victory that even the elders of the village could remember. The Eagle Dance was performed as usual. The two captives were tied to a stake, to wait to learn their fate. Titmouse's lodge was burned down, and her mother had the title of Honored Woman. Tanager didn't even speak to the captives. She ordered them to be burned at the stake.

Three Crows tended to Woodcarver's head. He would bear those scars for life no matter what anybody did. His father, Twisted Stick was full of hatred for the Muskogees, though he was far too old to fight them.

River Wolf, Buck and Panther helped Titmouse rebuild her lodge. It had been burned so severely that they had to tear it down and start from scratch. In two weeks, it was finished.

After the village had settled down from war and repairs, it was decided to hold a Booger Dance. River Wolf and other adults of the village gathered hides, masks and other things that the Boogers would need. They did this quietly, without telling any of the children.

That night, the villagers and children gathered at the heptagon. They told the younger children that they were expecting strange visitors who didn't know the Cherokee way of life, and they were not to be trusted. They were also told to show these people respect, for in spite of their sinister evil nature, they were still guests.

Six musicians sat on one end of the room. They functioned as callers. One was a drummer, and the remaining five shook gourd rattles. They sang six songs, and then the Boogers entered the building one-by-one.

The seven Boogers were clumsy and seemed to do everything backwards. They wore different masks, one of which was fashioned out of a gourd and had a phallic nose surrounded by animal hair.

The callers played and sang the seventh song, and the Boogers danced erratically as if they had never danced before. They approached the younger children, scaring them and teasing everybody. The older children and the adults pretended to be afraid, adding to the younger children's fears.

Then the song ended, and the Boogers rushed towards a log on one end of the building. They stumbled over each other as they scrambled to sit on the log.

Three Crows asked one of the Boogers, "Who are you?"

The Booger replied, "I am Rat Feces!"

"What do you want?" asked the Shaman, trying to maintain a serious expression.

"I want to fart in your face!"

Everybody was now laughing at this act of disrespect towards the Shaman. Then the Booger did a strange and awkward dance. He ran up to White Feather and River Wolf, turned around, bent over, and made sounds of flatulence. They just smiled and fanned the "smelly air" away.

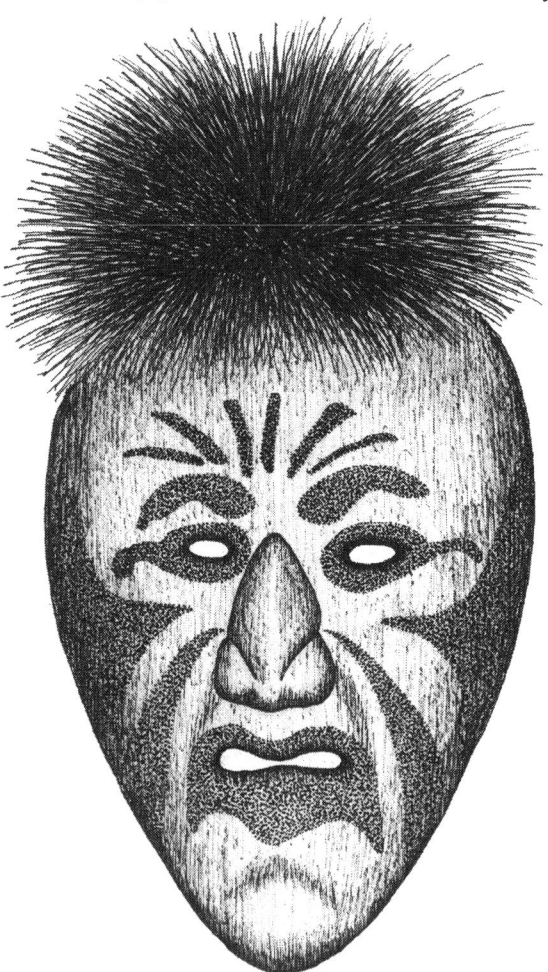

Booger Mask.
Redrawn from Lewis & Kneberg 1958.

One at a time, each of the Boogers went through a similar series of events. Each Booger had a different behavior and his own disgusting name. When Three Crows asked, the second one said his name was Raccoon Snot. Then there were Opossum Anus, Dog Spit, Bear Urine, Skunk Breath, and Wolf Vomit. By now the young children were on to them and were all laughing at them.

When all seven Boogers had finished each of their solo dances, they all were asked to do the Bear Dance together. This dance was performed by the Boogers and accompanied by any villagers who wanted to participate.

The Boogers danced clumsily and sometimes grabbed a screaming young girl and kissed her or made obscene gestures towards her. When the dance ended, the Boogers slipped away one-by-one and changed into their normal attire. Then they returned as normal people before they were missed.

Everybody was joyous and lighthearted. The Cherokee people were usually very polite, respectful and considerate towards each other, but the Boogers were always socially unacceptable and rude. The Boogers often did things that would normally lead to deadly consequences, but it was all in the name of good fun. It provided a temporary escape from the routine of everyday life.

"Who was your favorite Booger?" asked River Wolf.

"I liked Rat Feces," replied Snow Bear with a grin, "I think Mother liked him too."

White Feather blushed while they laughed at her.

* * *

The winter season came and went, along with the New Cycle and other ceremonies. It was a very rainy spring, and now River Wolf had plenty of stone carvings and effigy pipes waiting for the next trader to arrive.

River Wolf and Buck decided to go on a hunting trip together. They paddled upstream in River Wolf's dugout and, after a half-day, found a creek. They went up the creek until they arrived at a waterfall.

"This is a good place," said Buck.

They each took a drink from the clear water and began walking uphill with their bows, arrows, and axes. Before long, they heard a sound. They stopped and listened. It sounded like a bear scraping a tree trunk – marking its territory.

Quietly they crept up to the source of the noise. Through the brush they saw the bear. It got wind of them and began running away. They gave chase up the hill. When the bear arrived at the base of a cliff, he was trapped.

River Wolf saw the cliff and said, "He is cornered. Be careful."

They made their way closer and, when they were in range, they shot the bear with arrows. River Wolf cut its throat and paid his respects. It was a small bear, and they decided they could carry it back to the village themselves. They cut a pole and tied the bear's feet to it. Then they carried it, one person on each end, down to the dugout.

The bear was very heavy. They put it into the canoe, and River Wolf said, "We will have plenty of meat now!"

"Yes, we will," answered Buck as he caught his breath.

They rested there for a short while, and then shoved off for home. The canoe was low in the water from the weight of the bear. They were extra careful not to move around too much so they would not capsize it.

On the way, they reminisced of days gone by. "Remember that Yuchi warrior you killed with your axe?" asked Buck.

"I sure do. I especially remember going over that waterfall."

"You were crazy to do that, you know. But Eagle Medicine didn't think so. He thought it was the Spirits protecting you."

"I still believe it was the Spirits."

When they arrived at Birch Mountain, Snow Bear was there filling a water bottle for White Feather. They beached the canoe and carried the bear to Buck's lodge to butcher it. The dog stared at them as they cut up the bear.

"We are going to have a lot of grease," commented Tanager.

"Yes, we are," agreed Buck as he threw a piece of meat to the dog. The dog ran away with it so he could eat it in privacy.

Stone Axe came over to visit. "Titmouse says she is pregnant."

"Congratulations!" they all shouted together.

"Tell her that if she needs *anything* to come and tell us," said Tanager. "And that goes for you too."

Stone Axe thanked them and then went to tell his other friends the joyful news.

The next morning, River Wolf and White Feather were awakened by Snow Bear shouting, "The trader is here! The trader is here! Are you going to trade your pipes to him?"

"Not right now," replied River Wolf, as he wiped the sleep out of his eyes, "but I might trade a certain nine-cycle-old boy to him for some pretty shells."

"You mean me?" asked Snow Bear.

"Yes. You."

"Stop it, River Wolf," said White Feather, "We wouldn't trade you for anything, Snow Bear."

"Speak for yourself," yawned River Wolf as he got up.

"Tickle fight!" shouted Snow Bear, as he ran up and started tickling River Wolf.

River Wolf laughed and tried to get away. Then he pulled on his ears and stopped laughing immediately – even though Snow Bear was still on him.

"How did you do that? How come you don't laugh when I tickle you?"

"I pulled on my ears. It's an old Shaman's trick. An elder taught me that when I was your age. So, let's try it on you now." River Wolf immediately jumped up and tickled Snow Bear.

The child laughed and squirmed. He tried pulling on his ears, but couldn't stop laughing. "You were tricking me! I will get you back!" Snow Bear wriggled loose and got the water bottle and dumped the cold water over River Wolf's head. The entire village heard River Wolf screaming.

Snow Bear and White Feather laughed loudly. River Wolf was wide-awake now. "Okay for you two!" he said. "I'll get you back – eventually. You just wait."

"Now, Snow Bear," said White Feather. "Take the water bottle down to the river and refill it."

"Ah, Mother!" objected Snow Bear.

"You wasted it, now go and refill it."

"Oh, all right," Snow Bear said as he took the bottle and left. Soon he returned with the water bottle full.

River Wolf ate and then went to the river with Snow Bear to see what the trader had brought with him. He had some good clay and paints. He also brought plenty of seashells and woodcarvings. There was a sizable amount of flint nodules and preforms as well.

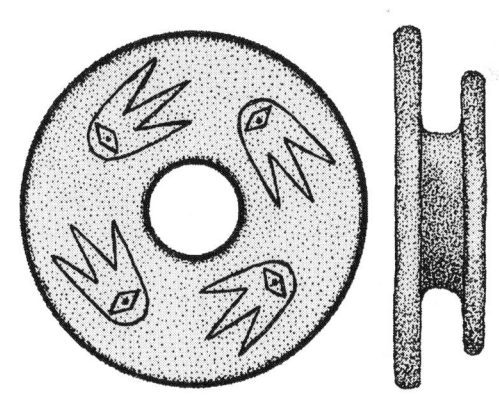

Frontal & Side View of Stone Earspool with Weeping Eye Motif.

River Wolf traded pipes for some clay and ochre paints for White Feather. Later that day, White Feather traded turkey feather cloaks for shell beads. She also traded for a pair of stone ear spools engraved with the weeping eye motif. These were gifts for River Wolf. She made necklaces with the beads, and gave one each to Snow Bear, Tanager, Titmouse, Moon, and Sand Dollar.

Panther traded for two large knives, and wrapped a rawhide handle on one of them. The other larger one he decided to keep and decide later what to do with it.

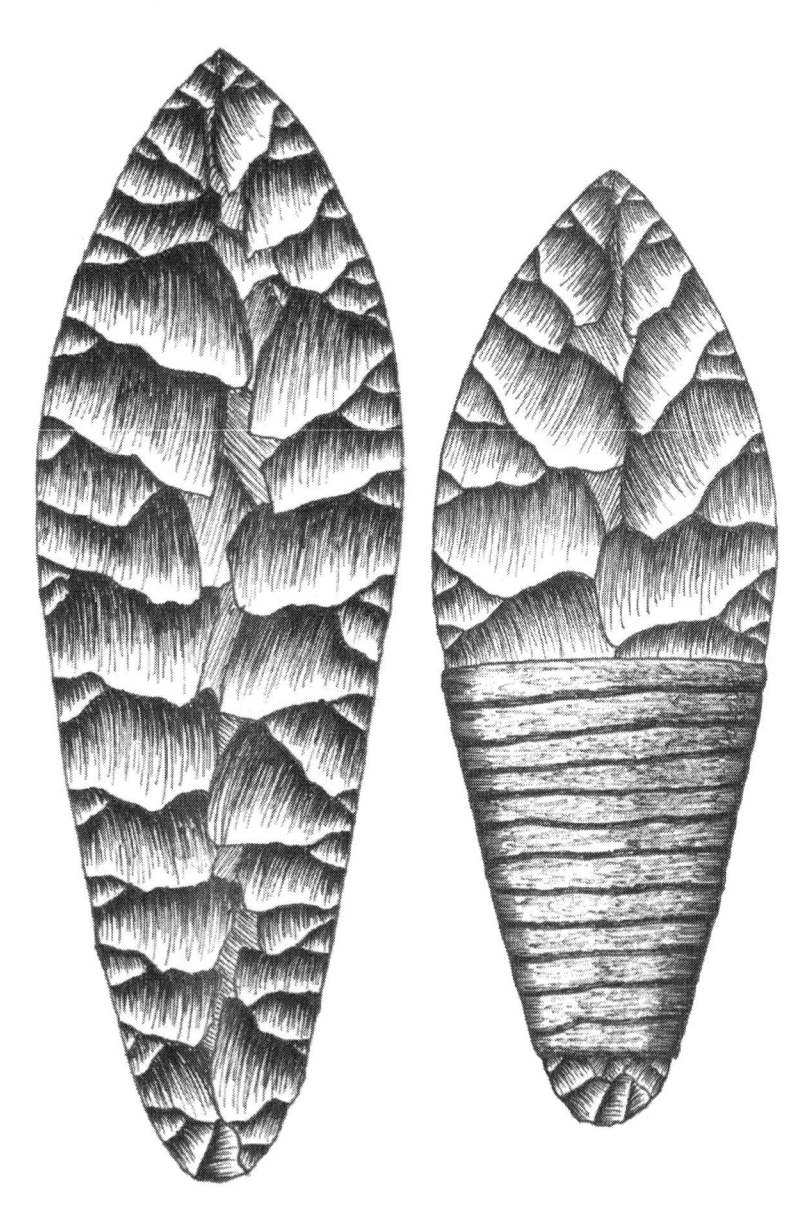

Panther's Two Flint Knives.

Buck traded flint knives and spear points he had made, for more flint. He was becoming the main supplier of flint flakes in the village. To him they were trash, because he usually only made the larger pieces and accumulated many flakes as a result. Anytime anybody needed flakes for making arrow points, they went to him. He was very generous and often just gave them away.

The trader stayed for two nights before leaving Birch Mountain. On the night of the day he left, a strong thunderstorm came up from the west. The river flooded, and almost reached the palisade of the village. The pond and the river were one large mass of water. Many of the villagers got diarrhea and were also vomiting from the dirty water. River Wolf was glad when the water dried up and things began to get back to normal again.

One day Buck gave Snow Bear a fine knife in an antler handle. Snow Bear was ecstatic. "Look at what Buck made for me!"

"Wow," said River Wolf. "That's nice!" It occurred to River Wolf that he should make his son a blowgun. He went outside the village to the canebrake and got the materials.

After several days, he had a nice blowgun with darts to give his son. He left it on his son's bed as a surprise for him. Later that day, Snow Bear returned from a war game and found it.

"A blowgun!" he exclaimed.

"It is yours," said River Wolf.

"Oh, thank you!"

The next day at around noon, Snow Bear brought home a rabbit he had killed and butchered. River Wolf couldn't help remembering, when he was a child, presenting his first kill to his father. "I am so proud of you! You even dressed it. Very good! White Feather! Let's eat this for dinner!"

White Feather smiled proudly as she took the rabbit from Snow Bear. Buck appeared in the doorway with a stranger. "River Wolf," called Buck. "My friend here hears that you are the best stone carver in the whole tribe. He wants to talk to you. His name is Blue Jay, and he has walked here all the way from Eagle Peak."

"Come on in," said River Wolf.

Blue Jay entered, while Buck returned to his lodge. "It's nice to meet you," greeted Blue Jay.

"What can I do for you?" asked River Wolf.

"We at Eagle Peak would like a pipe in the form of an effigy of a chunkey player. I am the Shaman's trainee over there. I have heard about your skill with stone, and we are hoping such a pipe might bring good luck to our village's chunkey players. Can you make one about this size?" he gestured with his hands.

"I can make one any shape or size. What color would you prefer?"

"We don't care what color it is."

"What position would you like the chunkey player to be in?"

"That's up to you. We know you are gifted. Use your imagination. I am sure it will be splendid."

"I can do it. I will go and find a rock from which to carve it. What will you trade?"

"What do you need?"

River Wolf glanced at White Feather. "What should I trade for?"

"We all could use some moccasins," replied White Feather.

"Will you trade three pairs of moccasins, and a deer hide with the head intact? What I mean is something to cover up with and use to get close to a deer?"

"That sounds fair enough," replied Blue Jay.

"It will take me about a moon to complete it. I will deliver it in person as soon as it's finished."

"That sounds good. I'd better get going, it was nice meeting you," said Blue Jay with a friendly smile, then he departed for Eagle Peak.

River Wolf drank some water and departed to find the right piece of stone. When he returned, he began whittling on it with a sharp flake of flint.

That evening, they ate the rabbit that Snow Bear had killed. River Wolf spent his time working on the pipe, and Snow Bear really began earning his keep, by bringing home two to three rabbits a day.

Whenever Snow Bear and the other village kids were involved in war games, the family ate dried meat and vegetables. One morning, the Yuchis attacked and shot fire arrows over the palisade. Two lodges were burned, but not beyond repair. The usual war party was sent out after them, but the enemies split up and slipped away. When the Cherokee warriors regrouped, they discovered that Stone Axe was missing. They tracked him and found him dead and scalped. He had been killed with an axe.

Titmouse was devastated when she heard the news. Her unborn child would not have a father. Buck and Tanager brought her meat and vegetables to eat. Stone Axe was buried under their lodge.

* * *

As he predicted, River Wolf finished the chunkey player effigy pipe after working on it for a moon. "Snow Bear, would you like to go with me to Eagle Peak?"

"Sure!" came the excited reply.

"We will get up very early. Make sure you are ready before you go to bed tonight. Bring along your blowgun and darts."

Before the Sun rose, they were on their way. Snow Bear had his blowgun, and River Wolf carried his bow and arrows. When the Sun came up, River Wolf realized he had forgotten the pipe!

They turned back and River Wolf was angry with himself for his carelessness. Just before noon they arrived back home and River Wolf grabbed the effigy pipe. They left again and began making their way up the ridge towards Eagle Peak.

Chunkey Player Effigy Pipe.
Redrawn from Mails 1992.

Late in the afternoon, they crossed the ridge and stopped to rest at a stream on the other side. River Wolf gave Snow Bear some dried meat and cornbread packed by White Feather.

They set out on their journey again. At sunset they arrived at Eagle Peak and looked for Blue Jay. They found him at the council house.

"Ah! My hero!" said Blue Jay when he saw the chunkey player effigy pipe. "My mother made your moccasins, and I have them and your deer skin, with the head still on, at my lodge. Do you have a place to spend the night?"

"No, we don't," answered River Wolf.

"You can stay at the guest lodge, but I will need to move some things out of your way. But we will worry about that later. Would you two like to eat dinner with my wife and me?"

"Yes, thank you."

They ate, and Blue Jay gave River Wolf the items he had traded for. Then they moved the things off of the beds at the guest lodge. River Wolf and Snow Bear went to sleep.

The next morning, River Wolf awakened Snow Bear and told him, "It's time to go. Where is your blowgun?"

"Oh no!" said Snow Bear. "I must have lost it in the forest! I know; I'll bet it is at the stream where we rested!"

"I hope it is. You should always treat your weapons with respect. Don't leave them anywhere except at home."

"I'm sorry. We could look for it at the stream – it should still be there."

River Wolf gathered the trade items and the two bade farewell to Blue Jay, and left for home. They arrived at the stream, only to see a bear cub playing around with Snow Bear's blowgun.

"Let's scare him away!" suggested Snow Bear.

"Shh! Snow Bear, we don't know where the cub's mother is," whispered River Wolf. "You should never mess with a baby animal unless you know you can kill the mother without getting hurt. You are young, and I don't want any trouble from that cub's mother. Be very quiet. We will leave the blowgun here and I will just make you another one. Let's go."

They drank some water from the stream, and then passed the cub at a respectful distance. When they were well out of any danger, they began talking normally.

"It sure is hot and dry," commented Snow Bear.

"I know. We had so much rain this spring. Now all the weeds are dying. I hope we don't have any forest fires – the conditions will be ideal for a fire if we don't get rain soon."

They arrived back home at sunset, and White Feather fed them dinner. She was satisfied with the new moccasins that they now had. They went to bed and slept well. The next day, River Wolf started making another blowgun for Snow Bear. When that was completed, he gave it to his son.

"Promise you will take care of this one," he told Snow Bear.

"I promise."

River Wolf now looked over his deer costume. The idea behind this was to be a human decoy so as to get closer to the deer to shoot them with an arrow. River Wolf had heard the idea all of his life, but had never tried it. He tried it on, and White Feather laughed at him in the costume.

River Wolf was not discouraged. He took it out into the woods. He sat for a long time and listened. He eventually heard deer snorting, and rustling in the dry leaves. He put on the costume and crawled on all fours near enough to where the deer were feeding. Once he was in range, he slowly got his bow and arrow and took aim. He released the arrow, and dropped a large, fat deer in its tracks.

When he returned with the deer, he asked White Feather, "Do you still think I am silly?"

"I really can't believe it actually worked!" scoffed White Feather.

"I told you," smirked River Wolf.

River Wolf's Deer Costume.

They butchered the deer and set out the meat to dry. White Feather gave one piece to Raccoon. The dog had been begging for it ever since River Wolf had shown up with the deer.

Some of the youths of the village went to Fire Arrow to request permission to raid the Yuchis. It was granted and they made ready to leave, eager to prove themselves in war.

Buck, Woodcarver, and many other warriors accompanied them. They wanted to make the most of the attack because Stone Axe's death had not been avenged, and his killers had escaped.

So, a total of sixteen departed on foot for Eagle Peak, where they hoped to recruit more warriors. Five warriors from Eagle Peak joined them – Eagle Peak was also subject to frequent Yuchi attacks.

They were gone for a week and-a-half, and then they returned triumphantly. They brought nine scalps, one prisoner, and the news that several Yuchi lodges had been burned to the ground.

The Eagle Dance was performed and the time came for the Honored Woman to decide the fate of the prisoner. Tanager had no love for enemies and, once again, she had the prisoner burned at the stake.

The youths were given adult names and were initiated into manhood. Two days later, a runner from Eagle Peak brought the news that the Yuchis had attacked his town. The runner stayed at Birch Mountain long enough to gather enough warriors for another raid. This seemed to be turning into an all-out war.

Panther asked River Wolf, "Why don't you come with us?"

"I am an artist, not a warrior," replied River Wolf.

However, there was still no shortage of volunteers, and a total of thirty-five warriors left with the runner from Eagle Peak. Their force doubled when they reached Eagle Peak, and this time they went far into Yuchi territory. They were gone for three weeks.

River Wolf hunted food for Sand Dollar, Tanager, and Titmouse. He was kept pretty busy doing this while the warriors were gone.

He spent a lot of time consoling the women and reassuring them that their husbands would safely return. Little Moon always cried when she saw her mother weeping. Titmouse worried about her father. Time seemed to go by so slowly.

River Wolf also worried about his brother and Buck. When they returned, they had three captives and thirty-two scalps. They had created much chaos among the Yuchis.

Buck and Panther told the story to River Wolf. "We went to a small village," said Buck, "and shot fire arrows and burned many lodges. Then when we left, we assembled in a "V" shape. The Yuchis ran right into our trap and we surrounded them. They fought fiercely, but we got the best of them without any casualties. One of the young men took an arrow in his leg. Three Crows is treating him now."

Panther spoke, "We split up and went to many other villages, using fire arrows. Then we caught the three prisoners and headed for home."

Buck and Panther went home, and River Wolf was getting uneasy. Things seemed to be getting out of control. His father's words echoed in his mind. *You should always be ready for combat... It doesn't really matter now, but someday you will have a family to protect, and you must be ready. You'd better practice now while you are young, or else you won't amount to anything, and your family will die!*

White Feather entered the lodge with a water bottle she had just filled. "What's wrong?" she asked him.

"Nothing," he replied, "I just have something on my mind."

"You seem very worried."

"It seems like a major war is beginning, and I am worried for your safety and Snow Bear's safety."

"There are always raids. Why would it lead to anything else?"

"Yes, you are right. I don't know why I worry. Do you need any help making dinner?"

"I think I have things taken care of. You have been very busy hunting for a long time. Why don't you just take a rest, now that the men are back?"

"Alright," said River Wolf, and he forced a smile so she would not worry. River Wolf took a nap. The next thing he knew, White Feather was waking him up for dinner.

"It's time to eat," said White Feather. "Where is Snow Bear?"

"I don't know," replied River Wolf sleepily. "Maybe he is playing with Moon. I will go and get him." River Wolf went to Panther and Sand Dollar's lodge and, sure enough, Snow Bear was there. "Come home with me; it's time to eat."

"Can I go too?" asked Moon.

"You must ask your mother," replied River Wolf.

"You may go," said Sand Dollar, "but be back by bedtime."

"I will."

They ate a good meal of dried meat and a stew of various vegetables. It was delicious. Then Snow Bear and Moon began playing around inside the lodge. Before long, they got rowdy and knocked over River Wolf's bow and quiver. It fell and broke a water bottle, spilling the water all over the dirt floor.

"You two go outside if you are going to play rough!" shouted River Wolf.

"I'm sorry," apologized Snow Bear as they left.

"You didn't have to raise your voice at them," said White Feather. "I can make another bottle."

"I know you can; you're good at it! But they need to learn to not be so rambunctious while they play inside."

Buck appeared in the doorway. "River Wolf, would you like to go hunting with me in the morning?"

"Yes, I will go with you. Maybe we will get lucky and get a large elk or bear."

"We will take my dugout and go upstream. I will see you in the morning."

"I will be ready."

Buck left and White Feather went out to call Snow Bear in for bed. "Snow Bear! Snow Bear!"

"What?" answered Snow Bear.

"Come in, it's time for bed!"

"Tell Moon to go home!" shouted River Wolf from inside the lodge. "Sand Dollar wants her back so she can go to bed also."

"Moon!" called Sand Dollar. "Come to bed!"

"Snow Bear," called White Feather, "come on."

The child returned to his home and went to sleep. River Wolf and White Feather talked quietly. River Wolf said, "We sure need some rain. The villagers are worried about a forest fire."

"We women have been spending a lot of time bringing water from the river for the gardens," agreed White Feather, "Have you noticed that the river is lower than it has been in a long time?"

"Yes, I have. It may even be at its lowest ever. I don't know what it means. It would be nice if we had a good rainstorm."

They went to sleep. Early the next morning, Buck and River Wolf got ready for their hunting trip. They left upstream in the dugout. They reached the creek and went up it for a while. Then they beached the dugout and went walking up the ridge.

River Wolf stopped and set some squirrel traps in case their hunting efforts were futile. Then they continued uphill and heard an elk calling in the distance. They followed the noise, but the elk was downwind of them and he caught their scent; they found tracks, but never caught sight of him.

Soon after, they heard sounds nearby in the woods. They were just about to go and investigate, when suddenly a flock of turkeys appeared.

"Let's each shoot one," whispered Buck. "That way we will get two."

River Wolf nodded in agreement. They took aim, and released their arrows simultaneously. River Wolf's arrow dropped one of the turkeys; Buck's arrow wounded another. The turkeys ran off, except for the one River Wolf had shot. Buck's turkey ran away with them.

River Wolf cut his turkey's throat and followed Buck after the wounded one. The turkey didn't make it very far, and they found it hiding in a thicket. Buck shot it one more time and then cut its throat and picked it up.

They started back down the ridge, and River Wolf grabbed up his turkey. When they came to the squirrel traps, they discovered five squirrels dangling from the nooses.

They killed the squirrels, paid their respects to them and the turkeys, and took them back to the dugout. They shoved off and drifted downstream towards home.

Buck and River Wolf arrived back much earlier than they were expected, but had killed enough for two days of food for each family. They were satisfied.

White Feather was busy, at the river, making another water bottle to replace the one that Snow Bear and Moon had broken. She looked up and saw her husband and Buck approaching in the dugout. "You are early!" she said. "If I would have known you would be back at noon, I would have cooked for you."

"We thought we would be gone all day," returned River Wolf.

"We heard an elk," added Buck, "but we were upwind and he caught our scent. He ran off. But we did get these turkeys and squirrels."

Buck took the turkeys and squirrels to his lodge to start cleaning them. River Wolf remained at the river to talk to White Feather.

"White Feather," he said. "You haven't been to the women's hut for a really long time. Do you think you are pregnant?"

"Well, I have suspected it. I am two weeks overdue for my moon time. I meant to tell you when you returned."

"Well, should I tell the village you are pregnant?"

"I guess so; I think I am."

Chapter 18: Warrior

The next day, River Wolf first told his brother, Panther, the exciting news.

"Congratulations!" said Panther.

Sand Dollar entered the lodge with a full water bottle from the river.

"Sand Dollar," called Panther. "Snow Bear is going to have a little sibling!"

"That's wonderful!" exclaimed Sand Dollar as she hugged River Wolf. "I am going to visit White Feather right away and see if she needs anything."

Next, River Wolf told Buck and Tanager.

"Go and tell Titmouse" suggested Tanager. "It will make her day. You know she has a new boyfriend, don't you?"

"No, I didn't. Happy news!"

"Well, you go and tell her *your* happy news."

"Alright, I will go and see her now." River Wolf left for Titmouse's lodge.

"Titmouse!" called River Wolf.

"Yes?" came the reply from inside her lodge.

"White Feather and I are expecting another baby."

"Wow! That is great!"

"So, how are you getting along?"

"I have my eyes set on Antler Tine. I want to marry him, and I am trying to show him what a good wife I can be."

"I can only imagine how you are doing that!"

Titmouse laughed and blushed.

River Wolf told everybody the joyous news. Finally, he went outside the palisade and set some squirrel traps. He returned later with five squirrels, and he prepared them for lunch. After eating, he took a long nap. When he awoke, it was around sunset. River Wolf went back to Buck's lodge and found him skinning a small bear. River Wolf helped him skin the bear and cut it up. Then they went to bed.

The next morning, before dawn, a choking smoke awakened the people of Birch Mountain. The strong wind was warm and heavy with smoke. In an unorganized and chaotic manner, everybody was going out of the palisade, and into the woods to see what was happening.

River Wolf told his family to remain inside the village while he investigated. He exited the palisade to look, and there was a peculiar red glow in the woods to the west. It was a tremendous forest fire, and the wind was blowing the fire straight towards the village!

He returned and told White Feather and Snow Bear to quickly gather as many things as they could carry, and were absolutely needed. He told them to meet him at the river. He couldn't believe this was happening.

They were quickly running out of time. The fire raced at a fast pace, fueled by the tall, dead grass. Before the villagers fully realized what was happening, and before they could get all the things they would need, the fire was already in the village.

Panther's lodge was on fire, as were many of the lodges on that side of the village. The fire intensified when it reached all of their dry corn crops. In the early morning light there were the sounds of women and children wailing and coughing.

River Wolf and his family waited at the river as the flames blocked their view of Birch Mountain. When the flames passed, they saw the charred and smoking remains of the Cherokee capital. The fire had spared nothing, except for the heptagon on the top of the ceremonial mound. Snow Bear began to cry.

"It's going to be okay, son," consoled River Wolf as he hugged him.

"Where will we live?" cried Snow Bear.

"Don't worry, Snow Bear," said White Feather. "We will build another lodge."

At least River Wolf's family was spared, but they were homeless, as were most of the other families. Many people died that morning because they didn't get out of the village soon enough.

Panther and Moon located River Wolf. "Sand Dollar! I can't find her! I tried to talk her out of going back, but she wouldn't listen!"

This was the first time River Wolf had seen Panther this upset. Moon began to cry. It broke River Wolf's heart.

Sand Dollar, Twisted Stick, Three Crows, Tanager, Titmouse, and many others were never found. At around noon, they looked over the destroyed village, desperately hoping to find survivors. The Uku, Fire Arrow had died inside of the heptagon. The heptagon itself was not damaged very much. Now the survivors set fire to it and burned it to the ground.

Meanwhile, scouts were sent in the direction that the fire came from, and they returned with some Muskogee and Yuchi arrows they had found. It appeared that they had joined forces and took advantage of the dry weather and the steady west wind to commit this terrible act.

Eight out of ten villagers had died, and now the survivors decided to head for Eagle Peak for refuge. Birch Mountain was abandoned forever. The trip was a very sad one; the men were silent, and the women were weeping for the dead. They couldn't even give them a proper burial.

"I never thought I would ever witness anything like this," White Feather said to River Wolf.

"I don't think anybody did," replied River Wolf.

"Why did they burn our village?" asked Snow Bear. "What did we do to them?"

"We have always been enemies of the Yuchi and the Muskogee," answered River Wolf. "The land to the south has been in dispute for many cycles."

The smoke from the smoldering village followed the survivors eastward up the ridge. Many of them were coughing and hoarse.

The refugees arrived at Eagle Peak, and members of the clans let their relatives stay in their lodges. A council of war was held, and runners were sent to all the villages in the Cherokee territory. Within two weeks, Eagle Peak was overcrowded with thousands of warriors. They split up and some of the parties headed for the Yuchi territory, while other parties left for the Muskogee land. Panther was among them. River Wolf stayed behind to hunt for the families whose fathers had left. New lodges were being built at Eagle Peak to accommodate the new residents.

White Feather, Snow Bear, and Moon went out to gather materials for a new lodge when, suddenly, they were shot and killed by enemy warriors. Normally, the warriors would have taken them captive, but they were so close to Eagle Peak, the enemies feared that the locals would hear their screams, and so they killed them.

They didn't scalp them, because there was no honor in killing women or children. They left them where they lay, and moved through the woods to a good location from which to attack.

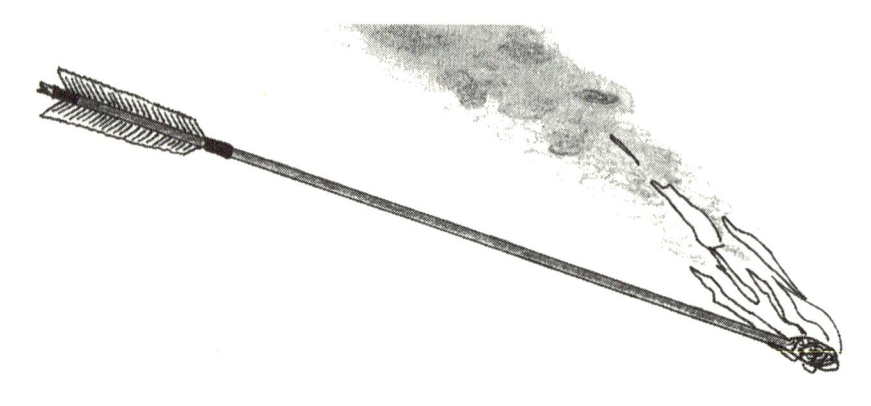

Fire Arrow.

Fire arrows went over the palisade, burning lodges in the village. Not many warriors were left to defend the village, as they were out in enemy territory. River Wolf and Buck went out to investigate, and found White Feather, Snow Bear, and Moon dead.

River Wolf was disbelieving. He just stood there numb, and almost in denial, looking over their bodies. White Feather still had the freshwater pearl necklace around her neck.

"Oh River Wolf," said Buck, "I am so sorry. Is there anything I can do?"

"I just want to be alone."

Buck understood, having recently lost his family at Birch Mountain. He left River Wolf quietly and said a prayer for his best friend.

River Wolf sat there for a long time shocked, sad and angry. Once again, he heard his father's words playing in his head. *You should always be ready for combat... It doesn't really matter now, but someday you will have a family to protect, and you must be ready. You'd better practice now while you are young, or else you won't amount to anything, and your family will die!* Too late, River Wolf realized that Elk Antler had been right. He was a failure in life, he thought. He prayed that the Spirits of his family would forgive him for his folly and neglect. He felt grief and wanted revenge. He vowed to become a warrior and kill as many enemies as he could.

Two days later, the warriors returned, and had many scalps. River Wolf told Panther about his daughter's death. Panther was stone-faced and showed no emotion except for the pent-up rage that seemed to burn inside every warrior.

Many of the residents from other parts of the nation helped in building a larger palisade to accommodate the growing village. This was a time-consuming task – and time was of the essence – so they worked hard, in day shifts and night shifts, to complete it as quickly as possible.

When the warriors heard about the most recent attack on Eagle Peak, they wanted to go back out again. They decided to leave some warriors there to guard the village. River Wolf insisted on going with the war party. The Eagle Dance was not performed this time because the last raid wasn't considered a victory.

So, they left and headed down Thunder River towards Yuchi territory. When they arrived at a village, they shot fire arrows over the palisade and then scattered. They returned to Eagle Peak one at a time.

River Wolf was alone on his way back to Eagle Peak. He heard people behind him – tracking him. He hid in a thicket and waited for them. Then two warriors came into view. River Wolf recognized one of them, by their buffalo horn headdress, as Winged Rattlesnake Chief, the Muskogee war leader. The other warrior appeared to be a Yuchi.

River Wolf aimed his arrow at Winged Rattlesnake Chief and shot. But the arrow sideswiped a tree branch, making a noise. Winged Rattlesnake Chief immediately ducked and the arrow struck the Yuchi warrior in the shoulder. The Yuchi groaned in pain.

Before they could react, River Wolf had loosed several more arrows, which fell all around the two enemies. They retreated, and River Wolf also left the area before they could return with more warriors.

He alternated running and walking so he could move fast without getting tired. As he passed by a particular place, he recognized it as the place on the river where he and Buck had camped cycles ago, on the night the Wolf Spirit had appeared to him in the dream.

Then he heard footsteps in the woods. Fearing it was more enemies, he hid in a thicket again and waited. He saw Buck and ran out to greet him. Buck made ready to shoot an arrow, but relaxed when he saw it was River Wolf.

"I almost killed Winged Rattlesnake Chief," said River Wolf.

"Really?" asked Buck. "What happened?"

"I tried to shoot him with an arrow but it glanced off a tree branch and made a noise. He ducked and the arrow struck his Yuchi friend."

"That's too bad. I never liked him. He is so sly and sleazy. He seems to always have that evil smirk on his face. And why he wears that buffalo headdress into battle has always been a mystery to me. It has nothing to do with his totem at all."

Winged Rattlesnake Chief.
Redrawn from Copeland 1997.

Just then, an arrow struck a nearby tree. It was Muskogee, but they had no time to ascertain whether or not it was Winged Rattlesnake Chief's arrow. Buck used signs to say, "Follow me."

They went back into the thicket, careful not to make a noise. They waited and listened for what seemed like an eternity. They could hear light footsteps, and they made ready their arrows.

Winged Rattlesnake Chief appeared, alone. He looked at his arrow, still in the tree, and then looked around, very alertly. He quietly approached his arrow so he could remove it from the tree. When he pulled it out, the flint arrow point stayed in the tree trunk. He mumbled something inaudible and looked around.

Buck nocked an arrow and when he drew back on the bow, it made a cracking noise. Buck let the arrow loose, but Winged Rattlesnake Chief had ducked after hearing the noise.

River Wolf had his bow and arrow ready, but Winged Rattlesnake Chief was long gone. There was a reason he was the highest-ranking Muskogee war chief. Buck and River Wolf listened intently until they heard the cracking of a twig some distance away.

River Wolf signed, "He is leaving. Your bow is broken. You go on ahead, and I will stay here for a while and make sure you are not followed."

"Be careful," signed Buck. "Take my arrows – you might need them. I will see you at Eagle Peak." Buck gave River Wolf all of his arrows. They were useless to Buck now that his bow had cracked. River Wolf gave Buck his axe and Buck silently departed.

River Wolf waited there in that thicket listening until sunset. Then he started back towards Eagle Peak. When he arrived at the village, he saw a woman filling her water bottle at the river. "Would you like me to help you carry that?" he asked.

"Thank you," she said with a smile. "I have seen you before! Are you from Birch Mountain?"

"Yes, my name is River Wolf."

"You're the man who made the effigy pipe! With the chunkey player!"

"Yes, that's me."

"You just came from a battle, didn't you?"

"More or less."

"Are you hungry?"

"Yes."

"Why don't you come to my lodge and eat dinner with me? By the way, my name is Redbird."

River Wolf followed Redbird to her lodge and they talked as they prepared dinner. She seemed like a very nice person to him.

"Did you have any family at Birch Mountain?" asked Redbird.

"All of my family was there. My pregnant wife and son were killed during the last attack on Eagle Peak."

"I am so sorry. My husband was killed one cycle ago while on a war party. So many people have lost loved ones. It seems that the whole Earth is just burning up. Just boiling over with hatred and rage."

"Yes, it does."

They ate, and then Redbird asked, "Would you like to spend the night here and talk?"

"I shouldn't," replied River Wolf. "I'd better go. But thank you for feeding me dinner."

"Please? There is nothing wrong with it."

He smiled for the first time in a long while. "Well, alright. I'll stay."

So they began to get to know each other. Redbird only had one bed in her small lodge, so they lay there side-by-side, just talking. They spoke late into the evening, till they finally fell asleep.

River Wolf's Disturbing Symbolic Dream.

River Wolf had a disturbing dream that night. He saw a silhouette of his hand, and in the center of his hand was a spiral that was coiled in the same direction as did a poisonous viper. Something told him this snake-like omen represented death, and that his hand represented his ability to do something about it. But he never did, and he never would. After all, he could have prevented everything that had happened to his family and people. But, even in his sleep, he wanted to run away from it like the big coward he was. He tossed and turned, trying to scream, but couldn't move or make a sound. It was a suffocating sensation. *This is how my dead family is feeling <u>right now</u>!* His moaning and shifting in the bed finally woke both himself and Redbird. She got up and rubbed his sweaty forehead, and he tearfully described his dream to her. She just listened, wishing he could somehow know none of this was his fault.

The next day, Redbird consulted with the Shaman, and he suggested the apparition may have been caused by the spirit of an enemy River Wolf had killed, but the Shaman had no time to treat him. Indeed, there were so very many wounded warriors to look after, so the Shaman had not a moment to spare for something as trivial as a bad dream.

In contrast, the next night, River Wolf dreamed of White Feather and Snow Bear. They seemed happy and were in a beautiful land. Then White Feather approached River Wolf and kissed him. She tenderly rubbed his arm while saying, *I love you, River Wolf. But you must now let go of me. You will father another child before you join Snow Bear, Beaver Pelt, and me.*

Then she began rubbing his arm, and he awoke and realized Redbird was caressing his arm. He was startled and got up quickly.

"Oh I'm sorry, River Wolf," she said. "I shouldn't have done that. It's just that you seemed to be having another bad dream. I didn't mean to upset you. I just wanted you to be comfortable. I am really sorry."

River Wolf calmed down and after some thought, he quietly replied, "I know. It's alright."

They went back to sleep. The next morning Redbird fed him breakfast after they did their morning bathing with the rest of the villagers. As they ate, they talked.

"I will go out and hunt some meat for you," said River Wolf. "You have been good to me."

"I will help you prepare it. There is not much corn or any other vegetables because of the drought. Otherwise I would cook some for you."

"You have done enough – letting me stay here and all."

"Do you think you could love a woman again?" asked Redbird after a long silence.

"No," replied River Wolf flatly.

Redbird's heart sank. She was silent the rest of the time they ate their breakfast.

River Wolf got his bow and arrows and headed for the woods. He walked up the ridge and when he got to the top, he could see the blackened landscape around Birch Mountain. It saddened him. Now that he was alone, he wept bitterly.

He set some squirrel traps and then followed a deer trail. Soon, he heard deer ahead and he began stalking them. When he got in range, he shot a yearling doe and cut her throat. Then he apologized to the doe's spirit.

He checked his traps and found he had caught two squirrels. Since he shot the deer, he had plenty of meat, so he decided to let the squirrels go. He removed the nooses from around their necks and said, "I do not need you two today, and I hope I won't need you tomorrow. I am sorry to have disturbed you. Go home to your families." He released them, and he went back for the deer. He carried the deer over his shoulders back to Eagle Peak. On the way, he thought about the squirrels. They never killed each other in battle. He wished he were a squirrel. Then all he would need to do would be gathering acorns.

When he arrived at Redbird's lodge with the deer, She helped him clean it. They cooked some and hung up the rest to dry. Buck and Panther arrived with the news that there was a new Cherokee capital. It was in a village far to the north, named Dogwood Creek. The new Uku was named Prancing Deer.

This news was of little comfort to River Wolf, though he was glad to see his friend and brother again. He said, "This is Redbird. She was kind enough to let me stay with her. Would you like some deer meat?"

"We just killed a bear," replied Buck. "In fact, we were going to offer you some meat."

"Thank you for your offer, but we have plenty."

"If you need anything, let us know. I am staying at that lodge over there," said Buck while pointing. "Old Linden is letting me stay there with him and his family."

"I am staying with Waterfowl," added Panther.

"I have your arrows, Buck," said River Wolf.

"That's good," said Buck as he took back his arrows. "Linden gave me his bow. It's a nice one. He said he wouldn't be needing it anymore. Thank you for looking out for me."

They left, and River Wolf and Redbird finished eating and went to bed. Over the next few nights, River Wolf continued to have nightmares.

During the days, much work was being done in Eagle Peak, and new lodges were being built. It was becoming crowded. The old palisade was left standing while the people built a larger one around it. It was a slow task that would probably take at least a cycle to complete. In the meantime, lodges were being built outside the old palisade. They were susceptible to enemy attacks, but there was little room left inside the old palisade.

Many scouts were constantly out in the woods to watch for signs of an attack. River Wolf, Buck and Panther were stationed together to watch the river. One day they saw canoes approaching. They quietly ran back to Eagle Peak to alert the villagers. This time they were ready for the intruders, and they killed all thirty enemies without any losses. After scalping all of them, they put their bodies in the canoes they arrived in, and sent them to drift downstream. This way their comrades would discover them after they passed into their territory. It served as a warning not to trespass.

River Wolf came home to Redbird, and saw her hanging up a strange object. It was a stick, tied into a hoop, and twine was woven in its center, not unlike a spider web. "What on Earth is that?" he asked her.

"It's a dream catcher I made! When you sleep, good dreams pass through the web, but bad dreams are caught in the web, and will not reach you. I learned about it from an Ojibwe trader from far to the north. I thought it might help you sleep better since the Shaman is so busy."

It meant a lot to River Wolf that she had gone through such effort to ensure he would be comfortable in her lodge. But he couldn't seem to bring himself to let her know he appreciated her thoughtfulness. They went to bed, and River Wolf did indeed sleep more soundly.

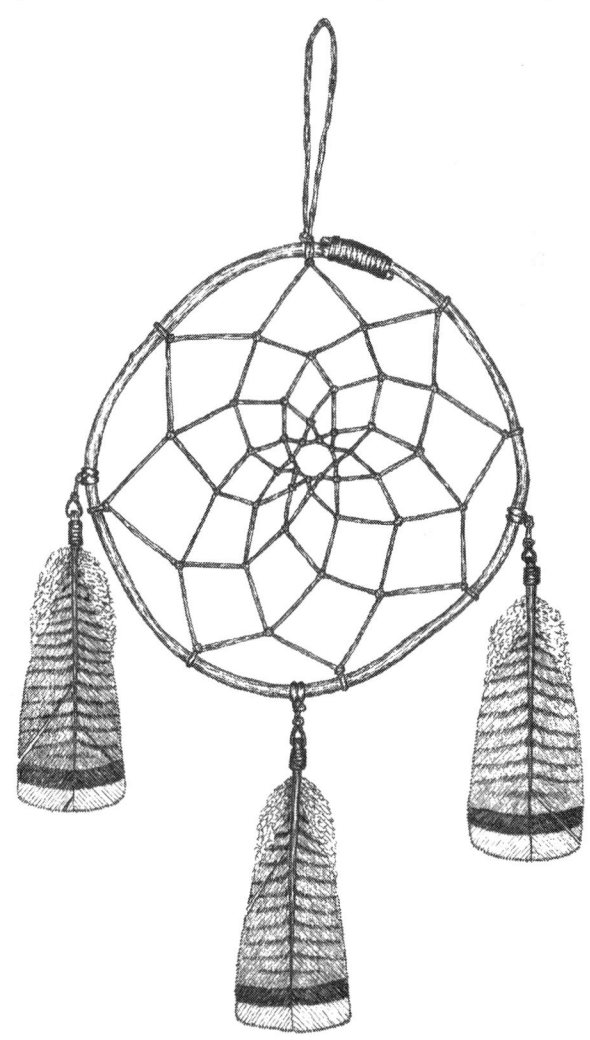

Ojibwe Style Dream Catcher Made by Redbird for River Wolf.

The next day River Wolf and Buck went out hunting, but killed no game. Fortunately, they had set some squirrel traps and brought home seven squirrels. The squirrels didn't last long, and the next day found them grinding black walnut rinds into a pulp. They used it for putting fish in a stupor like they had done cycles ago. In this manner, they caught all the fish they needed for several days.

When they arrived back at Eagle Peak, they heard the news that one of the guards stationed in the woods was found dead. Panther recognized the arrow in his chest – it belonged to his old nemesis, Winged Rattlesnake Chief.

Warriors were sent out after the intruders, but their trail was too cold. Now some of the village youths volunteered to make another raid, eager to prove themselves in battle. Tragically, none of the four returned.

One day, while River Wolf was making arrowheads to put on arrows, Redbird returned from the river with a full water bottle. "Wow!" she exclaimed. "How many arrows are you making?"

"I want at least forty in my quiver."

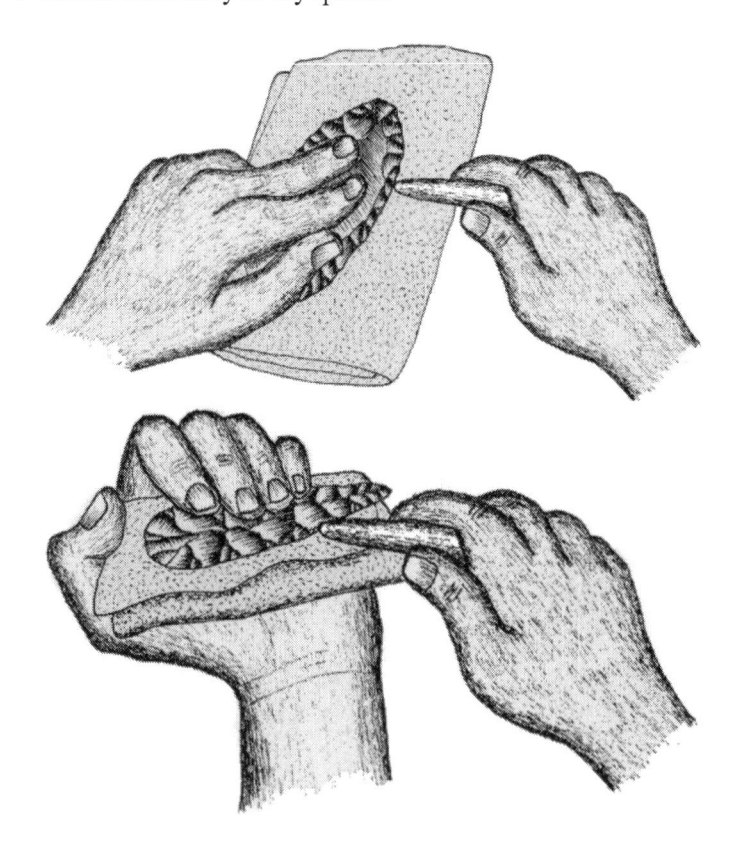

River Wolf Pressure Flakes Flint Arrowheads with an Antler Tine.

Then there was a commotion at the river. A trader had arrived. The warriors and guards were extra cautious and suspected mischief. The trader was offended at the way he was treated at first. He understood the reasons for their caution after they explained the situation to him.

For the first time, River Wolf had nothing to trade with. Redbird traded two turkey feather cloaks for flint – she knew the village would need the flint for arrowheads. She gave the flint to Buck, and Buck percussion flaked it into several large knives. These knives he planned on giving to warriors who had none. He also gave away the trash chips to anybody in the village who needed them for making arrowheads.

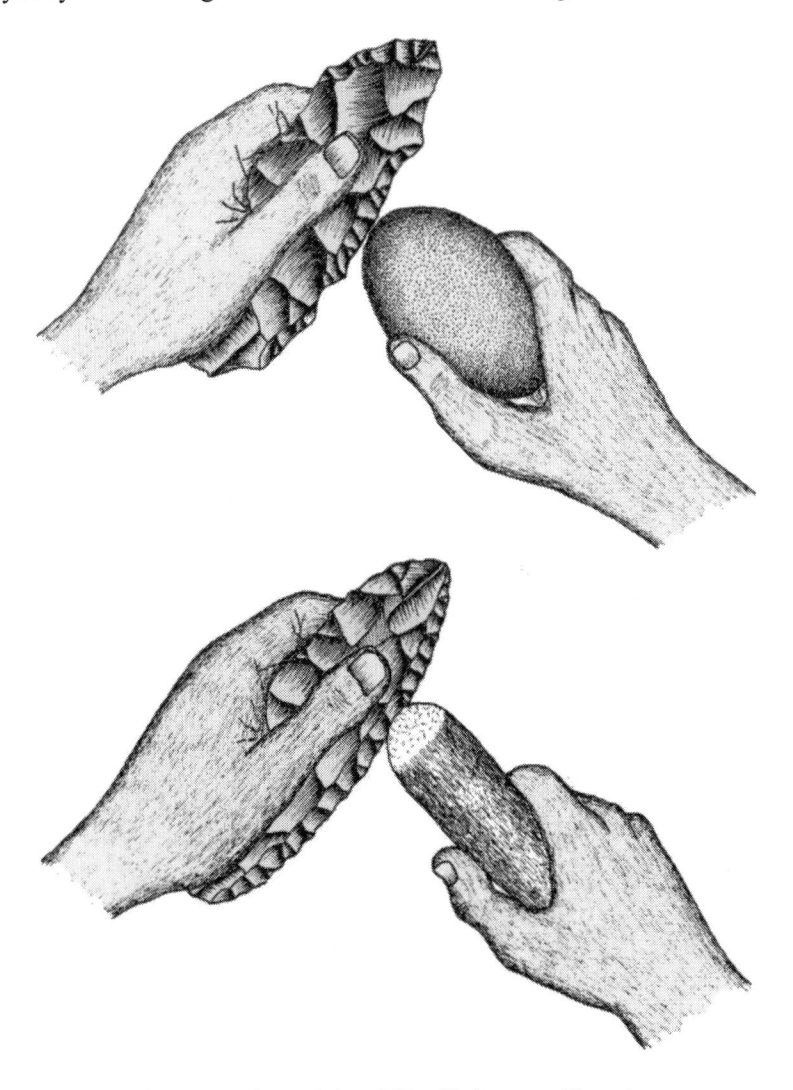

Buck Percussion Flakes Flint Knives to Give Away.

River Wolf managed to get his forty arrows in his quiver. There were flint-tipped and wood-tipped arrows. The wood points consisted of a simple foreshaft that was pointed on both ends. One end fit in the river cane mainshaft of the arrow, and these arrows were ideal for deer hunting because they could fit between the ribs and penetrated deeply. Some were barbed, while most of them were barbless.

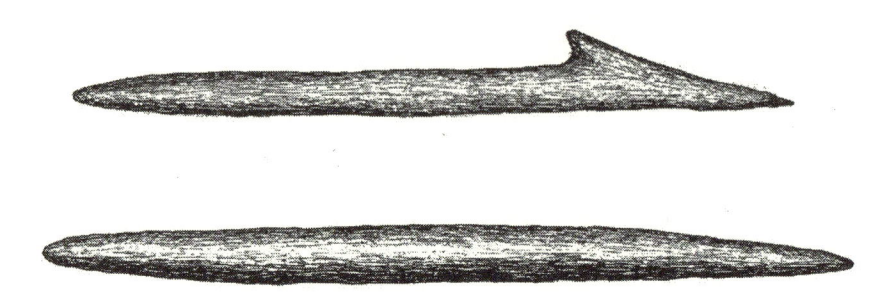

Wooden Arrowheads. Top: Barbed. Bottom: Barbless.

Finally, the long drought ended, and a massive thunderstorm brought plenty of much-needed rain. River Wolf and Redbird lay in bed as it rained all night. Inside, River Wolf was falling in love with her, but he chose to deny it. He was afraid to love again.

Redbird could sense his feelings towards her, but could do little. One night, in the heat of the moment, they made passionate love. They held each other all night. The next morning, Redbird told him that she had not drank any wild yam tea.

"But what if you become pregnant?" he asked, shocked.

"I want to have your child," she said.

"I already told you! I cannot marry you! What if I get killed in battle?"

"I know, and I don't expect you to take care of me."

"Of course I will take care of my child's mother. I wouldn't be a man if I didn't!" With that, River Wolf left angrily. He felt that she had tricked him. He went for a walk outside the village to decide what to do. As he walked down the path, he saw a person lying in the trail with arrows protruding out of his body.

He investigated and saw that it was his best friend Buck. He had been stationed there to watch for enemies. River Wolf returned to the village with the grim news. The Shaman and his assistants came and performed the burial of Buck, but River Wolf was too overwhelmed to be there.

He left the village and walked north over the mountains for a full day. He found a cave at sunset and slept in it. He was awakened in the night by the growling of a mountain lion that evidently had lived there and was returning home. River Wolf was too angry to be afraid. He picked up his axe and threw it, somehow striking the cougar on the head, killing him instantly. Then he cut its throat and went back to sleep.

The next morning, the buzzards feeding on the dead cougar awakened him. He chased them away and butchered the cat, cooked it and ate as much as he could. All the while his head was full of sad thoughts about his dead family and friends.

After two days, he had eaten every bit left of the mountain lion that was good, and he went hunting. Then he heard a noise that sounded like human footsteps. With his axe ready, he stalked the potential enemy.

River Wolf found a trail with fresh footprints and followed it. He was determined to kill this person if he was the enemy he hoped it would be. Then he heard talking, and it seemed to be getting closer to him. He stepped off of the trail, and waited in the woods, ready.

Two hunters appeared, and River Wolf recognized them as Cherokee. "Hello," he called.

The two hunters stopped, ready for anything.

"I am a friend," said River Wolf. "My name is River Wolf. I am Cherokee."

"Hello, River Wolf," said the older hunter, "I am Birch Trunk, and this is my son, Frog. Where are you from?"

"Eagle Peak. I was originally from Birch Mountain. My family is dead."

"I am sorry," said Birch Trunk, "We are from Dogwood Creek."

"The new capital?"

"Yes. You look so very tired! Why don't you come with us to Dogwood Creek and rest up with us?"

"Alright," said River Wolf, indifferent to where he went.

On the way north to Dogwood Creek, they shot a deer and River Wolf carried it over his shoulders with them to the village. They entered the palisade.

"They are making the council house into the new heptagon," said Birch Trunk. "See them working on top of the largest mound?" Birch Trunk pointed.

With minimal interest, River Wolf nodded, "Yes."

They arrived at Birch Trunk's lodge and Birch Trunk said, "This is my wife, Fishbone, and my little girl, Fawn."

"It's nice to meet you," said River Wolf.

Fishbone nodded and smiled in return. Fawn was timid, and was mostly hidden behind her mother. But she watched River Wolf.

River Wolf helped them prepare the deer, and then they ate a hearty meal. River Wolf tried to help out as much as he could. He knew that if he were idle, he would only have morbid reflections of his dead family and friends.

Fawn began to like River Wolf, because he made her a little soapstone deer. She loved it, and instantly overcame her shyness. The little three-cycle-old girl began following him around, constantly asking him questions. River Wolf taught her about the herbs of the forest, how he trapped squirrels, and how to put fish in a stupor with the crushed black walnut rinds. She watched him as he knapped flint arrowheads for her father.

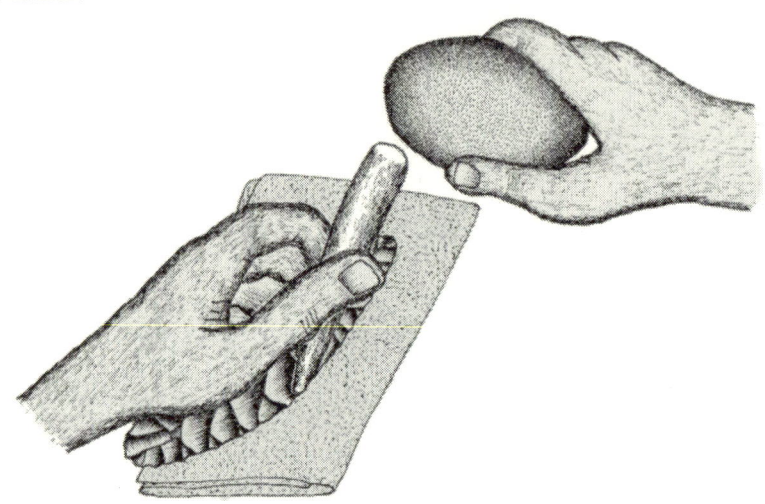

River Wolf Demonstrates Indirect Percussion for Making Arrowheads.

Fishbone and Birch Trunk were delighted that she had a new friend. She had been shy all of her life, and seldom played with other children of the village. River Wolf enjoyed the time he spent with her because it was like having a family once again.

He stayed with them at Dogwood Creek for two weeks, and then he began to feel like he should return to Eagle Peak to be with his brother. He bade farewell to his new friends.

Fawn was in tears. "Why do you have to go?" she cried.

"My brother needs me. I wish I could stay. You be a good girl and obey your parents."

"I don't want you to leave!"

"I know you don't, and I wish I could stay. It has to be this way." He hugged her, said goodbye to her parents and left. He was sad about leaving her. She reminded him of his son. By the late afternoon, he arrived at the cave where he had stayed before, and spent the night there.

The next morning, he woke up and resumed the long walk to Eagle Peak. His thoughts were on his dead family. He thought of Buck. They had been best friends all their lives. It didn't seem to matter though.

He heard noises in the woods. Then a black bear appeared ahead of him. The bear grunted and charged at him. River Wolf stood his ground, and when the bear got close to him, he jumped at the bear. The bear in turn jolted to a stop and retreated. It was common knowledge that black bears did "bluff charges," but seldom attacked a full-grown person.

After he gained some distance from the bear, he shot a turkey and camped at a stream. He ate as much of the turkey as he could, and went to sleep. The next morning, he was up and on his way early. It rained hard for most of the morning. He continued walking all day and into the night. Right at dark, he reached the top of the ridge and could see the fires of Eagle Peak below. He walked down the large ridge and slipped on a moist, moss-covered log. After getting up, he started walking again, this time more alert for slick spots.

He arrived at the village and entered the palisade. Now, he was feeling awkward at the thought of going to Redbird's lodge. What if she was angry with him? After thinking about it, he decided he didn't care if she was. *She* had tricked *him*. So, to her lodge he went. "Hello, Redbird," he called.

"Who is there?" she asked, sounding like he had just awakened her.

"It's River Wolf."

"River Wolf! We thought you were dead!" She ran out and hugged him with tears in her eyes.

Annoyed, River Wolf said, "Well, I'm not."

"Come inside, let's go to bed. It's late."

The next morning, River Wolf went to see his brother.

"I thought you were killed in the forest!" said Panther.

"I went north to Dogwood Creek after I found Buck dead. I just got back last night."

"Next time you leave, please let me know. I was worried sick!"

"I am sorry." Then River Wolf went out hunting. He had ventured far from Eagle Peak, alone. Suddenly Yuchi and Muskogee warriors surrounded him. They bound his hands behind his back with rawhide.

They gagged him with a piece of bloody deer hide so he couldn't warn his people. Then they threw him on the ground and left, leaving one young Yuchi warrior to guard him. River Wolf assumed that they were off on another raid against Eagle Peak.

He tried to work his hands free when the warrior wasn't looking, but was not successful. They had wet the rawhide and now, as it dried, it was shrinking tight. It cut off the circulation to his hands.

Late in the afternoon, the warriors returned with two scalps on their belts. The first thing their leader did when he saw River Wolf tied up, was walk up to him and kick him in the stomach. River Wolf could understand parts of what they said, though he didn't let on about it. It seemed that they had lost one of their own during the raid, and now they were taking it out on him.

They picked him up and they started walking south. River Wolf knew they would be followed, so he tried to slow them down by walking slowly. Then one of the warriors behind him struck him hard in the back with a club, muttering something that seemed to mean, "Hurry up!"

The party decided to split up and River Wolf went with the man who had hit him. He was terribly thirsty, but they deliberately stayed away from the river so they would not be discovered. Finally, they arrived at a stream and they threw River Wolf on the ground. Then they drank their fills, and dragged River Wolf to the water. When he lowered his head to drink, they pushed his face under the water. They did this repeatedly. The Yuchis seemed to enjoy this sport, and they even kicked him in the stomach while his head was submerged. When they let him raise his head, he coughed while they laughed at him.

Suddenly an arrow struck one of them and he fell with a gasp. The others immediately left, knowing their pursuers had caught up with them. They left River Wolf behind at the stream. His brother, Panther appeared out of the woods along with several other Cherokees. Panther cut the rawhide that bound River Wolf's hands.

"They took my bow and arrows," said River Wolf.

"Can you make it back to the village?" asked Panther.

"I think so."

"Go on then, we will catch up to those pieces of rat dung."

They parted ways, and River Wolf silently prayed that his brother would return alive. On his way back, he saw a single Yuchi warrior – perhaps a spy. He picked up a rock and threw it at the enemy's head. The warrior fell with a gasp. River Wolf ran up to him, and just as the enemy was starting to get up, River Wolf grabbed the bloody rock and finished the job with another swift blow to the head. The enemy warrior kicked and flailed about for a while, and River Wolf stole his knife, club, a bow and a quiver with around thirty arrows.

He killed a deer and began carrying it back to the village over his shoulder. He traveled along the river, knowing the enemies would not be seen in such an obvious place. His back hurt him badly from the blow of the war club, but he bore the pain, determined to make the trip productive.

He arrived at Eagle Peak and carried the deer to Redbird's lodge. The two butchered it and set it out to dry. Redbird fed him a meal of deer meat and mushrooms that had grown from the rain.

"Will you marry me?" asked Redbird.

"I told you, no!" retorted River Wolf. "I don't love you." Inside he knew he was lying, but also he was resentful. He felt very guilty as well, for treating her so badly. "I really don't love you."

Redbird had an expression of despair, but didn't say anymore on the subject.

They went to bed, and Redbird rubbed River Wolf's sore back until he fell asleep. The next day, around noon, Panther and the other warriors – one-by-one – returned from their excursion.

Panther came and visited River Wolf and presented him with a scalp. "This is for you," he said, "It belonged to the man whom I saw trying to drown you in the stream."

"Thank you, Panther – are you hungry?"

"Yes, I am very hungry."

River Wolf and Redbird made some venison for Panther. "Tell me your war story," requested River Wolf.

"We went running after the people who had you as a captive. They were running, and then they decided they had lost us, and slowed down. But we were hot on their trail and overtook them while they were walking leisurely. They are all now on the trail, dead. By the way, I recovered your bow and arrows, but couldn't locate your knife. The bow and arrows are at Waterfowl's lodge."

"I have a knife," said River Wolf. "I killed a Yuchi spy on my way back here. I took his bow and arrows and his knife. It's a really nice knife, but unusual. See it?" He pointed to it.

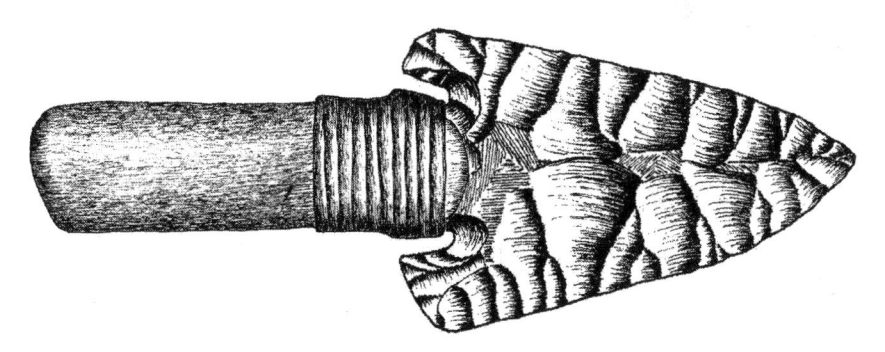

Knife in Wooden Handle.

Panther got up and looked at it. "That's a good knife! Not local. I wonder where it came from. Well, when I finish eating, we can go and get your bow and arrows. I hope you don't mind the Yuchi blood on your quiver."

"Not at all! In fact, the more, the better! Thanks also for the scalp."

Panther finished his meal of venison and then they went to Waterfowl's lodge to get the bow and arrows. Redbird went to the river to fill her water bottle. She heard a twig snap and turned to look. She saw a Yuchi stalking her. She let out a shrill scream, dropped the water bottle and ran back to the village.

Panther and River Wolf heard the scream and they ran to the river, accompanied by other warriors. The Yuchi warrior got away, and they never caught up with him. When they returned, they saw the broken water bottle that Redbird had dropped.

Many people were building lodges outside the palisade, while others were working on the new, larger palisade that would surround all of the new lodges. Panther and River Wolf began building a lodge for them to share.

The new palisade was showing much progress, and the villagers eagerly helped the refugees from Birch Mountain in their work, fed them, and provided lodging for them. The lodges of the village were so overcrowded, even the hothouses were cleared of the items stored inside them and used to house people.

Redbird began molding another water bottle from some clay she'd gotten from a trader.

"Don't you have better things to do?" snapped River Wolf. Although he didn't want to mention it, her working with clay reminded him of White Feather.

"The bottle I dropped was my only one," replied Redbird. "I am replacing it." She worked on it for most of the day, and then wrapped it in a deerskin to dry slowly. In a few days, it was dry and she fired it by digging a shallow pit and covering it with dry grass and twigs. She set it ablaze and, after it cooled, she had a new water bottle.

Redbird missed her moon time and she was suspicious that she was pregnant. But she told nobody because she wanted River Wolf to forget about it. She regretted not using the wild yam tea, and feared he would be angry if he found out. She had foolishly assumed that River Wolf would eventually marry her, but now she saw that he was firm in his decision not to. His heart had become frozen with the loss of his family. Now she thought of using mistletoe to abort the baby, but decided to wait to see if he would ever change his mind.

River Wolf forgot all about it; it had been more than a moon since she told him about not using the tea. He assumed she was not pregnant, or she would tell him if she was. He also decided to not trust her in this way anymore. He didn't want to marry, and he didn't want to bring any more children to raise in this unfair world.

River Wolf did, however, like children, and spent his free time carving toys for them. He made a soapstone fox for Linden's grandson, Fox Tail. Soon, the other children of the village coveted that little fox, and River Wolf was compelled to make toys for each of them as well.

Usually, he made toy blowguns and darts, and bows and arrows for the little boys, and stone beads, pendants and gorgets for the little girls to wear on necklaces.

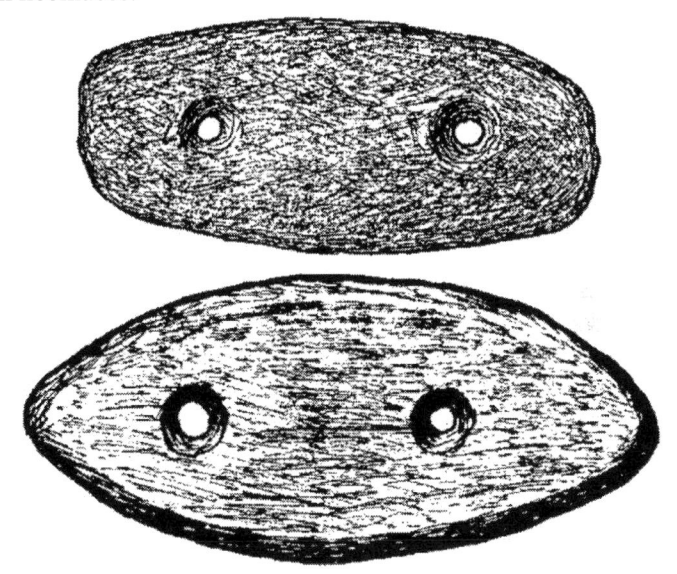

Stone Gorgets for the Little Girls.

But he also made plenty of animal figurines because the children sometimes fought over the few he made. It seemed that they were learning some bad behaviors from the battles that their parents were fighting. The children who were disobedient were scratched on their bodies by their clansmen, and the embarrassment of having the scars from them was their punishment.

This saddened River Wolf, and he made more and more toy figurines, to the point that almost every child in the village had one. Sometimes their parents would help River Wolf and Panther build their lodge, but River Wolf always told them it was not necessary.

He loved spending time with the children, and teaching them how to hunt while their parents worked on the palisade. River Wolf was rapidly gaining popularity among the villagers. They liked people who were nice to their children.

Redbird observed this, and was hopeful that River Wolf would change his mind and go ahead and marry her. Then she could be honest with him and tell him she carried his child.

River Wolf and Panther went out hunting one day and came upon a war party of five. They saw each other at the same time, and the Yuchis charged at them. River Wolf and Panther ran for their lives. The Yuchis followed them.

River Wolf and Panther split up and, while Panther went on ahead, River Wolf hid in a tall pine tree. He could smell the odor of the pines while he waited. The war party passed beneath River Wolf, and he noticed that Winged Rattlesnake Chief was their leader. When the war party passed, River Wolf climbed back down and followed them. He saw Panther fighting the war party. River Wolf shot arrows at three of them, killing them. Panther killed another one.

Winged Rattlesnake Chief and Panther were now engaged in one-on-one combat with their clubs and knives. They fought for a long time, while River Wolf ran to assist his brother. Before River Wolf arrived, Winged Rattlesnake Chief stabbed Panther in the ribs with his flint knife.

River Wolf saw his brother lying there and was filled with more rage and hatred than he had ever felt before. He threw his axe at Winged Rattlesnake Chief. It struck his head and knocked him down. But his buffalo horn headdress had cushioned the blow. Winged Rattlesnake Chief was getting back up, but River Wolf was on top of him.

Axe with Grown Handle.
Based on Leftwich 1970 & Mails 1992.

Winged Rattlesnake Chief grabbed the axe River Wolf had thrown, and swung it at River Wolf, trying to hit him in the head. It wasn't a direct hit, but River Wolf fell down next to Panther. Panther grimaced in pain while pulling the bloody knife from his chest. He started to give it to River Wolf. But he had no more strength left and died with his arm outstretched, clasping the knife.

River Wolf took the knife from his brother's lifeless hand. Winged Rattlesnake Chief was getting up with the axe planning to finish him off. He swung the axe at River Wolf. River Wolf caught the axe with his hand and stabbed him in the abdomen with the bloody knife. Winged Rattlesnake Chief sank back down with a groan. River Wolf stabbed him repeatedly until the flint knife broke in Winged Rattlesnake Chief's ribs. He couldn't believe what he had done, and lay there, for a long time, numb. Winged Rattlesnake Chief was dead. Panther's final act had saved River Wolf. *Thank you, Panther.*

He said a prayer for his dead brother, but that didn't stop the grief. He slowly made it to his feet and climbed down a cliff and got to the river. His head hurt. He saw a waterfall – the same one he had gone down during his Vision Quest so many cycles before. He visualized his broken canoe there, still lodged on the boulder. But it was gone.

Suddenly, River Wolf felt a powerful blow to his chest. He looked down and saw an arrow deep in his ribs. He collapsed and the Yuchis emerged from the brush, scalped him, and shoved off in canoes they had hidden. River Wolf surrendered to his fate, as he lay there in agony. He was afraid of what death would be like. He thought this was a peaceful place to die, the sound of Thunder River, the smell of the pines, and the mist from the waterfall. He heard the distant howling of the Wolf, and lay there until his consciousness, and his very life, faded away.

Everything was dark, except for a bright and beautiful light ahead of him. He saw the Wolf Spirit. The Wolf said, *Follow me...* He was walking the Path of Souls, or the Milky Way. As he followed this River of Death, his fear and pain left him.

Oh Long Being, nighttime has come upon my life. I have always been close to you. You have constantly guided my way and protected me. In life I have followed your River of Life. Now in death I follow your River of Death across the night sky, to the Darkening Land of the West. I bring with me the stories of my people - my mother and father, my first and second wives, and my son who died much too young, and my friends. I will tell these stories so that these fine people may not be forgotten. How I truly loved them all. Had I heeded my father's warnings, they would still be alive. I understand that I do not deserve to rest among them in the afterlife, or even have a proper burial. I am ashamed of my cowardly neglect. I will now tell you all of my stories...

River Wolf told all he could recall, from time's beginning, trying to include every detail. As he spoke, he traveled the River of Death in the night sky. He passed the star, Sirius – the Home of Agis'egwa, the Great Female Animal. He continued his story as he passed the star, Antares – the Home of Wa'hyaya', the Great Mother Wolf.

Then Elk Antler appeared. *My dear child, I look back and see that it was I who was wrong. You were but one person against thousands of enemies. Nothing you could have done would have protected your family. It was too much for you to save them by yourself. You have walked the path of a true human being. People for thousands of cycles will see the stone and shell carvings you made. They will someday be the only remaining testimony to our people's way of life on Earth. The rest will only crumble to dust. Through you, my seed will not be erased from the Earth. I love you and I am proud that you are my son.*

River Wolf was confused. *But my son and my pregnant wife were killed!*

You had a daughter with Redbird. She was born after you entered the Darkening Land. Her name is Mushroom. Our descendants will live on through her until the end of time.

Then River Wolf saw Beaver Pelt. She was more beautiful than she was the day he had married her. She was then accompanied by White Feather, Snow Bear, Squirrel Fur, Sparrow, Turtle Shell, Eagle Medicine, Panther, Buck and everyone else he had known and loved in his lifetime. Everybody seemed to have a glowing happiness and peace. A lush green valley appeared around them. A river of clear cool water flowed through the valley. There were towering mountains and green foothills teeming with game, and fragrant herbs and vegetables. River Wolf could hear the sounds of the birds, the calls of elks, and the gentle roar of the river. It was the most beautiful and peaceful place, beyond what River Wolf had ever imagined. He had finally arrived home.

Thunder River Falls.

Author's Note:

Writing a fiction story has its challenges, and this story was no exception. In doing so, it was my intention to breathe life into ancient cultures, in a most respectful way. I found it particularly challenging to write the point of view a fictitious character whose tribe was at war with others, without casting some of the characters in a bad light. It was never my intention to mock anybody, and I genuinely hope this story preserves the honor and dignity every person and/or group of people deserves.

There are three Native American tribes that are the primary focus of this book. These are the Cherokee, the Yuchi and the Creek Indians. But a certain tribe was often called by many different names by different peoples. There were the names they called themselves, the names that other tribes called them, and the names we commonly use for them today. For the sake of simplicity, in this story, I am calling the Cherokees and Yuchis by these names we commonly know them as today.

The Muskogee tribe is what the Creek tribe was originally known as, and they were speakers of the Muskhogean language. So, in this novel, the Creek Indians are being referred to as the Muskogee. Early English traders called the Muskogee the Ocheese Creek Indians, named after Ocheese Creek, which was their name for the Ocmulgee River, where a Muskogee village had once been located. Eventually, the name Ocheese Creek was shortened to Creek, which is commonly used today for the Muskogee Indians.

In ancient times, the people we call the Cherokees referred to themselves as the *"Ani-Yunwiya,"* which in Cherokee means "Principal People" or "Primary People." The name, "Cherokee" probably came from the word, *"Chalaque,"* which was the name of a territory that was visited by De Soto and his men in the year, 1540. Their guides, who spoke Muskhogean, identified the people of the mountains with the word, *"Tciloki"* which meant, "They speak a foreign language." *"Chalaque"* probably is a variation of the Muskhogean word. Many variations of this word were used as the name for these people, and "Cherokee" is the form that eventually was dominant.

The Yuchis called themselves the *"Tsoyaha Yuchi,"* which means, "Children of the Sun from a Faraway Place." *"Tsoyaha"* means "Children of the Sun" but their neighbors rejected this implied divinity, and simply called them *"Yuchi,"* which is used today. The word, *"Yuchi"* in their language meant "Faraway People." To the Cherokees, they were known as the *"Aniyuji"* or *"Aniyutsi." "Ani"* is a Cherokee word that means, "people," and *"Yuji,"* and *"Yutsi"* are the Cherokee pronunciations of the word *"Yuchi.* The Cherokees' word for the Muskogee Indians was *"Anigusa."*

The war between the Muskogees, Yuchis and the Cherokees for the most part ended years after River Wolf died. There is an old legend that says the area of Northern Georgia was under dispute, which was eventually resolved by a "ball game" between the Cherokees and the Muskogees. The Cherokees were said to have won this game. However, often war was referred to as a "ball game" since the ball game was often called "the little brother of war." It is therefore unclear whether they settled the matter with a real war or just a ball game. "Hit and run" raids were always common between tribes, and the Cherokees and Muskogees had an ongoing on-again/off-again relationship.

The Muskogees formed an alliance with the Yuchis and, eventually, the Yuchis migrated to the southeastern edge of the Appalachian Mountains, in the northeastern area of the Muskogee territory. The Muskogees were thought to have arranged this, so that they would be better protected from Cherokee attacks.

One common misconception about the Indians is about the practice of scalping. Many say that the Europeans taught this practice to the Indians. This rumor was started by the "hippie" generation, and is entirely untrue. Instead, the practice of scalping did indeed originate with the Indians of the Eastern United States.

The precise locations of the Cherokee villages of Birch Mountain and Eagle Peak are not known. These fictitious villages in this story are depicted as being located somewhere in the areas of eastern Tennessee and western North Carolina, in the Appalachian Mountains. It is thought the Cherokees could have migrated from the northwest into this area between 940 AD and 1,100 AD.

However, due to significant migration and trade during prehistoric times, it can be difficult at the least to say with any degree of certainty, which Indian tribes were located in a given location during prehistoric times. In my reference library are numerous books and, in these different publications, opinions differ (often greatly) from each other regarding these questions. So, consequently, there is a very good chance that this novel might be inaccurate, especially with what tribes occupied which locations.

It is unusual for a ten-year-old boy to have the skills needed to be carving effigy pipes, but Green Rock (River Wolf) had a divine talent. His fellow clansmen recognized this gift, and encouraged him in his career as an artist. Green Rock's father, Elk Antler – like probably most fathers in that situation – wanted to see him become a warrior. But discipline was the responsibility of the child's mother and her relatives. Cherokee kinship was a matrilineal-based organization. By custom, Elk Antler had no say in his son's behavior.

The drunken flint knapper, Stone Spear, brewed his drink from wild grapes that grew in the land to the south. I have never heard of the Cherokees brewing alcoholic beverages in prehistoric times, but since Stone Spear was once a traveling trader, I decided it was possible that he could have learned this recipe during his trading career. The Cherokees did brew a kind of beer from persimmons during historic times. Today, in South America, the natives still brew alcoholic beverages from various local fruits. So, it is possible it could have existed, albeit unlikely.

Every morning the ancient Cherokees went outside – or to the river – and sang the Morning Song, while facing the rising sun. They would often bathe in the river, no matter how cold it was. This ritual was performed to give thanks for the new day that was beginning. The Cherokees perceived a new day beginning at sunrise, and not at midnight.

The Cherokees had seven major ceremonies – six were performed each year, and the seventh took place only every seventh year. In this novel, I used the word "cycle" when referring to "year."

The ancients had no written language, and the dates of the ceremonies were based on observing the heavens. On the surface, the Cherokee calendar appears to be a lunar calendar. However, if this were true, the ceremonies would rarely have taken place at the same times of the year. The Cherokee calendar was a solilunar calendar – that is, it relies on both the Sun and moon. The Sun was used to keep track of the season, and the moon dictated the month. Every few years there would be a year with thirteen months. It should be noted that the Cherokee new moon was actually observed when the first crescent appeared, usually one to three days after the dark of the moon.

The Cherokee New Year began in the month of October. The ceremony – called the Great New Moon Ceremony – took place during the October new moon (the first new moon after the northern autumnal equinox, and when the Pleiades star cluster sets near the Sun). The Cherokees believe that the Earth was created during this time of year.

Ten days after the October new moon was the Friends Making Ceremony, in which friends and spouses settled their differences. The focus on this ceremony was bonding and love for each other. It also served the purpose of setting things right between the people and the Honored Spirits.

The Bounding Bush Ceremony took place during the first moon of the fall season – usually in September or November. This was a nonreligious ceremony that functioned similarly to our Thanksgiving holiday. It was the last major ceremony that took place before the winter set in.

The First New Moon of Spring Ceremony took place in March, when the new grass began to appear. The sacred fires were doused and rekindled, and the people thanked the Honored Spirits for the rebirth of the world that Spring brought.

The Green Corn Ceremony was held in August, when the first of the new crop was fit to eat. Nobody ate of the new crop until after this ceremony ended.

The Ripe Corn Ceremony occurred in late September, and was the last ceremony of the Cherokee year. It was performed to celebrate the harvest of the corn crops. Few Indian ceremonies lasted into modern times, but this one has. The reason this ceremony has survived is because it is not a religious ceremony that caused a religious conflict, as more and more of the Cherokees converted to Christianity. Many powwows take place this time of year, and they are remnants of this tradition.

And, finally, the Uku Dance took place every seventh year, in place of the Great New Moon Ceremony (in October). This was a ceremony of great rejoicing and giving thanks, led by the Uku (The principal Chief of the Cherokee Nation). In addition to the seven ceremonies described, the Cherokees had minor observances each new moon of the year.

It was unusual for a person who had not achieved his status as a man to have his family build him a lodge. But Green Rock's Vision came to him very late in his life, and his family and friends built him his lodge because he was impatient, and frustrated at not having his Vision. He was also kept extra busy providing meat for his family since his father was dead. Traditionally, a woman owned the lodge, and when they married, the new husband moved in with her. In many cases, a young man would build a lodge prior to marriage to show he could provide for a wife. The lodge typically became the wife's property upon marriage. After Green Rock received his adult name, "River Wolf," he married and his lodge became his wife's property.

River Wolf went with the trader, Bald Eagle. They portaged, and went over land for a distance, and then put in on the Coosawattee River in northern Georgia. They followed it down to the Coosa River. Southeast of what is now Gadsden, Alabama, they went up Big Canoe Creek – that is, after visiting Loner and getting flint. In this novel, the village of Rattlesnake Creek was on Big Canoe Creek. They portaged again over the ridge to a creek that led to the Black Warrior River.

The large Muskogee village – called Good Medicine in this novel – is known today as Moundville, where the Mound State Monument is located in western Alabama. The monolithic axe that River Wolf carved for Jaguar, the Shaman there at Good Medicine is an actual artifact that was found at the Moundville site. Also found there were the two engraved round stone tablets that, in this story, were owned by River Wolf's brother, Panther. In actuality, Moundville may not have been a Muskogee village. It could have very well been Chickasaw or another tribe; we can never know for sure.

From there, they went down the Black Warrior River to the Alabama River. They followed the Alabama River to Mobile Bay and headed east down the beach, after going around the narrow peninsula where Fort Morgan Historical Site is today. After the shark killed Bald Eagle, River Wolf met Medicine Wolf and his shy daughter, Sand Dollar, at their home on what is now Dauphin Island. Medicine Wolf helped River Wolf return to Birch Mountain afterwards.

It was taboo for a person to marry another of the same clan. River Wolf, of the Bird Clan, married Beaver Pelt, of the Long Hair Clan. Shortly afterwards, she died of an ectopic pregnancy. To ease his best friend's grief, Buck took River Wolf to see the giant metropolis known today as Cahokia.

They traveled the Hiwassee River and, from there, River Wolf and Buck followed the Tennessee River to the Ohio River near what is now Paducah, Kentucky. They followed the Ohio down to the Mississippi, and went up the Mississippi River.

When they reached what is present day St. Louis, Missouri, they went up Sun Creek (now known as Cahokia Creek) to the metropolis of Cahokia. Cahokia is located in Illinois, just across the Mississippi River from St. Louis. They visited Cahokia at the time before it was abandoned – due to their overuse of natural resources, and the lack of food that resulted from this.

They left in a hurry; so as not to become involved in the wars that Cahokia had endured before it was abandoned. Cahokia was the largest aboriginal village ever in North America, and some people now estimate that this city, and its outlying suburbs, could have once supported a population of 40,000 or more people. The well-known Monk's Mound at Cahokia was the largest Indian mound in North America, measuring 1,000 feet long, 700 feet wide, and 100 feet high. This mound, like all of the other Indian mounds, was built one basketful of dirt at a time. Cahokia reached its apex at around 1,200 AD, but was abandoned by the time the Europeans arrived.

After leaving the area, River Wolf and Buck followed the Big Muddy River (the Mississippi) towards the coast. They met up with the two Calusa traders, and headed down the river to what is now New Orleans. Then the four went out to sea, heading southwest until they were washed overboard in the hurricane.

River Wolf awakened on what is now called Matagorda Island, Texas, not knowing where he was. He went to the west side of the island and saw land. After finding a crude Karankawa dugout canoe, he paddled into San Antonio Bay, and then up the Guadalupe River. He met up with several bands of local cannibals, and kept following the Guadalupe upstream until he reached the canyon between what is now New Braunfels, Texas and Canyon Lake, Texas.

He met up with the Payayas, a Coahuiltecan band, and lived with them for ten years. The Payayas' territory was centered around what is now San Pedro Springs, in San Antonio, Texas, but they were nomadic, and wandered over a very large area of Central and Southwest Texas. After hearing about one of the Payayas plotting to kill him, River Wolf left that group of people and followed the San Antonio River back to San Antonio Bay, and Matagorda Island. There he met up with the trader, Large Fish, who guided him back to Mobile Bay.

This is where River Wolf met up with his long-lost brother and Sand Dollar on Dauphin Island. They returned home, and Sparrow helped Sand Dollar overcome her shyness by teaching her the Cherokee language and way of life.

River Wolf married White Feather – the infant he had rescued from the fire when he was a child. They had a son together, and another child on the way, when the war between the Cherokees, Muskogees and Yuchis began to heat up.

Birch Mountain was burned to the ground in an attack and, soon after, River Wolf's family was killed in an ambush. He became a warrior, and died in combat. After his death, Redbird gave birth to his daughter, Mushroom. Because of this, any modern person who has Cherokee blood in them could fancy themselves being River Wolf's descendant. I believe in after-death experiences (and so do many Native Americans), therefore, I wrote of River Wolf's entry into the afterlife.

All of my life, I have been interested in the Indian way of life. I carved stone and knapped arrowheads and spear points out of flint. I also made bows and arrows, atlatls and darts, and axes. I have made some pottery, baskets, and shelters like the one River Wolf built in Chapter 14.

My adopted father, who was part Cherokee and Sioux, always encouraged me in my Indian crafts. Sitting Bull was his great-great grandfather. Much of my understanding of these different traditional primitive skills I learned from my adopted father, and I have diligently attempted to use this knowledge to help breathe life into this story.

I have tried my best to make this novel as interesting, entertaining, accurate and true-to-life as possible. Writing this novel for me was a beginning of a journey towards understanding the traditional Cherokee religion and lifestyle. I hope you have enjoyed this novel, and have learned as much from it as I did while I was writing it. The Cherokees were (and still are) by nature very modest and polite. Their children were well-mannered, without receiving much discipline from their parents. Today, many people are rediscovering ancient religions. This is commonly referred to as the New Age movement. Many Cherokees today prefer to call it the Old Wisdom. May the Cherokee way of life never be forgotten!

Historic Period Cherokee Style Log Cabin.

Incised Blackware Pottery Beaker – Representing a Horned Rattlesnake.
Southern Appalachians.

Redrawn from Holmes 1898.

References & Suggested Reading

Access Genealogy 2021: *Creek Clans*, on Access Genealogy Website. Retrieved December 3rd, 2021. https://accessgenealogy.com/native/creek-clans.htm

Adair 1775a: *History of the American Indians* by James Adair, 1775. Second reprint, Blue & Gray Press, 1971.

Adair 1775b: *Out of the Flame: Cherokee Beliefs & Practices of the Ancients,* by James Adair, 1775 (reprinted in 1998).

Aid 2009: "Monolithic Axes of the United States," by Toney Aid, 2009, *Prehistoric American* Vol. XLIII

Allely & Hamm 1999: *Encyclopedia of Native American Bows, Arrows & Quivers Volume 1 – Northeast, Southeast, and Midwest*, by Steve Allely and Jim Hamm, 1999, Bois d' Arc Press.

Allely & Hamm 2002: *Encyclopedia of Native American Bows, Arrows & Quivers Volume 2 – Plains & Southwest*, by Steve Allely and Jim Hamm, 2002, Bois d' Arc Press.

Anderson 1989-1990: *Indian Artifacts of South Texas*, by Tim Anderson, 1989, second edition, 1990.

Anderson 2001a: *Arrowheads & Blades of South Texas*, by Tim Anderson, 2001, World Flintknapping Society.

Anderson 2001b: *Flintknapping Secrets*, by Tim Anderson, 2001, World Flintknapping Society.

Anderson 2004: *Arrowheads of South Texas*, by Tim Anderson, 2004.

Anderson 2006: *Indian Artifacts of South & West Texas*, by Tim Anderson 2006, Sweetwater Education Foundation.

Anderson 2014a: *How to Find Indian Artifacts*, by Bill Anderson, 2014.

Anderson 2014b: *The Life of the Cherokee* (Unpublished Manuscript), by Tim Anderson, 2014.

Anderson 2018: *Arrowheads: A Beginner's Guide 8th Edition*, by Tim Anderson, 2018.

Anderson 2019a: *Arrowheads & Artifacts: A Beginner's Guide* by Tim Anderson, 2019.

Anderson 2019b: *Monolithic Axes of the Americas: A Beginner's Guide*, by Tim Anderson, 2019.

Anderson 2020a: *Arrowheads & Artifacts: A Beginner's Guide 11th Edition*, by Tim Anderson, 2020.

Anderson 2020b: *How to Find Indian Artifacts*, by Bill Anderson, Revised Edition 2020.

Anderson 2021a: *Tomahawks & Hatchets: A Beginner's Guide*, by Tim Anderson, 2021.

References & Suggested Reading (continued)

Anderson 2021b: *Indian Pipes & Smoking Practices*, by Tim Anderson, 2021.

Anderson 2021c: *Builders of the Temple Mounds*, by Tim Anderson, 2021.

Anderson 2021d: *The Arrowhead & Relic Fact Book*, by Tim Anderson, 2021.

Anderson 2022: *Native American Bone, Antler & Shell Artifacts*, by Tim Anderson, 2022.

Andrews 1993: *Animal Speak: The Spiritual & Magical Powers of Creatures Great & Small*, by Ted Andrews, 1993, Llewellyn Publishers, Woodbury, Minnesota.

Apples 4 the Teacher: *The Plum Stone Game* – Retrieved November 23rd, 2021. http://www.apples4theteacher.com/native-american/games/hazard/plum-stone.html

Archaeological Analytics 2021: *American Artifacts Blog* – Retrieved November 20th, 2021. https://www.americanartifactsblog.com/blog/spatulate-celt-chickasaw-county-ms

Baldwin 1871: *Ancient America – The "Mound Builders,"* by John D. Baldwin, 1871. Reprinted by Caddo Press. Great information on the early understanding of North American archaeology.

Baldwin 1995: *Tomahawks: "Pipe Axes" of the American Frontier,* by John Baldwin, 1995, Early American Artistry-Trading Company.

Banks 2004: *Plants of the Cherokee,* by William H. Banks, Great Smoky Mountains Association, 2004.

Barnett 1973: *Dictionary of Prehistoric Indian Artifacts of the American Southwest*, by Franklin Barnett, 1973, Northland Press, Flagstaff, AZ.

Barrat 2015: *American Indians, Colonists Had Healthy Appetite for Crabs, Study Shows* by John Barrat, 2015, Smithsonian Insider – Retrieved November 22nd, 2021. https://insider.si.edu/2015/02/american-indians-colonists-healthy-appetite-crabs-study-shows/

Bauer 2013: *Arrowhead Adventures: The Ultimate Guide to Indian Artifact Hunting*, by William Bauer, 2013.

Beauchamp 1901: *Wampum and Shell Articles Used by the New York Indians*, by William M. Beauchamp, 1901, Bulletin of the New York State Museum No. 41, Vol. 8.

Beauchamp 1902: *Horn and Bone Implements of the New York Indians*, by William M. Beauchamp, 1902, Bulletin of the New York State Museum No. 50.

Bell 1958: *Guide to the Identification of Certain American Indian Projectile Points*, by Robert E. Bell, 1958, Special Bulletin No. 1 of the Oklahoma Anthropological Society.

Bell 1960: *Guide to the Identification of Certain American Indian Projectile Points*, by Robert E. Bell, 1960, Special Bulletin No. 2 of the Oklahoma Anthropological Society.

References & Suggested Reading (continued)

Bell 1980: *Oklahoma Indian Artifacts*, by Robert E. Bell, 1980. Stovall Museum, University of Oklahoma.

Bennett 2008: *Authenticating Ancient Indian Artifacts – How to Recognize Reproduction and Altered Artifacts*, by Jim Bennett, 2008, Collector Books. You can further your learning to spot fakes in this excellent book.

Best of Chips, The – Vols. 1-4 – Contains many of the best articles published in *Chips Magazine* – from 1989 – 2011. Can also be purchased with the 3 disc set containing the full archives of *Chips Magazine*. www.flintknappingpublications.com

Bierer 1978: *Indians and Artifacts in the Southeast*, by Bert Worman Bierer, 1978, Published by Bert Worman Bierer, Columbia, South Carolina.

Billard 1989: *The World of the American Indian,* Edited by Jules B. Billard, National Geographic Society, 1989.

Bonewitz 2005: *Rock & Gem* by Ronald Louis Bonewitz, 2005, DK Publishing. A very good identification guide to rocks, minerals and types of gems, with lots of high quality pictures.

Bostrom 2004: *Shark Tooth Weapons* – Retrieved October 21st, 2021. http://lithiccastinglab.com/gallery-pages/2004augustsharksteethpage1.htm

Bradford 1989: *Paleo Points: An Illustrated Chronology of Projectile Points Vol. 1*, by George Bradford, 1989, Caddo Trading Company, Murfreesboro, Arkansas.

Brain & Phillips 1996: *Shell Gorgets: Styles of the Late Prehistoric and Protohistoric Southeast*, by Jeffery P. Brain and Philip Phillips, 1996, Peabody Museum Press, Cambridge, Massachusetts.

Brand 1984: *How to Collect North American Indian Artifacts*, by Robert F. Brand, 1984. Printed by Nacci Printing, Inc.

Brandt & Guzzi 1985: *Indian Crafts*, by Keith Brandt, illustrated by George Guzzi, 1985, Troll Associates.

Brawner 1993: "The Southeastern Monolithic Axe" by Tim Brawner, 1993, *Central States Archaeological Journal*, Vol. 40, October, 1993.

Brehm & Smotherman 1989: *Tennessee's Aboriginal Art: The Monolithic Axe* by H.C. "Buddy" Brehm and Travis Smotherman, 1989, published by Mini-Histories. Has lots of information on authentic monolithic axes, as well as an entertaining account of the story of the Weatherly Monolithic Axe and how it was discovered.

Brehm 1981: *The History of the Duck River Cache* by H.C. "Buddy" Brehm, 1981, Misc. Paper #6, Tennessee Anthropological Association.

Britannica 2021a: *Corn*, Retrieved November 22nd, 2021. https://www.britannica.com/plant/corn-plant

References & Suggested Reading (continued)

Britannica 2021b: *Cahokia, Illinois*, Retrieved December 4th, 2021. https://www.britannica.com/place/Cahokia-Mounds

Brown 1996: *The Spiro Ceremonial Center* Vol. 2, by James A. Brown, 1996, Ann Arbor, Michigan.

Brown 2007: "Sequencing the Braden Style Within Mississippian Art and Iconography," by James A. Brown, 2007, *Ancient Objects and Sacred Realms*, edited by Reilly & Garber, University of Texas Press.

Bull 1931: *Monolithic Axe Found In Connecticut* by Norris L. Bull, 1931, No. 1 of Introductory Series, Connecticut Archaeological Appraisal. Contains photos and a description of a monolithic axe, found in an unusual area for monolithic axes.

Bunzel 1929: *Zuni Katcinas: An Analytical Study*, by Ruth L. Bunzel, 1929, 47th Annual Report of the Bureau of American Ethnology, Washington DC.

Burnett 1945: "The Spiro Mound Collection in the Museum" by E.K. Burnett, 1945, *Contributions of the Museum of the American Indian*, Heye Foundation, Vol. XIV.

Cahokia Mounds Museum Society 2015: *Mound 38: Monks Mound* – Retrieved December 4th, 2021. https://cahokiamounds.org/mound/mound-38-monks-mound/

Cameron 2020a: *North Carolina Projectile Points: Identification & Geographic Range* by Christopher A. Cameron – 2020

Cameron 2020b: *Georgia Projectile Points: Identification & Geographic Range* by Christopher A. Cameron – 2020

Cameron 2020c: *Florida Projectile Points: Identification & Geographic Range* by Christopher A. Cameron – 2020

Cameron 2020d: *Mississippi Projectile Points: Identification & Geographic Range* by Christopher A. Cameron – 2020

Canterbury & Hunt 2017: *Bushcraft First Aid: A Field Guide to Wilderness Emergency Care,* by Dave Canterbury & Jason A. Hunt, 2017, Adams Media.

Capps 1973: *The Indians*, by Benjamin Capps, 1973, Time Life Books.

Capps 1975: *The Great Chiefs*, by Benjamin Capps, 1975, Time Life Books.

Cavendish 1995: *Man, Myth and Magic: The Illustrated Encyclopedia of Mythology, Religion and the Unknown, Vols. 1 – 21*, edited by Richard Cavendish, 1995, Marshall Cavendish, New York, London, Toronto, Sydney.

Charles River Editors (Unknown Year): *The Arawak: The History and Legacy of the Indigenous Natives in South America and the Caribbean*, by Charles River Editors, printed in or before the year 2022.

References & Suggested Reading (continued)

Chickasaw Nation 2021: *Society: Clans*, Retrieved December 3rd, 2021. https://www.chickasaw.net/Our-Nation/Culture/Society.aspx

Clements 1945: *Historical Sketch of the Spiro Mound*, by Forest E. Clements, 1945, Museum of the American Indian, Heye Foundation.

Clottes & Lewis-Williams 1996: *The Shamans of Prehistory: Trance and Magic in the Painted Caves* by Jean Clottes and David Lewis-Williams, 1996, Harry N. Abrams, Inc., Publishers.

Coleman 2013: *Yes, You Can Find Arrowheads*, by Bill Colman, 2013.

Compton 1954 – 1963: "Duck River and Similar Artifacts" by Carl B. Compton, from *Tennessee Archaeologist* Vol. XIV, No. 2; reprinted in *Ten Years of the Tennessee Archaeologist/Selected Subjects*/Vol. II, 1954-1963.

Converse & Parker 1908: "Myths and Legends of the New York State Iroquois," by Harriet Maxwell Converse & Arthur Caswell Parker, *Education Department Bulletin*. University of the State of New York: 10–11.

Copeland 1997: *North American Indian Dances and Rituals*, by Peter F. Copeland 1997, Dover Publications, Inc. Mineola, NY.

Cordes & Diamond 2021: *The Ron Cordes Pocket Guide to Animals/Tracks*, by Ron Cordes with Andy Diamond, 2021, Pocket Guides Publishing

Cox 2009: "Monolithic Axes from the Spiro Site LeFlore County, Oklahoma," by Jim Cox DDS, 2009, *Prehistoric American* Vol. XLIII.

Crawford 2010/2017: *Stone Projectile Points Of The Pacific Northwest* second edition by F. Scott Crawford, 2017 (first edition originally published in 2010).

Crawford 2011: *What Is This Arrowhead? – Your Online Guide to over 57 Different Types of Stone Arrowheads Found Here in the Pacific Northwest* by F. Scott Crawford, 2011.

Crawford 2012: *Clovis: The First Americans?*, by F. Scott Crawford, 2012.

Crawford 2013: *How to Make Your Own Stone Arrowhead*, by F. Scott Crawford, 2013.

Culberson 1993: *Arrowheads and Spear Points in the Prehistoric Southeast – A Guide to Understanding Cultural Artifacts,* by Linda Crawford Culberson, 1993, University Press of Mississippi. Provides good background knowledge of Southeastern Indians.

Cushing 1880: *Zuni Fetishes*, by Frank Hamilton Cushing, 1880, Bureau of American Ethnology.

Davis (Unknown Year): *The Native American Herbalist's Bible: The Complete Native American Herbalist Remedies Encyclopedia*, by Maya Davis.

References & Suggested Reading (continued)

Davis 1983: *Points and Tools of the Texas Indians*, by W. R. (Pete) Davis, 1983, Published by Larry Davis.

Davis 1991: *Prehistoric Artifacts of the Texas Indians*, by Dan R. Davis, Jr. 1991, Pecos Publishing Company.

Dempsey 1984: "Archaeological Techniques," edited by Michael Dempsey, 1984, *Growing Up With Science*, Vol. 1. This 25 volume set is an excellent children's reference regarding the subjects of science and invention.

Dor-Ner & Scheller 1991: *Columbus and the Age of Discovery*, by Zvi Dor-Ner with William Scheller, 1991, William Morrow and Company, Inc. New York.

Downey & Angle 1961: *Texas and the War with Mexico*, by Fairfax Downey, in consultation with Paul M. Angle, 1961, American Heritage Junior Library.

Driver 1961-1969: *Indians of North America*, by Harold E. Driver, 1961, second edition 1969, The University of Chicago Press, Chicago, Illinois and London, England.

Drooker 1992: *Mississippian Village Textiles at Wickliffe*, by Penelope Ballard Drooker, 1992, The University of Alabama Press, Tuscaloosa, Alabama.

Dye 2004: "Art, Ritual, and Chiefly Warfare in the Mississippian World," by David H. Dye, 2004, *Hero, Hawk, and Open Hand – American Indian Art of the Ancient Midwest and South*; Richard F. Townsend, general editor, and Robert V. Sharp, editor. Has very good color photos of a few authentic monolithic axes and lots of related things.

Edey 1972: *The Missing Link*, by Maitland A. Edey, 1972, Time Life Books.

Erdoes & Ortiz 1984: *American Indian Myths and Legends*, Selected and edited by Richard Erdoes, and Alfonso Ortiz, Pantheon Books, 1984.

Ernst 1889: On the Etymology of the Word Tobacco, by A. Ernst, *The American Anthropologist*, 133-142.

Evert 2002: *Rocks, Fossils and Arrowheads*, by Laura Evert, 2002, Northword Books for Young Readers.

Fariello 2009: *Cherokee Basketry: From the Hands of Our Elders*, by M. Anna Fariello, 2011, The History Press, Charleston, South Carolina.

Fariello 2011: *Cherokee Pottery: From the Hands of Our Elders*, by M. Anna Fariello, The History Press, 2011.

Fewkes 1893: *Tusayan Katcinas*, by Jesse Walter Fewkes, 1893. 15th Annual Report of the Bureau of American Ethnology, Washington DC.

Fewkes 1899: *Hopi Katcinas*, by Jesse Walter Fewkes, 1899, 21st Annual Report of the Bureau of American Ethnology, Washington DC.

References & Suggested Reading (continued)

Filbrandt 1997: *Keokuk Axes,* by Bruce Filbrandt, 1997. Printed by Hynek Printing, Richland Center, Wisconsin.

Fink 1946: *Miniature Monolithic Axe* by Paul M. Fink, 1946, *Tennessee Archaeologist* Vol. II No. 4.

Fitzgerald 2009: *Mississippian Pottery: A Tribute to Roy Hathcock,* by Rick Fitzgerald, 2009, Phoenix International, Fayetteville, Arkansas.

Flintknapper.com 2017: *Shark's Tooth Clubs* – Retrieved October 21st, 2021. http://flintknapper.com/SHARKCLUBS/NEW%20SHARK'S%20TOOTH-I-2htm.htm

Fowler 1997: *The Cahokia Atlas* by Melvin Fowler, Second Edition 1997, University of Illinois at Urbana-Champaign, Studies in Archaeology No. 2. A very nice book that contains numerous maps of the Cahokia site and surrounding areas, and interesting information on the Mississippians as well.

Fox 2003: *Arrowheads of the Central Great Plains* by Daniel J. Fox – 2003, Collector Books.

Fulcher 2017: *Marbles Competitions,* by Bob Fulcher, 2017. Tennessee Encyclopedia, Tennessee Historical Society. Retrieved November 23rd, 2021. https://tennesseeencyclopedia.net/entries/marbles-competitions/

Fundaburk & Foreman 1957: *Sun Circles and Human Hands – The Southeastern Indians – Art and Industry,* Edited by Emma Lila Fundaburk, and Mary Douglass Foreman, The University of Alabama Press, Reprinted in 2001. This book is the "bible" of southeastern designs, motifs and background information.

Gallay 2017: *Native American Slavery,* by Alan Gallay, 2017. Mississippi Encyclopedia. Last modified on April 15th, 2018. Retrieved on November 21st, 2021. https://mississippiencyclopedia.org/entries/native-american-slavery/

Garrett & Garrett 1996: *Medicine of the Cherokee – The Way of Right Relationship,* By J. T. Garrett, and Michael Garrett, Bear & Company Publishing, 1996.

Garrett 2001: *Meditations with the Cherokee – Prayers, Songs, and Stories of Healing and Harmony,* By J. T. Garrett, Bear & Company Publishing, 2001.

Garrett 2003: *The Cherokee Herbal: Native Plant Medicine from the Four Directions,* by J. T. Garrett, Bear & Company, 2003.

Garrigue 1851: *Iconographic Encyclopedia of Sciene, Literature and Art,* published by R. Garrigue, 1851. Illustrations reprinted in *The Complete Encyclopedia of Illustration,* in 1996, by Gramercy Books.

Garton 2020: *The Oldest Fabric in North America,* by Christina Garton, 2020, Retrieved March 14th, 2022 from PieceWork Newsletter. https://pieceworkmagazine.com/the-oldest-fabric-in-north-america/

References & Suggested Reading (continued)

Goodman 2005: *Tobacco in History and Culture: An Encyclopedia*, by J. Goodman, 2005, Detroit: Thomson Gale.

Gooley 2014: *The Lost Art of Reading Nature's Signs*, by Tristan Gooley, 2014. Published by The Experiment.

Gottsegen 1940: *Tobacco: A Study of its Consumption in the United States*, by J. J. Gottsegen, 1940.

Gramly 1992: *Prehistoric Lithic Industry at Dover* by R. M. Gramly, 1992, Persimmon Press. Great illustrations of artifacts from Dover, Tennessee.

Gramly 2000: *Guide to the Palaeo-American Artifacts of North America*, by R. M. Gramly, 2000, Persimmon Press.

Gravelle 1994: *Early Hunting Tools: An Introduction to Flintknapping,* by Matt Gravelle, 1994. Pine Orchard Press.

Groves 1936: *The Indian Relic Collectors Guide*, by G. I. Groves, 1936, American Indian Books, St. Louis, Missouri.

Hail 2000/2008: *Cherokee Astrology: Animal Medicine in the Stars*, by Raven Hail, 2008, Bear & Company, Rochester, Vermont (Previously published in 2000 under the title, *The Cherokee Sacred Calendar: A Handbook of the Ancient Native American Tradition*. Destiny Books, Rochester, Vermont.

Hamel & Chiltoskey 1975: *Cherokee Plants: Their Uses – A 400 Year History*, by Paul B. Hamel & Mary Chiltoskey, 1975.

Hamilton 1952: "The Spiro Mound" by Henry W. Hamilton, 1952, *Missouri Archaeologist* Vol. 14.

Hammond 1958: "The Monolithic Stone Axe," by Owen Hammond, 1958, from the *Central States Archaeological Journal* Vol. 5, No. 1, July, 1958.

Hampton & Robertson 2016: *Arrowhead: Tool for Survival*, by Cecil M. Hampton & George Robertson, 2016.

Hanna 2007: *Antique Trader Indian Arrowheads Price Guide* by Jason Hanna, 2007, Krause Publications.

Harris 1995: *Easy Field Guide to Rock Art Symbols of the Southwest* by Rick Harris, 1995, American Traveler Press.

Harter 1988: *Plants: 2400 Copyright-Free Illustrations of Flowers, Trees, Fruits and Vegetables*, by Jim Harter, 1988. Republished in 1998 by Dover Publications, Mineola, New York.

Harwood 1986: *Arrowheads and Blades of Ancient California*, by Ray Harwood, 1986. Tekakwitha Institute of Ancient Man.

References & Suggested Reading (continued)

Hassrick 1974: *Cowboys and Indians: An Illustrated History*, by Royal B. Hassrick, 1974, Octopus Books Ltd.

Hathcock 2009: "The Morris Cannel Coal Monolithic Axe" by Roy Hathcock 2009, *Prehistoric American* Vol. XLIII.

Haywood 1823: *The Natural and Aboriginal History of Tennessee* by John Haywood, 1823 – Reprint, edited by Mary U. Rothrock, 1959.

Hellweg 1984: *Flintknapping: The Art of Making Stone Tools* by Paul Hellweg, 1984. Canyon Publishing Company.

Henschel 1996: *Prehistoric Tools, Points & Arrowheads* by Gary W. Henschel, 1996. Henschel's Indian Museum, Elkhart Lake, WI.

Hester 1980: *Digging into South Texas Prehistory*, by Thomas R. Hester, 1980, Corona Publishing Company, San Antonio, Texas.

Hester, Mildner & Spencer 1974: *Great Basin Atlatl Studies*, by T. R. Hester, M. P. Mildner & L. Spencer, 1974, Ballena Press Publications in Archaeology, Ethnology and History No. 2.

Highsmith 1985: *The Fluted Axe* by Gale V. Highsmith 1985, printed by Palmer Publications.

Hodge 1907: *Handbook of American Indians North of Mexico – Volume 1*, by Frederick Webb Hodge, 1907, Bureau of American Ethnology.

Hodge 1910: *Handbook of American Indians North of Mexico – Volume 2*, by Frederick Webb Hodge, 1910, Bureau of American Ethnology.

Hogberg & Olausson 2007: *Scandinavian Flint: An Archaeological Perspective* by Anders Hogberg & Deborah Olausson, 2007.

Holmes 1880: *Art in Shell of the Ancient Americans*, by William Henry Holmes, 1880, Smithsonian Institution – Bureau of Ethnology, Washington DC.

Holmes 1886: *Ancient Pottery of the Mississippi Valley*, by William Henry Holmes, 1886, Bureau of Ethnology, Washington DC.

Holmes 1891: *Prehistoric Textile Art of the Eastern United States*, by William Henry Holmes, 1891-92, Bureau of Ethnology, Washington DC.

Holmes 1897: *Stone Implements of the Potomac-Chesapeake Tidewater Provance* by William Henry Holmes, Bureau of Ethnology, Washington, DC.

Holmes 1898: *Aboriginal Pottery of the Eastern United States*, by William Henry Holmes, 1898, Bureau of Ethnology, Washington DC.

Honea 1965: *Early Man Projectile Points in the Southwest*, by Kenneth Honea, 1965, Museum of New Mexico Press Popular Series Pamphlet No. 4.

References & Suggested Reading (continued)

Horan 1972: *The McKenney-Hall Portrait Gallery of American Indians* by James D. Horan, 1972, Crown Publishers, Inc.

Hothem 1986a: *Arrowheads & Projectile Points*, by Lar Hothem, 1986, Collector Books.

Hothem 1986b: *Indian Flints of Ohio*, by Lar Hothem, 1986. Hothem House Books.

Hothem 1989: *Indian Axes & Related Stone Artifacts*, by Lar Hothem, 1989, Collector Books. Lots of very good pictures of axes, including a couple monolithic axes.

Hothem 1994: *North American Indian Artifacts – A Collector's Identification and Value Guide*, by Lar Hothem, fifth edition 1994, Books Americana. Features a monolithic axe.

Hothem 1999: *Collector's Guide to Indian Pipes – Identification and Values*, by Lar Hothem, 1999, Collector Books. Has a photo of a monolithic axe effigy pipe.

Hothem 2003: *Indian Trade Relics: Identification & Values*, by Lar Hothem, 2003, Collector Books, a Division of Schroeder Publishing Company, Inc.

Hothem 2006: *Antler, Bone & Shell Artifacts: Identification & Value Guide*, by Lar Hothem 2006, Collector Books, Paducah, Kentucky.

Hothem 2007: *Ornamental Indian Artifacts: Identification and Value Guide*, by Lar Hothem, 2007, Collector Books.

Howell 1965: *Early Man*, by F. Clark Howell, 1965. Time Life Books.

Hranicky 2015a: *North American Projectile Points* by Wm. Jack Hranicky, 6th edition – 2015, Author House.

Hranicky 2015b: *The Arrowhead in Virginia* by Wm. Jack Hranicky – 2015

Hranicky 2018: *American Arrowheads*, by Wm. Jack Hranicky, 2018, Virginia Academic Press.

Hudson 1976: *The Southeastern Indians*, by Charles Hudson, 1976. The University of Tennessee Press.

Hunziker 2004: *Exploring Burned Rock Middens at Camp Bowie*, by Johanna Hunziker, illustrated by Bruce Moses and Richard Young, April 18, 2004. Retrieved 7-29-2022. https://www.texasbeyondhistory.net/bowie/middenwhat.html

Hyde 1980-1982: *Living with Schizophrenia: A Guide for Patients and Their Families*, by Alexander P. Hyde, 1980, second edition 1982, Contemporary Books, Inc. Chicago.

Internet Public Library 2021: *Southeast Region Tribes*, by Unknown Author. Retrieved November 21st, 2021. https://www.ipl.org/essay/Southeast-Region-Tribes-FCYS2F536U

Jaeger 1945: *Wildwood Wisdom*, by Ellsworth Jaeger, 1945, Shelter Publications, Bolinas, California.

References & Suggested Reading (continued)

Jaeger 1948: *Tracks and Trailcraft*, by Ellsworth Jaeger, 1948, Second Edition printed 2001 by the Lyons Press.

Jensen 2015: *Totem Poles and the Lure of Stanley Park*, by Vickie Jensen, 2015, Westcoast Words.

Johnson 1981: *Prehistoric Caddo Indian Pottery*, by Sam Johnson, 1981, Caddo Press, Murfreesboro, Arkansas.

Jones 1873: *Antiquities of the Southern Indians* by Charles C. Jones, 1873.

Jones 1876: *Exploration of the Aboriginal Remains in Tennessee* by Joseph Jones, M.D., 1876; reprinted by the Tenase Company, 1970.

***Journal of the Illinois State Archaeological Society* 1949:** Unknown writer and photographer, October, 1949.

Kate 1999: *Big Book of Animal Illustrations*, selected and arranged by Maggie Kate, 1999. Dover Publications, Mineola, New York.

Keel 1976: *Cherokee Archaeology, A Study of Appalachian Summit,* By Bennie C. Keel, University of Tennessee Press, 1976.

Kelly & Larson 1957: *Explorations at Etowah Mounds near Cartersville, Georgia/Seasons 1954, 1955, 1956* by A.R. Kelly & Lewis H. Larson, Jr. 1957, Georgia Historical Commission.

Kennedy 1967: Preliminary Excavation of a Possible Early Man Site in Southeastern Florida. *The American Philosophical Society Yearbook* 1966. Philadelphia.

Kent 2011: "Dating Stone Tools" article by Dennis V. Kent, 2011, *The New York Times* Sept. 13, 2011 Issue, p. D2.

Knight 2000/2009: "The Dorroh Monolithic Axe," by James Vernon Knight, 2000, *Journal of Alabama Archaeology*, Vol. 46, No. 1. (Reprinted with color pictures in 2009 - *Prehistoric American* Vol. XLIII).

Knoblock 1939: *Banner-Stones of the North American Indians* by Byron W. Knoblock, 1939.

Kroeber 1961: *Ishi in Two Worlds*, by Theodora Kroeber, 1961, University of California Press.

Langford 2007: "The Path of Souls," by George E. Langford, 2007, *Ancient Objects and Sacred Realms*, edited by Reilly & Garber, University of Texas Press.

Leftwich 1970: *Arts and Crafts of the Cherokee,* by Rodney L. Leftwich, 1970, Cherokee Publications. Has a photo of a double-bitted Cherokee monolithic axe, along with other items, and interesting information.

References & Suggested Reading (continued)

Lehmann & Hunter 1927: *Nine Years Among the Indians, 1870 – 1879: The Story of the Captivity and Life of a Texan Among the Indians,* by Herman Lehmann, edited by J. Marvin Hunter 1927. Reprinted by the University of New Mexico Press, 1993.

Lewis & Kneberg 1941: *The Prehistory of the Chicamauga Basin* by Thomas M.N. Lewis and Madeline Kneberg, 1941, Anthropological Paper I, University of Tennessee.

Lewis & Kneberg 1946: *Hiwassee Island* by Thomas M.N. Lewis and Madeline Kneberg, 1946.

Lewis & Kneberg 1958: *Tribes that Slumber: Indians of the Tennessee Region,* by Thomas M. N. Lewis and Madeline Kneberg, 1958, The University of Tennessee Press, Knoxville, Tennessee.

Livoti & Kiesa 1997: *Adventures in Stone Artifacts: A Family Guide to Arrowheads & Other Artifacts,* by Sandy Livoti & Jon Kiesa, 1997. Adventure Publications.

Lossiah 1998: *The Secrets and Mysteries of the Cherokee Little People – Yuňwi Tsunsdi',* By Lynn King Lossiah, Cherokee Publications, 1998.

Lutgens & Tarbuck 1982: *Essentials of Geology,* by Frederick K. Lutgens & Edward J. Tarbuck, 1982. Merrill Publishing Company. This interesting book is the textbook we used while I studied geology in college.

Mails 1972: *Mystic Warriors of the Plains,* by Thomas E. Mails, 1972. Doubleday & Company, Inc.

Mails 1992: *The Cherokee People: The Story of the Cherokees from Earliest Origins to Contemporary Times,* by Thomas E. Mails, 1992. Council Oak Books. Contains a drawing of a Cherokee double bitted monolithic axe.

Marcom 2003: *Digging Up Texas,* by Robert Marcom, 2003, Taylor Trade Publishing.

Mason 1893: *North American Bows, Arrows and Quivers,* by Otis Tufton Mason, 1893, reprinted by Skyhorse Publishing, Inc, 2007.

Maxwell 1978: *America's Fascinating Indian Heritage,* edited by James A. Maxwell, 1978. The Reader's Digest Association.

McGaw 1965: "Tennessee Antiquities Re-Exhumed: The New Exhibit of the Thruston Collection at Vanderbilt" Pt. 1 by Robert A. McGaw, 1965, *Tennessee Historical Quarterly,* Summer of 1965.

McGuire 1897: *Pipes and Smoking Customs of the American Aborigines, Based on Material in the U. S. National Museum,* by Joseph Deakins McGuire, 1897.

Merriam & Merriam 2004: *The Spiro Mound: A Photo Essay,* by Larry and Christopher Merriam, 2004, Merriam Station Books, Oklahoma City, OK.

Miles 1963: *Indian & Eskimo Artifacts of North America,* by Charles Miles, 1963, Bonanza Books.

References & Suggested Reading (continued)

Moerman 1998: *Native American Ethnobotany*, by D, Moerman, 1998, Timber Press, Portland, OR.

Montgomery 2000: *Native American Crafts & Skills,* By David Montgomery, The Lyons Press, 2000.

Mooney & Olbrechts 1932: *The Swimmer Manuscript* by James Mooney and Frans M. Olbrechts, U. S. Government Printing Office, 1932.

Mooney 1891 & 1900: *James Mooney's History, Myths, and Sacred Formulas of the Cherokees,* By James Mooney, Bright Mountain Books, 1992.

Mooney 1900: *Myths of the Cherokee*, by James Mooney, 1900, Bureau of American Ethnology.

Moore 1905: "Certain Aboriginal Remains of the Black Warrior River," by Clarence B. Moore, 1905, *Journal of the Academy of Natural Sciences of Philadelphia* , 13: 125-244.

Moore 1971: *Stone Tools and Relics of the American Indian,* by Robert K. Moore, 1971.

Moore 1982: *Projectile Point Types of the American Indian,* by Robert K. Moore, 1982.

Moore 1988: *The Marshall Cavendish Illustrated Encyclopedia of Plants and Earth Sciences, Vols. 1 – 10,* edited by David M. Moore, 1988, Marshall Cavendish, New York, London Sydney.

Moorehead 1900: *Prehistoric Implements*, by Warren King Moorehead, 1900, The Robert Clarke Company, Cincinnati, Ohio.

Moorehead 1910: *The Stone Age in North America, Vols. 1 & 2*, by Warren King Moorehead, 1910, Houghton Mifflin Company, The Riverside Press Cambridge.

Moorehead 1932: *The Etowah Papers, Exploration of the Etowah Site in Georgia*, by Warren K. Moorehead, 1932, reprinted by the University Press of Florida, 2000. Features the only photo I know of, depicting the Moorehead axe.

Morgan 1995: *The League of the Iroquois, by* Lewis Henry Morgan, (1995). J G Press.

Morris 1963a: *Life History of the United States Vol. 1,* by Richard B. Morris, 1963, Time Inc. Book Division.

Morris 1963b: *Vicksburg Campaign of 1863: What Would have Happened if Present River Conditions (1963) had Existed in 1863?* By George A. Morris, 1963.

Morrison 2019: *The Shaman's Guide to Power Animals* by Lori Morrison, 2019, Four Jaguars Press.

Muench & Schaafsma 1995: *Images in Stone* – Photography by David Muench, Text by Polly Schaafsma, 1995, Brown Trout Publishers, Inc.

References & Suggested Reading (continued)

Murphey 1966: *How to Find Indian Arrowheads,* by Don Murphey, 1966, Canyon Publishing Company.

Myer 1927: "Two Prehistoric Villages in Middle Tennessee" by William E. Myer, 1927, *Forty-First Annual Report*, Bureau of American Ethnology.

Myer Unknown Date: *Stone Age in the Middle South* by William E. Myer (unfinished manuscript), on file at the Smithsonian Institution.

Newcomb 1961: *The Indians of Texas* by W. W. Newcomb, Jr. 1961, University of Texas Press.

Overstreet & Cooper 2018: *The Official Overstreet Indian Arrowheads Identification and Price Guide*, 15th Edition 2018, by Robert M. Overstreet (Edited by Steven R. Cooper & Matt Rowe), Krause Publications.

Overstreet & Pafford 2011: *Official Overstreet Identification and Price Guide to Indian Arrowheads,* 12th edition 2011, by Robert M. Overstreet, (edited by John T. Pafford), House of Collectibles books.

Overstreet, Cox & Cooper 2015: *Official Overstreet Indian Arrowheads Identification and Price Guide 14th Edition*, by Robert M. Overstreet, 2015 – (Edited by Sam W. Cox & Steven R. Cooper).

Owens 2009: *Arrowheads: Early Man Projectile Points of North America*, by Ken Owens, 2009, Collector Books.

Panther-Yates 2013: *Cherokee Clans*, by Donald Panther-Yates, 2013, Panther's Lodge, Phoenix.

Pastino 2016: *Ice Age Hunting Camp, Replete with Bird Bones and Tobacco Found in Utah Desert*, by B. D. Pastino, 2016. Retrieved January 3, 2021 from Western Digs: http://westerndigs.org/ice-age-hunting-camp-replete-with-bird-bones-and-tobacco-found-in-utah-desert/

Peacock 1954: *The Duck River Cache, Tennessee's Greatest Archaeological Find*, by Charles K. Peacock, 1954.

Perino 1968: *Guide to the Identification of Certain American Indian Projectile Points*, by Gregory Perino, 1968, Special Bulletin No. 3 of the Oklahoma Anthropological Society.

Perino 1971: *Guide to the Identification of Certain American Indian Projectile Points*, by Gregory Perino, 1971, Special Bulletin No. 4 of the Oklahoma Anthropological Society.

Perino 1985-1997: *Selected Preforms, Points and Knives of the North American Indians Volume 1*, by Gregory Perino, 1985 (second edition published in 1997), Points & Barbs Press. Features information on Duck River swords.

References & Suggested Reading (continued)

Perino 1991: *Selected Preforms, Points and Knives of the North American Indians Volume 2*, by Gregory Perino, 1991, Points & Barbs Press.

Perino 2002: *Selected Preforms, Points and Knives of the North American Indians Volume 3*, by Gregory Perino, 2002, Points & Barbs Press.

Phelen & Bones 1976: *Texas Wild*, by Richard Phelen with photography by Jim Bones, 1976, Excalibur Books.

***Pictorial Encyclopedia of American History, Vol. 1*, 1962:** Davco Publishing Company, Chicago, Illinois.

Prideaux 1973: *Cro-Mangnon Man*, by Tom Prideaux, 1973, Time Life Books.

Reader's Digest 1976: *The World's Last Mysteries,* published by Reader's Digest, 1976.

Reader's Digest 1978: *America's Fascinating Indian Heritage*, 1978, Reader's Digest Association.

Reader's Digest 1986: *Mysteries of the Ancient Americas*, published by Reader's Digest, 1986.

Reader's Digest 1990: *Magic and Medicine of Plants,* Reader's Digest, 1990, unknown authors.

Reader's Digest 1995: *Through Indian Eyes: The Untold Story of Native American Peoples*, Reader's Digest, 1995.

Reed 1993: *Seven Clans of the Cherokee Society*, by Marcelina Reed, 1993, Cherokee Publications, Cherokee, North Carolina.

Reilly & Garber 2007: *Ancient Objects and Sacred Realms*, Edited by Kent Reilly III & James F. Garber, 2007, University of Texas Press.

Russell 1951: *Indian Artifacts*, by Virgil Y. Russell, 1951. Johnson Publishing Company.

Salomon 1928: *The Book of Indian Crafts and Indian Lore*, by Julian Harris Salomon, 1928, Reprinted 2015 by Skyhorse Publishing, New York, New York.

Saville 1916a: *Monolithic Axes and their Distribution in Ancient America* Vols. 2-3, by Marshall H. Saville, 1916, reprinted by Sagwan Press, 2015. This is a book of around 500 pages, including Saville's piece about monolithic axes, which is only around 24 pages. This edition contains a better copy of Saville's piece than that listed below, but it is more expensive.

Saville 1916b: *Monolithic Axes and their Distribution in Ancient America* Vol. 2 No. 6, by Marshall H. Saville, 1916, reprinted by Palala Press, 2016. This edition contains only Saville's 24-page piece specifically about monolithic axes, but it is missing the first page. The advantage of this edition is that it is less expensive than the edition described above.

References & Suggested Reading (continued)

Schulz 1954: *Indians of Lassen Volcanic National Park and Vicinity,* by Paul E. Schulz, 1954. Loomis Museum Association, Lassen Volcanic National Park.

Secrist 1974: *Secrist's Simplified Identification Guide to Stone Relics of the American Indian*, by Clarence Secrist, Third Edition 1974.

Sedwick & Sedwick 1995: *The Practical Book of Cobs*, by Daniel & Frank Sedwick, third edition 1995.

Seed Change 2019: *Where Do Your Beans Come From?* Retrieved November 22nd, 2021. https://weseedchange.org/where-do-your-beans-come-from/

Seed Change 2020: *Where Does Squash Come From?* Retrieved November 22nd, 2021. https://weseedchange.org/where-does-squash-come-from/

Seever 1897: "A Cache of Idols and Chipped Flint Instruments in Tennessee," by William J. Seever, 1897, from *The Antiquarian*, Vol. 1 Part 6.

Shafer & Parsons 1986 – Painted Pebbles: Styles and Chronology by Mark L. Parsons, *Ancient Texans*, by Harry J. Shafer, 1986, Gulf Publishing Company, Houston, Texas.

Shafer & Zintgraff 1986: *Ancient Texans: Rock Art & Lifeways along the Lower Pecos*, by Harry Shafer, with photography by Jim Zintgraff, 1986. Gulf Publishing Company.

Sharpe 1970: *The Cherokees – Past and Present: An Authentic Guide to the Cherokee People*, by J. Ed. Sharpe, 1970, Cherokee Publications, Cherokee, North Carolina.

Silverberg 1970: *The Mound Builders*, by Robert Silverberg, 1970, Ohio University Press, Athens, Ohio.

Sizemore 1995: *How to Make Cherokee Clothing*, by Donald Sizemore, 1995, Cherokee Publications, Cherokee, North Carolina.

Sizemore 1999: *Cherokee Dance: Ceremonial Dances & Dance Regalia*, by Donald Sizemore, 1999, Cherokee Publications, Cherokee, North Carolina.

Skinner 1914: "The Charles S. Mason Collection," by Alanson Skinner, 1914, *The American Museum Journal*, Vol. XIV, No. 4.

Skinner 2019: *Ceremonial Use of Tobacco*, by A. Skinner. Retrieved January 2, 2021, from Milwaukee Public Museum: https://www.mpm.edu/plan-visit/educators/wirp/great-lakes-traditional-culture/tobacco

Smith & Dewey 1989: *All About Arrowheads and Spear Points*, by Howard E. Smith, Jr. – illustrated by Jennifer Owings Dewey, 1989. Henry Holt and Company, Inc.

Smith & Hunter 1927: *The Boy Captives*, by Clinton L. Smith and J. Marvin Hunter, 1927, Distributed by Allen Smith, Jr., P.O. Box 690, Camp Wood, Texas, 78833-0690, 1-888-926-1865.

References & Suggested Reading (continued)

Sonoma Valley Sun 2009: *Turning Stones: Civilization Emerges from City of the* Sun, Retrieved December 7th, 2021. https://sonomasun.com/2009/09/25/civilization-emerges-from-city-of-the-sun/

Spence 1994: *Myths of the North American Indians,* By Lewis Spence, Gramercy Books, 1994.

Squier & Davis 1847: *Ancient Monuments of the Mississippi Valley*, by E. G. Squier and E. H. Davis, 1847, reprinted by Alacrity Press, 2019.

Stanford & Bradley 2013: *Across Atlantic Ice*, by Dennis J. Stanford and Bruce A. Bradley, 2013. University of California Press.

Stevenson 1880: *Illustrated Catalogue of the Collections Obtained from the Indians of New Mexico and Arizona in 1879*, by James Stevenson, 1880. Second Annual Report of the Bureau of American Ethnology.

Suggs 2006: *From A Student's Notebook Vol. 1: Thoughts on Native American Spirituality*, by Tommy Suggs, 2006 (second edition published in 2014. Sweetwater Education Foundation, San Antonio, Texas.

Suggs 2007: *From A Student's Notebook Vol. 2: Essence of Lakota Sioux Spirituality*, by Tommy Suggs, 2007 (second edition published in 2014. Sweetwater Education Foundation, San Antonio, Texas.

Suhm Krieger & Jelks 1954: *Handbook of Texas Archaeology*, by Dee Ann Suhm, Alex D. Krieger and Edward B. Jelks, 1954. Texas Archaeological Society.

Sullivan 2001: *"Dates for Shell Gorgets and the SECC in the Chickamauga Basin of SE Tennessee,"* by Lynne P. Sullivan, 2001, Research Notes, McClung Museum, University of Tennessee, No. 19.

Swannanoa Valley Museum (Unknown Year): *History @ Home – Cherokee Games & the Cherokee Butterbean Game*. Retrieved November 23rd, 2021. https://www.history.swannanoavalleymuseum.org/wp-content/uploads/2020/06/Cherokee-Butterbean-History-at-Home.docx-1.pdf

Swope 1982: *Indian Artifacts of the East and South* by Robert Swope, Jr. – 1982.

Taylor & Sturtevant 1991: *The Native Americans: The Indigenous People of North America*, editorial consultant Colin F. Taylor and technical consultant William C. Sturtevant, 1991. Salamander Books.

Taylor 2002: *American Colonies, Volume 1 - Penguin History of the United States* by Alan Taylor, 2002. ISBN 9780142002100.

Tennessee Archaeologist 1957: "Editor's Notes" – *Tennessee Archaeologist*, Vol. XIII, No. 1 (Spring 1957).

References & Suggested Reading (continued)

The Best of Chips – Vols. 1-4 – Contains many of the best articles published in *Chips Magazine* – from 1989 – 2011. Can also be purchased with the 3 disc set containing the full archives of *Chips Magazine*. www.flintknappingpublications.com

Thomas 1935: *Chinook: A History and Dictionary of the Northwest Coast Trade Jargon*, by Edward Harper Thomas, 1935, Metropolitan Press.

Thomas 2000: *Exploring Native North America*, By David Hurst Thomas, Oxford University Press, 2000.

Thruston 1890-1897: *The Antiquities of Tennessee and the State of Aboriginal Society in the Scale of Civilization Represented by Them; a Series of Historical and Ethnological Studies*, by Gates Phillips Thruston, 1897, Robert Clarke Company, Cincinnati, Ohio.

Time Life Books Editors 1992a: *The American Indians- The First Americans*, by the Editors of Time Life Books, 1992.

Time Life Books Editors 1992b: *The American Indians- The Spirit World*, by the Editors of Time Life Books, 1992.

Time Life Books Editors 1992c: *The American Indians- The European Challenge*, by the Editors of Time Life Books, 1992.

Time Life Books Editors 1993a: *The American Indians- People of the Desert*, by the Editors of Time Life Books, 1993.

Time Life Books Editors 1993b: *The American Indians- The Way of the Warrior*, by the Editors of Time Life Books, 1993.

Time Life Books Editors 1993c: *The American Indians- The Buffalo Hunters*, by the Editors of Time Life Books, 1993.

Time Life Books Editors 1993d: *The American Indians- Realm of the Iroquois*, by the Editors of Time Life Books, 1993.

Time Life Books Editors 1993e: *The American Indians- The Mighty Chieftains*, by the Editors of Time Life Books, 1993.

Time Life Books Editors 1993f: *The American Indians- Keepers of the Totem*, by the Editors of Time Life Books, 1993.

Time Life Books Editors 1994a: *The American Indians- Cycles of Life*, by the Editors of Time Life Books, 1994.

Time Life Books Editors 1994b: *The American Indians- War for the Plains*, by the Editors of Time Life Books, 1994.

Time Life Books Editors 1994c: *The American Indians- Tribes of the Southern Woodlands*, by the Editors of Time Life Books, 1994.

References & Suggested Reading (continued)

Time Life Books Editors 1994d: *The American Indians- The Indians of California*, by the Editors of Time Life Books, 1994.

Time Life Books Editors 1994e: *The American Indians- People of the Ice and Snow*, by the Editors of Time Life Books, 1994.

Time Life Books Editors 1994f: *The American Indians- People of the Lakes*, by the Editors of Time Life Books, 1994.

Time Life Books Editors 1995a: *The American Indians- The Woman's Way*, by the Editors of Time Life Books, 1995.

Time Life Books Editors 1995b: *The American Indians- Indians of the Western Range*, by the Editors of Time Life Books, 1995.

Time Life Books Editors 1995c: *The American Indians- Hunters of the Northern Forest*, by the Editors of Time Life Books, 1995.

Time Life Books Editors 1995d: *The American Indians- Tribes of the Southern Plains*, by the Editors of Time Life Books, 1995.

Time Life Books Editors 1995e: *The American Indians- The Reservations*, by the Editors of Time Life Books, 1995.

Time Life Books Editors 1995f: *The American Indians- Algonquians of the East Coast*, by the Editors of Time Life Books, 1995.

Time Life Books Editors 1996a: *The American Indians- Chroniclers of Indian Life*, by the Editors of Time Life Books, 1996.

Time Life Books Editors 1996b: *The American Indians- Winds of Renewal*, by the Editors of Time Life Books, 1996.

Townsend & Sharp 2004: *Hero, Hawk and Open Hand*, edited by Richard F. Townsend & Robert V. Sharp, 2004. Art Institute of Chicago & Yale University Press.

Townsend 2004: "American Landscapes, Seen and Unseen," by Richard F. Townsend, 2004, *Hero, Hawk, and Open Hand – American Indian Art of the Ancient Midwest and South*; Richard F. Townsend, general editor, and Robert V. Sharp, editor. Has very good color photos of a few authentic monolithic axes and lots of related things.

Travis & Carlson 2019: *Arrowheads, Spears, and Buffalo Jumps: Prehistoric Hunter/Gatherers of the Great Plains*, by Lauri Travis, Illustrated by Eric S. Carlson, 2019, Mountain Press Publishing Company, Missoula, Montana.

Troost 1845: *An Account of Some Ancient Indian Remains in Tennessee* by Gerard Troost, 1845.

Truth Seeker 2013: *Cherokee Language and Dictionary*, by Truth Seeker, 2013.

References & Suggested Reading (continued)

Tully & Tully 1986: *Flint Blades & Projectile Points of the North American Indian* by Lawrence N. Tully with photography by Steven N. Tully, 1986. Collector Books. Contains photos of many large Mississippian flint pieces.

Tully & Tully 1998: *Field Guide to Flint Arrowheads & Knives of the North American Indian* by Lawrence N. Tully & Steven N. Tully, 1998, Collector Books.

Turner & Hester 1985-1993: *A Field Guide to Stone Artifacts of Texas Indians*, by Ellen Sue Turner and Thomas R. Hester, 1985, second edition 1993, Gulf Publishing Company.

Turner 2013: *Flint Knapping: A Guide to Making Your Own Stone Age Toolkit*, by Robert Turner, 2013, The History Press.

Turner, Hester & McReynolds 2011: *Stone Artifacts of Texas Indians* by Ellen Sue Turner, Thomas R. Hester & Richard McReynolds, 2011. Taylor Trade Publishing.

Ubelaker 1976: Prehistoric Population Size: Historical Review and Current Appraisal of North American Estimates – *American Journal of Physical Anthropology – Vol. 45, Issue 3: 661-65* by Douglas H. Ubelaker.

Ulmer & Beck 1951: *Cherokee Cooklore: To Make My Bread,* Edited by Mary Ulmer and Samuel Beck, 1951 (reprinted in 2014 by Coachwhip Publications).

Valle 1970: *The Illustrated Encyclopedia of the Animal Kingdom – Vols. 1 – 20*, by Antonio Valle, 1970, The Danbury Press.

Van Buren 1974: *Arrowheads and Projectile Points*, by G. E. Van Buren, 1974. Arrowhead Publishing Company.

Van Horne 2002: *Indian Warfare*, by Wayne Van Horne, 2002 – Retrieved November 21st, 2021. New Georgia Encyclopedia, last modified June 8, 2017. https://www.georgiaencyclopedia.org/articles/history-archaeology/indian-warfare/

Waldorf & Waldorf 1987: *Story in Stone, Flint Types of the Central and Southern U.S.*, by D. C. Waldorf, illustrated by Valerie Waldorf, 1987, Mound Builder Books.

Waldorf & Waldorf 1999: *The Art of Making Primitive Bows and Arrows*, by D. C. & Valerie Waldorf, New Edition 1999. Mound Builder Books.

Waldorf & Waldorf 2006: *The Art of Flint Knapping* by D. C. Waldorf, illustrated by Valerie Waldorf, fifth edition 2006. Mound Builder Books.

Waldorf 1997: Grey Ghosts and Old Timers by D. C. Waldorf, 1997, *Chips Magazine Vol. 9, No. 1.*

Walk 2020: *Human Sacrifices at Cahokia Mounds*, by Devin Walk, 2020. Memories of the Prairie Blog. Retrieved November 21st, 2021. https://www.memoriesoftheprairie.com/blog/2020/1/28/human-sacrifices-at-cahokia-mounds

References & Suggested Reading (continued)

Waring 1968: *The Waring Papers: The Collected Works of Antonio Waring Jr.*, edited by Steve Williams, 1968.

Watson & Zallinger 1960: *Dinosaurs and Other Prehistoric Reptiles*, by Jane Werner Watson, illustrated by Rudolph F. Zallinger, 1960, A Golden Book, Western Publishing Company, Racine, Wisconsin.

Weatherly 1969: "A Recent Monolithic Axe Find," by Raymond Weatherly, *Central States Archaeological Journal*, Vol. 16, No. 1, 1969.

Webb & DeJarnette 1942: *An Archaeological Survey of Pickwick Basin in the Adjacent Portions of the States of Alabama, Mississippi and Tennessee* by William S. Webb and David L. DeJarnette, 1942, Bureau of American Ethnology, No. 129.

Welsh 1995: *Easy Field Guide to Southwestern Petroglyphs* by Elizabeth Welsh, 1995, American Traveler Press.

Whisker & Whisker 1982: *Indian Artifacts Collection of the Late Major Simon Lutz at Old Bedford Village*, by Vaughn E. Whisker and James B. Whisker, 1982, Bedford County Press, Everett, PA.

White & Brown 1973: *The First Men*, by Edmund White and Dale Brown, 1973, Time Life Books.

Whiteford 1970: *North American Indian Arts*, by Andrew Hunter Whiteford, 1970. Golden Press. Contains illustrations of 3 carved monolithic axes, including a NW coast bird effigy axe and NW coast slave killer.

Whittaker 1994: *Flintknapping: Making & Understanding Stone Tools* by John C. Whittaker, 1994. University of Texas Press.

Wikipedia 2020: *Moccasin Game* – Retrieved November 23rd, 2021.
https://en.wikipedia.org/wiki/Moccasin_game

Wikipedia 2021a: *Mississippian Culture Pottery* – Retrieved October 18th, 2021.
https://en.wikipedia.org/wiki/Mississippian_culture_pottery

Wikipedia 2021b: *Culture of the Choctaw* – Retrieved December 3rd, 2021.
https://en.wikipedia.org/wiki/Culture_of_the_Choctaw

Wikipedia 2021c: *Cahokia Woodhenge* – Retrieved December 8th, 2021.
https://en.wikipedia.org/wiki/Cahokia_Woodhenge

Wilbur 1995: *The Woodland Indians: An Illustrated Account of the Lifestyles of America's First Inhabitants*, by C. Keith Wilbur, MD, 1995. The Globe Pequot Press, Old Saybrook, Connecticut.

Willey 1966: *An Introduction to American Archaeology – Volume 1: North and Middle America*, by Gordon R. Willey, 1966. Prentice-Hall, Inc.

References & Suggested Reading (continued)

Williams 1928 – *Early Travels in the Tennessee Country, 1840-1900*, by Samuel Cole Williams, 1928.

Wilson 1896: *Prehistoric Art*, by Thomas Wilson, 1896, Report of the United States National Museum.

Wilson 1899: *Arrowpoints, Spearheads and Knives of Prehistoric Times*, by Thomas Wilson, 1899. Reprinted by Skyhorse Publishing, 2007.

Wood, Vaczek, Hamblin & Leonard 1972: *Life Before Man*, by Peter Wood, Louis Vaczek, Dora Jane Hamblin and Jonathan Norton Leonard, 1972, Time Life Books.

Woods 1997: *American Indian Artifacts*, by Ellen Woods, 1997, Seven Locks Press.

Wormington 1957: *Ancient Man in North America*, by H. M. Wormington, fourth edition 1957. Denver Museum of Natural History.

Wright 1977: *Hopi Kachinas: The Complete Guide to Collecting Kachina Dolls*, by Barton Wright, 1977, Northland Publishing, Flagstaff, Arizona.

Yeager 1986: *Arrowheads & Stone Artifacts*, by C. G. Yeager, 1986. Pruett Publishing Company.

Yeager 2000: *Arrowheads & Stone Artifacts – Second Edition*, by C. G. Yeager, 2000, Pruett Publishing Company.

Yeager 2016: *Arrowheads & Stone Artifacts – Third Edition*, by C. G. Yeager, 2016. Westwinds Press.

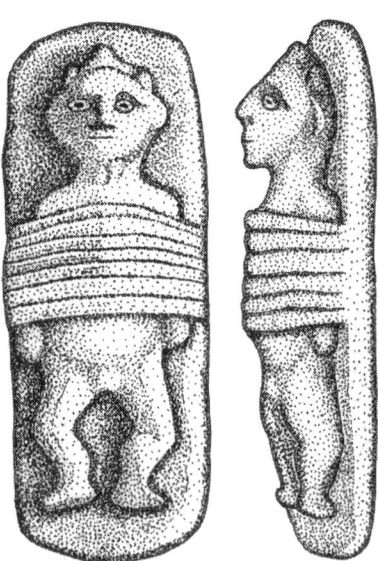

Pottery Baby in Cradleboard, Possibly a Child's Toy or Doll.
Redrawn from Thruston 1897.

Made in the USA
Columbia, SC
23 December 2022